THE EUROPEAN COLLECTION

Books by **David Cullen**

The Eye of Makarios
The Mesrine Conclusion
The Windsor Secret
Pick Up Sticks
Knock On My Door
The Baalbeck Decision
The Byblos Discovery
The Beirut Confession

Collections

The European Collection
The Eye of Makarios
The Mesrine Conclusion
The Windsor Secret
Bonus short story: *Shade*

The Lebanese Collection
The Baalbeck Decision
The Byblos Discovery
The Beirut Confession

DAVID CULLEN

THE EUROPEAN COLLECTION

THE EYE OF MAKARIOS
THE MESRINE CONCLUSION
THE WINDSOR SECRET

The European Collection
First published 2015

The author has asserted his right under the Copyright Designs
and Patents Act 1988 to be identified as the author of this work.

A catalogue record of this book is available from the British
Library.

ISBN: 978-0-9559911-7-2

www.lulu.com/davidcullen
Facebook: DavidCullenBooks

Published by Culpro Books
an imprint of Cullen Productions

THE EYE OF MAKARIOS

Ψ

DAVID CULLEN

Then (to be brief) the foreigners
Which the king found most dangerous
Hied them off, by every way
And, in short, they went away...

But ere their journey they had started
And from Limassol had departed
The king them all did recompense
And give them gifts at his expense:
Gold and silver, silken threads
Ships and jewels *and fiery steeds...*
- from *La prise d'Alexandrie*
by Guillaume de Machaut (1300-1377)

Ψ

To be tantalised is an experience almost sensual.
- Ilich Ramirov, in a written essay at the KGB
Academy Number 311 in Novosibirsk, Siberia,
April 16 1974

Ψ

Acknowledgements

For starting it all:
Pierre Rouan, who died because he told this story.

For their invaluable help:
Christina Cascianis
Mrs Margery Egginton (deceased)
Madame Sally-Anne Forêt (née Bowker)
Chief Inspector Johann Versleas (Amsterdam police)
Ms Charlotte Rapley
The ones who do not want to be identified in North America, Europe, Cyprus, Venezuela, Lebanon and Russia.

For their attempts at hindrance, and hence proving the story:
The British government
The French government

Finally my respect and admiration - but not necessarily my support - must go to the late Michael Mouskos, His Beatitude Archbishop Makarios III of Cyprus.

Ψ

Cast in order of appearance

Richard John Bingham - *7th Earl of Lucan (a patriotic fugitive)*
Commander Christou - *Cypriot Tactical Reserve Force*
Major Stavros Stavrou - *2nd In Command of EOKA*
Demetrakis Spourghitis - *3rd In Command of EOKA*
General George Grivas - *leader of EOKA*
Elizabeth O'Toole - *an Irish diversion*
Michael Mahoney - *an Irish opportunist*
Ali 'Akay' Al Khalifa - *Financial Controller of Black September*
Philomena O'Toole - *a second Irish diversion*
Khalid al-Wazir - *IRA liaison, Black September*
Ali Hassan Salameh - *Controller of Intelligence and Action, Black September*
Salah Khalef - *Consiglière, Black September*
Faisal Ibn Musaed - *PA to Ali Hassan Salameh*
Steve Graves - *an American on a quest*
Sally-Anne Bowker - *in love with Steve Graves*
Digenis – *an agent of Mossad Aliyah Beth*
Christina Cascianis - *a special lady*
Ilich Ramirov - *an itinerant terrorist*
Tony Verekelis - *a member of EOKA*
Old Mother Dimitri - *nurse to George Grivas*
Nicos Sampson - *the future President of Cyprus (however briefly)*
Raouf Denktash - *the future President of Southern Cyprus*
Takis - *a young helper*
Colonel Stanley William Egginton - *a traitor above suspicion*
Halil - *a restaurant owner*
Pan - *the spirit of nature and paganism (or just a local boy)*
Ekaterina Furtseva - *said to be Minister of Culture, USSR*
Annette Stewart - *junior executive of De Beers London*
Chaim Cohen – *Deputy Controller of Mossad, Israeli external security service*
Nathanson – *an agent of Mossad Aliyah Beth*
The Russian Ambassador to France *(perhaps)*
Georges Pompidou - *President of France*
Albert - *Pompidou's secretary*
Jim McKane - *a manager at Gulf, Houston USA*
Bishop Michael Rigakis - *aide to the Cypriot External Affairs Minister Ioannis*

Christophides
Costas - *an ogre*
Wilbur - *Air France, Houston Airport*
Sir Lovelock Armstrong - *Permanent Under Secretary, UK Ministry of Defence*
Ronald Arthur - *Security Officer MOD*
Eunice Tate - *PA to DoS MOD*
Dr Louis Thomas - *Texas Medical Centre*
Charlotte Rapley - *sculptor and artist*
Louise Petit - *fashion designer*
Claude François - *French singer*
Marcel Forêt - *friend of Claude's*
Matthew Ramm - *UK police Special Branch*
Ron Woods - *UK police Special Branch*
Don Metcalf - *UK police Special Branch*
An old Cypriot peasant
Michael Mouskos - *His Beatitude Archbishop Makarios III of Cyprus*
Andreas Papadopoulos - *a priest*
Sergei 'Hernandez' - *a Russian*
Melanie - *a masseuse*
The five Controllers of Israeli Intelligence
Alexei Nikolayevich Kosygin - *Prime Minister of the Soviet Union*
Roz - *UK police Special Branch*
Chief Inspector Johann Versleas - *Amsterdam police*

Ψ

FOREWORD

History would have judged it as a time of turbulence. A time when mankind had gone mad and the redemption of the Millennium was a quarter of a century away. But with hindsight, it is now seen as the time when innocence ended. A time when those with agendas of their own decided that they had the right to murder whomever they chose. A time when the causes - and the people - who created the horror of the early twenty-first century were in their formative years.

It was a time before the communications revolution. Mobile telephones required a battery the size of two shoeboxes, and only the select few had VCRs. 'Personal' computers were the size of a room, and Vinton Cerf was just devising the first workings of what was to become the Internet. Compact discs had yet to herald the digital age.

Germany was still divided and the Cold War showed no sign of thawing. The USSR was mighty and the cracks in communism had yet to appear. Terrorism was rife.

As far as the general public were concerned, the late summer and fall of 1974 were just like any other in that turbulent decade. The previous fall the fires of raging world-wide inflation had been stoked after the *Yom Kippur* war when the oil-producing countries had realised the power of the liquid weapon underneath their feet and had promptly trebled the price of their black gold. By September 1974 the economies of the West had assimilated this massive rise but not without the consequent affects on their 'growth' rates and retail prices. Inflation, too, was rife.

In France, Valéry Giscard d'Estaing successfully took over the Presidential mantle after the death of Georges Pompidou. In West Germany, Helmut Schmidt became Chancellor after the communist spy Gunther Guillaume caused the downfall of the affable Willi Brandt.

Indeed, it was not a year to take a bet on the security of any Head of State. Richard Milhous Nixon was finally forced to resign as President of the United States over the Watergate scandal, and Gerald Ford fell into his shoes. In Portugal, the repressive Dr Caetano was ousted and replaced by General Spinola who, in his turn, was forced to make way for Costa de Gomes. In Cyprus, the resilient Archbishop Makarios fled the island as Nicos Sampson and the Greek National Guard paved the way for Clerides and Denktash to partition Aphrodite's soil. In Greece, the seven year regime of the Colonels and General Ioannides dissolved into ashes and Constantine Karamanlis returned from an eleven year exile in Paris. In Britain Harold Wilson bounced back into power as Premier Edward Heath was defeated by a national miners' strike.

To a world-weary public, hardened by years of assassinations, terrorism and universal gloom, none of this warranted any particular attention. To them, 1974 was just another normal year in the cauldron of world affairs and the decline of their living standards...

Ψ

PROLOGUE

London, November 1974

When it came to it, the girl's head shattered easily and she was dead by the time her body hit the floor. It had been an instantaneous but very painful death, shards of skull penetrating deep into the brain. Sandra - the one person whom the police later thought might be able to name her killer for definite - never knew who her murderer was.

Richard John Bingham, 7th Earl of Lucan, looked down at the inert body and shivered. It was dark in the basement of his town house at 46 Lower Belgrave Street, but he could clearly see the dark patch which had once been the back of the nanny's head. Already there was an unpleasant smell.

His breath came fast and deep, and his hands were shaking. Strangely enough he did not feel sick, as he had thought he would. He felt somewhat relieved. Relieved that this part of it at least was over. But the worst, of course, was yet to come.

Thirty-nine year old 'Lucky' Lucan gathered himself together and got down to business. *They* had specifically instructed that everything must go according to plan. Ten minutes delay at any stage and it could all go wrong and land him in an English cell for life. He must get on with it.

Quickly he retrieved the sack from the darkened corner and began to shove the dead body into it...

When the top of the bag was tied and the macabre bundle propped back into the corner, Lucan left the murder weapon where it could easily be found - as instructed - and rushed up the stairs two at a time. His small bag was already packed with the very few things he was allowed to take with him, and now he just had time for the cosmetics. Then would come the chat with his wife, which the police would make so much of but which the Press would virtually ignore, and his escape in the borrowed car.

Everything went according to plan and soon Richard John Bingham, without the moustache which had been his trade mark around the gaming clubs of London, was driving south out of central London towards the suburb of Croydon. The night of November 7 1974 was crisp but not necessarily cold in London, and his thick Arran jumper was ample coverage against whatever the elements had in store. It was a dry night and rain was not predicted. This time Lucky Lucan hoped that the weather forecasters would be right. He had a long way to go.

His only regret was that he had to miss his dinner date at the *Clermont* with Greville, and without a word of apology or explanation. It was damn caddish of him. A gentleman really did not do such things.

He only hoped that, if the truth were ever known, England would be grateful...

One year earlier...

Cyprus, November 1973

Dawn came at 06:00 that morning. In Limassol, the five thousand year old town on the central southern coast of the island, a normal day had begun. Normal, that is, to the populus about to rise to earn their daily crust: working in the wineries or distilleries, or in the zoo or municipal gardens, or in the shops (anxious to start selling their lace or pottery or sheepskins to the low-season tourists); normal to the hotel workers or the rich, retired resident foreigners.

But in the very smart residential area in the north-east of the town, things were far from normal. Acting on information received from an EOKA guerrilla captured after wandering too far into the wrong part of Nicosia, ten men of President Makarios' Tactical Reserve Force were closing in on two houses. Inside one of the houses - and at that stage they knew not which - was Major Stavros Stavrou, codenamed Syros, second in command to General George Grivas, the leader of the island's guerrilla movement. *[For a brief history of Cyprus, see Appendix 1.]*

Commander Christou and his men were only too fully aware of what the death or, preferably, capture of Stavrou would mean to the wily Archbishop who governed Cyprus. The EOKA movement was tottering, their leader Grivas was old and it was rumoured that he was dying. To lose his Number Two now might be a blow from which he would never recover. And the promise of Stavrou's release (which, of course, would never actually happen) might secure the freedom of Justice Minister Kristos Vakis, taken by EOKA two weeks before.

The answer to Stavrou's location lay in the head of the terrorist now being interrogated in Nicosia. Christou only hoped that the boys at HQ extracted the answer soon. As it was, the rising sun would now force him to call seven of his men back to the discreetly parked English Army lorry - for word of 'The Red Priest's Men' in this, the main stronghold of Grivas, would spread like wildfire. That would leave just the two ununiformed lads to watch on a house apiece.

Christou removed his black beret and quietly opened the cab door and climbed out. He walked the ten metres to the corner with the main road, removed a khaki handkerchief from his pocket and wiped his brow. It was the signal for the seven in uniform to disperse and separately make their way back to the lorry.

Christou turned and walked back to the vehicle. The longer the transceiver did not crackle with the answer he wanted, the more irritated he would get.

The side street was still and lifeless. Unceremoniously he undid his trousers and began to pee up against the side of somebody's villa...

As it was, it took another six hours for the terrorist in Nicosia to crack, the final breakthrough coming only after his left testicle had been crushed to a pulp.

Just before noon the transceiver bleeped once. Christou grabbed it. The voice at the other end said just three words, "The grey villa," and the transmission ended. It was enough.

The wooden door gave with one mighty kick of Christou's boot. Four members of the Tactical Reserve Force stormed inside.

In the open living area, a woman of about thirty, dressed in only the flimsiest of negligées, was setting the table for lunch. Even before she had thought about screaming, Christou had leapt across the room and had grasped her throat so tightly that any exhalation of sound or air was impossible.

"Where is Stavrou?" he snarled garlic into her face. "Syros, where is he? Tell me woman and tell me now."

The woman's tongue poked out between her purple lips. She could not have answered even if she had wanted to.

"*Where is he?*"

Her eyes, almost bulging from their sockets, stared fearfully yet contemptuously at the TRF leader.

"Terrorist bitch!" He rammed her into the rough brickwork of the wall, following with one mighty slap with the back of his hand across her face. Her lower lip split in two places, blood jumping over her chin and negligée.

He let her fall and turned to his men. "Upstairs. And *don't* let the bastard get away!"

The first door upstairs was a lavatory, the second some sort of clothes cupboard. The third door was locked.

Again Christou's boot made contact with wood, and this time the frame shattered, splinters flying everywhere as the door crashed inward.

A man, dressed only in white Y-fronts, stood in the centre of the room. Next to him was a metal waste bin from which smoke was rising. He glanced up as the door slammed open and a reflex action made him start to his right towards a vicious-looking machine gun resting on a chair.

"Hold it, sir!"

In the split second the man had looked away from the door and twitched towards his gun, the soldiers had entered the room. Three 9mm sub-machine guns now pointed rigidly towards his body. Stavrou took this in and immediately realised it would be folly to resist. On Christou's bark he stopped dead in his tracks. After a moment, his whole body seemed to relax and he turned towards the soldiers and smiled. His resigned shrug spoke volumes.

Christou came towards him, staring at the tall rugged man with the rough-handsome features, jet black hair just greying at the temples. His body, once obviously athletic, was still powerful, but now his stomach jutted rather severely in a combination of middle-aged spread and too much *halloumi*. He almost looked pregnant, but the equally prominent bulge in the bottom of his Y-fronts proved that this would never be possible. On recounting the episode some years later, Christou was to liken him to "A massive, proud bullock."

The Commander walked over and picked up the machine gun from the chair. He looked at it for a moment and then threw it to one of his men and turned back to Stavrou.

The captive seemed to read his thoughts, for without being asked his brown eyes sparkled with pride and what almost looked like delight as he announced, "Yes, I am Syros."

"Of course," Christou said respectfully. "You could not be anybody else, Major." He lowered his gun and felt inside a breast pocket of his camouflage shirt. He pulled out a packet of *Camel*. "Cigarette?"

Stavrou laughed softly. "Why not? I am sure cancer is now the least of my worries."

"The very least." Christou put two cigarettes into his own mouth and lit them both. He removed one, and Stavrou, being wise enough not to move his hands from their position by his sides, accepted it with his mouth.

"Anybody else here?"

"Only me and the woman."

"I see." Christou walked back towards the door. "Guard him well," he ordered the three soldiers, as much for Stavrou's benefit as their's. "If he tries *anything*, kill him. I am just going to have a look around. If you will excuse me, Major?"

Stavrou inclined his head.

There were three untried doors in the corridor. The first was another bedroom, unslept in and devoid of human presence. The second door, opposite, was a third bedroom. This one showed signs of use the previous night, the bed unmade and two empty *ouzo* bottles next to it. There was nobody in the room, but presuming Stavrou and the woman had spent the night in the first bedroom, then there must be a third person about somewhere. And there was one room unchecked.

By logical deduction, Christou figured that this last room must be the bathroom. He threw his cigarette down as he approached, listening intently for any noise from within. There was none.

And then there was.

One soft, dull thud.

Christou smiled. He was now standing next to the closed bathroom door and the smell of burning was quite distinct.

Standing to one side, he gently knocked on the door.

"Good morning, my friend - or is it afternoon? This is Commander Christou, Tactical Reserve Force. I wonder if you would oblige me? Will you come out? Or does this nasty weapon I'm holding shred the door and you with it?"

There was no reply from within.

"And don't even think about going out the back way. There are a lot of bad men out there with even bigger guns." Cautiously, Christou turned the knob, making sure he was well concealed. A gentle push made the door swing slowly open.

Crouching low, he peered round the doorway. One look and he straightened up, laughter bursting from his mouth.

Standing there, metal waste bin with smouldering contents at his feet, was a man some five years or so younger than Stavrou. He was of the same rugged physical complexion, but without the pot belly as yet. And he was completely naked. And, most curiously of all, he had a semi-erection. Either that or he was hung like Priapus.

By the side of the waste bin stood a whole pile of intriguing-looking documents which he had not a hope in hell of burning even if he had not been discovered for another hour.

To the Commander it was an hilarious sight. He pointed his gun at the man's lower stomach. "Weapon cocked, I see ? Come on, let's be having you."

Christou's sense of satisfaction turned to euphoria later that day when it was discovered that the naked man was none other than Demetrakis Spourghitis, one of Grivas' top lieutenants, suspected of being Number

Three in the organisation.

To capture Numbers Two and Three of EOKA, Christou thought, was much much more than the health of General George Grivas could stand. In the last two days they - the Special Police and the Tactical Reserve Force - had captured twenty-six EOKA terrorists and over four hundred highly illuminating documents, including a detailed plan to assassinate Makarios on his daily journey from the Archbishopric to the Presidential Palace. The release by Grivas of Justice Minister Kristos Vakis must now be inevitable. Grivas had given and taken some beatings in the past but he could not, surely, ever recover from this?

As it was, Commander Christou was absolutely correct. Grivas was already consumed with a terminal heart disease, but it is still maintained by some that the shock of losing his Numbers Two and Three as well as twenty-four of his other top men was the straw that eventually broke his brave resistance to the illness.

With Stavrou gone, Grivas felt isolated from his organisation. He tried bravely to fight back, indeed the next day he issued a leaflet containing an eloquent personal attack on Makarios, 'Mr Mouskos' as he referred to him (for Grivas refused ever to recognise Makarios' title, either as Archbishop or President). In the leaflet he denied that there had been any plans to assassinate the Archbishop "That well-known arch-cook of black propaganda."

And even as the leaflets were being distributed on the streets, the remnants of Grivas' organisation were trying to ingratiate themselves with their now isolated leader by causing minor disturbances in and around Nicosia. In a pro-Grivas club in the city, a fifteen minute gun battle was waged; in a suburb a car was blown up by a crude bomb. Shots were fired at a petrol station in Larnaca, and other minor incidents occurred. But this violence was like the bite of a dog with its teeth removed.

Grivas was devastated. It was the end for him, the end of his life. By the time EOKA could blossom and grow again - as he knew he could make it do - he would be dead, and what would happen to his precious cause and followers then? *Enosis* - complete union with Greece - would probably fade away and Cyprus would be independent forever...

Had Grivas lived, the course of the 'coup' on the island the following July might have taken a turn far different from that which is now recorded historical fact. As it was, it was only a matter of weeks after the arrest of Stavrou, on January 27 1974, that General George Grivas, considered by some to be a terrorist and by others to be a hero, died.

But before his death he was to make one staggering last request. A request almost childlike in its spitefulness; for one last deeply personal victory against Makarios, to hurt Mr Mouskos for years to come. To give Grivas a triumph from beyond the grave.

And there was only one person in the world that Grivas wanted to carry out his request...

PART ONE

Ψ

OBJECTIVE

Ψ

Monday December 24 1973

"Independent Radio News, it is nine o'clock. The bombings in London. London was on full alert tonight after the bombs near Charing Cross Station and Whitehall two nights ago. Despite late-night Christmas Eve opening, Oxford Street, already a prime target for the bombers, was almost deserted by eight o'clock this evening."

Somewhere in the Irish Republic

With a bounce of her naked breasts, the girl sprang from the edge of the board and made a perfect dive into the deep end of the indoor swimming pool. Although the water was a pleasant twenty-two degrees celsius, the shock of the wetness on the naked curves of her young body made her nipples harden instantly.

Outside it was decidedly cold, as befits a Christmas Eve in Southern Ireland, but Michael Mahoney felt himself warming as he looked through the glass wall of the pool and admired the parting of the girl's legs as she crawled across the water. He smiled a wide, Irish smile and looked at the man standing next to him, heavily muffled against the chill of the two degree air.

"By golly, but she's a lovely girl."

The man nodded politely.

"I hope she... entertained you well last night?"

The man's face brightened as thoughts of last night flashed through his mind. He looked at Mahoney.

"Elizabeth was... what shall we say? Exquisite? Yes, that is the word. Purely exquisite. So charming, so... willing."

Mahoney beamed, cheeks rosy in the Atlantic breeze. He spoke quietly yet in exclamation. "Good on yer, Lizzie O'Toole. Yer a darlin' girl!" He looked at the other man. "Of course, she's available again for you tonight. And there's also a special gift for you, to mark what I hope will be the successful conclusion to our business."

The man raised an eyebrow. "Why, Mr Mahoney, I do believe you are about to offer me a bribe."

"A bribe? Me?" Mahoney's face oozed with geniality. "Heaven forfend, my dear sir. Indeed t'goodness, if it's one thing I've learned in my business it is never to offer a bribe to an Arab. Arabs are gentlemen, above that sort of thing."

The other man gave no indication that he knew the compliment was merely rhetoric sarcasm.

"No, no, listen," Mahoney continued, his breath smoking in the freezing air. "Yer've got t'stay until the twenty-sixth now before you can catch yer plane, so for the next two nights - whether our business is successful or not - I've arranged for Lizzie and her sister Philomena to entertain you in the evenings. My little Christmas present to yer. How's that?"

The bronzed skin of the Arab's face tightened as he smiled faintly. "Most... hospitable. You are the perfect host."

Behind the glass, the girl reached the side of the pool and stopped swimming. Her left hand held on to the metal bar as her right reached down between her legs. She smiled wickedly. Slowly, with circular motions, she began to rub herself...

The two men watched in silence. At the end, as the girl floated sated on top of the water, they turned away and began to walk towards the cliffs, a kilometre away.

After a while the Arab said, "And you own all this land?"

"Every last stone in the cliff." Mahoney put up his collar. "And I'd even have bought me own bit of the Atlantic Ocean if I could, but Eamonn de Valera wouldn't let me - and Childers ain't much help either."

The Arab sniffed. "I knew arms dealing was profitable, but your wealth surpasses anything I could have imagined."

Mahoney stopped in mid-stride. For just the slightest moment the guise of the simple, jolly Irishman slipped from his face and something cold and calculating was exposed. Then almost immediately the geniality was back. "Me? An arms dealer? What nonsense you do talk, Akay. I'm a businessman, that's all, and highly successful with it. Can I help it if the spirit of free enterprise has smiled on me? Painter and decorater, that's what I am." *Idiot wop.* Didn't he realise that there were such things as bugs and long-range voice detectors? Members of the Irish Special Branch, the sly boys of the *Garda*, could be listening to what they were saying from fifteen kilometres away.

The half-smile which seemed to be a permanent feature of the Arab's face did not falter at what was obviously an oblique slap across the knuckles. He gave a half-bow to his host. "Of course. Do forgive me."

Mahoney looked at him. Then he grinned and clasped Akay around the shoulders with a deceptively powerful right arm, an action which the Arab disliked intensely. "Nothin t'forgive, me ole stick," he put on his thickest brogue. "Of course, if it's business yer want t'discuss - and now's as fine a time as any, I must admit - then we'd best be getting back to the house. Constitutional over."

Mahoney steered the Arab in a tight semi-circle to take them back the way they had come.

To call Mahoney's abode a 'house' was an understatement. It was a mansion. Built from red-brick some five years before, it had cost Mahoney the best part of one hundred thousand punts, and in 1968 that had been a lot of money. It contained every domestic amenity money could buy, and included eight bedrooms *en suite*, spread across the three storeys. To any curious outsider, Mahoney would explain that he could afford such a luxury as this (and also his white Rolls-Royce Corniche, maroon Jaguar XJ6 and black and gold Mini Cooper) through sheer hard work and excellent management of his painting and decorating empire. This was only half true, the whole truth being much more sinister.

Born in County Cork in 1935, Mahoney had led a normal Irish childhood, progressing from teddy bears to toy cars to toy trains to toy soldiers to sport to books to dirty books to groping girls and finally to the ultimate anticlimax of a first sexual experience - just like any other male child in Ireland, or indeed the whole wide world. A spell in the British Army fighting the Mau-Mau in Kenya was followed by a return home and a job in a cousin's painting and decorating company. The company grew steadily and successfully.

Then one day, as they were painting the outside of someone's house, the cousin fell off the scaffolding, landed on his head and was dead before his feet had followed him to the ground. Michael was inconsolable - it could so easily have been him. The slightest wrong foot, *the slightest push*, and *he* could have been in the arms of the Lord right now. Still, his grief was not so great that it stopped him assuming full control of the company.

It was not long after when fate was to change his life and bring him money beyond even his wildest dreams.

He had been working one weekend decorating the house of a recently widowed neighbour. *God, but wasn't death everywhere?* There would be no charge, of course, as a sign of respect - and anyway what did a couple of days free labour matter when you already had over half a million in your personal account? The widow, a woman in her forties, had asked him to have a look through her late husband's things and if anything took his eye he could have it as she would no longer have any use for anything of her dear departed, God rest him. Mahoney did not really care for going through a dead man's belongings but, grimacing with distaste, he had done so just to please the woman.

Up in an unused bedroom there were shirts, suits, shoes, ties and various books packed into a large box.

The woman had gone downstairs to make some tea, and he was alone when he found the heavy brown paper bag in the bottom of the box. He had opened it cautiously. Inside, much to his astonishment, was a gun - a *Browning 1922 .32*, manufactured by *Fabrique Nationale* of Herstal, Belgium, as he was later to find out. It was in a bad condition, but he decided to keep it, smuggling it out of the house in his donkey jacket that night.

He had been an expert with arms in the army and it did not take him long to clean up the weapon and restore it to perfect working order. Casually mentioning it to an acquaintance in a bar one evening after work, he had been shocked when his drinking companion had asked him if he wanted to sell it.

"Sell it?" he had pondered. "Might as well. I've really no use for the thing."

Two days later, in his office in Duke Street off Grafton Street in Dublin, Mahoney had been visited by a rather dark-looking gentleman with a broad Belfast accent. He was keen to see the gun and, after a cursory initial inspection, he offered Mahoney one hundred punts for it. Mahoney had been staggered but, with his usual air of bluff confidence, he accepted the offer.

The visitor had asked him if he could get his hands on any more. Never one to miss a good business opportunity, Mahoney had said that indeed to goodness he probably could and would the honourable gentleman be wishing to place any orders with him? There had been no positive response, just a simple maybe. Nevertheless, Mahoney knew that he had found a way to make himself a very rich man, richer than he could ever be with his painting and decorating concerns. It was 1969 and the troubles in Northern Ireland were escalating horrendously. There was a market just sitting waiting for him, a whole new field to be conquered.

Using contacts from his army days, it had taken Mahoney six months to make the breakthrough on the supply side. Tentative feelers which had been put out in the direction of various embassies and other concerned parties - and which included two unexplained deaths and several trips to an undisclosed destination abroad - eventually paid off. Mahoney had been able to grasp the IRA and Protestants in both hands. He could supply them with arms, all sorts: big guns, small guns, bombs and bomb-making equipment and even field artillery and smaller, more sophisticated devices of death. Mostly Russian - either Russian from Russia, Russian from Libya, Russian from Africa - and, for much higher prices, arms from most other countries as well.

It had cost him all the capital he had, including three mortgages on his thriving business and two on his then semi-detached house in Howth, but in one year he was to recoup that investment ten-fold.

Now, four years later, he was considered one of the most trusted and reliable black market arms dealers in the world, and he had indeed cornered the Northern Irish market, supplying most of the needs of all the terrorist factions operating there.

His visitor that Christmas 1973 remains something of a mystery. His name was Ali Al Khalifa. At that time he was the Financial Controller, the Mister Fixit, of the military arm of the Palestine Liberation Organisation known as Black September. Apart from these few facts, nothing is known about him.

"Drink?" asked the Irishman, pulling open a drawer of the desk. They were sitting in Mahoney's office, a specially constructed windowless room in the basement of the house. In the background, air conditioning hummed with determination. "Oh no, I forgot. You don't, do you?" As he lifted the bottle of poteen, Mahoney's hand brushed against a small button in the side of the drawer. From that moment on, everything said in the room would be recorded.

Caring not for niceties, Mahoney swilled directly from the bottle. When he looked back at Al Khalifa, his manner had changed. The bluff Irishman had gone, the accent disappearing noticeably. "Now, I believe you were after something special?"

"Correct," responded the Arab. "And you have been recommended to us as being a specialist in providing what to most is unprovidable."

"God, but you're an expert in brown nosing Akay. If Kissinger was to give up his job tomorrow, you'd be his natural successor. The Belgian recommended me, so you said?"

"Yes."

"A good fellow is Jacques. Been in business far longer than I have. Knows his onions. And his Kalashnikovs. I'm surprised he has not tried to accommodate you himself."

"For Europe, he is excellent," nodded Al Khalifa. "But the event which our Operational Services is planning is to take place more to the north. We required a more local supplier and, once the Belgian had heard of our requirements, he said that you were the only possible man to help us."

"O'Connell will never let your boys into Ireland alive."

"O'Connell already knows all about it. We would not dare to approach his arms supplier without his prior permission. And we are not concerned with Ireland." The statement could not have been more blunt nor its implication more obvious.

A broad, crescent smile spread across Mahoney's face. "Well, well, well - so its The Bastards you're going for! You'll have a tough job, son, bloody tough. You were lucky to get Leila Khaled back alive, and you know it." He rubbed his nose. "And what use was she by the time they had finished with her?"

The Arab did not comment.

"Exactly what is it you want?" continued Mahoney.

"Some small arms for the personal defence of a unit of five men - "

".38 are my personal favourites. .44 magnums are quite handy little things too. I also do a nice line in the Russian Tokarev Model 30 - similar to the Browning."

"Preferably British Army issue."

Mahoney nodded. "They're yours. Actually, I can go one better than that. How about British *police* issue?"

The Arab permitted himself a full smile. "Excellent. Also we would like other personal weapons, knives and such like."

Mahoney held up his hand. "Leave it all to me. Complete personal equipment for a unit of five men. I'll give you the works." His hand came down via the bottle of poteen and he held it in his lap. "But you can get the equivalent of those items anywhere. You said you wanted something unprovidable. So hit me with it." He swilled from the bottle.

"Twelve pounds of plutonium."

The poteen sprayed backwards out of the Irishman's mouth as he shot forward in his seat.

"JEYSUS CHROIST!"

He began to cough violently, and it took a good two minutes of back-slapping by a concerned Al Khalifa to make sure that the Irishman did not pass on at that very moment. The first words Mahoney uttered when he had recovered were to do with the devil's domain and the sex act.

Ψ

Tuesday December 25 1973

"Reports are coming in from Norway of an accident involving a Hull trawler which is said to have hit the rocks in a fjord. Three trawlermen are unaccounted for."

Somewhere in the Irish Republic

Of the two men, Al Khalifa enjoyed that Christmas night the best. The pliable breasts, juddering thighs and pilose organs of the salacious sisters, Elizabeth and Philomena, had served him well. The last thing he remembered before the ever-wanting hands of sleep had dragged him forcibly away from the two Irish girls had been the lower half of Philomena's body descending onto his face.

Mahoney had slept alone - indeed, he had hardly slept at all - and he had arisen at 06:00. 'Twas Christmas Day and this afternoon his annual 24-hour party began. Some two hundred friends, relatives and simple hangers-on were expected to turn up.

But he had more important things on his mind. The staff could accommodate the thirty caterers especially employed for the party; but it was he, Michael Mary Mahoney, who had to accommodate Ali Al Khalifa and, by inference, Black September.

So, Black September was going to explode a nuclear device in Britain. The thought was outrageous, almost impossible to comprehend. Yet the idea was so simple. Just like that other simple idea the Arabs had recently discovered - the oil weapon (that had really shown the true face of most western nations when they had dropped their support of Israel almost overnight and had gone crawling to the Jews' enemies).

It is relatively simple to make a nuclear bomb. The Arabs undoubtedly had the right technical know-how, or could get hold of it (an Ivan perhaps? It was rumoured that they were behind the discovery of the oil weapon). The main ingredient required is forty pounds of enriched uranium or twelve pounds of plutonium; it will make a bomb capable of killing thousands.

And it is not all that hard for the right person to lay his hands on the right amount of the stuff. After all, Mahoney thought to himself, the Kerr-McGee Corporation in Oklahoma had at times been unable to account for upwards of sixty pounds of plutonium, and it could take as long as six months for such a loss to be discovered under the current detecting procedures of the American Atomic Energy Commission. That was just one possible source but, of course, with the inherent transportation problems he must try for a source nearer to Britain.

France perhaps? Now there was a thought. The ailing Georges Pompidou had, unknowingly, supplied him with arms on more than one occasion in the past. With the French so tetchy about world reaction to their own nuclear explosions in the Pacific, it might be possible to 'persuade' someone there to turn a blind eye whilst twelve pounds of a certain substance grew legs.

For four hours Mahoney walked about the green, rolling Irish countryside, pensive, swilling in vast lungfuls of the sharp Christmas air. It was not until 10:00 that he returned to the mansion, a much happier man.

It was about that time that Al Khalifa was waking up alone in the massive bed of one of the guest suites. He wondered if last night had been real or just a dream. There was no vestige of the sisters to be found, not even any naughty marks on the sheets, and it was only a dull soreness in a certain part of his anatomy where he had been rubbed raw that assured Akay that he had just spent one of the most pleasurable nights of his life.

Forty minutes later, as Al Khalifa walked down the stairs, fully washed, shaved and dressed (it was his custom not to breakfast), he was accosted by an ebullient Mahoney charging down the passageway,

"Akay! Akay, my dear, dear fellow. Merry Christmas to yer, and all that. God bless ye merry gentlemen!"

"Good morning, Michael."

"Yer just the person I wanted t'see. Come." Mahoney grabbed him by the arm and steered him downstairs to the office, ignoring the grimace on the Arab's face.

"Sit down, sit down," beamed Mahoney as he went around to his seat, the half-full bottle of poteen appearing in his hand as if by magic.

"You seem... happy," observed Al Khalifa, straightening his sleeve.

"Ah, indeed t'goodness," Mahoney nodded. "I had a long walk this morning, my friend. To think over your request and clear my mind."

"And?"

"Oh, I can get it, of course. I haven't contacted my friends yet - why should I worry them on Christmas Day, for God's sake?" He laughed. "For God's sake - good one, eh? But twelve pounds of the very best plutonium will be yours."

Al Khalifa nodded his approval. "That is good. Gratifying. But of course your ability to supply the item was never in doubt."

"Ah now I think there's just a touch of the old Arab camel shit there, Akay," said the Irishman warmly. "I think we can take it as read that if I could not supply the goods after what you had told me of your plans - or at least intimated even if no direct statement was made - Michael Mahoney would not have been long for this world. Not that I'm casting any nasturtiums upon the morals of your organisation, of course, heaven forbid."

"Of course."

Mahoney took a long swig from the whiskey bottle. "And now we come to the other side of this little arrangement."

"The other side?"

"My fee."

"Ah yes. We are prepared to give consideration to any reasonable quotation."

Sure and I bet you are, thought Mahoney, but you'll be surprised what I've got lined up for you, me ole stick. He asked, "Would you be wanting this... substance, within any specified time limit?"

"We have no deadline or time limit," answered the Arab. "But of course the sooner it is obtained, the less chance there is of other parties finding out about our arrangement and speculating upon its eventual use."

"True, true. Speculation can be a terrible thing. As soon as is practically possible then. Can we agree that we are talking in the middle term?"

"That is acceptable."

"After all, twelve pounds of the stuff just cannot go missing overnight - the British are not as lax about it as the Yanks are. But you need not worry on that score. That is my business." He read the question behind Al Khalifa's raised eyebrow. "Oh yes, I shall be getting it from Britain. That's the simplest answer, is it not? You want to use it there, so I obtain it there. Saves all the fuss and bother about transporting the stuff over sea - and I'm sure the British Customs would want something more than an end-user certificate for our little baby!"

Al Khalifa gave a polite quarter smile. "Of what price were you thinking?"

"Price? Two million pounds. Sterling."

The Arab was quiet, staring at a point far beyond Mahoney's head. The Irishman was able to savour two gobfuls of the wicked booze during the silence.

Then the Arab asked, "That does not include the guns or equipment?"

"Correct. Those can go on a separate account, to be finalised at a later date. Put it on the slate, as they say."

More silence. The Arab's eyes were glazed, far away. Finally he looked back at Mahoney. "Two million sterling is a highly satisfactory figure, Mr Mahoney. In fact we had estimated somewhat higher than that. Are you sure you will not be underselling yourself? Or us?"

"No, no, Akay," reassured Mahoney. "You are right, of course. It is a low amount. But I've no wish to bankrupt you - although, let's face it, I appreciate that if you were to pay me in cash the money would probably be Russian or Libyan."

"*If* we were to pay you in cash?"

"Well, I didn't say cash, my friend. You just asked me the price. I looks at it this way. I am, with all due modesty, a very rich man. What's another two million in one of my eight Swiss bank accounts? I'll probably never spend all the money I have in them already. Yes, I have undersold and I'll tell you why. I don't want your money. I want payment in kind."

"In *kind*?" The Arab looked perplexed. "And what might that be?"

Mahoney smiled. "In exchange for twelve pounds of plutonium, I want *The Star of Sierra Leone*."

Ψ

Thursday January 3 1974

"Demonstrations by Basque Nationalists continue for the second day in Spain, following yesterday's swearing-in of Señor Arais Navarro as Prime Minister. The ex-police chief takes over from Admiral Carrero Blanco who was assassinated two weeks ago."

Beirut, Lebanon

Looking back from the twenty-first century, it is hard to recall Beirut before the civil wars. Back in the early 1970s, before the madness took hold and the name of the city became synonymous with destruction and despair, Beirut was one of the most sophisticated and cosmopolitan cities, not only in the Middle East but in the whole world. Not for nothing was it called 'The Paris of the East'.

A chill winter's night had just begun, but upstairs in the *El Fateh* safe house near Sidani Street it was warm. In the dimly-lit room, five men were seated around a large oval table.

The men were: Ali Hassan Salameh, at that time controller of the intelligence and action arms; Salah Khalef (code-name Abu Ayad), co-founder of Black September and the group's *consiglière* (counsellor), and second to Arafat on the central committee of *El Fateh*; the number two of the *Fateh* intelligence agency, Jihad-al-Razd; Abu Jihad, the IRA liaison man; and Faisal Ibn Musaed, Hassan's personal assistant and protegé. *[For a brief history of Black September and* El Fateh, *see Appendix 2.]*

An atmosphere of tension, of expectancy, hung over the room. The five individual body odours were beginning to meet and meld into the stickly sweet-sour smell of humans *en masse*. It was 21:00.

"He should have been here by now." Abu Ayad, the second in command, darted his eyes from one to the other of his colleagues.

Nothing was said for a moment. Then the big, powerfully built Hassan looked up from the documents in front of him. He was chewing an item from a bowl of exotic candy on the table. He looked at his watch and grunted.

"He could have been delayed," suggested Abu Jihad, dragging on an over-stuffed cigarette which smelt distinctly of yak shit. "If he had to return via Britain he could have been delayed."

Abu Ayad turned to look at his small associate. "Yes, because of the trouble there. The 'Three Day Week' as they call it?"

"Quite."

"If only that stupid little country did not rely so much on coal." The intelligence man had spent three years at Oxford and therefore considered himself an expert on all matters Anglo. "*Oil.* That is their future power, their future prosperity. *Then* they will have no trouble with their communists."

Hassan kept his head down, but his voice was firm and definitive. "But you are forgetting, my brother. Once our operation is completed, Britain will have more, much much more, to worry about than any greedy miners or their future in oil. Indeed, if things go right - "

"Is there any reason why they should not?" snapped Abu Ayad.

Hassan looked up. The dark eyes flashed a warning. He said calmly, "Not in the execution of the operation, no. But who knows what the reaction of the British will be when thousands of them are... " He let the sentence float away. The merest trace of a frown flitted across his lined brow. He looked at his deputy. "You cause me concern, brother. You show an uncharacteristic caution." He stretched out a long, powerful left arm, extracted another candy from the bowl and crushed it between his teeth.

Abu Ayad glanced up at the leader and then looked away again. He sighed, talking to the centre of the table. "Yes, it is true. I have... a feeling that something... something..." He shrugged and raised his head. "It is nonsense, of course. It is this city. It was foolhardy to return here so soon after the murder of our brothers."

"This is, then, perhaps the safest place of all," ventured Abu Jihad.

The conversation continued for another twenty minutes. Only Musaed did not speak. He just sat there on the left of Hassan at the top of the table, taking it all in, his dark face confident, almost benign, as if he was the tolerant parent watching children at play.

It was nearing 21:30 when the door opened, flooding the room with brighter light from the staircase outside. The final guard of a six-man praetorian, each of whom were heavily armed, held the door open for Al Khalifa to enter hurriedly.

Hassan rose. "Brother!"

"I am sorry about the delay," apologised Al Khalifa after they had kissed three times. "There was some trouble at the airport here with some Christian faction."

Hassan burst out laughing and looked towards Abu Ayad. "Three Day Week, huh?" The Number Two was also smiling, his normal confidence returning with the advent of the sixth man.

Hassan motioned Al Khalifa to a vacant seat.

"How did it go?" asked Abu Jihad. "Did the Irishman prove to be to our satisfaction?"

"Oh, undoubtedly. He is the ideal man, he can supply all our needs."

"Even the most important item?"

"It would appear so."

Abu Jihad looked at Hassan in triumph. "What did I tell you, brother?"

Hassan nodded. "Indeed, your Irish contacts have served us good. We must offer our thanks and reciprocations." He turned back to Al Khalifa. "Now, my brother, what is the price involved?"

"Two million pounds."

The sounds of astonishment from the men were as one. Puzzlement flashed across each face.

"That is incredible!" exclaimed the intelligence man. "The face value of the stuff is much more than that." There were murmurs of agreement.

"Amazing indeed," nodded Hassan. "Why is he underselling?" The question was sharp and to the point.

The financier was unpeturbed. He gave Mahoney's own explanation. "He tells me he has enough money. To accumulate more would be simply to make it worthless, to add more figures onto a piece of paper somewhere. He wants payment in kind."

"In kind?" asked Hassan. "What *kind*?"

"He wants a diamond."

"A diamond?"

"It is called, apparently, *The Star of Sierra Leone.*"

The room was quiet again. Not even the sound of breathing could be heard as the five brains computed the news.

Outside on the stairway, the guard shuffled his feet and farted loudly.

Abu Ayad was the first to speak, shaking his head in bewilderment. "And where is this fantastic diamond that is worth two million pounds?"

Al Khalifa shrugged. "He does not know for certain. As he said to me, it is up to him to supply the goods, it is up to us to supply the payment. He has heard of this diamond and he wants it."

Hassan looked questioningly at Abu Jihad. The latter grimaced in embarrassment. "This was not something foreseen by my contacts. They said Mahoney was a cash-on-delivery man."

"This will delay the operation considerably," grumbled Abu Ayad. "*If* we should go along with it. Do we not have any other supplier?"

"Not in that part of the world," replied Abu Jihad. "It is new territory for us."

"He said it would take some months for him to obtain the substance," continued Al Khalifa. "But he can supply it *in England*. All we need is to have the diamond and our assembly team ready when the time comes. There will be no transportation problems. And the price, apart from the inconvenience, is incredibly cheap."

"In fact," suggested the intelligence man, "if we were simply to take the diamond from wherever it was, it would cost us nothing at all in cash."

Hassan nodded. His elbows were on the table, fingers steepled together in front of him. "It is an interesting proposition. One, I think, for the foreigner?" His semi-query was directed at Abu Ayad, who nodded in agreement.

Hassan helped himself to another candy and chewed it noisily.

They continued talking, slowly coming to agreement.

Only Musaed had no input. He sat silently in his place, scribbling on a scrap of paper, as if he was taking minutes. When he had finished he looked up at the other five men, once again with that curious benign expression. It was as if he was detached from the rest of the group, distrait and looking at the proceedings from afar. As if he was an observer.

Ψ

Tuesday January 22 1974

"The Dublin Court of Criminal Appeal today dismissed the appeals of Kenneth and Keith Littlejohn, who were jailed last year for their part in an armed robbery on a Dublin bank in October 1972. The Littlejohns have claimed that they were working for British Intelligence at the time."

Houston, Texas, USA

In the nineteenth century, two New York property speculators bought 6642 acres of swampland in the south at $1.40 an acre. It was their intention to build 'a great center of government and commerce'.

On January 10 1901, the first of the world's oil-gushers spewed forth just a baccy-spit away at Spindletop. There followed the building of an inland port, rising from the murky Buffalo Bayou. And in 1962 came the Lyndon B Johnson Space Center, putting the place firmly within the knowledge of most people of the western world. The great centre of government and commerce had become a reality: Houston, Texas.

It was a usual winter in Houston in 1974, mild but irritatingly damp. But, on that Tuesday, at least one person in the city had much more to concern him than the weather.

Steve Graves was a tall, powerfully built, first generation American-Greek. He wore the thick black curly hair and *Zapata* moustache that were the fashion at the time. An oceanographer with one of the 250 local firms involved in underwater activities, he had just completed a morning's session in the Public Library trying to garner research material on a particular project. *Trying* to, because frankly his mind had not been on the job.

In all fairness, he had to admit that the last three hours would have to be written-off as wasted.

And it was all the fault of that letter. That damn letter that had arrived at his apartment that morning.

Steve left the library and walked down to Lamar. This was a lunchtime for walking, for he had a lot of thinking to do. A decision had to be made.

He pondered on which way to go. Left along Lamar to find himself somewhere to eat, or right and cross over Brazo and Bragby into Sam Houston Park? The peace and solitude of the park were what he needed right now, but the hunger pangs just would not go away. He headed left into town. Four blocks down he came to the junction with Main. Just past Foley's he found a hamburger joint and ensconced himself inside.

He sat there, mechanically eating his quarter-pounder with everything, French fries and root beer, staring out unseeing at the top of the Exxon building beyond Capital National.

At precisely 12:56 he reached the decision.

It was clear what he had to do. There was no real choice. Accept that and the problem was solved.

He would have to take time out from his job. *Gulf*'s exploration of the Gulf of Mexico would have to carry on without him for a while. Anyway, as a fully qualified oceanographer and saturation diver he could find work anywhere. The decision was made. He would go.

Just to ensure that his imagination was not playing tricks, that he was not suffering from a belated attack of the bends, he removed the air mail envelope from his pocket for the umpteenth time. The flap was sharp where he had ripped it open earlier.

Inside was a single ticket on the following day's *Air France 747* to Paris, and a slip of paper with a short, unsigned, printed message:

Grivas wants you.

Sally would be the problem, of course. Sally-Anne Bowker, the girl who shared his cramped downtown apartment and who had been the mainstay of Steve Graves' life for the past two years. How could he tell her that out of the blue that morning had come a letter from a terrorist leader on the other side of the world? How could he tell her that the letter requested his immediate presence? And how could he tell her that he *had* to go?

Sure, he often had trips away, sometimes at short notice. But this time, more than any of the others, he could not reveal the real reason why. No one must ever know. Indeed, it would be better that she did not know where he was going at all. But he had to tell her *something*, he could not just walk out on someone who was part of his life. He loved her, as much as any man loves his woman, but Sally had her place in the scheme of things - and her place was not within ten thousand miles of General George Grivas.

Steve left the *Gulf* offices at his usual time of 16:30 after a rather patchy and unsatisfactory afternoon's work. Forty-five minutes later he reached the apartment, as usual half an hour ahead of Sally. Quickly, he showered and changed.

At 17:45 she arrived home. She breezed through the door, her usual lively self, short cut hair in no real semblance of order, make-up on eyes only, clothes bright and attractive in flower-power style but awry. Thick-rimmed glasses gave the true school-marm effect. Balanced in her right hand were two exquisite but greasy-looking specimens from the nearby *JC's Pizza Parlor.*

"Hi, baby!" She walked over to the table by the window and plonked down her purchases on the waiting plates.

Steve was coming through the kitchen doorway, mugs in hand. "Hi, kid." He admired the taut ass underneath the bright blue skirt. "How was school today?" He kissed her lightly on the cheek, put down the mugs and grabbed two handfuls of bottom. He rubbed up against her.

She turned to him, going with the embrace. "Mmm. Steady on there, tiger. I need a shower. Let me get nice for you."

"I got some news today," he said as she walked towards the bathroom.

"Good news?" She left the door open and he watched her skirt fall to the floor.

"Well... Kid, they want me to go to the Mediterranean."

"The *Mediterranean?*" Her blouse was tossed into the laundry.

"Balaeric Islands. A new project they've just started."

She unhooked her bra but did not take it off, letting it hang, loosely cupping her small breasts. She looked at him and then smiled. Walking over, she placed her arms about his neck. "Gee, baby, that's great news. All expenses paid trip to the Med. Fantastic! Any idea when you're going? How long for?" She licked his left nostril.

Steve's arms were around her waist. Their lower halves pressed together and she could feel him growing. He looked into her eyes. "Tomorrow."

Sally's smile weakened and then recovered bravely. "Tomorrow? Gee, that's some notice. What's so important that you have to go tomorrow?"

He raised his right hand under her bra and began making circular motions with his thumb against her nipple. It needed little excuse to corrugate. Before he could tell another lie, she again asked "How long for?"

"I don't know. A month. Two months. Maybe longer."

Again the smile held bravely. "Well, that won't be too bad, will it?"

He was relieved. The worst part was over. "No baby, no it won't."

"Listen, Graves," she pulled away. "You've got a lot of packing to do. We gotta organise things."

"Bowker..."

"Is all the laundry done? Have they delivered?"

"Bowker..."

"You must tell me exactly what you're gonna do. But first, the pizzas! Don't let 'em get cold - "

"BOWKER!"

"Yes, Graves?"

"Fuck the pizzas." He ripped her bra down off her arms, at the same time undoing his zipper. He pulled her to him, crushing her right breast with his left hand and grasping her hard bottom with the other. Their mouths touched and in a moment his tongue was down her throat.

Her glasses fell to the carpet. She made no attempt to retrieve them.

When they surfaced for air she said, "Why should the pizzas have all the fun? Fuck me, too."

For the next hour, he did.

Somewhere in the USA

He did not look like a Jew.

Which, of course, was the whole point. None of the world-wide network of Israeli Intelligence operatives – male and female – looked recognisably Jewish. The best operatives had to look like they belonged. They needed to fit in, not to stand out.

The agent known to his Controllers by the code-name Digenis was tall, but not too tall. Dark haired, but not too dark. Strongly built, but not too strong. Not too handsome, not too ugly. He *fitted in*. An ideal operative.

As night fell, he looked up at the fourth floor front left window of the apartment block. A light came on inside and he could see shadows moving about. Inside the block people would be going on with their normal, everyday lives.

And so would he.

Except he was a spy.

A new mission was starting. His subject had been identified, his instructions had been received.

He was prepared.

Ψ

Wednesday January 23 1974

"In Athens, two Arab terrorists, said to be members of Black September, have been sentenced to death for the murder of five people and the wounding of 50 others at Athens Airport last August. It is unlikely that sentence will be carried out in the immediate future."

Houston, Texas, USA
Roissy, Paris, France

"Hello, this is Sally-Anne Bowker."

"Hi kid."

"Steve? Oh, Steve honey, hi! Where are you?"

"I'm at Charles de Gaulle waiting for my connecting flight. Thought I'd ring my baby to tell her I miss her. Hope I didn't call at the wrong time. Are you in the middle of a class? It's ten at night here."

"No, honey, I was having a break. I miss you too, y'know, and its only been half a day. Seems like a lifetime already. Has your *Gulf* contact met you yet?"

"Just - he's outside the booth now, so I can't delay."

"Any more news of exactly where you're going? Which island will you be staying on?"

"Er... sorry kid, it's a bad line."

"Which island will you be on?"

"Oh, er, Minorca I think he said."

"You will write, won't you?"

"Sure I will."

"Phone if you can. And give me an address."

"The first thing I'll do when I get there."

"I love you baby."

"I love you too, kid."

"Take care of yourself for me."

"I will - and save *your*self for me."

"Why mah deeyer sir, what*ever* do you mean?"

"I'll show you when I get back. Bye now, Bowker."

"Bye Graves - I love you!"

Steve replaced the receiver and stood looking at it for a few seconds. He did not like lying, but in the circumstances he could do nothing else. She could never know the truth.

In fact, he had not been contacted by anybody as yet, and he now found himself at a loss as to what to do. If only that damn note had been more specific. If only that damn note had given him some explanation. If only that damn note had not come at all. If only it had said something other than *Grivas wants you*. But there had been nothing, just that and the ticket to Paris.

Well, he was here, now what? One thing was for certain, he could not stay staring at the payphone all night. He had to find somewhere to go. Charles de Gaulle Airport was a big, lonely and, on the evening of January 23 1974, very cold place.

After a few minutes wandering he found a far from busy snack-stall. He bought some delicious *café* and a packet of stale cookies, and found himself a place to eat on the transfer level (the mezzanine between the arrival and departure levels here in Terminal One).

He surveyed the people. There were the usual scurrying airline reps and workers, official-looking persons in uniform and the standard sluggish cleaners, all of which were synonymous with every major airport in the world. He looked at the other persons, the travellers, the meeters, the farewellers, most of whom were obviously French. The elderly men and women, heavily but elegantly dressed against the threatened snow; the middle-aged businessman, again sartorially immaculate, greying temples an appropriate frame to a slightly worried countenance, *Gauloises* being chain-smoked; the obligatory young man in denims, possibly from university, the customary scarf flung around his neck, reading some activist newspaper; the young woman with the long, glossy hair, almost devoured by an incredibly expensive full-length fur, obviously the mistress of someone with money. It was the embodiment of France on one concourse.

The cookies were eaten and the last dregs of coffee swilled down. Moments later he noticed a shapely pair of legs approaching from his left. Their owner was a dark, Mediterranean woman in her late twenties, straight black hair parted on the right and falling to just below her shoulders. Big eyes, black and mysterious, looked out from a handsome olive-skinned face. An ample figure was covered by a short denim skirt and a denim jacket fastened to the neck against the cold.

Steve crumpled his cup and scored a direct hit into a nearby waste bin. He smiled and pulled his own leather jacket tighter against his body and looked back at the woman. This one was definitely not French and, like him, had not come prepared for a stopover, however brief, in the middle of a Parisian winter. He wondered where she was going. Obviously to somewhere where the weather was more agreeable. Just as he would be.

What was she? Another mistress of some lucky bastard? An *au pair*? An *Avon* lady?

He frowned when he realised. Of course! She was coming directly towards him.

She stopped in front of him. Steve stood up. They looked each other in the eyes without speaking. The magic passed between them.

She said, "Stelios." It was a statement not a question. Her accented voice was deep, almost hoarse, and sensually feminine, but brittle, as if she was troubled by some deep emotion.

"Yes. What news? Why does he want to see me?"

"It iss not good, not good at all." A wetness rose in the two beautiful black eyes. "Come. Our flight leaves from Orly. There iss a taxi waiting."

Steve picked up his small bag and they moved off, their footsteps echoing off the synthetic flooring. "It is not good?" he queried.

She did not look at him as she spoke. "He would not send for you except for the final emergency, that wass the promise. Well, the final emergency hass arrived. Efen now it may be too late."

They reached the travelator and stepped into the totally enclosed glass tube. They stopped walking as the 'flat escalator' replaced their legs.

"So, the end is here, huh?" Steve's voice was sullen.

"We must pray that he holdz on, at least until you get there. He so badly wants you there."

Steve touched her on the arm. He looked at her, a million questions in his eyes. For a moment she seemed at a loss.

As they reached the end of the travelator, she said hurriedly "We must waste no time."

"Just a minute," he stopped her in mid stride. "What are you called?"

"*Tee?*"

"What is your name?"

"*Eh mee* Christina - Christina Cascianis."

"Christina Cascianis," he nodded.

"And you," she said softly. "You *are* Stelios."

And there, on the public concourse, she took his right hand in hers, raised it to her lips and kissed it.

Yeri, Nicosia District, Cyprus

The small lizard emerged from the cover of the long grass and froze in its tracks. It stared through the weak moonlight at the villa and outhouse a few hundred metres ahead. The place was in darkness except for the very faintest of diffused lights filtering through the shutters of an upstairs window. All was quiet and only the almost unnoticeable clicking of a group of cicadas disturbed the cool night air.

The lizard sniffed, realised there was nothing to interest it out here, and turned and scampered back into the grass.

The one softly lit room of the villa was a bedroom, but the two occupants were far from asleep. They were both nearing the ultimate ecstasy of orgasm.

The girl, the fifteen year old daughter of one of the farmers of the nearby village of Yeri, was unattractive facially and she even possessed the beginnings of a moustache. Nevertheless her body was ripe and of some substance, huge black-nippled breasts, plump but soft tummy and a down of the smoothest black fur trickling down from her navel and blossoming into a tropical forest between her legs. And big, rock hard thighs which were now spread far apart and were trembling as she thrust her pelvis up to receive the full length of the dick that was being rammed into her.

The owner of that organ was also of some substance, but in his case the body was powerful and solid, muscular without even a hint of fat. It was a body which had been trained well, in the special school at Ochakov on the edge of the Black Sea, and it was kept in perfect condition by regular and rather savage physical exercise of which the owner considered this two hour session of sex - which was just coming to a close with her sixth and his second orgasm - to be part. In contrast the face, now beaded with splashes of perspiration, was round and, to some eyes, chubby. It was a boyish face which served its purpose well by being the perfect camouflage for the power of the body underneath. The hair was short, black and wavy, pushed back.

On a table by the side of the bed were the tinted, plain glass spectacles which he always wore (except on occasions such as this), for his eyes were sensitive to the light.

The girl gave a half-scream half-sigh as she lost control as she climaxed. The man continued pushing for another fifteen strokes before he emitted a deep grunt and nearly ruptured her with a final thrust which held his organ tight inside her body until it had emptied itself.

He lay on her, his breathing fast and even. Then, abruptly, he rolled off, a job done.

The girl knew better than to talk at a time like this. She just lay there savouring the very last tingling sensations. She wondered if she would ever be able to move her legs back together again. Her anus was sore.

Ilich Ramirov put his hands behind the back of his head and brought his breath under control. His eyes were open, staring at the ceiling. He was twenty-four years of age, looked thirty-four, and had been born on October 12 1949 in Panfilovo, a village in central Russia. His mother had come from far-eastern Russia, near the borders with China, and his father, a man from

Rostov in the Ukraine, had liaised with his mother just once while passing through Panfilovo, and Ilich had been the result.

Although a normal-looking child, Ilich's ability to catch weasels and stoats with his bare hands - and his obvious pleasure as he slowly twisted their necks round and around until the whole head snapped off, or hung them up by their hind legs, made the smallest of slits in their necks with his knife, and watched them bleed so very slowly to death, writhing and squealing in agony - did not go unnoticed by his local party member. Word spread up the line from the local member to the district member to the area member and ever onwards. By the time he was ten years old, Ilich was being discreetly watched by two dark and nondescript gentlemen from Moscow.

As fate would have it (and it had it a lot in the Russia of the post-war), Ilich's mother died shortly after her son's eleventh birthday. She passed away from injuries received after part of a tree had fallen on her during a walk in the woods to the north of Panfilovo. The State descended with remarkable rapidity on the orphan boy and he was whisked away into care to a suburb of the capital.

For the next seven years, Ilich underwent specialised 'schooling', the subjects upon which it would be wise not to dwell. Suffice it to say that he emerged on his eighteenth birthday not only as a super-efficient killing machine but also a master-agent, co-ordinator, organiser, tactician and executioner, the top in the field of all things subversive. The greatest – and youngest – success story of Academy Number 311.

In the early nineteen-seventies he became the first 'itinerant agent', given carte blanche by his Russian masters to give every assistance he could to any 'resistance' group which requested it. His only restriction was that he had to submit a detailed monthly report on his activities to Moscow.

Ramirov was based in this comfortable but not opulent villa on the outskirts of Yeri village, entirely supported by the KGB's vast reserve of foreign currency - in this case Cyprus pounds. He was known only to a few select leaders of 'resistance' groups: the Arabs, the Japanese and the Germans being his main clients. In early 1974, Ramirov did not yet consider the IRA and the Italians worthy of his attention. Also at this time, his presence in the form of there being just one co-ordinating force behind the increasing global terror attacks was suspected by western powers, but he was far from being known in person.

Ramirov grimaced in distaste as the girl next to him began to snore. A fart slipped softly from her distended rectum. He considered his position. A meeting with Baader-Meinhof supporters two days ago in Bavaria had ended satisfactorily with plans - his own plans - for a *Lufthansa* hijacking carefully worked out down to the last detail. That would please Furtseva in the monthly report. Something would be said about the fact that he had failed to kill Sieff in London at the end of December, but he could gloss over that. Apart from that one little incident, things were going well.

So why couldn't he sleep?

It was not the noise of the girl or the insidious odour of her gas. It was nothing external. Something was going to happen, he knew. He had inherited this sixth sense from his mother and it rarely let him down.

It was not until 11:00 the following morning that he was to receive the first signs. A visit to the *poste restante* in Nicosia revealed three letters waiting for him under the name of Martinez. Two of the letters were of little consequence but the third, postmarked Roma, looked of great interest. Ramirov, always cautious, waited until he was back in his villa before giving the letter further attention.

He knew already what the Rome letter would contain, nevertheless he still opened it, inclining his head to one side as he did so, a curious habit of his. Inside was the expected blank sheet of sepia A4 parchment.

A letter from Rome was the signal that the Arabs wished to see him. The place would be one of three newly vetted safe houses in Beirut, dependent upon the value of the stamp furthest to the right on the envelope. It was 300 lire, therefore it would be the third of the three addresses he had. The date would be twenty-eight days from the date of the postmark, January 11. So the appointment would take place on Friday February 8 at the house in the district of Borj El Barajneh, Beirut. The time was always 21:00.

Ramirov permitted himself an inner smile. Good, he was glad action was planned. He did not like periods of inactivity. The Arabs only called when one of their own men could not handle the job, when they needed his expertise. Therefore, as always, it would not be easy. But those were the sort of jobs he liked best.

So, his feeling of the night before had been correct.

And, without further thought that his sixth sense was ever wrong, not even in the slightest, Ramirov began to formulate his travel plans.

Ψ

Thursday January 24 1974

"There have been more bombs in London this evening. Three bombs exploded in Chelsea, causing extensive damage. There are no reports of any casualties at this time. Earlier today, a parcel bomb was thrown into an Israeli bank in the City, slightly injuring a typist."

Above the Mediterranean

The Olympic Airways DC10 was twenty minutes away from touchdown at Nicosia Airport. In the rear seats on the left side, the young couple smiled at each other, their hands brushing as they reached for their drinks.

His questions had started just after take-off. "So, tell me about Christina."

He had learnt of the Cypriot girl who had longed to get away from her native island and see the world; who had great hopes as a singer, performing in all the clubs in Famagusta, Nicosia and the other main towns. She was a popular attraction in concerts given for the British troops who, fourteen years after independence, still maintained a presence on the island. Ten years ago, when she was nineteen, she had been offered club work in Athens. She had been about to leave the island when her father had been taken by Makarios's soldiers.

Although a hardened supporter of Grivas and EOKA, Christina's father had never actively indulged in any form of 'resistance' against the Makarios regime - but this had not stopped the Archbishop's men from torturing him for non-existent information and then summarily killing him. She had thought he was being held somewhere in Nicosia; she had not heard of his death until three months after he had been killed. Her mother had been shattered by the news, and Christina vowed to stay with her on the island and fight, in any way she could, for the overthrow of the black-clad priest and for *Enosis*, union with Greece, the cause for which her father had been murdered.

She had started off running local messages for Grivas sympathisers and helpers. Slowly, over the years, she had been drawn into the web of the organisation. With Makarios inflicting defeat upon defeat on the General, annihilating or arresting his top men, she became closer and closer to the old man. He tended to confide in her a lot, treating her as a daughter, and he began to seek her opinions on his various plans and strategies.

When Syros and Spourghitis had been captured last autumn, she had realised that there was nobody left above her in line of personal contact with the General. By the process of elimination by Makarios, she had become the person closest to her leader, his only trusted contact with the outside world now that the disease had confined him to bed for the last time.

Steve had listened to the story. On the one hand she was virtually a mouthpiece for the ailing leader of EOKA - a tough, uncompromising job for anybody. And on the other hand she was a woman, interested enough in the subject of life in the States to have interrogated him at length, and cheeky enough to have asked him "And what about girlz? Are there plenty of those in America? You haf a girl?"

He had grinned. "Yes, there are plenty of girls." He looked at her teasingly, saying nothing else, making her re-ask the question.

"Do you..." She hesitated. "Do you haf a girl?"

"Yes," he smiled gently. "I do have a girl."

Christina's face did not move a muscle, but he could sense the struggle within. She did not want to ask but she just *had* to. "And... and this girl off yourz... she iss good looking?"

"She's okay, as good looking as any other girl... Just as you are."

She looked away, reddening, but with that coy, satisfied grin that is taught to every female at birth. Then with a sudden coldness that shocked him, she said "You may haf to forget her. I do not know what he wantz you to do, but he said it would be tough and would not be done quickly. You may be here for some time."

Steve looked out of the airplane window into the nothingness of night.

"You will not disappoint him?"

He turned back. "Of course not, not under any circumstances. How could I? If it has to be, then it has to be."

Now the seat belts sign flashed on as they approached Nicosia, and they both finished their third drink and obeyed the notice.

"What happens when we land?" Steve asked. "Will you be safe?"

"Oh yes. The Priest's men know I am with Grivas, but they do not know exactly what I do. They probably do not consider me worthy of picking up."

He smiled. "On the contrary, baby, on the contrary."

She tried to pretend to ignore the remark, but that grin crept across her face again. "There will be a car waiting for us. It will be a journey of one hour and a half into the mountains. Do not be afraid to be seen with us, they will find out about you eventually anyway. There should be no danger at this time. But iff you could try to control your American accent a little, it would help with our own people. They haf a distrust off anyone they haf not known for years, especially foreigners." It was her turn to smile. "But then, you are not a foreigner, are you? You are Stelios."

Steve made a show of quickly hiding his hands in his pockets before she could reach them, and they both laughed softly.

She placed her hand on his thigh, lent over and lightly kissed his cheek.

Troodos Mountains, Cyprus

The room, normally so bright in the scented early morning, was in shadows. A pair of heavy black curtains barred the entrance of the sun.

Tony Verekelis, a short, thick Cypriot, heavily Greek, entered the room quietly and looked at the small, grey, emaciated figure on the bed. He had survived the night, that was good, but his breathing was harsh and irregular. It would not be long now. Soon he would be no more. Tony shook his head. It was distressing to see a great man die.

Tony walked softly across to the small bedside table. He deposited the fresh glass of water, with lid and special drinking lip, ready for old mother Dimitri to give on request.

Tony turned, and as he did so Grivas opened his eyes. They were clear and bright, and seemed so big against the wasted face. They were the only sign of life on the otherwise exanimate island of his small body. He was looking straight at Tony.

"They... they are here?" The voice was only a whisper but it was clear enough to be heard in the silent room.

Tony hesitated in case the eyes closed and he drifted back again. They did not, and so he answered. "No sir, not yet. But we have word that they have arrived safely and are now on their way."

"They come..."

"Yes."

"They come..." The eyes closed.

Tony walked silently out of the room, passing old black-clad mother Dimitri as she shuffled her way in.

They came at 09:00, travelling by jeep. As they wound up the tracks into the mountain, Steve's body registered tiredness for the first time. It surprised him to calculate that he had not slept since the flight from Houston yesterday. The flight from Orly to Nicosia had been completely taken up with Christina.

But he relegated fatigue to the back of his mind as he savoured the sheer pleasure of early morning in the Troodos Mountains. It was winter but there was still plenty of green about, and the temperature could only have been three or four degrees. There would be snow higher up, Christina had told him. The air was crisp, clean and fresh, and the smell of the pine trees was exhilarating.

Soon they turned between the trees into a discreet narrow road. About a kilometre along they came upon the house.

They climbed out of the vehicle, shaking their stiff legs. For a moment Steve paused to take in the place, the small clearing, the white stucco walls of the two storey house. Then he said sadly, "So, this is where it will all end."

Christina looked at him but did not speak. Behind them the driver of the jeep reversed, turned around and quickly drove off the way they had come. Nearby, two other vehicles were parked, a Land Rover and a battered old Ford Consul of the early sixties.

As they reached the front door, Tony Verekelis appeared. He looked at Steve in silence, staring intently at his face. After a moment he nodded and said, "My God..." Then he reached out and with an iron grip pumped the American's right hand in greeting. "Stelios, *kahloss.*"

"Hi."

"Stelios, this iss Tony, Tony Verekelis," introduced Christina. "Tony helps out here - in fact I do nott know what we would do without him most off the time."

"I do my best," shrugged the Cypriot. "What with the departure of Syros and Demetrakis, and now... this." He shook his head. "But come, come."

The front door led into a spacious, white-walled room, bright and warm with that pervading smell of fresh pine.

"Should we see him now?" asked Christina. "How iss he?"

"He fades. But yes, you must see him as soon as you can. He has been asking for you."

"This way Stelios."

Steve followed the girl over to the stairs at the far corner of the room. Her tread was swift but soft on the unadorned boards.

Upstairs, seven doors led off the passageway which stretched from the front to the back of the house. Christina headed for the door at the end to the left, the room looking out front, to the south. She tapped gently and entered.

Old mother Dimitri looked up from her knitting. Quickly, she rose to her feet and scurried out of the room, pausing to look long and hard at Steve as she passed. She crossed herself and then closed the door softly behind them as they looked at the pathetic object on the bed.

After a moment Steve said lowly, "My God. This... this is the man?"

"This iss he."

On the bed, Grivas' eyes sprang open. "Stelios!" For a second the voice was loud and clear, as it always had been. Quickly Steve moved into view at the side of the bed.

"I'm here."

The pain in the body was so great now, Grivas could not even turn his head. But his eyes, the sole vestige of the once great life, sparkled with excitement as they met the American's.

It was a traumatic experience for both men. Their eyes filled with tears as they looked at each other. Steve sat down on the bed and gripped the grey, wizened left hand. For a full two minutes neither of them spoke. Then, swallowing hard, Steve greeted him in faltering Greek.

Grivas' cheeks twitched infinitesimally in what was probably the best he could do for a smile. When he spoke his voice was again a mere whisper. "Stelios... well... a fine man..." It was a great, almost superhuman effort for him to form the words. Steve leaned forward to hear. "What... voice - accent... after... these... years... underst... ble... course... Thank... you... coming... You will... stay now...?"

Steve gently squeezed the old man's hand. "Sure I'll stay. This is my home - even if I do have a foreign accent!" His laugh was sad.

Grivas' head nodded ever so slightly. "Help... however you can... Christi... good girl... good girl... my girl..."

Steve looked behind, but Christina's head was turned away as she sobbed quietly into her hands.

Suddenly Grivas' fingers tightened with surprising strength. "Stelios!" The whisper was urgent. "Listen... in case... there is no further chance... You came... for me... get something..."

Steve leaned closer as the voice grew weaker and weaker. His left ear was close up against the dry old lips.

"When... Grivas gone... get it for me... you must get... from Mouskos... get it... you must, you must!"

"What is it? What do you want me to get?"

The voice was only just audible now and the eyes had closed. "From Mouskos... you, must be you... get it... get... The Eye of Makarios!"

Grivas exhaled violently and the hand grew limp.

"Christina!" Steve span round, but she was already up to the bed and pushing him out of the way.

She grabbed the limp wrist and put her right ear to his chest. After a while she straightened up. "He iss still here - but only just."

"Jesus Christ." Tears fell unashamedly down Steve's face. He shook his head. "Why must it be like this? Why can't he just go in peace without pain?"

She sighed. "Death iss never easy, Stelios."

"Don't I know that," he said.

In fact Grivas had fallen into his last coma and he was never to regain consciousness. But life was to remain in his body for another two and a half days before his heart gave out and the excruciating pain stopped forever. It was ironic and, in some ways, tragic that the last word he ever said was "Makarios".

PART TWO

Ψ

OBJECTIVE TRACED

Ψ

Tuesday January 29 1974

"In California, a Los Angeles Superior Court today ordered President Nixon to appear in person to testify at the trial of his former Domestic Affairs assistant, Mr John Ehrlichman. It is reported that the President, who tomorrow delivers his State of the Union address, will not obey the order."

Troodos Mountains, Cyprus

Makarios had forbidden Bishop Gennadios of Paphos from holding the funeral in Limassol Cathedral, therefore it had been decided to bury Grivas in the grounds of the house in Limassol where the body had been transported the day before. Thousands were expected to pay their respects.

The attack therefore was completely unexpected, and most of the occupants of the house in the mountains were still in their beds when it started at 06:30.

No stealth had been employed this time. Three lorries had pulled up on the main road, blocking the route from all directions, and thirty members of Makarios's Tactical Reserve Force had spilled out and immediately vanished into the trees. They had their orders, they knew what to do. The house and everything and everybody in it were to be razed. Now Grivas was dead, it was thought this final assault would eradicate the core of the EOKA movement forever.

The soldiers ran through the trees, sub-machine guns poised, ready to shoot anything that was not wearing the camouflage uniform of the TRF. Their Commander, Christou, was among the front-runners. It was he who fired the first blast, shattering the downstairs windows of the house, glass and stucco shrapnel flying in all directions. At the first sound of shooting, the soldiers began to roar, almost as one, a wall of horrific sound from the vectors of death.

A face appeared at an upstairs window and was immediately disintegrated by a shower of bullets and glass.

Christou reached the already bullet-ridden front door and sprayed the heavy locks. Three kicks of his right boot and the door crashed inwards noisily.

A young girl who had been preparing breakfast ran in from the kitchen and was peremptorily executed by the Commander, the impact of the bullets spinning her around, mouth spraying blood like some obscene fountain. Old mother Dimitri also appeared from the kitchen and she suffered a similar fate, her old apron being ripped from her body by the burning lead.

The soldiers gushed into the house, some charging upstairs, others moving through the ground floor to take up positions outside at the back.

There were a few shouts from up above, ominously cut short by the gun-fire as the iron-tipped boots thundered through the building. Downstairs, the ceiling shook.

It had only been ten seconds since the first burst from the Commander's gun, and the young couple were still in bed together upstairs. They sat up staring in shock and horror as two of the TRF burst into the room. The girl's breasts turned into deep red pulp and the man's face dissolved as their lives were sprayed away with no more concern than a child would have in treading on an insect.

Tony Verekelis had awoken five minutes earlier and was just putting on his pants when the invasion started. His feet and top were naked. He knew what was happening and he did not hang around to make sure his suspicions were correct. His room faced out the back, towards the mountain. Without thought for physical safety, he wrenched up the window and jumped the seven metres onto the grass below.

He felt his left ankle turn horribly as he landed, but it was a few seconds before the pain seared up his leg. He staggered upright, tried to run and fell, and he knew that the ankle was broken.

At that moment the first of the TRF charged through the kitchen and out into the garden. Tony was lying to the side of the door, not immediately visible. By the time the soldier spotted him, Tony's knife (which he always kept in a sheath around the waistband of his pants) was coming upwards from where he lay. It was rammed into the soldier's genitals, yanked sideways and pulled out again. The soldier screamed in agony, and his trousers were immediately stained by a spreading patch of dark maroon. He looked as if he had pissed blood.

Tony caught the gun as it fell and turned it on his attacker and a second soldier who was just bounding through the doorway. The first man was already dropping with his castration, and the second man fell like lead.

With a supreme effort, Tony forced himself to rise and run towards the far fence. God, his ankle! He couldn't do it, he just couldn't do it. But he must. He must! His run was nothing more than a hobble, a fast hop, but he had to reach them, to warn them.

He looked around and fired as another soldier came through the kitchen door. The first burst missed but a second chopped the soldier's legs from under him.

Beads of perspiration, of pain, of effort, broke from Tony's brow, and he forced himself forward. He reached the low fence and flung himself onto it.

He was just about to drop down the other side when the back of his head exploded.

He never even heard the burst of gunfire. One moment he was alive, the next moment all was blackness. He did not even have time to realise he was dead.

He stayed upright for a moment and then fell, the right leg caught over the top of the fence. The body dangled like some grotesque sacrifice with its brains dripping out.

In the doorway, Commander Christou sniffed in satisfaction. *Murderer! Murdering terrorist pig!* Two of his men dead and another losing blood at an alarming rate. *Murdering EOKA bastard!*

And again Christou was to have the satisfaction of a job well done. Nobody in the house was spared and soon, with some strategically placed charges, the house was blown up, bodies and all.

Six minutes and forty-two seconds after the attack had begun, the TRF men were walking back through the trees towards their lorries, leaving behind them a burning pile of rubble and an old, shot-up Ford Consul car.

The dead bodies, all except that of Tony Verekelis, were cremated where they had died.

They had risen at five that morning and had left the house while it was still dark, climbing into the Land Rover and driving off as quietly as they could. Their destination was the area higher up the mountain. They would not attend the public spectacle of the funeral. They had said their goodbyes to the body before it left the house yesterday. Now their objective was solitude amongst the pines, somewhere to think things out.

It had only been two days since Grivas' death but already the pressure was on from the remaining EOKA members for Steve to step into the old man's shoes. Present at dinner the previous evening had been Steve, Christina, Tony and three men from Nicosia: Raouf, Nicos and Lefteris.

"We need a man who is not only a leader but a person whom all the people can respect," Tony Verekelis had urged. "And they respect you, Stelios. They know about you and, in some ways, they fear you. You are a myth that has proved to be a truth. You have their respect sight unseen. If you do not step into his shoes, nobody else can. You will be the public face of EOKA."

The others nodded in agreement.

"This is all very hard for me to accept," reasoned Steve. "It is all so incredible. Just a few days ago I was an oceanographer in Houston, Texas - "

"But you were always aware of your background," put in Nicos softly.

"Sure. But now here I am being asked to take over an army of resistance in a country whose internal politics I don't really know too much about. It was part of The Agreement that he would not pull me into Cypriot affairs whatever happened. You must know that."

"Yes, but you are back and he has gone," argued Raouf. "This island is born into you, Stelios. Think what a figurehead you would be."

The pressure had been tough. The debate had lasted all evening, ending with discordance. The five EOKA members had pleaded, begged and cajoled, but Steve was not to be committed. Not in the best of humour, the three men from Nicosia had left for Limassol at 22:00.

As Steve, Christina and Tony were going upstairs, having bidden the others farewell, Tony asked, "Are you going back then, Stelios?"

Steve tried to sound reasonable. "I have another life to live - my own. I *cannot* step into his shoes. *He* knew that. He did not bring me here for that."

"When will you go?"

"Sometime. Indefinite. But not just yet, there is something I must do first."

Tony looked at the girl pleadingly. He knew she and Stelios had been lovers since the first night. "Christina? Can you not persuade him?"

She shrugged. "I haf no power over him, Verekelis. It iss hiss life as he says. My own opinion hass no bearing in this." She looked at the American. "What iss it that you must do first, Stelios?"

Steve hesitated at the top of the stairs, uncertain whether he should mention it. Had it been just the rambling of an old man on the point of death? Would they think he was a fool to give any credence to the request? Nevertheless, if he was to get anywhere, he had to talk to - and trust in - somebody.

He looked from Christina to Tony. "Tony, would you come inside? I think this must be said in private." He was aware that the young helper, Takis, was in a nearby room with his girl.

Once inside the room, Christina sat down on the edge of the bed, Tony remained standing by the closed door. Steve stood by the window, facing them.

"I didn't want to say anything in front of the others..."

"You have upset them, you know. They were looking to you. They will probably now arrange something by themselves."

"Sure Tony, I know, and I'm sorry to have to disappoint them. But I am *not* here to take over, and I will *not* be persuaded otherwise. Now listen,"

Tony opened his mouth to argue but shut it again when he saw the look in the other man's eyes. "Please! I want no further discussion on the subject. Lefteris seems a fine leader to me."

Tony shrugged in resignation. "They will not like it, you know, not one bit. Especially if you stay on the island. It *is* your place, you know - yes, yes, yes, I know. We have been over this a thousand times this evening. Anyway, what was it you were going to say?"

Steve looked at both of them long and hard. "Just before he slipped into the last coma, he whispered something into my ear."

"Yes, I saw that," nodded Christina.

"It was a request. He wanted me to get something. I might not even have been hearing right. Anyway, his exact words, as far as I could make out, were... 'Get The Eye of Makarios'."

He waited for any reaction. There was none.

"Get *what?*" said Christina.

"The Eye of Makarios."

Christina and Tony made puzzled faces.

"The eye of Makarios?" Mused the girl. "Eye as in eye - ?" She tapped her right temple.

"I guess so. Do you know what it means?"

"Apart from the obvious," said Tony. "No."

"The obvious being that he wanted me to kill the President? A sort of John the Baptist? 'Bring me the eye of Michael Mouskos'? Could be... Grivas *would* understand what he was saying, I presume? He seemed coherent enough. It would not be an old man's ramblings?"

"Never!" said Tony sharply. "Grivas would not 'ramble', *never!*" The two men looked at each other, a tension rising then falling again just as quickly. "Did he say anything else, give you any indication?"

Steve turned to the window, thinking. He gazed unseeingly at the diamante Mediterranean sky. "He talked generally for a few moments about the usual things," he turned back to face them. "About my accent! And then he became urgent, as if he knew the end had come. He said there was something he wanted me to get for him when he had gone."

"When he had *gone?*" repeated Tony incredulously.

"Yep, that's what he said. 'When Grivas gone'. He said that only I could get it for him, from Mouskos... The Eye of Makarios."

"When he had gone..." Tony pondered. "He wanted you to get this eye of Makarios for him when he had died..."

"A final hit against the hated priest from beyond the grave," concluded Christina softly. "That would be typical of the General, to get the last word. At least we know now he was not rambling. Only he could haf thought off something like this. And to ask *you*, Stelios, to do it. Don't you see? It iss a master stroke. A master stroke! *You* of all people to deliver Grivas' final snipe from beyond the grave." Her eyes shone and yet at the same time were clouded in memory of the General. "Oh brilliant, *brilliant!*"

They were quiet. Then Tony nodded slowly and chuckled. "It is good, yes. So, the General is not dead, even now. And it is *you*," he pointed at Steve, "who are to carry on his work. He has decided."

Steve's face erupted into a bright purple. "Dammit, yes, yes, yes, it's *me*, I know! Damn all of you crazy people. I will do as he has asked and no more. He had no right to expect anything else of me, no right at all. He knew that. The Agreement. By Christ, I will get this fucking eye of Makarios, I will get it and personally take it to his grave. And then as soon as I can I will return to the States, to my *home*, to live *my* life, and leave the lot of you feuding madmen to go on killing each other, which is what you seem to like doing best..." He realised what he was saying and forced himself to stop. Then he said, "I will *not* lead EOKA, but I *will* get The Eye of Makarios."

Tony looked at him without expression. The girl was staring at him intently. Then she smiled. She nodded slowly. "Ah ha, so there it iss. There at last iss the fire, eh Tony? The fire that shows he iss truly Stelios."

"Yes," grinned Tony. "Yes, indeed."

"And Stelios, my love," continued the girl. "I will help you. Whatever it iss, I will help you find 'The Eye of Makarios'..."

Now Steve and Christina were on the plateau high above the house, wrapped up against the chill morning air, watching the beautiful sunrise. They could see the snow on the slopes and peak higher up the mountain. People would be skiing up there later on.

"The thing is," remarked Steve as he surveyed the landscape, "we must find out what The Eye of Makarios is, otherwise we are thwarted before we start. Don't you have *any* ideas?"

"No," sighed Christina, drawing on the cigar she held between her lips. It was quite normal for women in this part of the world to smoke cigars or pipes. "But we shall find out, we must. Someone somewhere will know what it iss and, most importantly, *where* it iss."

"But you and Tony have been the closest to Grivas these last weeks. If you don't know, who in EOKA will?"

"I am nott saying anybody in EOKA will - and really Stelios, you upset them last night. We will be lucky to gett any help from them at all. Mouskos knows, and presumably some of hiss followers know. It iss just a matter off persuading someone to tell uss."

"That's all, huh?" Steve reached out to stroke her soft olive face. "Any idea what it can be?"

"No, none at all. It must be important - to Mouskos at any rate - for the General to want to take it from him, to warrant this last action. It probably hass to hurt Mouskos, almost like a slap in face. What more could it do?"

"But why, what is the point?"

"Haf you efer been slapped in the face by a dead man? An unbelievable surprise, I yam sure. And that iss why *you* haf to do it. Word will spread and Mouskos will know who sent you. Once you have The Eye of Makarios we will make sure that word spreads about who obtained it."

"Once I have it! You make it sound so easy, Christy - and perhaps it could be if I was trained in these things, in fighting, in tactics. But I'm a humble oceanographer, that's all, not a... a guerrilla." He knew it was a lie. She did not.

Christina gripped his arm tightly. "But it iss there, Stelios, it iss there. We saw it last night. Just remember who you are. It wass born into you. You are no stranger to danger. When you are under the water, you are in constant danger there."

"Yes, but..."

"You haf to haf your wits about you. Supposing you are attacked by a shark or some other predator, you know how to defend yourself and counter-attack."

"That is the world I know, under the water, I can handle those situations - in fact I can handle any situation, because I'm trained for it. This is different."

"*Why?* Why iss it? Iss it so different? Mouskos' men are the sharks, the barracudas, the moray eels. Cyprus iss your ocean. You haf to make it your world, just ass you would do the seabed. Efen iff you will nott stay, this island iss your world until you find what Grivas asked."

He leaned back on the grass and smiled gently. "Christy, you really do have a way of making it all sound so easy. Yes, and giving me confidence too, I like that. You are nice people."

She frowned. "I... I yam people?"

Steve found her confusion totally charming. "Yes, you are nice people, dear singer Christina, dear terrorist Christina. It is an expression, that's all. Means you're a nice person. That I like you. I like you a lot."

She smiled, shivering in the chill air, and leant down next to him, her face not far from his. "You, Stelios, you are... nice people, too."

She bent forward, cigar thrown aside, and they kissed.

"And do you know something?" he complained as he pulled out of the clinch. "I haven't heard you sing yet."

She grinned, the wide, lovely grin. "Well, maybe sometime soon you will."

At that moment the gunfire started from far below.

It was followed by the horrible, inhuman roaring.

"My God!" exclaimed the girl.

Steve dashed to the edge of the plateau and lay down. Christina grabbed some binoculars from the vehicle and threw herself down beside him, focusing quickly.

"It's the house!" cried Steve. "Jesus Christ, they're attacking the house! We must get back."

He was halfway to his feet before she peremptorily pulled him back down.

"Do not be a fool," her voice was hard and cold. "There iss nothing you or I can do. You do nott fight a shark unarmed."

The sound of gunfire thundered up the side of the mountain.

"But there must be *something* we can do! Surely to God!"

Christina lay on her elbows, not speaking, watching the devastation below. She saw Tony Verekelis jump out of the upstairs back window and try to run. It was obvious what was going to happen. Oh, Tony... Tony... She swallowed hard as she saw him die, and the tears filled her eyes. *The bastards!* The evil, evil bastards!

Steve snatched the glasses from her. It did not take him a second to recognise the body hanging from the fence. "Oh no, no...." His head shook in dismay. "Why?"

The girl had been resting her head on her forearms, and now she looked up, tears streaking her face. "The final blow," she said hoarsely. "Why did we nott think? We should haf expected it. Mouskos' final thrust against EOKA. Against hiss one-time comrades. He wass part of EOKA and fought side by side with Grivas and the others against the British. And now... now look what he hass done. He iss shit." She spat viciously over the edge of the ridge.

Gathering control of herself, she retook the binoculars. Down below, the firing had stopped. She looked for a moment and then said, "They are going to blow it up. The final insult. Bastards!" She looked at the American, her nostrils flared and mouth tight. "Yes Stelios, there iss something that you can do. Do what iss your destiny. Get it for him, Stelios. For Grivas. Get The Eye of Makarios."

Limassol, Cyprus

They had expected thousands to attend the funeral. In fact, tens of thousands turned up.

Limassol was at a standstill.

And one of those in the crowd – just another anonymous local male, *fitting in* – was agent Digenis of the Israeli external security service.

Ψ

Thursday February 7 1974

"There is to be a general election on February 28th, the Prime Minister announced in the Commons this afternoon. At the same time he appealed to the miners to postpone their national strike over pay, which is due to start at midnight on Saturday, at least for the duration of the election campaign."

London, England

It snowed that month in London, the first time the capital had seen snow for two years. At the window of the second floor of Stuart House in the south-east corner of Soho Square, Colonel Stanley William Egginton CBE stood gazing at the large flakes as they drifted slowly downwards, adding to the patina of white covering the trees of the Square. Inside the conference room it was warm, perhaps too warm, giving the lie to the weather outside. Egginton thought about the miners and how every decent man in Britain must despise this forthcoming strike.

At that time, the newly formed United Kingdom Standing Committee on Arms Sales Support (these were the days before witty acronyms) consisted of twelve permanent members. These were the Directors of the Service branches of the Ministry of Defence. Three of these men were suspect and their files were under scrutiny by the British Internal Security Service. Colonel Egginton, fifty-four, stout, with a veritable mop of iron grey-to-white hair, was not one of them. His bi-annual positive vetting was always quite thorough and showed him to be a man of the utmost integrity and loyalty, his trustworthiness never in doubt.

The morning session of the meeting of the Standing Committee had finished and the ten attending members now stretched their legs in preparation for lunch (a cold buffet set out in the room directly above) in five minutes.

Colonel Egginton puffed at his pipe contentedly as he looked out of the window (these were the days when smoking was permitted everywhere), his thoughts transferring from the miners to his daughter's forthcoming wedding.

"Sir, Colonel Egginton?"

The Colonel turned around. It was one of the ADCs who acted as receptionists at these meetings. In his hand he held one of the standard two-tone grey telephones, its wire dangling unconnected from the back.

"Mm?"

"Telephone call for you, sir. Gentleman wouldn't give his name, said it was personal. Shall I plug it in?"

"Damn and blast, just at lunchtime as always. Okay son, plug it in."

The young man plugged the wire into a socket in the floor under the radiator, presented the phone to the older man and retired. Egginton placed the phone on the windowsill and picked up the receiver, removing his pipe with his right hand.

There was a click as the switchboard responded.

"Egginton here."

"Just one moment please sir." Click, buzz, the noise of a camel breaking wind, and then, "Go ahead please."

"Hello, Egginton speaking."

"Stanley William me ole dahlin', and how are yer?" said the Irish voice.

The Colonel stiffened. He turned his back to the rest of the room and spoke lowly. "What the hell do you want? How dare you ring me here!"

"Now, now, is that the way t' treat an ole friend? I was over here on business an' oi taught how noice it would be if I took me ole friend the Colonel to lunch."

"Impossible, can't make it, engaged."

"This business is *profitable*, lunch will be on me an' all that. Make it a late lunch if yer busy right now."

"No - er - I have appointments for the rest of the day." Blustering.

"Break them." Joviality gone.

A pause, then resolution. "When?"

"Ah now, ain't that good t' hear, knew yer wouldn't refuse an ole pal. Any toime yer like. I'm just downstairs. Hurry if yer can, it's bloody freezin'."

"I'll be down shortly." Phone replaced brusquely.

Egginton had turned as white as the snow outside. He remained looking out of the window, trying to regain his composure before he turned around.

"Stan? Stan! Coming upstairs?" A gentleman almost identical to Egginton was calling from a metre or two away.

"Er, no... no," Egginton turned and tried to smile. "Something's just come up, have to see to it. About me girl's wedding. You go on, Douglas, I'll be back later. Sorry." He made a beeline for the door, leaving his pipe on the windowsill.

At that same moment, Michael Mahoney appeared in the Square having just left the telephone box in nearby Carlisle Street...

Egginton, dressed in a heavy grey overcoat, silk scarf and trilby hat, turned left, treading gingerly in the settling snow. Through the falling white feathers he could see Mahoney approaching from the south side of the Square.

There was no pretence of stealth from the Irishman. He raised his gloved hand and roared greetings.

"Stanley! Stanley, me ole bum-stroker! An' how are yer?"

Their paths merged and they began to walk down Greek Street. There was no shaking of hands.

"Do you have to?" snarled Egginton. "I know you for what you are, remember? You can drop the brainless Irishman routine."

Mahoney was undaunted. "Sure an' yer bein' very unkind t' me today, Colonel. Anyone'd think yer weren't pleased to see me!"

"The only place I want to see you is in hell."

Egginton stumbled in the snow, and the Irishman's hand came out to steady him. Brusquely, Egginton pulled himself away. "Get your bloody hands off me!"

Mahoney smiled, a big Cheshire Cat smile. But when he spoke his voice held the merest nuance of malice. "Such aggression, my friend. Especially when I've got a five card trick and you're payin' on seventeen."

"Crap."

"What?"

Egginton controlled the rage within. He snarled. "I prefer baccarat."

Mahoney frowned and then, slowly, the smile returned. "Ah, a little joke then, was it? A little play on words. Now, isn't that grand? Isn't that more like the Colonel we love and admire! Where d' you want to eat?"

"What do you want with me?"

They turned right into Old Compton Street, past the then Casino Cinema.

"What d' you fancy? French, Italian, Chinese?"

"What do you *want*?"

"All in good time, my friend, all in good time. Y' know, I fancy some seafood. Are oysters in season, d' you know? Worked wonders for me last time." Mahoney manoeuvred the Colonel across the road to the southern side. "But first I've got to go somewhere. Does the cold affect you that way, Colonel? Goes straight to me kidneys. I find myself weeing all the time. Any public bogs around here?"

Ψ

Friday February 8 1974

"Skylab 3 returned safely to earth today after a record eighty-five days in orbit. Splashdown was in the Pacific."

Beirut, Lebanon

In the district of Borj El Barajneh, the foreigner – Ilich Ramirov – met with Ali Hassan Salameh and the other core members of Black September, as planned.

Kyrenia, Cyprus

Early evening, the darkening sky stained a violet red. The sun was a gigantic, burning orb to the west, slowly descending to fizzle out its fire in the calm water of the Mediterranean.

In Kyrenia Harbour, a normal evening's festivities were getting under way in *Halil's Kebab Restaurant*. The huge Cypriot-Turk Halil was up to his usual tricks, striding between the already full candlelit tables, a metre-long kebab skewer in each mighty hand. At every table, he attempted to guess the nationality of the persons sitting there and address them in their own language, his eyes meanwhile drinking in the ladies. Apart from everything else that was big about him, Halil had a sexual appetite of mammoth and insatiable proportions.

A coach-load of thirty early-season English tourists occupied a long table down one side of the restaurant, and Halil entertained them with his 'dumb Cypriot' act, shouting "Cheers!" and "Thomas Cook!" as often and as loudly as he could. In fact his English was excellent, if heavily accented, but he wasn't going to let them know this. He had made some of his best conquests of the ladies by appearing to be the big, dumb, beautiful oaf. After all, not many foreign women knew how to say no in Turkish.

Steve and Christina sat at a table in a far corner. Far enough away so as not to get embroiled with the tourists and yet not so far as to be conspicuously separated from the other diners. They were enjoying the finest kebabs they had ever tasted.

After five more minutes of entertaining, Halil left his audience and lumbered over to where the couple sat. With a great fuss and bustle, he sat down and swiped one of the three bottles of wine on the table, a black *Mavro*. A full third of the litre bottle disappeared down his throat in one swill.

Christina was dressed in a blue cotton dress, a lilac garland (purchased on their way to the restaurant from a local urchin on a bicycle) in her hair. "Well?" she queried expectantly.

Another mouthful of *Mavro* was swallowed before Halil spoke. His voice was quiet, serious. "Why should I help you? I! Halil! Why should I help a Greek?"

Christina looked heavenward. He was in one of those moods! "Do not be stupid, Halil. And do not play games with me. This iss Christina, remember. Your old friend."

"You have sung for me at times, yes..."

"And other things."

Steve raised his eyebrows. Halil looked abashed, and then a smile of memory crept across his craggy face.

"So stop playing games," scolded the girl.

The Turk looked uneasy. "My darling, it is not easy..." He squirmed on the seat in discomfort and downed another gullet-full of wine.

Steve leaned forward impatiently. "Buddy, I think we're wasting our time here. Your food is excellent, but your loyalty is something else."

"Loyalty?" The tanned brow creased. "Loyalty? You can tell me nothing about loyalty, my friend. I am a Turk. Christina, she is a Greek. Loyalty does not - cannot - enter into it. It has been that way for centuries. It will be that way forever. You are welcome in my restaurant. You may stay. Enjoy. Are these not the finest kebabs in the world? Is this not the finest wine? And you will eat and drink free." A giant hand was raised to quell Christina's protestations. "I insist. But loyalty? That simply cannot be. There are some things you cannot understand."

As Halil swilled again, a trickle of the black wine rolling down his chin, Steve suggested "Then what about friendship?"

The empty bottle was returned to the table. Halil contemplated the flickering flame of the candle between them. He looked up and then frowned. The candle cast a very faint shadow across the American's face. He reminded him of somebody.

He asked quietly, "Who *are* you, Mr American?"

"I am - "

"A friend," interrupted Christina. "A close and loyal friend. It iss better that that iss all you know, my dear Halil."

The Turk looked at her questioningly. Her dark eyes and that low voice had lost none of their seductiveness. And none of their insularity either. She was her own woman, was Christina, and he knew that she was hiding

The Eye of Makarios

something. He also knew that he would never get it out of her, whatever it was, unless she wanted to tell him.

Halil decided. "Okay!" He slapped the table. "He is a friend. You are a friend. I am a friend! In friendship then. But I must tell you this," he leant forward, his faintly sour breath wafting across into the American's face. "I am a simple restaurant owner. Okay, so I know people. I have many friends. But I cannot become so involved. You will understand, Christina." The girl nodded to the plea in his eyes. "Certain of my friends... they may be able to help. I can promise nothing. Just maybe. I will make enquiries. This is for you Christina, because I love you. And for you my friend, because I like you."

"How long?" asked the girl.

Halil shrugged the mighty shoulders. In the background, three men began to play Turkish folk music on pipes and tambourines. "A week. Maybe two..."

"We will return in a week then."

"No! You must not return. Not for a long time. Not until at least the summer. It must not be thought I was involved."

The music insinuated, growing in insistence.

"Then where?" asked Christina.

Halil thought. "Be at Salamis. In *ten* days. At dusk. Someone will come."

The girl nodded.

Halil stood up. "And now I must see to my customers." He waved an all-embracing hand, joviality back. "My other friends, they need Halil!"

"Just one more thing," Christina grabbed his hand. Her eyes softened. "Be careful."

For the briefest of moments the Turk looked at her in silence. Then a broad grin split his face in two. "Careful..." His raised his left leg off the ground. "As my British friends would say, I will be discretion itself!" He twisted around and gyrated his hands and hips in time with the music. "Cheers! Enjoy!" His mighty feet crashed down onto the floor as he stomped off boisterously and was immediately swallowed by the throng.

As they left the restaurant a couple of hours later, heading for their make-do living quarters in an old house on the outskirts of the town, Steve asked "Why didn't you tell him who I was?"

"It wass not necessary, my darling." Christina slipped her hand in his. The evening was mild, balmy. The waters of Kyrenia Harbour were totally still, not a boat bobbed.

"Maybe he'd have been more keen to help us."

"And maybe he would have slit your throat."

He put his arm around her as they walked. Considering the time, the place and the woman, he was not really interested in maybes, but he asked "Do you really think so?"

"Oh yes." She leant her head on his shoulder. The soft black hair smelt fresh. "You must understand the Turks, Stelios. Like us, they are proud. Like us, they have long memories."

He pulled her up and raised her head, cupping her chin in his right hand. "Talking of which, my lady, what was that about you and he, hm?"

"Mm?"

"Well...? Did you...?"

Her smile revealed the perfect white teeth. "You would like to know, yes?" Coyly. "Well, I will tell you..." She walked a couple of paces away from him. "Maybe!" With a giggle she ran off along the harbour's edge.

"Why, you little..." Steve set off after her.

Taking Halil's advice, that night they enjoyed like they had never enjoyed before.

As if there was no tomorrow.

Ψ

Monday February 18 1974

"An army helicopter crash-landed on the lawn of the White House earlier today after being chased and fired on by two police helicopters. The pilot, a young army mechanic, has been taken under armed guard to a nearby hospital where he is being treated for gunshot wounds."

Tel Aviv, Israel

Chaim Cohen, Deputy Controller of the Mossad, the Israeli external security service, sat at his desk in the office in the non-descript building somewhere in northern Tel Aviv. Unlike his network of agents worldwide, Cohen was obviously Jewish – from his distinctive, hawk-like features, the hint of sibilance in his voice, right down to the fact that he wore a skull cap on his bald pate. He bore a distinct resemblance to the Director of *Mossad Aliyah Beth*, Zvi Zamir.

Cohen looked at agent Nathanson sitting in the chair on the other side of the desk. "They are planning something," he said. "Salameh and company. They have been meeting together too often and they would not present us with such a target unless they had something important to discuss. They think the house in Beirut is safe, that we don't know about it. The fools," his laugh held contempt. "The last meeting was ten days ago. And there was someone else present, someone we do not know. Not one of them. Possibly a freelance."

"Why would they want a freelance?" Nathanson smoked through a small, golden cigarette holder.

Cohen shrugged. "Why indeed. A freelance usually means one of three things. They need more man power – but the Arabs never employ mercenaries, they detest them as unclean. Or they are planning something with which they don't want to be identified - "

"Which would defeat their own object."

"Absolutely. Or thirdly, they need the freelance to do something they cannot do themselves."

Nathanson blew two perfect smoke rings. "And what might that be?"

"That's what I want you to find out."

"W-M-P?"

"Whatever means possible, yes. Discreetly."

"On my own?"

"Always better, don't you think? Especially with Hassan."

"Okay. Any links or fail safe?"

"All depends where you have to go. Digenis is back in the area if you need him."

Nathanson nodded.

"Find out what these fuckers are planning," scowled Cohen.

Salamis, Cyprus

Darkness. A deadly quiet, still, eerie darkness. High up in the bespeckled night sky, a quarter-moon shone lamely, casting barely enough light to see by.

Steve and Christina sat side by side in the centre of the third row of the Salamis amphitheatre, like the sole members of an audience come to watch the last performance of a closing play.

The amphitheatre dated from Roman times or even before. Behind the couple, the tiered, semi-circular seating area rose up to meet the stars. In front was the stone stage area behind a proscenium of air.

A torch sat patiently on the seat next to Christina, switched off to preserve its life. Steve hoped that it was the only life that would need preserving this chill, sinister evening. He sat on her left, his hand absent-mindedly rubbing the smooth surface of the centuries-old stone beneath him.

He sniffed. "Are you sure he'll come?"

"Halil? No. But he said someone would come." There was an edge to her husky voice.

"I don't like this." His eyes darted around what little of the stage he could see. "I don't like this one little bit. What a godawful place to pick for a meet."

"I think the theatre iss beautiful."

"Sure, but there is a time and a place, kid... And who the hell are we supposed to be waiting for? Suppose he tipped off Makarios's men?"

"He would not. Halil would *neffer*. Whatever else he may be, he iss not a traitor. He iss a Turk, remember?"

"Okay, okay, you're right. It's just that gradually I'm becoming aware of who I am and just what I might mean on this crazy island of yours."

"That iss good, my Stelios." A kiss was planted on his right cheek.

"And it scares me shitless." A dry chuckle came from his throat. "Jeesus... Got any chocolate left?"

"Yes." From a canvas shoulder bag resting at her feet, Christina produced some puce-wrapped offering.

Steve was not overstruck on Turkish chocolate, but he was quickly getting used to it. It was that or nothing in the confectionery line. Not a patch on

Hershey's.

He bit into the over-hard candy and stared out into the darkness. "I wish to hell they'd show."

As if on cue a voice said "Hello."

They both span round. Christina grabbed the torch.

Three tiers above them stood a youth of no more than thirteen. He had a mop of tousled hair and wore a sleeveless pullover with no shirt underneath, dark shorts, no socks and local leather sandals. In his right hand he carried a small musical pipe. On his face was the most disarming of smiles.

"I am sorry if I startled you," he spoke in perfect English. "It was not my intention."

Christina frowned. "What do you want?"

The boy's smile did not waiver. "They sent me."

"Who?"

"They. You are expecting a message, no?"

"Jees buddy," said Steve. "You sure have a way of approaching people."

"What iss the message?" snapped Christina.

"They cannot help you," replied the boy, a respectful trace in his voice but the smile still radiating full blast. Was he laughing at them? "You will have to try elsewhere."

Steve stood up. "They can't help us at all?"

"That is all I was told to tell you. They cannot help you."

"But didn't Halil say anything - ?"

"They cannot help you. That is all. You must not contact them again."

"Yes, but - "

"I must go now. The others get worried. Goodbye!"

"Hey now, just a minute fella - "

But the boy had clomped lightly up the steps and was enveloped by the darkness.

"Hey - !" called Steve.

Christina touched his arm. "Let him go, Stelios."

"But..."

"He iss only a messenger."

"Shit." He relaxed. "Yeh, I suppose you're right."

Christina picked up the bag. "More chocolate?"

"What? No, no thanks. So, what do we do now?"

"Now? Now we haf to try somewhere else." Resiliently. "Tomorrow we move on." The bag was slung over her shoulder. "Tonight we rest."

"We must be careful," cautioned Steve as they moved away. "The more people we ask, the more chance there is of Makarios finding out about our quest. Or even finding out about me - us. And that could be fatal."

She handed him the torch. "Yes, we must be very careful Stelios. Very careful. That was a warning."

As they reached the edge of the amphitheatre, Christina looked back to where they had been, to where the boy had been standing. It was a stupid thing to imagine, she knew, but she could not help the involuntary shiver that ran the full length of her spine. The tousled, closely curled hair of the youth; the pipe in his hand; the noise his feet made, almost like hooves...

If she had even an ounce of belief in her, she would have said that the boy reminded her of someone. Someone from mythology. But that was preposterous and ridiculous. Totally and utterly ridiculous. And she did not believe.

Did she?

And this was Cyprus. This was 1974.

Wasn't it?

[Not wishing to get involved, Halil has since admitted that he never did make the enquiries. Until the author's interview with him he had never mentioned The Eye of Makarios to any living soul, or even tacitly acknowledged that it existed. Who the boy was who spoke to Steve and Christina on the night of February 18 1974 is not known.]

Ψ

Saturday February 23 1974

"Reports are coming in of a robbery at Kenwood House on Hampstead Heath, London. Preliminary reports say that a painting - The Guitar Player by Vermeer, said to be worth over one million pounds - is missing.
"In Lahore, the Islamic summit conference, attended by the kings, presidents and prime ministers of the Moslem world, has opened. Items on the agenda include a discussion on how oil revenue should be used."

Moscow, USSR

To the western world she was known as the Soviet Union's most powerful woman politician. For several years she sat on the all-powerful Praesidium of the Soviet Communist Party, a feat seldom emulated by a woman in the *Soyuz Sovyetskikh Sotsialisticheskikh Respublik*. Her name was Mrs Ekaterina Furtseva, and at that time in 1974 she was presumed to be Russia's Minister of Culture, a post which she was supposed to have held for the last fourteen years.

In fact she was nothing of the sort. The Soviet authorities have always denied her true position, for it was considered not *kulturny* for a woman in the Union to rise to such a powerful and dominant rank. For this very same reason, western journalists have never bothered to question her status. Even the mighty American CIA is not aware of what she truly did.

For the last five years of her life *[she resigned on October 24 1974 and died in her sleep that same night, ostensibly from a heart attack]* Ekaterina Furtseva was none other than the overall head of a very special, self-governing division of the Committee of State Security, the KGB. Such was her division's autonomy that it was tantamount to a KGB within the KGB, and Furtseva reported direct to only Premier Kosygin himself (some said the division was his brainchild), by-passing even Shelepin and his cohorts. Furtseva was in total charge of her division, taking full praise for its successes - and full responsibility for its failures (which were very few).

At 09:00 that morning the temperature in snow-driven Moscow was a mild zero degrees, and by that time Furtseva had been in her office for an hour and a half.

She looked up as Ramirov entered, shown in by a minion. Ramirov was dressed in a floor-length coat with an incredibly thick fur collar, and a fur hat. The face, so young and chubby, was bright red with the cold. It would crack and chip if he was not careful.

Without saying anything, Ramirov slowly removed the coat and hat and went over to the blazing fire in the grate in the wall to the left. Thick fur mittens had completely covered his hands, but on removal he noticed that his fingers had still turned that almost translucent red, and they ached as they began to thaw in the heat of the flames. Even after the *déshabille*, he was still wearing a thick woollen jacket, heavy pants and two polo-necked sweaters. And he was freezing.

He looked over at the woman. She was dressed in a man's military uniform of indistinguishable, but very high, rank [*it has never been ascertained for certain what rank the woman held. Not that military rank at her level of the KGB was of particular worth, it was* political *rank that counted*]. It was buttoned to the neck, the colour a basic KGB green but with a stirring of brown, grey and khaki. Her grey hair was cut short above the ears and parted on the left. When, after a minute or so, she stood up to greet him, he could see that her pants fell over rugged leather knee-high military boots of at least a size 44. Ramirov grinned to himself; he always marvelled at the size of her feet.

Her voice was deep and totally masculine. "My God, Ilich, anyone would think you were not used to Russian winters. Is your body forgetting your motherland?"

Ramirov smiled, out of respect more than out of amusement. He had been back in Russia for almost twelve hours now and his mind had promptly adjusted to thinking and talking in Russian. "It could never forget its true home, Comrade Furtseva. It is just that these western climes are ruinous to the skin."

She laughed heartily and clapped him on the back. "Come! Some wodka?"

"Thank you."

She extracted a bottle of *Osoboya* and two tumblers from a tall cabinet behind her desk. She filled one tumbler to the brim and put it down on the front of her desk, then she proceeded to fill her own to a similar level. "Come! Pull up a chair Major and sit down."

Ramirov hated the stupid title and he inwardly winced, but he did as he was told, draping his wet coat over the back of the plain wooden chair. He sample the wodka. It was good.

"Saw that stuttering idiot Philby on the way in."

"Oh?" Furtseva sat down and lit herself a cigarette from a box on the desk. She pushed the box towards Ramirov.

"Thought he was supposed to be redefecting last year?" Ramirov shook his head at the cigarette box.

The woman raised an eyebrow at his impudence, like a mother with a naughty son. She said curtly, "Something went wrong."

"Oh." Ramirov knew better than to press the point. Changing his mind, he leant forward and took a cigarette and Furtseva's expensive lighter from the table. Immediately he lit the cigarette he wished he hadn't. Good God, what did they put in them nowadays? Peasant shit?

"And to what do we owe this unexpected but entirely welcome pleasure?" asked Furtseva, and before Ramirov could reply she went on, "Your monthly reports have been illuminating, most illuminating. Your success has been astonishing, greater than we could have hoped for. You are to be congratulated."

He inclined his head in that curious fashion of his as an acceptance of the praise.

"Even though you missed Sieff." The sting in the tail. "However, I presume some outstanding exigency brought you here into my office?"

"In some ways, yes." Ramirov, *even Ramirov*, felt intimidated by the woman - no, the *person*, the *hermaphrodite* - sitting opposite him. But he was damned if he was going to show it. "I am in need of your directions. As you know, the kidnapping of the British Princess Anne is scheduled for 20th March, three and a half weeks time."

"Yes, how is that coming along?"

"All the plans have been made, it is simply now a matter of execution. She and her husband are going to a film show that evening, they will be returning around 19:45. Our man intends to strike as they near Buckingham Palace."

"He is reliable, this 'man'?"

"I am satisfied. No one is completely as reliable as oneself, naturally, but he suffices. His name is Ball. I think perhaps he is... shall we be kind and say an idealist? Of course, it is my intention to leave Britain immediately I have disposed of the princess, her husband and Ball. The bodies should not be found for several days in the house in Kent, longer if I am lucky."

"Good."

"However, the Arabs have asked me to assist them in a little scheme they have cooking at the present time."

"They still do not know you belong to the Committee?"

"Oh no, not at all, no one does. My cover as Martinez/Ramirez is concrete."

"Good. Keep it that way."

"Naturally, Comrade. Anyway, I should assist the Arabs if I possibly can, but if I do it will mean my staying on in Britain, possibly for sometime after the kidnapping. I am confident that I am covered anyhow, Ball does not really know who I am. He considers me to be a fellow idealist, from South

America of course."

Furtseva nodded her satisfaction.

"Nevertheless, I feel that I should have your concurrence before I agree to the Arabs' request, as there may be just the slightest risk of danger if I stay on in the country."

"What is it that the Arabs are asking?"

Ramirov explained in full detail what he had learnt at the meeting in Beirut two weeks previously. How the Arabs planned to explode a nuclear device in Britain and how their supplier, an eccentric Irishman, wanted a two million pound diamond in exchange for enough plutonium to make the bang. It all sounded so ludicrous now, sitting in an office in the middle of freezing Moscow.

The woman listened patiently, gradually finishing her tumbler of wodka and refilling the glass. Ramirov's was still half full. At the end of his expatiation, she was grinning sardonically.

"They will never succeed, of course." (Ramirov inclined his head but did not comment.) "They have not a hope in hell. To try it in Britain of all places! It is almost impossible to commit a major act of significant terrorism there [history was, of course, to prove her wrong] they just won't have it - as we have discovered previously. The kidnapping and murder of a royal princess is one thing - she is of no consequence or political importance. But to set off a nuclear explosion, perhaps close enough to an atomic plant to cause a major disaster - HAH!" The cavern of her mouth revealed rotting teeth amongst the cheap single dentures. "It is ludicrous. They will probably all die of radiation before they even move the stuff."

Ramirov nodded. "Maybe, and I have no doubt that you are correct Comrade. I did not enquire of their exact *modus operandi*, whether they have the appropriate technicians available and such like, because it was none of my business, and it is not within my jurisdiction to ask such things. The Arabs are confident enough, therefore it must be left to them. What they want is for me to get this 'Star of Sierra Leone' for them."

"Tell me about this. It is a diamond, you say?"

"Yes, I have been doing some research. Apparently it was found not long ago - just one moment please." He turned in the chair and extracted a folded but crumpled sheet of paper from an inside pocket of his overcoat. He read from it. "It was found in the Diminico Mine in Yengema, Sierra Leone, which is state-owned. It weighs 969.8 carats and is the third largest uncut diamond ever found - larger even than our own *Orloff* - estimated value two million pounds sterling. Measures... let me see... two and a half inches long by one and a half inches wide. The Sierra Leone government asked *De Beers*, the mining company, to sell it for them. The transaction took place through their

London offices. Whom it was sold to will never be revealed publicly." Ramirov refolded the piece of paper. "Should you agree to me giving my assistance to the Arabs, it would be my task to find out who bought the diamond, to ascertain whether it has been cut or not and, if not, to take it."

Furtseva breathed in deeply. "Hmm... and what if this diamond has been cut? What then?"

Ramirov shrugged. "I do not know. Presumably the Arabs will come to some other arrangement with the Irishman. It is really a strange affair all round. They tell me that their supplier is well aware that the cash price for the amount of merchandise they require far exceeds two million pounds, but he has enough money, so he says, and wants this diamond. Almost like a child wanting a toy."

"Ardent Communists might call that the product of capitalism gone mad," commented the woman. She downed the remnants of the second tumbler of wodka and lit her third cigarette. "Well, Ilich," she ruminated. "You know that your brief is to help in whatever way possible. I suggest that you do that."

"Yes, Comrade."

"In fact on reflection, I like the Arab idea. I like it very much. It is amusing. Impossible, of course. But just supposing it did succeed, eh? Just supposing... I think we must help them in whatever way we can, Ilich, even to the extent of abandoning the royal princess plan. The very slim chance of the Arabs' plot coming off is worth much more than the simple assassination of a puppet."

Quickly Ramirov reached for his wodka and poured it down his throat to stifle his natural spontaneous reaction. The princess murder was his idea, his entirely. How *could* she expect him just to relinquish it? She had been so keen on the plan originally. The bitch.

But, of course, he knew better than to argue. It was literally more than his life was worth. He just replied "Comrade," acquiescently.

Furtseva pursed her lips, satisfied with her decision. "Let this man Ball continue against the princess if he so wishes. You will not contact him again. All your energy must be devoted to getting this diamond, if it is still in existence. Report back to me when you have succeeded."

"Comrade."

Ψ

Monday March 4 1974

"Mr Heath has resigned as Prime Minister. The fourteen new Liberal MPs this afternoon rejected Mr Heath's offer to form a Conservative-Liberal coalition government, and the Prime Minister travelled to Buckingham Palace almost immediately to formally tender his resignation to the Queen. Shortly after a subdued Mr Heath left the Palace, Mr Harold Wilson arrived to be invited to form a government.
"In France, it has been confirmed that all 345 persons aboard the Turkish Airline DC10, which crashed in the forest of Ermenonville near Paris yesterday, were killed. At least 200 of them were British. It is the world's worst-ever air disaster."

London, England

At that time *De Beers'* registered office in London was at 40 Holborn Viaduct. It was a round, eight-storey, typically depressing example of 1950's architecture. But *De Beers'* London business is of such a size and volume that this monolith could not contain all the necessary staff, and in nearby Hatton Garden (London's diamond centre) was a wide old building known as The Annex.

In the small office on the second floor of The Annex, Annette Stewart sat tapping figures onto a small mains calculator. Annette was a tall, well-built young woman in her mid-twenties, smart brunette hair cut to just below the ears, a pretty almost delicate face nearly smothered by a huge pair of spectacles, and make-up applied with taste although perhaps a bit too thinly on the lips. That day she wore a high-collared maroon dress, pinched in at the waist and falling to just above her knees.

After contemplating the answers given by the machine, Annette transferred the data onto a sheet of paper in front of her. It was part of her junior executive responsibilities to write a report of each Friday's bourse and to give detailed accounts of each deal involving *De Beers'* merchandise.

She was so absorbed in her work that she did not notice the time passing. When the telephone rang at 10:55 she visibly jumped and nearly dropped the short holder in which burned her *St Moritz* cigarette.

She put the cigarette holder between her teeth and mumbled into the mouthpiece. "Yes, Annette Stewart?"

It was General Reception downstairs. "Miss Stewart, your eleven o'clock appointment is here."

"Eleven o'clock! God, is that the time?" Her left wrist snapped up to her eyes and down again. "Okay, have him shown up will you please?" She replaced the receiver and hurriedly set about tidying up her desk. The calculator was unplugged and stuffed into a drawer, telephone straightened, papers assembled into two almost orderly piles and cigarette disposed of into an ashtray which also found its way into a drawer. She patted her hair and sucked her lips inwards. She wanted a pee but there was no time now. Why on earth hadn't she kept an eye on the clock?

There came a short tap on the door and it opened to reveal a tall, well-built man, wearing a rather out of fashion double-breasted two-piece striped grey suit, and carrying a small document case. His Latin face had a warm, permanent suntan and the jet black hair with shocks of grey at each temple was pushed straight back. A pair of golden-framed spectacles, tinted a pale brown, covered dark eyes.

"Mister Garcia," announced a voice from behind, and a hand reached out to pull the door closed as Garcia walked quickly into the room.

Annette rose. The hand that took hers was warm and the skin was hard, the grip powerful, the contact prolonged an iota longer than the norm.

"Good morning Mr Garcia, Annette Stewart."

"Miss Stewart, it ees my pleasure." He grinned, as if the last thing he was expecting was such a good-looking young woman. "Indeed, my pleasure."

"Won't you sit down?"

"I thank you." As he said it he inclined his head gently to the right and back up again.

"Now then, Mr Garcia," Annette pulled the chair in under her. "What can I do for you? Your secretary said you wished to talk about diamonds - any aspect in particular?"

"Perhaps I had better explain, Miss Stewart," an attractive, toothy smile added to the warm, accented voice. "Basically I would like to put myself in your hands." He opened his case and took out a small rectangle of cardboard. "My card."

Annette read: *Raimondo Garcia Martinez, President, Martinez Shipping, Cadiz, España,* together with telephone and telex numbers and the company crest, a golden filigreed M.

"Miss Stewart, the situation is that I own my own fleet of ships - in fact I will be truthful with you, I inherited the concern some ten years ago from my father. We manage a fairly lucrative business with cruise ships in the Mediterranean and cargo ships world-wide. I have nothing at all to do with diamonds. Frankly I possess no knowledge of them. I have some money - my own money - to invest, and I thought that in this age of uncertainty and inflation, diamonds would be - how do you say? - the best bet. I would like to use your good services, if it is at all permissible." He felt into his pocket and pulled out a packet of *Marlborough*. "Do you smoke?"

Annette smiled. "I do but not at the moment, thank you."

"It ees permitted?"

"Of course, please go ahead." She opened her drawer, surreptitiously tipped her own ash onto some important papers, and then withdrew the ashtray and passed it over to Garcia.

"I thank you."

She waited for a moment, looking at him light up (and noticing the crested lighter which looked as if it was 24-carat gold) and then she said, "Well, Mr Garcia, we can certainly help you. How much were you thinking of investing?"

His right hand flicked into the air. "Oh, that does not worry me. It ees all dependent upon what you have to offer me. I will be guided by your recommendations." Again the head inclined to one side.

Annette raised a mental eyebrow and went into her spiel. "You will find no better investment than diamonds - in the long term, that is. Prices are rising continuously, and quite sharply nowadays. But the retail mark-up is quite considerable and it will be years before a diamond will sell for what you paid for it. A good quality diamond - weighing a carat or over - is a good long-term investment.

"*De Beers Consolidated* owns and/or controls most of the diggings in southern Africa, mining some £91,000-worth of rough diamonds each day. Eighty percent of the diamonds aren't good enough to be gems and are used in industry. Our mines supply thirty-five percent of the world's new gem diamonds [*Russia supplied twenty-five per cent – a fact of which Garcia was well aware.*] Eighty percent of all diamonds mined are sent here to the Syndicate - the Central Selling Organisation. Here diamonds are sorted by weight, shape, colour and clarity.

"Now, I will be perfectly honest with you, we do not usually deal direct with customers in such a manner as this - we have our own list of 250 buyers who come to our five-weekly sights. However, your references *were* impeccable."

"Thank you." The head inclined. "Tell me, you mentioned that I should invest in diamonds of at least one carat. One hears of carats in diamonds and gold and such," he waived his cigarette, "but I am afraid that I do not completely understand their significance."

She smiled, her mouth wide and, beneath the formal British exterior, somewhat inviting. "Of course, please excuse me. Dealing with these things everyday one often forgets that the whole world does not know every facet of one's trade."

"No, no," Garcia's voice had become softer, even more friendly. The eyes smiled. "It ees I who must apologise for my ignorance."

She cleared her throat. "A carat is basically a unit of weight. Measured in points, there are one hundred points to a carat and one hundred and forty-two to an ounce *avoirdupois*. To give you an idea, most normal common or garden engagement ring diamonds average anything up to point five of a carat. Other rings with just one big diamond," she made a little figure of the size over a finger on her right hand, "are usually in the region of up to five carats."

"Intriguing. And to think that I have been living in ignorance all these years!" He chuckled and lifted his spectacles once off the bridge of his nose and then replaced them. He stubbed out the half-smoked cigarette. "Tell me more, Miss Stewart. Tell me how diamonds are discovered."

And so she told him, everything a layman would be able to understand about diamonds, their formation from carbon, discovery in the rough in kimberlite rock, the processing and reprocessing, the sorting at the Central Selling Organisation, the sights, the sawing and cleaving, the deals, the *mazel* and *brocha* (luck and blessing), the not so scrupulous activities of some members of the retail trade.

She found it easy to talk to this man with his intelligent questions and humorous interjections, and she found herself liking him more and more as the morning went on. Before she knew it, it had passed midday; a quick look at his watch made Garcia aware of this also.

Annette had just completed her lecture about the retail trade when Garcia asked, "Miss Stewart, please do not think it presumptuous of me, but I have taken up a lot of your time with my silly questions, and you are obviously a very busy lady. Would you do me the honour of allowing me to buy you lunch? Apart from an exquisite meal - which I can promise you - we can conclude our business and I need not take up any more of your time this afternoon." He suddenly looked abashed at his own audacity, and added quickly "Or perhaps you have another engagement?"

She had not and she hesitated only a moment. "Oh! Well, no, no, I have nothing on - I mean... yes, I'd love to! Thank you."

Outside, London was cold and grey and very windy, the pedestrians of Hatton Garden struggling bravely to keep their composure in the face of a wicked north-wester.

Garcia hailed a taxi which had just dropped a Jew in a large floppy overcoat outside number 87, the London Diamond Club, three premises up. They travelled not too smoothly through the lunchtime traffic, eventually coming to a halt opposite the *Warner* cinema complex in Leicester Square.

Garcia led the way into the *Trota Blu* restaurant.

Annette felt relaxed with the man and conversation flowed smoothly and easily. His occasionally stilted English added even more to his charm.

Garcia chose the meal: *Zuppa di datteri, Biscetta alla fiorentina con melanzane al funghetto,* followed, of course, by *tiramisu.*

They downed aperitifs of Martini, and went through two bottles of red *Lacrima Christi* during the meal. At the end, Annette had to firmly refuse his near insistence on another bottle of wine, compromising instead with a small brandy, the mellow *Hennessey.* Her head was spinning lightly but she felt good, and the food had been excellent.

Garcia had talked a lot during the meal, about his businesses in Spain and of his inherited wealth - which, Annette formed the impression, was immense indeed. Then he had asked about her, and she had heard herself telling him all about her private life, about Simon her fiancé, about where she lived, everything.

With the brandy downed and coffee being served, Garcia finally reverted to business. "Now, if I may, about my investment. Gem stones are, of course, beautiful but - and I must be honest with you - my investment will be purely for, er, how you say… financial expediency."

"I un'stand," Annette heard the faint slur in her voice and she quickly dragged on her cigarette. Garcia seemed unaffected by the alcohol, he was still his charming *good looking* self. Oh, that accent!

"So, from what you have told me, I was wondering if I should invest in rough diamonds rather than the finished article?" He smiled. "As you have explained, of course, a large rough could be worth several times its original price when cut - and, therefore, I presume the buying of rough diamonds is very much a closed shop. Quite simply, I would like to enter that shop." His head inclined to the left and the dim light of the restaurant reflected off his spectacles.

As the brandy's final assault on her system began to take effect, Annette's head became more and more fuddled. Garcia's voice was so deep, loud yet soft, as if it was only for her ears and her ears alone. She felt as if she wanted to go to sleep, to go to bed. She forced herself to pay attention, her eyes dreamily holding his.

"What I was thinking of," he continued, well aware of her state, "was that I should buy just one big rough diamond as my initial investment and then review the situation sometime afterwards. I would be prepared to spend in the region of five million pounds to start with."

That awoke Annette like a plunge into iced water. As with anyone being shot out of a near narcosis, she felt confused at the sudden alertness and she wondered if she had heard correctly. To cover her confusion and embarrassment, she blurted "We had a stone in not so long ago."

"You did?"

"It would have suited you perfectly. A 970 carat beauty. In fact, the third largest rough ever found. Sold for over two million."

"Pah!" Garcia slapped the heel of his hand against his forehead. He showed no sign of noticing her confusion. "And I have missed eet? Eet would have been perfect! Tell me, tell me who bought it. Please. Do you think they would sell?"

Annette giggled, a little girl with a secret. She leant forward. "Actually, I'm not supposed to tell, that information is s-strictly con-con-confidenshul."

His lips puckered. "But dear Miss Stewart, *please*." He also came forward, taking her right hand in both of his. "It ees just what I want. Perhaps I can persuade them to sell."

She shook her head, giggling. The booze spoke. "No chance, my dear Raimondo, no chance. It was sold..." She placed her left hand over her face in a wasted effort to contain a burp. "It was sold to the P-President of France."

Which was exactly what Ramirov wanted to know.

That night a terrible fire completely devastated Annette Stewart's home in Orpington, Kent. Her parents were away in Portugal, and only one charred body was found in the place the next morning. It was later identified (by the teeth) as Annette. So badly burnt was the corpse that the head just snapped off when the forensics attempted to bundle it into a plastic bodybag. Nobody ever detected the single needle mark on her chest where a full syringe of air had been injected directly into her heart.

Ψ

Wednesday March 20 1974

"Two British soldiers were killed and another seriously wounded in Ulster earlier today when members of the Royal Ulster Constabulary opened fire on them on the border with the Republic. Exactly what happened is not known at this stage but an official source has described the incident as 'a tragic accident'."

London, England

The attempted kidnapping of Princess Anne Elizabeth Alice Louise, GCVO, Chief Commandant Women's Royal Naval Service, Colonel-in-Chief 14th/20th King's Hussars, the Worcestershire and Sherwood Foresters' Regiment, 8th Canadian Hussars, Commandant-in-Chief Ambulance and Nursing Cadets, and only daughter of Her Majesty Queen Elizabeth II of the United Kingdom of Great Britain and Northern Ireland, took place at 19:45 that evening. What happened is a matter of historical fact, the Princess and her husband being saved by their solitary bodyguard, an Inspector in the police, who was shot three times and eventually awarded the George Cross, Britain's highest honour for peacetime gallantry.

Peter Sydney 'Ian' Ball was overpowered a few hundred metres away in St James's Park and was taken into custody to a cellar underneath the premises of the old police headquarters just off Whitehall. Despite harsh and stringent questioning, intimidation and plain torture, the police could glean no information from him as to there being an accomplice - although at one point, after a thin electrode had been inserted into the urethra of his penis, another into his anus and the current switched on, he did start rambling about the foreigner, the Peruvian who had helped him, who had set up the whole operation. However, no credence was given to this as the precipitate electric current had been greater than intended and, still tied to the chair, Ball had been flung across the room with the shock, his head landing with a terrible thud against the concrete floor.

Ian Ball was tried at the No 1 Court at the Old Bailey (the Central Criminal Court) on May 22 1974 and pleaded guilty to charges of attempted murder, wounding and 'attempting to steal and carry away Her Royal Highness Princess Anne'. It was ordered that he be detained in a special hospital under the Mental Health Act (in fact the top security Rampton Hospital in Nottinghamshire) 'without limit of time'.

That very same evening, and not a kilometre away from the incident in The Mall, Stanley William Egginton lay naked face down on the leather-topped massage table and cringed as the masseur's fingers gouged into his pectorals with what he considered unnecessary brutality. He was in his Club in Pall Mall.

In fact, the cringe was not only caused by the masseur's vicious administrations, but also by what was going on in Egginton's head. For over a month now he had lived on tenterhooks wondering what the Irishman wanted. The meeting on February 7 had been a pure and simple softening-up job. Mahoney had been as nice as pie, treating him to an expensive meal, wine and spirits, and an exquisite Cuban cigar, and only occasionally mentioning that he was after something big this time – a fact which Egginton had already worked out, as it was very rare for Mahoney to set foot out of Ireland to do business, let alone poach on another person's territory (and London was Bilbeisi's territory).

After the lunch with the Irishman, Egginton had made a brief appearance back at his meeting in the afternoon but had left after forty minutes giving 'a bloody migraine' as an excuse. Ten minutes walk away in Leicester Square, Mahoney had been waiting, and the rest of the afternoon had been spent driving around London, the Irishman marvelling with glee at the various sights. "Look, there's Westminster Cathedral, haven't been in dhere fr' ages – which remoinds me, oi must go t' confession. My God, Victoria Street's in a mess, hope all this rebuildin' is worthwhile."

And, in between the marvelling, Mahoney had been checking, asking Egginton if things were the same. How was his daughter? Getting married? Getaway! Did his wife Margery still have that very weak heart? ("Marvellous how she's lasted this long Stanley, me ole son of a donkey.") And did he remember those lovely and totally obscene photographs Mahoney had, locked away somewhere safe, of Egginton and two thirteen year old schoolgirls? And what a great pity it would be if they were accidentally to fall into the hands of Mrs Egginton ("I'm not sure her ole heart would stand it, yer know."). But that would never happen, of course, because Mahoney would look after them. And wouldn't it be possible for Stanley to supply him with an especial item he wanted at some unspecified date in the future? And sure, wasn't he a co-operative little Colonel to say of course he would get anything he was able to and sure didn't Mahoney know that indeed he was able to get *anything*? And wasn't the Colonel happy to know that this time, as the item required was extra-special, Mahoney would truly give him all the photographs and negatives and also a quarter of a million pounds.

Yes, he had heard right. A quarter of a million pounds. The item, you see, could not go missing overnight. It would have to disappear slowly, and subsequent investigations would be bound to point the finger if not directly at Egginton then at least in his general direction. The quarter million would enable him to get out, to save his neck, to spend his last remaining twenty years or so living as he had always wanted, anywhere in the world that suited him (except Britain). And think of all the thirteen year olds he could have then, all those ripe cheeky-pink bottoms and what was beneath them.

In his somewhat inebriated state (Mahoney supplying a bottle of whiskey on his guided tour of old London town), Egginton did indeed find the idea attractive. To get those photographs alone would be worth everything, for he loved his wife, deeply and dearly, and he would rather die (and even risk social disgrace) before he would let any shock or harm come to her. He would have to get what Mahoney wanted anyway, so he might as well relish the prospect of his rewards.

That night, Mahoney had treated him to a *VIP Special* at a certain well-known establishment in Kensington Church Street, and Egginton had spent the night, not with thirteen year olds this time, but with two of the juiciest whores West London had to offer.

And he had heard nothing from the Irishman since. Not a bloody word. And that was why on the evening of March 20 1974, Stanley Egginton had plenty to cringe about. Just when would that damn mick contact him again with details of his intended 'purchase'? It must be something colossal to warrant a payment of a quarter million. A brace of tanks, perhaps? A *Harrier* jump-jet?

He cursed roughly as the masseur dug a knuckle just a fraction of a centimetre too deep into his buttock, and he forced himself to fart sharply in retaliation.

Ψ

Wednesday March 27 1974

"The new Labour government announced today that it was suspending technical aid to Chile and no new arms deals would be made with the ruling military junta."

Paphos District, Cyprus

The waves came charging in towards the shore like wild fluorescent eels, laying end to end and stretching sideways on to the beach, threatening, only to peter out at the last moment with the weakest of liquid thunderclaps. The eels caressed the smooth white sand softly, like fingers on a body. Up above, the night sky was cloudless and the myriad stars shone like neon bulbs in the heavens. It was a full moon.

The situation was a kilometre or so to the north of the port of Paphos on the west coast, near the Tombs of the Kings.

The couple walked along the beach, arms around each other, like lovers do or wished they did the world over. They were lovers physically, and had it been another time, another place, another century, another planet, they might have been lovers in the full and true sense of the word: physically, mentally and spiritually. But this was Cyprus 1974. She was one of the remnants of a once powerful resistance organisation and he was a man with a mission. A mission that was proving most frustrating at that present time.

Her head was resting against his left shoulder, and they walked slowly, at a half-pace.

"I just can't understand it," Steve's voice contained neither resignation nor determination, he was simply stating a fact. "Two months. Two goddamn months. And no trace. Not a damn mention of this 'Eye of Makarios'. It's incredible. Nobody seems to have heard of it except Grivas – and he can't help us now."

Christina sighed. "I am forced to agree with your sentiments, dear Stelios. It iss not, how do they say, for the want off trying? We haf tried both EOKA and Mouskos people, both Greek and Turk," at that word she spat once, softly, onto the sand, "but nobody knows what it iss. I fear that it does not exist, this Eye iss not real. We haf discussed before about the General speaking in - what was the word you used?"

"Metaphor."

"Metaphor, yes. But he could not. He would haf known that his death-bed was not the place for riddles – especially for you. If you consider the search to be worthless continuing, Stelios, I will understand. Even Grivas in heaven would not hold it against you."

And they *had* searched. They had made surreptitious enquiry of nearly every person they had met; they had put out feelers, other persons had discreetly asked other persons, Greek had even asked Turk before slitting his throat. But everything had been met with a negative response. The only Eye of Makarios that was known were the two things on either side of the Archbishop's nose.

Apart from the frustrating quest, Steve and Christina had had to keep continually on the move after they had left Kyrenia. Word was out amongst Mouskos' followers that Cascianis and a male had escaped the final inferno of EOKA. And they, the final sperm of the movement, must be caught before they could fertilise a new generation.

The belief that EOKA was moribund was encouraged by the three gentlemen who split their time between Nicosia and Limassol – Nicos, Raouf and Lefteris. For it suited their purpose very well to have Makarios believe this. Little did the Archbishop know that EOKA was regrouping, without Cascianis and the male, and gaining strength day by day in preparation for something terrible that summer.

Steve and Christina had not stayed in one place more than three or four nights, and Christina had argued that even that was too long. But the followers of Grivas were still plentiful, and the couple had not as yet had to forego shelter when darkness fell. Washing facilities, food and clean clothes (sometimes badly fitting, usually on the larger side) had been provided when necessary.

For the first few days after leaving Kyrenia they had travelled around in the Land Rover which they had taken with them into the mountains on the morning of the attack. But they had decided that it was getting too well-known as word about them spread. The vehicle had had to be abandoned. Now their way was made in vehicles either borrowed or 'borrowed' or, for short distances, on foot. At that time they were lodging in a room in a house near the Church of St Kendias in Paphos.

They came upon some boulders separating the dry inland shrub from the beach, and they sat down. The noise of the waves made soporific musak.

Christina, rather fetching in a white billowing cotton top and a simple three-quarter length black skirt with a red and yellow flowered hem, sat open legged and withdrew a vicious-looking knife from a sheath around her left thigh. She did not lower her skirt but left it where it was, balanced at the top of her leg, plain white cotton pants showing a few centimetres away. Absentmindedly she began to churn the stones and sand with the knife.

Steve, who was wearing his own denim jeans and bomber-jacket with a borrowed black cotton shirt underneath, sat to her right and at an angle facing her. His listened to the rolling tide and the gentle patting of the girl's knife on the sand. He thought.

After five minutes he said, "No."

Christina looked at him. "Stelios?"

He smiled. "No Christy, I don't think continuing the search would be worthless. If the information will not come to us, then I – "

"We."

" – must go to *it*. It is time to look fate square in its goddamn face, kid. After all, that is the reason I am here. This…" he spread his arms wide to embrace the whole of Cyprus, " – is my destiny, the reason for my existence. I see it. It can be no other way. We *shall* find out what The Eye of Makarios is, even if we have to ask Mouskos himself."

He reached out and touched her soft black hair. "It's good of you to say you'll understand if I no longer wish to carry on, but I *must*. He would not want me to quit now. Grivas *will* have The Eye of Makarios – even if it kills me." He looked into her eyes as he said, "The least I can do after all these years is to obey my father's last request."

Ψ

Friday March 29 1974

"In Washington, President Nixon has agreed to hand over tapes and documents subpoenaed by the Watergate Special prosecutor Mr Leon Jaworski. Also in Washington, Dr Henry Kissinger today met the Israeli Defence Minister General Moshe Dayan to discuss troop disengagement from the Golan Heights."

Paris, France

Born July 5 1911 at Montboudif in the Auvergne

1934	military service
1935	teacher of classics in Marseille, married
1938	moved to Paris to teach at *Henry IV Lycée*
1939	40 Alpine Infantry regiment
1940	returned to *Henry IV Lycée*
1944	liaison work with the Education Ministry
1946	resignation of De Gaulle, stayed on in position but gradually became De Gaulle's close collaborator, became Treasurer of the *Anne De Gaulle Foundation*
1948	made head of the shadow cabinet by De Gaulle
1954	employed by Guy de Rothschild
1956	made director of Rothschild bank
1958	chief of staff to De Gaulle who emerged from retirement
1961	entrusted to join the broken threads of the Algeria negotiations
1962	nominated as Prime Minister, April 16
1968	resigned as Prime Minister
1969	elected President of France

Georges Pompidou became noticeably ill in the winter of 1972, Elysée spokesmen putting the President's sickness down to influenza and relapses. In May 1973 he appeared on television with Richard Nixon, the then American President. The whole world noticed the Frenchman's puffy features, hesitant manner and difficulty in expressing himself clearly.

By March 29 1974 his condition had worsened and his features had swollen to balloon-like proportions. Although his speech retained its hesitancy, his mind – as any of his doctors would attest – was as alert as ever. The disease would, of course, eventually prove fatal but no one that day imagined that the President would be dead in four days time – at least, not of his illness.

For the last year, Pompidou had spent whatever time he could in the modern (some would say futuristic) rooms in the east wing of the Elysée Palace, rooms he and his wife had personally decorated. There were four rooms, each brilliantly and beautifully layed out with modern furniture, *avant garde* ceiling and wall coverings and pictures by the time's top artists. *Les quartres salles* were completely out of place with the rest of the eighteenth century palace, but they were a magnificent anachronism.

At 11:45 that morning, the Russian Ambassador to France and his aide, a chubby-faced, curly-haired, Latin-looking fellow, were shown into the drawing room. They were keeping an appointment made at their behest some days previously. The President would not keep them a moment, they were told, and the private messenger scurried off, leaving them alone.

Neither man spoke, for they were well aware that even here there might be concealed microphones or hidden cameras. Instead they busied themselves admiring the paintings on the synthetic resin walls, offerings from Kupka, Delaunay and Matisse.

They were kept waiting only three minutes before the President arrived, wheeled in by his personal private secretary, a neat and thin fellow who had the aura of a mother hen.

Both the Ambassador and his aide were shocked as they looked at the grotesquely swollen facial features and the distended hands gaping out from the sleeves of the expensive dressing-gown. But it was the eyes that the Ambassador's aide noticed most. Yes, the eyes said everything. The eyes said there was still life in the President, a tenacious wonderful life that would not be relinquished easily.

The Ambassador recovered his composure quickly and smiled politely, speaking in French. "*Cher Monsieur le Président,* how nice it is to see you." He went to offer his hand in greeting but then thought better of it. Could Pompidou move his limbs?

The swollen face wobbled, and the President said, "*Messieurs, bonjour.* It has been... a long time since I have seen you, Mr Ambassador." The voice was deep, coherent without being clear, and held just an intermittent trace of hesitancy.

"The President cannot be troubled for too long, gentlemen," put in the secretary tartly. "He is unwell and has been advised to rest."

"*Pah,* do shut up Albert, for God's sake!" Pompidou half turned his head and slung the words over his shoulder. "Anyone would think I was a senile old man on his... death-bed. I am all right and I will probably see you in your grave. Now leave us."

Albert bridled and left. The three of them were left alone in the room, but the Russians were only too well aware that no more than a few metres away outside were guards with enough firepower to blow the flesh off their bones without even an effort. And they had, naturally, been discreetly screened before being admitted to the Palace.

Pompidou spoke. "You said the subject was of some… urgency. So, what is so urgent that the Russian Ambassador himself comes to visit me?"

The Ambassador smiled solicitously. *"Monsieur le Président,* may I present Alexei Mirzoff, my aide."

Pompidou looked at the younger man, who inclined his head in greeting.

Pompidou's head nodded gently as he said, "Please gentlemen… sit down." The right hand twitched in indication of the chairs. There were four in the room: two brown bucket divans to sit three apiece against two of the walls under the Matisse paintings, and two single chairs of the same design. The Ambassador sat on one of the divans, just a couple of metres away from the President. After a moment's hesitation, Mirzoff sat next to him.

The Ambassador looked uncomfortable. "Actually sir, it is about a diamond."

"A diamond…?"

"Oui monsieur, if you will excuse? It is a rather delicate matter," he leant forward in his seat, hands together, an unconscious supplication. "Recently my country's diamond, the *Orloff,* was stolen. This news has been kept secret, even from some members of the Praesidium, and you are certainly the first westerner to have been told about it. The persons who stole this diamond were members of a Ukrainian nationalist organisation known as OUM. They have since been captured and have been dealt with. However," he grimaced, displaying a definitely non-socialist gold filling in one of his left molars. "The diamond has not been recovered."

Mirzoff had remained silent and he now stood up and, with hands in pockets, strolled over to admire the Kupka and Delaunay paintings on the lateral wall.

"We managed to glean from the criminals that the diamond had been smuggled out of the Soviet Union," continued the Ambassador, "travelling via a *sympathique* captain on a Black Sea vessel, through contacts in Turkey, and eventually down to South Africa. Our agents suspect that the South African Security Service, the BOSS, then took a hand, but that is not a matter to concern us at this moment. Truthfully, we have not been able to trace *le diamant* further. However, we have strong suspicions that it was 're-processed' – by that I mean a large diamond was claimed to have been discovered, it was processed in the usual way and then sent as normal to *De Beers* in London. The history of it being concrete enough to fool that establishment, they took their proper action. Eventually the diamond was sold.

"This is only suspicion, of course. But it is very strong suspicion."

Pompidou's head wobbled. *"Très intéressant Monsieur l'Ambassadeur,* but what has this got to do with me?"

"Sources tell us that at the same time as the *Orloff* might have reached *De Beers,* they did in fact start negotiations on a large diamond. It was named 'The Star of Sierra Leone'. And we are told it was purchased by you."

"Ah!" There was amusement now in the President's eyes and the jowls wobbled some more. "Now I see." He looked towards Mirzoff, who was now standing in front of a Matisse two metres to his right. "I am indeed grateful for your prudence. Obviously you wish to ascertain whether The Star of Sierra Leone... and your *Orloff* are one and the same stone."

"My government has asked me to make discreet enquiries."

"And what do you propose to do if it is, *hein?* No, no, do not worry... I make fun." He stopped for a moment, thinking. Then he said, "Unfortunately I do not... have the diamond."

Both the Ambassador and Mirzoff looked up sharply.

"Monsieur le Président?"

"You see, my dear friend, I did indeed buy The Star of Sierra Leone – or the *Orloff* or whatever... I bought it in good faith with my own private and personal funds... and I bought it as a gift."

"The *Orloff* would make a very expensive gift."

"That is... my business."

"Mais naturellement."

"It was a gift for a friend. If you... want to see whether it is the *Orloff,* I suggest you ask him."

"I certainly shall, *Monsieur le Président, merci.* May I ask the name of your friend?"

"The President of Cyprus, Archbishop Makarios."

The Ambassador and Mirzoff looked at one another. Mirzoff inclined his head slightly and smiled. The Ambassador looked back towards Pompidou and stood up.

"Monsieur le Président you have been most helpful, I thank you..."

Mirzoff, just out of range of Pompidou's vision, removed a pen from his pocket.

"Naturally we will both treat this conversation in the strictest confidence," assured the Ambassador. "And, of course, the story of the *Orloff* will go no further than these walls."

"Of... course."

Pompidou did not notice the pen next to his right ear, neither did he have any heed of the two cubic centimetres of colourless, odourless, slow-acting cyanide gas that was squirted from the end of it. *[A more potent and immediate-acting form of this gas was used to kill Dr Lev Rebet in Munich on October 12 1952. The gas induces heart failure and is virtually untraceable upon post mortem examination.]* Pompidou felt no different from normal as Albert returned, and he bade the Ambassador and his aide goodbye.

Under one hundred hours later Georges Pompidou was dead.

Subsequent checks have shown that the Russian Ambassador did not visit Georges Pompidou at 11:45 that day. Neither did the Russian Embassy employ an aide named Alexei Mirzoff. It is suspected that immediately after the interview, the exact double of the Russian Ambassador was hastily driven into Belgium and from there onwards into the Soviet Union. It is a fact that he was seen in a suburb of Moscow on Sunday March 31. 'Alexei Mirzoff' was also seen in Moscow on the same day.

As for the link between Pompidou and Makarios, this has never been fully discovered. To this day, close family and friends believe their only affinity was that of two heads of two dissimilar republics. However, it is probable that in late 1973 Makarios struck up a friendship with the Frenchman during clandestine discussions on arms and agricultural sales, completely without the knowledge of France's EEC partners. It is also probable that the Archbishop was instrumental in obtaining the services of two Turkish and one Yugoslav specialist medical consultants who visited Pompidou in early February 1974. No allegory concerning a future French President and diamonds from an African 'republic' is to be drawn.

Ψ

Monday April 8 1974

"The joint Egyptian-British-American operation to clear the Suez Canal of debris from the Yom Kippur War starts tomorrow. Three Royal Navy minesweepers and one support vessel have today arrived at Port Said ready to commence operation."

Houston, Texas, USA

"Hi, this is Jim McKane."

"Ah, hello Mr McKane, you don't know me, my name is Sally-Anne Bowker and I'm a friend of Steve Graves?"

"Why Miss Bowker, of course, I recognize the name. Steve spoke a lot about you. What can I do for you, ma'm?"

"Well, actually, it was about Steve that I rang. He hasn't written or called me since he went off to the Mediterranean nearly three months ago. I kinda wondered if you could tell me how he was getting on and when he will be coming back...?"

"Well, I would if I could Miss Bowker, but how should I know?"

"Well, I – "

"Y' know it's strange the way Steve went off like that."

"Went off?"

"Without any notice or anything. Okay, he only worked for us on an assignment basis."

"An *assignment* basis?"

"Contract, you know. He was not on the payroll as an employee. Well, he just came back from lunch one day, a Toosday I think it was, did his afternoon's work and then announced that he could no longer complete his current contract and that he would be leaving immediately. He wouldn't explain further and none of us could understand it. He was brilliant at his work and he'd never complained about contract rates... So, he went off to the Med, eh? It would have been nice to receive a card or something from him. But if he hasn't written to you well then I guess there's no chance of him writing to us, eh? Heh, heh. We *would* like to know why he left, though – hope it wasn't something we said, heh, heh, heh. So I really can't help you on that score ma'm... Hello?... Hello, Miss Bowker?... Hello?... Well! And a Happy Easter to you too, you stupid broad...!"

Ψ

Friday April 19 1974

"The state of Bihar in north-east India was on full alert tonight after yesterday's dismissal of thirty-five government ministers by Mrs Gandhi. This followed the state government's formal resignation nine days ago over allegations of corruption. A new fourteen member cabinet has been formed."

Nicosia District, Cyprus

April in Cyprus is beautiful. It is a month of clear skies and a perfect temperature averaging twenty degrees. The citrus trees are in full blossom in preparation for the harvest of the summer, and the sweet, tempting, gorgeous smell of the orchards pervades the countryside. The tourist season is not yet fully under way, and it is a time of peace, a time to relax, a time when languor can be forgiven.

It is not a time for violence.

The Mercedes arrived at the house in Eylenja, south-east of Nicosia, at precisely 08:30, as it did every morning. The official government chauffeur did not alight or give any indication of his arrival, but nevertheless just fifteen seconds later the heavy wooden door in the side wall opened and the figure stepped out. He was dressed as usual in the long black flowing robes of a bishop of the Greek Orthodox Church.

Bishop Michael Rigakis was not an official Minister of State but an aide of External Affairs Minister Ioannis Christophides, and a close friend and confidant of the President.

Settling down in the back of the car, the Bishop closed his eyes and began to pray silently, as was his custom every day. Between his hands he held a silver crucifix which was tied on to a leather thong around his waist. The journey to the House of Representatives on Leophorus Omirou just outside the south-west walls of the old city of Nicosia would take twenty minutes.

Without a word, the driver engaged gear and pulled away. The roads were always quite clear at that hour of the morning, and he expected a short, uncomplicated drive.

They had been travelling for eight minutes and were on the main road to Nicosia when the attack happened.

It was the sound of the windscreen splintering that made the bishop open his eyes, just a split second before something hot and wet splashed onto his face. He screamed before realising he had not been hit, and he looked up to see that the left side of the driver's face had disintegrated into a ruby-coloured pulp. Only then did he hear the blast of gunfire.

The chauffeur leaned against the door, as if tired. The car swerved wildly as the dead hands fell from the steering wheel. The Bishop instinctively wiped his hands across his face and then pulled them away, covered with the driver's blood and brains.

The Mercedes thundered off the road, jumping madly up and down as it ploughed through the long grass. The chauffeur's body jogged up and down, almost hitting the roof, his flopping head painting firm, thick strokes of gore onto the closed side window.

The Bishop made to lean forward to grab the wheel but before he could do so the car came to an abrupt halt with an almighty *bang* from underneath as something broke and the undercarriage hit the hard, rocky ground. He fell forward and then sideways, cracking his head on the door. Dazed but conscious, he was aware of the door opening and then hands were dragging him out, His cassock caught on something, and for some stupid and irrelevant reason he found himself thinking that he would have to ask his housekeeper to stitch it for him later.

Then he was sitting on the dry, dusty ground, propped up against the side of the vehicle and facing away from the road. Any passing motorist would not have seen him.

An iron hand was clamped hard around his bearded jaw, puckering his features. The grip was so hard that he thought his jaw was going to be crushed. He winced in agony.

The owner of the hand was a huge beast of a man, totally bald but with a thick black moustache which contained various items that had fallen from his nose. His eyes were black and full of hatred, the one hatred that is worse than that of Greek and Turk: Greek and Greek. His breath was disgusting, and the Bishop would have turned his head away if it had been within his power.

In the extreme right of his vision, Bishop Rigakis could see another man. He was similar to the ogre, but this time not so fat and with more hair. A relative, possibly his son.

The Bishop made a noise, trying to ask the question, but he simply could not move his jaw within the grip.

"I'm glad you want to talk." A pair of blue-denimed legs entered his vision and their owner crouched down so that he was next to the ogre. "Because you've got something to tell me, fella."

It was a young face underneath a mop of tight, curly black hair. The face possibly looked older than it was because of a drooping moustache. The skin was tanned, but only recently so, as if the man had not been in Cyprus for long – which was really self-evident by his accent: it was American.

The priest's fearful eyes turned towards Steve.

The American's face was hard, yet it held none of the hatred of the ogre. "Don't worry, I'm not going to hurt you – providing you tell me what I want to know. Do you understand?"

The Bishop said nothing, he just looked scared.

"Do you understand?" The voice colder this time, menacing.

To help the Bishop's powers of speech, the ogre bashed the aching head hard against the side of the vehicle, then he released the jaw from the terrible grip.

The Bishop thought that two of his teeth had become locked together from the sheer pressure of the ogre's hand. He was vaguely aware that he had pissed himself with fear. "I… I understand," he managed to stutter.

"Good. Now tell me, Father: what is The Eye of Makarios?"

A dazed look came into the Bishop's eyes and his head twitched involuntarily. For a moment Steve thought he was going to pass out.

"The Eye of Makarios, Father. What is it?"

From behind the American a girl appeared, dressed in peasant clothes. Rigakis thought that her face was vaguely familiar. In her hands she held a rifle. So, it had been *she* who had killed the chauffeur.

He was about to speak when, without warning, the ogre's hand came down sharply across his face. He felt a nail rip the corner of his mouth.

"We don't want to have to use force," the young man sounded as if he meant it. "But we will if necessary. Tell me – please. We know you know. What is The Eye of Makarios?"

The Bishop's mouth moved in silence for a few seconds and then sound came out. "It… it… is that all? There is no need for all this – "

Again the hand across the face, blood in his beard.

"Please." The American.

"It… it is carried on his person at all times… in a pouch around his waist… I do not know where he got it… said it was a gift… I think it is a safe place for his money." He was finding it even more difficult to talk as his lips puffed and turned a wicked shade of purple. "He has not had it long…"

"Yes Father, but what *is* it?"

Rigakis managed to frown. Surely everybody knew what it was? "It is his name for it. It is a diamond… a big diamond."

Steve and Christina exchanged glances. Then he ordered, "All right, let him go."

Ogre and relative relinquished their intimidating positions and disappeared from view. Rigakis watched as the American stood up, said "Thank you, Father," and turned towards the girl.

"At last" he said. "Okay, let's go." He moved off.

The girl remained where she was for a moment, looking at the dishevelled bloody figure on the ground, all the pride and dignity of his ecclesiastical rank ground into the dust. She lowered the gun and fumbled in the folds of her skirt. She bent down and gently wiped the Bishop's forehead.

"Th – thank you." He noticed what deep, dark eyes she had.

She stared at him. Then Rigakis' eyes widened in total terror as he saw what was in her other hand. He tried to move but his limbs would not respond.

The finely sharpened meat skewer was inserted into the head behind the Bishop's right ear. It was pushed easily up into the brain. He died instantly with just the briefest flash of pain.

She arose and followed just twenty paces behind the American.

Half a minute later, a vehicle pulled out from behind the bushes and sped off down the road, away from Nicosia.

Back by the Mercedes, the Bishop's nervous system gave its final, convulsive twitch and he lay still forever. A fly landed on the swollen upper lip and began exploring the lower nostril hairs...

Ψ

Saturday 20 April 1974

"In Israel, it is now almost certain that the Labour Party will elect General Yitshak Rabin to succeed Mrs Golda Meir when it meets on Monday. Mrs Meir resigned ten days ago.
"Meanwhile in Greece, preparations are under way for the celebrations to mark tomorrow's anniversary of the colonels' military coup seven years ago."

Yeri, Nicosia District, Cyprus

The villa had been empty for over a month now – a fact which had not gone unnoticed by the locals of Yeri village. The businessman who owned the place must be off on one of his jaunts somewhere. Sometimes he had been known to disappear for up to half a year before arriving back out of the blue. He would stay for anything from ten days to ten months, and then he would be off again. One rumour had it that he was some sort of rich recluse who owned shipping lines. But the elders of the village knew better. They knew for a fact that his money came from crime. He was one of the leaders of the *Mafia* or the *Union Corse* and, they stated categorically, his periods away were on Family business.

Whether the people of Yeri village believed this to be true or not, they kept their distance from the house without actually isolating it, only speaking to the owner when spoken to and supplying the occasional domestic. They let him be and he let them be. It was an amicable, tacit understanding.

So far this time he had been absent for nearly two months. Whether it was by coincidence or design, he usually went away at this time of the year just when the tourist season was starting. If the past was anything to go by, he would not be back until September or October.

When the two Grivas people arrived unexpectedly two days ago, the idea had been discussed by the village elders. The couple were looking for a safe house while they planned some operation. The villa was perfect, isolated and well away from the village, empty and secluded. Why not? The man would not be back until the late summer, he never was.

Earlier that evening, a village elder had contacted Christina at the farm of Costas, the ogre. Suggestions had been made, heads nodded sagely. Not only did the place seem ideal but, in view of recent events, it also got them out of the village's hair.

Nobody in the village had spoken about what had happened yesterday, but the news of the Bishop's hijacking and murder had spread like wildfire throughout the island. Makarios had ordered a full alert, and three hundred members of the Tactical Reserve Force had swarmed into the area south of Nicosia.

The TRF expected to find nothing. The unit Commander, a man called Christou, reckoned that the murderers would be long gone, to a far part of the island if not to the mainland all together. It was this that Christina and Steve were banking on, that the centre of the storm was the safest place.

Their hypothesis had proved correct. The TRF had saturated the area, asked a few peremptory questions and had received well-rehearsed and totally false answers. Yes, people had seen them. Witnesses estimations of the number of persons involved ranging from ten to fifty, their escape route being towards Kyrenia, towards Larnaca, towards Morphou and towards Famagusta, all at one and the same time. Against this wall of well-prepared confusion, the TRF had withdrawn after just one day from saturation level to just a 'presence'.

Now Christina expertly picked the lock on the door of the villa. They entered by torchlight, not daring to try any of the light switches to see if the power was still on. These places usually had their own generator somewhere out back, and it would have been turned off by the owner before he went away.

The villa was cold inside, the windows closed and shuttered for the past two months.

Steve's torch played around the room. It was a big, split-level living area, tastefully furnished in contemporary Mediterranean style, tiled floor, honey-coloured stucco walls. At the far end was a door which would lead to the kitchen and thence to the back entrance and out into the grounds and outhouse.

"We shall explore more in the morning by natural light," said Christina, whispering even though they knew they were alone in the place.

"Sure," agreed Steve, his voice also instinctively subdued. "I think the best thing we can do now is find somewhere to lay our heads. C'mon, let's have a look upstairs."

On the floor above were three bedrooms and two bathrooms. A quick look in all the rooms revealed that the first one, on the southern side, was the one probably most used. The bed was stripped, as it would be if its usual occupant expected to be away for some time, but a convenient cupboard revealed sheets and pillows for the use of.

They prepared the bed together in the twilight of the torchbeam.

"God, I'm looking forward to a proper bed," said Steve. "Especially after that meal of old mother Makouri's. I've never tasted *stifatho* like that before."

"Haf you *effer* tasted *stifatho* before, Stelios?" Fold, flap, tuck.

"I have indeed, my child!" Indignant. "I'm not a complete freshman to the delights of things Cypriot, you know." He strained his eyes to see the curves beneath the blouse and skirt. "Especially women."

Christina straightened up. "I hope you arse miling when you say that, Stelios."

In the darkness he was in fact smiling broadly. As she went round to the other side of the bed, he stretched out and whacked the firm right cheek of her bottom. She squealed and ran out of reach of further discipline.

He chuckled, then changed the subject, "Y' know I'm surprised at all the help we're getting. EOKA seems to be more alive than ever, at least in support."

"In support yes, and in members too. Remember Nicos, Raouf and Lefteris? They are alive and active. We could haf been with them but we chose not to. But around here people know what Mouskos can do. And they are kind because you are who you are. The myth of Stelios, Grivas' long lost son, precedes you. Haf you not noticed the way they look at you, scrutinising and comparing?"

"Yes, I have."

"We should be thankful that it hass not got back to the TRF or Mouskos yet that Grivas' American son is one off the people they are looking for, or else we would stand no chance. Think what a pretty prize *you* would make for the Priest. The area iss crowded enough as it iss since yesterday."

The bed finished, she came over to him. He put his hands on her shoulders, looking down into her eyes. "And what a prize *you* are, beautiful lady. Now we must rest, for tomorrow we've got a lot of planning to do. Buddy Makarios carries that diamond around his waist. *That* is not going to be easy. I think I'm gonna need to take a few trips into Nicosia. Will Costas let me have the car?"

"There should be no problem."

"Good. This is gonna take some time, kid."

"But you will succeed."

"Oh yes, I will succeed. For my father."

"And then you will go away?"

"I don't know. Honestly, *I* cannot lead EOKA. I guess I will go back to the States."

"And to your woman – Sallyan?"

"Sally-Anne. Possibly. She's probably forgotten about me by now. But that's in the future, Christy. Think only of now. Think of what has to be done." His lips gently brushed against hers. "Think of us."

Her arms went around his neck and she pulled his head down firmly, her strong wet tongue forcing its way into his mouth.

Ψ

Monday May 6 1974

"Chancellor Willi Brandt of West Germany has resigned. Announcing his resignation this afternoon, he said that it was the only proper course open to him as he was politically responsible for negligence in the espionage affair concerning his former personal assistant Gunther Guillaume, who has admitted spying for East Germany.

"At home, the million-pound Vermeer painting The Guitar Player, *stolen from Kenwood House Hampstead on 23rd February, has been found in St Bartholomew's Churchyard in the City of London. It was wrapped in a newspaper."*

Houston, Texas, USA

Sally-Anne Bowker had spent a fretful weekend. The fact that it was her time of the month did not help, but she was well aware that the cause of her fretfulness was purely emotional, not physical. It had been a month since she had heard the earth-shattering news from that stupid man McKane. A month since she had been told that Steve, *her* Steve, had not gone off to the Balearics for *Gulf* as he had told her.

Just to confirm that McKane hadn't been lying, she had phoned *Gulf*'s Personnel Manager a few days after phoning McKane. She too confirmed that Steve Graves had simply upped and went that afternoon in January, breaking his assignment contract.

Sally was perplexed. She just could not understand it. Perhaps both the *Gulf* people were mistaken? No, stop fooling yourself sister. And what was this about him being on contract only? She thought he was a permanent employee. Something was obviously going on. Maybe it was national defense work and the 'quitting the job' story was just a cover? Steve had mentioned to her once that *Gulf* undertook certain undersea assignments for Washington (or for Langley, to be exact). Then again, maybe it was the old, old story – another woman. But Steve would not just load a pack of lies onto her and then walk out, it was not in his character. And anyway, it was not as if they were married. If he wanted to call it a day as far as their relationship was concerned, he would only have to say so, and he knew that. The fact that she was crazy about him would not enter into it.

What *had* happened to him? Had he met with some unearthly accident?

These thoughts had plagued her since her calls to *Gulf*. Up until a few days ago she had resigned herself to the fact that there was little or nothing she could do. However, her period depression had now instilled more determination into her, and she had gone into school that morning with her mind made up.

That lunchtime she dismissed her class immediately on time. What she had planned would take more than her allotted hour and twenty, but it just couldn't be helped. She jumped into her ancient Ford and quickly drove out to the airport, thanking God that the traffic was not too heavy.

It took her a while to find a place to park and then a further while to find what she was looking for. The middle-aged guy with the XXXecogn behind the *Air France* desk smiled pleasantly as she approached the counter.

"Afternoon ma'm," he was a local, not French as she had expected. "My name is Wilbur, I represent *Air France,* what can I do for you?"

"Hi, er... I wonder if I could ask you a question?" Like a lot of her countrymen, Sally spoke in continual question-marks. "It's a friend of mine? Well, basically, to tell the truth, he went off to Europe a few months ago and I haven't heard from him since, And, well, really..."

"You want to check whether he did in fact go?" Wilbur nodded knowledgeably.

"You got it."

"Well I think we may be able to assist you there. You have any details? Day, time, flight number an' all?"

"Hold on." She rummaged in her purse, coming up with a scrap of paper. "He went January 23rd, in the morning, on the direct flight to Paris?"

"Ah ha." Wilbur hastily scribbled down the details. "And he has a name?"

"Oh, sorry, yeh. Graves. Steven Graves?"

"Steven Graves... right. I can certainly check that for you. If you would like to wait over there ma'm?... Shirley, can you take over for a second please?"

A big-breasted, uniformed blonde squeezed out of a room behind as Wilbur went in. She gave a half-smile to Sally and then turned to attend to an elderly couple who, by the look on the wife's face, had something to gripe about.

It seemed like ages, but Wilbur was back in two minutes, a computer printout in his hand. He looked pensive. "Well ma'm, I'm afraid we had no Steven Graves on our morning flight to Paris on that day, it *was* January 23rd? Uh-huh... Oh, hold on... oh no, I guess not. The nearest we come to Graves is a guy called Grivas," he pronounced it Grivers. "Apart from that..." He shrugged his shoulders regretfully.

"Do you think I may just have a look at that list?" Sally smiled sweetly, pushed her specs up with a finger, and held out a tentative hand.

"Well, really I'm not supposed to, but..." He made a show of being circumspect. "I guess just a peek wouldn't hurt." He placed the sheet on the counter top and turned it in her direction.

She ran her finger down the column. He was right, of course, there was no Steven Graves, only this Grivas person. Stelios Grivas. Her eyes travelled down the other two hundred names. Nothing...

Hey now, just one minute... SG... Steve Graves – Stelios Grivas... it could be... No, could it?... Yes, it must be, it was too much of a coincidence. But why on earth...?

"Ma'm?"

She became aware that she was staring abstractedly into space. "Oh, er, oh, sorry."

"I said have you finished with the list?"

"Oh yes, thanks, yes."

"No Steven Graves, I'm afraid." The paper was taken back and slipped under the counter.

"No, no I guess not." She gave a false laugh. "Oh well, thanks for your help anyway."

"You're welcome ma'm. Thank you for enquiring of *Air France,* and you have a nice day."

"Mm."

PART THREE

Ψ

OBJECTIVE OBTAINED

Ψ

Thursday May 16 1974

"The stoppages in Ulster go on. Shops and offices, factories, public houses, clubs and hotels were closed today because of the Protestant Ulster Workers' Council Strike. Public transport in Belfast has been completely withdrawn. The strike is against the Sunningdale Agreement.
"In West Germany, the Bundestag today elected Herr Helmut Schmidt as the new Chancellor following the resignation of Willi Brandt ten days ago."

London, England

"And how are yer, me little piece of English mutton?"

"Oh it's you. At last. It's about bloody time you rang. Where in God's name have you been?"

"Ah, I have more important things to attend to than you, Stanley William me ole son. *The Bloomsbury* at one o'clock. Be there."

The Bloomsbury Wine Lodge was in New Oxford Street at the intersection with the southern half of Museum Street. It was a respectable single-bar establishment, rated as one of the best in the district by its clientele, many of whom were denizens of the nearby Ministry of Defence buildings.

Egginton arrived a little before 13:00 to find Michael Mahoney already seated at one of the tables against the wall, tucking into a large helping of shepherd's pie. The Irishman looked up as the shadow filled the doorway. He waved his hand, beckoning the Colonel over.

"Afternoon, Colonel. The usual?" Mahoney put his knife and fork down and felt in his pocket for money.

"I'll buy my own."

"Ah, t' hell with yer and don't be such a miserable sod. Hold it a minute." Mahoney slid off his seat and went over to the bar, returning two minutes later with a pint of bitter. "Place is filling up. That's good. The more people here, the less we are noticed. And we wouldn't want to compromise your distinguished position by having people see you talking to a mick now, would we ole son?"

Egginton mumbled something which came out like a growl. Mahoney attacked his food once more, deliberately stringing the Englishman along with silence. But Egginton was not to be baited. He had known Mahoney long enough to be wise to his tactics. Notice the imperiousness in the voice today, the dominance? That was a sign he was ready to make his wants known, to drop the bombshell. He was a fisherman at the point of heaving his catch from the water: it had been teased, played with and given line long enough.

It took a few minutes for Mahoney to finish eating, during which time Egginton sipped his beer and said nothing. You can make the running, you bastard, he said to himself, I'm not going to cue you one iota.

Mahoney downed half the contents of his pint glass of Guinness and then belched unnecessarily.

"Now then Stanley, t' business. Are yer game to my proposition?" He lowered his voice. "Remuneration as I stated. Quarter of a million and the negatives and all existing prints of the photographs."

"And you off my back forever?" asked Egginton too quickly. He must not seem eager.

Mahoney feigned hurt. "Well now, ain't that a nice t'ing to say! After all the good toimes oi've given yer, the women and children oi've paid for. That's gratitude for yer!"

Egginton sneered. "Stop pissing about you Irish bastard and get on with it, I haven't got all day. This is to be the last one."

Mahoney stared at him, all traces of geniality extinguished. "It's to be the last one when I say it is. But if you used yer brains you would realise that with the photographs in your possession I would no longer have a bargaining position, would I? And anyway, would you really stay around with a quarter of a million under your bed?"

"*If* I get a quarter of a million, *if* I get the negatives."

"I'm a man of my word, Colonel, you know that."

"Hmph, but I suspect the – "

Suddenly Mahoney leant forward, eyes slitting. "I don't give a fuck for your suspicions Egginton, okay? *I'm* fed up with *your* pissing about. Are you in or does your wife get the photos?"

"Damn you, you bastard."

Mahoney leant back. He smiled. "Great, well at least we've got that settled." The remainder of the Guinness was downed in one. "Come, walk with me."

Oxford Street, London's famous two and a half kilometres of every shop under the sun, is always at its busiest on a Thursday. With the anarchic shopping hours operating in Britain at that time, Thursday was the one day when all the shops stayed open to the unearthly hour of 20:00. The mass of beings ever eager to spend, spend, spend – and only the minority of whom were English – began to build up well before lunchtime, ready to observe the luxury of 'late opening'. Mahoney and Egginton were soon lost in the crowds.

For the first few hundred metres until they reached the intersection with Soho Street, the Irishman was silent. Then he said, "It's twelve pounds of plutonium."

At that very second a number 73 bus chose to thunder past, and the drama of the moment was lost. Egginton said "What?" brusquely.

"Twelve pounds of plutonium."

Egginton heard it this time and, on balance, he took it very well. He turned a nasty shade of grey, certainly; his hands started to tremble and his power of speech left him, without doubt; but he carried on walking with not a falter in his step. His eyes took on a strange, glazed appearance.

Mahoney smiled, recognizing the symptoms he himself had experienced five months before. "I know, it's horrible, ain't it me ole fella? I felt like it too. Don't worry, you'll soon get used to it. Twelve pounds of the beautiful stuff it is. Not an ounce less, not an ounce more. And as soon as possible – although my clients appreciate that such an amount just cannot disappear into thin air. Shall we say three months? Three months and you'll have a quarter of a million quid and the photos, and me off yer back forever. Don't worry about transportation, just let me know where the stuff is and when it is available, and I will arrange collection. Make it in Britain, of course. Here," an envelope was removed from his jacket and placed into one of Egginton's pockets, "a little something as a sign of good faith. I'll be in touch."

It was a full five minutes before Egginton realised that Mahoney was gone, and by that time he had walked as far as Argyll Street, next to Oxford Circus, the halfway point of Oxford Street at the junction with Regent Street. Egginton's brain was too numb to give his body anything but the most simple of commands, and it was certainly in no condition to think or evaluate.

He found himself entering *The Argyll* pub, and then he was at the bar and a voice which sounded like his own was ordering two triple brandies.

With the first triple inside him, his hands were sufficiently recovered to be able to reach into his pocket and extract the envelope the Irishman had deposited there. He knew what it felt like but it was not until he was in a cab travelling back along Oxford Street that he risked looking inside.

Mahoney's 'good faith' consisted of two thousand pounds and a print and a single negative of Egginton doing something particularly dreadful to a young person's nether regions.

Ψ

Sunday May 19 1974

"Preliminary statistics from yesterday's general election in Australia indicate that Mr Gough Whitlam's Labour Party has achieved a narrow victory over the Liberal opposition.
"And in France the final round of the French Presidential elections has been taking place. It has been a closely-fought contest between the two candidates: Monsieur François Mitterand and Monsieur Valéry Giscard d'Estaing."

Crimea, USSR

The villa was between the towns of Feodosiya and Yalta on the south-eastern coast of the Crimea, the mountainous part of the Russian Riviera. It was an official *datcha* reserved for the exclusive use of Very Important Members of the Party down for short spells from the capital. The villa itself was some thirty years old, but regular decoration and refurbishment made sure that it remained in prime condition for its honourable guests.

Ramirov had been at the villa for three weeks now, by order, and he was getting irritable. His mind and body were yearning for action again. He was not trained for a life of ease.

The first week of the current visit to Russia had been spent in Moscow with Comrade Furtseva. Ramirov had arrived direct from Paris under the guise of 'Alexei Mirzoff', and Furtseva had been deeply interested in what he had learnt from the French President. [*She did not know, nor would she ever know, about the incident with the cyanide gas. That was Ramirov's own doing. The only other witness, the look-alike Ambassador, had tragically had his skull caved in by a mugger in the Moscow metro two days after his return.*] After Furtseva had made a telephone call and then visited Someone, she had recalled Ramirov to her office and in no uncertain terms made him aware that he should be deeply honoured to be a party to what she was about to reveal.

Something was brewing in Cyprus, and as usual the *Komitet Gosudarstvennoi Bezopasnasti* was more than a little involved. An opportunity might arise soon when he could secure the diamond without any overt, singular attack on Makarios. Until she could give him more detail, he was to remain in the Soviet Union.

That had been nearly two months ago.

Three weeks at the secret KGB Academy Number 311 at Novosibirsk had followed, an enjoyable time for Ramirov who had to be warned about his zeal on the unarmed combat after a junior officer had had three ribs broken and had required no less than sixty-eight stitches in a head wound. There had followed another week in Moscow and then, on May 5, he had been told that the *datcha* on the riviera was available for him.

The weather had not been over-good (he would be getting more sun now back 'home' in Cyprus) and even this party palace was beginning to pall now that he was into his third week.

The one consolation, of course, was Natasha. To be very cruel, she could be described as an official whore supplied by the masters in Moscow for the privileged use of the *datcha* occupants (male or female). To be very kind, she could be described as a pretty local girl of some twenty summers, charming, always cheerful and an expert at all things carnal. She visited every third day, and Ramirov had to admit that he looked forward to her coming. She was due today.

Ramirov lay on his front on the grass feeling a welcomingly warm sun on his vested back. He listened to the soft, soporific sound of the sea mating with the beach not too far over the back wall. He smiled as he heard a vehicle pull up outside. She was right on time, as always. The key turned in the giant front door, and then the footsteps echoed across the tiled floor of the living-room.

Ramirov's head snapped up. Something was wrong. Something was not quite right. The weight of the tread was the same but the timbre of the echo was just the minutest bit different from usual. Only an expert would have picked it up. The shoes were not the usual ones. A state employee in Natasha's position would possess only one pair, so it followed that the person who had just entered was not her.

It took only a few seconds, but by the time the woman reached the patio Ramirov was up, gun in hand, and standing to one side of the door.

As the woman came through he seized her from behind, the barrel of the Polish *Radom .35* pointing straight into her left ear.

Then he let her go immediately.

"Comrade Furtseva!" He stood rigid, almost to attention.

The grey face looked at him without expression. "I see three weeks at the Academy have done you good, Ilich. I am pleased. A little refresher now and again hurts no one. Not even you. And," she moved her head up and down ruefully, "I am pleased that you are on our side."

"Thank you Comrade, and my apologies if I caused you any distress. Would you like a drink? Shall we sit inside?" The gun was tucked into the waistband of his slacks.

"No, let us walk in the garden, it is a lovely day." Furtseva was not dressed in her usual KGB uniform but in a grey dress of expensive material and probably of western manufacture. It was complemented by a light blue cardigan. The clothing was her attempt at looking casual, and with the short masculine grey hair and the hard features she looked utterly ridiculous.

They walked slowly, Fursteva observing the blooming bougainvillaea without interest. She spoke. "Have you been enjoying your rest here, Ilich?"

"To be honest Comrade, it has made a peaceful change but I cannot say that it has been enjoyable."

"Hnn! Always the man of action, eh? Always wanting to be in the thick of things!" She patted his arm, an almost maternal gesture. "Well, shortly you will champ at the bit no longer. I mentioned in Moscow about certain plans that were being formulated regarding Cyprus – of course, this will go no further than ourselves."

Ramirov inclined his head in agreement.

"Well, now I can tell you. You are aware of the organisation EOKA?"

"Naturally."

"Certain arrangements have been made between them and our own interest, the Akel Communist Party, on a little 'joint effort'. Sometime within the next two months there will be a coup on the island. Makarios will be killed. Your services have been offered. Neither EOKA nor Akel know fully what you are or who you represent, and I have no intention of them finding out. But I have told them that when the coup takes place we will have our own man on the island and his one specific task will be the President. Nothing, absolutely nothing, else."

"Is there anybody else involved?"

"Anybody else?" She smiled, looking like a harridan-coquette. She knew exactly what he was talking about.

"Any other... interested parties?"

She guffawed and slapped him mightily on the back. "I think that Academy is too good, Ilich. You will be wanting my shoes next!" Behind her laughter, her eyes gave him a piercing glance. Ramirov deliberately did not look at her.

"Yes," she continued. "There are other interests involved. Our comrades, the rulers of Greece. As you know, they have a presence on the island in the form of the National Guard. At a given date and time – which I do not yet know – they too will turn against Makarios. It is to be a concerted effort between EOKA and the National Guard, together with our interest."

Ramirov thought what an unholy, treacherous, potentially volatile alliance that would be, but like the good comrade he was he said nothing.

"The Colonels in Greece have leapt at the opportunity of your services. They still have some trepidation about liquidating the charmed person of the Archbishop. They are content to leave that up to you."

They had reached the wall at the end of the garden, and they turned to retrace their steps to the house.

"You *really* want me to kill him?"

The lips wrinkled. "Yes. In fact, Comrade Kosygin has expressly ordered it. Makarios has been a thorn in everyone's side for long enough. But get the diamond first. That is your priority. If it is at all possible to remove Makarios, then do so. But take no undue risks for his sake. There is excitement in the Praesidium over the Arab's plan. Let us not spoil our part of it."

"But if Comrade Kosygin has – "

"*I* will worry about him," she said tersely.

"Yes, Comrade."

A bird landed on the grass in front of them, looked around, crapped and then flew off again.

"When I have the diamond, should I report back?"

"No. You are not to contact me at all until the diamond is safely delivered and your part in this business is over. It must *never* be suspected that the Soviet Union was in any way involved with the detonation of a nuclear device in Britain. We must be grateful that your cover as a South American is so strong. If even the merest hint of Soviet involvement was ever made..." She looked at him stonily. "Then heaven help us *all*."

Ramirov returned the look. "I understand, Comrade."

They reached the villa.

"Now, Comrade Ilich, I think I will have that drink. You have wodka, of course."

"Certainly comrade. You wish anything with it?"

"Pah! Of course not. Perhaps some ice on this fine day, that is all. Natasha will not be visiting today," Furtseva continued as she sat down upon a well-upholstered leather couch and splayed her legs out in front of her. "So, after the wodka, we will see if we can improvise without her. Then afterwards you may cook me a delicious meal. Come, sit down here next to me and relax. I am in no hurry."

Ψ

Monday May 20 1974

"Five hundred more troops were flown into Northern Ireland today, the first full day of the Ulster Workers' Council strike. So far, two-thirds of the province is without electricity, and the delivery of essential food supplies has stopped."

Houston, Texas, USA

It had been another depressing weekend for Sally-Anne Bowker. And this time it could not be blamed on a period. This time it was purely the fault of Steve Graves.

Why oh why hadn't he written like he had promised? Had something happened to him when he had reached Paris? Had he, in fact, reached Paris at all? He had telephoned her, but that could have been from anywhere. What *was* going on? He tells her that *Gulf* are sending him on a project to the Balearic islands. *Gulf* say he just upped and left. Indeed she finds out that he didn't even work permanently for them. He phones her and says he will write. *That was four months ago and she had not heard a thing since.*

These thoughts and many others had been playing around in her head for so long now that it seemed they had made permanent camp there. They nagged at her as she drove to school that morning, windows open, arm resting on the side of her car, on a particularly warm May Monday.

Goddammit, she and Steve had lived together for two years so she should know a bit about the guy's character. It was not in his make-up just to leave her like that. But... there had been no contact.

Sally beeped her horn at an innocuous convertible and shouted "Bastard!" as her battered but powerful Ford thundered past. Most un-school-marmy. She felt aggressive to day.

Today was a day when she would be teaching the etymology of English sayings to some of her younger students. Well there was one that fitted perfectly the situation she was in now. *If the mountain will not come to Mohammed...*

Steve Graves was the mountain and he would not (or could not) come to or contact Sally-Anne Mohammed. So she must take things into her own hands. Two weeks ago she had checked that flight list at the airport, and the name Stelios Grivas had stuck firmly in her mind.

If she was going to play at all, she must play a hunch – and Graves/Grivas was the only hunch she had. It had taken a fortnight for her to reason it out and, if she were truthful, to pluck up the courage. After all, it took guts just to up and go off. At least she thought it did, but Steve Graves – whoever he was – seemed to have done it coolly enough.

Today was the day. Her summer break did not start until the middle of June, but with the sudden death of her favourite aunt up in Boston – no, make that her grandmother (or had she used that one before? No bother, it was her other grandmother if she had) she had to rush up to Mass immediately.

It would be frowned upon, of course. She would be called upon to explain to the Principal (miserable old sonbitch) how she *had* to go to arrange her grandmother's funeral and look after her estate, how her grandmother had brought her up since she was a bitty child and been like a mother to her, how she was deeply upset by Granny's sudden and unexpected death from a heart attack at the age of a hundred and twenty (now now kid, don't get frivolous) and how she was broken up and couldn't teach right now anyway if she was forced to stay.

She would be allowed to go, of course. Probably unpaid, but what the hell?

Her right foot eased fractionally off the accelerator as she neared her turning off the freeway…

It was the other driver's fault, of that there was never any doubt. But had Sally been concentrating more on her driving and less on her private thoughts, it was reckoned by the police afterwards that she could have swerved and saved herself.

Without warning, the other vehicle slewed across from the southbound lanes, crashed through the central barrier, and headed straight for the old Ford like a missile homing in on target.

Sally never even saw it. All she was aware of was the world outside suddenly spinning around. Then a horrible metallic crunching sound. The road above her where the sky should be. The edge of the seat belt gouging her chest like a knife into cooked cheese. A great splurge of something red and gooey on the cracked windscreen. A miasma of lights.

And then no lights at all…

Ψ

Thursday May 23 1974

"In India the railway strike continues into its thirteenth day. During violent clashes in many parts of the country, it is reported that up to forty-thousand railwaymen have been arrested."

Yeri, Nicosia District, Cyprus

Costas, the ogre who had helped in the attack on the Bishop's car, had brought round supplies that afternoon. It was enough to last for quite a while, paid for or stolen by local EOKA sympathisers. That evening Christina had cooked Steve a magnificent meze of *talattouri, taramosolata, dolmas, tavas, keftedes* and unbelievably delicious *lokmades* (hot doughnuts in syrup).

Now, with a half-bottle of *ouzo* inside him, Steve sat back on the comfortable couch and listened to an album by *Aphrodite's Child* playing on the old mono record player.

But, exquisite as the meal had been, beautiful as the music was, and contented as he felt thanks to the *ouzo*, he was also feeling edgy. For they had been here too long.

The hue and cry for the Bishop's murderers had long died off, but a month was a long time. And more and more people were beginning to know of their existence. Word was spreading that Grivas' son had come home to lead them to their glorious union with Greece, *Enosis*. It was a rumour that had been encouraged by the three men in Limassol.

Costas was the only person outside of Yeri village, to their knowledge, who knew of their presence in the villa. And that was the way Steve wanted it to stay. But tongues wagged, and if the TRF ever got even the slightest inkling that they were in the area it would not take long for them to 'persuade' a villager to reveal all.

A month had passed, they knew exactly where The Eye of Makarios was, and they still had to come up with a viable plan to get it. They had formulated and dismissed many theories. Excursions to the Presidential Palace (Steve as an American tourist) and to Makarios' home – the Archbishop's Palace – had produced many ideas on how Makarios could be intercepted. But it was the matter of physically getting the diamond from him without being blown to pieces by his guards that was the problem.

"You are looking worried again, my Stelios," observed Christina as she came though from the kitchen. "It iss the usual?"

"The usual," he nodded. "Shit, I simply can't see how I can do it Christy. Short of suicide."

But she wasn't going to listen. "Enough!" she snapped, and Steve looked up. "Get up!"

"What?"

"Come! Do not argue!"

She grabbed his arm tightly and heaved him from the couch. Deliberately, he fell against her, his face nuzzling into her soft and lightly scented neck.

"Will you get off me!" she scolded. "Come along." Drag. "And be unbuttoning your clothes... it would be futile to resist!"

"Yes ma'm. Whatever you say, ma'm."

Steve was dragged upstairs behind her (contriving to bump his face more than once into her bottom), and she pushed him into the bathroom. She stripped him and pushed him into the shower. Through the tingling water he watched her disrobe. She stepped in with him, kissed him firmly and then reached for the soap. She began to wash him, her hands tickling into the very crevices of his being. Then it was into the bedroom for a complete body massage.

An hour later she was just finishing. Steve, as relaxed as a rag doll, was both sleepy and aroused by her ministrations despite being attended to twice in that area.

She took her hands from him and hummed a tune from her half-forgotten repertoire as she wiped her mouth. Languidly, Steve leant over and rummaged in a drawer of the bedside cabinet. He produced a wrapped package which Costas had smuggled into the villa earlier.

Christina frowned as he offered it to her. "What iss this please, my darling?"

"C'mon, take it."

Like a child on Christmas morning, she proceeded to rip off the cheap paper. "A *komboloi!*" She grasped the amber beads of the rosary-like object between her fingers. "Oh Stelios, darling. Thank you, thank you so much."

His lips came down on hers and he pushed her backwards, pushing his way between her legs...

Three times a charm.

Afterwards they slept the wonderful cashmere-coated sleep that succeeds sex. By midnight they were both deeply gone. Christina was on her back with her arms above her head, provocative lips slightly parted. Steve was face down on her right, his right arm flung over her body and his face resting on her soft right breast, the warm breeze of his breath keeping the nipple erect.

They both dreamt of Makarios, but in different ways. Steve was on a long, dusty road with the Archbishop walking alone in front of him, a small bulging pouch on a rope around his waist. Every time Steve caught up with him and reached out to snatch the pouch, the Archbishop would disappear and reappear fifty metres up the road, still walking and unaware of Steve's presence. So Steve set off after him again. And again, and again...

Christina dreamt that Makarios was making love to her. He was still fully-clothed in his usual flowing ebony robes, but in place of a penis he was pushing a large and glittering diamond into her...

Their minds were that far removed from reality that they would not have heard the third person's arrival even if he had made a sound – which he did not. Three weeks at the KGB Academy Number 311 at Novosibirsk had seen to that.

Ilich Ramirov was always on his guard, his sixth sense permanently primed for the slightest thing untoward. Even at home here in the villa in Cyprus. He had parked his old Volkswagen Beetle car as far away from the villa as he could, around the side near his garage. Before getting out, he had removed the gun he always kept in the hidden compartment in the steering column, and he had then traversed the final fifty metres to his front door in total silence and complete darkness.

He knew as soon as he put his key in the lock that something was not right. As soon as he opened the door, the presence was obvious. The place, which was in darkness, should have smelt musty after four months of disuse. Instead it smelt of people, of use.

He closed the door behind him and stayed utterly still. The smell of cooking still lingered in the air and there was the faintest trace of a cheap scent. So, a female? And most probably accompanied by one or more males. Locals at play while the businessman was away?

He placed his suitcase down on the tiled floor and stood stock still. It took less than a minute for his ears to pick up the sound of breathing from upstairs. A man's breathing. With the even flow of sleep.

Whoever he was he had certainly made himself at home. And that told Ramirov that there was no immediate danger to his person. Professionals lying in wait would not have domesticated themselves.

He knew exactly which part of each stair to tread on without it creaking. In no time at all he was outside his own bedroom door, gun at the ready. He listened. The male breathing was still regular and heavy. He could hear no other, but then just as he reached out for the door handle the voice of a woman moaned once and then was quiet. The male breathing went on undisturbed.

Slowly the Russian's hand turned the handle...

Christina had to admit she was excited. The old, bearded, hated priest was on top of her, his breath reeking of *houmous*. He was pushing his diamond-hard organ into her. She had climaxed twice already and, although something in her mind told her not to for this was the man she despised above all living things, she found herself moaning, moaning for more and for him to stop, both at the same time.

Suddenly the sun came out and Makarios disappeared like a phantom of the night. The hardness was not pressing between her legs anymore but into her left eye. She awoke, just a fraction before Steve, as her hair was grabbed and the top half of her body was yanked a full metre off the bed. The gun was pressed so hard into her eye that she could not open it.

"Do not move, my friend," the voice spoke in Greek and was addressed to Steve. "Not even the tiniest muscle."

Steve was on his elbows, glaring in bewilderment at the unscheduled interruption of his sleep. It was a few seconds before reality came back. Then he saw a Latin-looking man in tinted specs sitting on the far edge of the bed. He had Christina's head in his left hand, her naked body across him, the gun pressed hurtfully into her eye.

"What the fuck!"

"I said do not move!" The voice was sharp and dangerous, and it had changed to English on hearing the American's oath. He pulled tighter on the girl's hair until she yelped. "Wake up! Wake up both of you."

"Oh, Jesus shit!" Steve was awake and he looked up at the ceiling in resignation. Then he looked across at the girl. "Please, please don't do that. You're hurting her. She's no threat to you."

"*I* will decided that." The gun remained where it was, and Christina grimaced in pain.

"But she is in pain. You could damage her eye!"

"So? If you want me to release your friend, talk to me. Give me a good reason why I should not kill you both right here and now."

Steve's eyes wandered around the room, up the walls, over the ceiling. "Look, you were away. We wanted somewhere safe, somewhere to stay. The place was lying empty... What can I say?"

Ramirov said nothing, he just stared at the American, his head inclined.

"Okay, okay," said Steve in what he hoped was a reasonable voice, trying to quell the anger that was brewing inside, anger at himself. He *knew* they shouldn't have stayed so long. Why hadn't he done something about it? It was against all his training. "We were looking for a safe hideout, see? The TRF are after us. We... we are members of EOKA."

The Russian snorted. "An American and a girl? Members of EOKA?"

"I am Cypriot by birth. My God, can't you see that?"

"Just because you *look* like a Greek..." The sentence was left in mid-air, but Ramirov pushed the girl back down onto the bed, glancing at the full bouncing breasts as she landed.

Her eye was bleeding. She sniffed once and was silent, her hand covering her eye, the good one glaring venom at Ramirov. "Bastard!" she spat the word like a true vixen. "So what do you do now? Kill uss in cold blood? *Mafioso* pig."

"*Mafioso?*" He laughed. "Is that what they say? The *Mafiosi* are mere children." The gun was lowered but remained in his hand. "I see that you are no threat to me." He looked about the room. "You have weapons?"

"Yes," said Steve. "There is a pistol underneath each of these pillows – " Ramirov raised the gun again. "There are no others."

"Please give them to me."

Steve passed his over and then fumbled under the girl's pillow. "Christy?"

She said nothing. She moved her left hand down and underneath the mattress. She pulled out her gun and threw it on the bed.

Ramirov emptied both the pistols with his left hand, letting them fall to the floor. He placed the bullets in his pants pocket.

"You are a sensible man, sir. The thought that is in your mind is correct. I will not have one moment's hesitation in killing both of you at any time I like. You will do well to remember that. Now, there are no other weapons. Are you telling me the truth?" The cold, black eyes bored into Steve's.

"Yes, I'm telling you the truth."

Ramirov continued to stare for another twenty seconds. Then he said, "Yes, you are." He stood up off the bed. "My friends, we have a lot of talking to do." He stood with his back against the door. "Both of you get dressed, and you see to her eye. Then we shall go downstairs – I take it you have stores in? Good. And you have got my generator working, I see. I would like some coffee and something to eat. You, my dear lady, will get it for me."

He looked at her as she raised her head and tried to look defiant. "My dear *Christina*. Christy, of course. Well, well, so it is you. I have heard you sing many times in *L'I* in Nicosia. I have watched you from afar." He seemed to amuse himself. "Before we are through you may be singing for me again. Now, get a move on both of you. I am thirsty."

Ramirov partook of his coffee and left-over *meze*, his gun remaining within millimetres of his right hand. The couple sat on the couch opposite, empty coffee cups next to them. The American was unshaven and rugged. The girl, eyelid distended and with a wicked-looking scab, glared.

Refreshed, Ramirov politely suggested "Talk to me."

Christina was reluctant. "You seem to know everything already."

Steve asked, "What do you want to know?"

Ramirov smiled disarmingly. "Why, everything, my dear sir. Everything. I do not even know your name. Let us start from there."

"My name is Stelios Grivas." Ramirov's eyebrows appeared over the top of his spectacles. "Yes, General George Grivas was my father. My mother was Amy Silver, an American journalist. She lived in Athens and she was the Greek correspondent of a national daily, in the late nineteen-forties. Do you really want to hear it all?"

"Of course."

"Okay. Well, to cut a long story short, she interviewed Grivas in his position as commander of the Greek forces in Cyprus. They hit it off. She became pregnant by him, the usual. I was the result. My mother told no one who the father was, not even the father. We lived on our own. Grivas did not find out about me until I was about four or five and my mother was sent back here to Cyprus to cover the worsening situation. Apparently he went into a rage when he found out – not because of my existence but because he had not been told.

"Anyway, after the rage he went into raptures. A son he never knew about! It was never revealed publicly that I was who I was, and Mom and I stayed here for two years, living on our own somewhere in the south in a place provided and kept by my father. He and Mom met up quite frequently, but the battle for *Enosis* took up most of his time.

"Things went on smoothly like this until the real outbreak of violence in 1955. My mother was on an assignment when one of EOKA's own bombs blew up the car she was travelling in. She lost both her legs."

Steve paused. There was absolute silence in the room.

He continued. "With her mobility gone, she was no use as a correspondent. Her agency – probably out of kindness than anything – offered her a staff job at their offices in Philadelphia. It was either accept that or stay here with the prospect of civil war looming." He sighed and shrugged his shoulders. "Of course she had no choice. And anyway she wanted out. Never, up until her death three years ago, did she completely forgive Grivas for the loss of her legs – although God knows it was not his fault. *He* was not responsible for the detonation of the bomb.

"He let us go, of course. It could not have been easy for him, but having never publicly acknowledged the existence of his bastard son things were not too bad. He would have no loss of face. He and my mother entered into some agreement. I do not know the finer details of it, but it seems that I was to lose my paternity. Grivas would never contact us again, and my mother would never reveal to anyone who my real father was. The agreement was kept.

"I never thought much about my father as I grew up, not until my mother's death. Then I decided to contact him. I felt he had a right to know about her passing. I had some contacts in the Press and, after months of enquiry, I came up with a *poste restante* address for the General down in Limassol. Apparently I was not to put his name on the envelope, just address it to some woman. I wrote him a short note telling him of Mom's death. I heard nothing until six months later when an envelope arrived. Inside was a scrap of paper with a hand-written message: *Thank you, G.* And that was all.

"I heard nothing else. He was obviously determined to keep his side of the agreement even though one partner to it was dead.

"Then in January this year I received another envelope. Inside was a plane ticket and a note that Grivas wanted to see me. So I came here, just three days before his death. He was almost gone when I reached him, but he made one last request, asking me to do something for him. He wanted me to get The Eye of Makarios. That was the last thing he ever said." He paused at the memory. He was aware that Christina and the man were looking at him intently.

"The Eye of Makarios?" prompted Ramirov.

"Quite. What the hell was it? He died before he could tell us. Since January we've been continually on the run. The TRF suspect that we exist, but they are not sure. So there's been no direct pressure, not until recently. That's when we took refuge here."

"On the assumption that they would not think of looking right under their own noses. Most sensible." He looked the girl. "And what part does Christina play in all of this?"

She bridled, tossed her hair back and spoke, reluctantly but with pride. "I was close to Grivas during the last months. When Syros and Demetrakis were taken last autumn he turned to me more than anybody else."

"So! That *is* something I did not know. But pray go on, you have more to tell me?"

Steve continued. "Just over a month ago we intercepted Bishop Rigakis on his way into Nicosia. He was persuaded to tell us what The Eye of Makarios was. And where it was."

"So it was you! No wonder the heat was on and you looked for refuge!"

"The Eye of Makarios," explained Steve, "is, we think, Makarios' personal investment, his pension. Although it could have been a gift. Whatever. It is a diamond. Must be pretty big. He carries it about his waist at all times."

That shocked even Ramirov. Was it *possible*? That fate should be so beneficent? That all the work and effort had been done for him? By this man and this girl? It appeared so.

He shook his head and then chuckled, a happy, throaty sound. "Magnificent. Magnificent!"

"You do nott belief uss!" snarled Christina.

"Oh yes, yes my dear. I believe you." His eyes filled with a few tears of mirth. "Please forgive me. It is an incredible story, but I believe it."

"And now what?" asked Steve. "Do you turn us in? Or kill us... or let us go?"

The laughing stopped abruptly and there was an ominous silence. Steve honestly thought the man was going to exercise the second option. He thought of throwing himself at the stranger, at least Christina might get clear.

But then to their great surprise Ramirov put the gun in his pocket and inclined his head. "My friends, I am certainly not going to turn you in or kill you. You may go if you want to. But I have a proposition for you. Stay here. Stay with me. I happen to know that there will be an opportunity coming up soon for you to get this diamond."

"How? We haf thought off everything."

"How does not matter. It is sufficient for you to know that there *will* be an opportunity. And I will help you. I will help you get this Eye of Makarios!"

Christina and Steve were stupefied. They looked at each other incredulously.

"Until the opportunity to take the diamond arises you may, if you wish, stay here – as my guests. It is very secure here."

"Well... that... hmm!... but why are you doing this? I don't understand," said Steve.

"Such matters need not concern you. It is sufficient for your purpose that I am. Consider me an old supporter of EOKA."

"Wh-who are you?"

"My name is Martinez. That is all you need to know. Further questions will be a waste of your breath. There will probably be some danger later on. You can handle a gun? We will have time, I will teach you how to use one properly. Both of you. You will be my pupils, I your master. Now," he stretched, his arms above his head. "How about some more coffee, my dear?"

Christina was still in a state of bewilderment. As she got up, she asked, "You – you don't happen to haf a cigar, do you?"

Ramirov would not sleep that night. Grivas and Christina could if they wanted to, but Ramirov had enquiries to make and people to see later that day and he did not want the inconvenience of sleep to dull his senses.

At 03:00 all was quiet and all was dark. Outside a half moon gave soft illumination and cast stark shadows. Earlier Ramirov had moved his car into the garage a few metres away from the villa. Now he walked soundlessly back across the gravel track. The garage door swung open with just a little resistance and no noise. Leaving it open to get the benefit of the moonlight, he stepped to the front of the car which, in a Volkswagen Beetle, was the trunk. The hood opened with a click, and he reached inside and removed a holdall. The contents clinked lightly.

He lowered the hood but did not slam it shut. Back outside, the door resisted again but then closed without a sound. Ramirov remained facing the door as he slipped the wooden bolt back over. He said quietly, "You could be as good as me. Except," he turned. "I knew you were there."

The person was in shadow, a little to the right. "If you say so."

Ramirov nodded back at the villa. "The son of Grivas, eh?"

"Apparently."

"We can hide behind that. Make them think it is all EOKA."

"Have they given the go-ahead?"

"No. It will happen. But not yet. Weeks, maybe."

"Should I report that?"

"That is for you to decide. We will not get the diamond until it happens. I just have to wait for instructions from Athens. Until the diamond is with the supplier, the materiel will not be available. So you have breathing space. That should keep Tel Aviv happy."

"Time for them to get people in place."

Ramirov inclined his head. "As you say." Saying no more, he set off back towards the villa.

Agent Digenis slipped back into the shadows of the night.

Ψ

Tuesday June 11 1974

"Three bombs exploded at the Strensall army training camp near York this afternoon. No one was seriously injured."

London, England

The two men sat in front of Colonel Egginton's desk in his comfortable office in Stuart House. They were representatives from the United Kingdom Atomic Energy Authority's Windscale Works in Cumbria in the far north, although their voices were strictly home counties stockbroker belt.

The Colonel had just sat down after greeting them on entry. "Well gentlemen, I am so glad you had a comfortable journey. I know what the ride from Windscale can be like. Has the transport problem improved?"

It was generally agreed that it had.

"That's nice to hear. Now, you know the reason I invited you here. Needless to say the matter is Top Secret and goes no further than ourselves. The Minister has asked me to undertake a little review of security matters at your establishment. While no disrespect to your current arrangements is intended, he feels that for the whole system to be looked at by an outsider not unknowledgeable in such matters would do it no harm at this present time. I must say I agree with him.

"He has asked me to look at one part of the set-up in particular: the security of the plutonium and uranium." Egginton dragged mightily on his *Dunhill* cigarette and swallowed all of the smoke. "I'll be honest with you. Strictly between ourselves, he hinted to me that the Defence Intelligence boys had got the wind up about a possible attack on one of our plants and the swiping of amounts of the stuff. Until they make the radiation level of plutonium lethal, how easy that could be given a concerted effort by a terrorist army. And we all know what could happen if that stuff got into their hands! It is feasible that the Arabs or the Japanese want some to convert into bombs for use in the Mediterranean somewhere. *[Egginton never knew how close his sheer fabrication had come to the truth.]* But that should really be no concern of ours. Official Secrets and all that, what!

"I'd like to discuss your security arrangements with you today, quite informally and without prejudice, of course. Then perhaps next week I can come up and visit you and have a look at the layout first hand. I've written down a few points here. Firstly, can you really account for every pound of plutonium at any given time…?"

Nicosia, Cyprus

That same day a telegram was collected from the main post office in Nicosia, sent from Vienna a few hours earlier. It read:

TO MARTINEZ POSTE RESTANTE NICOSIA STOP DESPITE EXHAUSTIVE CHECKS NO TRACE CAN BE FOUND OF THE TITLE MENTIONED STOP SUGGEST THAT AND YOUR OBJECT ARE THE SAME STOP PROCEED ACCORDINGLY STOP KATHERINE

Ψ

Friday June 14 1974

"With the results of the Australian general election now all in, the Labour government has failed to gain a majority in the senate.

Whitehall, London

Every non-elected civil servant in the United Kingdom is reported on annually. The report, at that time in the form of a standard ten page questionnaire, is completed by the reportee's immediate superior officer. It is then passed to the next person in the chain of command who is known as the 'Countersigning Officer'. The Countersigning Officer adds his or her own comments and then passes the report ever-upwards for eventual inclusion in personnel records.

Before he gets rid of the report, the Countersigning Officer may also interview the reportee in what is known in the service as a 'JAR' (Job Appraisal Review), a marvelous invention in which the discussion is supposed to be a no holds barred affair concerning the reportee's career prospects, job satisfaction, relations with colleagues, private life, right down to the clothes he wears and any unfortunate personal habits (like halitosis or the way he picks his nose).

Egginton's JAR that afternoon was of the friendly variety, his Countersigning Officer being the Permanent Under Secretary for the Ministry of Defence (Sales Executive) Sir Lovelock Armstrong. The interview lasted just fifteen minutes and was of the "Hello Stan – Hello Lovelock – How's the wife?" variety (for on more than one occasion the Eggintons had dined at the Armstrongs' in Denham, Bucks).

The interview ended with both men agreeing what a bloody waste of time these JARs were, and we must get together again sometime, my love to Margery.

Sir Lovelock Armstrong inked over his inked over his pencilled marking of 'Fitted' in the promotion column, signed his name on the bottom of the form, placed it in an orange *Confidential* envelope, and threw it in his Out Tray. His PA would see that it continued on its journey.

He picked up another piece of paper, the small *JAR Completed* form, and put a stroke through the *Comments/Suggestions Made* column and signed at the bottom. According to a recent DCI *[Defence Council Instruction]*, all *JAR Completed* forms on Assistant Directors and above had to be routed via

Security for a standard check. Bloody waste of time in this case, thought Armstrong, Stan was straight as a die, a damn good Director. But instructions were instructions, even for a Permanent Under Secretary.

Another orange envelope, addressed to the Director of Security, and that was that over for another year.

The Director of Security received the form via the internal mail shortly before he left for home at 16:30 that afternoon. He gave the contents of the orange envelope just a cursory glance, wrote the name of the Security Officer for Stuart House on the front in pencil, tossed the envelope into his Out Tray, picked up his case and walked out.

Ronald Spencer Arthur, Security Officer for the Ministry of Defence in Stuart House, received the form at 10:15 the following Monday.

Ψ

Thursday June 20 1974

"Israeli planes have again attacked Palestinian refugee camps in southern Lebanon. Reports say that at least sixteen people have been killed."

Reference DO/364/03

CONFIDENTIAL

Director of Security
Room 201
Main Building

DCI 36/74: SECURITY APPRAISAL ON COLONEL S W EGGINTON

Colonel Egginton was last positively vetted in November 1973 (see DI4's minute of 11 November at enclosure 42). Due to the nature of his work, he will continue to be positively vetted every 2 years. No interim vetting is recommended.

Ron Arthur

R S Arthur
SO Stuart House
20 June 1974

Whitehall, London

Ron Arthur was due at the regular fortnightly Heads of Security meeting in the MOD Main Building at 10:00 that morning. The Director of Security would chair the meeting, as always, and it would probably be stretched to lunchtime.

Arthur had decided to bring the minute on Egginton over himself, rather than waste the two envelopes needed to transmit confidential documents outside their parent building. He did not really want to meet The Old Man before the meeting, so it was with a modicum of circumspection that he walked along the corridor at 09:45 and nipped smartly in to the Director's PA's office.

"'Morning Eunice."

Eunice Tate was a thin woman in her menopausal late forties. She had been PA-DOS for the last two years (ever since the current DOS had been promoted from Assistant Director) and was disgustingly efficient at her job. She had the haughty, brisk manner one would expect from a professional spinster in such a position, but she was not a bad sort once she got to know you.

"Mr Arthur! Good morning. Off to the meeting?"

"Just thought I'd pop this in beforehand," Arthur handed over the unmarked, unsealed envelope. He looked furtively at the door leading to the next room. "Is he...?"

Eunice nodded, and as if on cue the door opened and the DOS strolled out.

"Signed 'em, Eunice," he dumped a bundle of letters down onto the desk. "Hello Ron. Business or pleasure?"

Eunice sniffed and pretended not to hear the remark.

Arthur smiled dutifully. "Just thought I'd pop up with Colonel Egginton's report, sir."

"Ah good, good. Coming to the meeting?"

"Of course, sir."

"Good, let's go then. Back this afternoon, Eunice."

As they were walking down the corridor, the Director asked "Anything, Ron?"

"On Colonel Egginton? No, sir," Arthur chuckled at the idea.

"Good."

They reached the lift lobby.

Arthur looked at the DOS. "There is one thing, sir... about the Colonel."

The DOS was about to ask what when a pretty young thing from the typing pool waddled along and pressed the UP button. She smiled coyly at the two men, who were now silent. They smiled inanely back.

The lifts came simultaneously. Arthur and the DOS were the only XXXecognize down, and before the doors had closed fully the DOS asked sharply, "What is this about Egginton?"

Arthur felt uncomfortable and he began to wish he hadn't opened his mouth. Really it was only something to say. "Nothing much, sir. Not worth reporting officially. But he seems to have been drinking a lot recently."

"Stan's always been partial to his wallop."

"Aren't we all, sir? But this has been more than usual, even for the Colonel. Just about every day now he doesn't come back from lunch until three and – well, you know the Colonel sir, he can hold it more than most of us. He never seems actually drunk, but... well, it *is* every day now sir... and considering his position..."

"Of course, of course, yes, you were right to tell me, Ron. And right not to make it official."

The lift reached the basement and they stepped out and turned right. Behind them another lift touched down and ejaculated three other building security officers. In between their mutual greetings, the DOS said as an aside "Let me sleep on it, Ron. Let me sleep on it."

The Director of Security must have slept during the meeting, for it was when he returned to his office that afternoon, after a double-whisky lunch, that he asked Eunice to get him a certain unlisted number over in Queen Anne's Gate.

Jamhour, Lebanon

The new Catholic church of Notre-Dame de Jamhour, above Beirut to the east, was only six years old. It was built in the round style of modern churches, long pews set in a decreasing semi-circle narrowing in to the wide, accessible altar. Beige wide-bricked walls held modern uplights at five metre intervals, discreet lighting which added to the calmness of the interior.

The church was quiet and empty as Nathanson stepped into the confessional.

"Bless me Father, for I have sinned. It has been... many years since my last confession."

Only the faintest of diffused backlighting entered through the grill that kept identities hidden, the sinner known only to God. The priest was just a dark shadow.

"And what have you to confess, my friend?" His voice was soft and low.

"My search for justice has made me many enemies."

"Vengeance is mine; I will repay, saith the Lord."

"I have managed to get close," said Nathanson. "To the financier. I am – how should I put it? – in his employ."

"Good. And you are not suspected?"

"No."

"Digenis has been involved also. We now know what the Arabs are up to. It is not good." The priest spelled out the Arabs' plan. Then he said, "But they need to get the diamond first."

"Should we finish them off?" asked Nathanson. "Do you want me to retreat?"

"No, not yet. Stay in place. You will be useful on the inside. We will do nothing yet. We must let them proceed. The world will not believe us unless we expose them red-handed with the evidence."

"I understand."

"Confess regularly."

"Of course."

"In nomine patre, filis et spiritus sancti."

"Amen."

Five minutes after Nathanson had left the confessional, Monsignor Chaim Cohen stepped out of the priest's side and closed the door behind him. He nodded paternally to two ladies (Madame Renée Ibrahim and her daughter Violette) who had started decorating the altar dias for a forthcoming wedding on Saturday, and, without pausing for them to wonder who he was, walked out of the main door and into the warm darkness of a Lebanese evening.

Ψ

Saturday June 22 1974

"Tension is still high in the Middle East after the Israeli air attack on Palestinian refugee camps in southern Lebanon two days ago. Sixteen people were killed and more than forty injured in the attack. A Palestinian spokesman has threatened dire revenge for what Palestinian sources call 'This cowardly attack by Zionist warmongers on innocent women and children'."

Istanbul, Turkey

Ramirov, dressed in a white cotton shirt and grey slacks, stood in the hot midday sun without perspiring. He was waiting on the quayside on the European bank of the Golden Horn, looking out over the water and watching the ferry approach from Asia. His head was cocked slightly to one side.

Behind him, people of every nationality milled about noisily, a hum of excitement rising as the ferry came nearer. Istanbul, the New York of the east, smelt of spices, sun and body odour.

He looked at the gold Rolex Oyster Perpetual on his right wrist. It showed five minutes after noon. His appointment was late, but never mind. He half closed his eyes and enjoyed the sun.

Two minutes later a voice said, "I apologise for my lateness." 'Akay' Al Khalifa, the financial controller of Black September, appeared beside him from thin air. Any person other than Ramirov would not have been aware of his approach.

Ramirov waited.

"Did you enjoy your recent visit to Cana?" asked the Arab.

"Very pleasant but the Jordan is vast and mysterious."

"Who knows where a river ends?"

They spoke in French and made customary greetings, but they did not shake hands or make any form of physical contact. They both faced the water and gave the impression of speaking casually, as if exchanging pleasantries about the view.

The Russian said, "It has taken time, but I have now discovered the location of the item."

Al Khalifa sniffed with the beginnings of a summer cold. "My colleagues will be pleased with your news. You are able to obtain the... item?"

"Yes." He pointed out over the water as if indicating a point of discussion. "There will be a certain amount of difficulty but nothing that cannot be handled."

"Good. It will take long?"

"Hard to say. Not too long. One week, five weeks. It all depends on various circumstances."

There was a moment of silence, and then Ramirov asked "And what about your supplier? Is he ready? I would advise you not to have the item on hand for too long once I get it for you. But that is, of course, your business."

"Indeed, but we are always glad of your counsel."

"I will contact you to make the arrangements just before or just after the item is secured."

"Please do."

Without further ado, both men turned and disappeared into the crowds.

Ψ

Friday June 28 1974

"Reports are coming in of a coup in Ethiopia in north-east Africa. Members of the Ethiopian army have taken over control of two radio stations in the capital Addis Ababa. The fate of Emperor Hailé Selassié is not yet known."

Houston, Texas, USA

"You've been lucky, young lady. Very lucky. Drive more carefully in future." With a shake of the hand, Dr Louis Thomas of the *Texas Medical Center* turned and walked back into the main area of the hospital.

Sally-Anne Bowker walked slowly and carefully down the two steps and across to the waiting cab. She gave her home address to the driver who, once he realised that his attempts at joviality or conversation of any sort were being met with silence, remained quiet for the length of the journey.

As Dr Thomas had said, she had been lucky. Lucky to have survived at all. Most people would have been killed. More than anything, it was the old broken seatbelt that had caused the damage, nearly pulping her left breast and helping to fracture four ribs on the left side and one on the right. Her chest was scarred for life with deep stitching lines where the breast had been sewn back into some semblance of a tit, and various evil-looking lacerations stretched from shoulder to shoulder. As well as that, her skull had been fractured in three places, albeit the breaks were only 'hairline'. Her head had been shaved and now, some six weeks later, her hair had regrown into a short cropped style, masculine and some two years ahead of its time fashion-wise.

Her huge, school-marm glasses had shattered in the crash and she had been told that she had been very fortunate that the glass had missed her eyes and only caused deep cuts and painful bruises in the cheeks and forehead. Thankfully these had healed completely after a month. Now she had broken in a pair of pure plastic contact lenses.

Yes, the general opinion of everybody in the hospital was that luck had been with her on that fateful May 20th.

Well, fuck that. If she had been so lucky the accident would not have happened in the first place.

One can measure the amount of physical damage inflicted by a car crash but, without very careful examination and knowledge of the patient's previous condition, it is hard to determine the amount of mental damage sustained. Sally had been visited by two psychiatrists who had both pronounced her a mentally normal, if somewhat bitter, young woman. The bitterness would pass, they had decreed, it was caused by latent shock.

So to all intents and purposes Sally-Anne Bowker was a healed human being both physically and mentally when she signed off from the hospital that fine June day.

But she had changed. Physically the change was obvious: hair shorn, no more the huge glasses, sixteen pounds in weight lost, and a predilection for wearing denims to hide her scarred legs. Mentally, it was not so obvious. Determination had set in. Where once there was tolerance and concern for others (under other circumstances she would have returned the cab driver's banter) there was now impatience and concern only for herself.

Apart from the bastard and dead out of town farmer who had been driving the other vehicle, there was one person and one person alone who was responsible for her being in that hospital: Mister Steven Graves – or Stelios Grivas or whatever he called himself and whoever he was. If it had not been for him, her mind would have been more on her driving six weeks ago. If it had not been for her concern for his safety, she might have avoided the other vehicle. If his whereabouts had not been bothering her, she would not have ended up cut to pieces in a hospital bed. If she had not been so damn much in love with him...

At least there was one consolation – she would not now have to lie about the death of her grandmother to have time off. She had the perfect excuse for absence from school! She was not to return to work until at least September, by order. So she had the best part of three months. It would take all her savings and probably more so, but, goddammit, she had decided she would find Steve Graves wherever he was.

Even if it killed her.

The cab deposited her outside the apartment block and, after telling the driver to go fuck himself after he had made some sarcastic remark about her cheerfulness, she walked very slowly into the building.

Ψ

Monday July 1 1974

"From Ethiopia it is reported that most of Emperor Hailé Salassié's advisers have been arrested, but the new controlling army have renewed pledges to the Emperor himself."

Over the Atlantic Ocean

The *Air France 747* lifted into the clear azure sky above Houston, banked sharply to starboard and set course for its direct run to Paris. In the final seat on the left in the first class compartment, Sally-Anne Bowker relaxed the tense muscles of her neck and breathed a sigh of relief. She did not mind flying, it was the take-off and landing that she could not, literally, stomach.

"There now honey, that wasn't too bad, was it?" smiled the woman next to her.

"Guess not, but I'm always glad when we're up." Sally tried to sound amiable but, as usual nowadays, she just did not feel like it.

The woman next to her was a butch-looking character who had introduced herself as Charlotte Rapley, "Call me Charlie." Dressed in a tweed three-piece suit, hair short but fluffier than Sally's crop, face framed by large agony-aunt spectacles, she had been one of the last to arrive in First Class, making an ostentatious display of breathlessness as she entered. The seat next to Sally had been empty and she had just *known* that this loud lesbian would be heading for it. She had been right.

Charlie had tried to strike up a conversation straight away, but Sally had been even less responsive than usual. However, bowing to the continual verbal pressure, she had eventually had to say *something*.

Charlie was unputoffable and, to be fair, Sally knew what the obvious attraction of herself was: short hair, rather hard face, bra-less tee shirted chest (on doctor's advice) and denim jeans. Charlie was trying her out to see if she was one of her own kind. Sally knew that she was not but, after twenty minutes, she had to admit that she did not dislike the chatty, blowsy, personable female.

Charlie was a sculptor and artist, in that order. She came from New York and had been in Houston for the past month conducting an exhibition of her works. Perhaps Sally-Anne had heard of it? ("Well, actually, no.") She was now on her way to Paris to organize a similar showing.

By take-off she had all but told Sally the story of her life, and Sally had reluctantly reciprocated with a few forced details of her own. Charlie had been most concerned when she had heard about the accident.

Now they sat high in the air over Texas, ready for the long flight ahead of them. Charlie smoked on a *Peter Stuyvesant*.

"Gonna watch the movie, Sal?"

"Guess so, not much else to do. Wonder what it is?"

"Dunno, hope it's something good. Something with a bit of spice, know what I mean? Ever seen any of those movies?"

"No."

"Dunno what you're missing, babe. You must come and see me when we hit gay Paree, I'll show you some celluloid to open your eyes – and your legs." She guffawed. "Hey, wanna drink?"

"I don't think so."

"Shit, of course you do. Hey miss!" A stewardess, with a catchy wiggle which did not go unnoticed by Ms Rapley, appeared from somewhere. "Two double scotches on the rocks please honey – no, nothing with it."

Sally looked out of the window and inwardly sighed. It was going to be a long flight.

"*Chinatown*. Shit, what kind of movie was that?"

"A very good one, what was wrong with it? You don't like Polanski?"

"Argh Sally, you're too nice, y' know that? Certainly wasn't my kinda movie."

"So you keep telling me. Never mind, you'll be able to see plenty of those when you hit Paris – as you keep telling me."

"Right. How long – God, two more hours yet! Want another drink?"

"Really no, not this time Charlie. Four is enough."

"Well, p'raps you're right."

They travelled on above the clouds of a rainy Atlantic.

"So, when you get to Paris, what you gonna do?" Charlie broke open her second packet of duty-free *Peter Stuyvesant*. "How you gonna find this guy of yours? If you ask me, you're putting yourself to a lot of trouble over nothing. No man is worth it."

Sally sighed. "Quite honestly, Charlie, I'm not too sure what I'm going to do. Try the airline desks and check their flights to the Balearics for January 23rd last, I reckon. See if they have Steve down."

"Or this crazy 'Stelios Grivas'. One heck of a name that – don't sound unfamiliar though. You got somewhere to stay?"

"Nope, I didn't reckon I'd need anywhere. I'll check the airlines and I'll either be on my way forward or back home again."

"Heck, you're one hell of a devoted gal. But what do you do for sleep, hm? Or hadn't you thought about that?"

"I've slept on the plane."

"Shit, you don't call that *sleep!* Just a doze. Everyone knows that sleep on a plane's not restful. It's not *sleep,* just a way of passing the journey." She drew on her cigarette.

Sally looked out at the milling clouds. For the first time she had a feeling of doubt about what she was doing. *Screw* this woman! Or, she thought cynically, is that exactly what she wanted?

"First time in Paris?" the smoke rolled back out of Charlie's mouth as she spoke.

"Yep."

"And you're just gonna land, touch the wall and fly off again? Shit girl, do you know what you're missing? This is Paree, honey. The City of Light."

"*Gay* Paree?"

"It simply won't let you ignore it. Everything you've read about it is true, and more so." Charlie frowned. Her sales pitch did not seem to be making any impression. She grabbed hold of a soft hand. "Listen, if you don't have anywhere to stay, you can come with me to my friend's place for the night."

The offer was not unexpected. "Oh no, really, I couldn't." Sally moved her hand away.

"Sure you could! Louise won't mind. You've been through a lot recently, you need your rest. This plane ride's enough for one day. You can stay the night at Louise's and then tomorrow we'll maybe help you make those enquiries about this precious Steve of yours. How's that?"

"But, Charlie – "

"Great, that's settled. We'll be glad of your company." She patted Sally gently on the right knee, and Sally wondered what she had now let herself in for.

Paris, France

Much to Sally's surprise, Louise was a small, slim, dark-haired Parisienne of around twenty-five. Quiet and elegant, her features were gamin and Gallic and would appeal to both sexes. She lived alone in a plush apartment at 46 Boulevard Exelmans in the 16th Arrondisement, and was a fashion designer by trade. She welcomed Sally as if they were old friends.

The three women enjoyed *omelettes à la poulard* cooked to perfection by Louise, and they then finished off two bottles of *Sancerre* while a Pink Floyd cassette played on the expensive stereo.

"Don't let Claude hear that or he'll be down like a shot," joked Charlie. "Don't s'pose you know Claude, Sal. He's a singer. Lives on the top two floors of this building. Good friend of Looey's. *Clo-Clo* they call him. You'll have to meet him. Hell of a nice guy. For a man."

La Française was deeply interested in Sally's story of her missing lover, which she retold with prompting, interruptions and embellishments from Charlie. Louise offered whatever assistance she could during tomorrow's enquiries at Orly.

Although only early evening, Sally and Charlie were obviously weary after their journey, and so the three women retired early. Each, surprisingly, sleeping in a separate bedroom.

Ψ

Tuesday July 2 1974

"A state of national mourning has been declared in Argentina following the death yesterday of General Juan Perón. General Perón relinquished his third presidency to his wife, Señora Maria Martinez de Perón, just three days ago because of his failing health."

Orly, Paris, France

Orly Airport was invaded early that morning. Sally and Charlie assailed the *Iberia* desk while Louise tackled *Air France*. They then rejoined to assault any other airlines flying south from Paris.

The airline clerks were, on the whole, helpful. But helpfulness is not necessarily synonymous with success, and it was three disappointed ladies who drove away from the airport at midday. They had tried every airline flying to the Balearic Islands and the Spanish mainland, all to no avail.

They travelled back in silence, Louise driving her new green Opel with the motoring ferocity which comes naturally to the French.

As they turned off the A6 autoroute onto the Boulevard Périphérique, south of the city, Charlie broke the sullen silence with a forceful "Shit!"

"Shit is right," agreed Sally, looking out of the front passenger window and the fast moving motley of vehicles heading west.

"*Et maintenant?*" asked Louise in between *merdes* aimed at the unprepossessing form of a Fiat in front.

"Well, I guess that's it. Home to the good old US of A and goodbye Steve. Damn." Sally stared unseeingly at the graceful metal giraffe, *La Tour Eiffel*, thrusting its way heavenwards between the 15th arrondisement office blocks in the distance.

Louise exchanged glances with Charlie via the rear-view mirror.

"Perhaps it's just my imagination," Sally continued, "but my scars seem to be aching more now. Probably outta disappointment." Oh damn you Steve, damn you, damn you, damn you.

"Well you just tell them to quit," ordered Charlie, herself just a trifle more subdued than usual.

"But he couldn't have disappeared into thin air, surely?" reasoned Sally, clutching at straws.

"Seems he has done just that, honey. If Stelios Grivas was Steve Graves in the first place."

"Mm."

"As I said yesterday on the plane, no man is worth losing sweat over. Tell you what! Heck, you don't have to go home straight away. Why not stay here with us for a while?"

"I couldn't."

"Zat is ze good idea!" exclaimed Louise. "You will be no problem. *Bâtard!*" They overtook the Fiat.

"You can help me set up the exhibition if you like," suggested Charlie. "But nothing too strenuous, mind. You'll meet some interesting people."

"All our friends would love to meet you. Per'aps even find you a man to take your mind off Steve, hah?" The French girl smiled.

"What say we do the town tonight? Say Looey, how about if we asked Claude – he's not on tour, is he?"

"*Non.*"

"Good! And maybe he could bring along Michel too."

"Michel will be off preparing for his programme tomorrow."

"Shit, yes. Well how about that guy at Isabelle's party?"

"Oo? Guillaume?"

"Guy, yeh. Claude and Guy, wee, they could accompany us an' I'm sure Claude'll have a friend for Sally. We can all make up a sixem – or a sexem as you French would say, heh, heh."

"But I thought you two…" Sally smiled and frowned at the same time.

"Listen, honey," explained Charlie, leaning forward from the back seat, her hands on Sally's shoulder. "Why just sample the rosebuds when there's beefsteak to be had as well? Huh? I'm not purely queer, y' know. Now whadya say? Will you stay on for a while? Are you game for a good time?"

They drove over the Pont du Garigliano and paused at the traffic lights at Rue Chardon Lagache.

Sally looked from one to the other of them: Louise's pretty French face intent on the lights and Charlie's face alive and swashbuckling.

The lights changed and they pulled away, made a quick right into Rue Boileau and parked. Further up the street an armed policeman stood guard outside the Vietnamese embassy.

Both the women looked at Sally. She made up her mind. She smiled broadly, something she had not done for a long, long time.

"Hell, yes, dammit. I'll stay. I'd love to!"

Claude's friend was called Marcel, and in the early hours of the following morning, after a fantastic time at *Don Camilo,* he followed Sally into her room by invitation and, using great care because of her recent injuries, he made sublime love to her.

Ψ

Friday July 5 1974

"The Queen has been at the Edinburgh Academy today to mark its 150th foundation anniversary."

Queen Anne's Gate, Westminster, London

Queen Anne's Gate is a smallish thoroughfare, a tangent from the Westminster Abbey end of Victoria Street. It runs for only half a kilometre to St James's Park underground station and then loses its identity to the narrower, curiously-named Petty France. In 1974 a vast portion of Queen Anne's Gate was in the process of being demolished.

At the western end of the street, opposite the underground station, the modern monstrosity that is Number 50 was nearing completion. Part of this monolith was destined to house the security section of the police Special Branch, but until it was ready for occupancy the security section was dotted about various parts of Westminster.

Special Branch Security (Operations) Division 1 was based on the top floor of the ancient, but very secure, Queen Anne's Mansions, just across the road.

The Special Branch of the British police is a curious organisation, a cross between the American FBI, CIA and National Guard but without the overt thuggery. In addition to its well-known roles of Diplomatic Protection and Diplomatic Investigation, it also handles certain internal security matters and many other concerns subversive. And it does it without treading on the toes of MI5, MI6, DI6 and the SIS. *Almost.* For the Special Branch are a strange mob.

And there were none stranger than the unfortunately titled S(O)D 1. For a start, it was rumoured that they harvested their personnel from spent SAS men, the most elite soldiers in the world. For another thing, they never referred to each other by their police rank. They always used 'mister'.

Thus it was that at 10:30 that Friday, Mr Ramm and Mr Woods (in fact Detective Inspector and Detective Chief Inspector respectively) were summoned into the inner sanctum of the S(O)D 1 suite at the behest of Mr Metcalf (in fact a Detective Chief Superintendent).

"Come in, lads, come in." The bald-headed Metcalf was a good boss, but he had one embarrassing habit: when he addressed you he would always unconsciously touch his genitals.

The two men approached the desk and sat down, exchanging 'Good mornings'. They looked nothing like coppers, which of course was the whole idea. The bespectacled Mr Ramm looked like a rather shabby pin-striped civil servant from the lower echelons of Whitehall. Mr Woods would not have looked out of place on a building site.

"How's Janet?" asked Metcalf solicitously.

"A week overdue now," nodded Ramm. "And still no sign. I think she's got a bloody elephant up there."

"Told you you shouldn't have gone to Kenya last year," quipped Woods. "Never know what those witch doctors get up to. Mind you, you could always sell its tusks. Worth a bob or two."

"And we could certainly do with that. Can't go on fiddling expenses forever, can we Mr Metcalf?"

"Quite," Metcalf brought his hands up from his lap and opened a buff file in front of him. "How's the workload?"

"As ever," reported Woods. "No further forward on the Sieff shooting. Coupla reports on IRA activity in Kilburn – I think they're building up for Christmas. A certain Central African diplomat fucked four suburban housewives in one night last week, paying their husbands five ton each for the privilege."

"God, I wish he'd come to me," grumbled Ramm. "I could just see five hundred off nicely. And Janet wouldn't feel a thing in her condition."

"Apart from that, the usual irons in the fire."

"Hmm," Metcalf nodded, one hand disappearing again beneath the table. "I've got another little job for you. Long-term effort. Surveillance job probably."

"Phone tap?" Woods.

"Not at this stage."

"Who's our client?" Ramm.

"Chap at the MOD. Probably nothing. Straight as a bat for years. Still is. Just something that came up during a routine security check. Been imbibing to excess. We've been asked to have a little look. Over the OBN [*Old Boy Network*]. Leave Five out of it."

"A big boy?"

"Big as they come," Metcalf threw the file across the desk with his one available hand. "One of the defence sales directors. Colonel Stanley William Egginton..."

Ψ

Saturday July 6 1974

"There is growing concern in America over the role of President Nixon in the Watergate scandal. Pressure is mounting in Washington for his impeachment. On Monday, the Supreme Court will hear arguments concerning the President's claim that he had a right to withhold sixty-four White House tape recordings."

Paris, France

That night Sally and Charlie and Louise slept together, forming a bond of friendship in a very special way.

Ψ

Friday July 12 1974

"In America, President Nixon is still retaining the controversial sixty-four White House tape recordings, which were the subject of a Supreme Court hearing during the week. He awaits the final report of the Senate Watergate Committee which is due to be published tomorrow."

Paris, France

It had been a wonderful week. Helping Charlie set up the exhibition at the gallery in the Avenue Matignon had been fun. Sally, the new alive Sally, had no intention of leaving her friends and the wonderful city for a long while yet. And there was no pressure on her to do so. Her lovers, both male and female, had asked her to stay, if not forever then at least until the passion on both sides had abated. And that could take a long, long time.

But fate was to move its prophetic hand that Friday evening.

Sally had stayed home in the apartment that afternoon, it being her turn to prepare the evening meal (*boeuf en daube*). Louise arrived home at her appointed time of 16:30, and she and Sally supped *Dubonet* and talked about the events of the day to a stereo background of their neighbour Claude François. Charlie had promised to be home "at least by five" but, knowing Charlie, Sally had scheduled dinner for 18:30.

As it was, Charlie burst upon the scene at 17:15.

The door slammed open with such force that it rebounded off the stop and stood trembling on its hinges. "Sally! Sally! It suddenly came over me on the way home!"

Sally looked up, startled. "What? Who did?"

"Whadyamean *who*? You sex mad or sumpn? No," Charlie threw herself down into an armchair. "Remember I said I thought his other name was familiar? Y' know, the *Grivas* one?"

"Yes, I do."

"Well, I've been so dumb! I've known all along but it didn't occur to me till just now, as I was parking. Grivas. He was that guy in Cyprus, y' know that terrorist leader. Died not so long ago. January I think it was."

"January! But that was when Steve - !" Sally sat bolt upright. "Do you really think - ?"

"Holy shit, it seems logical! Why it should be, I don't know. Why the hell he should travel under that name in the first place, d' you know?"

"No, but that doesn't matter right now."

"We must find out." Louise picked up the excitement. "Flights on *vingt-troisieme Janvier* to Cyprus or that area."

"Let's do it *now!*" Charlie jumped up, loose change rattling in the pockets of her tweeds.

"But what about the *boeuf en daube?*" Louise was forever practical.

"Shit the berf on dowb, Looey," Charlie reached down, snatched Sally's glass and swilled down the remaining *Dubonnet* in one. "This is love we're talking about. C'mon, let's get moving!"

Their joy, however, was short-lived. Again a descent on Orly, again all the airlines most helpful, again nothing. No Graves or Grivas on any flight to Nicosia, Istanbul, Athens, Beirut or any other likely place on January 23rd or in the week following. They noticed a Mr Golkadas and a Miss Casceri on the early morning flight to Nicosia on January 24th, but it meant nothing to any of them.

It does not need recording that the most prevalent word in the volcabulary of Ms Charlotte Rapley on the morose journey back to the apartment that evening was one consisting of just four letters and associated with the movements of the bowels.

That night Sally asked Charlie to sleep with her, out of need for comfort and to quell her feelings of loneliness and abandon, rather than out of any need for sexual gratification. Charlie understood this and, although she touched the intimate parts as they held each other in their arms, nothing more happened between them.

They must have lain awake for two hours, talking spasmodically in between long periods of silence. This time the older woman had nothing to offer, no hope, no optimism. They both knew they had tried everything. The final inspiration had failed.

Outside, the late evening chatter of a summer Paris gave way to the stillness of night.

It was nearing 01:00 when Sally said, "I'm going anyway."

"Mm?" Charlie had been dozing off, and her bedmate's voice startled her back to consciousness. "What, honey?"

"I'm going anyway, Charlie. To Cyprus. I just *know* that's where Steve is."

With an effort, Charlie sat up in the bed, her full baggy breasts wobbling as she turned to switch on the dim bedside light. "Shit kid, is that wise? Whadya gonna do when you get there?"

Sally also sat up, and the woman in Charlie winced as the raw scars on the girl's chest came into view.

"I don't know, I just know I have to go. I have ample money, I'll find a hotel or something. I don't even know how I'm going to set about finding Steve, but he's there, Charlie, he's there. And I'll find him."

For a moment Charlie was silent. Then she smiled a big, warm, friendly-bear smile. "Y' know, I think you're right. It's probably the best thing you can do. It'll either kill or cure you." She looked again at Sally's scars and thought that perhaps that was not the right expression to use. "I mean of this love you have for this guy. I only hope he'll appreciate what you're doing."

A rueful look crossed Sally's face as she said wistfully, "So do I, Charlie. So do I."

Ψ

Sunday July 14 1974

"The new Prime Minister of Portugal is Colonel Vasco Goncalves. He was named yesterday following the resignation of Professor Adelino Palma Carlos last week."

Nicosia, Cyprus

At 21:30 that evening, Ramirov met someone in a secluded corner of the noisy *Picnic* nightclub in northern Nicosia. Few words were exchanged and Ramirov left the club just twenty minutes after he had entered it.

Yeri, Nicosia District, Cyprus

Steve and Christina were in the bath together when Ramirov returned to the villa. Without even the courtesy of a warning knock, the bathroom door crashed open. They made no attempt to cover themselves, but Steve frowned angrily at the sudden intrusion. "What the hell, Martinez!"

"My partners," Ramirov knelt by the side of the bath, addressing the couple like old and trusted friends. "The time has come. It is to be tomorrow. Tomorrow Grivas, you will have The Eye of Makarios!"

"At last! What exactly is going to happen? What do I do?"

"Later. Tonight we have a lot of work to do and a lot of planning. Come, we must not waste time." He had hold of Steve's arm and he was literally lifting him from the water.

The American fought him off with a series of splashing slaps. "Hey buddy, do you mind!" He had never seen the other man like this before. Was he high? "At least give me the chance to finish my bath!"

Ramirov's eyebrows narrowed and then rose. "My goodness! I am sorry! Of course. But downstairs as fast as you can, Grivas. We have a long night ahead of us!"

He went out, bubbling with excitement. The bathroom door slammed behind him.

Steve paused to get his breath back. "Jees, I don't even think he knew we were naked. So our cold, hard teacher *can* get excited. I wonder what's coming down?"

Christina shrugged. "Excitement is not necessarily a good thing, Stelios. If a man gets too excited he can make foolish mistakes."

"And a woman?"

"What?"

"A woman can get too excited and make foolish mistakes too, you know."

"Ah, but for a woman it is different."

"Cascianis?"

"Yes?"

"Think, will you?"

"Of what, Stelios?"

"Just think of this afternoon."

"This afternoon…?"

"About a woman getting excited…?"

A cat-with-the-cream smile oozed across the olive face.

"Now," continued Steve. "You're thinking, right?"

"Oh yes Stelios, I am thinking." She closed her eyes dreamily.

He picked up the soap and lathered his hands. "Well now, gorgeous Christy, don't you give me any of your Cypriot bullshit about women not getting excited, huh? I can still feel your nails in my back."

"Just the claws of a pussycat, my Stelios."

He reached forward and lathered both her breasts simultaneously, the soft-yet-solid mounds quivering beneath his palms. "A pussycat or a tiger?"

She kept her eyes closed. "Maybe both."

Very gently, with the softest of caresses, he rinsed the soap off. "But tigers can bite."

"So can pussies."

He bent down and took her hardened left nipple between his teeth. He sucked at it and then bit it sharply.

She squealed and pushed his head down her body. The water lapped at her pubic line.

"I didn't think pussies liked water," he said as she forced his head down and between her legs.

It was the first saturation diving he had done since January.

And the excited Martinez/Ramirov had to wait quite some time for them to come down.

"And what do I do?" asked Christina with a pout. They had been talking and planning for two hours now. Ramirov had informed them that tomorrow a great turmoil would be unleashed on the island as history took its ineluctable course, but he would not be drawn on specifics. "The diamond is your only concern. You and I, Grivas, are going to attack Makarios."

Christina had tried to bully, coax and seduce further information from him, but he was not to be drawn. That had started off her sulks and she had moodily puffed her way through three pungent panatelas which looked and smelled as if they had been made out of the eviscera of a rotting goat corpse.

Now the man they knew as Martinez was giving Stelios his instructions. They were to raid Mouskos' palace. And this had prompted her question of her involvement.

Ramirov looked towards her, his mouth smiling but the black eyes behind the tinted glasses remaining cold. He inclined his head. "You, my dear, do nothing. You remain here and prepare for our return. Be ready to move if things do not go according to plan. If things go all right, there should be no necessity for us to move. But we must be prepared just in case. Every circumstance must always be catered for."

"But that ees not right!" Her accent became more pronounced with her increased emotion. "I must comma weeth you. You *cannot* leaf me here!"

The look Ramirov gave her would have turned anybody to stone. She stared back at him, but then her resolution began to waiver and her eyes faltered from the stare, came back again, then away again. She rammed the butt of the panatela back between her teeth.

"Best do as he says, babe," counselled Steve. "He's the master, don't forget. Our *sempi*. And besides, we do need you here as he says. You never know what might happen."

"So, the two off you are going to raid the Presidential Palace, take a priceless diamond and comm back and liff happily effer after, hah? You will need help, you know. You cannot do itt on your own effen if you are supermen like Meester Martinez here seemse to think he iss. You must get help from somewhere." She scowled at Ramirov. "Why will you nott tell uss exactly what iss going on?"

"Baby, I think – "

"Shut up, Stelios! You will be risking your life tomorrow in somsing that seemse bigger than oll off uss, and *he* will not tell you what you are getting involved in." The eyes glared again. "Just who are you anyway, to come with your threats and then leaf uss again for a month and come back and order uss about with the promise of geeting The Eye of Makarios? I think Meester Martinez that you are using uss. How can we be sure that we will effer see thees diamond - ?"

It happened so suddenly that Steve did not have time to move.

All Christina was aware of was a black blanket descending over her eyes. Ramirov had been sitting with his hands clasped together on his lap, head tilted to one side, taking in the woman's vitriol. Suddenly his right arm shot outwards, hand and fingers rigid, slicing sharply through the air. It met Christina's right temple with a sickening thud. She dropped back on the chair immediately, totally limp, the panatela rolling onto the floor.

For a second Steve was speechless, then he leapt over to her, grabbing her wrist to feel for a pulse.

"For Christ's sake man!"

"She is alive," Ramirov announced with an air of total disinterest. He walked over, picked up the panatela and killed it in a rush of effervescence in her half-empty glass of local champagne. "If I had wanted to kill her I would have aimed thirty millimetres lower."

Steve let her wrist drop and turned to look at the other man. "You callous bastard."

Ramirov spoke as if scolding an errant schoolboy. "I said when I first met you that there would be no questions, that you would do as I say. I could have killed you both that night, please remember that. Do you *want* this diamond? Or is this little piece of Cypriot ass worth more to you? In five hours time we will get The Eye of Makarios. May I suggest you also get some sleep? Shortly we will both be very busy."

"What kind of animal are you?"

"The kind that is helping you fulfil your father's last request. She will awake with a headache, nothing more. I will take my rest in the outhouse. I have things to do. Five hours, my dear Mr Grivas, that is all. Five hours."

Outside, two hours later.

"Do you want this?" Digenis held up the syringe. "For the woman?"

Ramirov shook his head. "I can use the cyanide gas."

"No. We're not into death – "

"I am."

"Maybe so. We are not. This will keep her out for a few hours. Use it, please."

In the darkness, Ramirov actually looked disappointed. He took the syringe.

"It will keep her out long enough for you to be on your way," Digenis continued. "Get the diamond and she will never see you again. And she does not know your real identity."

"Nobody does," said Ramirov.

Except you, he thought.

For a summary of the events leading up to the attempted coup in Cyprus on July 15 1974, please see Appendix 3.

Ψ

Monday July 15 1974

"Reports are coming in of a rebellion in Cyprus. No details are available as yet, but it is known that members of the EOKA terrorist organisation have taken over Nicosia radio. Unconfirmed reports say that President Makarios has been killed."

Cyprus

The Presidential Palace is on the south-western perimeter of Nicosia, just over two kilometres from the southern walls of the old city. To reach it direct from Yeri village it is not necessary to enter the city itself, passage can be made via Strovolos and round the back of Engomi.

But Ramirov had one last piece of business to attend to that morning, and in the early hours his battered grey Volkswagen Beetle was seen thundering through Athalassa and heading straight on for Eylenja.

"Hey, it's that way!" shouted Steve above the roar of the supercharged engine as they swept over the intersection. He shifted in his seat, uncomfortable with the weight of the sub-machine gun on his lap.

"Not yet my friend, just one last thing. How do you think we are going to reach the Presidential Palace in an old Volkswagen and looking like two stupid tourists who just happen to be carrying a whole arsenal of weapons?"

Steve said nothing but looked grimly out of the window. It was hot inside the car, but even hotter outside, even at this early hour, and the window remained closed against the heat and the dust.

He thought of his life. Of his *lives*. The one people knew about, the one they didn't. He thought of the madness of the last months. He thought of his father.

He said a silent prayer for the soul of George Grivas.

Eylenja was reached in no time, and the Volkswagen pulled up outside a ramshackle old dwelling on the eastern side of the town.

"Wait here." Ramirov climbed out and ran into the house without bothering to knock.

Inside it was dark, and it took just a second for Ramirov's eyes to adjust from the glare of the early morning sun before he could make out the old peasant waiting patiently in a wooden rocking chair by the bare wooden table.

The old man looked up as the door burst open.

"Martinez," snapped the visitor. "You have something for me." He spoke in Greek.

"I have," said the old man calmly, and he reached down the side of his chair and handed over a brown package tied up with string, like a bundle of laundry.

"My thanks, old man," Ramirov leant forward as if to kiss him on the cheek.

The old man was surprised by the action. He was even more surprised as he felt the knife slide into his body just below the breastbone and push upwards into his heart. He died immediately.

After two jerks up and down to ensure death, Ramirov removed the knife, wiped it on the old man's dirty trousers, and replaced it in its sheath.

Back in the car, Ramirov slit open the parcel, yanking off the brown paper and string. Two uniforms were revealed.

Steve sniffed in irony. "Well, well, the Tactical Reserve Force. I'd XXXecognize *that* uniform anywhere."

"Not quite the TRF, but they were the best official uniforms they could get hold of."

"Who are 'they'?"

Ramirov did not answer. Roughly he rewrapped the uniforms and tossed them onto the back seat. He gunned the car into action and took a quick left at the end of the road, heading into the capital.

"Martinez, who are 'they'?" Steve repeated.

"EOKA, of course," Ramirov answered smoothly. "More precisely, EOKA B."

"But I thought they were finished?"

Ramirov was searching the road on the right with his eyes, and they had slowed down to a reasonable speed. "You are a fool if you believe that and such thoughts are not worthy of the son of Grivas."

"But we were told – "

"You were told nothing. You refused their offer of leadership, therefore you were excluded. You were not required – you and that meddlesome female. You are Grivas' son in name only. The two of you had your own little mission and they were content to let you get on with it. EOKA has grown stronger since the death of Grivas. People revere his memory. And today is their day, today is *the* day of *Enosis!*"

Steve remained quiet. Two minutes later, Ramirov cried "Ah, here we are!" and he turned the car sharply to the left between two rows of old and not very well kept houses.

About a hundred metres along, three men waited anxiously beside an old jeep. They were wearing the uniform of the Cypriot National Guard. They tensed, hands on their holsters, as the Volkswagen approached. Then, at a word from one who must have been the senior officer, they relaxed as the Beetle came to a halt and Ramirov could clearly be seen.

"Our way into the Palace," explained Ramirov. He reached into the back seat. "Get out and change into one of these uniforms and sit with me in the back of the jeep. Talking will be superfluous. They are genuine members of the National Guard and under orders. They know who you are and not so long ago would have shot you on sight. Today you will be quite safe. Prepare your gun and pistol for action. From now on it is kill or be killed. Come, Grivas, let us go."

Stelios Grivas stepped from the vehicle and did as he was told.

As the jeep with the five men on board drove swiftly through the streets of Nicosia, Grivas noticed how quiet everything seemed. It was not that there was a lack of activity – for the majority of the people who were not in on the coup would not know what had happened until it was all over – but there just seemed *something*, something almost tactile in the air, as if the Gods from high up on Olympus knew exactly what was going on and disapproved.

And it was hot. So, so hot. Grivas' shirt was saturated and it stuck to his back uncomfortably. The back of his curly hair was matted and gritty. And, he had to admit, he stank. Yet Martinez next to him did not seem to be sweating at all.

They took the main Dhiyeni Akrita, hooting the tourists out of their way.

And then he saw her.

Or at least he thought he saw her.

Or it was someone who looked like her.

But it could not be her, of course.

They had flashed past her in a moment, and Grivas was too cramped between Ramirov and one of the others to turn around. He laughed to himself. His mind was playing tricks on him! That tourist they had just hooted out of their way looked like Sally, the girl he had left behind in Houston. Wasn't her, of course. This one had cropped hair, was decidedly skinnier than Sally, and the glasses were missing. Also she looked wan, as if she was not well or was just recovering from some illness. No, it was not her. But just for one moment, one crazy moment, he thought he had seen someone from another, forgotten world…

They travelled on.

Michael Mouskos, His Beatitude Makarios III, Archbishop of the Autocephalous Church of Cyprus and President of the Cypriot Republic, had not slept well that night. And he had good reason. For he knew of the probability of the attempted coup that morning and, worse, of his proposed assassination.

Makarios was a man of vast intellect and personal charisma. He prided himself on the intricate intelligence network he and his intimate counsellors had built up over the years. It was only natural that he had known of what would be attempted that day nearly two weeks in advance.

After spending many nights alone in the Archbishop's Palace considering the avenues open to him, Makarios had come to an important conclusion. During the four previous assassination attempts he had been able to meet threat with force, either prior to or shortly after the event. This time it would be different. This time, if his intelligence was correct, it would be himself against the army. Odds much too numerous. This time he would not be able to meet force with force. This time, in all probability, he would not even be able to defend himself.

Needless to say, he had been particularly circumspect that morning during his daily four kilometre journey from the Archbishop's Palace within the old city wall of Nicosia to the Presidential Palace on the south-western outskirts.

Some ten days previously, as soon as Makarios had evaluated all the possibilities of this rumoured new attack and had decided on his action, he had summoned someone from Kykko Monastery, his own home monastery in the district of Marathasa, Paphos. That someone was a priest Makarios had used before.

Makarios was a commanding figure. Over six feet in height, he looked even more imposing than his size already allowed due to the combination of the tall hat, the flowing black robes and the Greek Orthodox bishop's long staff. His eyes were sharp and penetrating, and he wore the thick greying black beard. He was, therefore, very hard to impersonate with any conviction. Hard, but not impossible. And that was his little secret.

Makarios had stumbled across the priest many years before on one of his return to visits to the monastery that he loved. The priest was younger than Makarios, but he was of the same height and identical build. His facial features were roughly similar, at least to withstand perfunctory examination, and his black beard was the same shape. Dressed in identical robes to the Archbishop, beard greyed with powder, Andreas Papadopoulos could have been a twin brother.

He had been used successfully in the past when it had been necessary for Makarios to be in two places at once: once during an assassination bid (when a forlorn EOKA attempt on the President's life had missed even his stand-in by metres) and, more notably, on the famous occasion eighteen years previously in 1956 when Makarios had supposedly been taken from the island into exile in the Seychelles, escorted ashore by the Chief of Police Trevor Williams. [*Makarios was, in fact, stripped of his robes, shaved and immured by the British for over twelve months in Limassol, unbeknown to the rest of the world. Whether he underwent deliberate physical intimidation or just the discomfort of gaol is not known.*]

Andreas Papadopoulos had not been used for a while, but today The Red Priest would need his services like never before…

In the cramped, bumpy rear seat of the jeep, Ramirov raised a suntanned arm and looked at the Rolex on his wrist.

"One minute," he said. The head inclined itself a few degrees to the left.

In front of him, a member of the National Guard blocked his right nostril with his finger and snotted over the side of the vehicle.

Archbishop Makarios looked up from his desk and responded quietly to the knock on the door. "Come in."

The priest entered diffidently.

Makarios smiled. "Ah, Father Andreas, come in, come in. I believe we do not have much time…"

The tanks of the National Guard had just started firing into the Presidential Palace as the jeep turned the last corner of the main drive and screeched to a halt. There were people everywhere, those in uniform heading towards the palace, the rest fleeing for their lives.

The five occupants of the jeep leapt out. Ramirov and Grivas headed as planned directly for the huge main door, which had already been blown apart from a blast from one of the tanks.

There was noise everywhere.

And it was hot.

And it was dusty.

And it was hell.

When the tanks started firing, Makarios and Papadopoulos were together in the palace on the broad landing looking down onto the wide main lobby below. Anybody seeing them at that time would have thought they had suddenly been inflicted with double vision. Here was Makarios in duplicate. Both men were fully robed and standing erect, holding themselves with the Mouskos calm, the Mouskos self-assurance. The only difference was the eyes. One held the charm, the cunning, the slyness, the greatness, that was the embodiment of the genuine Makarios.

The other held almost nothing.

The second tank blast shattered the main door, and Makarios sprang into action. While his double watched, the Archbishop flung down his staff and pulled off his headgear, revealing his bald pate. The black robes were whipped off carelessly and left in a bundle on the floor. Underneath, Makarios wore a pair of old brown cord pants and a dirty white shirt with beige stripes. The transformation had taken only four seconds, yet no one would now have recognised the world-famous priest.

"All right," Makarios busily tucked his shirt into the pants. "Give me half a minute's start and then flee yourself, dear Andreas. I fear this time we may indeed be in serious danger." He paused for the briefest moment. "And may God be with us both."

Papadopoulos grabbed the Archbishop's hand and kissed the ring of office in genuine devotion.

"Goodness, yes." Makarios tugged the ring off his finger and grabbed Papadopoulos's hand. The ring slipped onto his finger, a macabre marriage of souls.

Papadopoulos's eyes held tears. "He will protect you, your Beatitude."

The eyes of Makarios watered also. A swift blessing, a smile, and then Makarios was gone, down the wide staircase and out of sight somewhere into the back of the palace.

Dust began to fly in all directions as more tank shells thudded into the walls and through the shattering windows.

Papadopoulos stayed his ground and silently prayed as he allowed thirty seconds to pass. On the thirtieth second, amid the noise of the tanks and the chatter of machine guns, a shard of the ceiling directly above fell away and exploded on top of his head. It shook him but he did not collapse. His head hurt but he was alive. Now he must escape, and quickly...

The masonry had stunned him, and instead of running deeper into the palace as would have been expected, Papadopoulos went full pelt down the stairs, head on into the firing. Halfway down his foot caught in the hem of his robes and he fell, his knees thudding on the stairs, his face ripping against a piece of rubble as he came to rest at the bottom, knees oozing warm liquid.

His face was cut just below the left eye and was bleeding savagely, but the smash on the head had dulled his sense of pain. He staggered to his feet, bent down, picked up the fallen headgear and jammed it back into place. Then he turned to head for the back of the palace.

Just as he did so, two men charged over the shattered main door, their guns blazing. One was swarthy and had a chubby face, the other tall and with a black moustache and - *my God!* Didn't he look like the young Grivas! No, it couldn't possibly be!

Papadopoulos turned away to run, but he knew it was hopeless. His feet slipped across the heavily polished tiled floor and he tried to reach a door.

"MOUSKOS!" shouted an accented voice from behind.

But he kept on running.

One of the machine guns fired and for a moment it seemed to the priest that the bullets had missed. But then all life went from the right side of his body and his right leg was whipped away from under him. He span around, robes swirling, in a wild, macabre pirouette. He saw the tall man's mouth move and flames shoot from his gun.

Papadopoulos never heard the fire of the gun, and at his moment of death - as pieces of his chest flew away at all angles and the floor came up to meet him - he heard the man shout "FOR GRIVAS!".

Then all was tranquility.

Ramirov and Grivas dashed over to the body. Ramirov was mumbling to himself. Above the din, Grivas heard "You did it. My God, you did it!"

Ramirov's hands scrabbled frantically at the clothing, ripping the bloodsoaked cloth away.

"Where the hell is it?" shouted Grivas. "It's not here. For fuck's sake, it's not here!"

"Wait." Ramirov's hand withdrew something from near the body's genitals. It was a small leather pouch connected to a leather cord still around the waist. Ramirov's knife appeared and the cord was instantly cut. Quickly, he opened the pouch.

The Star of Sierra Leone slipped out into his hand, a huge but ungainly rough diamond.

"The Eye of Makarios!" said Grivas. "Holy God!"

Without a word Ramirov replaced the diamond in the pouch and went to put it in a top pocket. Grivas grabbed his arm, the barrel of his gun pointing between Ramirov's eyes.

"Mine I think."

Their eyes locked. Then Ramirov let the diamond and the pouch be removed from his hands.

Then he said, "Come on, quickly!" and the American rose and followed him through the back of the palace.

Two civilians appeared from an office, and Ramirov shot their faces away without thought.

They reached a side door, already gaping open like a corpse's jaw, and ran out of the palace and into the grounds. They did not know that just two minutes before the real, live Michael Mouskos, Archbishop Makarios III, had fled this very same way.

The firing into the palace did not last for long. The first genuine members of the National Guard to enter the building found the body of the fake Makarios, hence the radio reports later that day that Makarios had been killed. It was not until the body was moved some hours later that the headgear fell off to reveal Papadopoulos's full head of jet black hair, the main feature that had distinguished him and Michael Mouskos in mufti. And by that time Makarios had hitchhiked into the mountains and would soon be picked up by the British troops. Two days later he was in London.

Christina Cascianis surfaced slowly from the man-made oblivion. She had the worst headache of her life. It began at the cranium and travelled upwards over the top of her skull to erupt above the eyes in a whirlpool of ache, pain and nausea. The side of her head hurt like hell. She touched the spot gingerly as she moved herself gently into a sitting position. And what was the bruise on her arm?

How long had she been out? Where was Stelios and that bastard Martinez? What had happened? The last thing she remembered was berating Martinez over something, and then... nothing.

What time was it? She had no watch. Carefully she straightened her stiff neck and moved her head to look around the room. She had been in the villa long enough to know that there were no clocks about the place, but one of the men might have left a watch somewhere.

There were no watches, but there was something else. A person.

Standing just inside the half-open front door was a man. A tall, broad man with dark brown hair and a sallow, gaunt face which was distinctly out of place above the broad and obviously muscular body. He was dressed in a lightweight brown suit of old-fashioned design, and ancient brown brogues. A small-collared once-white shirt and thin knitted brown tie completed the ensemble.

"Who - who are you?" she stammered in Greek.

The main raised an eyebrow and looked quizzically at her. The eyes held no trace of comprehension.

She tried again in English. "Who are yoo?" She could almost hear his brain computing the language.

After a moment he said, "Ah! In-gleesh. Mine not good. Turk?"

Christina spat unladylike on the floor. The man paused again, computing the gesture. Then his cheeks twitched upwards, once, and then down again, and he walked over towards her.

"In-gleesh not good. I... friend of Ramirov. He here not yet no?"

A sharp stab of pain pierced the back of her skull and came out through her right eye. The stranger was standing three metres away. "Who iss Ramirov? I do nott know heem."

"This howse hiss," the gentleman gestured.

"Martinez. His name iss Martinez."

Information computed once again, then the gaunt face turned even paler as he realised his error. "Oh... I wait. You... well?" He came nearer.

He was just a metre from Christina when she snarled. Without warning, her right hand shot out and grabbed him mercilessly in the groin. She could feel the balls beneath the cheap cloth of the pants. She squeezed with all her might.

The man screamed with the sudden agony. His hands fumbled ineffectively at her wrist, trying to pull her off, but she was not going to let go. He tried to kick her but found it impossible to move his legs up. He screamed again and again, spittle flying from his mouth, until the red haze overcame him. His legs gave way.

Christina maintained her emasculating grip as he fell, and she twisted the balls wickedly for good measure. The screams had died off into a whimpering gurgle, and the spittle has changed to drool oozing from the corners of his mouth.

Christina released the organs, stood up, swung her right foot back and brought it down heavily into the man's crotch. He grunted and rolled over onto his stomach, his knees raising themselves in protection.

She wasted no time. Disregarding her complaining head, she ran over to the door and out into the hot, dazzling sunlight. As she went through the doorway, a gun cracked from behind and the lintel splintered above. But she did not pause, she just kept on running, running...

On the floor of the villa, the gun slipped out of the Russian's hand, all strength gone, and, crying in sheer agony, he rolled his face to the left and spewed all over an expensive rug.

The old Volkswagen pulled up outside the villa two hours later. Ramirov and Grivas, both now back in their own clothes, climbed out. The sub-machine guns were in the front in the trunk of the vehicle; Ramirov carried a simple pistol tucked into the waistband of his pants. The American was unarmed, the diamond buttoned safely in his shirt pocket.

The mood of both men was euphoric.

"Did you see the way that son-of-a-bitch's back exploded?" asked Grivas as they walked towards the house. "Do you *see* it, Martinez? Jees, I only hope my father did. Revenge is so, so sweet."

"It was remarkable, all of it," nodded Ramirov. "Not a hitch. And Makarios just where I thought he would be. Stunned and stupefied and running like a frightened animal. Well, he will run no longer."

He turned the handle of the front door and they entered the villa. Ramirov was not at all surprised to see the gaunter than usual visitor sitting uncomfortably in one of the armchairs, and he greeted him with "Sergei!".

Grivas stopped in his tracks just inside the front door. "Who the hell...?"

Ramirov totally ignored him as he walked towards the other man. "All is ready?" he asked eagerly.

Sergei nodded and said something in Russian.

"Hey Martinez, who *is* this guy?" Grivas continued on into the room. Again he was ignored.

"What happened here?" asked Ramirov in Russian, indicating the big damp patch on the rug.

"There was some bastard woman here."

"Oh yes, a minor hindrance which I had to put to sleep."

"Not permanently enough."

"I told him that."

"She was just waking when I arrived. She attacked me. In the bollocks." A weak gesture towards the rug explained everything else.

Ramirov could not resist a guffaw. "I think a spell at Novosibirsk would do you good, Comrade! But I am sorry about the female. As you say, I should have made it permanent."

The foreign tongue was aggravating Grivas. "Do you two mind? Who *is* this, Martinez?"

Sergei sniffed. "And what about him? This is the famous Son of Grivas, huh? When will you deal with him?"

"Martinez, will you *answer* me?"

Ramirov turned and looked at the American, his head inclined to one side. He said in English. "Now is as good a time as any."

"As good a time as any for *what?*"

Ramirov drew the gun from his waistband and shot Stelios Grivas through the heart from a distance of only two metres.

PART FOUR

Ψ

OBJECTIVE DELIVERED

Christina kept running. Running and running. Wildly at first, the pain in her head increasing with each stride until she thought she would pass out. The wide ethnic skirt entangled itself around her legs as she moved.

After half an hour her legs began to tire and she slowed to a walking pace, her breath coming uneasily. In a further fifteen minutes she had reached the village of Laxia. People seemed to be going about their business as normal, but there was an eerie quietness about the place. She accosted a villager and asked what had happened that morning, but the old woman just gave her a stony stare and hobbled on.

Christina came to the main Nicosia-Limassol road. The traffic seemed unusually thin, and what little of it there was was heading for Limassol, away from the capital. She had a nasty feeling that she knew exactly what was going on in Nicosia. Stelios had probably got embroiled in an attempt to overthrow Mouskos. She only hoped that he and Martinez had been successful, because such was the nature of their mission - to steal a diamond from the very person of Makarios - that they must either succeed or lose their lives.

Resting under a tree by the side of the road, she realised that her best bet lay back at the villa. Stelios would need her help - *if* he came back. *If it was ever Martinez' intention to have him come back.*

She accepted her thoughts with resignation. She had been near death too many times for the thought of it to horrify her any more, even the death of General George Grivas's son, her lover. But she must not run away. She must return to the villa to see what she could do.

As she arose a jeep thundered past her on the road, heading towards Nicosia. In the back she thought she saw one of the old EOKA members of the good old days, but the jeep had gone in a second in a cloud of dust, and she could not be certain. Not until days later did she realise that she had seen Nicos Sampson on his way to take up his short-lived Presidency.

She returned to the villa by the route she had come, half walking, half trotting.

Arriving back an hour later, the first thing she noticed was that the door of the place was ominously open, and there was not a sound from within...

It was evening by the time the Volkswagen arrived at its destination, Sergei driving, Ramirov asleep in the front passenger seat. They had gone south from Yeri to Athienou where they had turned east, heading through Arsos, Lysi and Kondea. They had followed the road for Famagusta, turning south about two kilometres out and then picking up the main road through Dherinia and Paralimni. They were now stopped to the south of the village of Ayia Napa in a secluded spot to the east of the Nissi Beach Hotel.

The evening was warm and still, a calmness which belied the events of the day.

Ramirov awoke immediately the car's engine was switched off. "We have arrived?"

"Just beyond the trees," confirmed Sergei.

"And now we wait." Ramirov touched the inside pocket of his cord waister jacket to confirm the safety of The Star of Sierra Leone. "Till dark?"

"Immediately it gets dark we descend to the beach. A motor boat will pick us up. It is arranged."

"And you are sure we will not be seen from the hotel?"

"There is a small headland on the way, it will give us sufficient cover. And anyway, the tourists are evacuating, they will be much too preoccupied to notice us."

"That is true. If only we had a radio to know how things were going. If it has gone according to their plan, things will be over by now. Makarios is dead, that I know."

"You can get all the news you want on board the yacht." Sergei opened the door.

Abruptly, Ramirov reached across and grabbed him by the forearm. "Where are you going?"

"Piss."

"We do not want to risk attracting any attention now. Can't it wait?"

"I have just driven over seventy kilometres non-stop, Comrade. No, it cannot wait." He pulled his arm free.

He was back in a couple of minutes. "There was blood in it and the balls are a deep purple."

"We must get you to a doctor. There will be one on board the yacht?"

"Yes. He was thought necessary in case anything happened to *you*."

Ramirov chuckled. "Such are the vagaries of life, Comrade. It is causing you much pain?"

"Discomfort, the pain has subsided. You should have killed that bitch, you know."

"Quite, but I was talked out of it. I did not expect you to arrive so early. I had planned to deal with her and the American at the same time. Still, wherever she went she will be of no trouble now. I have what I want and her beloved EOKA now has power. Why, she should thank me and the late Mr Grivas for our part in it!"

Ramirov's good humour lasted for the half hour until darkness had settled. Then the two men simply left the vehicle where it was, for all intents and purposes abandoned by fleeing tourists.

There was little moon and it was almost pitch black on the beach, sparse and intermittent illumination being provided by a pencil torch carried by Sergei. The sibilant waves slid along the sand towards them and then crept away again diffidently.

They did not have to wait long before they heard the sound of an outboard motor approaching from their right. Sergei raised the pencil torch and gave three flashes of five seconds duration and one of two seconds. It was answered by three flashes of two seconds duration and one of five.

The small motor boat contained two men in crew uniform. With simple acknowledgements, Ramirov and Sergei waded out twenty metres through the undertow and climbed in. They hardly had a chance to sit down before the boat had been pushed around and they were off, raking into the night.

They travelled in an easterly direction for ten minutes, Cyprus lost in the darkness behind them. Then all of a sudden the yacht loomed up from nowhere. Only a few lights were on but Ramirov could tell that it was huge, much bigger than the normal rich man's vessel. *[The vessel belonged, and still does belong, to K – a very influential Arab.]*

On board they were met by 'Akay' Al Khalifa, smart in dark suit and white polo-necked sweater. This time he shook Ramirov's hand. "My friend, congratulations! Mr Hernandez, welcome once again." He spoke in French. "Did you enjoy your recent visit to Cana?"

"Very pleasant, but the Jordan is vast and mysterious."

"Who knows where a river ends?" Al Khalifa smiled. "Please excuse the lack of illumination, for obvious reasons. And this night air out here leaves something to be desired in warmth. Come, I will show you to your cabin." The three men passed through a doorway and down some steps. "You know, of course, that Sampson is now President?"

"I guessed as much, that was their plan. Everything appeared to go extremely well, entirely as arranged. What happens now is up to them."

They were walking on thickly-piled carpet, and the walls were tastefully finished off in well-polished wood. Through another doorway and down some more stairs. Al Khalifa opened the second door along, and Ramirov followed him inside.

"Your cabin," said the Arab. "Mr Hernandez is situated just next door."

"I must see the doctor," said Sergei from the doorway. "He is awake?"

Al Khalifa looked concerned. "No, but I can wake him. You are hurt, unwell?"

"Both," sniffed the Russian. "Some accursed female attacked me."

Al Khalifa raised an eyebrow but pursued the matter no further. "I will see that he comes to your cabin immediately."

Sergei walked away, and the door to the next cabin could be heard opening and closing.

The Arab turned back to Ramirov. "The item is safe, I trust?"

"Of course, and it will remain in my care for the time being."

"*Mais naturellement.* We can talk further in the morning. I will have some hot food brought in to you and something to drink. There is also a bar," he indicated a cupboard set into the wall next to the wide and extremely opulent bed. "Is there anything else you wish at this time?"

"Just to relax, that is all. What time do we arrive in Beirut?"

"We are scheduled to dock at noon tomorrow."

"Good."

"Relax well, my friend." Al Khalifa left the cabin, closing the door noiselessly.

A few minutes later the muted hum of the vessel's engines increased as it picked up speed, and by this time Ramirov was lying on the bed, naked except for a black jock strap, and gazing up at his reflection in the mirrored ceiling, willing himself into a state of relaxation.

Another few minutes passed. There came a gentle tap on the door. "*Venez!*" called the Russian.

The door was pushed open and a trolley was wheeled in by an attractive red head. She was dressed in a green knee-length kaftan, nothing adorning her legs. She smiled, natural gaiety in her green eyes. "Good evening," she said in English, her voice deep, lilting.

Ramirov raised himself up on one elbow. "Good evening. You are English?"

"That's right. Akay - Mister Al Khalifa - has sent this food along for you."

"You are the waitress?"

She chuckled. "No, I was coming this way anyway. I believe you wish to relax? I am a qualified masseuse." She left the trolley behind the closed door and walked over to him, red hair bouncing, green kaftan rustling. "May I help you relax?"

Ramirov smiled and removed the tinted glasses. "But certainly."

"My name is Melanie."

"And I am - "

"You are... to relax." She undid the kaftan and let it fall from her body. Underneath she wore just the smallest pair of red G-string pants. Her breasts were firm and stood out from her body without support; they wobbled gently as she knelt down on the edge of the bed.

She put her hand firmly on the front of his jock. "You have far too many clothes on. May I remove them?"

Tel Aviv, Israel

At the same time that Ilich Ramirov was surrendering himself to the ministrations of the delectable Melanie, a very special meeting was taking place in a room on the top floor of an office block in northern Tel Aviv.

Usually the Controllers of the five branches of *Mossad Aliyah Beth* (Israeli intelligence) met informally in this room once a week on a Wednesday morning. This week, however, an extra-special meeting was being held on Monday night.

They sat at a round table, each man in his shirtsleeves and no tie. All were in the forty to sixty age group, each one a tanned, anonymous-looking Jew. Outside of government circles few people, if any, would have guessed their occupation.

Up above the table the blades of an old and only partly effective fan moved around noisily and reluctantly, a token effort against the heavy summer heat.

The mugginess of the evening did not aid the men's collective testiness at having to meet extra-ordinarily. They did not want to be here, but they had to be. It would be a short meeting, that was for certain.

They had started by expressing regrets over certain events in Cyprus.

Then the Controller of *Sherut Bitachon Klali*, or *Shabak*, the Israeli internal security service, gave a short discourse on the effects of an attack the previous week by Arab terrorists on an apartment block in Nahariya, a town near the Lebanese border. Now the other four men digested the information about the dead and mutilated.

"Are we certain it is the work of Black September?" asked the Controller of the external security services branch (also known under the title of *Mossad*), who was the overall Controller of the other four men.

The Controller of *Aman*, the military intelligence unit, cleared his throat. "I have reports that Hassan had a private meeting with Qadhafi only two days before. You can bet your mother's life that baby Colonel is behind it, either directly or indirectly."

"I see. Any other proof?"

"We do not need proof!" hissed the *Shabak* man stiffly. "Let us hit them as we did last year."

"But not too much," said the sixth man in the room, Chaim Cohen the Deputy Controller of the external security services. "They are planning something big. We have people in place. We need to catch them in the act."

"But their actions cannot go unpunished," argued the *Shabak* man.

"Of course not. But let us not over react."

The overall Controller blew his nose on a large white handkerchief. Then he asked, "Can we agree then on a limited but effective response?"

The *Shabak* man reluctantly nodded, as did the other three.

"Right. I will arrange it. I should have something to report on Wednesday. Thank you, gentlemen. I am sorry to have kept you."

Ψ

Tuesday July 16 1974

"Archbishop Makarios is alive. Following yesterday's rebellion by Greek-backed members of the Cypriot National Guard, it was reported that the Archbishop had been killed in a dawn raid on his palace. In fact he escaped and was taken by RAF helicopter to the British base at Akrotiri on the southern-most tip of the island. Today he was taken by RAF plane to safety in Malta."

Beirut, Lebanon

The yacht docked at Beirut at 12:30. Ramirov and Al Khalifa were on deck to observe the intricate manoeuvring.

It was a hot, musty day in Beirut, not even the slightest breeze from the Mediterranean to take the edge off the heat. The smells of Lebanon rose off the dock to greet the vessel.

Ramirov was dressed in the same clothes as the night before. Al Khalifa was smart, as usual, in a crisp white short-sleeved shirt and cream slacks.

"You are sure you're not known?" asked the Arab as the vessel moved sideways to position itself correctly.

"No, it is all right," said Ramirov. "I have been here on two occasions in the past, both times as a guest of the Palestinian exiles. Why should anyone be worried at my coming?"

"Look at those faces down there. Any one of them could be Israeli."

"And what of it? I have done nothing to interest the *Mossad*. Yet. Worry when worry is due, *amigo*, not before. This is your home territory. I am safe."

"Of course," nodded Al Khalifa, but he wished tonight would come and he would have this foreigner off his hands. He was an organiser and accountant, not a minder.

"Go over it just once more," instructed Ramirov. "The meeting is at nine tonight?"

"Correct. Until then you and Mr Hernandez are requested to remain in the Hotel Phoenicia where separate suites have been reserved for you. I am to stay with you and this evening I will take you to the place."

"In other words, you are to watch me like a hawk."

"That is not in my instructions. You are trusted, surely that is not in doubt? Once the item was in your possession you could have gone anywhere, but you chose to complete the mission. Of that we are grateful and eternally in your debt."

"You are not in my debt. You are indebted to the cause of peace and justice."

"Of course."

"Just one thing..."

"Yes?"

"The English girl, the masseuse. She comes to the hotel with us."

Al Khalifa knew argument would be pointless. "I see."

"You can stay in Mr Hernandez' suite. I am in need of more relaxation."

Moscow, USSR

It was sunny that day in Moscow, but the warm rays hardly penetrated into the courtyard of the Arsenal. It was a chilled Ekaterina Furtseva who pulled up in the black, chauffeur-driven limousine.

At that time the Arsenal was the one-third of the Kremlin that was totally forbidden to both tourists and most Russians alike. Only the upper echelons of the Soviet hierarchy, their workers and their guards were permitted to enter the area. It consisted of a rectangle of office blocks surrounding a central courtyard. On the third floor of the six-storey eastern building was the room which housed the most powerful caucus in the world at that time: the *Politburo* of the Central Committee of the Soviet Union. Every Thursday the *Politburo* met in the room, and only a very select few (including three transcript secretaries) knew exactly what went on around the huge T-shaped table.

That Tuesday afternoon the room was empty save for one man. He stood at the window, gazing down onto the courtyard below as the limousine pulled up.

Alexei Nikolayevich Kosygin had been Prime Minister of the Soviet Union for ten years. Born in 1904 in St Petersburg, the son of a turner, he had fought with the Red Army in the revolutionary war, but it was not until 1927 that he became a party member. From then it had taken him just eleven years to rise to mayor of his home city, by then called Leningrad. In 1940, aged only 36, he was made Deputy Premier in Stalin's wartime government. Just after the end of the war, further elevation saw Kosygin into the *Politburo* where he shone with his expertise on economics. His career remained dormant during the reign of the peasant Nikita Kruschev, with whom he never saw eye to eye. With the ousting of Kruschev, Kosygin became Premier. His economic brilliance did much to remould the structure of Russia's ailing industry, but he was destined to become the quiet, stern half of the partnership with the showman Brezhnev.

In 1974, the craggy, severe Premier was still a force to be reckoned with, and an unexpected summons from him could make even a hard-faced bitch like Furtseva tremble in her Y-fronts.

Kosygin turned from the window as Furtseva was shown into the room, her shoes - which looked as though they were made of cast-iron - echoing on the floor.

"Comrade Prime Minister," nodded the woman bravely, holding the edge of concern from her voice.

Kosygin nodded. "What are you up to in Cyprus, Comrade Ekaterina?"

"Prime Minister?"

It was not Kosygin's habit to repeat himself, and he did not do so now. He just looked at her.

"The coup was known about," she explained. "We spoke about it. It was not the direct responsibility of my division."

"Of course, of course," he said gruffly. "But there's something else going on, isn't there Comrade? Something you have not told me about." He walked forward to stand on the opposite side of the baize-topped table. He did not ask her to sit down.

"My division has certain... interests in the area, Comrade Prime Minister."

"And you did not see fit to tell me, your Controller? What are they?"

She stared at the iron jowls. "One of my agents is assisting certain middle eastern factions."

"The Palestinians?"

"Among others, Comrade. They are formulating certain plans which necessitated their obtaining a diamond which was in the possession of Makarios. My agent has an assisting brief, and I authorised that he use the coup as the opportunity to obtain it."

Kosygin scowled. "The orders from the *Politburo*, from this office, were that Makarios was to die."

"And according to the reports - "

"The reports are wrong! It has now been confirmed that Makarios is alive and well and with the British." He raised his right fist and brought it crashing down onto the table. "And I have been told by impeccable sources that a certain gentleman, *unknown to me*, led the attack on him. And yet Makarios is not dead. The instructions from the *Politburo* must never be interfered with, do you understand that *Comrade?*"

"Yes, I - "

"As it is, your man's meddling could have wreaked untold damage. We wanted Makarios out of the way forever. Now he is still around our necks." He turned sharply back towards the window, biting off whatever else he was going to say.

Furtseva remained still and said nothing.

When Kosygin spoke again, his voice had subsided to normal, the hysteria vanquished.

"It is... unfortunate." He turned to face her again, motioning to a chair. "Sit, sit, Comrade, please."

They sat facing each other on opposite sides of the table. The Premier's hands were clenched together, resting on the baize top. Furtseva's hands were in her lap.

"Tell me about this 'secret' agent of yours. What exactly is he doing? What is his brief?"

Furtseva opened her mouth and then closed it again. There was so much she could say to the man. How Ramirov had been her idea, not even known by the head of the KGB. How she had been briefed about the planned activities in Cyprus and had considered it within her discretion to authorise her own man to become involved to his own particular ends without the authority of her Controller. How she had stressed that killing Makarios would be a bonus but the diamond must come first, despite Kosygin's ruling to 'other parties' that Makarios was to die at all costs. How she accepted the kudos for her division's many successes. How she must now accept the responsibility for its interference. How she was getting old...

Instead she told Kosygin in detail what she had outlined in private to certain members of the *Praesidium,* about the Arabs' plan to explode a nuclear device in Britain, and also (garrulous now, hoping to save face) about her future plans for Ilich Ramirov. How it was her intention that he should become a discrete entity in the co-ordination of world terror, with only a tenuous umbilical connecting him to the KGB. How her plan was succeeding and how Ramirov was within a year of permanently adopting the South American cover. How it was hoped that he would have untold successes in, say, the next decade.

At the end of it all, Kosygin was quiet. After a while he nodded. "I see," he did not expand on the comment. Then, rising, he said "All right, Comrade. Thank you. But in the future you are to inform me of all your little escapades in advance. No more discretion. The only initiative in the Soviet Union is taken in this room."

"Yes, Comrade Prime Minister." Furtseva leapt to her feet, snapped to attention and turned away.

"Oh, Comrade Ekaterina?"

"Yes, Comrade Prime Minister?" She turned back, puzzled.

"I wish you continued luck with your Ramirov. *But keep me informed.* Always."

She almost smiled. "Thank you, Comrade Prime Minister." She turned and left the room.

Kosygin returned to the window. The basic premise was good, he had to give her that. Ekaterina had a brilliant brain for subversion, that was why he had agreed to giving her her own division in the first place. An itinerant agent with an open ticket... And it would be easy enough for him to persuade the *Politburo* that the failed assassination of Makarios was just another example of the extraordinary fortune that surrounded the magical priest.

But Ekaterina Furtseva - was she really now the right person to run such an agent? Should it not be put in the hands of someone younger. Or perhaps, because of its international delicacy, in the hands of only Shelepin himself? Was Furtseva getting too old?

He watched from the window as, three floors below, the woman left the building and climbed back into the limousine.

Was it time she was retired?

Beirut, Lebanon

The same members of Black September met in the safe house near Sidani Street that night as had met there the previous January, when Michael Mahoney's request for the diamond had been revealed to them by Al Khalifa: Ali Hassan Salameh, controller of the intelligence and action arm; Abu Ayad, the IRA liaison man; the man from the Fateh intelligence agency, Jihaz-al-Razd; and Hassan's quiet personal assistant, Faisal Ibn Musaed.

They met at 20:30, for they had other matters to discuss before the arrival of Martinez and the diamond at 21:00.

As it happened, Al Khalifa, Ramirov and Sergei were to be late that evening. That afternoon, after two hours of sex and massage in the sumptuous suite in the Hotel Phoenicia with the delectable, wanton and genuinely red-haired Melanie, Ramirov had foolishly (for he was usually so careful about everything) ordered oysters from Room Service. A dozen prime, and incredibly expensive, specimens had been promptly delivered, and Ramirov had swallowed his way through seven of them.

About thirty minutes later the stomach cramps had begun, and he had spent the rest of the time in self-incarceration in the bathroom, defecating. It was a final ten minute shit that had delayed the three men leaving the hotel that evening. Had it not been for the oysters, Ramirov would have delivered the diamond and been away before the major events of that night took place. But fate, God, chance, call it what you will, had decreed differently.

It was 21:15 before the three men arrived at the house, by which time the nervous Abu Ayad was extremely worried. He still harboured the feeling that to return to Beirut after the massacre of his brothers last year was folly of the highest order. However Hassan, as overall leader on these matters, had overruled him.

The five members of Black September were waiting patiently when Al Khalifa entered, accompanied by Martinez and followed by Sergei Hernandez. They all rose in welcome to much scraping of chairs.

"My friend, my dear, dear friend! My brother!" effused Hassan, swallowing a candy and gripping Ramirov in a tight embrace. "Welcome, it is good to see you again. And congratulations! I hear the coup in Cyprus has been one hundred per cent successful." He nodded greeting at Sergei, who remained by the door. "The island is rid of the devil priest at last. But there are rumours, you know, that he is not dead. Sit down, please, sit down. Faisal!"

Musaed pulled out a chair next to Hassan and on the opposite side of the table to where he himself was sitting.

"But still," continued Hassan, "that is not our concern, is it?" He took another sweet from the candy bowl on the table.

"He is dead," assured Ramirov. "I saw his back explode with my own eyes. And," he removed what looked like a chunk of glass from the breast pocket of his shirt, "I took this from his corpse." The diamond was placed on the table in front of Hassan.

The Arabs looked at it in awe. The room was still, no man daring to move or speak, as if paralysed by some force emitting from the rock.

Then Abu Ayad picked it up. "It does not look much," he sniffed. "Can this really be worth two million pounds?"

Ramirov inclined his head and gave a false smile of respect. He kept the intolerance from his voice. "That is The Star of Sierra Leone, otherwise known as The Eye of Makarios. It is an uncut rough diamond, that is why it does not sparkle. That," he nodded at the stone, "is a piece if natural magnificence."

Abu Ayad replaced the piece of natural magnificence on the table.

From the corner of his eye, Ramirov noted that Faisal Ibn Musaed was staring at the stone in a curious, trance-like manner. Still, the peccadilloes of the Arabs were no longer his business. His task was completed.

"Well gentlemen," he said chirpily, "my task is complete." He made movements to rise. "I would advise you not to hang on to the diamond for too long. But, as always, that is your business. Your plan is progressing?"

"We have not heard from the supplier for a time," commented Al Khalifa. "But then, neither has he heard from us. I must chase him."

"Just take care of the stone," Ramirov flashed another insincere smile, "there is no other like it. Now, I must leave." He rose and Sergei came over to join him.

"Both so soon?" frowned Hassan amicably. "You will not join us in celebration? We know a place where there is good food... and good women..."

"You are kind," again the inclination of the head. "But I must refuse." His bowels twitched ominously and he had a silent breaking of wind. "I have an urgent engagement."

"Whatever you say, my brother," Hassan rose and clapped him on the shoulders. "How can we ever thank you? The Palestinian people will be forever in your debt."

"Just win, my brother," said Ramirov and meant it. "Just win your fight."

"Oh, we will, we will. It may take some time, but the Zionist war machine -"

It was at that moment that the attack started.

The first blast of gunfire echoed from downstairs and, although the men in the room did not know it, the first two of their six bodyguards were already dead. The guard on duty immediately outside the door began firing as he screamed hysterically *"Israelis, Israelis!"*

They all jumped to their feet. "Bastards!" screeched Abu Ayad.

Ramirov and Sergei had guns in their hands.

"The window, quickly!" instructed Hassan.

It opened out onto the back of the building, and there was a drop of four metres to the roof of the extended ground floor, then a further drop of an equal distance to the ground.

"Hurry, hurry!" snapped Hassan. "Quickly!"

Ramirov grabbed the stone and replaced it in his pocket, knocking the candy bowl over. "I have the diamond!" *Damn* this intrusion!

The roar of gunfire from the stairway was deafening. From a building nearby, a woman screamed.

Musaed was the first through the window, quickly followed by Abu Ayad, the intelligence man, Abu Jihad and Al Khalifa. All landed safely on the roof and scrambled down to the ground. Swiftly they dispersed into varying, pre-planned directions.

Up in the room, Hassan stood by the window ushering Ramirov and Sergei through. The firing was louder, and a torrent of Arabic and Hebrew obscenities could be heard through the din. The stench of cordite swept its way into the already stinking room.

As the two foreigners jumped, Hassan pulled a set of keys from his pocket and leapt over to a small, triple-locked cupboard set into the wall. He swore as he dropped the keys, picked them up, and then opened the door. His hand darted inside and emerged with a cold, pineapple-shaped object. He slipped back to the window, swung one leg over the sill and waited.

The door of the room started to splinter as the final guard outside lost his battle.

Hassan pulled the pin from the grenade with his teeth, and threw it as the door slammed inwards. He jumped into the darkness as the room exploded behind him. [*One member of the four-man Israeli hit team died in the explosion and another died of his injuries back in Israel two days later.*]

As he slid over the ground floor roof and down onto the ground, Hassan saw the foreigner in the shadows bending over the wriggling figure of his gaunt companion. The man's left leg was twisted at an hideous angle. Hassan bent over and rasped into the foreigner's ear "Rome. We will contact." And then he was up and away.

The room upstairs was now burning, but that did not prevent a shot being fired into the shadows near where Ramirov crouched. His left hand was pushed tightly over Sergei's mouth, and he looked straight into his comrade's agonised eyes. Both of them knew what had to be done.

Ramirov positioned his gun pointing upwards behind the left ear. He fired once, the sound muted by the hair and skull. With a final twitch, Sergei was still, the agonised eyes still starting at Ramirov, all life extinguished.

Ramirov did not dally. Quickly feeling to ensure that the diamond was safe, he moved away, blended with the shadows, and was gone.

Ψ

Friday July 19 1974

"General Franco has stood down as Spain's head of state. The health of the general, who is eighty-one, has recently been deteriorating. The heir to the vacant Spanish throne, Prince Juan Carlos, who is thirty-six, is taking over as provisional head of state."

London, England

Pandemonium. Or possibly mayhem. Or turmoil. Whatever it was, it was happening in the S(O)D 1 suite in Queen Anne's Mansions that morning. When Detective Inspector 'Mr' Ramm entered through the main door at 10:00, it was a fact that not one member of the staff was sitting down or even in a stationary position. Papers rustled as if a window had been left open, telephones rang, the drawers of filing cabinets banged incessantly, and bodies flitted in all directions.

"Bloody hell!" murmured Ramm to himself. He intercepted a passing WDC. "What's up, Roz?"

"A biggun." She hurried on.

He didn't know whether it was a comment on the state of affairs or a dream of her boyfriend.

"Boss in?" he shouted into the air.

"Yeh," came an unidentified voice from beneath a mountain of paper.

Ramm passed through the two general offices, knocked on Metcalf's door and entered. At least the Boss was sitting down, but he was talking excitedly to someone on the telephone. His free hand came up from beneath his desk, where it had been comforting his willie, and motioned Ramm to sit down.

"Yes... yes, sir. Right away. Any staff? Right." Metcalf replaced the receiver. "By crikey!" he blew out imaginary steam.

"Something up, Mr Metcalf?"

"Makarios. Sir Robert's ordered additional protection. Apparently there've been threats to get him while he's here. An iron curtain has been ordered around him. He's not even gonna be allowed to pick his nose without us looking up there first. And because of shortage of men, I'm to co-ordinate it."

"You, sir?" It was not meant to be rude and it was not taken as such.

"Right. So I'm just having a swift run-through of our current workload before I nip across to the Yard. I'll be working from there."

"Who - ?"

"Mr Woods will take over here. Where is he, by the way? Shouldn't take more than a few days until all the fuss dies down. Sooner we get Makarios out of Britain the better. Still, we've got our obligations, I suppose." He fiddled with some papers.

"Mr Woods is out on reccy. Actually, that's why I came - "

"I'll call him. What's the state of play on your jobs?" A sandwich appeared from a drawer and was crammed into Metcalf's mouth. His left hand reached for the mug of steaming tea on his desk.

Ramm briefed him on this three current assignments: a certain embassy using the diplomatic bag to import nasties, a junior government minister's unusual sexual proclivities, and Egginton.

"It's Egginton I've come to see you about, sir."

Metcalf grunted through a piece of fruit cake.

"We've come up with nothing. Certainly he's been taking the booze, lunchtimes and evenings. But he's able to handle it. No question of a security risk. He's been working on some hush-hush job for the Minister. Been up north a lot at the nuclear place. We can't make out what's causing the drinking. The only thing is that his wife has a chronic heart condition, and his daughter's got a wedding coming up. Maybe he's just anxious."

Ramm thought he translated Metcalf's words as "Want to call it off?" but they got caught in a mouthful of apple.

"There seems to be nothing," said Ramm. "However, I want to be safe than sorry. I want your permission to tap his phones. You said it probably wasn't worthwhile before."

A young member of the civilian clerical support staff entered, handed a buff file to Metcalf, nodded to Ramm and withdrew. Metcalf studied the front of the file, frowned, and then looked back at Ramm, distinctly preoccupied.

"Er... you think a tap'll reveal something?"

"No, sir. No, not at all. But we want to be sure."

"Hmm... " Metcalf was thinking more about the file than the Inspector's request. Then he said, "Yes, yes okay."

"Thank you, sir." Ramm rose to leave.

"Oh, Matthew?"

"Sir?"

The applecore sailed through the air, bounced off the edge of the wastebin with a dong and flew off across the room.

"Don't forget, this is all over the OBN. Unofficial. Five or Six not to be involved. Why cast doubts on the poor sod when it looks like there's nothing there? Home phone only."

Bugger it, thought Ramm. Out loud he said, "Yes, sir."
But Metcalf already had his nose deep in the intrusive file.

Ψ

Wednesday July 31 1974

"Watergate. President Nixon's former chief adviser, Mr John Ehrlichmann, has been sentenced to twenty months to five years imprisonment for his part in the break-in at the office of Mr Daniel Ellsberg's psychiatrist.
"In France, the prison riots continue and the death toll has now reached seven."

London, England

Colonel Egginton was depressed that morning. In fact, he had been descending into such a state for the past month. In his guise of working on a hush-hush review for the Minister (a guise which no one had thought to check), he had visited Windscale Works twice for informal meetings and checks on security, and had also had three meetings here in his office in Soho Square.

Security was first class at the place. There was no way, simply no way, that any fork from the canteen could go missing, let alone any plutonium. Not one hardly-radioactive ounce of it, let alone twelve pounds. Short of hiring a battalion of mercenaries to raid the place, there was no way he could get in.

And Windscale was his only hope. He was not sufficiently known at any of the other British nuclear establishments to start even the most initial of enquiries without attracting unwanted attention to himself.

He could have gotten Mahoney any armoury he wanted. Absolutely anything. He had done so in the past. But plutonium was out of the question. Mahoney was asking the impossible.

So what could he do? If he could not come up with the stuff, Mahoney would send the incriminating photographs to Margery (and he would, of that Egginton was sure). And that would kill her.

He was at a loss. Mahoney had given him three months on May 16th. That meant that in just fifteen days time the evil Irishman would be in contact again. And it seemed to Egginton that he was helpless. All he could do was sit and wait. Thursday August 15 1974 was to be his day of reckoning.

Egginton took his pipe out of his mouth and gently laid it against the ashtray. Then he pressed a button on the intercom and instructed his secretary that he would be engaged to callers until lunchtime.

He leant back in his chair, arms lifelessly dangling towards the floor, and stared at the opposite wall. His eyes became vacant and his mouth opened just a fraction. His mind switched off.

Slowly, a dribble of snot ran from his nose and settled on his upper lip...

Ψ

Monday August 5 1974

"No one has yet claimed responsibility for the bomb which killed twelve people and injured forty-eight others aboard the Rome-Munich Express yesterday. It exploded as the train passed through a tunnel in the Apennines, thirty miles south of Bologna."

Paris, France

Charlotte Rapley and Louise were in bed together and sleeping when the doorbell rang at 04:00. Neither woman heard it the first time, but Louise began to surface after the second ring, suddenly snapping into consciousness when her brain realised that the ringing had become continuous.

With great difficulty she awoke Charlie who, swearing, dragged herself from the bed and pulled on a robe. They fumbled in the dark, reaching the front door before putting any light on.

"Okay, okay, who the shit is it?" shouted Charlie. "Key est eel? Take yer finger off the goddamn bell!"

"Charlie?" The voice from outside was weak and distant. "Please let me in."

"*Sally?*"

Bolts withdrawn and dead-locks undone, the door was hurriedly opened. Charlie stood staring at her fellow-American, not believing what she saw. "Oh shit."

"*Sacré Maria!*" gasped Louise. "*Ma chère Sally, entrez, entrez!*"

Sally-Anne Bowker was dressed in torn denims and a filthy white T-shirt made of the thinnest material. Her nipples showed through the shirt without any concealment. Her hair was untidy, and there was dirt on her face mingled with what could possibly be blood.

"I - I'm sorry for wakening you, the *concièrge* let me in," she said emptily.

"For shit sake, don't worry about that," said Charlie. "C'mon inside, honey, c'mon."

Sally was ushered into the lounge. Sitting down on the couch, she at once began to cry, heavily and uncontrollably.

The two other women let it come, not saying anything, not even touching her in consolation for whatever grief had caused the tears. Look at the state of her, poor kid, she looked... as if she had been through a war.

It took five minutes for Sally to take control of herself, and she readily accepted a large brandy offered by Charlie. Louise had gone into the kitchen to prepare a pot of strong, sweet black coffee.

Sally dabbed her eyes with a tissue donated by the older woman. "Oh, I'm sorry. Whatever must you think of me? I'm sorry to get you up like this, but..." Her face creased and she almost started again, but instead she leant forward and put her head in her hands. Charlie's face was creased with anxiety but she said nothing.

They stayed like that until Louise reappeared with the coffee. "*Ici ma petite*, drink zis, it will do you good."

Sally accepted the hot mug and cringed as the liquid burnt her lips. Charlie came over and sat next to her. "It's all right now, baby, you're with friends." She put her arm around her, but it was roughly shrugged off.

Immediately Sally regretted her brusqueness. "Oh, I'm sorry Charlie, I'm sorry, really I am. Whatever must you think? It's just... I... I can't be touched. Not at the moment."

"I understand honey." Then: "You want to talk about it? Or do you want to get some sleep? We can talk in the morning if you like."

"No! No, I'd rather talk now. You deserve an explanation, of course. I - I don't know where to begin..."

"Don't rush it, hon. In your own time."

"Try some *café*," suggested the French girl. "You would like *crème*, per'aps?"

"No, no this is fine," she made an attempt at a smile.

A minute later she took a deep breath and said, "I didn't find him."

Charlie gave a resigned nod, as if she had known it all along. She tried consolation. "Aw, gee, that's nothing to get yourself so upset about, sweetheart. At least you got back. We were worried when we heard of the trouble out there."

"It - it's not that. I didn't find Steve, but there really wasn't much chance that I would - oh God, you just don't know... When the fighting began, I - I was in the capital, Nicosia. My first morning. I saw the army vehicles speeding through the streets, even thought I saw Steve in one of them, wasn't that crazy? I wondered what was happening... " She sipped the coffee. "There was panic. I tried to find somewhere to go, in case shooting started in the streets... I don't know, somehow I managed to get back to my hotel. They advised me to pack up and leave immediately, all the rest of the tourists were going and some of the residents. There was a coach leaving for Limassol, where the British are. I went up to get my bag, which I hadn't even unpacked, but by the time I got back downstairs the coach was gone. There wouldn't be another one. They said it was everyone for themselves. I didn't know what to do... so I just stayed there." She stopped, the fact of remembering painful. So, so painful. Steve, where are you?

"The next day things seemed to be getting back to normal. I heard rumours that President Makarios had been killed. There were a few other tourists left in the hotel the same as me. We got together and began to help out in the kitchen. Only some of the staff were left, the others had fled. There was a sort of... camaraderie, all helping together, you know? Well, there was nothing we could do, all transport was at a standstill. It was reported that the British were coming, but they never did. I heard they had reached southern Nicosia, but I was in the north.

"And then... a few days later, we heard that the *Turkish* army was coming... That same night a group of men raided the hotel – I don't know who they were or what they wanted – they just seemed to want trouble... to hurt, to steal... One old man, I think he was Dutch, was hit across the head with a pan full of hot oil. They... they killed him with it, just hitting and hitting him...

"And then... three of them... they grabbed hold of me... there, right there on the kitchen floor, and they... they fucked me. They just pulled my denims off and... did it... one after the other... Then some others came and... while one was doing it, another ripped off my shirt, and when they saw my scars, they... they started to laugh and spit at me and call me names, said I was a freak... and then they started to punch me and kick me... and then something wet started to splash on my tummy and I opened my eyes and one of them was... was pissing on me... oh God... " The tears came again, and they fell without interruption. Louise was crying openly too, and Charlie fought a losing battle with her twitching lips.

A while later, with half the mug of coffee inside her, Sally continued her story. "I - I passed out, at least I think I did. I can't recollect anything happening. I remember walking... buildings either side of me... then no buildings... and then I was in a truck with some other people, mostly Greeks I think, and then a soldier and a guy in a white coat were helping me out... I don't know...

"Anyway, I found out later that I had been picked up by the British in southern Nicosia. They said I was lucky as I was in the last truck out before the Turkish army arrived. We were all taken to the British base at Akrotiri. They guessed what had happened to me - I don't think I was able to speak right then - and I was hospitalised and given a good clean-out inside. I think I stayed there for two or three days. But they said they were evacuating and there was a place reserved for me on one of their air force planes. They told me after that I was in shock and couldn't walk at this time.

"Well, they took me to Malta, and I was in hospital there until last week. Then they offered me a flight to some air force base in England, and I accepted.

"They'd washed my denims and T-shirt for me and, so they said, found a hundred dollars folded inside a back pocket - really I think they were just being kind. They gave me some sort of identity card, said they weren't supposed to as I wasn't British, but they thought it would stop any problems on arrival. Anyway, we landed in a base in... Wiltshire, I think it was called? No problems. And they fed me and gave me a warrant to get a train to London and precise directions on how to get to our embassy.

"I went to London, but didn't go to the embassy. I used the hundred dollars to come here. There was some blockade on at Calais, a strike or something, and we were delayed for five hours, that's why I'm here only now. The train arrived an hour ago. It's too late for the metro, so I walked from the *Gare du Nord*." She sighed and downed the rest of her coffee.

Really there was nothing Charlie or Louise could say. Words or sympathetic clucking would have been superfluous. Charlie lit her third *Peter Stuyvesant* and stared into the exhaled smoke. Louise dabbed a moist eye.

It was Sally who broke the silence after five minutes. "So here I am." A little laugh, totally devoid of mirth, jumped from her lips. She was aware of the French girl frowning at her.

"But your clothes, your face, the condition," said Louise. "Somsing must 'ave 'appened after they were washed."

Sally looked down at the torn jeans and filthy T-shirt. She laughed again, pathetically. "This? *This?* I was looking up at your window and I fell up the kerb outside here. Can you believe it?"

Again silence.

Then Charlie rasped "SHIT!" forcefully.

Ψ

Wednesday August 14 1974

"As a reaction against further Turkish military incursions into Cyprus, the new Greek Prime Minister, Mr Constantine Karamanlis, today announced the withdrawal of all Greek armed forces from NATO, and he has threatened to take suitable measures against what he calls 'The Turkish menace to world peace'."

Crowthorne, Berkshire, England

Stanley William Egginton stayed up until all hours that night in a state of total anxiety. He had kissed Madge goodnight at 22:30 and had then retired to his study in a final vain attempt to think something out. By midnight he was quite despondent.

To beg, borrow, steal, hijack or even buy twelve pounds of plutonium in Britain was just impossible. Security in this country was watertight. Two days ago he had made yet another visit to Windscale, and he had even made a half-hearted attempt to offer a couple of employees a bribe (which, when refused, had been passed off as a security test). Then, to top everything, when he arrived back at his office yesterday morning, he had been telephoned by the Head of Accounts over in Shell Mex House. His frequent trips to Windscale had been noticed and he was asked for an explanation. Being in charge of defence sales security, he had managed to fob the fellow off with some extemporaneous story which he had even by now forgotten.

So, it was not on.

And tomorrow the Irishman would call.

And it would be the end. The photographs would be sent to Madge, and it would kill her. Or if not, it would at least mean the end of their thirty-year marriage. How could thirty years be shattered just like that by some stinking, blackmailing, conniving Paddy bastard?

By the time the clock dragged round to 01:00, Egginton's mood had changed. As usual with over-stress and over-anxiety, his mood had swung from one of concern through deep depression to sublime insouciance. He had realised, quite suddenly, that there was nothing he *could* do. The Irishman would just have to do his worst. To hell with him.

Even this realisation gave the Colonel great relief, and he decided that it was now time to go to bed. At least he could catch six hours sleep before the moment of reckoning.

With the Irishman still in his mind and another "To hell with him" on his lips, Egginton turned out the study light and left the room, closing the door softly behind him. Then he froze in his tracks. My God, *why hadn't he thought of it before?*

Quickly going back into the study and closing the door, Egginton switched the light back on and nipped over to his antique mahogany bureau which held all his paraphernalia. *It had completely slipped his mind!* He unlocked one of the four drawers and pulled it out nearly to its limit. With his right hand, he rummaged in the back. Ah! There it was.

He pulled out a plastic bag wrapped tightly around something and secured with sticky tape. Mumbling to himself, he ripped the plastic off the greasy old *Colt .455* automatic, a keepsake (unlicensed) from his field activities in the fifties.

He examined the gun and decided that it was in good working order, the grease and the plastic had preserved it well. Now, somewhere in the back of this drawer was an old box of ammo... yes, there it was.

Egginton wiped off the surplus grease with a tissue and slipped the safety catch off the gun. He practised firing at a picture of his old regiment on the wall. The gun clicked ominously as the pin fell on the empty barrel.

Satisfied, he loaded the maximum seven rounds into the magazine, replaced the box of ammunition and closed the drawer. Always tidy, he picked up the torn plastic and screwed-up tissue and put them into his waste bin. The daily would see to it in the morning.

Placing the gun in his jacket pocket, Stanley William Egginton, a much happier man, left the study once again and went up to bed.

For some incongruous reason, his mind took that moment to remind him to ring the Post Office in the morning. There was something wrong with his phone. For about a month now there had been a click on the line every time he picked it up. And when he spoke down it he could hear a strange hollow echo...

Ψ

Thursday August 15 1974

"Today is Princess Anne's twenty-fourth birthday, and it has been announced from Buckingham Palace that the Princess has been made a Dame Grand Cross of the Royal Victorian Order for her 'calm and brave behaviour' during the attempt to kidnap her in March. Her husband, Captain Phillips, has also been admitted to the same order for his 'excellent conduct' during the same incident."

London, England

Michael Mahoney telephoned Colonel Egginton at his office promptly at 10:00 that morning. Perhaps the jauntiness, the actual eagerness in Egginton's voice should have warned him, but Mahoney thought it was because the stuff was available as required. An appointment for 12:30 was arranged, and Egginton turned up five minutes ahead of time, tapping on the side window of the brown Cortina parked at a meter in Greek Street.

Mahoney let him in and he could sense at once that the Colonel was different. "You seem happy today Colonel, good news is it?"

"Get driving," ordered the older man peremptorily. Mahoney raised an eyebrow but made no comment.

"Where to?"

"How about... let me see... Hyde Park. Yes, that will be an ideal place. Nice day for a trip to the park, don't you think?"

"Okay, here he comes." Mr Ramm nodded towards Stuart House, just a little to the south of where they were parked in Soho Square.

"Wonder what pub it'll be today?" mused Mr Woods dryly as he threw his half-finished cigarette out of the open side window.

Ramm sniggered. "Last day, guv. Might as well make the most of it. I've been doing this on my jack for the last four weeks while you were made up." He gunned the white, unmarked Rover 2000 into life. "You on foot? You've got a nice day for it."

"Bloody well suppose so." Woods climbed out. "Keep in sight."

He sauntered past the front of Stuart House and fell into a deceptively casual stroll some twenty metres behind Egginton. What with being in charge of S(O)D 1 these past weeks in Metcalf's absence, this was the first chance Woods had had to 'meet' the Colonel in the flesh. Egginton was more jauntier than Woods imagined he would be, and the heavy drinking had not taken one iota of toll. Looked like S(O)D 1 was on a fool's errand, just as they had expected all along.

Egginton disappeared round the sharp corner into Greek Street. No rush, thought Woods; all his drinking emporia were within five minutes of the office.

By the time Woods reached the corner, Egginton was just climbing into a brown Cortina a little way down the road. There was somebody at the wheel, but Woods could not clarify any descriptive features. It looked like a man.

Bloody hell! He turned back and signalled frantically to Ramm. The white Rover had only just pulled away from the kerb, but when Ramm saw his partner turn back he shot out into the traffic, thundered down the road, and pulled up sharply by the corner.

"He's bloody got into a car!" Woods jumped in.

"He's *what?* Which?"

"Brown Cortina."

Ramm frowned, focussed on the vehicle now at the far end of the street, and sped off after it.

"Anybody in it?"

"Someone. Couldn't see. Male."

They saw the Cortina turn right, heading south on Shaftesbury Avenue.

"Get the number?"

"No." Woods could feel the unspoken criticism. "For Christ's sake, it was all too sudden. *You* didn't expect him to get into a car, did you?"

"No, sir."

"Thought he was going to the pub as always, didn't we?"

"Yes, sir."

They arrived at the junction with Shaftesbury Avenue. The traffic was heavy and there seemed to be an inordinate number of taxis about. Ramm nudged the Rover out and to the right, to the background of a complaining cacophony of horns.

"Don't make yourself too conspicuous. Where is the bugger? Ah, there." Woods pointed unnecessarily ahead. The Cortina was just passing the Queen's Theatre, heading towards Piccadilly Circus. There was a group of four taxis between hunter and hunted.

"This is a turn-up for the books," continued Woods. "I wonder where he's going. And who *is* that driving?"

"Could be just an MOD driver," suggested Ramm. "If we had the number…"

"If those buggering taxis would get out of the way we could see the bloody number!"

The Cortina made the then compulsory left turn into the Piccadilly one-way system in front of the Eros statue, heading down the Haymarket.

The four taxis turned, followed by the white Rover.

"C'mon, c'mon," mumbled Woods impatiently.

Then, outside the London Pavilion cinema, the taxis stopped. Right there in the street, two abreast, completely halting the flow of traffic.

"What the hell - ?" Ramm slammed on the brakes. No sooner had he done so than another black machine pulled up to their left.

"Christ!" shouted Woods. "I don't believe it!"

Both policemen turned around in their seats. More taxis and a couple of other vehicles had stopped behind them, completely pinning them against the railings of the Eros island.

Ramm banged on the horn irascibly. The vehicles in front did not move even though the road was clear ahead of them. People were beginning to look.

Woods had his head out of the window. "Move you bastards, move!"

A friendly, lived-in face rolled down the window of the cab next to them. "They can't, mate."

"What?"

"They can't. This is a cabbie stoppage - in protest over Wilson's refusal to raise our rates."

"It's what?"

"You won't get out of here until three o'clock," chuckled the cabbie.

"What?"

"Might as well sit back and relax, mate."

"But we're police officers!"

"Good! Per'aps you can put in a good word for us with the PM."

"I demand - !"

"Our Association advised the Yard this morning. Didn't they tell yer?" He stretched out his right arm. "Wanna Polo mint?"

Woods looked at him aghast and then turned back to Ramm. The Detective Inspector was staring resignedly ahead. He did not look at Woods as he spoke. "He's clean anyway. It might have been an official trip - you know he's been travelling all about the country recently. Or it could have been just a friend. We'll pick him up back at the office this afternoon... after three o'clock."

"Sure," fumed Woods. "Sure."

"If only they'd've let us tap his work phone..." mused Ramm.

A moment later, Woods leaned back out of the window and shouted at the top of his voice, "Fuck your bloody Polo mint!"

Mahoney became more and more bemused by the Englishman as they drove west through sunny Piccadilly, unaware of the stoppage behind them. Around Hyde Park Corner and into the park. Egginton matched the Irishman's usual patter, but he was not to be drawn on the subject of the plutonium.

It was not until they were on the main road by the Serpentine that the Colonel suggested they pull over. Mahoney did so with alacrity.

Mahoney shifted into neutral and turned off the engine. "Now, me ole Colonel, yer hoigh spirits must mean yer have good news."

Egginton shifted so that he was facing Mahoney, his back against the door. He beamed.

"Oh, I have good news all right, but not for you, you stinking Irish bastard."

Mahoney frowned. There was something not right about the Colonel's eyes, something that told him this time it was no joke. "What?"

"The news is splendid, you blackmailing lump of crap. Shall I tell you what it is?" Egginton's left hand went into his jacket pocket. "The news is that I don't have your plutonium. Not one single fucking ounce of it. And I am so, so pleased."

Mahoney's face was stone and he was tensed in caution, his eyes riveted on the other man. He spoke softly and with deep menace. "Well, you know what this means Colonel."

"The pictures you mean?" grinned Egginton. "You know what you can do with them. I don't give a damn. To hell with the pictures. And," he said calmly, "to hell with you." His hand came out of the pocket with the pistol. It was pointing straight at the Irishman.

Mahoney shrank back in his seat, his hand reaching for the door handle. "You fool. I should have guessed something like this. You mad English prick." Beads of perspiration broke out on his brow. "You'll never get away with it, you know. Yer might kill me, but you'll have a lot of talkin' to do. D' yer think oi haven't left a letter in case I die under mysterious circumstances? It'll all come out and you'll be finished."

"Oh shut up - *and take your hand away from that door!* Mahoney, I am sick, sick, sick of hearing your haunting bloody voice. I have had enough of it, do you hear? Enough!"

Mahoney said nothing.

"Now, where are the rest of the pictures?"

The Irishman swallowed, freely perspiring now. "I - I don't have them on me."

"No, no you wouldn't, you little runt. Well, never mind. I just wanted to see what they were like, that was all. It doesn't matter."

"Perhaps we could still do a deal, Colonel? The photos *and* you keep the two thousand you already have."

"Shut up! The time has come, runt. You will never blackmail me again." His finger tightened on the trigger.

"Now Colonel, wait, please…"

"There's no more to say."

"Stan - !"

"Irish bastard!"

"Colonel - !"

Egginton raised the gun, by-passed Mahoney and, turning his wrist, pointed the gun into his own mouth. He fired once, up into his brain, and slumped…

Mahoney sat there staring, mouth open, lips quivering. He tried to move or say something to the corpse, but only animal grunts came out of his mouth. His bowels moved violently and the immediately rising smell told him he had shit himself.

"B… b… but… "

Tiny rivulets of blood trickled from Egginton's nose, and with a thud the gun slid from the dead fingers onto the floor. The head slipped a few centimetres, and Mahoney could see brain, light and pink, smeared on the window.

But…

Then there was a scream. A loud, piercing scream which shocked Mahoney back to his senses. Outside, a woman with a pram was staring into Egginton's side of the car and pointing.

"Oh Jesus, Mary and Joseph!" Mahoney was out of the vehicle in a flash and running. A voice from somewhere shouted "Hey, you, stop!" but stop was the last thing he was going to do. He ran and ran and ran…

Back by the car, the woman with the pram had been joined by other people, mostly office workers out sunning themselves in the lunch-hour. More than one lunch was brought up by the side of the road before the police arrived to clear the area. One lunch, regrettably, even ended up spewed into the baby's pram. The child, who was happily playing with teddy, could not have cared less, and it splashed merrily amongst the diced carrots and tomato skins…

The irony of it all was that Mahoney had no other negatives or photographs. His collection of eight had been accidentally destroyed back home about a year before. Only one photograph and its matching negative had survived, and that was the one he had already given to Egginton with the two thousand pounds.

Ψ

Wednesday September 11 1974

"In trouble-torn Ethiopia, Princess Tenagne-Work, only surviving daughter of the now virtually powerless Emperor Hailé Selassié, has been arrested. Today is the country's New Year's Day."

Somewhere in the Irish Republic

With Egginton's suicide, the worry, concern and anxiety shifted like an evil spirit from the body of the Colonel into the soul of Michael Mahoney. The Colonel's death had been widely reported in the newspapers on the first day, with wild speculations about the identity of the man seen running away. Then it had died the death of most newspaper stories. An inquest had been opened and adjourned indefinitely.

After fleeing from the car, Mahoney had travelled immediately to Heathrow Airport by the most inconspicuous route: underground from Hyde Park Corner to Hounslow West and then express bus *[The Underground link to Heathrow was not yet open in 1974. The* Heathrow Express *overground rail link was nearly a quarter of a century away].* Just three hours after the incident in the park and before the body had even been moved by the police, he was landing at Dublin Airport. His Mini-Cooper awaited him in the long-term car park, and by early evening he was back home in his mansion, somewhere in the south.

His worries had started on the plane after the anaesthesia of the initial shock had worn off. He could not be connected to Egginton's death, of course, he was too careful for that. The car had been hired under the name of Christopher Whelan, and his travelling alias for this trip had been Thomas Doherty. His fingerprints were not on any police file, so he was clear there.

No, the source of his worry was the Arabs. They would very soon want him to produce the goods, the infernal twelve pounds of plutonium, and there was no way he was going to be able to do so. He had been so sure Egginton would supply him. And, although the Arabs understood that sometimes there had to be failure (not like some of his other customers), they would not forgive him on this one, they had too much at stake - especially as they were probably going to a lot of trouble to get that diamond for him. Mind you, he had not heard from them for nine months: was it too much to hope that their plan had been abandoned?

Black September had not forgotten. That Wednesday morning the telegram arrived for him. Al Khalifa would be arriving at Dublin the following Saturday; transport would, of course, be waiting for him?

Throughout that Wednesday afternoon Mahoney tried to lose himself in the soft, delectable body of Lizzie O'Toole, who had now moved into his mansion permanently. But he just couldn't get business out of his mind, and he knew that he did not perform well (although the girl did not complain).

Then, at 18:00 that evening, whilst swilling poteen in his office, it came to him like a bolt from heaven.

Glory t' Jaysus, Moichal, he thought, *yer nothin' if not Oirish!* Why hadn't he thought of it before? It was really the only course open to him, if he did not want to be immediately exterminated. *He would bluff it out.* Take it all the way and see what happened. If it came off, it would be the biggest ever con trick played on the Arabs. And if it didn't...

He had nothing to lose but his life.

Ψ

Friday September 13 1974

"A bomb exploded in a restaurant in Madrid earlier today, killing at least twelve people and wounding forty more. No one has yet claimed responsibility."

Frascati, Italy

It had been nearly two months since the affair in Beirut, but Ilich Ramirov had not been idle. The diamond had been deposited in a sealed package in a bank on Rome's Via del Corso, and from his house in Frascati, fifteen kilometres south of the city, Ramirov had spent his time organising certain other matters. That very morning he had had to leave Madrid in something of a hurry.

It was waiting for him when he arrived back at his house. Posted in London six days before, the envelope contained a small piece of sepia paper with just three typewritten words:

MILANO. GCONTINENTAL. 2MARDI.

The meeting was to take place at the Grand Continental Hotel in Milan on the Tuesday of this month whose date fell in the twenties. Ramirov consulted a small pocket book. That would make it 24th, eleven days hence.

Right, he had a few other things to settle and then he had to pay a visit to his bank manager to reclaim a very special package. Then he would drive to Milan to enjoy a few relaxing days seeing the sights (hopefully there would be a race meeting on), with perhaps one or more of Milan's prostitutes for carnal company, before getting down to business again on Tuesday 24th…

Ψ

Saturday September 14 1974

"The three members of the Japanese Red Army terrorist organisation who yesterday took Count Jacques Senard, the French Ambassador to Holland, and ten others prisoner in an attack on the Ambassador's office in The Hague, have now made their demands known. They are asking for the release of a member of their group who is held in a Paris jail."

Somewhere in the Irish Republic

"Akay, my dear, dear friend!" Michael Mahoney rushed from the front door of his mansion as the Arab stepped out of the chauffeur-driven Rolls-Royce. "How are yer? Goodness, yer lookin' well!"

All the charm was there, and the empressement sickened Al Khalifa, but he smiled pleasantly. "Michael, how are you? It gives me pleasure to see you again."

"Indeed it should," winked the Irishman, "indeed it should. Come insoide, come insoide. Fitzgerald'll take yer bag. Did yer have a pleasant flight? Weather's still very warm for mid-September, isn't it? What's it like in your country?" These and other banalities poured from Mahoney's lips as he led the way to his office.

Mahoney plonked himself behind his large mahogany desk and produced the ubiquitous half-drunk bottle of poteen. He also switched on the hidden tape recorder.

Al Khalifa sat down in the gigantic maroon leather armchair in front of the desk.

A shot of the whiskey inside him, Mahoney wiped his mouth on the back of his right hand and spoke, the exuberant culchie gone. "You have the diamond?"

"You have the plutonium?"

Mahoney stared into the Arab's black eyes and then said, "I think we can take the answer to both questions as being positive."

"That is good. Then we are in business."

"Right. When and where do you want the stuff? It can be delivered anywhere in mainland UK."

"We will notify you. It will not be where you think. The fact that the plutonium is available is sufficient for now. I take it that there is no immediate urgency to remove it from wherever it is?"

The Irishman thrust the bottle at the Arab. "A drink? Oh no, of course, I forgot, you gentlemen don't, do you?" Swig. "No urgency whatsoever, my friend. In fact it is being looked after by none other than my very good friends the British government." He saw Al Khalifa's look of consternation. "Over the past nine months, twelve pounds of the stuff has been spirited away, bit by bit - *on their books*. In fact, it has remained exactly where it is, so they now have twelve pounds more plutonium than they can account for. And, because my men are very clever, it does not show up on any audit or security inspection. How about that for brilliance?" It was brilliant, he thought. If only it was for real.

Al Khalifa was frowning. "If the plutonium has not in fact been moved then you are sure you will have no problems in transportation?"

"None whatsoever." Total confidence. "My contacts are good, you just name the place and date you want it and... Seamus is your uncle!"

"That is good Michael, and very clever too, as you say. I will advise you of the collection and delivery details. A date early in seventy-five has been suggested for the operation. Therefore we will have to take delivery - when? Late November or early December? That is what I am told, it is not really my department."

"Then late November or so it will be, Akay. Now, about my little gift...?"

"The diamond can be delivered as soon as you like. You will wish it brought here, naturally."

"Not on your bloody life, boyo! Here is the last place oi want a two million pound diamond. I already have the *Garda*, the income tax boys *and* the VAT gestapo on my tail. If they ever got a whiff that oi had such a magnificent and expensive jewel - glory be! They would have it off me before you could say 'distraint'."

"Then where?"

Mahoney pondered for another mouthful of gut-rot. "I'm due in Amsterdam soon, deliver it to me there."

"That can be done."

"My meeting is on, let me think... the fifth of November. Then I'll be stayin' for a few days after. Make it on the eighth, a Friday I believe?"

Al Khalifa was writing in his small pocket book. "A Friday is indeed correct. When and where?"

"I always stay in the Park Hotel, Stadhouderskade. Have someone contact me there, say eight o'clock that evening. I'll be in the bar."

"Good. That shall be done." Al Khalifa finished writing and put the pocket book away.

Mahoney exhaled deeply. The thick accent returned. "And now Akay, me ole friend, come wit' me."

He led the way from the room, talking as they walked.

"To celebrate the successful conclusion of our business oi have a little surprise for yer. D' yer remember those two friends of mine who were here last time, Lizzie and her sister Philomena? Well, they're here again, and positively oozing at the chance to entertain yer after dinner. Philomena's been working out and my God you should see the superb arse she's got on 'er now..."

Ψ

Tuesday September 24 1974

"Australia and New Zealand have both devalued their currencies, Australia by twelve per cent and New Zealand by nine per cent.
"In Honduras, the number of people killed during the recent Hurricane Fifi has now been estimated at between seven and eight thousand. Six hundred thousand people have been made homeless."

Milan, Italy

"Water."

"Signore?"

"Water."

"Certainly, *signore.*" A glass was produced and filled.

"No ice."

"As you wish, *signore.*" The barman sidled off to serve some other customers.

Ilich Ramirov turned on his stool and gave the impression of casually looking around the adjacent tables. In fact he was scrutinising very closely every one of the twenty or so persons in the plushly decorated bar of Milan's Grand Continental Hotel.

He sipped his water slowly and inclined his head to one side as he surveyed the legs of an Italian girl seated at one of the tables. Whores, even high class ones, were not usually allowed in hotels But hotel managers did not know every girl who plied her trade in the city. Perhaps she was new on the job?

His answer came two minutes later when a man who was undoubtedly her husband approached, and she arose and walked out with him. Ramirov gave a mental shrug. He could not be right all the time. Anyway, to him all women were whores. He pushed the tinted glasses up on his nose and waited...

Just before 21:00 Faisal Ibn Musaed, Hassan's aide and the silent member of the Black September caucus, walked in. He stopped, picked out Ramirov and walked over. He spoke in French without preamble.

"Did you enjoy your recent visit to Cana?" His voice was soft and low, and Ramirov realised that it was the first time he had heard him speak.

"Very pleasant but the Jordan is vast and mysterious."

"Who knows where a river ends?"

Musaed, tall, olive-skinned and with long tight curly hair, stood looking down at Ramirov on the stool. "Sheikh Hassan sent me and bids you greetings. He asks if you would come with me."

Ramirov did not move. "Where to?"

Musaed's voice became even softer. "There is a house. To the south of the city. It is safe."

Ramirov said nothing but he slid off the stool. The Arab led the way out into the street and to a white Lancia parked nearby.

It was an acceptably warm Italian evening and the stars in the heavens had turned out in full force, a scintillating celestial panorama.

The journey took twenty minutes and during that time the two men uttered not one word. Ramirov stared out of the passenger window, smelling the countryside, remembering every detail of the route, and secure in the knowledge that his favourite blade was strapped on the inside of his right forearm. Occasionally he moved his left arm to check on the security of the diamond in an inside pocket of his leather jacket.

Musaed concentrated on his driving, now and again casting cautious glances at the man to his right. He well knew this man's reputation. He was the man behind a great many of the operations of the world's freedom fighters, and he was, first and foremost, a lethal killer.

The 'house' was a low, rambling, two-storey villa set at the end of its own drive at least two hundred metres from the road. It had been built in Roman style and was brilliantly illuminated by two floodlights which stood to either side of the turn of the drive. Ramirov was surprised and not a little vexed by the glowing advertisement of their presence.

"If you will come this way?" asked Musaed politely as they stepped from the Lancia.

They entered the villa by the main double doors. Two huge, smelly eastern types with ominous bulges under the left armpits of their jackets patrolled inside the main hallway. At a nod from Musaed, they allowed them to pass without hindrance. Musaed knocked gently on another double door to the right, and they entered.

Three people were sitting with their backs to the door watching television, hoots of canned laughter coming from the box. Musaed coughed and the occupant of the chair on the left turned quickly and then stood up smiling.

"My brother, again we meet!" Hassan came over and embraced Ramirov. "This time in a more friendly climate, I hope. I do apologise for that little incident on the last occasion. As you will appreciate, it was beyond my control. At least we escaped with our lives, for that we must give thanks."

"Indeed." Ramirov smiled politely and tried not to show his distaste for the embrace.

"Come, sit down," ushered Hassan. "You know Akay Al Khalifa of course."

The occupant of the furthest chair nodded in greeting.

"And he has brought along a mutual friend of yours."

Ramirov came level with the centre chair and looked down at the smiling freckled face of Melanie, the English girl from the yacht. He smiled back in genuine pleasure and bent and gallantly kissed her proffered hand.

"Melanie, it is a renewed pleasure."

"Hello again." The green eyes sparkled with that wicked promise.

Musaed had pulled over two more high-backed chairs and Ramirov sat down between Hassan and the girl, Musaed placing himself on the other side of Hassan.

Al Khalifa switched off the television.

"You will drink?" asked Hassan.

"Just water, please. No ice."

"Good man. Faisal."

Musaed rose and walked over to a large refrigerator against the far wall. He began to pour liquid.

"This place is new to me," commented Ramirov. "I thought I would have known about it."

"You like it, eh?" Hassan with a new toy.

"The little I have seen of it."

"A new *Fateh* purchase, just finalised last week. As far as the Italians are concerned it belongs to a Saudi banker."

"I see." Ramirov accepted the cool tumbler from Musaed. He declined a toffee from the bowl offered by Hassan. The big Arab could not resist temptation so easily.

"My dear," he chewed and smiled at the same time. "I wonder if you would be kind enough to leave us while we discuss our boring business? I will not keep our brother here long."

"Certainly." Melanie stood up, looking totally desirable in her green baggy fisherman's jumper and incredibly tight blue denims. Her hand brushed Ramirov's shoulder as she passed him.

They waited until the door had closed, then Hassan asked "You of course have the diamond?"

"Safe and sound." Ramirov produced the small leather pouch and pushed the diamond out into Hassan's big, hairy right hand.

The Arab felt it awkwardly, like a giant caressing a new-born babe. "Magnificent!" he grinned.

PART FIVE

Ψ

OBJECTIVE
RELINQUISHED

"Magnificent. Not its looks but the fact that this one stone could be worth so much."

"Indeed." Ramirov did not really care about that side of things.

"Cut, it will be worth even more," explained Al Khalifa. "Our supplier has chosen his reward well."

Ramirov took a mouthful of water and then said, "That, I think, concludes our current business. You know how to contact me for future assistance. I would not be prepared to involve myself in the exploding of the bomb in Britain, but if you have anything else more in my line you have only to let me know." He moved to rise.

"Actually, there is something," Hassan sounded just a shade sheepish. "Still to do with this diamond. We have to hand it over to our supplier in Amsterdam on November 8th." He looked embarrassed. "Normally it is a task we would undertake ourselves. However just a week ago, as you probably know, two of our brothers were arrested by the Dutch police. They were in Holland quite innocently, as it happens, but we fear that our network in that country is split open. Except for Faisal here, my face and those of my brothers are too well-known in northern Europe since the Olympics [*the Olympic Games in Munich in 1972 during which Black September murdered most of the Israeli competitors*] for us to attempt it." He smiled ingratiatingly. "We wondered if you would undertake to deliver the diamond for us?"

Ramirov was irked. This diamond was beginning to weigh heavily around his neck. He was getting tired of it. But he had offered his services so, after reflection, he agreed. "November 8th is some five or six weeks away. Yes, if you would feel happier, I will deliver it for you. You will need to keep the diamond safe, I suggest you put it in a safe deposit box in a bank."

"So public?" queried Musaed softly. The three other men were surprised to hear him say something, and for the briefest of moments they stopped dead in their verbal tracks.

Then Ramirov explained. "Yes, indeed. The chances of the bank being raided are remote - even in Italy. Thousands to one against. Admittedly, the chance of your safe here being robbed is remote also but the odds are not quite as good. The diamond has to go somewhere for five weeks and I suggest a bank. It is only my counsel, of course. Really it is up to you what you do with it."

"Oh I agree with you," nodded Hassan, looking reprovingly at Musaed. "Who is to say that the *Mossad* will not find out about this place and raid it? We hope not, of course. Then what would happen?"

"I agree," said Al Khalifa. "Our brother's suggestion is sound."

Musaed frowned sulkily.

"Now gentlemen," Ramirov looked at each of them. "If you have no further use for me this evening...?"

"We know somebody who has!" laughed Hassan. "Enjoy yourself, my friend. Come, I will show you to your room." The diamond was still in his hand. "I will put this in our safe tonight, then in the morning you may care to accompany Faisal and myself into the city?"

"Of course - but I hope you will not be up too early!"

Both men roared with laughter as they left the room.

After the door had closed, Musaed looked at Al Khalifa. "You trust him?"

"The foreigner? Of course, he has never let us down or cheated on us. There is no reason why he should now."

"I am unhappy. Not just because of the bank. Why must it be *he* who takes the diamond to Amsterdam? He is becoming too involved in *Fateh's* personal affairs. I do not like it."

"Then why do you not have a word with Hassan?" suggested Al Khalifa with just a trace of scorn.

Musaed looked back towards the closed door.

"Maybe I will. Yes, maybe. Things have progressed too far to be ruined at this stage."

Al Khalifa sniffed and leaned forward and turned on the television. Musaed stayed staring at the door, frowning.

Ψ

Thursday October 24 1974

"In Greece, the four army officers who seized power in 1969, among them former President Papadopoulos, who were arrested yesterday, have been banished to the island of Kea in the Aegean Sea."

Moscow, USSR

Ekaterina Furtseva died that night. The official version is that she died in her sleep of a heart attack, having resigned earlier that day. How much credence is given to this should be measured against the fact that the official version of her career, as previously stated, was that she was Minister of Culture and had been so for fourteen years.

Precise facts about her death cannot be ascertained. It is known that Kosygin was displeased over her meddling in Cyprus. It is known that for the past thirty years the Russians had employed, on numerous occasions, the untraceable cyanide gas which induces heart failure. It is rumoured that the only way out of the KGB was death.

Exactly what happened concerning Ekaterina Furtseva must be a matter for conjecture.

Ψ

Wednesday October 30 1974

"Finally, sport. Muhammad Ali has regained the world heavyweight boxing title. His bout with George Foreman in Kinshasa has just ended with a knockout for Ali in the eighth round.
"These have been the headlines from Independent Radio News. The time is three minutes past nine."

Milan, Italy

"My brother, greetings again!" Hassan's huge face smiled welcome as his hand pumped Ramirov's. They were in the wide hallway of the villa, the two hear-nothing see-all guards by the front door. Hassan motioned the Russian into the room on the right and then bade greeting to Faisal Ibn Musaed as he came in, having parked the Lancia. The young Arab closed the door and followed them into the room.

"I hear your other activities have been meeting with success," conversed Hassan. "Long may it remain so. Drink?"

"Just water. No ice. Indeed, I have been successful with certain matters in Syria." Ramirov's voice sounded clipped. The matter of the delivery of the diamond was now an irritating inconvenience.

He was more concerned about the death of Ekaterina Furtseva five days before. He could not have cared less about the woman, it was the future of his own position he had to look out for. And she had died of a heart attack. So sudden. And rumour had it she had *retired*. If so, why had she not informed him beforehand? It was suspicious, but he knew better than to fan embers. He had yet to contact his new Controller - whoever that might be.

"Now tell me," Hassan handed over the water. "When will you be leaving for Amsterdam? Contact has to be made with this Irishman in the bar of the Park Hotel, Stadhouderskade, at twenty hundred next Friday, the eighth."

"I will leave tomorrow and I shall travel by car, so avoiding any airport security checks."

Hassan's brow creased. "But what about the borders?"

"Customs do not worry me, they are no threat. I will stay overnight in Frankfurt, arriving in Amsterdam late Friday. That will give me a full week to reconnoitre, to get the *feel* of the city. It is a long time since I have been there."

"Just as you wish, we place the matter entirely in your hands. You wish to collect the diamond tomorrow?"

"Today. Preferably right now. It can remain in your safe here overnight."

"Are you sure that is wise?" asked Musaed softly.

Ramirov looked at him, his head inclined to the right. "Yes."

"I am sure our brother does what is best, Faisal," scolded Hassan. "We need no quibbling at this stage."

The young Arab said no more.

Ramirov removed the glass of water from his lips. "You will accompany me, Hassan? Now, to the bank? Or I can do it on my own. It does not need both our signatures, either will do, though I would prefer it if you were there."

Hassan looked a little put out. "Actually, my brother, I had not planned on going into the city today. I did not expect you to want to collect the diamond so soon. I have made other arrangements for this afternoon."

"So be it. Faisal can drive me."

Musaed remained silent.

"I have hunger," announced Ramirov. "When we get back, there will be food ready?"

"Whatever you wish," Hassan spread out his hands.

"And I have another hunger," Ramirov smiled. "Melanie is here?"

Hassan chuckled. "Indeed, my brother, indeed. I believe she is upstairs bathing right at this moment."

"That is good," Ramirov's head was inclined and nodding at the same time. "That is good."

In fact Melanie was not bathing but was waiting patiently in Hassan's bed, for she was his 'other arrangement' for that afternoon. A fact which, in the light of subsequent events, was to cause Ilich Ramirov great anger.

It took three hours for Ramirov and Musaed to travel into Milan, complete the necessarily strict formalities at the bank, and return to the villa. By this time Hassan had completed his gyrations with the English girl and felt much the better for it. Although powerful and bulky of physique, the Arab was a five-star performer when it came to matters carnal, and it must be said that Melanie felt much the better for it also. She had bathed, douched, and was waiting with Hassan when Ramirov entered, Musaed as always on his tail.

There were smiles all round, Ramirov's reserved mainly for the girl. Her hair had been permed into a frizz since he last saw her, and she wore a one-piece full-length black pants suit, unzipped provocatively so that a glance from the side would receive a generous view of her magnificently taut breasts.

"All went well?" asked Hassan, suddenly realising, and for no apparent reason, that he was always the first to speak. The foreigner never opened a conversation.

"Of course," the reply was confident. Ramirov now seemed in good spirits, sullenness ebbing. "Here is the..." He remembered that the girl was not party to these matters and he changed verbal course deftly, placing the pouch back into his pocket. " - item. I shall have a relaxing night and then tomorrow things can get under way." He smiled. "How are you, Melanie?" he asked in English.

She smiled warmly. "Absolutely radiating with health. But I think I feel lonely."

"That is a situation that must certainly be remedied," He reverted to French. "Hassan, there is food?"

"The dining room is ready. We have a woman - dear old Signora Garofalo - who is cooking something delicious for the kind Arab businessmen. Come we must not keep her. I believe she has a husband and seven *bambini* to go home to."

As they walked from the room, Musaed asked. "What about the di- the item? Should it not be put in the safe?"

Hassan thought and then said. "Perhaps you are right, Faisal. We do not wish its security to mar our evening's enjoyment. You are in agreement, my brother?"

"I intended leaving there overnight, so yes, let me be rid of the thing now, at least for tonight," agreed Ramirov.

"The safe is in my office. Faisal will show you. He knows the combination."

The office was to the rear of the villa, behind the stairway. It was a small room containing a filing cabinet, desk, three chairs and two telephones. On the far side a pair of French windows led out onto the back patio and then to the villa's spacious garden.

The safe was a small standard house-safe set into the wall at head height behind the desk.

Ramirov closed the door of the room behind them. Faisal stood in front of the safe, and Ramirov said "Open it please."

Musaed began. Five or six turns to the right to clear the combination and then the first of the turns to the left. He deliberately blocked Ramirov's view so that he could not read the numbers. What he did not realise was that Ramirov had been taught at a very special training school to *hear* the combination of a safe.

It was open in moments and Musaed stood back to let Ramirov pass.

Inside the safe were various sealed envelopes and substantial amounts of different currencies. There was also a solitary key, for what Ramirov did not know. He walked past the young Arab and took the pouch from his pocket.

His back was to Musaed for only three seconds, but that was all it took. Ramirov heard the sound of the phone being lifted, but he turned too late. The instrument came crashing down onto the left side of his head, he heard a mighty bang like a volcano erupting, and then he fell into total darkness...

His rage was white hot, an emotion he had not experienced for years. But as always he kept his feelings under control and he sat at the dining table tight-lipped. His glasses were off and in front of him was a plate of *caponata* which was receiving the bulk of his visual venom. It had been two hours, and Musaed and the diamond were long gone.

Melanie also sat at the table, her meal devoured, but she knew better than to say anything to this unusual and frightening man. She had tried to administer to the cut under his hairline earlier on when Hassan had led him into the dining room dazed, but she had been brushed off with a curse in some language she did not know.

Hassan now entered the room, his face grim. "Well, that is done. All airports and seaports east of Greece are under surveillance. He will be held immediately he sets foot in any of them, the diamond will be retrieved and he will be executed. We cannot cover everywhere, of course. If he decides to go west we will have no immediate pick-up. My men are covering the airports here, as you know, but it is just possible for him to have got out before I found you and signalled the alert."

"How long was it?" The voice was tight.

"Fifteen minutes at the most, no more."

"Fifteen minutes!" Ramirov's hand smashed down onto the table. The *caponata* jumped into the air.

Hassan sat down two seats away, shaking his head. "I just cannot understand it. It is not like him. I have known Faisal since he was a youth. He is dedicated to *Fateh*."

"But he is not Palestinian."

"No, he is Saudi. But he believed deeply in our cause. He has been involved in many of our campaigns. He was the reconnaissance man for our Japanese brothers at Lod Airport, in fact he was still in Tel Aviv when the incident happened. He was fortunate to get out of the country. I - I just don't understand. He was truly Palestinian, even though he was not of our nationality. He believed in world revolution. Why would he do such a thing? Just for money?"

Ramirov replaced his glasses, wincing as they touched the left side of his head. He said nothing.

Melanie looked from one to the other of them. "Excuse me, but may I say something?"

They both looked at her, Hassan realising with horror that he had been speaking in English.

"Well," she shrugged nervously, "it might not mean anything, but, well, Faisal has said on more than one occasion recently that he doesn't trust you." She looked at the visitor.

"Does not trust me? *Me?*" Ramirov's index finger jabbed into his own chest. "That, my dear, is *ironic!*"

She continued. "Well, if he doesn't trust you - sorry, but that is what he said - if he doesn't trust you and he is as dedicated and fanatical as Hassy tells us... could he not have taken the diamond to its destination himself?" She went on quickly, "You just said it was a diamond Hassy, that's how I know."

The two men were silent. Slowly their heads turned towards each other.

"Well?" asked Ramirov.

Hassan was almost speechless. "That... that is amazing! It had not occurred to me. But of course! *That* is totally in line with his character." He gave a sharp half-laugh. "That *must* be what he is up to!"

Ramirov stood up. "In that case I will follow. He is a fool. An Arab face in Amsterdam would be sure to cause suspicion if seen in the wrong quarters, especially at this time. I must get the diamond before he gets picked up." He brushed a scab off the side of his head. "Or no, he is no fool as you say. In fact, looking at matters objectively, one might say that he was brave and intelligent to take such action if he did not trust me. One *might*. I believe he knows all the risks involved. He will not let himself be taken. Yes, the first thing he will be concerned about is the security of the diamond. He will no doubt bank it, just as we have done here, until contact can be made with this Irish supplier, this Mahoney." He was nodding his head in rumination. "He will have gone by road?"

"Most probably, for the same reasons as you." Hassan also rose.

"I will need a car, fast and in good condition."

"I have an Audi sports available, full tank."

"Ideal. I want you to alert the German Fraction. Musaed is not to be intercepted but I want him located and tailed as soon as he enters that country. I will call at the addresses in Stuttgart, Frankfurt and Duisberg. I expect someone to be waiting with news. And I need a good map."

"There is one in the car."

"Right. You have any food I can take with me?"

"There must be something in the kitchen. I will see while you prepare yourself."

Both men left the room, leaving Melanie on her own. She stared at the empty doorway. "Well, thanks a lot boys," she said. "Nice to be appreciated."

Ten minutes later Ramirov was in the car at the front of the villa, Hassan leaning in through the open window.

"You are sure you are in a condition to travel?"

"Yes."

"Then I wish you well, my brother. For the sake of us all."

Ramirov nodded and turned the ignition key. The engine purred into life. "I will report back here if anything happens or, if not, on safe delivery of the diamond. There is one thing, of course."

"My brother?"

Ramirov's right arm moved fractionally to touch the gun in his jacket pocket. "Good intentions or not, I will not have my authority undermined. Musaed dies."

With a kick of gravel the Audi shot away, off down the drive, and turned north for Milan, leaving Hassan nodding his head reluctantly in the half-light of evening.

That night, while Hassan snored loudly beside her, Melanie crept out of bed and walked quietly to the office downstairs. She was naked, but there was no one about. At night, the guards were on duty outside the villa.

She dialled a thirteen-digit number on the telephone. It was answered after one ring.

"It's Melanie. How is our friend? Good. Listen, I have some very interesting news..."

At the end of the call, she replaced the receiver softly and went back upstairs.

Melanie Nathanson, one of the many female operatives of Israeli intelligence, climbed back into bed with the leader of Black September. She prayed to God he would not wake up, her sex was raw enough already.

Ψ

FINALE

Ψ

Thursday October 31 1974

Italy/Switzerland/West Germany

Ramirov travelled fast but remained within the speed limits at all times. To be picked up by the police was the last thing he wanted to happen.

He took the E9 from Milan and had reached the Swiss border in just over an hour. His Swiss passport (one of fifteen supplied by his masters) saw him safely across.

He stopped once, just outside Chur, to relieve himself, and he munched cold pizza, bread and crackers as he drove. There was not too much traffic about and he found driving through Switzerland at night quite peaceful, if a little chilly. The heater was off in the car and would remain so. He did not want himself getting drowsy. And his head still throbbed with what was possibly a mild concussion.

He reached Zurich by 03:30 and here he had to slow his speed down from the motorway maximum of 130 to the town limit of 60. He entered the city along Mythen Quai, Lake Zurich lambent in the still moonlight.

Through the city and then out into the suburbs towards Winterthur. As he hit the motorway again he willed the car forward. He wanted to get to Stuttgart quickly and receive a report. Once he knew that this was the way Musaed had come then he could relax and take it easy, let the Arab do all the work.

He reached the E70. Now it would be a straight run, across the German border and up to Stuttgart. Swiss passport again, a cursory couple of questions by a bored Customs Officer, and he was through.

He arrived in Stuttgart at 06:30 and made his way through the awakening city to the apartment up near Hohen Park. Parking was easy, and he was greeted like an old friend by the woman and two men who met him. They were members of the German Fraction. [Sometimes known as the Baader-Meinhof Gang, named after two of their leaders – Andreas Baader and Ulrike Meinhof – both of whom were later to be executed whilst in their prison cells.] He was given the news straight away: Musaed was indeed heading for Amsterdam, the white Lancia had been picked up immediately it crossed the border. He was two hours ahead and was at that moment nearing Mannheim.

Ramirov was pleased. That was all he wanted to know. He could now take his time.

He was given a rough but filling meal consisting mostly of potatoes and some green vegetable, he drank vodka with his colleagues and then he settled down on the couch to sleep solidly for twelve hours.

Ψ

Saturday November 2 1974

Somewhere in the Irish Republic

Oh God, what time is it? Half-eight already?

I knew I shouldn't have taken *mavourneen* Lizzie to me bed last night - Lord, but she's gorgeous though. Look at her, lying there fast asleep, tits on display like two beached jelly fish. Wish she'd close her mouth though...

Well Michael, me ole fella, it's no good lying around here, yer've a plane to catch in Dublin this afternoon. And in just seventy-two hours from now you'll be meeting with Eyskens. Then you'll have three nights to enjoy yerself until Friday.

Friday...

It will be yer day of reckoning, boyo. Take the diamond and run, that's yer best bet. Whatever yer do, it's too late to worry about it now. Yer in lad, up to yer neck. Play it as it comes.

Come on now, yer lazy git. Up outta this bed... that's me boy. God, it's cold this morning. Must have a pee. Funny how a good session always makes yer want ta pee. Let's just have a look at yer face in the mirror here...

My God, but yer a handsome bastard, d' yer know that?

Amsterdam, Holland

Ilich Ramirov arrived in Amsterdam at 16:00 that afternoon. He had received his last report about the Lancia two and a half hours before in Duisberg. Musaed was now over a day ahead of him. He could be anywhere, of course. And it was that fact that had decided the Russian's course of action.

He would do nothing in the way of trying to find the treacherous, misguided Arab, nothing at all. All he would do was check into the Park Hotel, where the meeting was to take place next Friday, and wait. It was simply a waste of time and effort to try to trace Musaed in the city. He would wait, look around the town (he had not been to The Red Light District for years) and then on Thursday night (just in case) and Friday night he would be waiting in the bar of the hotel.

He entered the city on the E9 and turned left into President Kennedy Laan and up Ferdinand Bol Straat.

He turned into Van Baerle Straat, passed the Stedelijk Museum on his right, and then he was there.

At last, the Park Hotel...

Ψ

Tuesday November 5 1974

Amsterdam, Holland

Ramirov left the hotel early that morning to reconnoitre an area up by West Docks. He arrived there around lunchtime. It was good to see the old warehouse was still in use. Ostensibly it was a front for a firm of flower wholesalers; in reality it was a convenience for the KGB. Earlier he had picked up the keys to the place from a travel agency (also with KGB connections) on Kalverstraat in the centre of the city.

The warehouse was still in good condition, and it was the ideal place for what Ramirov had in mind: the death of Faisal Ibn Musaed. There were a few rats in the dingy corners but, he thought unemotionally, they could gnaw on the Arab's bones.

Ramirov caught a tram back into the city. He did not notice the man who got on the tram directly behind him, who walked past him and sat in the back. He was a tall man, slim with a noticeable hunch in his shoulders. His hair was iron-grey and it was beginning to fall out at the front. He wore a full beard which was just a shade darker than his hair.

And his eyes were something else. For he had no whites, none at all. Where the whites should have been was, quite simply, blood. As if all the blood vessels in his eyes had burst simultaneously, through some strain, shock or traumatic experience.

The Man was pleased the Russian had not recognised him. His Controller in Israel had been right. They had given him his chance and it must be taken. But not here, not now. It was too public.

The Man got off three persons behind Ramirov. He followed him to the Park Hotel and up into the foyer where he saw him ask for his key.

The Man walked over to Reception. "You have a room?" His voice was a raucous croak, devoid of any accent, and with a constant rasp as he breathed.

The hotel was always busy, of course, but *ja* there were a few vacancies at this time of the year *mijnheer*. How long would the gentleman be staying?

"Not long. Maybe three days." It would take no longer than that.

A room was booked and The Man, smiling all over his ashen face, went off to retrieve his luggage from the safe house. The clerk frowned at him as he walked away. The man moved slowly and seemed to have to gasp for breath before every step. A modern Quasimodo.

On his way out of the hotel, The Man passed a jovial Michael Mahoney entering, but as neither knew each other they hardly even noticed their mutual presence, although Mahoney did wonder what the sudden gasping noise was.

The Man was back at The Park within the hour. As he was signing in, he rasped to the clerk casually in English: "I believe you have a friend of mine staying here. A Mr Martinez?"

"Martinez?" The clerk consulted his records and tried not to stare at the ghoul in front of him. "N-no sir, no one by that name. We have a Swiss gentleman, a Mr Martini." He chuckled. "Not the sort of name one forgets."

"Martini! Of course, that's the guy. So he *is* here, that's good."

"Shall I tell him you are enquiring after him, sir? I can have him paged."

"No, no! Whatever you do, don't do that. I want to surprise him when I'm good and ready. What room's he in?"

"Er... on the floor below yourself, sir. Room 203."

"Thanks. You've been a great help." The clerk was rewarded with a magnificent fifty guilden tip.

"Thank *you*, sir !" Perhaps he was not so bad after all, thought the clerk. The poor man could not help the way he looked. But his breath was so rank! It smelled of dried blood and grit...

Ψ

Thursday November 7 1974

London, England

When it came to it, the girl's head shattered easily and she was dead by the time her body hit the floor. It had been an instantaneous but very painful death, shards of skull penetrating deep into the brain. Sandra - the one person whom the police later thought might be able to name her killer for definite - never knew who her murderer was.

Richard John Bingham, 7th Earl of Lucan, looked down at the inert body and shivered. It was dark in the basement of his town house at 46 Lower Belgrave Street, but he could clearly see the dark patch which had once been the back of the nanny's head. Already there was an unpleasant smell.

His breath came fast and deep, and his hands were shaking. Strangely enough he did not feel sick, as he had thought he would. He felt somewhat relieved. Relieved that this part of it at least was over. But the worst, of course, was yet to come.

Thirty-nine year old 'Lucky' Lucan gathered himself together and got down to business. *They* had specifically instructed that everything must go according to plan. Ten minutes delay at any stage and it could all go wrong and land him in an English cell for life. He must get on with it.

Quickly he retrieved the sack from the darkened corner and began to shove the dead body into it...

When the top of the bag was tied and the macabre bundle propped back into the corner, Lucan left the murder weapon where it could easily be found - as instructed - and rushed up the stairs two at a time. His small bag was already packed with the very few things he was allowed to take with him, and now he just had time for the cosmetics. Then would come the chat with his wife, which the police would make so much of but which the Press would virtually ignore, and his escape in the borrowed car.

Everything went according to plan and soon Richard John Bingham, without the moustache which had been his trade mark around the gaming clubs of London, was driving south out of central London towards the suburb of Croydon. The night of November 7 1974 was crisp but not necessarily cold in London, and his thick Arran jumper was ample coverage against whatever the elements had in store. It was a dry night and rain was not predicted. This time Lucky Lucan hoped that the weather forecasters would be right. He had a long way to go.

His only regret was that he had to miss his dinner date at the *Clermont* with Greville, and without a word of apology or explanation. It was damn caddish of him. A gentleman really did not do such things.

He only hoped that, if the truth were ever known, England would be grateful...

Ψ

Friday November 8 1974

Across England

Everything had gone according to plan and Lucan's nervousness had now abated. He had met with the inconspicuous member of the British SIS as instructed, outside a public house in the suburban town of Crawley, fifty kilometres south of London. The SIS man had said nothing to him, he had simply given Lucan a set of keys, pointed to a red Morris Mini parked on the opposite side of the road, and had then climbed into Lucan's car and driven off. He would get to Newhaven on the south coast in under two hours, and there he would abandon Lucan's car and travel back by another waiting vehicle. The police would find the deserted car and the false trail would be laid.

Lucan, on the other hand, drove the Mini back into London, up through Streatham, across the river into Chelsea, Knightsbridge, Oxford Street, Swiss Cottage, Hampstead, Highgate, and out of the capital once more, heading north-east.

He arrived in Harwich three hours later, right on schedule, and he had only gone wrong once in finding his way to the docks. His instructions were to wait in the car outside another specified public house and he would be contacted.

Five minutes after his arrival, there was a single rap on the passenger window. A man in a grubby mackintosh, cap pulled down to his eyes, looked in. Lucan wound down the window. There were no introductions, and the voice that came from underneath the cap had a Northern Irish accent.

"Leave the car here, it will be taken care of. Get yer things and come with me."

Harwich was quiet at that hour of the morning. As soon as Lucan stepped out of the car, it started to rain. The forecasters had been wrong.

He was led through a maze of backstreets, some so narrow as to be sinister. The rain became heavier, so that by the time he came out on the quayside it was lashing the street with some force.

"Not a very nice night for it, what?" He tried to make conversation as they crossed the deserted road. The street lighting was poor and clouds obscured all traces of the moon. He nodded at the rain. "This wasn't forecast."

"No." The reply did not invite any further exchange.

Lucan shivered as his sopping jumper finally gave up the fight against the rain and the water oozed through to his skin.

They walked to the edge of the quay. The other man climbed down an unsafe iron ladder and stepped into a small boat with an outboard engine, moored below.

Halfway down the ladder Lucan dropped his bag, but he was relieved to hear it thump into the bottom of the boat and not splash into the sea. The craft was unsteady and he sat down quickly, facing the other man.

The mackintoshed figure pulled two oars from underneath their feet. "Here, sit next to me. We'll row out a little before startin' the engine. Don't worry about the rain, I believe it's quite calm out there. For the North Sea, that is."

They were about a kilometre from the shore before he decided that it would be safe to start the engine. Then they were off, carving through the water, the tangy mixture of the now dying rain and the salty spindrift of the North Sea splashing into Lucan's face and completing his drenching.

The North Sea

They met up with HMCC Venturous as planned, five kilometres out.

[The original manuscript of this book contained a detailed description of the vessel and its activities in the guise of a UK Customs cutter, together with details of the short discussion which took place on board, and the truth – finally – about Richard John Bingham. The material has been deleted at the 'request' of the British security services.]

The final briefing completed, Lucan settled down inside and began to dry his hair with a towel. Soon, in Holland, it would be styled and dyed to disguise his appearance even more, and then he would continue on his pre-planned way eastward.

He suddenly felt quite tired and he leant back against the bulkhead and closed his eyes, only to be disturbed by one of the crew offering him a mug of steaming hot tea, which he accepted with his usual urbanity.

He thought of England and of what he was doing for her...

Amsterdam, Holland

Interpol Amsterdam received news of the Lucan murder by telex at 09:00 that morning. By midday, a copy of the telex and a preliminary description of the Earl 'wanted for questioning in connection with' was on the desk of every senior ranked member of the Amsterdam-Amstelland police.

The preliminary description was: 'Tall, about six foot, aged 39, hair black parted on right and pushed back, well built, special feature thick black moustache probably removed." A wire photo would follow, it was promised.

Middle-aged, world-weary Chief Inspector Johann Versleas assimilated this information on his return to his office at 41 Constantijn Huygensstraat at 13:30, hmphed to himself that the description could fit anybody, and put the copy telex to one side.

The Man entered the bar of the Park Hotel at 19:45. His grizzly eyebrows raised as he saw the unmistakable back sitting on the stool at the bar.

He walked over, stood deliberately close, and ordered a *John Collins*. The seated man did not give any sign of recognition.

"Nice evening," said The Man in the flat, dry rasp. "I find Amsterdam in late fall most beautiful, don't you?"

The eyes behind the tinted glasses turned to look at him. The head inclined to the left.

"I - I am zorry," said the familiar but deliberately deeply accented voice. "My Inglish, not good." The eyes turned away without even a glimmer of recognition.

The Man smiled. "Ah, forgive me. I understand."

He paid for his drink and found himself a seat by the wall. He sat staring at the Russian's back and occasionally sipping his sharp drink (too much lemon), pondering.

A sudden, sharp pain shot across his chest, and he held his breath and concentrated on not letting the agony show on his face. The pain subsided and he exhaled, safe again this time. But one day, he knew, the pain would not stop. Well, it would – but forever.

At 19:50 Ramirov vacated his stool at the bar in favour of a seat at an empty table near the entrance, his back towards the wall.

Seconds later, Michael Mahoney entered and strolled over to the bar, plonking himself down on the very stool Ramirov had just left. Ramirov heard the thick Irish accent order a whisky and then begin to pass the time of day with the barman, making casual enquiries about a girl who was on her own at the end of the bar.

They waited, The Man watching Ramirov, Ramirov watching the Irishman, who in turn was intent on the generous tits of the young lady who, as anyone but Mahoney could see, was a whore of the highest order. If Mahoney had not had other business that evening, he would be over there now whispering sweet begorrahs into her ear.

By 20:05 a third glass of whisky was being swallowed, the *John Collins* was just a trace in the bottom of the glass, and the water, no ice, had gone completely.

Musaed appeared at 20:06.

He stood in the entrance surveying the occupants of the place, not noticing Ramirov right underneath him. He went over to the bar. Three men and the whore were there, two of the men talking in German and one man on his own.

"Mijnheer?" The barman.

"For me, nothing," said Musaed in French. "But the same again for that gentleman there." He nodded at Mahoney who, as he knew no French, sat in ignorance of the attention given to him - until the drink was placed in front of him and he looked up questioningly.

"From the gentleman," explained the barman in English, with a nod towards Musaed.

Mahoney frowned, and then comprehension dawned. He said, "Ah, yes! My friend. Thank you!" He held the glass up and smiled at the Arab. The contents disappeared in one. "Won't you join me for a drink, sir?"

Musaed came over. "No drink for me, thank you."

"Oh no, of course, I'm always forgettin'. You fellas don't, do yer?"

"But I believe we have some business together?"

"Indeed we do, me ole son."

"You are Mr Mahoney?"

Mahoney put a hand inside his jacket pocket and threw a green Irish passport down onto the bar. "I sure am meself," he grinned.

Musaed gave the passport a cursory look and handed it back.

"Please excuse me, but this is not my regular area of employ. You know of a discreet place where I may make delivery?"

Mahoney sniffed and looked about. "Here's as good a place as any, oi reckon, don't yew?"

"As you wish."

Musaed's hand went to his jacket pocket. He tried to pull it back out with the diamond but something had suddenly gripped his forearm, as if a dog's jaws had tightened around it, and the arm was paralysed. He looked to his right and gasped with shock as the bespectacled face of Ramirov glared angrily at him.

For a moment the three men were silent. Musaed staring in fear, Ramirov glaring in hatred, Mahoney, mouth quivering, wondering what was going on. Was his plan going to fail at the last minute?

Ramirov stared down Musaed and then turned towards the Irishman, his grip not diminishing on the Arab's arm. "You must excuse me, Mr Mahoney," he said in almost unaccented English. "This gentleman and I have a little unfinished business."

The Irishman was alert, alarm bells ringing. "What's going on?" he asked softly. "If this is Arab against Arab I'm out of it, you can keep the sodding stone." He went to get off the stool but Ramirov's other hand restrained him.

"There is no need for alarm, I assure you. The stone is yours. But I do not think it wise that these things are done in public. If you will come with my friend and me, we will give you the diamond."

"Really, I don't - "

"Please." Ramirov's hand had left Mahoney and was now in his right jacket pocket, the unmistakable outline of a gun poking outwards underneath the cloth.

It was done so discreetly that only Musaed and Mahoney knew anything was wrong. Not far away, the barman went about his business, and likewise the whore who was now being propositioned by a small, balding American.

Ramirov stood back to let Mahoney off the stool, pulling Musaed back with him and laughing as if it was the meeting of old friends. With one hand on the gun in his pocket and the other still painfully gripping Musaed's arm, he ushered the party out of the hotel and into Stadhouderskade.

A chill had descended and their breath turned to vapour in the Amsterdam air. They walked southwards.

Musaed's Lancia was parked just along from the hotel.

"Into the back if you would, Mr Mahoney," directed Ramirov. He pulled Musaed to a halt while the Irishman climbed in. "You are unusually quiet tonight, Faisal. Cat got your tongue? No opinions to express? You will drive. Follow my directions."

The gun was produced from his pocket and he pushed the Arab into the driver's seat. Ramirov got into the back, next to Mahoney and directly behind Musaed, all the time the gun pressing hard into the young man's head.

Ramirov gave instructions and they were off, Musaed nervously jerking them out into the traffic towards Constantijn Huygensstraat.

None of them, not even Ramirov, noticed The Man with the grey hair, beard and stoop, come out of the hotel, hail a cab, and climb into it, giving instructions as he did so. The cab pulled out in the wake of the Lancia...

It had been a long day and Chief Inspector Johann Versleas was tired. Ever since his transfer to the Drugs Squad his working day had been getting longer and longer, some days melting into the next without pause. And, of course, this did not please his wife. She was going through the change, so he received little or no physical attention these days, but she was one of those women who objected to her husband being away from home and yet could not tolerate him when he was there; the ball-crushing vicious circle.

Versleas' day had started at 08:00 that morning and now, over twelve hours later, he was on his way home in his old Opel. Home to a couple of hours of nagging while he tried to watch television, and then seven hours merciful oblivion in his single bed. Oh well, roll on Christmas when his children would be home from school. He had lots of trips and visits to the theatre lined up which he hoped they would enjoy - he would, at any rate.

Versleas smoked placidly on his *Ritmeester* cheroot and drove up Biderdijkstraat, pausing at the intersection with de Clerq Straat for a chance to turn right into the busy traffic.

A white Lancia pulled up next to him, the driver - a young Asian-looking type - trying jumpily to edge his way into the flow, but with little success.

More intent on the traffic, Versleas gave a casual glance into the back of the vehicle where two men sat. One, on the far side, thin, long faced, looked very sombre and absentmindedly picked his nose. The other, on this side, looked well-built, from what little Versleas could see of him, and had dark hair, probably black, parted on the right and pushed back. He looked to be in his thirties, and he wore a pair of tinted spectacles, unusual and quite unnecessary in Amsterdam at this time of year and at this time of night. This one was speaking to the driver, possibly giving him directions, and he had his hand on the back of the driver's seat.

Versleas found a gap in the traffic and neatly slipped out into de Clerq Straat. In his rear-view mirror he noticed the white Lancia also take the same opportunity, then the gap in the traffic was closed before a cab could pull out.

Versleas took the cheroot from his lips and held it between the first two fingers of his right hand as he steered. He drove with the traffic along Rozen Gracht and thought of nothing in particular.

It did not hit him until he was waiting at the traffic lights at the next intersection.

My God! The man, the one with the dark glasses in the back of the Lancia. Well-built, in his thirties, black hair parted on the right. It was almost an identical description to the one he had read that afternoon of the missing English Lord! What was his name? Lew... Loo... Loosen? Loo... Lucan, that was it! Otherwise known as Bingham.

Could it be? Could it actually be the fugitive earl in the back of the Lancia? No, absolutely not. Yet it would certainly explain the incongruous dark glasses. The history of police detection was rife with chance incidents like this. Could it be?

Versleas felt a tingling in his stomach.

The lights changed and Versleas drove on, keeping an eager eye on the car behind. The traffic began to thin at Raadhuis Straat, and he pulled over to the side and stopped, forcing the Lancia ahead of him. As it went past he took a good look at the man in the back. This second look did nothing to allay his suspicions. He let a cab go past and then pulled back into the traffic, eyes glued on the Lancia two vehicles ahead.

He noticed that it had begun to rain, and he switched on the Opel's wipers...

The Lancia kept to the main streets and Versleas kept with it, the cab still separating him from his quarry. By the main Post Office the Lancia made a left turn, then left again a few hundred metres on. Curiously enough, the cab did too. Versleas was now deeply interested. This seemed to be a two-man tail. If it was, who was in the cab?

The Lancia turned right and continued on under the railway bridge into the West Dock area. The smell of the city decreased as the smell of the docks and the sea overcame the gentle odour of the canals.

Soon the Lancia began to slow down. It turned right into a narrow lane and stopped a little way along. The cab did not turn but went past the intersection and then pulled suddenly to a halt. As he drove by, Versleas saw a tall grey man with a beard and marked stoop shuffle out and quickly hand over money. Versleas pulled over a little way along. As he turned to look back, the now passengerless cab shot past him.

The rain was heavy now, coming from the west, and it tappy-tapped on the roof of the vehicle like the fingers of a thousand devils. Versleas peered through the back window into the darkness. The sinister, stooped figure had crossed the road and was just entering the lane which the Lancia had pulled into.

Reminding himself that he was unarmed, Versleas sat and wondered what he should do...

"Right, if you would be so good as to step outside and accompany us, Mr Mahoney, this transaction will not take too long."

"But it's pouring down with bloody rain, oi'll be soaked!"

"As you are about to receive a diamond worth a considerable amount of money, I should think that would be the least of your worries. Please. Faisal - out!"

Swiftly Ramirov climbed out of the Lancia, gun still pointing doggedly at the forlorn Arab. Mahoney clambered out after him, being extra careful not to get in front of the gun as Musaed nervously joined them on the narrow, puddled sidewalk.

"Walk," ordered Ramirov. He looked at the Irishman. "You no doubt wonder what is going on, Mr Mahoney. Unfortunately it is not my province to offer you explanations. This is an internal matter, which I shall resolve shortly. Meantime, I apologise for the inconvenience caused."

"I don't want to be involved in no internal matters, thank you very much."

"Just bear with me."

"Hm."

They walked for one hundred metres, the lane dark and illuminated only by the moon which peeked through the rainclouds at irregular intervals. Mahoney became wet and he did not like it one bit. If he was honest with himself, he had to admit that he was as scared as hell. What *had* he got mixed up in?

Ramirov stopped them outside the entrance to some sort of warehouse and motioned them inside through a wicket-gate. It was dank inside, seemingly through years of unuse, and but for a few old soapboxes and straw on the floor it was empty.

Leaving the wicket-gate ajar, Ramirov went over to the wall on the left and switched on a dim lightbulb which was suspended by a hideously worn wire from the high ceiling. All the time his gun was trained on Musaed, who had turned and was looking at him.

As the light went on, Mahoney could have sworn he saw something with four legs dash for cover into the darkness of a far corner. Then he too turned to face the man with the gun. God, this place stank of cats.

Keeping at least four metres from the other two men, Ramirov came back over and stood with his back to the open doorway. The gun jerked at Musaed.

"The diamond."

Musaed hesitated, fear in his eyes as he again tried to stare down the foreigner and failed. His hand came up to his jacket pocket and he slowly pulled out the familiar leather pouch.

Ramirov inclined his head. "Good." He kept his speech in English for the benefit of the Irishman. "Now please remove the diamond so we can see it." *What was that strange smell?*

The top of the pouch was pulled open and the diamond was tipped out, filling Musaed's left palm.

Mahoney was staring wide-eyed at the huge stone. "Jesus, Mary and Joseph, look at the size of that!" A wicked, greedy gleam came into his eyes. Sheer avarice. "The Star of Sierra Leone."

"I THINK NOT!"

The satanic rasp came from no more than half a metre behind Ramirov. The Russian went to spin round but he was halted by the unmistakable hardness pressing into the small of his back. Musaed and Mahoney looked up in shock.

For a moment there was silence. Then the man with the beard and stoop said in his flat, grating, lifeless tone, "No sudden moves, eh? Especially you."

The gun jabbed painfully into Ramirov's back, but he showed no reaction whatsoever.

The demonic eyes looked across at Mahoney. "You, put the stone back into the pouch... That's good... Now keep it in your hand where I can see it. Hold it up! Good." Again the jab in Ramirov's back, "You, drop the gun onto the floor at your feet - don't lower your arm, just let it go."

Thud.

"Kick it behind you. Careful now, my finger isn't as steady as it used to be."

Ramirov kicked the gun behind him. Slowly he turned. He frowned as he looked at the man with the lifeless grey hair and beard and the nasty stoop which made him look as if he was permanently raising his head. For the first time in a long time, Ramirov felt a pang of apprehension as he looked at the eyes, black and surrounded with blood.

The Man caught the frisson and grinned. "Scare yer, huh? Well, so it should - *you* did this to me, Martinez."

Ramirov frowned again. He had never seen this man in his life before the casual meeting at the hotel, yet the man knew one of his aliases.

Now a laugh came from The Man's lips. "Don't recognise me, huh? Well, how do you think I came upon you without you sensing me, eh? You told me in Cyprus you knew I was there – well you didn't this time, did you?"

"I do not believe it," Ramirov almost smiled in admiration. "Mr Digenis. I indeed would not have recognised you."

"Why should you?" growled The Man. "Last time you saw me, I was a normal human being. I had a *life*. In Cyprus, remember? And you, you shit, shot me through the fucking heart. Call me by my real name. I AM GRIVAS. STELIOS GRIVAS! You shot me, you double-crossing bastard. You. You did this to me!" The horrible sound as he breathed in. "You shot me through the heart but you forgot to check that I was dead. Now I have a bullet in there and I have to stoop to ease the pain, and it has sent me grey. And they tell me that the bullet only has to move one centimetre to complete its work. One centimetre, Martinez. One fucking centimetre..."

The hand with the gun whipped upwards into the Russian's face. Ramirov staggered back and fell into a sitting position. The tinted glasses had shattered with the impact of the gun, and he brushed them off his face.

Glass had entered his right eye and blood began to roll from it.

"That's from Christina Cascianis, bastard! Stand up. Stand up NOW!"

Ramirov did as he was ordered.

"Now come back over to me."

Ramirov walked slowly over and straight into another smack with the gun, three teeth spinning from his mouth as he fell back again onto the straw.

Grivas looked at the other two men. They were stiff with terror. "The diamond," he ordered.

Musaed weakly proffered the pouch.

The inhaling gasp. "It is for my father. Give it to me. The diamond is The Eye of Makarios."

Musaed went to pass it over.

Grivas reached out a hand.

At that moment a wet, unstoppable figure came hurtling through the doorway, bowling Grivas over with a tackle.

Then all hell broke loose.

The gun fired as Grivas fell, the bullet narrowly missing Mahoney's left ear. Ramirov was up in an instant and he kicked the fallen gun out of the reach of the grasping Chief Inspector Versleas.

Versleas pushed himself off the top of Grivas and grabbed Ramirov's right ankle, jerking the bloodied Russian down as he went for the gun. Ramirov's nose hit the floor with an almighty crack, but he turned around and rammed his heel savagely into the face of the policeman.

Mahoney took two steps and planted a foot firmly into the Russian's testicles, then he saw Musaed sneaking around the edge of the warehouse and leapt over after him.

"No yer don't, me boyo." A push, and the pouch was snatched away.

Cringing with pain, nose broken and face completely covered in blood, Ramirov rose, looked once at Mahoney and once at the gun, saw the man beneath him grabbing for his feet again, and decided on the diamond. He leapt over and aimed a blow at the Irishman's head.

Mahoney ducked but not sufficiently. The top of his head was struck and he was knocked off balance, dropping the pouch into a dim corner.

Musaed jumped forward and grabbed hold of both sides of Ramirov's bloody, chubby face, wrenching downwards. This time the pent-up scream burst from the Russian's lips.

Versleas had shaken his cut forehead and was now coming out of his momentary daze. He saw the gun three metres in front of him and he began to crawl towards it.

Ramirov lashed out at Musaed but his fisted chop was knocked off target as Mahoney rammed his head into his stomach, lifted upwards with all his might and sent the bulky Russian right over the top of him. Mahoney fell back down with the effort, but then he dragged himself to his feet again, chuffed...

Versleas could see two of everything. His two right hands stretched out and made contact with both the guns...

Mahoney had Musaed by the collar when he saw the other man pick up the gun.

"He's got the gun!" He and the Arab almost fell over each other as they dashed from the warehouse and out into the rain. Mahoney tripped over the bottom slat of the wicket-gate, sprawled across the wet, dirty sidewalk, pulled himself back up and was away...

Versleas turned in a seated position with the guns in all four hands...

Ramirov saw the Irishman go and, not realising he had dropped the diamond, he staggered to his feet and headed for the doorway, blood pouring from his eye, nose and mouth, dripping off his chin and staining the old straw red...

Versleas fired.

Ramirov span around and then sank to his knees, right hand clutching his left collar-bone. He got up once more, then fell back again, then got up again, staggering towards the gateway...

Versleas pulled the trigger again.

There was no report.

Ramirov stumbled out into the lane and away...

Versleas threw the jammed gun towards the gateway and shouted "Lucan! LUCAN!"

He tried to get up but nausea overcame him and he fell back down. He heard a car start up outside and skid away, and he knew it was too late...

All was now quiet again in the dank, seedy warehouse.

In the middle of the floor, Stelios Grivas lay motionless. As he had fallen, the bullet had been jogged that one feared centimetre, and by the time Versleas had crawled off of him he was dead of a myocardial infarction.

Versleas succeeded in getting to his feet. It did not take him a moment to realise that the stooped, sinister man was dead, although quite why he did not know at that stage. He noticed something on the floor in a far corner and he walked gingerly over to investigate. It seemed to be a pouch or something.

Cautiously he picked it up. Hmm, leather... He pulled open the top and looked at the contents, laying the object in the palm of his hand.

It looked like an opaque, roughly-cut chunk of glass...

Ψ

POSTSCRIPT

There the story fades. A few more facts are known and, under the UK and US Freedom of Information legislation, some of them have now been incorporated into this second edition of the book.

And what of the protagonists?

Michael Mahoney died just three months after the incident in Amsterdam. Working on a tip-off from a very high up grass in the IRA, the Gardai (Irish police) were already two months into an investigation of his activities when Mahoney went to Amsterdam. While he was away, the Gardai took the opportunity to raid his mansion 'Somewhere in the South'. The place was ransacked, gutted of every moveable object. The hidden tapes of most of Mahoney's recent business deals were discovered, and all the police had to do was sit back and await his return. When the dishevelled and weary Mahoney landed at Dublin Airport in the morning of November 9 1974, he was immediately arrested.

Mahoney knew that he would be under threat from his suppliers and customers, he had even more to fear from them than from the police. For this reason, he said not one word throughout the whole of his trial. He was, of course, found guilty and sentenced to life imprisonment. On his way to his internment at Port Laoise prison, a bullet from a gun - some say it was Catholic, some say it was Protestant - entered his brain via his right eye and ended his existence.

Sally-Anne Bowker now lives permanently in Paris, in Neuilly, and is married. With this book, she reads the full story for the first time.

Michael Mouskos remained a 'troublesome priest' until the end. He died in 1977 of a heart attack… possibly genuine. He lies in the Kykko Monastery in Cyprus.

Christina Cascianis is now based in Athens and owns property in various parts of the Hellenic Mediterranean which she lucratively leases to holiday-makers. To this very day she visits Cyprus at least once a month and lays flowers on the joint grave of George and Stelios Grivas. Occasionally she works for the *Mossad*. She is an exceptional lady in every way. She meets Ilich Ramirov again in *The Windsor Secret*.

Ilich Ramirov, with a slight adjustment of his name and his South American cover strengthened, went on to become one of the most feared and famous terrorists (or freedom-fighters) of the nineteen seventies. The Press gave him the nickname 'Carlos The Jackal'.

Cast off by his Russian masters on the fall of the USSR, he became a freelance. At the turn of the twenty-first century he was supposedly spending the rest of his life in prison in France. But Ramirov had never been arrested by the French. Using the Makarios precedent, it was a double the French had unwittingly incarcerated.

Ramirov continued to live in freedom in Venezuela, foraging into the northern hemisphere when his special talents were required. He had gained a certain perverse respectability and was employed as necessary by governments and royal households. His more notable later successes included a car crash in Paris in August 1997 and a plane crash off Cape Cod in July 1999. He meets Christina Cascianis again in *The Windsor Secret*.

Faisal Ibn Musaed had perhaps the most macabre fate of all. He was publicly decapitated with six hideously painful strokes of the executioner's sword in April 1975 after he had assassinated his uncle, King Faisal of Saudi Arabia, the previous month.

The Eye of Makarios never left the possession of Michael Mouskos. It was taken with him in the pocket of his pants when the British flew him out of Cyprus in July 1974. It stood to reason, after all, that Papadopoulos being a duplicate Makarios, the 'diamond' carried around his waist would be a duplicate as well. The item held in the hand of Chief Inspector Johann Versleas in Amsterdam on the night of November 8 1974 was indeed an opaque, roughly-cut chunk of glass...

The Star of Sierra Leone. It has never been conclusively proven that this and The Eye of Makarios were one and the same. Its fate is uncertain. Rumour has it that, after the death of Makarios, a Swiss jeweller spent three years supervising its cutting, and the stone was eventually cut to become the 170 carat *Star of Peace*. If this is true then it gives this story its final irony - for the person who bought the three million pound diamond in early 1981 was a prominent, and subsequently famous, member of an Arabian Royal Family.

Ψ

REFLECTION

At the time of writing, neither Black September nor any other body has yet exploded a nuclear device in Britain or, within these terms, anywhere else. However:

"We undertake not to drop it on anyone, but if someone is going to drop it on us or someone is going to threaten our existence and independence, even without the use of atomic weapons, we should drop it on them."

Colonel Muammar Qadhafi
Leader of Libya
in a televised lecture, June 1987

It was to take thirteen more years before Someone realised that they did not need to make their own nuclear devices. Objects that would create similar devastation and loss of life were already flying in and out of airports every day of the year in every country in the world... and they were their's for the taking.

Ψ

APPENDIX 1

CYPRUS

The Island

The island of Cyprus in the eastern Mediterranean is 805 kilometres from the Greek mainland and just 65 kilometres from the Turkish coast. It is one of the world's tiniest countries. In 1974 its population of 650,000 was composed of 78% ethnic Greeks, 18% ethnic Turks and 4% other.

Greek colonies were established in Cyprus over 3000 years ago, and the island later formed part of the Roman, Persian and Byzantine empires. It became a Frankish kingdom in 1193, a Venetian dependency in 1489 and was then conquered by the Turks in 1571.

Under a convention concluded with the Sultan of Constantinople on June 4 1878, the island was made over to England for administrative purposes. Great Britain annexed the island on November 5 1914, and it was given the status of a crown colony on May 1 1925.

Michael Mouskos

Michael Mouskos was born on August 13 1913 in Ayia Panayia, a village in the remote south-west of the Paphos District of Cyprus. In 1926, at the age of 13, Michael became a novice at the famous Kykko Monastery, in the Paphos District. In 1942 he took his divinity degree at the University of Athens and then continued to live in Greece. He was ordained in 1946.

Two years were then spent on a scholarship in the United States, and while he was still there he was elected Bishop of Kitium (Larnaca). In 1950, at the age of 37, Michael was elected head of the Greek orthodox Church of Cyprus upon the death of Archbishop Makarios II (Makarios means 'blessed'), and, like his predecessors, he also assumed the role of Ethnarch, national leader.

On April 1 1955, a Greek Cypriot terrorist organisation known as EOKA began a campaign against the British in Cyprus. They wanted *Enosis*, complete union with Greece. Mouskos himself was suspected of being the instigator and real leader of EOKA.

Mouskos was arrested in March 1956 and deported to the Seychelles. He was released in 1957 with freedom to go anywhere but Cyprus. He chose Greece.

Although exiled from the island, Mouskos twice attended the General Assembly of the United Nations, and, although he initially demanded *Enosis* and nothing but, he was pressured into acceptance of a compromise solution guaranteeing independence for Cyprus. On February 19 1959, the London Agreement was signed, which meant that Mouskos and Cyprus had renounced *Enosis* forever. Once the Agreement was signed, Mouskos was allowed to return to the island.

Cyprus became an independent republic on August 16 1960 (although Greece, Britain and Turkey still maintained an interest). Mouskos had been elected President the previous December.

However, there were those who were opposed to the renouncement of *Enosis*. EOKA lived...

George Grivas

General George Grivas, a strong supporter of *Enosis* and a good friend of Makarios before the London Agreement, was in charge of all Greek Cypriot forces on the island. He was withdrawn by the Greek Colonels in 1967 at the urging of the Turkish government.

By 1971 Grivas, as head of EOKA, was in hiding. EOKA's terrorist attacks increased and occupied most of Makarios' time.

The Cypriot National Guard

The Cypriot National Guard was a force of about 12,000 conscripts led by some 650 officers on loan from Greece.

Ψ

APPENDIX 2

BLACK SEPTEMBER/*EL FATEH* IN 1974

El Fateh, the largest and strongest of the many Palestinian resistance organisations, was born out of the smouldering ashes of the Arabs' defeat in the battle for Palestine in 1948. One of the many lives lost in the fight was that of Sheikh Hassan Salameh, the legendary Palestinian leader and a hero to his followers both in life and in death. At the time, the entire Palestinian people mourned his untimely departure. Little notice was taken of his then young son, a son who was to become even more famous than his father, and who was to spread the word TERROR throughout the world - Ali Hassan Salameh, co-founder of Black September.

The word *Fateh* is based on the initials of the Palestinian Liberation Movement and means 'Victory'. The name 'Black September' is commemorative of the massacre in Jordan in September 1970 of *El Fateh* guerrillas. Not all died, and the survivors - headed by one Yasser Arafat - slipped across the northern borders of Jordan into Syria and Lebanon. The group was bent on revenge and on righting the injustice they considered to have been done to the Palestinian people.

They first came to the world's attention in Cairo, Egypt, on November 28 1971 when four gunmen shot dead Jordanian premier Wasfi Tell at the entrance to the Sheraton Hotel. One of the gunmen - as was seen on television screens throughout the world - bent down and licked the still-warm blood of his victim from the hotel steps. Although arrested for appearance's sake, the four gunmen were fêted as heroes, and they were eventually released by the Egyptians.

Black September flourished. Many idealists from other countries joined them or announced affiliation. The united groups performed acts of terror, spreading throughout the world, going from strength to strength, reaching an all-time high in atrocities in 1972 with the massacre of the Israeli athletes at the Munich Olympic Games.

However, in games with high stakes, tides easily turn. In the spring of 1973, an Israeli assassination squad raided a certain house in Beirut. Inside, a core of Black September's leaders and advisers had been planning a series of military spectaculars to take place in Europe that summer. Three of the top men died: Mohammed Yusuf Al Najjar, Kamal Adwan and Kamal Nasser (who went the way all men would wish - in bed with two naked girls). As well as this stinging blow, the Israelis also seized a vast amount of Black September/*El Fateh* documentation. Now it was Black September's turn to have its back to the wall.

It was because of this depletion that the remaining powers of the organisation had decided that a military act so grand, so spectacular, so *terrible* had to be committed within the next year. It would be designed to let the world know that their cause was not dead, and to raise them once again in the eyes of their Iraqi, Syrian, Libyan, Algerian and Russian backers.

It was this resolve that led to Black September's liaison man with the IRA, the Maoist Khalil al-Wazir (code-name Abu Jihad) arranging, through the Belgian, the meeting of Michael Mahoney and 'Akay' Al Khalifa.

Since the Israeli raid the previous spring, the core of Black September had kept themselves well hidden and protected from the jubilant *Mossad* (the Israeli Secret Service). No meetings had been held and no contacts made; no direct military act had been perpetrated at their instance. [*The incident at Rome's Leonardo da Vinci Airport on December 17 1973, when Arab terrorists killed 31 people, was not a direct action by Black September/PLO. Likewise the shoot-out at Athens Airport the previous August, when 5 people died, was committed by two young hot-heads without the official backing of Black September.*]

It was seven months after the Israeli bloodbath that the remaining three core members had met in secret at Zahlé, near Lebanon's eastern border with Syria. There they formulated their plans for the ultimate military act.

The three persons who met in Zahlé were Ali Hassan Salameh, at that time controller of the intelligence and action arms, and who was feared even by Yasser Arafat; Salah Khalef (code-name Abu Ayad), co-founder of Black September and the group's *consiglière* (counsellor), and also second to Arafat on the central committee of *El Fateh*; and a gentleman who has never been positively identified but who is thought to have been the number two of the *Fateh* intelligence agency, Jihad-al-Razd.

These three persons were also present at the subsequent meeting on January 3 1974 (originally scheduled for October 1973 but delayed for three months because of the *Yom Kippur* war) which is related herein. Also in attendance were Abu Jihad, the IRA liaison man, and Faisal Ibn Musaed, a young Arab whose origins were uncertain but who had risen quite suddenly over the past year to become, effectively, a personal assistant to Hassan. Hassan held the young man in great esteem and it was thought by the other core members that Musaed was being groomed to take over should Hassan's demise come suddenly and unexpectedly - which was more than an even bet when you were the leader of the world's most prominent, if currently faltering, 'liberation army'.

Ψ

APPENDIX 3

A Summary of Events Leading Up To The Coup in Cyprus on July 15 1974

The coup was organised by Brigadier Dimitrios Ioannides, head of the Greek military police and on the outer circle of the Colonels who seized power in Athens in 1967. Through his own efforts, Ioannides assumed total power in Greece in 1973. He operated completely behind the scenes, and few people in Greece even knew what he looked like.

Stationed in Cyprus in the 1960s, Ioannides developed a hatred for 'The Red Priest'. Ioannides had under his control the 650 regular officers of the Cypriot National Guard and elements of the old EOKA (known to some as EOKA 'B') to whom Mouskos was a traitor for having abandoned *Enosis*. The intention of the coup was to rectify this.

When Ioannides gave the signal, the National Guard and EOKA brought down Makarios.

THE MESRINE CONCLUSION

DAVID CULLEN

*"If thou, O Lord, should mark our
iniquities, Lord, who would survive?"*

- from the Requiem Mass of
Jacques Mesrine in the church
of St Vincent de Paul, Clichy,
Paris, November 1979

‡

*"I have a story to tell you. A true story.
About a cop, about the most wanted man
in Europe and about a document
containing a secret."*

- Claude Gerard,
Tuesday 23 October 1979

‡

Acknowledgements

For their invaluable help and assistance I would like to thank:

Veronique Lensens, who knows but will not tell;

and

Sylvie, who doesn't really know but wants to tell.

Finally, my respect and admiration – but not necessarily my approval – must go to Jacques Mesrine (you couldn't make it up).

‡

PRÉFACE

L'histoire de Mesrine

L'occupation, France, 1944

It was glorious. An azure sky, sun high but not overbearingly hot as befits an early summer's day.

It was quiet in the village of Château-Merle, near Poitiers in western France. A tranquillity which gave the lie to the circumstances. For people were joyful, but they could not show it. They wanted to cry in triumph, but they dare not. For the news had come through that the Allies had landed in Normandy. France was again, very soon, to be free. The German occupying forces were retreating. June 1944 was going to be a month to remember.

When the convoy of German vehicles left Poitiers that day for the last time, the people carried on their normal routine, only quietly, subdued. For one smile, one hint of the volcano of jubilation within, could bring untold reprisals from the departing forces. And no one wanted that at this stage, now that it was nearly over after four years.

The boy, Jacques, was seven years old. He had been staying in a farm outside the village with relatives after fleeing from Paris with his mother, brother and sisters at the start of the occupation. Despite coming from a large family, Jacques was a lonesome child, never wanting to play with the local children, never becoming involved in any of their games or adventures, never speaking to them if he could avoid it, ignoring the encouragement of his aunt to "Join in, Jacques. Why do you not play with the others? It is not right, a boy of your age..." He preferred the company of just his one friend, Georges.

In fact Jacques was not lonely at all. He liked it that way. Why should he play with the stupid village children? He always had a nicer time on his own or just with Georges. But grown-ups never understood that, did they? They always thought children had to have 'friends'.

He was playing ball with Georges in the field opposite the farm when he first heard the rumble. He listened, letting the ball roll to a stop at his feet.

Georges looked at him, a question in his eyes.

"Hear that, Georges? Hear that noise? What is it? Thunder? Is it going to rain?"

Georges shook his head.

"What can it be? It's getting louder. It's coming this way! *Allons-y*. Let's go and see!"

They ran across the field towards the road, Georges' loping stride taking him ahead of his *copain*.

The road from town turned sharply half a kilometre back, before it reached the farm. There was nothing to be seen yet but both of them could feel the trembling of the track beneath their feet as the rumbling grew louder and louder.

Then there was another sound. A rapid *rat-tat-tat* which, even for his tender years, Jacques knew well. He had seen his uncles and older cousins practise with their guns many times. They were supposed to belong to some secret group that would drive the Germans out of France, but in four years they had not succeeded.

The slightest pause in the rumble, a staccato response, and then the convoy appeared in sight, the sun glistening off the leading jeep. There were many of them. The front jeep and the first lorry seemed to be going faster, pulling away from the lorries following.

Jacques was not old enough to understand that he should not like the Germans. Indeed the few he had come across had smiled and spoken kindly to him in harsh Teutonic French. Some had even given him pieces of *chocolat*. But this was different. This gave him a troubled feeling in his seven year old gut. The approaching jeep contained four uniformed men; one of them in the front was half lying over the side, arms flopping like a marionette.

Georges was transfixed, staring at the vehicles down the road.

"Georges? Georges!" said Jacques urgently. "Quick! Come. We'd best get out of here. I don't like it."

Uncle's farm was on the other side of the road. Jacques did not run to the farmhouse where he knew he would find Auntie, Great Aunt and a few cousins not old enough to work the land. Instead he headed for the barn, instinctively seeking solitude.

Georges pulled himself out of his reverie and followed hard on his heels.

Jacques gave his pal a hand up into the hayloft and they lay still, flat out on the sparse hay.

Georges' breath rasped through his teeth and Jacques whispered for him to be quiet. He peeked out through the small window and saw the jeep and lorry turn towards the farm, the dead man bouncing as the jeep hit the cobbled dirt track. They pulled up beyond the front door.

Great Aunt, still a stout and formidable woman despite her eighty years, appeared from the farmhouse, wiping her hands on her pinafore. She mumbled something Jacques could not hear and motioned with her arms.

The back flap of the lorry was flung back. There were soldiers inside.

Without hesitation a soldier raised his machine gun and blasted Great Aunt from their path. She performed a pirouette, bits of pinafore and something red spraying outwards, before she fell heavily.

The Germans leapt from the vehicles and charged into the farmhouse. There were few shouts or screams from within, just the eerie *crack-crack-crack* of gunfire.

A cat ran from the front door. A single *crack* from within and it somersaulted and lay still.

To the boy watching fascinated from the hayloft it seemed like eternity, but it was in fact just one minute later that the Germans came back out. Their faces were business-like, a job that had to be done, vengeance for their dead *Kamerad* in the jeep. Death to the Resistance! How long till we reach the Fatherland?

A horse grazing near the barn looked up at the men just ten seconds before its eyes and brain were blown away by another gunburst. It fell to the ground, legs stiff and shaking in its death throes.

Jacques quickly pulled away from the window. Beside him, Georges had his face buried into the floor, whimpering in fright.

There was a minute's dreadful silence, then he heard a few foreign voices. Did they know he was there? Were they going to come for him? He heard the vehicles start up and pull away.

He risked a look out. The whole thing had taken so short a time that the main convoy had only just reached the farm entrance. The jeep took its place at the head, the lorry eased its way into line, and they drove off as if nothing had happened, save for the dead man in the front passenger seat.

Jacques could not count more than the fingers on his hands, so he could not say how many lorries, jeeps and cars passed, but it was at least three handfuls.

After the rumbles had faded into a distant hum, Jacques roused Georges and together they descended the wooden ladder.

Hesitantly Jacques looked out of the main door of the barn. All was quiet. The sun still shone, the trees still rustled in the breeze, a bird flew nearby. Life went on. But in the farm there was now only death. A crow screeched.

In front of them the horse still trembled, excreta flowing unrestrained from its arse like lava from a volcano.

Out by the track Great Aunt lay in a heap, her blood running wetly over the grey cobblestones, in some places already settling between the cracks, a macabre grouting.

Jacques looked at the scene. He did not faint or feel sick, in fact he did not feel anything. He was not afraid of the death all around him, he was fascinated. He could see a small, dead hand poking out from the farmhouse doorway.

Georges dashed over to Great Aunt. He stopped and stared, bewildered. He cried softly. Then he sniffed and bent down and began to lick her warm, fresh blood.

"Georges!" cried Jacques, his face stone. "Georges, stop that! Come here! Bad dog, Georges! Bad, bad dog..."

Algérie, 1958

They say that at the moment of death, life flashes before your eyes. At that moment, staring up into the darkness at the twin glints from the Arab's knife and sneering teeth, Jacques believed it.

And it had been such a marvellous day, as well. First a thirty kilometre forced march over the uneven, sandy terrain of Algeria. The big, burly Jacques Mesrine had relished the trip while his French army colleagues had weakened under the debilitating sun. Then, while the others collapsed in their bunks exhausted, an illicit AWOL from barracks for an evening's pleasure at the local brothel. He had enjoyed three journeys inside Camilla, the hundred and ten kilo darling of the establishment, noted not only for her size but for the profusion of hairs on her breasts, up her belly and down the inside of her thighs.

Perhaps it was that that had put him off his guard, made him less careful than usual. After all, a French army uniform in the seedy quarter of Constantine in the spring of 1958 was inviting trouble.

It was in the darkest part of the darkest alley where the Arab, a member of the FLN [*Front de Libération Nationale*], struck him from behind. The blow would have broken the skull of a normal man but, although he was sent sprawling to the ground, Mesrine's hair was not even ruffled.

The Arab swiped downwards with the knife. Mesrine scuffled back on his rear. *Merde alors, Jacques, you let yourself in for this one...*

Expelled from the Oratory School, Juilly, in 1951.

Expelled from the Lycée Chaptal, Paris, in 1953.

Asked to leave technical school in 1955. Troublemaker, they said, ringleader of the bully boys. Ha! He wanted to see life. He wanted adventure, excitement. If everyone else wanted to sit behind a desk reading boring books or being lectured at all day, that was fine, each to his own. But not him, not Jacques Mesrine...

Mesrine lashed out with his right foot but it was deflected by the Arab.

Married Lydia. Ah, ma belle Lydia, big and black from Martinique - and already one month pregnant with another man's child when he met her. But Lord, how she could love...!

Mesrine leapt to his feet, avoiding another stab from the blade and punching the Arab in the right eye.

Then the staleness setting in, the drunken evenings with Lydia in the Latin Quarter. Evenings which always ended in a blazing row. Then making-up, then visiting heaven in that exquisite ebony body...

The Arab staggered and Mesrine broke his hooked nose with one expert chop, following up with a kick to the groin. The Arab gasped and dropped the knife, clutching his balls.

Her jealousy, her laziness. Expecting him, him Jacques Mesrine, to earn money to keep her. She even gave up her university course. The baby was born. How he hated it, it was not even his, the half-black little bastard...

Mesrine swooped down for the weapon, but as he went to rise the Arab leant forward and butted the back of his head.

Mercifully call-up. Quick divorce. Army life...

Mesrine sank to his knees, groping again for the knife. It was gone. He looked up as it came spearing towards his throat. This is it, Jacques. The end -

The Arab's hand exploded.

Literally, when it was only centimetres away from his face, it blew up, blood and shards of bone splattering over Mesrine's head and into his mouth. Only then did he hear the report of the gun.

A scream from the Arab as the Frenchman chopped his legs away, kneed him twice on the nose and then stood up, his hobnailed right boot pushing hard across the man's throat.

The Arab gurgled. The stump of his shattered hand pounded uselessly on the ground as his good hand clawed in vain at the Frenchman's leg. His feet flailed in the dust.

Mesrine stood victorious, hands on hips, confident, tough face beaming. He spat out pieces of the other man's bone, wiped his mouth and looked around.

The alley was dark, deserted and noiseless. He could see or hear no one. The shot had obviously driven any observers away or indoors. *No comprendi effendi*, hear nothing, see nothing, say nothing, slit your throat for a *sou*.

A little way back, a dim lamp hanging on the wall creaked in a sudden breeze.

Mesrine looked. Nothing. If there was anyone there they were hidden in the darkness beyond. He chuckled and spoke without raising his voice. "M'sieur, whoever you are, wherever you are, I like your style. That was an amazing and efficient piece of shooting." He looked down at the Arab still clawing uselessly at the boot that was slowly crushing his windpipe. "And you saved my life. I, Jacques Mesrine, will not forget that. May I have the pleasure of knowing to whom I am indebted?"

Silence. Did something move in the shadows?

"I feel like a gladiator," Mesrine was now playing to the audience he knew was there. "You are my Emperor. What shall I do with this shit melon beneath my foot? Does it live or does it die? You threw me the lifeline, you must decide the fate of the vanquished."

This time there was a definite movement. A shadow appeared, but Mesrine could not make out any distinct features. There was just a dark silhouette in front of the wall lamp.

Mesrine gave a half bow. "*Ah! Bonsoir m'sieur, ça va?* Of whom do I have the pleasure?"

There was silence. Then a voice said, "Richer."

He was French and he appeared to be in uniform. Rank? Couldn't see. A conscript like himself?

"Monsieur Richer?"

"Captain Richer."

"Ah." Mesrine nodded. "*Alors, Capitaine.* What is your answer?" A dry wheeze ruckled from beneath his foot as he applied more pressure on the Arab's windpipe.

The figure in the shadows remained still. The voice said, "You are a Frenchman, he is an Arab."

"Yes...?"

"That is your answer."

Mesrine smiled. Slowly he took his foot from his assailant's throat. The Arab looked up in disbelieving relief. He did not even have time to cough once before the heel of Mesrine's boot smashed back down again, instantly breaking his neck with as much concern as a child treading on an ant.

The death was instantaneous but the limbs still twitched for a full thirty seconds afterwards.

"You should be careful, my friend," said Richer from down the alley. "You have been very lucky."

Mesrine looked up from the now still body and wiped more of the dead man's blood from his face with the back of his hand. "Very lucky?"

"Lucky that there was only one of them, they usually hunt in packs."

"Like the animals they are."

"Lucky because you should not even be out, you should be in barracks."

"Pah! Rules, regulations. Why waste a night? We are not prisoners, we are not in jail. We are French soldiers on French soil." He held himself erect.

"You were lucky for another reason."

"What was that?"

"Look in his robes."

Cautiously he bent over. He came back up with a .45 automatic in his hand.

He concealed his surprise carefully. "Hah! He probably didn't know how to use it. These *fellaghas* never do."

"Maybe. Maybe not." The figure moved back into the shadows, out of sight. Mesrine just caught a glimpse of a tall, fair man in uniform as he passed beneath the light, then he could see nothing.

"Hey, Captain Richer!"

"You seem to like danger, Mesrine," came the voice from the dark. "You are not frightened of it, hmm?"

"Me? Frightened?" Mesrine guffawed. "Jacques Mesrine is frightened of nothing."

"You would be interested in getting involved in something a bit different, perhaps? Something dangerous?"

Mesrine smiled. "What did you have in mind, *mon ami?*"

"At the moment, nothing. But we may have a use for you in the future."

"We...?"

The question floated unanswered into the air and was carried away on the night breeze. The silence of the night had descended again.

"Captain? Captain! Are you there?"

Silence. No one, just Mesrine and the corpse. Time, reflected the Frenchman, to make himself scarce. He turned to go.

"Just one more thing," came Richer's voice, but from further away, almost distant. "You had one final piece of luck."

"Really, *Capitaine*, and what was that?"

"I saw the Arab was about to kill you. I thought you would rather die at French hands than at a melon's. I was not aiming at his hand, I was aiming at your head."

France 1958 - 1960

Mesrine left the army as a fully-trained soldier, an adept combat machine, expert both unarmed and with weaponry. He took with him the Military Cross for Valour, the Commemorative Medal for Operations for the Maintenance of Order - and a certificate of good conduct.

But life in civvy street did not come easy. Army life with its tough physical demands had fitted Mesrine like a glove. Back in the real world, the job his father had lined up for him (a travelling salesman for a lace manufacturer) grated and rubbed like a too-tight shoe.

But he always had his gun, the one he had taken from the dead Arab that night in Constantine. Each night in the privacy of his room in his parents' home in Clichy, Paris, he would dismantle the weapon, clean it, oil it and put it back together again. It made him feel good.

There were women, plenty of them, but nothing permanent, nothing more than the casual lay. He had one marriage behind him and was determined not to make the same mistake again.

Money was transient. It came on pay day and went on wine, women, food and gambling.

He began to meet people he had met in the army, some of the more undesirable conscripts, people to whom crime was a way of life.

Jacques was restless, unsettled... and depressed. Normality was not the life for him, not Jacques Mesrine. He did not always want to have to scrape to make ends meet. He was not like the others, the professional poor of Paris who would not know what to do with one thousand francs if they had it. He did not want to order *vin ordinaire* when *Château Rothschild* was his to be had. If only he had one thing: more money.

He began quarrelling with his mother. God help it, he didn't want to, it wasn't her fault, but he couldn't help himself, she was just getting on his nerves. Her scolding, her chiding, "You are a grown man. What are you going to do with yourself?" Followed by the contradiction of her constant concern, "I love you, you are my son. I want the best for you. You must do something with your life."

Inevitably it got too much. Soon he left home with only the clothes he stood up in, and his gun. He stayed with his army 'friends', and to pay for his keep helped them out with little 'odd jobs'.

He found the little odd jobs easy, almost boring – and, frankly, the beating of a shopkeeper for being late with his 'insurance' payments was not his style (although a unilateral helping of a handful of cash from the till for himself helped ease his *ennui*). But this work did have potential. If he was allowed to do it *his* way, if he was to work for himself, this could be his future. This could feed his craving for adventure, give him that adrenalin rush, pay for the good things of life - and satisfy his demand for *style*.

And it was style that formed the backdrop to his first crime, as it would every crime he ever committed - a breaking and entering, in broad daylight, carrying a huge bunch of flowers. Whilst it could be argued that such an approach, rather than the usual stealth in the darkness, would be a perfect disguise, it was also true that anyone noticing the big, burly man with the big flowers would not fail to remember him...

Europe 1960 - 1978

The crisis in France began around 1960 when relations between the de Gaulle government and the army deteriorated.

Algérie Française, said the army - and they had hoped that the supposedly supreme patriot Charles de Gaulle would support them. But after echoing the cry, he reneged. He wanted a 'political solution' to the Algerian problem, and everyone knew what that meant. As always, for 'political solution' read 'sell out'. A negotiated independence was mooted.

Many members of the army considered de Gaulle a traitor. They did not want independence for Algeria, not at any price. They would fight to keep Algeria French. Together with the French settlers in Algeria, they formed the OAS *[Organisation Armée Secrète]*. It was headed by General Raoul Salan.

Inevitably with his army and criminal background, Mesrine was recruited. Little is known about his OAS activities, but it is thought that the Organisation sent their prized, brave, skilful, flamboyant recruit back to Algeria to fight in Degueldre's notorious Delta Commandos. He might also have been involved in the standard OAS activity of demanding money with menaces from known right-wing sympathisers in France.

What is known is that in the autumn of 1961, in the still hours of the night, Mesrine climbed one of the towers of Notre Dame Cathedral in Paris and hoisted the OAS flag. A daring and courageous feat in itself, made even more outrageous when one realises, of course, that Notre Dame is just two hundred metres opposite, and facing square on to, the *Préfecture* - police headquarters. *Encore le style Mesrine!*

Through his army experiences, both legitimate and secret, Mesrine had learnt everything there was to know about weaponry and things subversive. The OAS had within its web some of the best criminals, smugglers and craftsmen of things illegal, not only in France but in the whole of Europe and beyond.

Again women came and went in Mesrine's life. Another marriage, for five years to the beautiful latin Soledad who gave him an equally beautiful daughter, followed by a succession of girlfriends, usually innocents dragged into Mesrine's criminal circles and, once there, captivated by the man.

Mesrine tried on several occasions to go straight, but one of the requisites to leading a normal life is that you must be at least part way normal yourself. Jacques Mesrine was never normal, indeed he would have scoffed at the suggestion. He was *special*. He knew it, the police knew it and, by the end, nearly the whole world knew it. Going straight would not give the lifestyle this special man required. Crime was the only job that not only paid well but also gave Mesrine his regular fix of the only drugs he ever needed:

excitement, danger, adventure.

In March 1962 Mesrine was arrested for burglary. Eighteen months later he was released from Orléans jail. Through the next sixteen years his crimes were to become the talk of Europe. The kidnappings, the burglaries and especially the bank robberies, all carried out with the Mesrine flair, the Mesrine panache, the Mesrine style. Such as stopping to chat with a cashier of a bank he had just robbed whilst the hysterical alarm bells deafened all around him, then a casual stroll outside, turning his reversible jacket inside out, producing a hat, perhaps walking with a limp, certainly altering his expression and posture to look twenty years older, and mixing with the ever-growing crowd looking to see where the din was coming from. Even, it is said, some minutes later approaching the policeman now guarding the doors to the bank to ask him what was happening. Of such stuff, which would not be tolerated in a work of fiction, was the real-life Jacques Mesrine.

It is not the purpose of this book to detail the life and times of Jacques Mesrine. That has been brilliantly done by others, including Mesrine himself in his autobiography *L'Instinct de Mort [Editions Jean-Claude Lattes 1977]* and Carey Schofield in *Mesrine - The Life and Death of a Supercrook [Penguin 1980]*. Some questions which remain unanswered to this day – such as the ease with which Mesrine obtained official identity documents, his smooth escape from jail on 8 May 1978, and the fact that some areas of public authority appeared not to want him recaptured in 1979 – might be answered herein.

Suffice it to say that by 1978 Mesrine genuinely merited the often misused expression 'notorious'. Secretly admired by the public, openly loathed by the police and the Establishment of whom he constantly made fools, Mesrine was truly France's Public Enemy Number One...

Majorque, les îles Baléares 1965

In view of the story that follows, one other incident in Mesrine's career must be mentioned.

On 2 December 1965, Mesrine broke into the residence of the Governor in Palma, Majorca. He was arrested therein. He had entered the house to steal a document, concerning what and for whom he was never to reveal, which was unusual for the great self-publicist. Perhaps it was something to do with the OAS, perhaps it was not.

When questioned by the Spanish *Guardia Civile* he claimed he was just a simple thief. The *Guardia* suggested that he was an agent of the French government. Mesrine fell into paroxysms of laughter. He was seen by the

French Ambassador, brought to court, given a six months suspended sentence and then deported to Paris.

But despite Mesrine's laughter, he never did deny the suggestion made by the *Guardia*...

Subsequent to his breakout from prison on 8 May 1978, Mesrine committed many crimes, some of which are not even known to this day (and some have been attributed to him which he could not possibly have committed). In order for this account to be seen in the perspective of the time, many of the crimes have been reported herein as they happened.

Although the OAS was considered to have collapsed in the sixties with the arrest of General Raoul Salan and the banishment of his successor, Georges Biddault, in 1978 it was still alive in France. No longer an overt terrorist organisation, it had gained the respectability of age and familiarity, a brotherhood who considered themselves the only true Frenchmen. Its members belonged to every major profession, including the public services.

1^{IÈRE} PARTIE

‡

L'ENLÈVEMENT

‡

1. Voleurs

Au cours de l'hiver passé

At 02:00 in the morning the streets of the 16th Arrondisement in Paris are still and almost deserted. Occasionally a taxi might cruise past carrying home a resident of this most exclusive quarter of the French capital. Here and there a solitary figure may be walking, having missed the last metro. Once or twice a week revelry may be heard from within one or other of the fashionable residences, an all-night party which the givers could not afford but had to hold for appearances' sake: for even in this day and age, appearances among the super, nouveau or manqué rich were everything.

That night a lone figure hurried nervously down the wide Avenue Henri Martin. He was self-conscious, aware, for he knew that this area of Paris was not a place for a 190 centimetre, 125 kilo black man. He looked up at the occasional still-lit windows and bared his teeth, embracing all the residents of the *quartier* with that one sneer of hate. He was a man with a mission: he was going to collect his pension.

Thirty years he had worked for them. *Thirty years!*

He had been their darling, their pet nigger, picked up in the Caribbean during the 40's and brought back to Europe, their butler-cum-handyman-cum-bodyguard. He had served them well. And, he had to admit, they had served him well: good food, good clothes, good accommodation for half a lifetime. Not so good wages, but they were noted for their parsimony.

The boss, 'The Little Man' as lady-boss sometimes referred to him, had died six years ago. But 'Peaches', lady-boss, had kept him on even though the cost of upkeep of the rented house grew year by year. He saw his fellow servants 'let go' one by one until only a minimum had been retained.

Then it had happened. At the beginning of this year. He had heard word that his only brother was dying in Florida. Politely, he had asked lady-boss for time off to go and see him. Her reaction had been to dismiss him summarily. Not even a reprimand, not even a chance to retract his request. *Out.*

Okay, so she was old and frail, half the time *non compos mentis*, living in the past, the Europe of the late 40's and 50's. But that did not excuse her. She had had three facelifts that had tightened her throat so much that she could swallow nothing exceeding one centimetre in width. A hairdresser came in every day to paint over any grey hair that might show, lest she wake (some days she did not), look in a mirror and have a raving fit.

He could allow her her tetchiness, her meanness, her lapses of memory ("Who are you, nigger? Get away from me, get away! I'll call my husband!"), but to be sacked after thirty years with no pension, no severance pay, nothing, was not on ("Be grateful I'm letting you keep the livery you're wearing. Now get out of my sight.").

Okay, so he had been lucky and had found immediate employment on the staff of a diplomat up in Neuilly, but that did not assuage the wrong that had been done. Tonight he would have his pension.

And how would he have it? He touched the bump in his pocket. By the simple expediency of the keys. One by one she had picked off her staff until now she had only one secretary, three contract cleaners and two caterers, and six nurses (two at a time on a 24 hour basis). As each employee had gone, he had retrieved their keys. In the end, the old woman had more keys than staff. When he went he had handed his in - but nobody had asked him for the collection of spares. He had a key to every lock in the house.

Not for him a breaking and entering. He would enter through the door he always used to use, round the side. There were three mortice locks on it but no bolt. From there it was a simple walk up to the old lady's bedroom and the single key safe (no dial or combination) where his pension lay.

He reached the Place de Colombie. Over at the Porte de la Muette, leading into the Bois de Boulogne, a man was propositioning a tart dressed as a nun. Her skirts were open, revealing the goods, and a wad of money changed hands.

As he headed south on the Boulevard Suchet, it began to spit with rain. The house he wanted was on the south-eastern corner of the junction of the Boulevard and the Square des Écrivains Combattants mort pour la France. Number 24...

It was dark, but the night entering from the unshuttered window gave a diffused greyness to the regal ornateness of the bedroom.

The old lady lay flat on her back in the centre of the wide double-bed, painted hair spread out roughly on the bolster, mouth hanging open. Her throat was too tight to permit any snoring. She looked dead, only the slow rise and fall of her chest showed that life was still present. She looked like a queen lying in state – something history had decreed she would never be.

The safe was free-standing against the wall opposite the bed. It opened with a click which reverberated around the large, ornate room. He froze, slowly turning his head.

She did not move.

Carefully he pulled the door open, praying it would not creak.

He shone his pocket torch inside and smiled at his pension. Resting the torch on a bundle of letters tied with pink ribbon, he began to empty the jewellery boxes, fondling each expensive piece in his black-gloved hands as he put them into his pockets.

He did not hear anything, but when he was halfway through he turned and looked back at the bed. He got the shock of his life.

The old woman was sitting up, staring straight at him.

Could she see him? He remained still, but his hands began to shake and he almost dropped a diamond-encrusted gold lizard.

In the dimness he could see her lips moving, and then the voice spoke, croaky but almost girlish in manner. "David? David, is that you?"

He was confused. Could she see? Should he keep quiet, pretend there was no one there?

"David?"

He spoke in a whisper, but he could not disguise the Caribbean accent. "Yes... P-Peaches?"

"What are you doing, you naughty boy? At the bar again? Well, pour me a vodka while you're there, then come to bed, I'm cold."

"Y-yes, P-Peaches."

"What have you been up to, my little man? Out with that floosie again? Little tramp! You know what the doctor said last time. Put on the light and tell me all about her. I'm awake now."

She sank back on the bolster.

He did not move. After half a minute he said, "Peaches?"

There was no response.

"Peaches?"

Her chest rose and fell. She was asleep again.

Holy Mother of God! He grabbed the torch, picking up some tied letters with it, and swiftly but silently closed the safe door.

By the time he was back out in the street, he was perspiring freely, despite the chill of the early morning. A-*men* to that! Still, he had his pension and plenty of it. But can you believe that old woman! If she had not gone back to sleep, what would he have done? The thought that he might have had to get into bed with her did not bear thinking about. The paparazzi would have had fun with that had they been around, but even they had deserted her in the twilight of her life.

He turned left into the Square and walked quickly into the Bois, resisting the urge to run.

It was the last mistake he ever made.

The Bois de Boulogne runs down the entire south-western side of Paris. During the day it is a huge, welcoming, attractive park with something for everybody, from duck ponds and playgrounds for children, through cycle and horse riding, to the race courses of Longchamp and Auteuil. It is always heavily populated, especially at weekends when Parisians descend *en famille*. But even the most novice of tourists knows not to frequent the park at night. Come dusk, every element of Parisian low life crawls out of the woodwork, and you do not go there. Unless, of course, you are after vice in any form, in any position, with any animal from human to aquatic, and are willing to pay for it - in which case it is the place for you.

He should have known that. He *did* know that, so the fact that he went there is even more inexplicable.

He still held the torch and letters in his hand as he crossed the Avenue du Maréchal Maunoury and scurried through the line of trees. The threatened rain had not materialised, but nevertheless it was damp under foot...

They picked him up as he reached the Allée des Fortifications and began to walk north. There were two of them, blatantly homosexual, one tough and aggressive, the other a bitch-queen. They followed the big, black hunk across the appropriately-named Allée des Dames and made their move as he walked along the edge of the Lac Inférieur.

He was aware of nothing until something grabbed his crotch in the darkness. "*Bonsoir, petite,*" said an effeminate voice. "Who's a big boy then?"

"What the - ?"

He felt his genitals being pulled savagely downwards and he had no alternative but to sink to his knees. As he went down, something hit him in the neck.

He drew his left arm back to hit out but stopped as he felt something wet on his chest. He dropped the torch and letters and raised both hands. Something was spraying. *God, was he being pissed on?*

He was not, and as his head flopped the last realisation he had before he fell was that his throat had been cut.

The one with the knife wiped it on the victim's suit as his mate complained. "It was too quick, idiot! You hit the jugular. He's sprayed all over me!" He knelt down and began feeling the pockets, the body still twitching underneath him.

"I'll spray all over you later, sweetie, that's a promise." The one with the knife stood up. "What's he got?"

"A big one."

"Bitch. Find his wallet."

While one searched, the other picked up the torch and letters.

The one kneeling down gasped. "My God, look!" He held up a diamond necklace, glittering even in the faint light from way down the road.

The other stopped undoing the ribbon on the letters and grabbed the necklace.

"Is it real?"

"How the hell do I know? Has he got anything else?"

The rest of the jewellery was removed, two double handfuls in all.

"Je-SUS! We've hit it here, LouLou. If this stuff is real, we're rich bitches!"

"What've you got there?"

"Just his torch and some old papers, nothing. C'mon, let's get out of here. Chances are this stuff is hot, and now we've got it it's hotter still. We've gotta get rid of it and quick."

"What about him?"

"In the lake, he'll never be found. Give me a hand."

"But he's all messed up."

"You're usually not so fussy, sweetie. Come *on*."

It was an effort. In death the black man seemed to weigh a ton. But eventually the body slipped into the water with barely a splash.

They left the Bois at the Porte de la Muette. Under a street lamp, the girl dressed as a nun exposed herself to them until she realised they would have no interest in her.

They shuffled across the Place. As they took a right into Rue de Franqueville, LouLou's chum dropped the bundle of letters. He turned to retrieve them.

"Leave them, Butch," urged LouLou. "Come *on!*"

"Okay, okay," Butch grabbed the bundle. "You never know, there might be something here. If not, I'll chuck them later. And take your jacket off, there's blood all over it."

"What? Oh fuck, another job for the dry cleaners! I suppose red makes a change from white!"

Holding hands, they hurried off.

‡

2. Flics

Mercredi 12 Avril

To call 11 Rue des Saussaies in Paris a turn-of-the-century apartment building would be wrong, although it looks like it and once was. To call it a police station would be wrong, although in effect it is. To call it simply a government building would be wrong, although it could be argued that it is. In fact, the whole of the north side of the Rue des Saussaies is part of the Interior Ministry, each building inter-connecting and in turn joined to the Ministry's *hôtel particulier* (main building) in the Place Beauvau at the southern end of the street. The building that is number 11 is the headquarters of the Sûreté Nationale.

Although staffed by police, the Sûreté Nationale is an administrative unit which at that time controlled the five divisions of France's national crime force: the *Police Judiciaire* (PJ), *Renseignments Généraux* (RG), the *Bureau de Sécurité Publique* (BSP), the *Corps Républicain de Sécurité* (CRS) and the *Direction de la Surveillance du Territoire* (DST). The head of the Sûreté is the Director-General.

As well as the administrative unit, there was one other branch in the Rue des Saussaies. A relatively new section, born just at the end of the presidency of Georges Pompidou, it was known as the *Bureau de la Coopération Politique* (BCP). It was responsible for the protection of, liaison with, and the general comfort and happiness of all foreign government interests in France, primarily the embassies and the consulates and also the various Important Foreign Citizens granted residential status (either short or long term depending on their political ambitions). The BCP was a small section, officially coming under the DST but in fact independent, reporting directly to the Minister, by-passing even the Director-General.

The BCP was the only section in the whole of the Saussaies complex to have detectives on its staff. Even these, it was argued by the five 'proper' divisions of the Sûreté, were simply glorified public relations men with guns. (There is never any love lost between the police units of France.)

Chief Inspector Paul Richer walked down Rue du Surène, crossed Saussaies and walked through the iron gates of number 11, passing the public entrance on the right. At that same time, Commissaire Charles Fleury-

Goujon closed one of the tall wooden doors of the office of the Minister of the Interior in the main building and walked less than enthusiastically back down the maze of corridors that led through to the Saussaies building.

The Commissaire sighed and hefted the file under his right arm, a treatise on the curious sexual proclivities of a certain senior Italian civil servant at the embassy. The Minister had not been interested, "I leave it to you, Charles." Instead he had wanted to talk about the phone call he had received that morning from a certain house in the Bois de Boulogne.

Fleury-Goujon listened to what the Minister had to say and wondered why on earth it should concern a Commissaire of Police let alone a Minister of State. It was a simple theft, and even if the articles were valuable she could afford it. But, as on several occasions in the past, when *Le Bois* barked Saussaies or des Orfèvres (or sometimes even The Elysée) jumped.

"Take care of it, Charles," the Minister had instructed. "Personally if you are able. If not, assign your top man. I want this cleared up, quickly and quietly. And with no publicity. She doesn't often kick up a fuss nowadays, so when she does we must accommodate her."

Chief Inspector Paul Richer entered the elevator and jabbed the button for the sixth floor. Something, he had decided, must be done. He did not like working in a school playground.

It was all the fault of that bastard Claude Gerard. Ever since Richer had joined the section on promotion three months ago, Gerard had made his life hell. They had started off on the wrong foot, Gerard lambasting and Richer strenuously defending Richer's previous section, the CRS anti-riot squads. And they had been at loggerheads ever since. Gerard, also a Chief Inspector, had carefully contrived to leave the messy assignments to Richer, either deliberately not being around when a particularly sticky case was looming, or feigning overwork to the Commissaire at the daily briefing.

After the initial contretemps, Richer and Gerard had hardly spoken to each other, except on official necessity, a supreme example of the testy sulkiness of middle-aged men.

Two days ago had come the last straw. Richer had been in the lavatory, trousers down, when he had heard two others enter. One was Gerard, he could tell instantly, and the other was young Inspector Bauer. They were laughing as they entered.

"Bent as a six franc note," Gerard was saying. "Must be."

"*Mais Monsieur l'Inspecteur - !*"

"Consider." There was a double zzzz followed by faint splashing. One of them farted. "Mid forties, unmarried, lives alone *and* in Montmartre. I ask you! Never mentions any women friends."

"Well, he has never troubled me."

"Pray he doesn't."

"He seems to be a very fair chief."

"At a work level. But keep him at arm's length, Victor, do you hear? Or is a promotion worth a prick up the rear?"

"I will keep your advice in mind, Inspector."

"It's not your mind you have to worry about, son."

Richer had gritted his teeth and ignored Gerard when he returned to their shared office. For an instant he considered taking Gerard outside and teaching the fat, lazy slob a lesson he would never forget. So, he had never married. That did not mean he did not enjoy women, many and various, even *les girls* of the Rue St Denis or Pigalle whom he frequented whenever he felt lonely. Who wanted to be married with a nagging wife and five kids like that *con* Gerard?

But violence would achieve nothing. Gerard was the senior man, and whatever justification there might be, whatever extreme provocation, as in all government departments throughout the world seniority would decide the victor.

But it had got to the stage now, after three months, when something had to be done.

Richer had just put paper in the typewriter when the Commissaire poked his head round the door. "Morning Paul, Claude in?"

"Morning Commissaire. He's not on till this afternoon. Could I see you for a - "

"*Merde*. Paul, come in will you?"

Richer sat opposite the Commissaire, the window looking out onto the Rue des Saussaies behind the chief's left shoulder.

"Something urgent has come up, from ministerial level. Cigarette?" The Commissioner indicated a silver box on his desk.

"*Merci*." Richer shook his head.

"Usually I would give the case to Claude, he handles these problems," the Commissaire blew smoke out between pursed lips. "But as he is not here and the Minister has stressed the urgency... well, it will be something for you to cut your teeth on."

Richer nodded dutifully. "Actually sir, I wanted to discuss - "

"You may have heard Claude talk about our resident in the Bois de Boulogne, *oui*? He has successfully handled matters there in the past."

"You mean La Dame?"

"*Naturellement*. Well, there's been a hue and cry on. Some sort of robbery. At least, things have gone missing. Only just discovered. Possibly a break-in."

"Light fingered staff?"

"Not likely, she has so few. But you will check, of course."

"No other information?"

The Commissaire shrugged and spread out his hands. *"Non.* One hopes she is not wasting our time, it has been known. She might have put whatever it is that's gone missing into another drawer."

"Je comprends."

"As quickly as possible, Paul. This very morning. Drop whatever you've got on, leave it for Claude. I'll have a word with him when he comes in."

"He's not going to like it. She's his lady."

"Too bad. La Dame cannot suit her domestic distress to his hours. Let me know tonight how you get on. The Minister will probably be content just to have her off his hands, but you never know. Bonnet is noted for picking on the most innocuous of things and blowing them up into a proportion they do not deserve."

Richer rose.

"And Paul?"

"Sir?"

"I needn't stress the need for the utmost tact and diplomacy. Humour her if you must. And above all keep it quiet. You do speak her language, I recall?"

"Rusty, but yes sir."

"Bon. Now, you wanted to see me about something?"

The Commissaire did not notice the briefest of pauses before Richer replied, "No sir."

"Alors, I'll see you this evening."

"D'accord, monsieur le Commissaire."

When the portly, balding Chief Inspector Claude Gerard came on duty that afternoon he was, predictably, less than pleased that the upstart Richer was trespassing on his territory. La Dame and her problems always fell to him, not to some bungling novice who wouldn't know how to handle her.

Nevertheless, he put on his bravest, most ingratiating face when the Commissaire casually mentioned it *en passant,* and he agreed that the experience would do Richer good.

Back in the privacy of the office, he kicked over a waste bin in petulant disgust and sulked for the whole afternoon.

‡

3. Flic et Victime

Richer walked east along Rue du Ranelagh. It was an overcast day and, to be on the safe side, he had put on an open fawn raincoat above his brown suit.

A train thundered overhead as he passed under the railway bridge. He crossed diagonally across the grand Avenue Ingres and turned right into the Boulevard Suchet. He was surprised to see that the Louis XVI-style *grand maison* on the corner had no driveway to separate it from the road. The front door was right there, accessible to all. He would have expected some form of security, or at least some privacy from prying eyes. He looked up as he pressed the bell next to the large, black wooden door. No cameras.

After an age he was ushered inside by a smooth, well-outfitted gentleman who announced himself to be madame's secretary. Madame's hairdresser was with her. Monsieur l'Inspecteur would wait?

Richer looked around the large foyer. La Dame had always been noted for her sense of design and decoration, and it had not left her even in her later years (he hesitated at even thinking the word 'dotage'). The place was plush and tasteful. Above his head a chandelier tinkled.

Some minutes later a thin, wiry Italian bounded down the stairs, case under arm, and let himself out. The secretary appeared and indicated that Richer should ascend and follow.

As the secretary knocked on the bedroom door and opened it, he said quietly "Please do not take too long."

The lady looked younger than her 82 years. Propped up in bed by pillows too numerous to count, her hair was jet black, dropping down to touch her black housecoat. Her face was heavily but expertly made-up. She stared at Richer as the door was closed behind him.

She held out her right hand, but it dropped back before Richer could reach it. "Monsieur Gerard, how nice of you to come." Her voice was high, speaking in her original language, still with a trace of American accent.

"Madame - "

"It is such a long time since we've seen you - "

"I - "

" - but you have not changed. Do sit down." She indicated a space near the foot of the bed. There was no chair.

Richer stood in the space allocated. "You called the Minister, madame?"

"Yes. How are your wife and children?"

"Fine. Fine, thank you."

"Good. I would so loved to have had lots of children myself, but it was not to be." Her eyes clouded over at her memories.

Richer fidgeted. *Christ.*

She came back into the present. "Well, what can I do for you, monsieur?"

"The Minister?"

"Oh yes, how is he?"

"You rang, madame. Something has gone missing."

"Ah." She sat forward, a tangible change descending on her, another spirit entering the body. "Yes indeed. In fact Robert - my secretary, you met him - phoned you. I discovered the loss yesterday evening. Or was it the day before? Anyway, the long and short of it is, someone's been at my safe."

"A burglary?"

"Must have been."

"Without you knowing?"

A sheepish expression passed over her face. "I sleep a lot, you know."

"You keep this door locked?"

"No, my servants come in and out."

Richer sensed that he had to keep the questions coming before he lost her. "Are there any - how do you say? - signs of a break-in?"

"You will have to check with Robert, I don't think there was any trace of breaking and entering."

"I noticed you have no cameras. Do you have alarms?"

" Alarms? I think we used to have them..."

"Madame, what has gone missing?"

"Missing...? Has something gone missing...?" Momentarily she looked bewildered. "Oh, yes. Jewellery. Two diamond necklaces, a gold watch and - what was it? Three gold bracelets set with diamonds. And my lizard."

Her *lézard?*

"What is their value?"

"Value? Heaven alone knows. That doesn't worry me, they're of sentimental value, presents from my husband. The two necklaces were handed down from his great grandmother."

Richer raised an eyebrow. Her husband's great grandmother? That was easy to work out. And that would make the necklaces alone priceless.

La Dame moved a weak hand to indicate the bedside table. "Pour me a drink, there's a good boy."

Richer poured what looked like water from a jug. It was vodka.

"Thank you." She wetted her lips with the liquid, hand shaking. "How are your wife and children, Monsieur Gerard?"

"Was anything else taken, madame?"

"What?"

"Taken. From your safe. Anything else besides the jewellery?"

"My God, yes." A dribble of liquid ran unnoticed down her chin. "For goodness sake sit down monsieur, I can't keep looking up at you, it will strain my neck."

Richer made a pretence of looking around for a chair, and remained standing.

"Some documents," continued the lady. "Mostly letters from David, my husband. You know him, of course."

"*Naturellement, madame.* They were of value, these letters and documents?"

"To me, yes. But there was a document which, if it was made public, would give the game away. And we can't have that, can we? Not after all these years. Not when everything has become normal again."

He frowned. "Game, madame?"

"That's why I called you in, Monsieur Gerard. The jewellery is precious. But I can do without it. But the document... It has an importance greater than you could possibly imagine. You must find it. It *must* be returned!"

Shakily she drained her glass. Quickly Richer refilled it. Taking a tissue from a box on the bedside table, he leant forward and wiped her chin. She did not seem to notice – or perhaps she was simply used to people tending to her.

She looked quite frightened. "My family have never known. David's sister-in-law knows the secret, the rest of his side are dead. No one else must know."

"Madame," said Richer gently, placing the tissue back next to the jug. "What is it? What is this game that must not be given away, this secret? What is this document?"

Her eyes were clear, all faculties intact. "I shall tell you..."

Halfway through her story, Paul Richer involuntarily sat down on the edge of her bed. It was either that or fall down. He could not believe what he was hearing, but he was convinced it was true. At that moment she was completely in control, lucid and cogent. Perfectly sane.

At the end he sat there stunned, unable to say a word. What *could* he say...? One thing was certain: the document must be found, whatever it took, whatever had to be done.

Its value was incalculable.

After a while Richer realised where he was and on whose bed he was sitting.

He leapt to his feet but offered no apologies.

"*Madame, qu'est-ce qu'on peut...?*" His voice was hoarse as he lapsed into his native tongue. "What can one say?"

La Dame squinted her eyes as she stared up at him. "Nothing. Precisely nothing, monsieur. You are very privileged to have heard the story. Nobody else must know, especially not the Minister. There must be no police snooping around here. You may not ask my staff questions. No investigations whatsoever are to take place in this house."

"But madame - "

"You will do as I say." Her voice was sharp and nasty. "Do I make myself clear? Nothing is to happen that indicates in any way that anything has gone missing from this house."

"But the jewellery is priceless!"

"I don't care. The document is the only consideration. It must be found and in complete secrecy. Here - more."

She held out her glass.

Richer poured more vodka.

He looked at the lady. When she took the glass away from her lips, her face had changed. She smiled sweetly up at him. She asked in a little girly voice, "How is Madame Gerard and your children?"

‡

4. Flics

It was a serious and thoughtful Richer that returned to the Rue des Saussaies late that afternoon. He was in no mood for Chief Inspector Claude Gerard, who was gleefully awaiting him.

"Well, well, so the blue-eyed boy is back!"

"Stuff it, Gerard."

Gerard took his feet from the desk top and flicked ash from his Disque Bleu. "Have a nice time? Sort it out? Mountain out of a molehill as usual?" He frowned in momentary discomfort and then reached down with his left hand and pulled at his balls.

Richer stared at him.

"Did she give you tea and biscuits?"

Richer sat down, drawing a pen from his pocket and tap-tapping it on his notepad.

Gerard came round, shook his left leg and sat on the edge of his own desk. "Hope you didn't upset the old baggage, she needs careful handling at her age."

"Hmm."

"Tell you what, as a special favour to you, how about if I took it on? Hush hush, Fleury need never know. You'll get the credit."

Richer looked at him in silence, not caring if Gerard saw the contempt in his eyes. Then he asked, "Is the Commissaire in?"

"Think so. What about my offer?"

"He's given it to me. I'll have to see it through."

"What's it about? Her cat escaped again?"

"You could say that." Richer picked up the phone and tapped out three figures. He said to himself, "If *this* cat ever got out of the bag... Richer, sir. Is it convenient? *D'accord.*"

"Hey!" complained Gerard as the door closed. "Aren't you even going to tell me what it's about? She *is* my case, you know!" He stood with his hands on his hips, cigarette in his mouth, squinting as the smoke went into his eyes.

Bastard. Damn CRS bastard. Should stick to his riots, that's all he was good for. Well, we'll see about this...

"Everything all right?" Commissaire Fleury-Goujon looked up from the thick file in front of him as Richer entered.

"Yes, sir. Some jewellery missing, nothing much. She's not too worried. I think she just wanted someone to talk to."

The Commissaire humphed and sipped coffee, Arabica with cream. "As always. So I can leave it in your hands?"

"Absolutely."

"*Bon*. I'll tell the Minister we have it under control. Well done, Paul."

"Thank you, sir."

He saw Richer was not moving to go. "Was there anything else?"

After a moment, Richer nodded.

‡

5. Flic

Lundi 17 Avril

Five days later. A sunny but cool Parisian spring morning.

Richer left the headquarters of the Police Judiciaire at the Quai des Orfèvres, turned left and swore softly to himself. His final lead, his only lead, had just gone up in smoke.

Despite La Dame's instructions to the contrary, during the end of last week he had interviewed the small staff retained in Boulevard Suchet and had examined the place for any sign of a break-in, all unbeknownst to herself who stayed in her room, asleep for most of the time.

Having no date for the alleged robbery did not help, but he was convinced the staff knew nothing. The house was normal, no sign of forced entry.

Therefore the thief or thieves had keys, it was the only possible explanation. Therefore who had keys? It had not taken him long to learn of the dismissed black butler. Tracing him to the diplomat in Neuilly was easy.

But the suspect had disappeared nearly two months ago. Simply upped and left one night, leaving his few personal belongings behind. No note, not a word to anyone.

Richer had felt a nasty sensation in his stomach. If the man had *taken* his things, he would have been elated, and the case would have become a simple manhunt. As the man had *not* taken his things, it probably indicated that he had intended to return. Why then hadn't he?

Now the PJ had just confirmed that a black Jean Dubois had been fished out of the Lac Inférieur in the Bois de Boulogne three weeks ago in a state of ripe decomposition. No identification, indeed nothing at all, in his pockets. Cause of death? The autopsy report said basically that it appeared he had bled to death as a result of a knife wound – consistent with his throat being cut. As with all deaths in the Bois, it had minimal investigation and had been recorded as person unknown murdered by persons unknown.

Thank you PJ. Richer had not told them the reason for his enquiry, but he knew he would have to help them clear their books sooner or later. Make it later.

So, the black butler, peeved at being sacked, had returned to help himself to the old woman's jewellery and some letters. Why the letters? Did he have a market or was it just *en passant*? Richer would check into his background, but the chances were that the letters were just grabbed in the rush. It was the jewellery that he would be interested in.

On his way from his crime he had cut through the Bois de Boulogne - and met his death. The mugger had been mugged, the fear of every investigator, for it meant a short, sharp and often permanent halt to any enquiries. The lead had run out.

So, Richer knew what had been taken and he knew who had taken it. But he did not know who had it now. It could be anywhere.

As he crossed the Pont au Change a *Vedettes du Pont Neuf* pleasure boat passed underneath him, only half full with tourists.

The situation reminded him of one of the adventures of the supercriminal Jacques Mesrine. During a chase with the local gendarmerie somewhere in the north, Mesrine had stolen a car. It had been traced once it had been reported missing. But then Mesrine had ditched it and had stolen another vehicle - a vehicle that was already stolen. Obviously the first thief did not report the theft, so end of trail. Mesrine had got clear away.

Richer glanced over at the Tour St Jacques on his right as he headed towards the Rue de Rivoli.

So now what? The document was esoteric, and the chances were that anyone in the criminal underworld in possession of it would not know or understand what they had. Maybe it had simply been thrown away with the letters. But if it still existed it had to be found. Speed was not of the essence – the document had been around for a long time - but secrecy was.

Not only had La Dame insisted that he worked alone, but the information – the secret – she had imparted to him could not be told to anybody. La Dame was asking the impossible. She didn't need the police, she needed a private detective (but, of course, she would have to pay for that). She wanted someone with deeper underworld connections than any *flic* in the country, even those lucky few with their own supergrasses. Someone who could move where no *flic* could. Someone -

He stopped, staring back over at the Tour St Jacques. Fifty-two metres high, it was a tower without a church. A curious incongruity. Originally the belfry of St James-the-Butcher's, the church had gone in 1802 but the tower had survived.

An idea had occurred to him, linked to his previous thoughts. An idea so preposterous, so outrageous, so *impossible*...

An impossible person for an impossible task?

He was aware that people were looking at him, and he walked on. He turned right into the Rue de Rivoli and caught a bus 72 heading west.

‡

6. Flics

"Two hours!" moaned Chief Inspector Claude Gerard. "Two hours and all you've done is sit there with your diary open in front of you tapping your bloody pen."

"Do I annoy you?" Richer did not look up.

Gerard sat back, hands clasped in front of his protruding stomach. "You look like a man with problems."

"Nothing I can't handle."

"That's what Napoleon said on the eve of Waterloo."

"Hmm."

"What is it? La Dame?"

Richer did not reply.

"She's an awkward cow if you don't know how to handle her. Look," ash fell down Gerard's tie from the cigarette in the side of his mouth, "final offer, no strings attached: shall I take it on?"

Richer still did not reply.

"Hey!"

Richer looked up. "What?"

"I'm talking to you."

"Look, I've got work to do, do you mind?"

Gerard shrugged. "Up to you, sunshine."

Five minutes later Richer tidied his desk, locked the diary in the drawer, scribbled something on his notepad, ripped off the top sheet and went out of the office.

Gerard sighed irritably and lit another Disque. Then he frowned, got up and went over to Richer's desk. He picked up the notepad and stared at it closely. Then he snatched the blank top sheet off the pad, stuffed it into his pocket and hastily returned to his own desk.

‡

7. Flic et Voleur

Vendredi 21 Avril

In some ways Rue de la Santé, which forms the boundary between the 13th and 14th Arrondisements in southern Paris, is ironically named, almost with a sense of the macabre. *'Santé'* means 'health' and for sure the *Groupe Hospitalier Cochin* and the *Clinique Chirurgicale Péan* are situated at the northern end of the long street. However, just to the south, on the corner of the Boulevard Arago, is *Maison d'Arrêt de la Santé*, La Santé Prison, the most famous prison in France.

Said to be escape-proof, La Santé is the home of some of France's most notorious criminals. Only fitting then that in the spring of 1978, La Santé housed the most famous criminal in the whole of Europe: Jacques Mesrine.

Mesrine was at the beginning of a twenty year stretch for crimes ranging from murder to passing dud cheques (at the trial it had taken two days to read the list of charges against him). Even as he was being taken down at the end of his trial, Mesrine had vowed to escape from the inescapable La Santé, if it was humanly possible - and one of the several tenets Mesrine lived by was that everything was humanly possible, at least for him if not for mere mortals.

The prison authorities had taken his outpourings seriously and a special top-security wing had been built in which Mesrine now languished.

At 09:50 that morning, Mesrine was on his way to the exercise yard when he was intercepted by three warders. He was wanted in the interview room. Who was it? Who knows? Probably one of his many lawyers conducting his many appeals.

The interview room would have been better termed an interview cupboard. Two metres long by one and a half wide, it contained a small plank table which could be raised flat against the wall on hinges, and two chairs. Nothing else. A reinforced plate glass window looked out onto the corridor.

The plank table was down and a tall, fair man stood behind it.

Mesrine arrived, more like a king attending an audience than a convicted criminal. *"Merci mes amis,* I won't be needing you now," he grinned at his retinue of screws.

"Allez Jacques," retorted one, nodding at the room. *"Et ferme ton bec."*

Mesrine stopped as he entered, frowning at the man on the other side of the table. *"M'sieur?* Do I know you?"

Richer nodded to the guards. The heavy steel door was closed. One guard remained outside by the window, the others dispersed.

The two men stood facing one another, only the table between them. Richer pulled a full packet of *Gauloises* from his coat and threw them onto the table. He followed it with another package, similar in size but heavier.

Mesrine did not touch either. *"Naturellement, Monsieur Le Flic.* As if I did not know. Broussard send you?"

"Sit down, Jacques," Richer indicated the cigarettes. "Help yourself."

"Filthy habit," Mesrine took the packet as he sat down, opened it and threw one back at Richer. "But, like so many filthy habits, enjoyable. You have a light?"

Richer lit his own cigarette and swallowed smoke into his lungs. Then he took back Mesrine's cigarette and lit it from the tip of his own.

"A cautious man," observed Mesrine, taking a full centimetre off the *sèche* with one inhalation.

"With you, Jacques, always. Keep the packet."

"I was going to."

"And, if you don't mind..." Richer nodded at the other item.

Mesrine opened it. "A remarkably recent picture, Chief Inspector Paul Richer," he tapped the card. "Which tells me one of two things. Either your old photograph was out of date and needed replacing, or you are new to... to what?"

Richer accepted the wallet back. "Very good, Jacques, very good. Very perspicacious. Still as mentally agile as ever - "

"As *agile* as the *lapin*."

"I'm glad a couple of years in jail, with eighteen more still to come, has not weakened your faculties."

"Only the bromide does that."

Richer gave a rueful smile. He said, "So tell me, you are content to spend another eighteen years here, huh? You'll be - what? Nearly sixty when you come out."

"Inspector, Inspector," Mesrine's voice held the patience of one talking to a child. "I will not be here for another eighteen years. Not even for another eighteen months. I have told them all, even the Governor himself. There is not a gaol that can hold Jacques Mesrine."

"But no one has ever escaped from La Santé."

"There is not a gaol that can hold Jacques Mesrine."

"Hmm! Are you a little - forgive me for saying this - foolhardy for publicising your intentions?"

"Hah, everyone knows!" Mesrine pushed out his chest. "Some of my previous escapes from custody - "

"I know, I know. The Master of Invention, the Master of Disguise, *et cetera, et cetera.*"

"You mock?"

"As if I would! You - yes, even you – cannot escape from La Santé alone. You will need help."

Mesrine stubbed out the cigarette on the table top. Smoke drifted from his nose and mouth as he said, "Maybe. But, *Monsieur l'Inspecteur*, we are getting into the realms of name, rank and serial number. What do you want? I am a busy man."

Richer sat back. "What do you know about La Santé, Jacques? You've obviously done a lot of research, seeing as it's taken you two years already and you haven't escaped."

Mesrine chuckled. "What do you *want?*"

"Is this room clean?" Richer looked up at the ceiling. "No fleas? Swept every day?"

"Ha! You, monsieur, are a member of the Establishment. Don't give yourselves credit for more guile than you have. No, this room is not bugged."

"*Bon.*" He looked into Mesrine's dark, deep set eyes. "I want to help you escape."

Mesrine's face was expressionless. He looked at Richer coldly. For thirty seconds he did nothing. Then his brow creased in the slightest of frowns. He took another cigarette from the packet. He did not offer it up to be lit but instead he began rolling it between the fingers of his right hand, gangster-style. It seemed to take up all his attention.

Richer just looked at him.

After a while, Mesrine asked "Am I being set up?"

"No."

The cigarette moved back and forth, Mesrine staring at it.

"Am I being mocked?"

"No."

"I do not like being mocked. Makes me angry. Makes me want to kill."

"You are not being mocked."

With a flick of Mesrine's right thumb, the cigarette jumped from his right hand to his left. Immediately on landing it began rolling between the fingers.

"Then why?" He stopped moving the cigarette and looked up at Richer.

Richer kept his voice low. "I need a man with special talents."

"You have maybe one or two in the whole of the Sûreté."

"I need a man with *extra* special talents. Someone outside the police. Someone with contacts, someone with connections in the criminal world that a *flic* can only dream about."

"There are more criminals out there than there are in here."

"I need *you*."

"And no free lunch."

"*Comment?*"

"There is no such thing as a free lunch. For what do you need *me*, m'sieur?"

"To retrieve something."

"To retrieve something?" Mesrine looked bewildered. "Kidnapping, theft, robbery, even murder - those I can understand. But *retrieval?*"

"In return I will assist in whatever way I can, in whatever way you want me to, in your escape."

"And what makes you think I need help?"

Richer sighed. "Don't piss me around, Jacques. I too am a busy man. A damn sight more busier than you. I'm giving it to you straight."

Mesrine sat, eyes half closed. "And what," he asked at length, "is to stop you and a whole army of *flics* mowing me down in the road outside? How do I know this is not an Establishment plot to finish Mesrine once and for all? Why the hell should *I* trust *you*? What the hell *is* this? Monsieur, I think I have heard enough!" The chair scraped back as he stood up.

"Sit down, Jacques, sit down. And don't be so bloody dramatic." Richer flapped his hands. "For Christ's sake."

Mesrine eyed the other man suspiciously. Only when Richer looked away did he resume his seat.

Richer then said, "You owe me, Mesrine. I've come to collect."

He frowned. "*Owe* you? *I* owe *you*? Monsieur, I have never met you before in my life. How can I possible *owe* you?"

Richer blew out smoke. "I saved your life."

"*You?* You saved the life of Jacques Mesrine?"

"You don't remember? Think back. Algeria 58. We were both in the army. The Arab. In the alley at night, when you should have been in camp..."

Mesrine held up the cigarette. This time Richer came round the table and used his lighter.

"You told me then, Jacques, that you liked danger. That you would be interested in something different. Well, we recruited you and trained you, did we not? But you never repaid me personally for saving your life. Now I'm calling."

Mesrine's voice was soft. "It was *you* that night?" He thought back over the years. He could hear and smell Algeria of twenty years ago. "Richer...

Richer... *Richer! Captain* Richer!"

"I was then. I am now, as you know, Chief Inspector Richer."

"But... you belonged to the Organisation."

"I did. I still do."

"And you are truly a Chief Inspector in the Sûreté?"

"*Oui.*"

"And you belong to the *Organisation Armée Secrète?*"

"*Oui.*"

"Then you are one of us!"

"Not quite, Jacques, not quite. My beliefs still concern France. I work for France, not for my own ends."

Without warning, Mesrine was up. Richer did not even have a chance to move his arms before the big man had hold of him. "*Mon ami, mon ami*, after all this time." The bear hug was excrutiating. "*Mon dieu!* I do not believe it. But I know it is true! Comrade! *Capitaine!*"

"Jacques - " Richer tried unsuccessfully to avoid the double kiss on each cheek. "Jacques, sit down please. Christ Almighty. Mesrine, sit down!"

"Sir! *Mon Capitaine!*"

Richer made the thumbs-up sign to the warder frowning in at the corridor window, hand on the door.

"I will give it to you straight," Richer straightened his tie. "At this moment I am talking to you as a Chief Inspector of the BCP. There has been a robbery. Something has been stolen. I want you to get it back."

"That's all?"

"Let me finish. This robbery took place about six or seven weeks ago at a house in the Bois de Boulogne."

"A house?"

"*The* house."

"Ah!"

"Something very important was taken. *Very* important, Jacques. So important that I cannot tell you what it is."

Mesrine raised his hand. "*Un moment, mon ami, un moment.* If I understand right, you want me to retrieve something and you won't even tell me what it is!"

"Correct."

"*Mais c'est impossible.*"

"For the police and for most other people, yes. But not for Jacques Mesrine."

He grinned. "True, true. You know me well. What leads do you have?"

"The only thing we know is that this robbery took place. And I think I know who did it."

"You know who did it? I am confused."

"He was found dead in the Bois. It's pretty certain he died the same night as the robbery."

"Killed by his colleagues?"

"I think he worked alone."

"*Alors*, I am beginning to understand. He tried to take a shortcut through the Bois at night?"

Richer nodded.

"*L'imbécile*."

"*Oui*."

"And you have a trail that vanishes."

"*Oui*. He took jewellery worth easily ten million francs, probably a lot more. La Dame is not too worried about that. But he also took some letters. In those letters was a document. I cannot tell you what is in that document. That is between me and La Dame. I do not believe the thief knew the significance of what he was taking. He probably just grabbed the letters along with the ice."

"Can't you give me any clue as to what it is?"

"All I can say is that if it fell into the wrong hands its disclosures would cause chaos in France and Britain. It would damage both governments - no, both *countries*. It would cast black clouds in America. And - needless to say - it would upset La Dame.

"That's it, Jacques. That's what I've been asked to recover. That's what I'm asking *you* to recover. I cannot tell you anything further about what is in it, in case you don't find it. It is dangerous to have the knowledge. All I can offer you in return is assistance in your already well-notified escape from here. I can give you no immunity from recapture or future prosecution, not even a guarantee for your safety. And it *will* be an escape. I can, of course, assist with any hardware you might require, any contacts you may wish to make. You will not be assisted by the police, you understand. You will be assisted by the OAS.

"Just one more thing. If you find the document, take no chances with it. Bring it back at all costs, and only to me. Our mutual friends may have an interest in it."

Mesrine stared at the table, running a nail along the grain of the wood. He said, "So what you are saying is that I will ostensibly be working for the Sûreté on behalf of the government, but in reality I will be working for the OAS?"

"If you like. From your point of view you should regard yourself as working only for Jacques Mesrine. To everyone except me and our friends you will be just an escaped criminal. You will have to watch your back. It will not be easy. But if it was, I wouldn't be asking Jacques Mesrine."

Again the flattery, albeit the truth, pleased Mesrine. He drew on his cigarette. After a minute he said, "Under no circumstances would I do it for the Sûreté."

Richer said nothing.

Mesrine continued. "I might possibly do it for the French government - I am, after all, as patriotic as the next man."

Richer knew the game was being played out now. He watched as Mesrine finished the cigarette.

"I *will* do it for the man who saved my life, and for the OAS."

"Thank you."

"But you must understand, *Capitaine*, that it is my intention to escape from here anyway. I will pursue the document in my own time and at my own pace. I will not be hurried, I will not be intimidated. Neither will I delay any other activities I have planned."

"I understand. I will come to see you again next week. Let me know what you need and what you want me to do. I will see our friends. Once you are out, we will not meet until you have the document. And Jacques?"

"*Inspecteur?*"

"I trust you. I trust you to do it and do it well. In effect I am paying you in advance, with no way of recollection if you default."

"No way? How about a bullet in the head?"

"How will I know where you are? How will I know *who* you are? All I ask is for a regular progress report. I have two telephone numbers, one at Saussaies, one at home. Try Saussaies first. I will answer with my name. If I do not, or if it is someone else, hang up. Then try me at home. At all times use a false name - which?"

"Bruno."

"Okay, Bruno. Memorise the numbers, do not write them down." He gave him the Saussaies number first then the one of his apartment in Montmartre. "Got them?"

Mesrine repeated the two seven-digit codes.

"Good." Richer stood up and walked round the table. "The best of luck, Jacques."

They shook hands, Mesrine's broad back hiding the action from the sight of the guard outside. "Who needs luck, *mon ami*? I am Mesrine. I am luck itself!"

"Of course you are." The steel door slid back upon Richer's rap on the window. Richer said, "You haven't heard the last of this Mesrine. You did it and you know you did. I shall be back."

"*Sale flic!*" spat the prisoner. "You want to pin every unsolved crime in

France upon me, huh? Shitehawk!"

"Shut up Jacques, for God's sake," advised the guard as Richer turned and went down the corridor.

"Bastard!" shouted Mesrine over his shoulder as he was led off in the opposite direction. "Damn bastard pig!"

‡

8. L'Organisation

The three men sat in a row behind an old wooden table that had long since seen better days. Paul Richer sat in front of them. The bare room was dingy and smelled of dust and rotting meat. It was a place rarely used nowadays, but in the fifties and sixties the room above the butcher's in Rue Fessart in the 19th arrondisement was a frequent meeting place of the OAS High Command. It had never been discovered to this day.

A lightbulb hung above Richer's head. The men on the other side of the table were in shadow.

"What you are suggesting is preposterous," scoffed the man on the left, the one wearing the cap. "We have not indulged in active operations for years."

"I do not see that as a hindrance. Or as an excuse," countered Richer.

"Oh you don't, do you?"

"Captain, I think you should remember where you are and whom you are addressing," advised the man on the right, the chain smoker.

"If I appear insubordinate sir, that is not my intention. However, we have here a golden opportunity. If we could secure this document for ourselves, I promise you it would give us leverage beyond anything we have hoped for in the past. We would have a direct line into our own government and the governments of at least two other countries."

"But you won't even tell us what this supposed secret is!" complained the man in the cap. "How do you expect us to order active duties when we do not even know what we are after?"

"Sir, I have already explained. It is better that you do not know. Not until the document is ours. It is not safe. The fewer people who know, the better. With the knowledge I have now, even only verbally, I might be in danger."

"So you do not trust us?"

Richer took a deep breath. "I find that comment insulting, both to me and to everything this organisation represents. Of course I trust the High Command. But you have lives outside of this room. You could be vulnerable. I am protecting you. This is literally a case of what you don't know can't hurt you. When the document is ours, all will be revealed. Do you, sirs, trust *me*?"

"Now who is being insulting?"

"Gentlemen, gentlemen," soothed the man in the middle, the Colonel, the head of the OAS. "Please. Let us not get into squabbles. I know Captain Richer - we all do. I trust him. So do you." It was not open to debate.

The man on the right dragged on his cigarette. "Two questions," he said.

Richer turned to him. "Sir?"

"What about La Dame? She is expecting her document back, *non*? I do not think she would be pleased with just a photocopy. And we would want a provably authentic original."

"She is old, as you know. I have interviewed her. She is very frail, not always there. Leave her to me."

"What will you do?"

"If she proves a problem? I will kill her."

There was silence. The men looked at each other.

The Colonel breathed out very slowly, very audibly. After a while he said, "You will take no action in that respect unless it is first authorised by the High Command."

Richer nodded. "As you wish, sir."

"My second question," continued the man on the right. "Why on earth Mesrine? Of all people. Why can't we use one of our own, someone whom it is not necessary to break out of jail?"

"Mesrine *is* one of our own. He served us well in the troubled years. We used him before, in Spain. As you said, sir," he addressed the cap man, "the Organisation has not indulged in active operations for years. Who else is there? I've explained the problems of tracing the document. Who else can do it if even the police cannot? I believe there is only one man. Unless you know of any alternatives? In which case I would be pleased to co-operate with them."

The question hung in the air with the smell of the meat from downstairs.

Richer continued. "As to breaking Mesrine out of jail, that is not what I am asking. He has vowed that La Santé will not hold him - *merde alors*, that is why they built the wing especially for him. For sure he will attempt to escape. Rather than have him killed in a battle with the guards, let us help him. Then he will help us. Help, that is all I am asking for. Subtle help, untraceable help. I am not asking for a battalion of OAS veterans to storm the gates of La Santé. I just want help. A door open here, a key in the exact place it should be, some equipment to hand, that sort of thing. With your authority I will organise it." He looked along the table. "Gentlemen?"

The Colonel sat with his hands together in front of him. He looked at his colleagues and then at Richer. He said, "We will need time to consider your proposal, Captain. Return in two hours."

Two hours later, Richer entered the room when beckoned. There was a full liqueur glass on the table and a bottle of calvados. The OAS High Command were standing, glasses in their hands.

The Colonel handed the remaining glass to Richer. He nodded. "It is agreed. Assistance will be arranged. After that it is just you and Mesrine. This is a gamble. Do not fail us, Captain."

"The consequences," said the man with the cap, "might be severe."

"I will not fail," said Richer. "And neither will Mesrine."

"Then gentlemen, a toast," proposed the Colonel.

The four men stood in a circle and raised their glasses.

"Charles de Gaulle," said the Colonel.

They spoke together. "May the traitor rot in hell."

‡

9. Flics

Mardi 25 Avril

Claude Gerard was on duty an hour early that day, a most unusual occurrence. His arrival coincided with Paul Richer's return from his second visit to La Santé Prison. Richer kept the look of surprise from his face as he entered the office and saw Gerard lighting up his first Disque Bleu.

"Afternoon Paul, how's things?"

"Busy. How's things with you?"

"Managing, managing. There's rumbles of an embarrassment with a South American diplomat, got a bit too excited with the gee-gees, lost a packet, might have to go home. Did you clear up the business with La Dame?"

"Yep," Richer sat down and pulled a file and a notepad from a drawer.

"Clever boy."

"Thank you."

"What was it about? Usual something about nothing?"

"Yes."

"Pussy up a tree?"

He was fishing, but Richer's silence told him there would be no biting.

Gerard said, quite calmly, "She was - is - my case, you know. Just because you happen to get *one* job - "

"Yes?"

"Why not confide in me? We're both Chief Inspectors in the BCP, for Christ's sake. Maybe I can help you write it up. In *my* file."

"Don't want you spouting about La Dame's business in the lavatory, do we?"

"What?"

"You heard. Fond of giving advice to junior officers in there, aren't you?" Gerard understood. "You shit."

"Precisely. And that's what you should have been doing too, arsehole. Rather than slagging off your colleague to a junior. Is Fleury in?"

"See for yourself." The half-smoked Disque was crushed into the glass ashtray.

Richer went to tear off the top sheet from his notepad then changed his mind and picked up the whole pad. Without a further glance at Gerard he left the room, leaving the door swinging open behind him.

On his own, Gerard cursed again, stood up, closed the door and went over to Richer's desk. There was a file in the In Tray and he flicked it open, scanning it briefly. It concerned a grass Richer had contacted in République, something about a plot to bomb Marks and Spencer in Boulevard Haussmann. Nothing about La Dame.

Quickly, Gerard went through the drawers of the desk. Nothing of consequence. But the top drawer on the left was locked.

He swiped a paperclip from the tidy on the desk top, twisted it into shape and bent down level with the drawer.

Richer came back in.

"What're you after?"

Gerard was on his hands and knees looking under the desk.

"Nothing."

Richer snatched the file from the In Tray. "What do you mean 'nothing'?"

"I dropped my fucking pen and it rolled across, don't mind do you?"

"You should use it to write with and not keep tossing it about and playing with it." Richer hurried back out.

"*Con.*"

With two or three deft twists Gerard had the drawer open, eyes lighting like Aladdin in his cave of treasure.

The light soon went out. All Richer had under lock and key was an English *Parker* fountain pen, twenty francs in small change, a packet of tissues, an apple and his leave chit. *Shit!* Hold on, what was beneath the tissues? A diary!

Quickly flicking through the pages, Gerard's eyes skimmed over the entries, mostly appointments both official and social. The letter 'M' appeared on 21st, today and Friday 28th. Around Friday 5th May was a faint red circle.

Gerard replaced the diary and locked the drawer as skilfully as he had opened it.

He picked up his own telephone and keyed the front office. "Chief Inspector Gerard. Can you tell me where Chief Inspector Richer was this morning?" He heard the thumbing of a page.

"He was logged down as being at La Santé, sir."

"Right. Is he back yet?" Cosmetics.

"Saw him in about twenty minutes ago, sir."

"*Merci.*"

You bastard, what are you up to? A visit to La Santé... The letters 'M' in the diary... A mark for ten days hence...

Gerard pulled the folded piece of paper from inside his pocket, the one he had taken from Richer's notepad last week. He opened it. From a distance, where he had lightly rubbed his pencil over the surface, it looked like a drawing of a grey rain cloud. Only close up, peeking palely through the cloud, could he make out the two letters. The first was a J, definitely a J.

J.M.

‡

10. Flic

Samedi 29 Avril

Richer was not on duty that day, so Gerard had time to rifle his desk at leisure.

For a long time he examined the diary, turning the pages back and forth, staring at the entries again and again in case they might change. It was only a fit of coughing that made him realise that he had smoked half a packet of Disques and that the room was getting heavy. Lighting another, he stood up, stretched and coughed again. He pulled his left butt cheek outwards and farted. Quickly he opened the window.

What he was thinking was crazy, preposterous. He had not an ounce of proof. 'M' could stand for *'mère'*. Perhaps Richer had been visiting his mother a lot? As CI with responsibilities for personnel, Gerard knew that the lady was in her eighties and was permanently ensconced in a clinic in Issy. But that would be giving Richer the benefit of the doubt. It was too easy. Richer had been at La Santé last Tuesday. Richer's mother was not in La Santé! But someone with the initials J.M was.

Was there a link, either in the present or in the past, between the two men? Couldn't be, Richer would never have risen to where he was today had there been the slightest doubt about his background.

Gerard went over to his own desk and opened the big envelope that had arrived for him in the last internal post. Inside, in another sealed envelope, was a pink personnel file. He took it out.

From a locked drawer of his desk he removed a thick blue casework file he had obtained from central registry that morning. It was one of a series of files with the same number.

He sat staring at the two files. As he lit another cigarette, he opened the blue file labelled *Mesrine J R* and began to read.

It took him an hour to get to 1956. When he did, he put the file still open to one side and pulled over the pink file. The label on the cover read *Richer P J.*

‡

11. Le Directeur

Mercredi 3 Mai

The direct telephone line to the office of the Governor of La Santé prison was at that time 336-40-50. It rang that afternoon, logged at 14:30 hours, and was answered by the then Deputy Governor Monsieur Jean Fagianelli.

The message consisted of fourteen words.

"Mesrine will escape on Friday 5th May. I repeat, Mesrine will escape on Friday."

Naturally the caller did not identify himself.

The Deputy discussed the matter with the Governor, Monsieur Hubert Bonaldi. It was decided to note the call but to take no further action as a consequence. Nobody had ever escaped from La Santé, and the grey world of the Parisian criminal fraternity (from where it was thought the call had originated) is always rife with rumours, plots, counterplots and tip-offs which come to nothing.

‡

12. Voleur

Vendredi 5 Mai

A discreet extra watch was kept on Jacques Mesrine on 5th May, but he did nothing out of the ordinary.

The authorities of La Santé prison never knew that the only reason he did not escape that Friday was that it rained all day.

Lundi 8 Mai

[The following is a factual account of the escape of Jacques Mesrine from La Santé prison.]

At that time there were only three other men considered dangerous enough to share the top-security wing of La Santé prison with Jacques Mesrine. Two of them, François Besse and Carman Rives, were taking their exercise with Mesrine at 09:50 that morning.

At 09:55 two guards came into the exercise yard and escorted Mesrine to the interview room. Madame Giletti, one of his many lawyers, awaited him on legitimate business.

Prisoner Besse was taken back to his cell at 10:00. Rives, who was not in on the escape, followed, suspicious of this break from routine.

After a few minutes in the interview room with the lawyer, Mesrine knocked calmly on the inner window. One of the two guards opened the metal door.

"Albert," smiled Mesrine as if speaking to a close friend. "Forgive me, I need some papers. They are in a file I left in François' room. I wonder if you would be so kind as to get them for me?"

"Certainly, Jacques." The guard was only too pleased to assist. "Excuse me, madame," he nodded at the lawyer.

Besse's cell was a mere ten metres along the corridor.

"François, you have some papers of Jacques'? He needs them." Albert unlocked the outer wooden door.

Besse was fiddling with a toothpaste tube. *"Papiers? Ah, oui.* That Jacques is an idiot! Why did he leave them here?" He took a large box file from the table in the corner and tried to push it through the bars of the inner door. As intended, the box was far too big.

"Pah! Hang on, hang on." Albert unlocked the inner door. As he pulled it open, Besse simultaneously whacked him on the chin with the box and squirted soapy water into his eyes from the toothpaste tube. Albert shouted out. Besse kneed him in the groin.

Although talking to his lawyer, Mesrine's gaze was glued on the window. He saw the second guard dash to his left.

Besse saw the second guard coming and quickly rammed his foot into the face of the moaning, prostrate Albert. The moaning stopped.

"Madame, this room is bugged!" To his lawyer's astonishment, Mesrine suddenly jumped up onto the plank table.

Pulling a pair of nail scissors from his shirt pocket, Mesrine undid the retaining screw of the ventilation grill in the ceiling with one fluid twist.

"Monsieur!" gasped the lawyer.

From inside the shaft, Mesrine pulled two pistols and a grappling iron with blue mountaineering rope attached. "Madame," he announced triumphantly, "the bugs in La Santé are huge!"

Besse struggled, pinned against the wall by the big, beefy second guard. Albert was still on the floor but slowly moving. Besse kicked out, trying to make contact with the second guard's shins or more vital areas.

The guard held him tightly. "What the fuck's got into you, François? Want to get rough, hn?"

Then he felt something hard press into the back of his neck.

"Do not move." There was no mistaking the voice of the most dangerous, most notorious killer in France. "Let him go."

The guard relaxed his grip.

"Sensible, Charles, sensible."

"Jacques, you'll never - "

"Silence!" The gun pushed against his skull.

Besse grabbed the guard and swung him into the cell. Albert was now on his knees, perplexed and bewildered.

Mesrine filled the doorway. "Right, messieurs, take off your clothes."

"What?"

"*Vite!* Or are you in such a hurry to meet your maker?"

Mesrine and Besse covered the guards in turn as the other stepped into the discarded uniforms of navy blue jacket, pants, cap and tie, and light blue shirt.

Charles' clothes fit Mesrine with a stunning exactness. The criminal was transformed, every inch the warder. Once Besse was ready, Mesrine said "*Adieux, messieurs.* One way or another, you will never see me in here again." He slammed the cell doors shut, locking each of them.

Besse had the mountaineering rope and grapple wound round his shoulders. "*Allons, Jacques.*"

"*Oui, François, oui.* But remember, we are warders. Warders do not hurry."

They headed for the staff office at the end of the corridor, passing the cell of Carman Rives. The convict was at the bars of the locked inner door, staring out. Mesrine had an idea.

"You want to come?" he asked the astonished Rives, unlocking the door. Rives was out in an instant.

At the staff office, Mesrine calmly opened the door and walked in. Inside were two assistant governors, the Chief Warder and five of his men. A convenient meeting at a convenient time.

"Good morning, gentlemen," greeted the unmistakable moustached figure. Quickly and deliberately he gave the nearest warder a savage smash around the head with the butt of his gun. The man staggered and then sat down untidily on the floor. "That is a warning. If anyone tries anything they will be shot."

While Besse covered the men and Rives looked bewildered, Mesrine relieved them of their guns, keys and papers, and ripped the telephone wires from the wall.

He was handing a gun to Rives when the door to the office opened. Two nurses from the prison infirmary came in, their smiles dropping to looks of horror. They froze.

"Mesdames, welcome," greeted Mesrine. "Close the door and be quiet."

One of the nurses looked at the warder sitting on the floor, his head bleeding. "He will live," said Mesrine. "And so will you if you behave."

Besse tugged at his sleeve. "Take them hostage, *Le Grand.*"

"No." The look in his eyes said more than the simple negative. "Ladies, if you will excuse us?" The prisoners backed out of the office. Mesrine locked the door and threw the key down the corridor.

He knew exactly which of the other keys would fit the main double doors of the top-security wing, and the three men were out into the yard in moments.

On the other side of the area, the Chief of Works was standing at the base of a ladder. Up above, a workman was fitting new bars onto the window of an empty cell.

The Chief of Works was aware only that two warders and a prisoner were approaching across the yard. He thought nothing wrong with the request of the big warder, the one with the moustache, to move the ladder into the outer courtyard between the inner and outer walls. It was needed urgently.

Exchanging banter with the warders, the Chief of Works and the workman dutifully carried the ladder between them.

As they approached the iron door in the inner wall, five men came round a far corner: three prisoners escorted by two genuine guards.

Rives gasped a nervous warning, but Mesrine and Besse already had their guns raised. "Gentlemen, good morning," Mesrine gave a little bow. "Yes, it is I, Mesrine. If you would be so kind as to join our little group?" It was an invitation they could not refuse.

The door leading to the outer courtyard was open. Mesrine looked at the Chief of Works. The Chief of Works looked back at him blankly.

Across the courtyard, a sentry box stood in front of the outer wall. Although prison regulations forbade sentries leaving the reinforced bullet-proof box whilst on duty, the man was already outside, rifle slung casually over his shoulder, smoking a cigarette. He saw four warders and assorted other men approaching.

"*Merde alors*, what is this?" He made no move for his gun, but the half-smoked cigarette was stamped out.

The largest of the warders strolled over to him, smiling. The smile disappeared as he raised the pistol in his hand. "I am Mesrine. You may have heard of me. Hand over your gun or I will kill you."

As he passed the surrendered rifle to Rives, Mesrine ordered the other men to place the ladder against the wall. He did not notice that one of the warders had gone missing, sneaking back through the inner door...

Besse climbed the ladder first, reached the top of the wall and straddled it. Fixing the grappling hook in place, he went down the outside with the aid of the rope and jumped the last couple of metres into Rue Messier, narrowly missing some dustbins by the foot of the wall. He looked up, waiting for the next man to come over.

Then an alarm began to scream.

"*Merde! Vite!*" Mesrine nodded for Rives to climb the ladder.

The young man hesitated, his nerve failing at the last moment. "I don't know, *Le Grand*."

With a curse, Mesrine climbed the ladder himself. He reached the top of the wall and looked back. Armed guards were rushing into the courtyard. A bullet skimmed past. "Carman. Carman!" he shouted. "Now or never!" He disappeared over the top.

Making the decision, Rives ran up the ladder. Wood chipped off the rungs as the guards fired. He had the sentry's rifle and, as he reached the top, he stopped to return fire. Then he threw the rifle into the road below and began to slide down the rope.

As Mesrine hit the street, armed policemen appeared from the front of the prison. A little way down the road, Besse was running. He stopped abruptly as he saw the policemen.

As far as the policemen were concerned, they saw two armed warders in the street.

"Quick, over here!" shouted Mesrine. "It's Mesrine trying to escape!"

Rives was halfway down the rope.

Mesrine raised his pistol and fired, deliberately missing Rives. Rives stopped to look round, holding onto the rope with both hands.

Besse had resumed his run.

"I'll cover the front!" Mesrine screamed at the policemen. "He should give you no trouble. Take him back, will you?" He nodded at the frozen figure halfway up the rope.

As Mesrine disappeared left into the Rue du Faubourg St Jacques, completely in the opposite direction to the front of the prison, one of the policemen, in a state of panic, fired at Carman Rives.

In the Place St Jacques, Besse was waving down a white Renault 20. The driver stopped the car sharply for the rather anxious-looking man in uniform.

Mesrine ran up, fury on his face. "They shot Carman. The *bastards!*"

He pointed the pistol through the side window and his finger tightened on the trigger. "OUT!"

Paul Richer obeyed.

With Mesrine driving, the Renault shot away, across the Place and through the red light at the intersection of the Rue St Jacques. Overhead a metro thundered along the railway, its passengers oblivious to the drama below. Soon enough they would read about it in the papers and see it on the television.

The Renault headed south on the Rue de la Tomb Issoire. Although furious about Rives, more than anything furious with himself for involving the young man, the driver managed to smile. Jacques Mesrine and François Besse had done it.

They had escaped from 'the great unbustable', La Santé prison.

The 7.65 bullet hit Carman Rives in the chest, probably killing him instantly. His head lolled and bashed against the wall of the prison with a dull, hollow sound that echoed halfway down the road. His grip on the rope slackened and his body crashed to the street below, landing on the dustbins and scattering them like tenpins.

The policeman who had fired the shot came over, his panic turning into a triumphant grin. Was this Mesrine? Had he actually shot Mesrine? If not, those two warders would get the bastard round the front.

The death rattle groaned from Carman Rives' throat and his dead eyes stared upwards. He seemed to be looking at something. On the wall, just above where his dead head had hit, was a plaque. It remembered eighteen men of the Resistance executed inside La Santé by the Germans in the Second World War. It read:

EXECUTED ON THE ORDERS OF A GOVERNMENT SERVING THE ENEMY.

2IÈME PARTIE

‡

LA POURSUITE

The escape of Jacques Mesrine from La Santé prison is timed at 10:25 on Monday 8 May 1978, the time that Mesrine's feet touched the ground outside the prison.

The police were in a state of panic. In the aftermath of Mesrine's escape, roadblocks were set up on all major routes out of Paris, and railway stations and airports were hastily put under surveillance. One thousand extra police were immediately called into the capital, and in the coming days others would be recalled from leave.

Commissaire Serge Devos, on his very first day as the new Head of the Brigade de Répression de Banditisme (BRB) *was given the task of recapturing Mesrine and Besse.*

All French television and radio programmes were interrupted with news of the escape. Special programmes on Jacques Mesrine were hastily assembled.

Soon the switchboards of every major police headquarters in France, both regional and national, were jammed. People had seen Mesrine. By 13:00 he had been seen in Lille, Dunkirk, Bordeaux, Lyons, Marseilles, Nice – and even Vienna.

‡

13. Flics

"Have you heard?" Commissaire Fleury-Goujon poked his head round the office door. "Mesrine escaped from La Santé half an hour ago."

"*What?* Bloody hell!" Chief Inspector Gerard stood up, ash falling from the cigarette in his lips. "I didn't actually believe it."

"When's Paul on?"

"He's on now. Out somewhere. The office'll have it logged. Shall I - " He reached for the phone.

"No, no. I'll see him when he comes back. *Merci.*"

Gerard followed the Commissaire out into the corridor. "Broussard taking it on?" [*Broussard was Head of the* Brigade de Recherche et d'Intervention, *the man who had arrested Mesrine in September 1973.*]

"No, they've given it to Devos and his new gang."

"The BRB?"

"Yes. Poor bugger. Apparently Peyrefitte [*the Minister of Justice*] is breathing down his neck already. Giscard's taken an immediate personal interest. He wants Mesrine caught and caught now. Paris will be saturated. Everyone remotely suspicious will be questioned. All his old haunts and old cronies will be watched. If someone so much as mumbles Mesrine's name in their sleep, they will be arrested."

"Easier said than done with the resources we have. And Mesrine is popular, there will be plenty of people willing to help him. It is *us* the public doesn't like. He's a d'Artagnan. Or who's that English fellow... Robert Hood?"

"*Oui.* Except Mesrine robs the rich to give to himself." The Commissaire stopped by the door to his office. "Was there anything, Claude?"

"No, sir, no. Got to wash my hands."

"What about that South American diplomat?"

"Think we sorted him out. It'll be in my weekly report, or you can have a special sooner if you like."

"No, it's your case. Ask Paul to see me when he's back, will you?"

"Yes, sir."

Gerard pushed by a civilian clerk coming out of the WC, and unzipped in front of the nearest porcelain. He pissed like an elephant.

You bastard, Richer. Did you actually do it? Did *you* spring Jacques Mesrine from La Santé? No, that was impossible. *N'est-ce pas? Ou pas n'est-ce pas?* And if so, why?

What are you up to?

Gerard rezipped, flicked the pee off his shoes, didn't even think about washing his hands, and went back to the office.

‡

14. Voleur

"Forgive me for asking, monsieur, but may I use your bath oil?"

In response, the kindly grey head of the seventy year old homosexual looked round the kitchen door and smiled. Mesrine was naked except for a short towel around his waist, and he was wiping away the dredges of shaving foam after taking off his moustache. Behind him the bath water ran furiously, splashing the portable television that he had balanced on top of the bidet.

"But of course, *mon ami,*" said the homosexual, quietly admiring the big, muscular man. "This apartment and the things in it are yours for as long as you wish. Dinner will be ready in one hour."

The master criminal had known the old queer Marcel (or Marcelle as he liked to be known) for some years, he was a friend of a mutual friend. A swift phone call by someone on Mesrine's behalf yesterday afternoon had ensured that Marcel was prepared for his special guest.

The apartment in the Rue Jean Nicot, near Les Invalides, was a typical piece of Mesrine cunning. Les Invalides is on the western edge of Paris' *quartier* of central government. Nearby is the Assemblée Nationale and just to the north is the Quai d'Orsay itself. Mesrine's principle of never fleeing but sheltering in the eye of the storm had seen him through on many occasions. The police would think he was well away from the capital by now - and even if they didn't, the apartment was clean. Mesrine knew for certain that the police did not know of the place or of Marcel.

Similarly, Mesrine always believed that searching for one needle in a haystack was harder than searching for two, so he and Besse had split up after abandoning the commandeered Renault 20 in the Rue André-Theuriet down near Malakoff. The police would establish it as a hired car and their enquiries would reveal that the hirer had used false papers. End of trail.

He stepped into the bath and lay back in the *Floris*-scented water. He felt pleased with himself. It had all gone smoothly, as he had been promised. Keys, people and things had been in the right place at the right time - except for poor Carman Rives. He should never have invited him along, it had been a foolish impetuosity. He had never intended for Rives to escape, of course. He was to be a decoy, to be recaptured and throw attention away from the 'warders'. He had obviously underestimated the venom of authority. To shoot Carmen in cold blood. Somebody would pay for that. In the meantime, Mesrine would ensure that Rives had the best funeral money could buy.

And at some stage he would have to figure out how to obtain a document. An anonymous document, subject unknown. How would he know if he had the right item? *Merde alors,* if it was that important he would certainly know it when he saw it.

Now, plans. He would phone the *Capitaine* and confirm his safe arrival. Then he would lie low for as long as it took for the immediate fuss to die down. He reckoned on a month. Marcel would be accommodating. Money would be needed, though, and he might have to make one small excursion out at sometime.

He let the water flap around his neck and grinned as he saw his face flash up on the television screen. Not bad, taken a couple of years ago, moustache, no beard.

"*Marcelle, cherie,*" he called over his shoulder, "you don't have such a thing as a cigar, do you?"

He settled down to listen to details of his past exploits in the news bulletin. If they got any facts wrong he would contact the producer in the morning.

Mardi 9 Mai

The second casualty of the Mesrine escape (after Carmen Rives) was Monsieur Pierre Aymard, the Director of Prison Administration. While the hunt continued, with police forces throughout France visiting every address of every person who had ever known Jacques Mesrine, Monsieur Aymard received a call from the Chief Secretary's Office of the Ministry of Justice that morning.

As Aymard looked for the last time out of his office window over the Place Vendôme, he was told that he had been removed from his post. The escape had damaged the credibility of the French penal system and the reputation of the Ministry of Justice.

‡

15. Flic et les Anglais

Lundi 15 Mai

At 14:30 on the day that Jacques Mesrine entered the second week of his self-imposed seclusion, Claude Gerard entered foreign territory over on the Faubourg St Honoré. The Chief Inspector had been asked, if he would be so kind, to pop across to the British Embassy when he had a spare moment, on a completely informal basis, naturally.

Behind the diffident, reserved Anglo-Saxon manner, Gerard recognised a summons when he heard one. He did not like 'visiting'. Meant he had to do his shirt collar up. Nearly bloody strangled him.

"Claude, old chap, how nice to see you." Small, stocky Ron Becker came to meet him at the ornate Reception.

"Ronald, 'ow are you?"

"Can't complain, old duck, can't complain." Becker was Gerard's usual liaison. Supposedly just a normal Foreign Office executive officer, beneath the veneer that fooled no one Becker was a member of the British security service.

"There is somesing I can do for you?" queried Gerard. "You are 'aving problems?"

Becker smiled at the slovenly Frenchman with the dog-end hanging from his lips. His collar looked tight enough to strangle him. "Problems? No, no, not at all. Just something that's come up from back home. Nothing much. Actually, not really my baby. There's someone who'd like a word, Claude old love."

"A word?"

"Or two. This way."

Gerard was ushered upstairs, along plushly carpeted corridors with old paintings of long-dead Englishmen on the walls, and into a small but comfortably-furnished office.

The man who stood up from behind the large desk was tall and immaculately dressed. His woollen suit probably cost what Gerard earned in a month. But he was almost painfully thin, suspicious eyes sunk into his skeletal face. "Chief Inspector," he shook Gerard's hand with the warmth of a midwinter's day. He did not introduce himself but apologised in surprisingly good and well-accented French for asking him to call on a public holiday and please would he sit down?

As he sat, Gerard turned to see Becker leaving the room. Gerard shifted back, noticing the examination he was getting from the sunken eyes. He pulled out his cigarettes.

"I'd rather you didn't." It was the statement of a man used to being obeyed.

Gerard stopped with a fresh Disque halfway to his lips, the old *mégot* between his fingers. Who was this damn *rosbeef*?

He lowered his arm and replaced the Disque and butt tenderly into the packet.

Without preamble the man said, "I believe you have special responsibility for La Dame?"

Gerard replaced the packet into his pocket. "I think you had better ask my superiors, m'sieur, through proper channels."

The face did not react. "You *are* the BCP official charged with UK interests?"

"Among many others, yes."

"Then these are the proper channels."

"Nevertheless - "

"Nevertheless nothing."

Gerard inhaled, bit his tongue, and just decided against standing up and walking out. Instead he asked, "What do you want, m'sieur?"

"You have not answered my original question."

"And until I find out what this is about, neither will I."

This time an eyebrow was raised. "I see." Then he asked, "A drink?"

"I beg your pardon?"

"Would you like a drink?" The man actually smiled.

"Er... thank you." Gerard's fingers fiddled with an imaginary cigarette. "Do you have cognac?"

"Certainly." The man stood up and walked over to a glass-fronted cabinet. He spoke as he selected and poured. "Word has reached us from London that La Dame lost something not so long ago. Something important."

"I see."

"We have been asked - very discreetly and unofficially you understand - to (a) see if the rumour is true and (b) ask what is being done about it."

"I see."

Gerard accepted the generous glass of liquor.

The man waited, standing in front of him. Gerard sipped the drink.

"Well?"

"M'sieur?"

Lightning flashed in the eyes and then was replaced by amusement. Now it was the Englishman's turn to say, "I see."

Gerard put his glass down on the rim of the desk and again reached for his cigarettes. This time no curt command stopped him before he lit up.

Through smoke Gerard said, "I thought you people regarded La Dame as purely an embarrassment, the sooner she departed this life the better. I am surprised you have taken an interest."

"Therefore you are confirming my point (a)." The man sat back down.

"Possibly." Gerard surveyed the top of his Disque and blew on it. "I am still surprised at your interest."

"Frankly, so am I. But I am a mere pawn of my masters, I simply do as I am bidden."

And I'm the Sun King, thought Gerard. He said, "Monsieur, I will confirm your point (a). There was a robbery, things went missing. But I am interested to know how you found out."

"The walls, monsieur, have ears."

Gerard looked around.

"Oh no, not here. I was speaking in metaphor."

"Ah. One of your little British *tournures familières*, hmm?"

"The loss has got to the ears of someone in London. Cards on the table - "

Gerard glanced at the desk top.

" - I know nothing about this other than what I am told. La Dame has, apparently, lost something. London is asking questions. So, if you wish to enlighten me further...?"

"Monsieur, with respect, I do not."

"I see. Just as well, perhaps. As to my point (b)...?"

Gerard put down the empty glass, noting that there was no offer of a refill, and looked around for an ashtray. Finding none, he tapped his Disque into his cupped hand. "As to your point (b), I am not in charge of the enquiry."

"You are not?"

"*Non.* Usually I would be, but on this occasion a colleague was assigned the task."

"Oh."

"However, I can tell you that the matter is being looked into. But, to be frank m'sieur, robberies occur every day, throughout France, throughout Europe, throughout the world. Notwithstanding the owner of the goods in this instance, enquiries are enquiries and the chances of a successful outcome are... remote."

The man was nodding. "Naturally, I understand. Which brings me to point (c)."

"Point (c)?" Gerard sat with a palmful of ash in one hand and his cigarette stub in the other.

"Point (c). I am to ask, unofficially, that London - through me - is kept informed of *any* developments, and that if it is humanly possible the missing articles be retrieved."

"I understand."

"And I hope that means more to you than it does to me."

"Really, m'sieur, no. I have said that it is not my case. You are speaking to the wrong man."

The man sniffed. "I think not. You are our BCP liaison officer. When your department was set up at the instigation of your late President himself, we were promised the fullest co-operation from yourselves. A report to the contrary at ambassador level would not, I am sure, be well received."

Nasty.

Gerard was silent.

He made a show of looking around. Then he calmly tipped the palmful of ash onto the carpet. "I understand, m'sieur. So your point (c) is?"

"Keep us informed, Chief Inspector, keep us informed."

"*Bien.*" Gerard stood up, resisting the urge to stub out the cigarette on the polished desk top. "*If* I find out anything, I will let you know. For whom shall I ask?"

"Becker, your normal contact."

They walked over to the door and out.

"Not you?"

"Becker will know even less of what it is about than I do. Just leave a sealed report with him.

"Shall I address it to you?

"No, just leave it blank, he'll know."

They reached the top of the stairway which led down into the wide, echoing foyer. Three steps down, Gerard turned. "Monsieur, I do not know your name."

"No, you don't," said the Englishman as he turned and walked away.

Jeudi 18 Mai

Ten days since the escape. The hunt for Mesrine continued. The failure of the prison officials and the police was discussed in Parliament. The Press showed the authorities no mercy.

The police were angered by the negative publicity. But what could they do? Everyone whom they thought Mesrine might contact was being watched – there were even police marksmen on the roofs of buildings surrounding the home of Mesrine's daughter, Sabrina.

To cover their embarrassment and plunging morale, the police made frequent announcements that Mesrine was about to be recaptured.

But in reality there was nothing. All the sightings had proved false. There had not been one reliable tip-off.

Mesrine had vanished into thin air.

‡

16. Voleur

Samedi 27 Mai

Deauville is a stylish resort in Normandy, a meticulously clean seaside town much frequented by well-to-do visitors from both France and throughout Europe. The place is littered with high quality, expensive villas, usually open for only three or four months a year when their rich owners take their summer break.

As with most haunts of the wealthy in France, Deauville is heavily policed, a state protection which the residents are only too pleased to pay for because of the ever-present threat of robberies or, worse, kidnapping.

The casino in Deauville is a huge, ornate building redolent of times when fortunes could be made or lost with the spin of a wheel or a turn of a card, and horse-drawn carriages would pull up outside to collect their ecstatic or suicidal owners. Fortunes could still be won or lost, of course, but in the more careful and less dramatic late twentieth century the chances were that the gentleman, or sometimes lady, win or lose, would still drive away afterwards in his/her Audi or Lamborghini, not too worse for the experience.

Fortunes can not only be won or lost, they can also be taken. It is recorded that on 27 May 1978 Jacques Mesrine and François Besse robbed the casino in Deauville. Their haul was a mere thirteen thousand francs, small even by working class standards. By Deauville standards it was nothing more than petit monnaie.

‡

17. Flics

Mardi 30 Mai

Paul Richer handed over a ten franc note, accepted his two francs change and the kilo of early strawberries, and walked further up through the crowds on the Rue Lepic, Montmartre's food market. It was a warm, pleasant day and, as usual, the old artists' quarter of Paris was swarming with tourists.

He stopped at another stall for carrots, beans and mushrooms, then popped into a boucherie for his weekly treat of a small steak, and then into a boulangerie for a crusty loaf and tomorrow's breakfast croissants.

Shopping complete, he turned right and continued up the hill. On his left, tourists posed beneath the Moulin de Galette.

He first became aware of the vehicle as he turned right into Rue de l'Abreuvoir. There were always vehicles, of course, trying to negotiate the narrow, cobbled streets of the *butte*; usually experienced residents or careless taxi drivers. Therefore one more white Peugeot should not seem out of the ordinary. But this driver was not experienced or careless, but cautious and careful - a sure sign of a novice on the streets of the hill. And he was moving slowly, keeping a steady but regular distance.

Richer nipped right down Rue des Saules. The car followed.

Richer walked on again and then stopped abruptly, pretending to adjust his parcels of shopping. The vehicle stopped.

Shit.

He walked on.

Richer stopped to look in the window of a clothes shop. The car slowed.

Who could it be? Why would they be following him? His CRS days were behind him, he had retired from this sort of skulduggery. Perhaps he was being too suspicious, the paranoia of his last days at des Orfèvres creeping back. It could just simply be a Parisian who happened to be going his way. Not.

Hell, this was ridiculous. Montmartre, mid-afternoon, in late spring, and he, a Chief Inspector of the Sûrêté, was being followed.

Not breaking pace but casually looking around as he stepped off the kerb, he crossed Rue Saint Vincent. Now it became quieter, off the tourist track. A little way along he turned right, descending the steep steps of the Cimitière

Saint Vincent.

No vehicle could come down here, the road was twenty metres above and behind. Whoever it was would have to alight and follow on foot.

It was silent among the graves. The little tombs were about the height of a man, all different in design but each with the same sombre purpose. Some had doors leading into vaults, others were simply exaggerated headstones. Some of the more recent ones contained framed photographs of their occupants.

As in all Paris cemeteries, there were cats; some looking suspiciously from behind the stones, others brazenly walking about and eyeing the intruder with feline contempt. One dozed on top of the tomb of Utrillo. Over in a corner, a ginger tom pissed his territorial boundary.

Richer came to a stop halfway in, in a position facing the steps. Above one side of him was the road, above the other the back of a block of apartments out on Rue Caulaincourt. He rested his bags behind a vault and crouched down. He wished he had his gun with him.

He could just see the wheels of the Peugeot, stationary on the road above. Someone in a raincoat - stupid for such a lovely day - came from the far side. With no attempt at stealth the person walked down the steps, almost falling down the last three where they were broken.

Richer grunted in annoyance and stood up. "What the bloody hell do you think you're doing, you stupid bastard!"

Claude Gerard jumped as his colleague appeared from nowhere. His cigarette popped out of his mouth and fell onto the grass. He bent down, picked it up and replaced it in his mouth without so much as blowing the dirt off. He smiled. "God, this place smells of piss. *Ça va, Paul?* Wanted a word."

"Why all the cloak and dagger?"

"You've been on leave."

"Exactly, and I still am until next week. Can't I have a rest, for Christ's sake?"

"I was coming to see you at your apartment, and I noticed you in the street."

"Ever heard of the telephone?"

"Truth is, I wanted to get out of the office. Fleury's been on my back about our resident Iranian."

"What is so damn urgent?"

"Paul, I..." Gerard actually looked shamefaced. "I wanted to apologise. Make amends. I've been thinking about it while you've been off. You know, we haven't exactly started off on the right foot."

"And whose fault is that?"

"Okay, okay. But I thought we might try to patch things up. Look, do you fancy a drink?"

"Patch things up? Gerard, you were the one who started the aggression in the first place... Oh fuck it, this is bloody ridiculous! Two grown men, two Chief Inspectors of police, skulking about in a cemetery. If one of our lads comes along he'll have us up for gross indecency in a graveyard. Look - Claude - I'm on my way home. Can't it wait until Monday?"

"If you like..." Gerard turned to go.

"No, hold on." If it was an olive branch, Richer did not want to reject it out of hand. But the chances were this *con* was up to something. "I can't go for a drink laden down with shopping. Come back to my apartment if you like. For a quick *Napoléon*." He shook his head at the proffered packet of Disques.

"Rue Lamarck you live, isn't it?"

"Number forty-eight." As you know damn well. "You'll have to drive out onto Caulaincourt and round."

"*D'accord.*"

"And here, you can take one of these bloody bags as well."

Richer's apartment consisted of four rooms on the top floor of the block, facing south. Rue Lamarck skirts the northern side of the Montmartre *butte*, so one half of the view from the *salle de jour* was obscured by the huge whitestone magnificence of Sacré Coeur on the crest. But just to the east, where the Basilica did not extend, one could see at an angle over the ridge with a view sweeping across to the towers of Notre Dame and beyond.

Gerard insisted on helping to unpack the shopping, dropping the mushrooms onto the kitchen floor. As he bent down to pick them up, something black and furry shot out from underneath the fridge and stopped a rolling champignon in its tracks.

"Jesus Christ!"

Gerard jumped back, squashing two mushrooms under foot.

Richer looked round nonchalantly. "Chivas! *Bonjour petit*. No, that's not for you."

"I didn't know you had a cat," said Gerard.

"No? Claude meet Chivas. Chivas meet Uncle Claude." Richer smiled. One brown trouser to you Gerard.

"Er..." Gerard nodded to the animal. "*Bonjour*."

Richer poured two double *Napoléons* and asked if Gerard would like something to eat. "If we are burying the hatchet, let us bury it in a tournedos."

"*Merci bien, Paul*. But will you have enough? Surely you shopped just for one?"

"I can stretch it."

"*Non, non, pas de probleme!*" Gerard stood up. "I will be back in a moment. You - er - prepare the mushrooms." Before Richer could say anything more he was out of the door and his feet were thumping down the stairs.

Richer looked at the cat.

"What do you think, Chivas?" The cat jumped up onto the worktop as Richer opened a can of beef and chicken liver. "What is he up to? We must watch ourselves with him." He forked the food into a bowl. "No doubt his intentions will be revealed in due course."

In reply, Chivas thrust his backside into his flatmate's face and began to eat.

Gerard was back within twenty minutes with an additional steak, two bottles of Le Piat d'Or rouge and some cat treats. "Three bachelors together, hmm?"

Richer busied himself in the kitchen while Gerard admired the comfortable, cosy apartment and enthused over the view.

Thirty minutes later the two men sat down on the easy chairs in the living room and devoured the rarely-done tournedos, lightly fried mushrooms, carrots and beans, bread and special sauce upon which Richer would not be drawn as to the contents. Already with two double brandies inside them, they now had a bottle of the Piat d'Or each.

They mellowed.

The conversation became quite pally.

"I can understand why you've never married," Gerard leant back in his chair and rubbed his generous gut. "You cook superbly, you have Pigalle within walking distance. Why be saddled with one woman permanently? Why the expense of a wife? What one would cost you you could spend once a month on a full night with one of the local lovelies. Now as for me, well I don't mind telling you, sometimes Mathilde and the four brats get me down. That's why I'm enjoying this evening so much."

"But your children must be growing up now."

"In their teens - and that is the most dangerous age, especially for the girl. You know why. One of the boys is at university, he's okay, outgrown it. But the other two are yobs, potential or actual... It's good to get out."

Richer sympathised and cleared away the plates which Chivas had been giving a pre-wash with his tongue. Gerard poured wine into both their glasses and broke open a packet of Disques. He sauntered over to the floor to ceiling window and quietly watched the lights of Paris come on beyond the Basilica.

Richer came back in.

"Want help with the washing up?" Gerard turned.

"It's in the machine."

"Ah! All mod cons. Here," he held out the Disques. Richer took one and accepted a light. "Love this view. If you ever leave here, let me know. I'll ditch Mathilde and move in myself. My own little bachelor pad."

"You'll have to ask my co-occupant."

"Does he go out?"

"I leave a window ajar for him. Perfectly safe. He loves the rooftops."

"More wine?"

"Sure. Coffee's on."

Gerard exhaled a lungful of smoke. "Look, Paul. I honestly wish to apologise for the way things have gone. It was an unfortunate start. I admit there is no love lost between the CRS and, well, any other branch I suppose, but I shouldn't have put it on a personal level. Genuinely, I'm sorry."

Richer waved his cigarette in the air. "Forget it, Claude. Harsh words were said on both sides. We have to work side by side, so..." He extended his hand. Gerard took it. They shook.

Later, over their third cup of Maison du Café, the air heavy with the combined odours of the evening, Gerard asked, "How's things with La Dame? Everything seems to have gone quiet."

Richer drew on his Disque. Ah, here it comes. "It's going to take time, probably a long time," he said.

"Usually she's on the Minister's back if it's not settled within a day."

"This is special."

"What is it?" It could not have been more ingenuously put.

Richer surveyed the empty cup on the arm of his chair. "Another coffee?" He reached for the jug on the warm plate.

"Why not? Any more of your superb brandy?"

Richer held up the bottle. "Should be enough for two. In the cup?"

"Great."

Richer poured the coffee on top of the *Napoléon* and sat back. He felt relaxed. He felt good.

"What about La Dame?" repeated Gerard.

Richer stifled a burp and then said, "She's lost something..."

Claude Gerard left Paul Richer's apartment at 22:30. He was more than a little pleased with himself.

A fruitful evening Claude, you old dog. A very fruitful evening. He had heard the story of the robbery at Number 24. So, the old woman had lost a fortune in jewellery. But was that all it was? Of course she would want it back.

If and how Mesrine fitted into all this he had yet to establish. It was unwise to strain the new détente at its birth. Perhaps he was reading things into things which just did not exist. He had no proof that Paul Richer had anything to do with Mesrine, let alone his escape from La Santé. His presumptions had been guided by two letters scribbled on a piece of paper, some hieroglyphics and a date marked in red in Richer's office diary, and the fact that both men had served in Algeria at the same time.

So? Many men had served in Algeria at that time. And the date in the diary was a day on which Mesrine had *not* escaped.

He climbed into his white Peugeot.

In a way the evening had gone as planned. In another way it had not. He had confirmed part of the information. La Dame had lost some jewellery and wanted it back. That gave him a base from which to work on the request of the British. But also he had modified his opinion about Richer, which he had not set out to do. The bastard had become at least semi-legitimate. He wasn't such a bad bloke after all. And that would make Gerard's task all the harder.

He must cement the new friendship.

He wondered if Paul would fancy going to the next Paris St Germain match?

‡

18. Voleur

Lundi 12 Juin

Jacques Mesrine climbed the steps from the Guy Moquet metro station, looked around casually and began to walk up the Avenue de Saint Ouen. He walked slowly, enjoying the freshness of freedom, letting the hazy sun caress his face. It was his first time out of doors since his excursion to the north coast two weeks ago, and he had forgotten how good the open air tasted, even the open air of a city.

He entered the first bar he came to, just past the Rue Collette, and ordered a kir at the *zinc*. It was mid-morning and there was only a handful of people in the place. No one took any notice of the man with glasses, clean shaven, hair parted in the centre, slightly protruding chin, dressed in a crisp dark blue two piece suit.

Leaning on the bar, Mesrine began to read yesterday's *France-Dimanche*. On page 9 was a picture of himself and an article on his love life. Lurid stuff. If only he had had half the women they alleged! But that would still be ten times as many as normal men!

"Some man, that Mesrine," grunted the proprietor behind the bar, nodding at the paper.

The customer looked up, almost diffidently. "I've never really followed his exploits myself."

"But you've heard of him?"

"Oh yes."

"Naturally, everyone has heard of Mesrine. Here," the proprietor leant forward conspiratorially. "He used to live around these parts."

"No!"

"*Mais oui!* Down in Clichy. Occasionally he would come up here."

"Heaven! In this actual bar?"

"*Oui.* In fact, he has stood right where you are standing now."

Mesrine, who had never been in the place before in his life, gasped.

"But did you feel safe with a murderer around?"

"Pah! Mesrine a murderer? Never. He's killed people, certainly. Thirty-nine of them - "

"Thirty-nine!"

"*Mais oui. Trente-neuf.* But he's not a murderer in the sense we know it. He does not go out to kill. Only if people get in his way. Well, it is understandable, *n'est-ce pas?*"

"*Oh oui, oui.*"

"You're not from these parts?"

"I'm from Nice. I've just been posted to Paris."

"What do you do? No - don't tell me, let me guess. It's a hobby of mine." The proprietor stared long and hard at Mesrine's face. There was not even a flicker of recognition, no mental connection between the customer and the face he had just seen in the newspaper. "I know! You work in a bank? Am I right or am I right?"

There was admiration in the customer's eyes. "How can you tell?"

"Ah, I have a nose for these things. You develop it after years behind a bar."

"And you are so right! I mean, I could have been anything!"

"Ah!" The proprietor nodded knowingly and tapped the side of his nose. "This never lets me down."

The banker asked, "Don't know of any apartments to let round here, do you? I'm in an hotel at the moment, but I'd like to get my own place. No hurry, the bank's paying, but an hotel's not the same."

"Nothing like your own roof, eh? Another kir?"

"*Oui merci.*"

The proprietor poured one for himself also. "Not many places about nowadays." He made a show of thinking as the banker paid for both drinks with two one hundred franc notes and indicated that he did not want the change. "Try further up near the Porte."

"That's up that way?"

"*Oui.* Out and to the left."

"*D'accord, merci bien monsieur.*" Mesrine raised his glass. "*Salut.*"

"To Mesrine!" said the proprietor.

"Mesrine?" said the banker. "And why not?"

After five places had proved negative, a shopkeeper (with the help of some innocent charm and the purchase of a rather expensive *Cardin* silk tie) directed him to the concièrge of 124 Passage Charles Albert, near the Porte de Saint Ouen.

It was lunchtime and the aroma of coffee floated from a saucepan on an old gas stove in the corner of the *loge*. The concièrge - Madame La Salle, an old harridan with a gruff manner - was about to start on a baguette and a slice of camembert. She did not take kindly to being disturbed, but the charming, apologetic manner of the smart businessman eventually won her round (although she would never admit to it).

Monsieur Lenoir, the banker from Nice, that afternoon paid three months' rent in advance and took possession of the keys to a ground floor studio apartment.

‡

19. Flics

Jeudi 15 Juin

The telephone on the desk of Chief Inspector Paul Richer rang at 10:39 that morning. He answered with his surname.

The voice on the other end was muffled. "Bruno."

Richer looked across at Claude Gerard. His head was stuck in a file and surrounded by a halo of cigarette smoke.

"Oh yes, hello."

"I am now on the move."

"You are in the city?"

"No questions please. I will set things in motion."

"Good. Things are calm."

"I am pleased to hear it. But remember the terms. Me first, you second. In my own time. I will call you as and when. I must go."

"I'm not tracing."

"Of course not, *chef*. But there are half a million other people who might be." The line went dead.

Richer replaced the receiver and lit a Gitanes, throwing one over to land on Gerard's desk.

"Cheers." Gerard did not even look up.

The telephone on Gerard's desk rang. He answered with a grunt.

The voice at the other end said. "Hello Claude old stick. Ron Becker."

Gerard looked across at Richer. He was staring out of the window.

"Oh yes, hello."

"Any news on La Dame's lost possessions?"

"I'm working on it."

"Of course you are, old fruit. But any news?"

"I have progressed. When I am satisfied, I will report."

"You do that, old son. You do that." The line went dead.

"Want some coffee?"

Gerard looked up with a start to see Richer standing over him. Had he been listening?

"Hmm?"

"I'm getting coffee," repeated Richer. "Want some?"

"Yeh, sure, sure."

"You're bloody engrossed. What've you got there?"

Gerard flicked the file. "An English diplomat, involved with a fancy whore."

"Oh? It's not only a stiff upper lip the *rosbeefs* have then? Going to warn him off?"

"Probably. Doesn't seem like anything sinister, no photos or anything. He just likes to screw." He lit the Gitanes. "Fancy coming to football sometime?"

Richer turned, halfway out the door. "Football?"

"There's a pre-season friendly soon. St Germain against some English club with a funny name."

"You got a spare ticket?"

"I can get one."

"Okay, if I'm not on. Tell you what, we'll see the match then you come back for a meal, huh? Mathilde won't mind, will she?"

"Mathilde can go bugger herself. She didn't even hear me come in the other night."

Richer chuckled and left the office.

Gerard smiled, noted the time and wrote something in the file.

‡

20. Flic puis voleur

Samedi 17 Juin

The knock rebounded between the four doors, echoed along the corridor and fell headlong down the stairway. The second knock did the same. And the third.

Claude Gerard looked through the letter box. "Chivas? Chivas!"

Everyone, it seemed, was out on Saturday night.

He popped a few cat treats through the letter box, slipped a *bonbon* into his mouth and walked back downstairs. To call at Richer's apartment on his way home after a day's shooting out near Boissy had been a spur of the moment decision. He should have realised that the bachelor would be out. Wonder if he was with a woman?

Well, no *levant le coude* with Richer tonight. He would have to get back home to his beloved and the offspring.

Downstairs, even the concièrge was out.

It was getting dark as Gerard drove away, forced along the cobbled sidestreets by the *butte*'s one-way system. He had only a vague recollection of the route as last time he had been, if not drunk, certainly *sous l'empire*.

Eventually he came out under Sacré Coeur in the Boulevard de Rochechouart. He turned right and followed the main road along into Pigalle. In the Place Blanche, opposite the Moulin Rouge, he nearly ran down a maniac pedestrian crossing over on a green light. He slammed on his brakes.

"Watch where you're going, *imbécile!*" Gerard shouted through the side window. "*Andouille!*" He wrenched his gear stick into second and without a second glance drove off west towards his home in Levallois-Perret.

"Up yours, drunkard!" shouted Jacques Mesrine at the disappearing Peugeot, thrusting his middle finger into the air.

Mesrine's crisp new slacks gave the lie to the cap and shabby jacket above, but no one would notice. With the cheap Algerian cigarette hanging unlit from his lips, he would pass as any of the other members of Parisian lowlife hanging around the *quartier*.

As ever, Pigalle was Pigalle. It never changed. The smells of coffee and booze and exhausts, the new heavy frying odours from the hamburger joints, the warmth of the interminably flashing neon lights, the calls of touts outside the topless joints and sex clubs. The hooting of the vehicles and the chattering of people. And the girls.

The girls paraded their wares openly on the street, in amongst the African street traders (handmade goods spread out on the ground in front of them) and the inevitable pickpockets and chancers. Most of the ladies of the night left nothing to the imagination. Some stood in doorways in their night clothes, complete with the obligatory suspenders and jangling keys. Others paraded encased in studded leather, their tight garments revealing every crack and crevice of their body. Some walked dogs, whether for protection or purchase was debatable. Inevitably there were also men for sale, some macho studs, some high-rouged slags.

"Like some?" asked an enormous-breasted girl from a doorway, wiggling her orbs. There was a distinct love bite on one of them.

Mesrine grinned. "Later, *chérie*. You keep it hot for me, eh?"

"Hot? It will be roasting!"

"Good girl!"

Already she had turned to someone else.

This was Paris as Mesrine remembered it. His Paris. Lewd, dangerous but, in its own way, honest. You got what you paid for. But he could not remember there being so many people in Pigalle before, even on a Saturday. There seemed to be more traders, more girls, more customers, even more traffic like that *batârd* who had nearly knocked him over.

He walked into a bar on the south side of the Place, near the small church. It was busy and nobody took any notice of one more punter. Men sat around solving the problems of the world amongst the heady atmosphere of alcohol, tobacco, sweat and stale food. Two pinball machines *ping-pinged* near the front window as some kids in leather jackets tried the impossibility of topping the invented Highest Score on the fascia. At some of the tables girls did business, persuading clients to take them to hotels in the sidestreets where rooms were let by the hour and the porters were on a percentage.

Mesrine ordered a large calvados then sat down near the front window, facing sideways into the bar but with easy access out. Across the Place Blanche the electric lights on the mechanical windmill on top of the Moulin Rouge rotated and flashed, causing alternate red and white dotted reflections on the window and on Mesrine's face.

He waited.

‡

21. Voleur et poule

She came in about 23:30, looking for what was probably her fifth trick of the evening. Tall and of dark complexion, coarse-featured but in an attractive sort of way. She glanced casually at Mesrine, but his shabby appearance obviously dismissed him as a worthwhile client. She settled on a loud and patently drunk couple of Dutchmen at a table further in.

Mesrine watched and admired the way she did business. In twenty minutes she had persuaded them to buy four more rounds (she would be on a percentage), the last supposedly vintage champagne, certainly highly-priced and even more certainly *vin blanc* diluted fifty-fifty with *Perrier*. But the Dutchmen were too drunk to notice, they would have enjoyed it even if it had been sparkling dog's piss, which was not outside the bounds of possibility.

Ten minutes later the *ménage à trois* rose and left. Drunk or not, one of the men, the younger of the two, had a distinct bulge in the front of his jeans. She was going to have to earn her money this time.

Mesrine followed them out, keeping at a safe distance, strolling casually, looking for any watching eyes.

They turned right out of the bar and right again into Rue Fontaine. An argument was developing as they reached Rue de Douai and one of the men, with a dismissive wave of his arms, continued down Fontaine, leaving the woman with the one with the hard-on.

They entered a hotel in Rue de Douai.

Mesrine hung around in the street, knowing he would not attract attention from passers-by. A lot of men hang around in doorways and on corners in Pigalle at night.

He gave the woman and her client enough time to complete the formalities with the porter. The Dutchman would have to pay as much for the room for the hour as he would for the night in a good three star hotel in the 16th. The porter would give him a clean towel for which he would expect another *pourboire*, not obligatory but you would get your balls kicked in on the way out if you did not subscribe.

Another few minutes to get up to the room and for the woman to obtain her money immediately they went in. Then Mesrine entered the hotel.

In his years in the place, the porter had seen it all and his face was trained into showing no surprise or emotion at whatever might come into, or go on in, the hotel. So when Mesrine entered, the porter's face registered nothing. But he looked. He looked at Mesrine hard. And Mesrine looked back.

"*Ça va?*" asked the porter lowly.

"*Ça va,*" replied Mesrine.

"Congratulations."

"*Merci.* What room?"

"*Vingt-et-un.*"

"*Bien.*"

Five hundred francs (from a wallet lifted from an American tourist two hours earlier) sped across the countertop and was gone.

"I do not exist."

"*Naturellement, Le Grand.*"

Mesrine climbed the uncarpeted stairs to the second floor. The stairway and corridors were only dimly lit and the place stank of the familiar bleachy smell. Every fourth step did not creak.

Muffled noises came from three of the five rooms on the corridor. He stood outside 21 for a second, listening. Then he smiled, stepped back and kicked the door in.

A frozen tableau greeted him. The woman was naked except for white suspenders and laddered black stockings. The Dutchman still had on his shirt and socks, but the rest of him was bare. They were by the sink, the woman in the process of washing the man's jutting member. She screamed, once, as the door crashed open.

Mesrine had never seen an erection go down so quickly. One second it was there, the next it was gone, like an icicle in a furnace. The woman was left holding a limp sausage. The Dutchman gasped fearfully and tried to cover himself, like a schoolboy caught fiddling in the toilets.

"Out!" shouted Mesrine, picking up the man's trousers and flinging them into the corridor.

"But - "

"OUT! Now!" He grabbed the man by the hair and propelled him across the room.

"I have paid good money - " began the Dutchman in broken French.

"Shut it, Frans. *Deux s'amusent, trois s'embêtent.* Be thankful I don't take the rest of it off you, you bloody foreigner!" With a shove, Mesrine had him in the corridor. Kicking his trousers halfway down the stairs, he counselled "And don't let me see your face around here or anywhere ever again!"

He stepped back into the room and slammed the door behind him.

He waited, his back against the door. There was a rapid *thump-thump*ing down the stairs outside.

The woman was still by the sink, drying her hands on the towel. She looked at Mesrine expressionlessly.

"How much did he pay you?" he asked.

"A thousand."

"A thousand? But the summer sales don't start till next month."

"Needs must."

Mesrine admired the still firm body and remarkably jutting hard-nippled breasts. He held her eyes with his. "I would pay you a million."

"I didn't think you were coming." Her voice was deep and hard. "Any later and I would have had to have seen him off into the sink."

Mesrine pouted. "You are two floors up. I was as quick as I could be."

She stared at him. Then she smiled warmly. "Jacques."

"Janou."

She came across. Putting her arms up around his neck, she kissed him tenderly, something Parisian prostitutes reserve for friends, not clients. "I knew you would come to me, my love," she said softly into his ear. "My apartment is being watched, but I knew you would come to me."

"Of course. The only woman I have ever really loved." He took her face in both his hands. "I have need of you, *ma fille*."

She touched his inner thigh. "Of course you do."

Moving her hand up over his hardness, she unbuckled his belt as she pulled him towards the bed.

She lay in Mesrine's arms, head on his chest as he smoked. The place was peaceful, the only sound the muffled thumping of the bed and the occasional grunt from the room next door. It had been two hours and the porter had not come to tell them time was up. Nor would he. They had all the time in the world.

Outside, trade still went on in the streets of Pigalle but now it was muted in deference to the early hour, like a market winding down before closing. Lights gradually turned off, there were not so many noises, life began to fade.

"Janou?" said Mesrine, softly in case she was asleep.

"*Oui, mon Jacques?*"

"It was marvellous. As always. Soon you will retire. We both will. I will set you up with a house of your own."

"With a room reserved especially for you?"

" *Mais naturellement.*"

"And you will test all the girls before they enter my employ?"

"Rigidly."

Her hand moved from its place on his groin and scratched across his lower stomach. "Bastard."

"Ah, you little cat! Stop that!"

"Cats can be vicious." She bit and sucked on his nipple, causing simultaneous pain and pleasure.

"Wicked, wicked girl," he growled. "I shall thrash you."

"Go on then," she turned in the bed and rubbed her rump against him. "I dare you!"

Mesrine gave each cheek a firm slap and then forcibly turned her around. "Listen, you minx - no, no, don't mess, listen. There is something I want you to do for me."

"Mm? What is that?" Her tongue tickled the corner of his mouth.

"You still know the old gang?"

"Of course. But I will not mention you. The streets are riddled with grasses." The tongue darted into the corner of his eye, then made its way down his cheek like a little wet fish.

"I want some information."

"What sort?" The sharp hairs on the shaving line of his neck pricked her tongue.

"There was a robbery. Sometime this year. Don't know when. Certainly before the middle of April. It was kept quiet in the press. From the house in the Bois."

Her mouth worked its way down his breastbone, licking the blood from the nipple she had bitten. "I think I did hear something on the street."

"I want to know who is involved and, more importantly, where the goods are. There is something of importance to me."

Her head was on his stomach which was firm and muscular despite the time in jail. She kissed his navel, mumbling "I will see what I can do. How can I contact you?"

"You cannot."

"You will contact me?"

"Sometime, yes. At work, not at home."

She moved across his pubic line.

"And Janou?"

"Yes, my love?"

"Be discreet, my child. I do not exist. Listen. Only ask if necessary. Be the model of circumspection."

"Am I ever anything else, *mon petit chou*?" She took him in her mouth and manoeuvred her hips over his head.

‡

22. Voleur

Vendredi 30 Juin

After eight weeks the hunt for Mesrine finally cooled in Paris. The police acknowledged that it would have been suicidal for the master criminal to have stayed in the capital after his escape. As a consequence of both their failure to find him and his appearance in Normandy - and although it had done nothing for their flagging morale - they had already widened their net to take in the whole of France, especially the areas Mesrine had been known to frequent: Lyons, the north coast, the Riviera.

Mesrine knew things would quieten, but he also knew that the hunt for him would never *be called off. The cry had gone out. The infamous Mesrine had to be caught. It was nothing more nor less than a grudge match between him and the Establishment. With every crime he committed, the grudge became deeper, more bitter.*

He could not contact his family or friends, not for a long, long time. It was something he just had to face and accept. Even contacting Janou had been a risk, but his expertise had ensured his safety. Janou was not being watched on the street: he could smell a flic a kilometre off.

Monsieur Lenoir, the banker from Nice, came and went each day at the studio apartment at 124 Passage Charles Albert. He would leave at 08:00 and take the metro, ostensibly to his office in the 8th Arrondisement. At night he would return at 18:30. Sometimes he would go back out in the evening and Madame La Salle, the old concièrge, would smile knowingly. Well, he was a man alone in Paris, wasn't he?

In fact, during the day Mesrine would use the apartment in Invalides. Marcel(le) would ask no questions, naturally, and half the time the old poof was out on adventures of his own anyway. From Invalides, Mesrine would set out into the city in any of his many characters. They were not disguises, for the clean-shaven giant rarely used false items or other things theatrical, except the occasional beard or wig which, on their own, would fool nobody. No, the character came from within. From posture, that could vary his height by as much as thirty centimetres; from facial expression, that could make him a youth or age him twenty years. That was the secret. When he was in full character, no one would instantly recognise him.

It was, Mesrine acknowledged, just one of his many talents.

Thievery was another. On 30 June, Mesrine and Besse raided the home of Monsieur Jean-Claude Martigny at Noissy-le-Sec, to the east of Paris. Monsieur Martigny was a bank employee. Whilst Besse held Madame Martigny hostage,

Mesrine escorted her husband to collect money from his bank, the Société Générale in Le Raincy. The total haul was four hundred and fifty thousand francs. Nobody was hurt during the operation.

‡

23. Flic et les Anglais

Lundi 3 Juillet

Claude Gerard nodded at the security guard on duty just inside the main doors of the British Embassy and walked across to the pretty receptionist. She smiled in recognition.

"Bonjour, mam'selle," said Gerard politely. "Is he in?"

"I'll see, *m'sieur,"* she replied in French. *"Un moment, s'il vous plait."* She picked up the handset of her complex-looking telephone and keyed a three-digit number. The other end was quick to respond.

"Reception here, is Mr Becker available? I have Mr Gerard for him." She listened, nodded, then held the handset against her shoulder. *"Je regrette, m'sieur.* Monsieur Becker is in a meeting at the moment. Can I arrange an appointment or get him to call you?"

The policeman did not look too happy. "No, it does not matter. Just see that he gets this, will you?" From an inside pocket he withdrew a white, sealed A4 envelope. There was no name written on it.

The receptionist looked at it. "This is for Mr Becker?"

"Oui. He will know what to do with it."

"Any reply?"

"I do not think so."

"D'accord m'sieur. I will see that he gets it."

"Merci bien, mam'selle."

The receptionist watched him go. Then she put the handset back to her ear. "Hello? Tell Ron that report he's been waiting for has arrived..."

‡

24. Voleur et poule

Vendredi 21 Juillet

The English tourist sheepishly entered the bar on the south side of the Place Blanche, looking around with the apprehension of a married man let off the leash alone in a foreign city. He was probably a Tottenham Hotspur supporter still lingering after their defeat by Paris St Germain the previous Wednesday. Usually such men travelled in (drunken) packs, but the occasional stray was not unknown.

Not wishing to draw attention to himself, he sat down cautiously at a table for two near the doorway, looking out at the neon lights of the Place, tonight refracting from the puddles of a rainy Paris. He undid his sports jacket and adjusted the cravat at his neck. His suede Hush Puppies streaked dirt onto his slacks as he crossed his legs.

Taking the last of his pack of Players No 6 cigarettes, he lit up, put the match into the empty packet and crumpled it into the ashtray.

The pinball machine opposite was unoccupied. From further inside Claude François, the recently dead pop star, sang *Magnolias For Ever* from the jukebox.

"*Monsieurquestcequevousdesirez?*" The waiter used the usual Parisian trick of speaking at such velocity that the foreigner had not a hope in hell of understanding what he said.

The man blinked up from behind his British National Health spectacles and guessed what the question must have been.

"A-avey vooz urn beer?" he asked with the dead accent of the English.

Without a word the waiter walked away, giving no indication that the order was received, understood or accepted.

Nevertheless ten minutes later a full litre glass of French beer was delivered, together with a till receipt. Making the mistake of every tourist, the Englishman hurriedly placed a note underneath the bill. The waiter ignored it and walked away.

The tourist took a swig of the beer, blanched at its harshness, and took another. Distorted over the rim of the glass, he noticed the tart at a nearby table. The tough, man-of-the-world expression he adopted fooled no one, but the tart returned his smile.

She came over, the scrape of tightly denimed thighs beneath the open rubber rainmac, low cleavage in the cheap blouse.

They spoke the usual introductory platitudes, the mild flirting before the encounter's inevitable conclusion. The Englishman had trouble with his French, but the intent of the exchange was universal. Perhaps the tart spoke a little too loudly, but no one noticed.

A bottle of the sparkling plonk was in equal parts cajoled, moued and extorted, the tart ensuring that the client drank most of it.

Soon they were out in the street, the Englishman nervous and diffident but forced to huddle against the woman in the rain. Her perfume wafted into his face. She led him into the backstreets.

"God, that champagne!" laughed Jacques Mesrine, still in accent. "I've tasted better stuff out of the sinks in La Santé!"

"I have to drink at least one glass of that every time I'm in that place!" complained Janou. "Think of that!"

"*Ah, ma pauvre petite,* soon you will not have to. I do not forget my promises." As he was still in character, he resisted the urge to hug her.

The hotel porter knew Janou but this time he did not recognise the man with her. The usual procedure of payment for the room plus the 'free' towel went smoothly, Mesrine handing over money like an innocent abroad.

In the room they made love.

Later, as they smoked together, he asked about the robbery on the Boulevard Suchet.

"I had to be careful," said Janou. "I couldn't ask just anyone. And I was being discreet as you asked."

"Good girl."

"The word is that it was not a local job, possibly someone new or the crew from up north."

"The Nenesse mob? I've done a few jobs with them recently - you may have seen it in the papers. They would have told me."

"Apparently not them then. Could be a new outfit. Could be someone from outside France all together, maybe from Holland. It's uncertain, but not local. Not much is known."

"Any mention of some letters or a document?"

"*Non.* But it was quite a haul in jewellery. Actual value some two or three million, according to the *téléphone arabe.*"

"So I understand. You heard nothing else?"

She turned so that she lay flat on the bed. In the half-light from the street lamps outside, he could see a wicked smile on her coarse face. "I did hear something else, but I don't know whether it would be of interest." Coyly she ran her finger up her right breast and made circular motions on the nipple, making it harden.

"What did you hear, you tease?"

"They got rid of the stuff here."

"What!" Mesrine pulled her towards him, her breasts flopping sideways as she leant on her elbow above him. "Where? Tell me."

"I knew you would be pleased," she giggled. "In the shop near the Gare de l'Est."

He said the name.

"That's right."

"So, they come from out of town, fence the stuff *here*, and then have it away with the proceeds. Little risk of being caught with the ice on them. Very good. Worthy of *me*. Janou, you are wonderful." He crushed her to him, his lips enveloping her whole mouth, tongue darting between her teeth. After a full minute kissing he beamed, "What on earth would I have done without you?"

"But I love you, Jacques," she reasoned with an innocent naiveté, that one principle explaining everything.

"And I you, my princess. Here," he reached over the side of the creaky bed and dragged his jacket from the floor. "A little something I obtained for you earlier on." He handed over a sizeable wad of rolled money, mixed denominations.

"Jacques! There must be - "

"I don't know how much is there. I haven't counted it. What do you think a grocer's in Neuilly takes in a day?"

As she opened her mouth to respond, there came a sudden banging at the door. "Hey in there, your hour is up!"

Janou slid from beneath the sheets, peeled two one hundred franc notes from her roll, bent down from the waist and slid them underneath the door. There was a grunt from outside and then the sound of footsteps retreating.

Mesrine admired her rump as she straightened up, the cheeks contracting with a powerful grip. It was still firm, but not too firm. It would not resist probing.

"Now," she came back over. "We have at least another hour. How would you like me to say thank you?"

He thought of the desirable buttocks. "Take me somewhere Greek," he said.

‡

25. Voleur et receleurs

Mardi 25 Juillet

At 10:15 that morning there were no customers in the small gunsmith shop on the Rue du 8 Mai 1945, up by the Gare de l'Est. The owner was busy polishing his stock while his brother fiddled with the window display of pistols, revolvers and hunting guns.

The shop's busiest days of the week were Friday and Monday. Friday for the legitimate sales and rentals of firearms prior to a weekend's shoot, and Monday for quite another purpose. For the shop was also a launderers, frequented by members of the Parisian underworld. On a Monday they would bring the weekend's spoils, money for laundering at a fifty per cent exchange rate, articles for fencing at a maximum of ten per cent of their true value.

The man in the blue anorak and cream cap who now entered had avoided the busiest days and, having sat on the metre-high wall outside the station opposite for an hour, had avoided any early morning callers.

The owner looked up from his polishing, decided the caller was buying not selling, and smiled *"M'sieur"* in greeting.

"Bonjour messieurs," said the customer jovially. "A pair of handcuffs if you please."

An unusual request, but often such things were required by gamekeepers and such like, and there was no law against selling them.

"Certainly m'sieur, any particular type?"

"It is for a play. I am a teacher, you see. The nearest you've got to standard police issue."

The owner bent down and began to sort through a drawer underneath the counter. He was aware of his brother coming over. He extracted an appropriate pair of cuffs and straightened up. He found himself facing the barrel of a .38 Smith and Wesson.

He stared, not saying a word, handcuffs dangling from his right hand. His brother was already next to the gunman, hands in the air.

"Go round," ordered the man to the brother, softly but firmly. *"Vite!"*

Brother joined brother behind the counter.

"Closer."

They moved together.

Holding the gun actually touching the owner's right eye, arm outstretched, the gunman said, "*Alors messieurs,* if you would be so kind as to put the cuffs on."

"What?"

"The cuffs. Put them on. One on you," he tapped the gun on the owner's nose as he spoke. "And one on you." Tap. "Then put your other hands flat on the counter top, palms up."

It was quickly done, the owner fumbling with the catch on the cuffs but getting it at the third attempt.

When their hands were in position, palms up and open, the gunman relaxed. "*Merci bien.* Now gentlemen, considering your line of business I am sure you do not have any alarms connected to the *gendarmerie* down the road. Why should you? You are well protected with all these guns around!" He laughed. "So I will give it to you straight. Behave and you will live. One false move, even to scratch your nose, and you will die. I cannot say fairer than that now, can I?" He actually seemed to want a reply to the question.

"N - n – n - " said the owner.

Next to him, beads of sweat draped his brother's white face.

"Now then, if you please…" The gunman's first task was to come round and open the till. Inside was twenty thousand francs. He tut-tutted. "So much, at such an early hour! You're just asking to be robbed. Let me look after it in case any thieves come in."

He then went round the shop at his leisure, examining guns, looking down their barrels, experimenting with the safety catches, firing at invisible objects. All the time he kept the two men expertly covered.

Some housewives walked past outside, their loud voices complaining about the price of the loaves they had just purchased from the *patisserie* further along. The owner of the shop looked across, fearful lest they look into the place and raise the alarm. He could tell this man was a professional, an expert – look at the way the arms were being examined. One intrusion and somebody would surely end up dead.

The gunman chose two Smith and Wesson 9mm pistols, seven hundred rounds in boxes of one hundred, and a wicked-looking hunting knife, usually used for skinning. He took a sports bag from the shelves and packed the guns and ammunition into it. He kept the knife in his hand.

"Thank you, gentlemen," he looked across, satisfied. "Very kind of you. I'd love to stay and enjoy your company longer, but you know how it is. I've enjoyed our little chat." He flung the holdall over his right shoulder and made for the door. Then he stopped as if something had just occurred to him. He turned back. "Oh, one other thing. You had some jewellery in here sometime during the last months. Very expensive jewellery."

The brothers looked nonplussed.

"Don't look so bloody stupid!" The friendliness vanished with a frightening suddenness. His right hand holding the gun swept through the air and knocked a display flying. "Jewellery stolen from a house in the Boulevard Suchet. From La Dame. You bought it. Right?"

"What?"

Without a second's hesitation, the gunman's left hand moved upwards then down. With a thump the knife sliced through the brother's left palm, pinning his hand to the wooden counter. There was a scrape of bone as the knife went in and one squirt of blood. It made a pretty red pattern over a display of shotgun cartridges.

The scream echoed round the shop. Instinctively the brother pulled his hand, but it was pinned firm. More blood flowed thickly from the pulled wound.

The owner began to shake as he stared with shock at his brother's hand.

"Now," said the gunman sadly, "that was unfortunate and unnecessary, wasn't it? Be quick or they will find two bodies here. Answer me, you handled the stuff?"

"Th - there was some s-stuff that w-would fit - " The owner was very pale.

"Well I am not interested in it. Something else was taken at the same time. Some letters which might be of interest to me. You have them?"

"Of course not. I never keep things." He spoke softly now, in monotone.

"But you handled them."

"A wad of old letters, m'sieur. Nothing important. But I noticed one or two signatures. I thought they might be of value to an autograph collector or someone."

"Who did you sell them to? Quickly please."

"It - it is a specialised area. I undercut myself. There is a dealer," he stole a glance at his brother who was staring, equally ashen, at his own hand. "In the Boulevard Montmartre... in the arcade."

"Thank you, m'sieur. You will, of course, not be so silly as to phone the arcade?"

"Monsieur, I have no interest. I disposed of them to my gain - just."

"Has anybody else been asking about them?"

"We have our regular visits from the police. They look around, but we never keep things here. We pay them our insurance. They go. They did ask about some jewellery – but, as always, we were found to be innocent."

"And the letters?"

"No, they have never mentioned them."

The gunman drew ten thousand francs from his pocket and put them on the counter top. "You are a man of honour, I can see that. Well so am I. This is to compensate your brother. It will pay to have his hand seen to."

The brother looked up at him, unable to speak. His legs were shaking.

(It was not until many hours later that the owner was to realise that the gunman had given him back his own money and had still kept half the contents of the till.)

The gunman removed his cap. Both men looked at him, expecting something more. All he did was smile. "Messieurs, continue with your good work. You will remember this day." He backed to the door. "Naturally I ask you not to contact the police. I do not think you will. But if they arrive as a result of the scream, I will not hold it against you." He turned and was gone.

The brothers stayed motionless. After five minutes the owner fumbled for a key to the handcuffs. Two minutes later the brother, still attached to the counter and unable to move, had recovered sufficiently to say, "H-he looked familiar. Wh- who was he?"

The owner thought for a moment. "God knows," he said.

God knew that Jacques Mesrine left the shop, turned left and walked quickly down the steps of the southern entrance to the Gare de l'Est metro station, his bag of guns in his right hand, ten thousand francs in his anorak pocket. He paused to buy a *tarte aux fraises* from a little shop in the underground complex and scoffed it in two bites as he queued behind a man renewing his *Carte d'orange*. When his turn came he bought himself a *carnet*.

Ligne 4 to Strasbourg - Saint-Denis, then Ligne 8 to Rue Montmartre. The journey on the most efficient underground system in the world took less than ten minutes. By car it would have taken an hour at least.

It did not take him long to find the shop in the Galeries Montmartre in the Passage de Panoramas.

Pulling himself up to his full height, he adopted a cock-sure pose, made certain the bag with the cap and guns was zipped up, and entered the small premises.

The place was warm and musty, books lining all three walls from floor to ceiling. A bespectacled, middle-aged man was seated at a desk. He looked up over his *pince-nez* as a police identity card (complete with proper photograph) was thrust at him.

He sniffed. *"Monsieur l'agent?"*

"Monsieur...?"

"Buisson."

"Monsieur Buisson, bonjour. I will not keep you long. We believe certain documents recently came into your possession, to wit a bundle of letters

containing some famous signatures."

"Whose signatures, m'sieur?"

The policeman told him a name.

Buisson removed his spectacles and absentmindedly began to clean them on the end of his tie. "I think I recall the items. Nothing wrong was there? Not forgeries or anything? The seller seemed genuine, said he had owned them for years."

"No, no," the policeman, sensing co-operation, relaxed his voice. "We would just like to have a look at them. We believe something might have slipped in there by mistake. Something that was not for sale."

"He hasn't complained, has he?"

"Who?"

"The vendor. He did accuse me of being a criminal, an extortionist. Said I only gave him a fraction of their worth."

"And did you?"

"Naturally. I am not a charitable organisation." The bookseller put the *pince-nez* back on, blinking up at the policeman.

"Did you examine the letters?" asked the policeman.

"I examined the signatures. Seemed genuine. But you can never be one hundred per cent sure. Never. It's like finding a completely unknown Renoir. Is it or isn't it? Majority acceptance decides."

"You did not actually read the letters?"

"I went through them superficially. Nothing much. Mostly letters she sent to and received from her husband. Love letters. Some others. She is a meticulous lady. All on plain paper."

The policeman pondered. "Hm. Doesn't sound as if it's what we're looking for. You don't still have them, I suppose?"

"No. I have a mailing list of clients. There is an Anglophile in Normandy. He snapped them up."

"At a hundred times what you paid for them?"

"Twenty."

"I'll contact him anyway. Can you let me have his name and address?"

Buisson turned and rummaged through a box index. Withdrawing a card, he transferred the information onto a sheet of yellowing headed paper.

The policeman read the name and address and frowned. "You don't happen to know what he does, by any chance?"

"Actually I do. Funny coincidence…"

Buisson told him and it was all Mesrine could do to stop himself exploding with laughter.

‡

26. Flic et l'Anglais

Lundi 31 Juillet

Claude Gerard sat on the benches in front of the *Jours de France* buildings on the south side of the Rond Point des Champs Elysées, facing north, watching the traffic manoeuvre back and forth across the circular crossroads. He sucked on a liquorice-tasting cachou and simultaneously smoked a Disque. The hot sun beamed down on the back of his head. He hoped it would not be as hot as this in Ostend, upon which the Gerard family would be descending at the end of next week.

For the third time he looked at his watch. 13:35. His meet was late.

It was another ten minutes before he saw him, walking past the Matignon Drugstore on the far side of the Point. Gerard rose, stubbed his cigarette under his right foot, and walked round to meet his man as he crossed over the Avenue des Champs Elysées at the lights.

"Afternoon, Claude old stick," greeted Ron Becker of the British Embassy. "Sorry I'm late."

"*Pas de probleme,*" said Gerard. "Sometimes it is nice just to sit and reflect."

"Quite."

"You wanted to see me?"

"Yes. Shall we walk?"

They began to walk up the Champs on the southern side.

"Wondered how things were coming along re the little problem," said Becker without preamble. "It's been a while."

Gerard raised his eyebrows. "I gave you a report."

"Not good enough, old son, not good enough. So I'm told. I didn't read it. Passed it on to the man as instructed."

"Who *is* he?"

"Just a civil servant."

"Of course. Aren't we all?"

"Cigarette?" Becker proffered a packet of Peter Stuyvesant.

"*Merci.*" Gerard shook his head. "Cachou?"

"Trying to give them up."

They passed the Le Paris cinema on their left, at that time twinned and, as usual, not doing very good business (it was to be demolished in the mid-eighties).

"Exactly what is it that you want?" asked Gerard gruffly. "What do you mean, my report was not good enough? I told your superior that he was talking to the wrong man - and now I'm telling you. It is not my case."

Becker chose to ignore the point of contention. "I had a little chat with my superior, as you call him. He put me in the picture, as far as he was able. In fact, he is pleased that there's been no publicity. He says that shows that whoever has whatever it is does not know its significance - whatever that significance may be. Even he does not know. Do you?"

"No. What can be so significant about stolen jewellery? *Alors, bien sûr,* I know it is worth a lot, and there could be some historical interest – "

"It was more than jewellery."

"*Pardon?*"

"Something else was taken as well as the jewellery."

Fuck. "I am not aware of this. What is it?"

"That, old sport, I don't know. I just know it is of great significance. There is firm pressure being applied from somewhere. My *superior* has asked me to remind you of point (c)."

Gerard furrowed his brow. "Point (c)... point (c)? Which one was that? There were so many points."

"Come on, Claude," sneered Becker. "Don't act the innocent. For God's sake be reasonable. You're our liaison man, and we have passed on a reasonable request. The request comes from a very important person in London. Doesn't that mean anything to you?"

"You know what we did to royals in this country, m'sieur."

They stopped outside the *Aéroflot* offices.

"So," said Becker. "You are refusing to co-operate?"

Gerard sighed and looked everywhere but at the Englishman. He said, "*Non.* I will co-operate. I *am* co-operating. I have given you a report. All I knew was that some jewellery was stolen. I will pursue things further. I will give you another report as and when I know something. Monsieur, things take time. Your royal cannot expect results within a day. If I may tell my colleague of your interest, he can liaise with you direct - "

"No, my son, no." Becker stabbed his cigarette in Gerard's direction. "No one else is to know of our interest. It's in your hands. As long as you have our interests at heart, that's all that matters."

"Of course."

Becker looked at his watch, took a final drag on his cigarette before throwing it away, then said "Okay, keep in touch. I must go, I have some shopping to do. Just keep us informed, old fruit." With a nod, he disappeared down the Marignon entrance to the Franklin D Roosevelt metro station.

For a minute Gerard stayed looking at the magazines on display around the nearby kiosk. He muttered, *"Rosbeef* arsehole," then he crossed the Champs and walked off down the Rue du Colisée.

"Stupid frog," mumbled Becker as he waited for his Ligne 9 train to take him to Havre-Caumartin. Absentmindedly he looked at the Pont de Sèvres train standing at the opposite platform. A blonde, middle-aged man looked back at him from inside the train. Their eyes met and then quickly looked away, as strangers' eyes always do.

Paul Richer turned from the window and began to read the adverts inside as the train pulled away towards Alma Marceau. He read the same advert over and over again - details of the *Billet de Tourisme* - until he was distracted by a bunch of tourists alighting at Trocadéro for Chaillot and the Eiffel Tower. He knew this route well but still he looked up at the linear map above the doors. Three more stops to Ranelagh. Then the short walk and he would be at the Boulevard Suchet.

‡

27. Flic et victime

Soon Richer was being ushered into La Dame's bedroom. He had booked his appointment two days in advance, so this time there was no delay for cosmetics (or, as he thought cruelly, for the cracks to be plastered over).

She looked the same as when he had visited her before, propped up in the centre of the bed, housecoat matching her jet-black painted hair. Make-up heavy but tasteful. It was as if she had not moved since his last visit, as if she had been turned off when he left and only switched back on again a few minutes ago.

"Madame," he gave a little bow and spoke in English. "I regret to disturb you. I thought you would like a report on my progress."

Her clear eyes looked at him. She gave a quizzical little smile. "Who *are* you, monsieur?"

Richer coughed. "From the BCP, madame." He pronounced it Bay-Say-Pay. "The Sûreté."

" The Sûreté... the Sûreté..." She frowned. "But where is Monsieur Gerard?"

"He could not come, madame."

"Such a *nice* man."

"Indeed, madame. I thought you would like to know how things were progressing."

"What is *your* name?"

"Richer. Chief Inspector Richer."

"We have never met?"

"Once, madame."

"Oh, you must forgive me. I am an old woman." She giggled like a little girl. "Now, what can I do for you, Chief Inspector?"

"About the document, madame. I thought you would like a progress report - "

"Document? What document?"

"The robbery."

"What robbery? Oh never mind, never mind. Come here, will you? Pour me a drink."

Richer did as he was bidden and stood on the spot he had occupied three months before.

She sipped the vodka. "Sit down, monsieur, I cannot look up at you. I will get a pain in my neck."

Not even bothering to look for a chair, Richer squatted on the edge of the bed. "Although we have had no success yet, madame, I have a good man on the job."

"Monsieur," a feeble hand was raised and then fell back on the bed. "What *are* you talking about?"

"You called us last April, madame. About the robbery. The jewellery that had been taken."

"I did? *Jewellery!*" Another giggle twinkled lightly from her old lips with the incongruity of a mountain stream in a desert. "Did I *really?*"

"*Et je pense que - Pardon.* And I thought that you would like a progress report seeing as August is now upon us."

"Monsieur," she spoke kindly, on the edge of condescension. "Monsieur *Gerard*. I do not know anything about any robbery or jewellery."

"Or the document, madame? The game that must not be given away?"

"I... game? I have a feeling... that this... is a game... monsieur..." She closed her eyes and Richer quickly caught the glass as it flopped from her fingers.

Putting the glass back on the bedside table, he rose, keeping his eyes locked on La Dame. She did not stir.

Silently he walked across to the door. It opened without a sound.

"Thank you for coming," said the old woman's voice suddenly, loud and clear.

He looked back.

She was wide awake, looking at him. "Do call again. It has been so nice talking to you. I hardly have anyone visit me nowadays, you know. Not since David left me." She sighed.

Richer nodded and turned to leave.

"Tell me," she said. "How *is* Madame Gerard and your children?"

That evening Richer sat in his favourite chair in his *salon*, brandy in one hand, stroking Chivas on his lap. A current affairs programme was on TRF1 but, although his eyes stared at the screen, nothing was registering. He was deep in thought.

La Dame could remember nothing. To be more correct, *at this moment* La Dame could remember nothing. But she was notoriously inconsistent. Tomorrow she might remember all.

But if she did not?

Chivas turned in his lap for a belly stroke.

If she did not, then there need be no further police involvement other than a filed report. There need be no lies about the document being destroyed, no stealth.

Tipping Chivas off his lap, he went across to his jacket and removed the article he had taken to the Boulevard Suchet that afternoon. A woman's stocking.

He twisted his hands between the ends and snapped the stocking out sharply.

And he need not murder La Dame, the very important American lady: Wallis Warfield Simpson, the Duchess of Windsor.

‡

28. Voleur

Vendredi 4 Août

It is difficult for the non-French to understand the significance of an August in France. August means vacation. Many factories and offices close for the whole month. The cities close down, the coastal resorts come alive.

Even in Paris every third shop is closed and every second restaurant has the 'Fermeture Annuelle' sign on its locked doors. It is truly a month when Paris is populated only by tourists and the thieves who prey on them.

No self-respecting Frenchman remains in Paris in August unless he has to through personal, occupational or other fiscal necessity. If it was one trait of Jacques Mesrine it was that he was self-respecting. Thus August and most of September saw him on holidays with friends, first touring in Italy then Algeria. Then he left the friends and took a lady to London, staying in an hotel near Marble Arch.

On Friday 4 August, while Mesrine was enjoying himself in Italy, Paris Match *published an interview he had given to a freelance journalist a couple of weeks previously. It caused an uproar, embarrassed the police and the Establishment, and led to the arrest of the magazine's publisher Daniel Filipacchi on charges of condoning murder and theft.*

The interview put Mesrine back on the front pages and renewed pressure on the police to find him. Frequently the police stated that they had new information, new leads on the master criminal's whereabouts. Undoubtedly at the time they thought they had. But their failure to produce him led to them being pilloried in the press for incompetence and laziness. The press, of course, had their axes out and finely honed after the arrest of Filipacchi, one of their brethren.

Public demand for Mesrine stories was rekindled and satisfied (August is a noted news-less month throughout the western world).

Mesrine was away from the furore, but he kept in touch with events, taking French newspapers at whatever town, whatever address he happened to be staying. He was pleased that he was back where he considered he belonged, on the front pages.

By the time he returned to Paris, at the end of September, things had quietened down again...

‡

29. Flic

Samedi 30 Septembre

Paul Richer stood by his window, brandy in one hand, Gitanes in the other, and watched the floodlights of the Sacré Coeur Basilica blink on. It was mid-evening and the sun was leaving Paris for another day, bequeathing a clear sky which augured well for the morrow. Chivas slept on top of the television.

Richer was busy at work, but thank God his rank and job were sufficient to ensure he never worked nights as a matter of routine. He left that to his staff. Young Inspector Bauer seemed hardly ever to be off duty.

Things were quiet on the Mesrine front. No longer did his picture appear in the newspapers *every* day as a consequence of the Paris Match fiasco last month. No longer were there extended accounts of his exploits in the nightly news bulletins. It was generally accepted in police circles that Mesrine was once again well away from Paris, probably out of France.

But one man in the force knew differently.

Because just a few moments ago Richer had received a phone call. A quickly-terminated phone call from Bruno to say he was back and would soon be taking 'further recovery action'.

At 21:46 on Saturday 30 September, Paul Richer raised his glass in a salute from his window and swallowed his brandy in one.

‡

30. Voleur et flics

Vendredi 6 Octobre

In keeping with the quiet opulence of the rest of the town, the police station in Deauville, Normandy, looks anything but what it actually is. It is more like a cottage, quaint and gabled, with six stone steps leading up to the front door. Inside, the hallway has a mosaic floor, wood panelling on the walls and wooden furniture.

That night, as usual, two officers were on duty in the public reception area. All had been quiet for the first hour of their 22:00 to 06:00 shift.

At 23:00 the outside door opened. The officers looked up from their newspapers to see a big man dressed in a neat but slightly crumpled serge suit, document case under his arm, striding towards the counter. He looked angry.

"Chief Inspector Dorner, Internal Affairs, Paris. Is Inspector Le Bouthillier in?"

Quickly the officers straightened themselves up. "He's not on duty, sir," replied one.

"*Merde alors!*" Chief Inspector Dorner's eyes blazed. "It is imperative that I get hold of him. I have been travelling all day."

"*Je regrette, monsieur -* "

"Why did he not wait for me? Did he not get my message?"

"Your message, sir?"

"Yes, my message! I telephoned from Paris this morning. He wasn't in *then*! Some rookie took a message. By Christ, this is *typical*! Bloody provincial *gendarmes*." His fist clenched and unclenched around the bottom of the document case, bottled fury on the point of exploding.

"*Monsieur, je regrette -* "

"Yes, yes, yes. Well I'm here and I want to see him. What's his home address?"

"I have his telephone number, sir." The officer who was doing the talking thumbed through his book while the other officer went over to a card index. "Here it is."

"What about his address?"

The second officer called over his shoulder, "I have it here, sir."

"Right." Dorner accepted both the number and the address. Then, as if the thought had just struck him, he looked at his watch. "Hell. Do you have a private phone in a private room? I had better call him first considering the lateness of the hour."

The officers were the personification of help and assistance, not wishing to displease the already irate Chief Inspector from Paris.

"This way, sir."

Dorner was shown into a small unoccupied office behind the reception area. Next door he could hear muffled voices in what must have been the general office.

Left on his own, he moved quickly, dialling the number he had been given. After three rings a man's voice answered, muffled, as if he had been asleep.

Dorner put down the receiver. He did not, however, replace it in its cradle but balanced it on the body just above. Anyone looking in casually would presume the receiver was down, only close examination would reveal otherwise.

It was one of the oldest tricks in the book. The incoming call that could not be cut off. Now, even if Inspector Le Bouthillier replaced his phone, as he would do imminently, the connection was made. If he picked up his receiver again, he would be connected back to this office. And, of course, any incoming calls to the Inspector would receive the engaged tone.

Dorner came back out, closing the door behind him. "*Merci*." His temper was abating. "The Inspector will see me."

"Do you wish a car, sir?"

"No, no. I have my own. Which way do I go?" He was given directions. "*D'accord*." He paused by the front entrance. "Oh by the way, is the Inspector married?"

"Sir?"

Dorner actually smiled. "It is late. I wish to disturb his wife as little as possible."

"Oh yes, sir. The Inspector is married."

"Children?"

"Grown up, not at home."

"*Bien, merci messieurs*." And Dorner was off through the doors.

Like a thief in the night.

It was not until the officers were nearing the end of their shift six hours later that one, the younger one who had done most of the talking to the Chief Inspector, said suddenly, "That man was Mesrine."

"Who?" The other officer was engrossed in a cup of hot chocolate.

"That Chief Inspector earlier on. It was Mesrine."

"Rubbish. You're going mad."

"It was Mesrine I tell you."

"Mesrine would never return to Deauville after the casino job. The Chief Inspector was fatter and younger than that shit. Besides, Mesrine is out of France by now – haven't you read the reports? You're getting tired, Pierre, hallucinating. I think you'd better go home."

"He didn't show any identification."

"True..."

"I think I'll ring Le Bouthillier."

"What! You *are* mad! He'll have your bollocks. It's five o'clock in the morning, man!"

"But what if it *was* Mesrine? I'll ring him anyway."

But by then it was too late.

‡

31. Voleur et flic

The stolen blue Simca crossed the Pont de Belges and, keeping within the speed limit at all times, passed through Trouville. The street lighting disappeared on the edge of town and Chief Inspector Dorner drove through the quiet, dark lanes of Normandy on full headlights.

A mélange of intermittent farms and houses passed by until he found the one he wanted, a thatched, single-level cottage, with sizeable gardens front and rear, out of shouting distance of anywhere else.

And out of screaming distance.

He cruised the Simca the last few metres with its engine off, parking it off the road, blocking the small driveway but facing outwards. With the headlights off, Dorner had only a half moon for illumination. He climbed from the vehicle, leaving the keys in the ignition and the door unlocked, and strode purposefully up to the double front door.

He gave the bell three short bursts and then kept his finger on it.

After two minutes a light came on inside and footsteps could be heard approaching.

"*Alors, arrêtez, arrêtez!*" shouted a gruff, disgruntled voice. "*Qu'est-ce que c'est? Qui est-là? Merde alors, c'est minuit!*"

"*Monsieur l'Inspecteur?*" called the man outside. "Inspector Le Bouthillier?"

"*Qui est-là?*"

"Dorner. Chief Inspector Dorner. Sûrêté Nationale. It is vital that I see you at once."

"From Headquarters? Caen?" There was a fumbling of chains. A bolt was pulled back.

"No, not Caen. Paris."

The door was opened.

"Paris!" Le Bouthillier was a squat, balding man in his early fifties with a surprisingly aristocratic hooked nose. He frowned at the official ID thrust into his face. He gawped at the 9mm Smith and Wesson that followed it.

"Inside and shut your mouth *tight!*"

"What the - ?"

"Shut up, *con,*" Mesrine pushed the dressing-gowned policeman against the wall as he forced his way in. "Shut up and you *may* live to see tomorrow."

"What - "

Mesrine pushed the gun savagely up Le Bouthillier's left nostril. His eyes glared death. The policeman closed his mouth without further sound.

Mesrine span him around to face the wall as he kicked the front door closed behind him. He grabbed the Inspector's right arm and bent it excrutiatingly up his back, held in place by the closeness of his body. He wrapped his left arm around the Inspector's neck and pressed the gun firmly into his right temple. Le Bouthillier struggled but the big intruder was strong, and another hard jab from the pistol pre-empted anything silly.

Mesrine marched him along the smartly-carpeted hallway and into the first room on the right, the *salon*.

"Your wife." Mesrine's hot breath blew into his ear.

"What?"

"Your wife. Where is she?"

"In bed."

"Where's the kitchen?"

"The what?"

"The kitchen - for Christ's sake man, are you deaf? Ah, I know what your little game is! Bedroom, quickly!" He released the neckhold and grabbed a clump of hair at the back of Le Bouthillier's head. The gun moved round from the temple to press into the ear.

The Inspector was pulled into the hallway. Mesrine was breathing deeply, almost snarling. "Madame Le Bouthillier!" he called. "Madame! It is no good. Your telephone is blocked. Please come out. I will have no hesitation in shooting your husband."

There was a silence lasting half a minute. Mesrine said, *"Madame, s'il vous plait.* I will not ask you again. In thirty seconds you will become a widow."

Slowly a door down the hallway creaked open. A middle-aged woman, frightened but defiant, stepped hesitantly out. She was dressed in a flowery pink robe with a nightdress poking out at the neck and ankles.

"Bonsoir Madame." The intruder gave a broad grin which, at another time, in another place, would have been received as a charming smile. "I out-thought you. But do not be down-hearted. There are not many people who get the better of Jacques Mesrine."

The Inspector stiffened. "M - Mesrine?" He tried to turn to look but he was still held tight. "What on earth - ?"

"Silence. In a moment, Inspector. *Madame, s'il vous plait.* Where is the kitchen?"

She nodded to her right. *"Là."*

"Then if you please, madame."

Madame Le Bouthillier led the way, instinctively flicking on the light switch. Two flourescents flashed into life.

Just before he entered, Mesrine paused, the Inspector held in front of him. "The blinds. They are drawn?"

"They are drawn, m'sieur," confirmed the lady.

The two men shuffled in. Mesrine swiftly sized up the place. Traditional, oak beams, old stove, solid wooden table and chairs, newer cupboards and worktops, a few modern appliances.

"Madame, please sit down. Put your hands flat on the table top, palms upwards. Thank you. Please do not move, not even to scratch your nose. If you do, something terrible might happen."

The Inspector tried again to turn round but he was still held fast. "F - for goodness sake, what do you want Mesrine?"

"Be patient Inspector, please," said the voice next to his ear. "In a moment. Now, I want you to go and join your good lady. Sit opposite her and adopt the same posture. Please believe that I will not hesitate in shooting both of you if the need arises. I *beg* you not to be foolish." He let go of the hair and took a quick step backwards.

But the Inspector was not foolish. He did as he was instructed.

With husband and wife seated at the table, hands in view, Mesrine said, "Now then, I must apologise for calling at this ungodly hour, but I am on a quest. A quest of the utmost delicacy. And it is better perpetrated under the cover of darkness."

Inspector Le Bouthillier frowned across at him.

"I shall not keep you long. Inspector, you recently bought some signed letters from Monsieur Buisson in Paris. Letters of the American lady. I want them."

The Inspector's jowls wobbled as he shook his head uncomprehendingly. "That is all this is about? They are not worth what you might think, you know. Fifty thousand at the most."

"I am not interested in their value. Do you have them?"

"You are not interested in their value? Then why - "

Mesrine moved like a lynx. With two steps he was across the room. His gun slammed down onto the fingers of Madame Le Bouthillier's right hand.

The lady gasped and went very pale but, through what must have been terrifying pain, she retained her composure. The fingers were black and swollen within two seconds.

It was the Inspector who screamed. "You fucker!" His hands lifted off the table.

Mesrine pointed his gun straight between Le Bouthillier's eyes.

"Easy, easy. I did advise you, m'sieur. Now look what you have done to your poor lady wife. Calm yourself. Please. Come on, calm down."

The Inspector was breathing deeply. He glared at Mesrine.

Mesrine smiled at him, like an old friend. "Better, *non?* Fancy making me do that to the woman you love."

Le Bouthillier let his hands fall back onto the table, palms upwards. Two tears ran down Madame Le Bouthillier's cheeks.

Mesrine went over to the worktop and, with his left hand, unravelled the flex on an old liquidiser. The Inspector, now sweating profusely, looked perplexed. Mesrine pulled the flex from the worktop to the table, satisfied himself that it stretched, and brought over the liquidiser. He plugged the cable into the socket in the wall.

The liquidiser sat, blades glistening, in front of Madame. Mesrine tested it. The machine roared viciously, like a wild beast disturbed from its rest. Both the Inspector and his wife jumped.

"Madame, your self-control is admirable," complimented the gunman as he turned the liquidiser on its side. "I am sorry for what your husband did to you. *Monsieur L'Inspecteur*, please. No more delays, questions - or lies. *Madame, permettez-moi.*" He took the woman's now paralysed black fingers. She tried to tug her arm back but did not have the strength.

As casually as if he was loading meat into a mincer, Mesrine pushed her hand into the liquidiser. He held the wrist on the table and, gun pointing in the Inspector's direction, held the ON/OFF switch with the third finger of his right hand. "*Monsieur?*"

The Inspector was open-eyed. "You - you *animal*, Mesrine. How *can* you? Everything they say about you is true."

"And more so. Believe it, m'sieur. Now, let us make this unpleasantness as brief as possible. You have the letters?"

Le Bouthillier was staring at his wife's hand in the obscene machine. "In - in the *salon*. I - I am a collector of autographs - in a small way, you understand. More out of interest than any financial investment, though they could be a hedge against inflation. I have others also. There's a Pasteur, a Piaf - take them please. Take them all." A nervous giggle jogged from his lips.

Without warning Mesrine thumped Madame Le Bouthillier across the back of the neck. She slumped forward soundlessly, head on the table, hand still in the appliance.

"You bastard!" The Inspector leapt to his feet. By the time his legs had straightened, the gun was pressing into his left eye.

"Easy!" snapped Mesrine. "Easy, Inspector, easy. She is asleep, that is all. Control yourself, you're a police officer."

The men stared at each other.

"She will be fine," continued Mesrine. "A dull headache when she awakes, no more. The letters, if you please."

"But - "

"Please."

The Inspector led the way back into the *salon,* all the time covered by Mesrine's gun. No words were spoken as he fumbled in the top of an escritoire for a key and then unlocked a drawer lower down.

"Be careful what you pull from that drawer, m'sieur." It was wise counsel.

A bundle tied with pink ribbon was held out to Mesrine.

"Into my hand please. *Merci bien.* Now Inspector, if you would be so kind, remove your dressing gown."

"*Quoi?*"

"Please do as I ask. Let us not spoil our new-found co-operation."

With a sigh, the Inspector did as he was asked.

"Now, sit down on the couch. *Bon.* And wrap the gown around your ankles. Come along. Thank you."

Mesrine sat on a chair behind the couch next to the escritoire, the back of Le Bouthillier's head a mere metre away. "I do not have to tell you, *Monsieur L'Inspecteur,* that a bullet from this range would ensure that your widow would need to completely redecorate this room."

Mesrine untied the ribbon and began to read the letters. Occasionally the silence was punctuated with comments like "You know, you really should keep these somewhere safer. There are thieves about." And, "It is a pity your wife is not awake, she could make us some coffee."

There were nine of them in all. Mostly from 'Peaches' to 'David' and back. They were all in English. He read each one carefully. He did not fully understand some of them, but his time in Canada had given him a fair command of the language.

At the end of the ninth letter, he frowned and then read them all again in reverse order. Then he held each one up to the light and then shook each envelope out, the ageing glue complaining and parting.

They all seemed straightforward, completely non-controversial, nothing earth-shattering. It would help, of course, if he had some idea of what the hell he was supposed to be looking for. But the Captain had said he would know it when he saw it. Well, he hadn't seen it here. *Merde.*

Then he asked sharply, "Where are the others?"

Le Bouthillier jumped at the sudden breaking of the silence. He began to turn his head until he felt the coldness of the gun against his face. "Oth - others?"

"You heard what I said."

"I have no others - "

"*D'accord!*"

Le Bouthillier was pulled upwards by the collar of his pyjamas. He stumbled with the dressing gown still round his ankles and Mesrine dragged him into the kitchen on his knees, the cotton of the pyjamas tearing, the opening in the front gaping, exposing him lewdly.

Mesrine let him fall at the feet of his unconscious wife. "I have had *enough!* Let us see how your wife looks without her fingers."

Le Bouthillier snuffled, trying to cover himself and rise at the same time, still entangled in the robe. He slipped, his head landing on his wife's lap.

The liquidiser roared as it was switched on.

"NO!" screamed Le Bouthillier above the roar. "IN THE NAME OF CHRIST!" His head came above the table, eyes half closed, not wanting to see what he must see. "I'll tell you. Let me explain. *Oh my God!*"

His wife's hand was intact. Mesrine held her wrist, the fearsome blades one centimetre from her fingers.

Mesrine said nothing for a full minute, letting Le Bouthillier appreciate the drama of the moment. Then calmly, almost amicably, he said softly "Please do not think that this reprieve is any sign of weakness on my part. I switched the machine on without looking. Madame's hand must somehow have fallen backwards. I will not miss this time."

"You *bastard*. You *cunt*. You're a madman."

"It has been said. Now, you were going to explain?"

"I thought you must be after those. My dealer advised me to sell. Said the police had been enquiring after them. But how did you know? How could you have possibly found out?"

"Where are they?"

"*Ecoutez!*" There was desperation in the Inspector's voice. "Perhaps we can do a deal. I belong to the - "

He never had time to complete the sentence.

Mesrine was always to swear that it was an accident, that he never had any intention of doing it. Whether his finger slipped or not, the result was the same. The liquidiser roared again.

The top of Madame Le Bouthillier's second finger disintegrated, and her whole hand disappeared from sight as the centrifugal force coated the sides of the jug in blood. She moaned in her unconsciousness.

Le Bouthillier screamed and leapt for the gunman.

Mesrine, shocked himself, stepped back and easily knocked the policeman to the floor. On his back, Le Bouthillier made a wild sweep for his legs. Mesrine kicked his arm away and stepped on his throat.

Memories flooded back. Memories of years ago when he had had an Arab in exactly the same position. That night in Algeria. The night he had met, and been saved by, Captain Paul Richer. The man who was responsible for him being here in Normandy tonight.

The smell of Africa came back to him.

He pointed the gun straight down into Le Bouthillier's face. "One chance, melon," he murmured. "One chance before I blow you away."

Le Bouthillier's face was turning purple, water streaming from his eyes, breath cracking.

"Who has them and where?" Mesrine eased his foot just enough.

The Inspector gasped a name and a place.

"Repeat," ordered Mesrine, leaning forward to confirm his ears. "*Encore.*"

The Inspector repeated the name and the place.

Then it happened.

Mesrine had not even been aware of a movement, let alone the sound of any drawer opening. Perhaps it had not. Perhaps she had had it on her all the time. Whatever, it did not matter. What mattered was that at that moment, with a speed belying her age, Madame Le Bouthillier lunged forward and stabbed Jacques Mesrine with a carving knife.

‡

32. Flics

Samedi 7 Octobre

"Did you hear?" Claude Gerard burst into the office, tossing a bag containing a slice of warm quiche at Paul Richer. It was 14:00 on a sunny Parisian day. Gerard was on lates.

"Hear what?" Richer laid the greasy bag down gingerly on a piece of scrap paper and tore it open.

"Mesrine. He's surfaced."

Richer looked up sharply. "Where d'you hear this?"

"On the radio. One o'clock news."

"What did they say?"

Gerard attacked his quiche with gusto, a piece of onion lodging on his chin and bouncing up and down as he spoke. "Killed an inspector and his wife up in Normandy last night."

"A *police* inspector?"

"*Mais oui.* Strangely enough, nothing seems to have been taken."

"Then - ?"

"A straight case of murder. Revenge probably. You know what a vengeful bastard he is. Always swearing to get even with those who put him inside. He robbed the casino up there in May."

"They didn't give the inspector's name?"

"No, but we can find out." The last half of the pie was crammed into his mouth. Richer had not even started on his.

"How do they know it was Mesrine?"

"No details," mumbled Gerard. "Seems he was recognised by a young officer earlier that night."

"Earlier? *Je ne comprends pas.*"

Richer picked up the telephone as Gerard asked him if he wanted coffee.

"Something stronger." Richer tapped out the three figures of the General Office. "Fancy coming downstairs? - Hello, Bauer? What's this I hear about Jacques Mesrine? You don't? Okay, leave it, *merci.* I'll be out for about half an hour."

Gerard was grinning. "You're starting early today. Just afternoon and you want to booze already."

"You complaining?"

"No, let's go. What's up? Something wrong? You had a shock?"

"I just fancy some cognac, that's all. If you don't shut up you can buy your own."

The telephone on Richer's desk shrilled. Both men turned from the doorway. Gerard looked at him inquiringly. He nodded at the phone.

"Leave it," said Richer bluntly.

They went out.

Commissaire Fleury-Goujon put down his telephone then picked it up again immediately, keying the General Office.

"This is the Commissaire. Where's Chief Inspector Richer?"

"Just logged out sir."

"Did he say he'd be long?"

"Half an hour, sir."

"I want him immediately he returns."

"Yes sir."

They stood at the *zinc* of the bar at the corner of Rue de Penthièvre and Rue Cambacérès.

"Anything wrong, Paul?" asked Gerard as he lit their cigarettes. "You seem... pre-occupied."

Richer opened his mouth to say something, thought better of it, paused and then said, "No, I'm having problems, that's all. On a case." He swilled his drink down in one.

"Can I help?"

Richer smiled. "Claude, you offered already. *Henri! Encore!*"

"La Dame? Is the old bitch causing trouble again?"

"No, just trying to retrieve her damn jewellery. Enquiries drawing a blank. You know how it is."

"I thought you'd written it up as closed."

"I did. To keep the Minister happy. I lied."

"How many men you got on it?"

"Just one. And you know it can't be full time. There are other, daresay more important, things."

"Of course there bloody well are. I told you, it's a PR job. Smooth her over, charm her up. Chances are she'll forget about it."

Richer stared at the bottles on the shelf behind the bar. For some reason his eyes rested on an ornately-designed bottle of chocolate mint liqueur. On its label was an ebony maiden carrying a pannier on her head. Why on earth did she remind him of Mesrine?

He called to the barman. *"Henri! Deux petites!"*

As they tucked into the sausages and bread, they spoke about other things: about Claude's case of the British diplomat and the whore that was occasioning frequent visits to the embassy; about the vicissitudes of Paris St Germain; about Mathilde Gerard; about Jacques Mesrine.

Lydia.

It hit Richer like a bolt from the blue. Mesrine's first wife, the black girl from Martinique. That's who the girl on the bottle reminded him of. How strange.

He asked, "Fancy another meal sometime?"

Gerard was halfway through his *petite*, crumbs down his tie and over the *zinc* in front of him. He nodded. "That's good. I'd like to. When?"

"When are you free?"

"God, any time. Mathilde probably thinks I've got a woman anyway. You know what she said to me the other day?" A piece of half chewed sausage shot out of his mouth and landed like a limpet on the side of his glass. "That I was turning queer, spending all my time with you. *All my time!* I ask you! I only go round your place - what? - once a month? And already we are lovers!"

Richer slapped Gerard on the back. "Come along then, *chéri*, let us finish off with a beer. *Henri! Deux bieres!* What do you say? Tomorrow night?"

"Suits me, *mon ami*," Gerard wiped his mouth on his sleeve. "And wear your suspenders and that wispy little thong, there's a good chap."

The young officer heard the chatter of the two Chief Inspectors in the corridor and poked his head out of the General Office. "Chief Inspector Richer, sir?"

"Oui?"

"The Commissaire, sir. Wants to see you immediately."

"Shit."

"Yes, sir." The officer disappeared.

"La Dame?" asked Gerard.

Richer shrugged. "Shouldn't be. But I'll soon find out."

Fleury-Goujon motioned for Richer to sit down. "Heard about Mesrine?"

Richer accepted the proffered cigarette and reciprocated with his lighter. "Third hand, sir. From the radio."

"Strange happenings," the Commissaire swallowed most of the smoke, a trickle flowing down his nostrils like a resting dragon. "Apparently it was quite a deliberate act of murder. The Inspector was shot once through the heart at a distance of no more than one metre. The wife was different. She was battered brutally about the head and then shot behind the left ear. Seems she put up a struggle. Also the top of one of the fingers of her left hand had been chopped off."

"Torture?"

"Possibly. But the strange thing is, there was not a drop of blood anywhere but on the bodies. Not a speck. And nothing was out of place. The whole house was neat and tidy. They were discovered stretched out on the kitchen floor next to one another. Had it not been for the manner of their deaths, it could have been a suicide pact."

Richer stared at the top of the cigarette in his hand. "No weapon?"

"*Non.*"

"And nothing missing?"

"*Non.* But two unusual things. Firstly, there were deep marks on the Inspector's neck - "

"Attempted strangulation?"

"Boot marks. And secondly, placed on the floor next to the bodies was… a melon."

Richer stared at the Commissaire. "A melon?"

"A melon. And underneath that melon was an old letter, written some forty years ago. From La Dame to her husband."

Richer did not react. His face was stone.

"Devos has been on to me already," continued Fleury. "Wanted to know if we knew anything about it or if it meant anything."

"What did you say?"

"I said no. Our only interest was in some jewellery that was taken many months ago."

"How exactly do they know it was Mesrine?"

"He went into the local station earlier asking for the Inspector. Passed himself off as a *flic*. You know he's noted for doing that. It was only hours later that one of the lads on duty realised who he was. They'll have the poor buggers balls, of course."

Richer sniffed. "The Inspector anyone we know?"

"An Inspector called Le Bouthillier."

‡

33. L'Organisation

"An Inspector called Le Bouthillier," answered Richer to the question from the man in the cap. "Just a provincial *flic*." They were seated as before in the room above the butcher's in Rue Fessart.

"So Mesrine has the document?"

"I don't know. This murder may not even be connected with the quest. Remember, Mesrine said he would get it in his own time. He might have been leaving me a sign with the melon. I don't know. He will let me know when he has it."

"Meanwhile we just sit and wait," grumbled the man.

"Is there no other way we can get it?" asked the chain smoker on the right.

Richer shook his head. "How? The reason I involved Mesrine in the first place was because of his special talents. If something needs sniffing out, he'll sniff it. If something needs retrieving, he'll retrieve it."

"And you're sure this letter under the melon was not the document we are seeking?"

"Absolutely not. Mesrine would not do that. He is contracted to bring the document to me."

"And you trust him?"

"Mesrine is a man of honour." Richer ignored the cap man's cynical laugh. "He has a quest for which he has been paid in advance. He would not play games. And he would not take kindly to being withdrawn - even if I could contact him, which I cannot."

"So all we can do is sit and wait," echoed the chain smoker.

"And what if this secret - which you have deigned not to let us in on - breaks?" The cap man. "The document will be no good to us then. All will be lost, and we will have freed Mesrine for nothing."

"The secret will not break." It was the first time the Colonel had spoken. "If it was going to break it would have done so long ago, long before La Dame even got round to reporting the theft to the Minister. No, whoever has it is keeping quiet for his own purposes."

"Or does not know what he has," said Richer.

The Colonel nodded slowly. "*Oui.* That is the alternative."

"I still think we should try some other way to obtain it," said cap man.

"How?" Richer could not keep the contempt from his voice. "Who do you suggest? Some OAS geriatric?"

"Captain!" The Colonel frowned.

"Pardon me, gentlemen," Richer looked at each man in turn. "All I'm saying is Mesrine's not only the best we have, he *is* the best. But we must be patient. He is looking for a needle which is not even in a haystack. It could be anywhere."

"What about La Dame?" asked the chain smoker.

"I visited her two months ago. She remembers nothing."

"You are certain?"

"I will, of course, make further visits. But she cannot even remember losing her jewellery."

"Then it will not be necessary to kill her?"

"It is an option we must keep open," reasoned Richer. "But I don't think so, no."

"That," said the cap man, "is a pity."

‡

34. Concièrge

Mardi 10 Octobre

Madame La Salle, the concièrge of 124 Passage Charles Albert, stood in front of the old sink in her *loge* preparing some potatoes for her evening meal. Her shaky, arthritic hands could barely hold the knife, let alone peel, but somehow she managed, the chopped skins falling onto the newspaper in front of her. It was yesterday's *Le Figaro* which she had picked up from one of the tenants this morning.

She never read the headlines. An old woman could do without the wars, the crimes, the accidents, the rapes. She read the inside pages, particularly the stars and agony columns (for neither of which was *Le Figaro* noted). Consequently she had not noticed the picture on the front page and the report of the killings in Normandy.

She noticed it now as a piece of potato peel fell onto the photographed face. Had she had her reading glasses on, the face would have appeared fully in focus and she would have thought nothing of it. As it was, she saw a blurred image of a round head, hearty, confident face, deep set eyes and a moustache.

The image reminded her of someone, but she could not put her finger on it. She brushed away the piece of peel and squinted.

No, she would have to get her glasses. But later, it was not important, do the potatoes first.

The next piece of peel fell onto the picture, covering the blur of the moustache.

She stared again.

Good heavens! What a remarkable resemblance!

With the moustache covered up, the blurred image looked just like Monsieur Lenoir from the ground floor studio!

She chuckled. With her glasses on, of course, the picture would look nothing like him. But what a coincidence! Monsieur Lenoir was a charming man, always ready with a quip (if she had been thirty years younger!). He would see the funny side of it when she told him. He was back home in Nice for a time, but when he returned she would have a little joke with him. Would he laugh when he found out who he looked like!

‡

35. Voleur et filles

Mercredi 11 Octobre

It was a dream.

He lay on the bed, eyes half closed, trying to recapture the sleep that was quickly fading - but at the same time trying to focus on the dream in front of him. They were hazy at first, just two blurs, but slowly they came into focus. He must be in Heaven.

There were two women standing at the end of the bed. And they were both completely naked.

Jacques Mesrine smiled and winced at the same time as he moved onto the tender spot.

Janou came over. *"Bonjour mon amour,* you are feeling better?"

"Bonjour ma petite." He reached out and caressed her smooth thigh. "How long have I been asleep?"

"Off and on for four days. You had a fever." She smiled towards the other woman. "You remember I introduced you to Sylvie?"

Sylvie pulled a robe across her shoulders - an act which concealed nothing - and grinned. There was naughtiness in her eyes. "Hello. It is nice to have you back with us again. We were worried about you."

"Hush!" said Janou. "He'll get big headed!"

"But it is true!" Sylvie's voice was rich and golden. "You should have seen her. She was worried to death about you."

"Sylvie, *hush!* Go and prepare breakfast, you wicked child."

Sylvie moued at Mesrine, poked her tongue out at Janou and went out of the room. Mesrine saw a beautiful, full round bottom beneath the diaphanous robe. He could have sworn it blew a kiss at him.

"How is it?" asked Janou. "Let me see."

"Bloody sore, but I'll live." Mesrine turned onto his front.

Janou pulled back the bedclothes. She could not help grinning but she dare not let Jacques see her. Of all the places to get stabbed! "Looks better this morning," she commented. "But we must keep the cream on it like the doctor advised."

"Pah! It is not deep!" he mumbled into the bolster. "A flesh wound, that is all."

"Six centimetres is not a flesh wound. As he said, six centimetres anywhere else could have been fatal. In your arse it was nothing more than a cut. But still a severe cut. And you have had a fever and shock reaction." She slapped on the ointment. Mesrine flinched.

"And you are very bruised," nagged Janou. "I ask you, fancy driving all day with a stab wound underneath you!"

"Shut up woman. You are worse than a wife. Nag, nag, nag. If I didn't love you, I'd marry you!"

But he had to acknowledge that what she said was true. He had driven the two hundred and forty kilometres from Deauville to Paris all day Saturday after spending a total of three hours cleaning up after the unfortunate 'accident'. He had not intended to harm either of the Le Bouthilliers, not even Madame's finger, but after she had attacked him and the old man had foolishly joined in... well, instinctive self-preservation had taken over.

He had arrived in St Germain-en-Laye to the west of Paris late in the afternoon. The long distance had taken even longer as he had to drive with one cheek off the seat and an increasing temperature. An RER Ligne A train to Charles de Gaulle-Etoile and then metro Ligne 2 to Pigalle and into the bar to wait for Janou.

She had not come in for two hours, during which time Mesrine had become very restless, ill and just a little drunk. When she had appeared she had made no pretence of picking him up, she had come straight across, shocked at his appearance. She knew better than to ask questions, but it was obvious that Jacques needed a doctor and fast.

Even after all this time it was likely that the *flics* were watching her place, so she could not take chances. Her friend Sylvie had a place in Rue du Ponceau off the Rue St Denis. She would put them up. No fear of any clients calling as she was a visiting girl.

Once they were safely in the apartment, a *médicin* of dubious character from Belleville had been called. He was used to treating the combatants of Parisian street fights and he had no reason to believe *le m'sieur* was anything else. He did not recognise the face that in the past months had been plastered over every newspaper and TV screen in the country.

A tetanus jab, an undisclosed tablet and a jar of ointment in exchange for a donation of one thousand francs, and the doctor was on his way, silent for ever.

"Breakfast!" called Sylvie from the kitchen. "Shall I bring Jacques' in?"

"No," called Mesrine rising. "I am not an invalid. I shall have it in there." He rose very carefully from the bed, trying not to show his dizziness. "Do you have a robe?"

"Only a flimsy nightgown of Sylvie's, my sweet," grinned Janou. "I'm not sure it would suit you."

"But I cannot sit down at the table like this!"

"Of course you can," said Sylvie from the doorway, a pot of hot coffee in her hand. "We do not mind. We have seen boys before, you know."

"But I am stark naked!"

"No! Really?"

Mesrine hobbled into the *salle*, trying unsuccessfully to keep one hand over his dick without looking as if he was being modest. The delicious smell of the coffee and warm croissants reminded him how hungry he was. Over by the window, the pot was full and the plate was high.

Janou produced a cushion. "Here, sit yourself down and eat. And behave yourself. We are Sylvie's guests."

Mesrine smiled at his pretty, blonde-haired, big busted hostess. *"Mais naturellement."* He sat down, poured the coffee into his *bol* and dipped in his first croissant. "I like your place, Sylvie. All yours?"

"Oui. Originally I rented it, but when my man took me off the streets and moved me up, he bought it for me. I have the deeds."

"That was remarkably kind." For a pimp, he added to himself.

"He was a remarkably kind man." Sylvie had her bowl in her hands and was sipping from it. "He really did love me."

"Did?"

Janou explained. "Sylvie's man was killed last year. Outside on St Denis. A disagreement with a customer over the rates for one of his other girls. A knife…" She shrugged.

"So who protects you now?" asked Mesrine.

"No one." Sylvie put down the bowl and broke a roll. "I run my own business from here. That," she nodded at the white telephone in the corner with the answering contraption beneath, "is my sole employer."

"But this is a rough area. Beaubourg, the old Halles, the street is famous for its girls in doorways. Wouldn't a business be better run from, say, Neuilly or somewhere in the sixteenth?"

"Maybe. But I like it here. I was brought up here, introduced to the trade here. I could move if I wanted to, I make enough. But I shall not go until I retire."

Mesrine looked at her face, surprisingly soft and innocent for a whore. "And when will you do that?"

"When I am thirty or when I marry, whichever is the sooner."

He poured his second bowl of coffee. "You are a woman who knows her own mind. I like that. You have done Mesrine a great favour by accommodating him here. He must think of a way of repaying you."

Janou nudged her friend. "Careful Sylvie, I think he likes you."

"I am grateful to you beyond words, Sylvie. You know who I am. The infamous Jacques Mesrine! Thief! Murderer! The most wanted man in Europe. The most wanted man in the world. Yet you take me in. I will not forget this."

Sylvie smiled. Not the false, lecherous smile of the professional tart, but the smile of an attractive, intelligent woman. *"Tu es très gentil, Jacques."*

Janou began to clear away the bowls, leaving Mesrine's as he refilled it for a second time.

The telephone rang.

"Shall I get it?" he asked.

"No, no, the machine will take it," said Sylvie. "Probably somebody fixing for tonight."

"Ah." Mesrine licked his finger and began lifting crumbs from the table and popping them into his mouth. "You never bring your customers here?"

"I always visit. *Pourquoi?*"

"I may need somewhere to stay. I have a couple of places, but until I see how the land lies may I stay here?"

Janou's voice came above the sound of the running water from the sink. "That's it. You'll never get rid of him now!"

Sylvie laughed, stood up, bent over and kissed him on the top of the head. "He may stay here for as long as he likes," she called back to her friend. Her eyes met his.

She walked away, the gown open down the front, concealing nothing, not even the fact that she was not a natural blonde.

At that moment Mesrine wanted her. Her wanted her very much. It was only after feeling the first stirrings of arousal that he remembered he was stark naked. As his erection peeked above the top of the table, the two women looked at him and giggled.

Jacques Mesrine blushed red as an edam cheese.

Sylvie's phone rang regularly throughout the day. Although Mesrine expected it, he was surprised. If all the calls were for that evening, she was a hell of a busy lady.

In mid-afternoon she had a private session with the answering machine, transferring the messages from the headphones to dates in her notebook. Mesrine would have loved to have heard the messages, but he thought it unwise even to make the suggestion.

One thing he had decided: sometime he would have her. She was gorgeous. Wonder how much she charged her clients? However much it was not enough, not for that body.

Janou returned from shopping as Sylvie was going out to work at 17:30. Sylvie had what she termed a 'double-nighter' - somebody had booked her for two nights and days - and she was carrying a small overnight case. They bade farewell to each other and soon Mesrine and Janou heard Sylvie's car start up downstairs and the friendly ribald comments of the girls out on the street as she drove past.

"Here," Janou handed over *Le Figaro* and *France-Soir* and watched his face fall as he saw that he was not on the front pages. *"Et voici te pantalon."* She held out the distinctive red and white *Monoprix* bag. "It was all they had in your size. It is not a very big branch in Sebastopol."

Mesrine pulled out the grey slacks. "They are fine, *ma petite*, fine. You had enough money?"

"Certainly."

"Good. But I must get some more. Maybe a spectacular stunt is called for. It would get me back on the front pages. How dare they take the great Mesrine off after only one day!" He was trying to make light of it, but Janou knew he was serious.

"Also I got you these." With a flourish she held up a pair of bright scarlet underpants.

Mesrine guffawed. *"Merde alors chérie,* but you think of everything!" He pulled her to him and kissed her.

"How are you feeling?" she asked after the embrace.

"Pas mal, in my self. Physically my arse is sore and, strangely enough, my leg feels a little stiff."

"You should rest, perhaps for a few weeks."

Mesrine looked around. "I might do just that. I like this place. It is safe. I like - "

"You like Sylvie."

"You mind?"

"Of course not! My dear boy, I do not own you. I love you. And I know Sylvie likes you too."

He grabbed her round the back of the neck, pulled her to him roughly, and kissed her again, long and hard. "You are a hell of a woman, Janou," he said softly after the embrace.

"Nonsense." She licked the tip of his nose. "I am a woman, *simplement.* We go back a long way."

He nodded. "A lot of water has flowed through the stable doors since then."

"Oui, beaucoup d'eau."

"But I have things to do. There are places I must be seen in."

"*Je comprends.*" Janou understood, and she would not ask questions. She did not want to know. She had not even read the weekend's newspapers which had yet again splashed his name and picture over their front pages. It was the best way.

"What about food?" she asked.

"If I had my wardrobe from Marcel's, we could go anywhere. I would like to take you out. I have not been to *La Tour d'Argent* for some time. But perhaps going out is not wise for the moment. I shall eat here. Sylvie's freezer is well stocked."

"Shall I prepare you something?"

"*Non, non,*" he took her hand. "I will do it later. When are you going to work?"

"Soon. I need to go home first."

"Then we have time." He raised her hand and kissed it.

"Time? For what?"

"Well, I told you. I have this stiffness…"

‡

36. Voleur et concièrge

Vendredi 13 Octobre

Despite the date, that day in Paris was glorious. Not a cloud in the blue autumn sky. A gentle breeze wafted the smells of the city together: the *patisseries*, the *boucheries*, the fruit on the market stalls, the cigarette smoke, the coffee, the traffic fumes, the musty boiled rice smell of the sewers from the metro ventilation shafts, all forming to make a not unpleasant scent that was uniquely Parisian.

The Passage Charles Albert runs roughly north to south up in the 18th Arrondisement and, as with all roads that run off at an angle from the direction of the Seine, the even numbers are on the right as looked at from the river. Thus it was that the sun did not shine directly on the entrance to number 124 until late afternoon.

Madame La Salle was sitting on a creaky old wooden chair outside the doorway, pinafore over two thick cardigans, glasses on, trying to read last week's edition of *France Dimanche*.

It was quiet in the Passage, but now and then noise would drift through from the Rue Jules Cloquet further up where the shops were. Pedestrians passed by, some (usually the older ones, not these roughneck young) occasionally stopping to pass the time of day.

With her glasses on she could see him clearly when he was still some way down the road. Monsieur Lenoir had returned! At least - ?

It *was* Monsieur Lenoir, she could not mistake him, he was a big man. Yet he seemed different. He was limping noticeably, and he kept looking about as if he was searching for someone. But it was the clothes, that's what made him look different. Short jacket and grey *pantalon*, shirt but no tie. She was used to seeing him in his business clothes, not dressed casually. But what could she expect? The man was just returning from a break with his family, he would not be dressed for the Bourse!

She chided herself for being a stupid old woman, and watched him approach. She wondered about the limp. The poor man had probably hurt himself playing with the children. It always happened. The unfit father!

The big, charming smile spread across his face as he saw her sitting outside. What a *nice* man he was.

"*Bonjour Madame La Salle!*" he called. "A lovely day!"

"*Bonjour Monsieur Lenoir*, welcome back." Good Lord, he did not look at all well. He was as white as a ghost. "How was Nice?"

"Nice was fine, fine."

"You do not look too brown, monsieur."

"Ah," he nodded sadly. "A little accident. With the dog, you know? I was inside with my foot up most of the time." He helped her to rise, her old elbow shaking in his powerful hand.

"Pah! Men of your age should be careful," she reprimanded. "You try to do too much. You go on vacation and wear yourselves out, so you are none the better for it." They walked slowly into the dark foyer. "Look at me. I have eighty-six years and I have never taken exercise in my life. It is a killer m'sieur, mark the words of an old woman who intends to live for a lot longer yet."

"Madame, you are right. Undoubtedly right."

They stopped by her little *loge*. She patted his arm. "I have something to show you," she confided, the gleam in her eye made all the more mischievous by the gruff expression beneath. "I think it will amuse you. *Ici*."

Lenoir pulled open the hinged counter and they entered her little sanctum. "What on earth can it be?" he put the incredulity into his voice to humour her. Sweet old biddy. But he hoped it would not take too long, he did not feel good.

A newspaper lay on the small table, wrinkling at the corners where it had been screwed up and then flattened out again. It was *Le Figaro* of a few days ago.

"Look!" she pointed.

Lenoir looked. The headlines were about the Mesrine slayings. The most recent picture (moustachioed, longish hair) stared up from next to the text.

"The picture," enthused Madame La Salle. "Look!"

"I cannot see anything unusual, madame. It is that murderer Mesrine."

"Ah, but watch!" She was excited now, like a child with a secret. From a drawer beneath the table she produced a knife and placed it over the upper lip on the picture. "Now!"

Lenoir hoped it was not what he thought. "*Madame, je regrette mais -* "

"True, true. But if you screw up your eyes, so..." She pulled off her glasses and squinted. "Do you not see? It is *you*, it is you! Isn't that funny! You'd best be careful of people who have not got their glasses on, m'sieur. What a catastrophe to be mistaken for *this* man!"

"Oh, madame," Lenoir sighed quietly, despondently. "Oh, madame..."

His hands went to her throat and he murdered her with the least possible pain.

‡

37. Voleur et fille

Samedi 14 Octobre

Sylvie did not return to the apartment in the Rue du Ponceau from her double-nighter until after the early hours. She entered quietly, turning the light on in the kitchen rather than in the *salle* which would reflect into the bedroom.

Opening the door of the *frigo*, she decided against making an omelette and instead grabbed the final piece of a chocolate gateau. Coffee was still warm on the hot plate and she poured a cup.

Carrying her food into the *salle*, she sorted through her bag while she ate. Usually she would make neat piles of the cash, cheques and credit card slips, ready to pay in in the morning, but after two days with one client she just had one, rather sizeable, wad of cash, English money from her diplomat friend.

After working out the current exchange rate (hmm, not bad for two days' work), she tidied up her plate and cup and then walked soundlessly to the bedroom door, pushing it open. A smile spread across her face as she saw what she wanted to see. He was in the bed. Fast asleep and snoring gently.

And the two suitcases in the corner (which, in fact, contained the last mortal traces of Monsieur Lenoir) showed that he had come to stay - at least for a while. She was pleased.

The shower was off the bedroom so she could not avoid some noise as she washed and douched and then rubbed herself with body lotion.

He was awake when she came back in. His sleepy eyes roved over her naked, glistening body, lingering on the large breasts which were suspended at an impossibly horizontal angle but irrefutably were without support.

"Hello," she whispered, the sheets rustling as she slid in next to him.

"*Bonsoir.*"

"I'm glad you are staying."

"Staying?"

"You have your cases."

"*Ah, oui.* You had a nice couple of days?"

"Work is work."

"Of course."

She bent forward and kissed him tentatively, her lips becoming stronger and more confident as he responded.

"You are not tired?" asked Mesrine as he ran his lips over her nose. His right hand came across and grasped one of the amazing breasts. It was solid.

"Not for you, my hero."

Her touched her lips with his index finger. "I'm no hero, I am just - "

"A hero." She sucked on the finger.

" - a man. I have talents, true - but I'm as mortal as anyone else. I have needs, I have hungers, I have - "

"Desires?"

"*Oui.*"

"Then, mortal hero, prove it to me. Or are you too sore?"

"I am *never* too sore. But be gentle with me. Don't hurt me."

She straddled him, her breasts on his head, the rock hard nipples demanding to be sucked. She straightened up, one tit in his mouth, the nipple being pulled. As she guided him into her, she gasped. "That," she said, "is not a mere mortal."

Gently she began to move her hips up and down.

‡

38. Flics

Lundi 16 Octobre

"I have an idea!" enthused Claude Gerard as Paul Richer let him into the apartment. They shook hands.

"*Bonsoir Claude,* and what is that?" Richer looked quite at home in his apron depicting brassiere, pants and suspenders on the front. It had been a gift from Gerard last time they had had a *soirée.*

Gerard nodded at the apron. "Just that! What say we see some of Pigalle tonight?"

"You're joking."

"No I'm not. Not to indulge, you understand. Just for a stroll about."

"If you feel like even *moving* after the meal I've prepared I shall feel highly insulted!"

Gerard sniffed the air. "*Alors,* smells delicious. *Qu'est-ce que c'est?*"

"Moussaka."

"My God, you will make someone a perfect wife one day!" From a brown paper bag he handed over a litre of Monoprix's best and a bottle of *Napoléon.*

"*Merci bien.* You proposing?"

"You'd probably be better than Mathilde. At least you can cook."

"Ah, but what about the other pleasures?"

"What other pleasures?"

Gerard sat down, loosened his tie and broke open a new packet of cigarettes. Chivas came over and flopped by his feet.

Richer called for him to pour two brandies. "And put some music on if you like."

Gerard studied the collection of about fifty cassettes as he poured the drinks.

A few moments later, Brel began to sing about the port of Amsterdam and the bellies of whores. Deciding that perhaps Brel was, after all, a bit on the depressive side, at least for so early in the evening, Gerard stopped the immortal man in mid-crochet and replaced him with Liberace, the American pianist.

"Want your cognac in there?"

"No, leave it there, I'll be out soon. I'll have one of your *sèches* too."

"You're the *chef*." Gerard sat back down in the comfortable armchair, angled towards the window, and gazed at the byzantine magnificence of Sacré-Coeur on the *butte*. His mind wandered.

He mused on his case of the British diplomat and the whore. On the pretence of other matters, he had spoken to the man personally, explaining how the French government did not like to see a representative of an ally (ally! The British!) compromising himself like this.

The man had made self-deprecating clucking noises, understood completely, and had promised to behave. He had not. He had seen the tart on at least two more occasions to Gerard's personal knowledge, the last time being closeted away with her for two days and nights in a small hotel out near Torcy.

So, it was time for the photographs. Which would mean the man's removal from the embassy. But that was his look-out. Rather removal because of compromising ally photographs than blackmail by Red photographs -

"Fuckit!"

Richer's oath snapped him out of his reverie.

"Paul?" Gerard was on his feet. Chivas jumped away with a squeak.

Richer's furious face appeared in the doorway. "Know what?"

"What?"

"I'm out of eggs."

"Out of eggs? Is that all? I thought some catastrophe had happened."

"It *is* a catastrophe. I cannot make a roux without eggs! What time is it?" He wiped his hands on his apron.

Gerard looked at his wrist. "Mickey's big hand is just poking up Minnie's skirt. Eighteen forty-five."

Richer yanked off the apron. "I might just make it. There's a Co-Op down the road, closes at seven."

"I'll go." Gerard put down his cognac.

"No, no. My own fault. I'll go." Richer pulled on a jacket. "You just relax. Look after Chivas. You can wash up after, as usual." He went out.

Gerard settled down. Chivas leapt silently onto his lap, and Gerard absentmindedly stroked the cat while he stared out of the window. The room slowly darkened as the sun was obscured by the church above. He found himself on the verge of sleep.

Richer had been gone five minutes when the telephone rang.

The sudden, prolonged shrill startled Gerard back to awareness and the cat fled from the room. Bloody hell, the one moment Paul was not here and it had to ring. Should he ignore it?

It trilled again.

Could it be Paul from downstairs? No, he would come up. Could it be Mathilde? He had told her where he was going.

Ring.

He picked up the receiver.

"'Allo?"

"Bruno."

"Yes?"

"I had problems at Trouville, you probably heard. I did not intend to kill them."

"What? I'm sorry?"

The line went dead.

‡

39. Voleur

Mesrine slammed down the telephone. *Merde.* What had happened? A wrong number?

It was this infernal bloody machine of Sylvie's, all strapped up to this glorified tape recorder. She had told him to leave the phone alone if it rang, but she had not said anything about not using it to call out.

You were an idiot, Jacques, an imbecile. The Captain had *said* he would answer with his name.

After five minutes he began to see the funny side of it. Had he got through to one of Sylvie's clients? Now that would have perplexed whoever it was. Could it have been that British diplomat she had been telling him about, the one with the taste for conservative blue knickers, the one she had spent the double-nighter with in Torcy? Serves him right if it was. Shouldn't associate with young girls. After all, Sylvie was *his* -

He stopped himself. Heaven! Had he actually thought that? *His* Sylvie...?

It was an idea. She was a lovely girl. But he had tried permanency before with Lydia and Soledad, and it had not worked. Why should it on this occasion? And what about Janou?

But if you were on the run you were less noticeable with a woman by your side...

‡

40. Flics

By the time Richer returned, Gerard was on his fourth cognac and was feeling the warm, mellowing effects.

"She was closed," said Richer. "But there's a Felix Potin down in Rue Yvonne-Le-Tac, that's why I've been so long. Just caught her." He held the eggs in the air like an Olympian with the torch and hurried through into the kitchen.

Claude blew out a lungful of smoke and assaulted the cognac as if it was going out of fashion. "Had a call while you were out."

"Oh yes?"

"Weird. Think it was a wrong number. Somebody called Bruno."

There was silence. Slowly Richer's head came round the door.

"What?"

"Know him?"

"What did he say?"

"He hung up when he realised it wasn't you."

"He's… one of my snouts."

"Ah, that explains it. He mumbled something about some killings in Trouville. Mean anything?"

"Don't know. Hunting. He goes hunting. Did he say anything else?"

"No, he hung up like I said."

"*D'accord.*" Richer went back into the kitchen.

"Funny," said Gerard above the music, the smoke and the effects of the alcohol. "Trouville should mean something to me, but I can't for the life of me remember why."

Richer grimaced wryly. God, Jacques, what a time to ring! Of all the seconds in all the days you had to pick one when he wasn't there and someone else was. And what a someone else!

And, my dear Claude, what an expression for you to use. *For the life of you.*

He hoped it wouldn't be.

With half a bottle of cognac inside him (not to mention the half litre of wine, two whiskies from Richer's cabinet and the delicious moussaka), Gerard was too far gone even to walk down the stairs. At around 23:00, in the middle of an intense discussion on the merits or otherwise of women shaving their pudendas, he keeled back in the chair and began to snore deeply.

Richer, not feeling over energetic himself, put the older man's feet on a pouffe, covered him with a blanket and left him to it. He shut Chivas in the kitchen and then went to bed.

Trouville. Would Claude remember in the morning? He hoped not. If Claude put two and two together… but he would not. He might realise the recent Mesrine murders had been committed there, but he could not possibly even guess at the link between Richer and the supercriminal. He had said nothing. There was nothing written down.

There was no way Claude could make the connection.

No way.

‡

41. Flic et voleur

Jeudi 19 Octobre

Richer had a briefing with Commissaire Fleury-Goujon that morning. The Commissaire had hinted that a trip to England might be on the cards. Whitehall were getting snotty about some photos Gerard had of one of their diplomats and a Parisian whore. They needed smoothing over. The personal touch. Couldn't send Gerard, of course, not on a public relations exercise.

The phone was ringing as Richer re-entered his office. He lit up a Gauloise.

"Richer," he mumbled half-heartedly into the mouthpiece.

"Bruno."

"Jesus! Where have you been?"

"I know, I know. I am sorry. There have been difficulties, you've no doubt read about them. Listen, I cannot stay - you know why."

"It's not tapped."

"I still have matters under control. It has been passed about. If only you'd tell me exactly what I am looking for - "

"Bruno, listen! We should meet - "

"No chance, Captain, the heat is on. I must drop out for a while. I am ill and I need a rest. I will contact you when I return."

"When?"

"I do not know. But I do not forget an agreement. I will go now."

"Wait! Jacques - "

He was gone.

‡

42. Voleur et fille

Dimanche 22 Octobre

Mesrine never worried, it was not in his character. So the best way to describe the emotion was *concern*. It had been caused by a simple incident that had happened when he was returning to the apartment last night.

The Rue St Denis has been described as 'the hottest street in Paris'. While recently, with the removal of the market in next door Les Halles to Rungis on the southern side of the city, the hottest street could be said to have cooled a bit, ladies of pleasure still paraded their wares in the doorways nearly 24 hours a day.

It was one of the pretty ones, nipples peeking over the top of her baby doll nightie, small G-string, and the incongruous but ubiquitous bag over her shoulder, who said hello to him as he passed by on his way to the apartment.

It wasn't what she said, it was the way she said it. It was not a come-on greeting, it was a greeting of neighbours. And it was that that concerned Mesrine. For it meant that he was becoming known. Sylvie's guy. And that was dangerous. Tongues wag.

So there was only one logical conclusion. Move. He needed a new pasture.

But what about Sylvie?

Over breakfast he announced that the time had come for him to look for a new place.

A sad smile passed over Sylvie's face, but she had been expecting it. This man, of all men, she could not hold on to forever.

She came over and sat on his lap, raising her negligée as she sat down so that her bare bottom rested against his flesh. Putting her arms around his neck, she kissed him.

"It had to happen," she said softly. "Janou warned me not to get involved, that you would have to leave some day. But I was hoping you wouldn't. At least, not so soon."

"Believe me, *ma petite*, there is nothing I would like better than to stay here with you. But I am a man on the run, and I have things to do. You must appreciate that. I am becoming known. 'The man who lives with Sylvie.' They cannot recognise me from the published pictures, but all it needs is a *flic* to overhear something in the salad basket *[the police wagon used to round up streetwalkers]* and come nosing."

Lightly, he stroked her thigh, the skin smooth and warm and inviting. She smelled of desire.

A tear filled her left eye but did not fall. "I shall miss you," she said at length.

"Really?"

"Really. In my business you do not have chance to become fond of men. Since my man was killed I have had nobody to love me, nobody to love. Not until you. And now you will leave me." Reluctantly, the tear fell.

He licked the tear, licked a dribble of snot from her nose, and licked the valley between her breasts. He caught the faintest of traces of last night's body oil.

"Come with me," he said.

It took a moment to sink in, then she pulled his hair back savagely. "*Qu'est-ce que tu dit?*"

He grinned. "Come with me."

She slammed his head back into her chest, pressing him hard into the solid mounds. "But... I cannot!... I mean... you would not want me... what you say is true... you are important... you are a hero... you do not want to be saddled with *me*..."

"Mmgurph," said Mesrine.

She wrenched his head back. "What?"

"Calm down, my child, calm down. I have already discussed it with Janou. She thinks it is a good idea."

"Jacques - my love - how can I? Do you *mean* it? Honestly mean it?" She pouted suspiciously. "You would not joke with me?"

"Of course I mean it. But it will mean leaving all this, all your clients."

"Fuck them."

"Exactly. But it is your living."

"*Was* my living. As of this moment Jacques Mesrine is my living. *Tout compris.*"

"But think of your future! With a criminal. With a man on the run - "

"With a man I love! Oh, do not change your mind Jacques. Oh say you mean it, please say you mean it." She was jumping up and down on his lap, with the consequent profound effect on a certain part of his anatomy.

"Sylvie," he said softly. "I promise you. I mean it."

With a whoop of joy she leapt from his lap, went over to the wall and yanked the telephone and answering machine from the socket. "*Voila!*" she dropped the lot on the floor with an almighty thud. "Sylvie Jacquot, call-girl, no longer exists. I am *yours*."

She bounced back, threw a leg over and squatted on his naked lap. "Let us begin the way we mean to carry on."

He feigned astonishment. "Here and now? At the breakfast table?"

"Here and now. At the breakfast table."

"You little animal."

"I have never denied it."

She manoeuvred herself so that he slipped up into her.

Between bites at her breasts, he mumbled "I've heard of having a roll for breakfast, but this is ridiculous!"

‡

43. Flics puis Voleur

Lundi 30 Octobre

"Nice arse, don't you think? I wouldn't mind slipping that one myself."

"Personally I'm a tit man, Chief," said Inspector Bauer looking over Gerard's shoulder.

"She's generous with those as well," Gerard shuffled through the packet of photographs and produced a top torso shot. A bald headed, middle-aged man was hanging by his teeth from her right nipple.

"The Brits don't want to know," sniffed Gerard. "They're even kicking up a bit of a fuss because we took the pictures in the first place. I'll never understand them. They pretend they're the height of sophistication yet underneath they alternate between strict prudery and unabashed savagery. I think the whole country needs to see a shrink." As he spoke he was laying the photos out one by one across his desk.

Bauer was smiling. Work or no work, it was still a pleasure to see a girl getting well and truly shafted. "So no action?" he asked.

"Not against him. But I've found who the girl is." Gerard turned over the last photo - a particularly raw and slightly blurred shot of anal intercourse - and read the particulars. "Sylvie Jacquot, 3 Ponceau, just off St Denis."

"Form?"

"Picked up six times when she was on the streets. Nothing since she moved indoors."

"Want me to pull her?"

"Put the frighteners on. Scare her off the *rosbeef*. If she doesn't co-operate, show her these." He selected three photos and gave them to the Inspector.

"*D'accord.*"

"Take a couple of lads in case you have trouble with her pimp."

"Know who he is?"

"No. Some new guy, so rumour has it. Once he sees their uniforms he'll be off like a shot. It'll be the worse for this little darling when he comes back later of course, but that can't be helped. She shouldn't be a naughty girl."

"Right."

"And Bauer?"

"Yes Chief?"

"No fucking, not even for free."

"Thanks a lot, Chief. How about a blow job?"

"Kind of you to offer but I've just eaten."

Bauer had been hammering on the downstairs door for three minutes with no answer. The two uniformed men remained in the unmarked car with the tinted windows.

Once again Bauer stepped back and looked at the upstairs window. There was no abrupt movement, no curtain quickly closing. The place was still.

A female voice said, "She's gone."

Bauer turned. A little way along, on the corner of Rue St Denis, a girl in a baby doll nightie lounged against the wall.

"Gone?"

The girl pushed herself upright and walked towards him, high heels clicking, handbag over one shoulder, keys jingling in her hand.

"She left this morning."

"When will she be back?" Bauer's eyes rested on her nipples jutting over the top of her nightie.

"No, she's left. Moved. She's never coming back."

"Did she leave a forwarding address?"

The girl laughed. "What do you think, *mon amour*? You'll have to find yourself another friend."

"Fuck," said Bauer.

"Five hundred francs," said the girl.

"Forget it," said Gerard when Bauer reported back. "She could be traced, no problem. She owns the apartment. But why bother? If the *rosbeefs* don't care, I'm sure I don't. She's not worth a toss." Which, considering what he had been doing with the photographs in the lavatory that afternoon, was a lie.

Earlier that day, Monsieur and Madame Renoir ("No, no relation, I cannot even paint by numbers!") had taken over the lease of an apartment at 7 Impasse St François in the 18th Arrondisement. The concièrge had been struck by the charm of *le monsieur*, a tall man with a beard and a mop of curly hair.

‡

44. Voleur

Vendredi 10 Novembre

On this day Jacques Mesrine made a bungled attempt to kidnap Judge Petit, the presiding judge at his last trial.

Whether it was due to lack of planning, underestimation of what the job would entail, or just downright ill-health (Mesrine's knife wound simply refused to heal completely and he was still subject to spasmodic bouts of fever), or a combination of all three, is debatable, but the outcome was a fiasco in which the police were alerted and Mesrine only narrowly missed being recaptured.

He came face to face with the police as he was fleeing down the stairs from the judge's apartment after realising his game was lost. He used his usual trick of becoming one of them. Gun in one hand, handcuffs (which had been meant for his victim) in the other, he shouted that the intruder was still in the block and ordered the advancing men upstairs. As they rushed past him, he continued downwards.

The only policeman to recognise Mesrine was a young officer who had been left to guard the entrance to the building. And it was this recognition which caused the fear that froze all his bodily functions except his bladder, that saved his life. He was found later, handcuffed to a nearby lamppost, sobbing quietly. His pantalon *were saturated.*

Although the attempt had been a farcical flop, when the story burst in the following day's papers Mesrine was again a hero thanks to his lenient treatment of the young officer.

Samedi 11 Novembre

Armistice Day celebrations in Paris always put a great strain on the capital's police forces. With the knowledge that Mesrine was certainly back in town, and the hunt for him now renewed with avengeance, the strain that year was almost at breaking point. But for that weekend all available men were on crowd control, so the hunt for Mesrine would have to wait at least until Monday.

So it was that Jacques Mesrine was able to visit the Gare du Nord that Saturday and book two tickets on tomorrow morning's train to London without so much as a second glance from anybody.

He was displeased with himself. A displeasure bordering on the fury. All right, the newspapers were lauding him, he was popular again. But the popularity did not assuage the fact that he had failed. He had failed himself, as the ransom for Judge Petit could have seen him through many a month.

And he had failed the Captain as he had not yet gotten the document, the item he had to retrieve without even knowing what it was.

He was unwell and he needed to get away, out of Paris, out of France. He loved London second only to Paris. He needed to go there. Maybe he would rent a flat. Sylvie would like the town. They would live well, but not extravagantly. And when the money ran out... Well, he would face that bridge when he came to it.

He was getting tired. If only he had enough money to retire, to settle down, to spend the rest of his life with Sylvie. He would be able to end his life of crime. He would be able to *try* to live like a normal person.

If only...

‡

45. La visite

Vendredi 15 Décembre

"Inspector Richer?"

"Chief Inspector Richer, madame," he said in heavily accented English. "From the Sûreté, in Paris."

"So you said on the telephone. Please, won't you sit down?" Julie Bayfield was an attractive woman in her late thirties, hair long but tied up, dressed in a classic but tight-fitting blue two piece. The Frenchman liked what he saw.

She accepted his offer of a cigarette, *Ma Griffe* wafting in his direction as she leant forward for a light.

"So," she said as she sat back in her swivel chair. "What brings a French policeman all the way to London on a cold winter's Friday? It must be something important."

"Something which needs... discretion, madame. Firstly, my thanks for seeing me at such a time. I am duty bound to point out to you that I have no authority as a police officer in your country. I am here on other business. For the purpose of this conversation I must be regarded as being here as a private citizen."

"Intriguing. Well then, would you like some tea *Monsieur* Richer?"

"That would be nice, thank you."

She spoke into an intercom on her desk and then smiled back at him. "So, in a private capacity, what can I do for you?"

"Madame, I believe you have in your possession certain documents which were stolen from a French resident almost a year ago. I am investigating the crime."

"And what makes you think I have these documents?"

"My investigations have shown me that since the theft these documents have passed through many hands. The last possessor of them confessed to me that he sent them to an auction house in London. Both Phillips and Sotheby's deny any knowledge of the documents and both suggested I contact you. You specialise, I believe, in books, manuscripts, letters, that sort of thing."

"I see. Well, Chief Inspector - " There was a tap on the door and a young boy entered carrying a tray. "Thank you, Clint."

"Miss." Clint put the tray on her desk and ambled off.

"Milk and sugar?"

"Black, just as it comes, please madame."

"Unusual." She poured.

"You know us French!" he laughed as he accepted the china cup and took a chocolate biscuit from the proffered plate. "Do you have the articles, madame?"

She sipped her tea. "We are a small, family firm. Not in the league of the major auction houses."

"An ideal situation if someone wanted to sell something unobtrusively."

"You are not, I hope, implying some sort of criminal action on the part of this house?"

"No, no, no, madame, not at all."

"Good. In which case I will look in our records. You realise if we do find something I am not going to simply hand it over to you."

"Proper procedures will be followed madame."

"Right. Now what are the documents about?"

"I have no idea."

She looked at him quizzically. "Well then, were they signed? Who was the originator?"

"The Duke of Windsor, the Duchess of Windsor."

She smiled. "Oh yes. In that case I do not have to look in our records."

"Madame?"

"There were a bundle of letters and assorted documents."

"You read them?"

"No. I did not have time to. I just looked at the top one. It was an old love letter. Authentic enough, but there really is no market for them. Not in this country, anyway."

He put his cup and saucer down on the edge of her desk. "So you still have them?"

She moved his crockery onto the tray, next to hers. "No. I was going to include them in my spring catalogue but I had an enquiry for them. From your country actually. From France. The offer was reasonable, so I let them go."

"The offer was only reasonable?"

"I told you, they were of little value. And she is notoriously litigious. To trade in her letters while she is still alive might be inviting trouble. I made a small profit." She shook her head regretfully. "I'm sorry Chief Inspector, but it seems your trip here was wasted."

"Not at all, madame," he smiled a big, charming smile. "I have met you, have I not?"

She looked away coyly.

"And London at Christmas time!" he continued. "All those pretty lights! Might I presume to ask to whom you sold them?"

"Ah, the six-four thousand dollar question."

"Madame?"

"These documents were stolen, you say?"

"They were. And the lady wants them back."

"It is a question of ethics, you see. I sold them to a dealer in Paris. If I tell you his name, will I be implicated?"

"Madame, I can assure you. The French police have no authority here. You bought the goods in good faith - and from a French policeman, Monsieur Le Bouthillier, *non*? Acting in good faith is not a crime. And you have your money."

"Yes. That is true." She tapped a pencil against her desk. "Do I have your word, Chief Inspector, that I will not be implicated?"

"Madame, your only offence is to unknowingly deal in stolen goods from another country. There is no reason for you to fear. I will not implicate you. The lady wants her letters back. She is not after retribution."

Julie stood up and took a small, thick book from a cabinet against the wall. She flicked through it, transferred certain details onto a sheet of paper and handed it to him.

He looked at it. "You know this man?"

"Not personally. I have occasional dealings with him."

"You would not, for example, be tempted to ring him and tell him of the Surêté's interest?"

"Now why should I do that? It is none of my business."

"No, of course not." He stood up. "Madame, I have taken up far too much of your time. You have been most gracious." He slipped his scarf around his neck and pulled on his gloves. "And most helpful. My thanks." He held out his right hand.

She came around the desk. "You are welcome, Chief Inspector. I always try to stay on the right side of the law." She went to shake his hand but somehow missed it.

"So do I, madame." His raised hand lunged for her throat. She gasped as the fingers sunk into her neck. Before she could even raise a hand in defence, she was lifted off her feet by the big, burly policeman. She tried to grab his arm for support. Her legs flailed. One of her shoes fell off.

His face was no more than half a metre away. He watched as her cheeks turned purple and her bulging eyes went from shock to incomprehension to pleading and to terror. They began to roll and fade.

"Forgive me, madame," he pleaded softly. "One day you will understand.

I can take no chances."

His hand made a sudden movement as if turning a key in a lock. Her neck broke with a sharp *crack*.

Gently he placed her back down in her seat behind her desk. Slowly he lowered her forward so she looked as if she had fallen asleep.

Outside, he popped his head into the General Office. Clint was talking to a young popsie sitting behind a typewriter.

"Madame has asked not to be disturbed for one hour," said the Frenchman.

"Okay guv," nodded Clint. "Mind 'ow yer go now."

"I will." Jacques Mesrine turned up his collar and went out into the cold, blustery English wind.

‡

46. Voleur

Mesrine returned to France after only two months in London.

1979 was to become known as 'The Year of Mesrine' in Europe. How many petty crimes he committed is not known, but with each incident to which his name was linked (either properly or by certain members of the police who had no one else upon whom to pin the particular crime) the pressure for his capture increased.

In early January, Mesrine sent a threatening letter to Jean-Claude Lattes, the publisher of his autobiography, claiming that he was owed two hundred and thirty thousand francs. This was rather a forlorn attempt (it has been suggested by some that it was done purely for publicity) as Mesrine well-knew that the profits from the book had been frozen on the orders of the French government.

On Saturday 20 January he held up a supermarket in Massy and came away better off to the tune of four hundred thousand francs. This, together with the proceeds of the many robberies he committed in the second quarter of the year, went towards financing The Big One.

It was planned for months, to the exclusion of everything else. He planned down to the last detail, including intricate notations on the phases of the moon and whether or not leaves would be on the trees at any particular time.

The Big One happened on Thursday 21 June. Impersonating policemen, Mesrine and an accomplice [the rumour that this was Chrastny, his protegée, has never been proved] kidnapped Henri Lelièvre from his house in the village of Maresche near Le Mans. Eighty-two year old Monsieur Lelièvre was an ex-banker and industrialist, one of the richest men in France.

At a rented house in Breuil, near Blois, the victim was held for over five weeks. On Saturday 28 July he was released safe and well near a taxi rank in the 17th Arrondisement in Paris. The ransom paid was six million francs in used fifty franc notes.

Never one for modesty, Mesrine was pleased with himself to the point of jubilation. He had done it. This time he had really pulled it off. For the first time ever he felt financially secure. He could fulfil his dreams, he could plan his retirement. He would buy a property somewhere. He would marry Sylvie.

But later.

First there was a slate that needed to be wiped clean.

3IÈME PARTIE

‡

LE RECOUVREMENT

‡

47. L'Organisation

Vendredi 15 Juin

"How do you know he hasn't given up?" asked the man on the right, the chain smoker.

"I know him," answered Richer. "He will fulfil his debt. I told you it would take time."

"It is all a con," snapped the cap man. "He tricked us into getting him out of jail and now he is laughing at us. All these crimes he is committing, without one word to you. He will not fulfil any debt. There is no honour among thieves."

"But there is honour," said Richer calmly, "amongst the OAS."

There was silence. Then the Colonel smiled. "*Touché*, I think."

"Why don't we send someone else after it?" asked the chain smoker. "I don't mean some OAS James Bond. Just someone who knows about the subject."

"Someone who could make discreet, knowledgeable enquiries," suggested the cap man. "Someone who will not run amok over France and have the entire bloody judiciary gunning for him!"

Richer finished his cigarette and immediately lit another. "That is at your discretion, of course. But Mesrine wouldn't take kindly to it."

"Mesrine wouldn't take kindly to it!" scoffed the chain smoker. "Fuck Mesrine. He is a simple conscript - like yourself, Captain. He obeys orders. Like yourself, Captain."

"Could you call him off?" asked the Colonel.

Richer shook his head. "I have no way of contacting him. He contacts me. And in the present climate, with everyone wanting his blood, he is not likely to. He suspects my phones are bugged."

"And are they?"

Richer shrugged. "You tell me. There is no reason why they should be." He held the Colonel's eyes.

"Tell us what the secret is," urged cap man. "Then we can ask someone else to look for it."

Richer transferred his gaze. "That order must come from the Colonel himself. Otherwise my answer is no."

The Colonel looked from cap man to Richer. Then he looked at the man on his left. He said to Richer, "You do not want to tell us?"

"Not yet, sir. Not till we have the document. Be patient. Let Mesrine get on with it. He will not fail."

"He'd better not," came a mumble from the left.

The Colonel breathed out long and slow. "And La Dame?"

"She is unconscious most of the time now. I have managed to speak to her twice this year. She doesn't know who I am or what the hell I am talking about."

"*Alors,*" the Colonel nodded. "For now, Captain. For now we will leave it. But our patience is wearing thin. We must have a return on our investment soon."

‡

48. Voleur et receleur

Mardi 31 Juillet

It was overcast, warm yet with a sharp breeze that whistled along the boulevards and gave spasmodic reminders that summers can never be guaranteed. The big, tall man with the dark, deep set eyes did not look out of place in the open beige trenchcoat as he walked along Boulevard Montmartre and turned into the Passage de Panoramas.

He had expected the shops in the Galeries Montmartre to be closed for the 'Fermeture Annuelle', but a phone call earlier that morning had revealed that the one he was interested in did not shut until the end of the week.

The bell on the door *ting-a-ling*ed as he entered the small, musty premises. The lights were on, there was the smell of cigarette smoke, yet no one was there. He closed the door behind him and looked around.

A scuffling sound came from somewhere. As if by magic some papers rose in the air from behind the desk. They were followed by a mumbled "Oh dear", and then the bespectacled Monsieur Buisson came into view.

He jumped as he noticed the visitor. "*Ah, monsieur! Pardonez-moi!* I did not realise there was anyone here. What can I - ?" He frowned at the man on the other side of the desk. "Do I not know you?"

The visitor's hand went towards the right pocket of his trenchcoat, the one that looked like it had something heavy in it.

"Undoubtedly."

"Let me think," Buisson looked hard into his eyes. Then he nodded. "Oh yes. I know you."

The visitor's hand went into the pocket.

"It was a while ago, wasn't it? Sometime last year..." His upper lip wrinkled, then his face cleared and he said, "The police."

"The police?"

"I am not wrong, am I? Are you not from the police? Were you not here before?"

The visitor laughed. "You remember?"

"Indeed. I am right then."

"I was here last year making enquiries about autographs of La Dame."

"La Dame... yes, I recall. Didn't something happen? Did I not read...?"

"Yes, the name you gave me. Inspector Le Bouthillier. He died."

"Yes, yes. That is right. Poor man."

"Well, you know how it is," said the visitor chattily. "When people don't co-operate."

"Yes indeed. Well, what - " The smile fell from Buisson's face as he realised what had been said.

The visitor still grinned at him.

"Y - you mean the *police* killed him?" The shopkeeper removed his pince-nez and began rubbing them on a dirty handkerchief.

"No, no, you're missing the point. Not the police. *Mesrine.* Jacques Mesrine." The hand came out of the trenchcoat pocket holding a gun - a weird-looking object with a round, bulbous knob on the end which resembled the glans of a penis. "You may have heard of me."

Buisson's mouth was open. It stayed that way, a single strand of spittle joining his upper and lower teeth.

"Let me introduce you to my little friend," said Mesrine.

Buisson went cross-eyed as he stared at the gun no more than thirty centimetres from his face. His jaw trembled.

"Although her beauty leaves something to be desired, her physical performance is excellent. She is a foreign lady. Russian. You have not met her like before, hmm?"

"N - n – n- "

Mesrine ran the circular tip down the edge of Buisson's face. "She likes you. I can see that. Pray that she does not want you. She is like a Black Widow. Deadly. And she is silent, did you know? She doesn't go *bang,* she doesn't even go *phut.* She just goes *click.*" He came round behind the shopkeeper. He could smell his fear as he said softly into his ear, "*Click,* monsieur. And if you are her mate, you do not even hear it."

An involuntary fart shot out from the seat of Buisson's chair. "I - "

"You will co-operate, yes? Then you need soil yourself no further."

"Y - yes."

"*Très bien.* Now, m'sieur, you have been very naughty, have you not?" The gun tapped lightly and rhythmically around Buisson's face. "After I had been here last year – my God, what did you have for breakfast? - you contacted your client, the late lamented Inspector Le Bouthillier. You told him, no doubt, of the police interest and you advised him to sell the document. Make a quick profit before the police seized them."

"I did not - "

The gun prodded sharply into his lips, breaking two of his front teeth. The obscene bulb slid into his mouth like a cock. "Do not talk to me if you are going to lie." Buisson screwed up his eyes in agony. "Now, the Inspector took your advice. He sold them to a dealer in London. He told you. And here you pulled what you thought was your master stroke. After the fuss of the death had died down, you contacted the dealer and bought them back. You realised that if they were important enough for a thief - a thief identified publicly as the great Jacques Mesrine - to kill for, then you were onto a very, very big profit margin indeed."

The gun came out of Buisson's mouth and slowly wiped spittle and blood across his cheek. One of his front teeth had been snapped at the gum.

"But you came unstuck, did you not?" continued Mesrine. "You couldn't shift them. Weren't you surprised at the price the London dealer let them go at?"

"I didn't - "

"Shut up. Did she not tell you they were of very little value, especially over there? People look at the signatures you see, and they do not want their's. They are not fashionable. People do not look at the contents of one document slipped among a handful of namby-pamby love letters. I suspect you have not been able to sell them, m'sieur. I believe they have been here, in this shop, for the last seven months. Am I right, m'sieur?"

At last that horrible, tormenting gun left Buisson's face. His mouth was swollen and sore. His throat was dry and tight. "N - n - near enough, m'sieur. You are correct. Yes."

"Good. Then I will take them off you now, if you please."

"No."

"I beg your pardon?" The gun came back towards him.

"Y - you were almost right. They hung around here for ages. But I sold them. Two weeks ago."

"*You did what?*"

"A collector. I had offered them to him before but he was not interested. Then two weeks ago he changed his mind."

"Why should he do that?"

"Said something about a wedding present for his daughter."

"And you sold them to him for ten times what you paid for them."

"Only d - double this time."

"I do not believe this," Mesrine spoke to himself.

"It - it is true, m'sieur. I swear."

"This is simply impossible. These letters are more elusive than a virgin in Pigalle. *Alors, monsieur,* a simple request then you will never see me again."

A piece of paper was placed in front of Buisson.

"Name and address please."

Slowly, Buisson's trembling fingers picked up his pince-nez from the desk. He got them onto his nose at the second attempt. Carefully he stood up, all the while keeping an eye on the gun. A rivulet of blood was running slowly from his mouth and pooling on his chin.

Under Mesrine's close supervision he searched through his index. About halfway along he pulled out a card.

Mesrine reached over and grabbed his hand, holding it steady as he looked at the details on the card. Then he gave a soft, ironic laugh.

"*This* man?"

"*Oui.*"

"This *is* impossible. Someone up there is playing games with me. *This man?*" He stared at the card for a few more moments, shaking his head. "It is so ridiculous, I believe you. *Bien.* Now, please sit down, m'sieur - No, no, take the card with you." He stood behind him again. "Now, I want you to make a little phone call, do you think you can do that? To that gentleman there."

"Him?"

"Yes. Can you do it without sounding unnatural? I can always impersonate you, but it would be much better coming from the real thing."

"Im - impersonate me?"

"It is always easy to impersonate the dead."

Buisson wiped his mouth and sighed. "What do you want me to say?"

"Make it chatty. Talk about the weather. Ask after his family. You know. Then I want you to ask him whether he still possesses the autographs. Ask him whether he still has them and, if so, would he sell them back to you? Haggle if they are for sale, complain if they are not, the usual thing. You know, what you are expert at."

"That is all, m'sieur?"

"Yes. Don't enter into any agreements with him. If it comes to it, say you will have to confer with your client and get back to him."

The shopkeeper nodded that he understood.

Mesrine squatted beside him, the gun pressed snugly into his ribs. "Hold the telephone between our ears so that I can hear."

It took the shaky fingers three false starts before they managed to dial the number fully. A switchboard answered and put him through to a secretary. After explaining who he was and that it was a call regarding investment, Buisson was put through to the gentleman himself.

Mesrine listened and was pleased. The man confirmed to Buisson that he still had the papers in question but no, they were not for sale, not at any price.

After some concluding platitudes, Buisson terminated the call. He turned to Mesrine as the criminal stood up from his crouching position, rubbing his right buttock. The stab wound still nagged.

Mesrine smiled. He was pleased with Buisson. He had performed well. He could not have asked for better.

Which made it even more of a shame to kill him.

Mesrine looked at Buisson.

Buisson looked at Mesrine.

Click.

‡

49. Voleur

Jeudi 2 Août

The Avenue Alphonse XIII is a small residential avenue off the Rue Raynouard, just to the north of the church of Notre Dame de Grace de Passy in the select 16th Arrondisement of Paris. The buildings in the avenue are typically Parisian, between six and eight storeys high, tall narrow windows, daunting three metre high double black front doors, some leading into courtyards beyond.

As with most of these elegant buildings in the capital, those in Alphonse XIII have been converted into apartments, nonetheless luxurious and spacious for that. The apartment in question on this day was at number 5.

The clean-shaven man with the large, square spectacles, hair short, almost cropped and pushed straight back from his forehead, dressed in T-shirt and jeans, ambled along the Avenue. A man with a purpose but in no hurry to complete it, blatantly unhappy with his surroundings. He would have been more at home in the 14th across the river.

Standing outside number 5, he looked up at the building as if making up his mind that this was indeed the place he wanted. The decision made, he walked inside.

Although his rubber-clad shoes made no sound on the tiled floor, he was spotted by the concièrge immediately.

"Yes? Where do you think you're going?" snapped the man from his *loge*, adapting his tone to suit the person in front of him.

"Ah," the visitor turned as if he had only just noticed the kiosk. "*Bonjour m'sieur*, I am looking for - " He fumbled in his pocket and produced a scrap of paper, folded in half. "Er - " He passed it across.

The concièrge frowned at the rough, uneducated writing, and held the scrap of paper with the tips of his fingers. "What month is it?" he asked disdainfully.

The visitor was taken aback. "*Comment?*"

"The month. What is it?"

"Er," he fiddled nervously. "August?"

"*Exactement!*" The concièrge threw the piece of paper back, point made. It fell to the floor. "How do you expect such a man to be in Paris in August? He has gone away, dolt. Always does this time of year. Won't be back till the end of September at the earliest, maybe later. What did you want to see him about anyway? What would the likes of you want with him?"

"That, m'sieur, is my business."

The concièrge looked up, surprised at the sudden change in the man's tone. The man was staring at him. The concièrge felt angry but also, for some reason, very much afraid. Damn upstart working classes, didn't know their place nowadays. "Was there something else?" he asked.

"No."

"Then I think you'd better leave."

"Yes." The man turned and left.

The concièrge stared after him.

Only later, when he was leaving his *loge*, did he notice the piece of paper on the floor, lying where he had thrown it.

‡

50. Flics

Lundi 3 Septembre

This day in 1979 was noted for two reasons. Firstly, it was the fortieth anniversary of the outbreak of the Second World War. Secondly, and more importantly, it was the day Paul Richer made the mistake.

It had been such a fine summer as well, in all ways. Richer was deeply tanned after three weeks camping on the Côte d'Azur. In the two weeks since his return he had sorted out four major problems concerning diverse foreign interests and was well on his way to organising the deportation of a certain Middle Eastern religious leader who had only been admitted to France on the strict understanding that he would engage in no political activity and had then proceeded to do just that.

Richer felt good, both physically and professionally. And it was probably this that led him into the blunder.

It was 15:00. Richer, brown and open-necked, sat smoking in the office as he completed a report on the suspected bestial proclivities of the son of a German industrialist baron resident up north. Across the room Gerard, peeling pink from his annual week in Ostend, could just be seen through a haze of Disque Bleu, writing in a file.

Richer's telephone rang. Absentmindedly he stretched out a hand, still concentrating on the report in front of him.

"Richer."

"Bruno."

He said it. "Bruno who?"

Gerard's head shot up as if he had been hit in the back by an RER express train.

"*Bruno.*"

"Oh! Yes!" Richer looked across the room. His colleague was fumbling in a drawer, coughing. He appeared not to have heard. "Sorry. It's been so long. Thought you'd given up."

"I've had other things to do."

"So I've read. Congratulations. A good job. But you know the numbers were noted?"

"So I have discovered. I have had to have them laundered. And that is expensive. I wanted to retire but now there must be one more job."

"Who?"

"Don't be silly. One more, then I can retire. But I never forget an agreement, *Capitaine*. I am very close now. Shortly the item will be yours."

"I have authority to end it. You can stop if you want to."

"An agreement is an agreement. I will contact you soon."

"*D'accord.*"

The caller hung up.

Richer sat, his eyes on the report on the desk.

Mesrine had had to launder the six million francs ransom paid for Henri Lelièvre because the bank had recorded all the numbers before handing them over. At the most he would get forty per cent of the true value. So he was not as rich as he had hoped to be. Now he was tying up loose ends prior to his final job and his retirement. And Richer was a loose end.

Across the room Gerard calmly picked up the telephone and, with no pretence of stealth, keyed the British Embassy.

"Meester Becker if you please." He spoke in English. A few moments later he said, "Good afternoon, Gerard BaySayPay."

"'Afternoon Claude old son. How's things?"

Without even looking at his colleague, Gerard said "A matter has raised its head again."

"Oh yes? And which matter would that be?"

"A matter of some time ago."

"Can't you - ? Oh, I see. Is someone there?"

"Yes."

"Right, so what matter concerned us some time ago? Not our man and his fancy lady, the one in the photos with nipples like coathooks? The bit of stuff that disappeared?"

"No."

"No, he's back in the UK now. The secretary who kept taking fees off casual enquirers?"

"No."

"Some time back?"

"Yes. Serious. The man upstairs."

There was a long pause, then Becker said lowly "I think we should meet."

"So do I. Soon."

"Tomorrow morning? At ten?"

"At your place."

"Right."

"*D'accord.*"

Gerard replaced the phone and stretched. Arms behind his head, he looked over at Richer. He was writing.

"Hey!" Gerard smiled as he attracted the other man's attention. "Fancy a snifter?"

"Later," said Richer. "Fleury's just buzzed."

‡

51. Le Colonel

Commissaire Charles Fleury-Goujon looked out of his window at the mid-afternoon traffic moving smoothly along the Rue des Saussaies. Across the road and a block beyond, he could see the top of the Palais d'Elysée.

He turned as Richer knocked and entered, and he said without preamble "La Dame."

Richer was stone faced. "What about her?"

"I've decided. I want to know."

Richer's eyes travelled around the room. "Not here."

The Commissaire looked at his watch. "I have an appointment over in d'Orsay in half an hour. Travel with me."

The chauffeur-driven Citroen pulled out of the gates of the Interior Ministry, crossed the Place Beauvau and purred down the tree-lined Avenue Marigny. In the partitioned, sound-proofed back, Commissaire Fleury-Goujon lit a Gitanes and blew the smoke towards the ceiling. He turned to the man next to him.

"*Alors*, Captain Richer. I want to know. What is this secret that has been kept hidden all these years by the Duchess of Windsor?"

The vehicle pulled up in the courtyard of the imposing building on the Quai d'Orsay. Both men sat in silence.

At length, Fleury-Goujon said, "*D'accord*. I now understand. Who would have thought? De Gaulle was worse than any of us imagined."

"He was only a minor part of it."

"Yes."

"Will you tell the others?"

"No. I agree with you. Not until we have the document. As your Commissaire I have not heard a word you said. As your Colonel I instruct you to carry on. Let Mesrine get the document. We have been waiting years for this opportunity."

"Yes sir."

"The car will take you back."

Without further word, the head of the OAS climbed out of the vehicle and walked into the building.

‡

52. Flic et les Anglais

Mardi 4 Septembre

"We are very grateful to you for contacting us."

Gerard shrugged with due diffidence and wondered for the umpteenth time if he had done the right thing. He was sitting in the chair in the small office at the back of the British Embassy. The thin, anonymous man with the sunken eyes, and the small, lively Ron Becker each sat on a corner of the desk facing him.

This time Gerard smoked with full permission, an old saucer for an ashtray balanced on his knees. Underneath his legs was a large, and obviously full, holdall at which Becker kept casting curious glances.

The man thanked him again. "Very grateful."

Gerard waved his cigarette and narrowed his eyes as he exhaled smoke. "Last time, monsieur, you indicated that I was being unco-operative. I told you then that you were wrong."

"You've always been a good lad, Claude," Becker sounded disgracefully insincere. "We've always had faith in you."

Gerard looked at him but said nothing.

The man pushed himself up from the desk and walked round to sit behind it. Becker quickly shoved himself off the corner and stood in proximity to Gerard.

The man joined his hands together in front of him. "After you rang yesterday I contacted Clarence House."

"Clarence who?"

"Clarence House."

"A place not a person, Claude," explained Becker.

"Oh." The reference to the residence of the matriarch of the British Royal Family meant nothing to the policeman.

"In London."

"Ah." He nodded, absolutely none the wiser.

"Had to disturb our lady as she was dressing for a film premiere. Wasn't very happy."

"Ah."

"Anyway, she has now told me more. It is not the jewellery that we are after. It is a *document*."

"A document, m'sieur?"

"A document."

"What sort of a document?"

"She is being cagey. Wouldn't amplify. A document, that is as far as she would say. A document containing a secret. And the short of it is she wants a point (d)."

"A point (d)?"

"Situation as before - but she would now like the document herself."

"*Quoi! Mais c'est* - " As Gerard straightened himself in the chair, his legs parted. The saucer of ash plummeted downwards, bounced off the side of his holdall and spilt its contents all over the thick carpet. All three men looked at the mess.

" - *impossible*," said Gerard.

They all looked back up.

"*Impossible*, Claude?" queried Becker. "Surely not."

"Surely yes, m'sieur. I can keep an eye on things, advise you, as agreed. But to actually get it myself! How am I to know what it is when you don't? A document? Could be anything. A laundry bill? A theatre programme? There are millions of *documents*. That is an impossible task. There is no one that could find a document without knowing what it is!" He made a dismissive motion with his hand. "*Non*."

"In that case, how about point (e)?"

Gerard sighed, tired of this stupid Anglo-Saxon way of talking. "Point (e)?"

"If you cannot obtain it yourself, suppress it."

"Suppress it?"

"Our lady has instructed that at all costs the information in the document must not become public. The document can be returned to the Duchess if needs be, but even that would be inadvisable considering the state of her mind. But all information as to its contents must be suppressed."

"We are very discreet in the BCP, m'sieur."

"Of course, of course. But..." The outward movement of the man's hands said more than words.

Gerard pulled out a grubby handkerchief and loudly blew his nose. He mumbled, "I will do what I can do."

Surprisingly, the man accepted it. "All right, so be it. I appreciate we cannot ask the *impossible*." (Gerard raised an eyebrow at the piss taking.) "But all points (a) to (e) are extant. Please keep us informed. And bear in mind point (d), won't you?"

"*Certainement. Messieurs*, may I ask? Do you have *any* idea what this secret is?"

The man snorted and shook his head.

Becker spoke. "We know no more than you. This document - and we're not even too sure exactly what it is - contains something important about or concerning the Duke and Duchess of Windsor. Other than that we know nothing. Perhaps it's not our place to know."

"Perhaps," put in the man, "it is better that we do not know."

"Whatever it is," continued Becker, "it is important enough to warrant the personal attention of our lady in London. And that means important with a capital 'I'."

Gerard picked up his holdall as he got to his feet. "I will keep you informed of anything I find out. And if I can do anything, I shall."

"Thank you," said the man, rising. "We are pleased with your help and co-operation, monsieur. It will not go unforgotten."

Gerard gave a formal little bow and turned away. Becker followed him out.

"If only we knew what this secret was," said Becker as they walked along the corridor.

"Does he know?" Gerard nodded backwards at the room.

"No, I think he's on the level."

"Will we ever find out what it is all about?"

Becker stopped at the top of the stairs as Gerard continued on down.

"Oh undoubtedly," he said. "Undoubtedly."

Back in the office, the thin man was sitting, fingers forming a pyramid. "Do you trust him?" he asked when Becker returned.

"That shifty-arsed frog? No way."

"But he did alert us to the renewed activity."

"He was duty bound."

"Ron, I have to tell you that Her Majesty has instructed us to take an active interest. No more back seats."

"Are you sure that's wise? Activity in a foreign country?"

"We no longer have any alternative. She thought that the document had gone and the secret was safe forever. H M has issued strict orders. It must not get out. The only way she can be certain is if she has the document. No suppression like I told him. She wants the document. And if anyone knows the secret they are to be *persuaded* to remain silent."

"I see."

"She has said that *whatever* needs to be done must be done."

"I understand."

"Do what needs to be done, Ron."

"Yes, sir."

‡

53. Flics

The door to the Chief Inspectors' office opened with a thumping crash. Claude Gerard came in lugging a heavy-looking holdall. Richer looked at him absentmindedly and then looked at his watch. "Claude? Thought you weren't on till later."

Wordlessly, Gerard nodded at the bag. Richer glanced at it and then looked up into the other man's face. For a moment he did not comprehend. Then realisation hit him. "You're joking!"

Still not saying a word, Gerard went across and hefted the bag onto his desk.

"You *are* joking," repeated Richer.

Gerard stood there with his hands on his hips.

"You have *got* to be joking!" insisted Richer. "Tell me you are!" Thoughts of Mesrine had temporarily taken a back seat to the horror that now confronted him. "I *cannot* believe it."

"You'd better, *mon ami.*"

"Come on! It's one of your little comedies, right?"

"No."

"Permanent?"

"Who knows?"

"*I* don't. Tell me. Spell it out."

Gerard spelt it out. "Mathilde's thrown me out."

"Don't tell me! Christ! But I thought you were talking again?"

"We talked too much. Sharp words."

"What're you going to do?"

Gerard shrugged, a lost orphan.

Richer groaned at the creeping realisation. He rubbed his right hand down his face. "No way. No fucking way. It won't work. Look, I don't... You *are* serious, right?"

Big puppy dog eyes.

"Oh, dam*nation* Claude..." He stood up, shaking his head. "Shit. Okay, okay. But only temporarily. A week at the most. Then you'll either have to effect a reconciliation or find a place of your own."

His rotund, overweight colleague grinned like a simpleton. "*Tu es un vrai copain.*"

"*Un vrai idiot!* I'll do the cooking, but don't expect extravaganzas every night. Some days it'll be Burger King."

"Of course."

"You can do the housework. And you can damn well give me some money for the grub."

"Whatever you say."

"And the bed is mine. You get the couch."

"*Naturellement... et merci.* I'll buy you a drink later."

"You'll buy me a bottle. And why not now?"

"Got to see the old man. Is he in?"

"You might catch him. He's going to lunch somewhere. Important?"

"Just something that's come up. Need some guidance."

"Anything I can do?"

"Get me the document you've got Mesrine looking for," thought Gerard. He said, "Just an embarrassment the *rosbeefs* want hushed up. You know, if fucking hadn't been invented the world would be a much happier place."

"It would be full of bloody wankers. Like the Brits," said Richer.

‡

54. Voleur et le pouvoir

Mesrine spent the remainder of September planning his last crime: the kidnapping of broadcaster and journalist Philippe Bouvard, a man with many political connections and one of the most famous figures in France.

Mesrine found it difficult to plan the operation with the detail he required. He knew that he was on his own. Apart from Sylvie, he could trust no one. He could not even visit Janou, the hunt for him now was too intense.

Mesrine knew that the underworld would not deliberately betray him, but with the Press and the police now totally obsessed with him to the virtual exclusion of everything else, slips could occur. One wrong word by someone somewhere could do it. He had to work alone.

Commissaire Devos and his Brigade de Répression de Banditisme *and Commissaire Broussard and his* Brigade de Recherche et d'Intervention *had conducted the biggest criminal manhunt Europe had ever known – but without success.*

All three police forces of France had been looking for Mesrine. The Paris Préfecture *of Broussard and Devos. The* Sûreté *and its own* Office Centrale de Répression de Banditisme *under Lucien Aimé-Blanc and Charles Pellegrini. And the provincial police forces, the* gendarmerie.

And Mesrine had not been found.

The President of France, Valéry Giscard d'Estaing, had indicated that he wanted l'affaire Mesrine *ended once and for all. In private (which meant that it was reported in* Le Figaro*) he had confided that he did not even want Mesrine brought to trial. He issued an ultimatum. Either Mesrine was found or Christian Bonnet, the Minister of the Interior, would be replaced.*

It was time for innovation. For a fresh initiative. A new man was called in to take overall charge of the national hunt for Mesrine: Maurice Bouvier, one of France's most eminent and successful career policemen. Bouvier's notable triumphs included the breaking of the OAS campaign of terror in France in the early 1960s, and the arrest of Lieutenant-Colonel Jean-Marie Bastien-Thiry and the others responsible for the assassination attempt on President de Gaulle at Petit-Clamart on 22 August 1962.

It was hoped that a combined national unit under Bouvier could succeed where the fragmented efforts of the others had failed.

‡

Mesrine had moved again, now ensconced with Sylvie in a third floor apartment at 35-37 Rue Belliard in the 18th Arrondisement. Some of the proceeds of the Lelièvre kidnapping had bought an unfurnished apartment in a luxury block in Marly-le-Roi near Versailles, to which he intended to take his bride. Unbeknown to Sylvie, he had spent a lot of time decorating and furnishing it, hopefully to her taste.

By October he was ready on all fronts. Ready for Marly-le-Roi, ready for Philippe Bouvard. And ready for a certain Monsieur Lensens.

‡

55. Voleur

Vendredi 12 Octobre

This time the concièrge at 5 Avenue Alphonse XIII was charming. He knew class when he saw it. The caller was a tall man with spectacles and a three-piece suit, hair parted in the centre, too prominent chin and with a hint of an effeminate manner. He reeked of money.

Yes, there was someone in the Lensens apartment, please go on up, fifth floor.

The doorbell of the apartment *ding-dong*ed in expectation. After a moment the door was opened by a distinguished, late middle-aged lady.

"Madame Lensens?"

"*Ah non, monsieur,* she is away. I am just the maid."

"*Oh, pardon.* Actually it was *Monsieur* Lensens I wanted. I'd best explain. My name is de Guy, Guillaume de Guy, from de Guy Rare Books and Prints. Monsieur Lensens ordered some special manuscripts from us. I just wanted to advise him of the state of his order. Is he in?"

"*Je regrette, monsieur,* nobody is here. The family always goes to the house in the country on a Friday for the weekend."

"*Ah, quel domage!* Never mind, madame, my own fault. I should have telephoned, but the order just came in as I was leaving the office. No problem. In fact, Monsieur did mention about his country house, now I reflect. Out near Versailles, is it not?"

She smiled. "Wrong château! Fontainbleau. La Ferté-Alais."

Monsieur de Guy slapped himself on the forehead. "Of course! I knew it was one of them! Well, I hope he has a pleasant weekend. I'll see him next week. Oh - I wonder... Should I deliver the order to the house or here? Does he keep his books and papers here?"

"*Non, monsieur,* the house is the true family home. None of his collection is here."

"Do you have the exact address, madame?"

"Of course. *Un moment, m'sieur.*"

She returned momentarily and handed him a slip of paper.

"*Alors,* you have been very helpful. I am sorry for having disturbed you, madame."

"Pas de probleme, monsieur. Bonsoir."
"Bonsoir madame, et merci!"

Guillaume de Guy knocked politely on the door of the apartment in Rue Belliard. It was opened by the demure, plainly-dressed Madame Mercier.

"Madame Mercier?" enquired the caller.

"Oui?"

"de Guy - Rare Books and Prints. About your husband's order?"

"Ah oui, entrez, monsieur, entrez..."

No sooner was the door closed than de Guy's hand was grasping Madame Mercier's left buttock brutally as she forced her tongue against his tonsils. When they broke for air, they were laughing.

"It's funny, this play acting," said Sylvie.

Mesrine pulled off the glasses. "One can never be too careful. There didn't seem to be anybody out there, but one never knows nowadays. The casual, moustachioed Monsieur Mercier lives here. Questions would be asked if the smart, bespectacled, clean-shaven Guillaume de Guy marched straight up with a key to the door."

"You are right, of course." Sylvie pressed herself against him and mussed up the slick hair. "I missed you."

"My child, I have been gone but two hours!"

"Seemed like two years. And I am hungry."

"But we ate before I went out!"

"Not that sort of hunger."

"You are insatiable!"

"I have never denied it."

He swept her off her feet with one movement of his mighty arm, tossing her over his shoulder, her bottom next to his right ear. He smacked it with his free left hand. The cheek wobbled.

She squealed and playfully kicked and punched as he carried her to the bedroom. He was pleased to feel that underneath the plain dress Madame Mercier wore suspenders and stockings and - he moved his hand in verification - no panties.

"My darling," he mumbled into her right butt cheek. "How would you like to spend next weekend in the country, near Fontainbleau?"

Very late that night, the body of a man was found at the foot of a staircase at 5 Rue Alphonse XIII. It was the concièrge of the block, the one who had been so rude to the *parvenu* in August. Apparently he had slipped on the top step, broken his neck with the backward whiplash as he fell, and was dead before he hit the bottom.

‡

56. L'opération

Dimanche 21 Octobre

La Ferté-Alais is some forty kilometres south of Paris in the *département* of Essonne. It is a small, peaceful town living contentedly in the shadow of the nearby larger town of Milly-la-Fôret and the sprawling forest known as Fontainbleau.

At 18:30 on Friday 19 October, Monsieur and Madame François had checked into the hotel in the town square, fulfilling their reservation made earlier that week by telephone.

The staff of the hotel remember Monsieur François as a big, charming man, close cut receding hair greying at the temples, with a neatly trimmed moustache. Every inch the businessman. His wife was a petite woman with huge breasts, long black hair and minimal make-up, who looked exceedingly young. Common opinion agreed that *le monsieur* was in fact having a weekend of naughties with some waif from the typing pool. The staff sniggered knowingly and left them to it.

Jacques and Sylvie enjoyed their weekend. The weather stayed clement and, once they forced themselves from bed in the morning, they roamed the surrounding countryside, more than once laying together in some quiet, sunny field.

They had been booked in for two nights, the Friday and the Saturday, so after a superb meal in the hotel's small restaurant at Sunday lunchtime, *les François* bade a bashful farewell and drove off in their hired car along the N191, heading for Paris.

However, at Baulne just outside la Ferté-Alais they made an abrupt right onto the D87 and, five kilometres further along, turned right again onto the D83, facing La Ferté-Alais from the east. It was now evening and they pulled off the country road near the crossroads at Chêne-Bécart.

Mesrine switched off the car's lights and they sat in the penumbra of dusk, watching the remarkably quick nightfall. Now and again they kissed, occasionally they whispered something. They were far enough off the road not to be seen, but Mesrine had already explained that they would not tempt fate by playing the radio to pass the time.

When it was dark enough, Sylvie removed the black wig, scratching and fluffing her blonde hair. In the close confinement of the vehicle, Jacques could smell her perfume as she moved her body.

"How romantic," she whispered. "Just you and me and the starlight."

"And a job to do." Mesrine ran his finger gently down the centre of her face, from hairline to chin. "Shortly." Again they kissed and his hand crept up the softness of her left thigh to the warmth above. She was damp.

For a while he let his fingers play with her. Soon her deep, quiet sigh indicated at least partial satisfaction.

Two minutes later he reached over the back seat for a holdall. "Time to say *au revoir* to Monsieur François." He stepped out of the vehicle.

Quickly he changed from François' formal suit into black slacks and runners, shirt and black windcheater. With one rip he pulled off the false moustache and discarded it in the grass, a petrified caterpillar. Before packing away the suit, he took one last item from the holdall: a hood.

Opening the trunk, he placed the holdall inside and removed a shotgun. He came back round, leant in the side window and kissed Sylvie firmly on her half open lips.

"Now then, my love, you have food in the *sac* there, yes? You may play the radio now, but if you do, play it *softly*. No one will disturb you, absolutely no possibility. I hope to be back within the hour, but give me until midnight. If I am not back by then, return home - and listen to the radio in the morning."

"Jacques, I am worried for you. Please won't you tell me what you're going to do?"

"*Non.* What little girls don't know, won't hurt them."

She pouted. "You wouldn't hurt me, would you?"

He grinned and flicked her chin. "Only in lust, my darling, only in lust. Remember, one minute past midnight you leave. But I will be back long before then."

With one final kiss he disappeared soundlessly into the darkness.

Sylvie wound up the window, turned out the light, checked that all the doors were locked, and sat there in the silent starlight.

A couple of minutes later, she reopened the door, got out, had a pee, then got back in. Rummaging in the *sac*, she pulled out a litre of *Perrier* and a roast leg of chicken and began to tuck in.

The house had a gravelled driveway curving up the front and disappearing around one side. It was a big place, probably with at least six bedrooms, but the land had obviously been sold off over the years and it seemed an incongruous giant in relation to the small gardens.

Mesrine made no pretence of stealth, walking up the pathway, feet crunching on the gravel, hood on with just eyes, nose and lips protruding, shotgun held casually under his right arm.

Lights shone from various windows. He reckoned on there being two servants, Monsieur et Madame and, perhaps, an *enfant* or two. That was why he had decided on the direct approach. Stealth and deception were too dangerous when there were many people about. Fear was the key, as somebody had once said.

He walked around the building, looking in each window, whether it was illuminated or not. In one room to the side, a maid was putting the finishing touches to a cold collation, spread out attractively on a long table.

Mesrine frowned. There was more food there than for the number of people he had estimated.

Turning the corner to the rear, his suspicions were confirmed. There were about ten vehicles parked in a neat row, and from here he could hear the muffled sounds of merriment from within. There was a party going on!

The sounds were coming from an open window a little way along. Inside about twenty people were standing in a circle around a young couple, glasses raised in a toast.

He pulled himself back quickly as the girl in the centre seemed to look straight at him. There was no change in the sound from within, no shout or scream.

A distinct voice was raised. *"Michel et Veronique.* May their marriage be long and happy!" The other voices were as one in salutation.

Mesrine nodded grimly. *Merci, Michel et Veronique.* You have made the job that much harder.

There was movement and he pressed himself into the wall. Someone opened the windows as music started playing. The party was getting under way now, formalities over.

Up above, a balcony stretched the width of the house, connecting the four rooms on this side.

Holding the shotgun in his left hand, Mesrine leapt, grabbing the iron trellis with his free hand.

For a moment the huge, hooded figure swung in the air, then he eased the shotgun through the ironwork and swung himself up and over.

He looked through the windows at each room in turn. As he had guessed, they were four bedrooms. And each full-length window was fractionally open, letting in air. And letting in Jacques Mesrine.

He squatted at the far end of the balcony and waited. Whatever room was entered first would be the one he would choose. Fate would decide. He rested the shotgun on his lap. He hoped fate would not keep him waiting long.

‡

Half an hour.

And that was too long. He was becoming stiff and irritable. But at last there came the sound of muffled conversation from the second room along.

Before rising, he checked over the railings. Noise and music still came in equal volumes from downstairs. Nobody was outside.

He stood up, stretched, and then walked to the window as silent as death. He smiled. There were no lights on in the room but he could now hear the familiar grunting, groaning, giggling and sighing of copulation.

The window opened outwards noiselessly.

Mesrine walked across the room in the dark. The couple on the bed were oblivious, the body on top giving the body underneath a massive pounding.

Mesrine flicked on the light switch, and in one stride was across to the bed.

The female's scream was blocked as both barrels of the shotgun were thrust into her open mouth.

Apart from their genitals, both of them were fully dressed. Mesrine looked down the barrels of his gun into the bewildered, terrified face of Veronique, the girl whose engagement they had been saluting downstairs.

The man on top of her, face awash with perspiration blended in equal amounts from fear and carnality, was not Michel.

Mesrine gave them a full minute to appreciate the situation. Then he said politely, "Mademoiselle Lensens?"

"Gng." Her head moved up and down as much as the obscene phallus in her mouth would allow.

"Get off please," said Mesrine to the male. "And lay down beside the lady."

The male obliged.

"And please adjust your clothing. Your winkle is wet, it will catch cold."

The male flopped his now shrunken penis back into his fly.

"Thank you. And my condolences - but I'm told size doesn't matter. Mam'selle Lensens, I am sorry for this unpleasantness, but I wish to speak with your father. You are my instrument. I am going to move this weapon from your mouth. Please do not emit one sound, for you must rest assured that I will have no hesitation in blowing your pretty little brains out if you do. You understand?"

"Gng."

"All right."

Slowly, the barrel withdrew. She lay there without moving, eyes wide, mouth still open, gaping at the hooded man in front of her.

"Put your legs together."

She did as she was told.

"Close your mouth."

She did as she was told.

Mesrine stepped backwards. "Now off the bed please."

Hesitantly she rose.

The man moved to rise also. Without the flicker of an eyelid, Mesrine hit him in the face with the butt of the gun. As the girl gasped, her lover fell back onto the bed unconscious, flat as a deadweight. His front teeth had disappeared in a welter of blood and horrible white pieces.

"I will pay his dental bill," said Mesrine. "Now, we will go outside together. You will go to the top of the stairway. The first person you see, tell them you want your father. Say you do not feel well - you certainly don't look it. But insist it must be your father. If anyone else comes, I will kill you. If you say anything to alert your father or anyone, I will kill you. Look at your friend on the bed. LOOK AT HIM!" He grabbed her by the hair and wrenched her head round. She cried out. "Believe I mean it! He is alive. You will not be. Now, if you please."

Standing in the lee of the doorway as he opened it, he motioned Veronique outside. She moved out, walking stiffly as if her legs were about to give way.

Mesrine nodded for her to go to the top of the stairs while he stood forward and to the left of her, out of sight from below. He raised the gun and aimed it at her head.

Considering the circumstances, she performed well. Yes, whoever it was would get Papa, *vitement*. Too much Beaujolais, eh? Yes, something like that. Did she want Michel? No, no, just Papa.

Mesrine indicated for her to come back to him. "Is that your room?" He nodded at the one they had come from.

"*Ou - oui.*"

"Which is your father's room?"

"*Là,*" she nodded at a door further down.

"*Venez.*"

Mesrine positioned her in the doorway of her father's room and stood behind her out of sight, the shotgun firmly at the base of her spine.

It took five minutes before he heard the reassuring *thump-thump* on the stairs.

When Monsieur Lensens turned onto the landing, Veronique could not contain herself. "Papa," she cried. "Oh, Papa!"

Mesrine held her roughly by the back of the dress so she could not run out.

She began sobbing uncontrollably, certain in her own mind that she was signing her father's death warrant.

"My darling, what is the matter?" Lensens hurried along the corridor, puzzled at why his daughter was standing there, arms loosely by her side, apparently unable to move.

He was but two metres from her when she fell backwards through the doorway, out of sight. "Veronique?" He rushed into the room and then found himself going sideways involuntarily. Something was pressing against his head and forcing him to the wall.

He heard the door slam behind him. Veronique was on her knees on the floor in total distress.

Lensens turned slowly, realising the inevitable. His grey eyebrows rose just slightly as he saw the gun and the hooded figure holding it.

"*Bonjour* Monsieur Chief Prosecutor," greeted the hooded Mesrine.

"*Bonjour* Mesrine," nodded Lensens. "I have been expecting you. But not tonight. Only *you* could have picked a night when I would be surrounded by people."

"Although good for the image, a pure coincidence I assure you. As is this whole affair."

"Get it over with then. But don't let my daughter see it."

"You were the man who was instrumental in having me sentenced to twenty years. At the time I swore vengeance. And I still might have it. But not now, not tonight. Tonight I am on different business."

"Really? Why don't you just shoot me and get it over with? Why should I believe a convicted murderer?" He looked at his daughter on the floor. "What did he do to you, Veronique? Or need I ask? Tell me, so I can damn him in hell."

She looked at her father, her bottom lip quivering.

"Tell him," urged Mesrine. "Go on. I simply disturbed her with a friend." The eyes beneath the hood looked coldly at Lensens.

"Is it true?"

"Y - yes, Papa."

"He didn't touch you?"

"N - no."

"A sign of my good faith." The hood lifted in a smile. "The friend, alas, is having a good sleep. But your daughter is unharmed."

"What is it that you want? Kidnap? A ransom? Not me, they'll never pay. I'm no Lelièvre."

"You delude yourself, monsieur. You are not even worthy of it. No, you have something which does not belong to you. I want it."

Lensens was perplexed. "I have not the faintest idea what you are talking about."

Mesrine thrust the gun into Lensen's neck. "You recently bought something. From Buisson, the bookdealer ."

Fear shot through Lensens' eyes. "So his death *was* connected. I couldn't believe it when I heard he'd been killed. You were after the document?"

"Yes."

"And you killed him. Tortured him first, I suppose."

"I will kill *you* if you are silly - and I will shoot the whore-hole of your charmingly promiscuous little girl here. Give me the document and I shall go. And you can call the police and the Press and tell them what a brave man you've been, fighting off the infamous Mesrine, who came to kill you. Naturally, you would not mention the document, for your own sake."

"Naturally. But do you think you can get away - "

"ENOUGH!" The shout made both father and daughter jump. "Enough talking, monsieur. Where is the document?"

"It is in my safe."

"And the safe is downstairs, I suppose?"

"No, it is here in this room."

Mesrine's eyes roved. He frowned. There were no pictures on the elegantly-papered walls for it to hide behind, nothing else obvious that could conceal a safe. "Mam'selle Lensens," he said. "If you would be so kind. Please lay on the bed."

Veronique looked at her father, who nodded. She did as bidden.

"Good. Now raise your hands above your head... *Bon*... please stay in that position. Now monsieur, if you please. The document."

"It is not worth that much now, you know. I bought it as a long-term investment for Veronique and Michel - "

"*Please.*"

With the gun pressed into the back of his skull, Lensens led the way over to the wardrobe. Watched every centimetre of the way by Mesrine, he unlocked the double doors and pulled them open. Inside there was still no indication of a safe, simply clothing and, down one side, a set of open shelves holding such items as handkerchiefs, underwear and socks.

Lensens put his hand under the middle shelf and pulled. The entire top half of the shelving unit swung outwards to reveal the safe in the wall behind. It was a small affair, no more than thirty centimetres square, and was controlled by one of the modern press-button combination devices rather than the standard dial.

Lensens pressed an activation switch and then keyed five numbers. The steel door clicked open.

"Hold it!" snapped Mesrine, prodding the gun into Lensens' head. "Just don't move."

"Oh for goodness sake!" sighed Lensens, but he obeyed.

Swiftly, Mesrine transferred the gun from the father's head to the daughter's groin. He ordered the Chief Prosecutor to observe what he had done. "Just in case you feel brave."

"You are a pig, Mesrine."

"I have never denied it. Now, if you please..."

Lensens took a buff envelope from the safe and held it out.

Still with the gun pointing at the girl, Mesrine stepped back a couple of paces. "Now do exactly as I say. Keep the envelope where I can see it and come to the bed... Lay on top of your daughter. Face down."

"*What?*"

"DO IT!"

The grotesque incest took place, the father laying gently on his daughter, trying to take his weight on his elbows.

"Now both of you. Roll over so Mademoiselle is on top."

It took an effort but it was accomplished, Veronique's dress rising in the manoeuvre to reveal two petite, but far from modest, cheeks.

"Forgive the indelicate position," apologised Mesrine. "But I am sure you understand." He snatched the envelope from Lensens' fingers. Sitting on the far edge of the bed, away from any lashing feet but with an enviable panorama of the delights of Veronique, he cradled the gun and carefully opened the envelope.

The paper had yellowed at the edges, but it was good quality stuff and far from brittle. He read it slowly, eyebrows rising beneath the mask.

He understood the implications immediately. It was unbelievable. There it was. About de Gaulle, about the agreement. About Elizabeth.

He read it again, shook his head in amazement, and then popped it back into the envelope, satisfied. "At last," he said softly. "At last. Debt paid, Captain." The envelope disappeared into an inside pocket of his windcheater.

He was pleased. In an effortless movement he leant to his left and slowly French-kissed the join of Veronique's cheeks through the mouth gap in his hood, his tongue intimate and probing. Then he stood up from the bed. Her father was not witness to the violation, as from his prostrate position with his daughter on top of him, all he could see was the ceiling. And Veronique never told him, but she was later to confide to a friend that it was the most erotic experience of her life.

Mesrine helped himself to some wads of diverse currencies from the safe and a handful of what appeared to be gold coins. "Monsieur Chief Prosecutor," he announced. "You have pleased me. Because of your co-operation, I will consider the matter of the twenty years cancelled. I will not bother you again. But please be sure to cry from the rooftops that the great

Mesrine was here. Say I stole all your cash and jewellery - you can even claim on your insurance, no one will know.

"Now, one final favour if you would. Both of you, please. Into the wardrobe."

They moved hesitantly. Stiffly. The man with a defiant expression he patently did not feel, the girl with a look in her eyes a mixture of fear, admiration and downright animal lust.

"Your party is still in full swing," chatted Mesrine. "But someone will miss you soon. And your knocking might even attract someone passing by. Monsieur, I thank you. We will never meet again. Mademoiselle," the eyes beneath the mask smiled, "it has been a pleasure." He closed the doors and turned the key.

Over to the window, out onto the balcony.

From inside the bedroom, the banging started on the wardrobe door.

Effortlessly, he swung out over the railings.

He landed perfectly on the gravel. Straightening up, he pulled off the hood and stuffed it into a pocket. The shotgun was covered by his jacket and held there by his left arm.

Smoothing his hair, he walked leisurely away, calling *"Au revoir!"* to a small group of people outside the front door.

They shouted goodnight and waved goodbye, not one of them querying the fact that he left on foot instead of by car...

4IÈME PARTIE

‡

LA CONCLUSION

‡

57. La suite

Mardi 23 Octobre

Monsieur Lensens did it well.

Unfortunately for the destiny of Jacques Mesrine, too well.

It was reported in the newspapers as the kidnapping that had been foiled. Each publication had its own version of the events, but the general story was that Mesrine had gone to the house to kidnap the only and beloved daughter of the Chief Prosecutor upon whom he had publicly sworn vengeance. The Chief Prosecutor himself had caught the supercriminal in the act of abduction and, although he had been overcome by the raider, he had caused enough of a diversion to thwart the kidnapping. Instead, the criminal had settled for jewellery worth half a million francs. *[Mesrine's experienced eye reckoned the value at nearer fifty thousand francs – but the insurance companies could afford it.]*

Had the story stayed at that, Mesrine could yet again have come out of it with his Robin Hood image intact. But there was one distasteful codicil. It was claimed by the Chief Prosecutor that Mesrine had been caught in the act of sexually assaulting Mademoiselle Lensens.

Although any true student of the exploits of Jacques Mesrine would have realised that this was out of character, indeed downright untrue, the casual follower - as most of the public were - was stunned. In the two-faced, hypocritical world of the late nineteen seventies murder, robbery, extortion and kidnapping were acceptable; *un morceau* of unilaterally consented sex was not.

Public opinion does not change over night, but the initial outrage when the story broke that Tuesday was encouraged by the Press whose diverse leaders were as one in their opinion: the time had come, Mesrine *must* be caught.

In Montmartre, Paul Richer read of the incident in *Le Figaro*, and he thought it was just another Mesrine attempt at revenge not connected to La Dame's document.

In a cubicle of the *WC* on the sixth floor of 11 Rue des Saussaies, Claude Gerard read about it in *Le Matin*. *Le Matin* was the only paper that included in its biographical details of Chief Prosecutor Lensens that he was a collector of rare books and manuscripts.

On Tuesday 23 October, Claude Gerard put two and two together. With perverse accuracy it made four. Now he knew something Richer did not yet know.

Mesrine had the secret.

‡

58. Flic et l'Anglais

It was noisy on the southern side of La Madelaine, cars roaring down on the right, up on the left, and meeting in mayhem in front at the top of Rue Royale. Down the rue, above the traffic, Claude Gerard could see the *obélisque* in the Place de la Concorde.

A cloudy sky was fulfilling the forecast of overnight rain. He shivered. It was chilly.

He farted softly. A moment later a voice said, "Doesn't get any better, does it Claude?"

He turned around to face Becker. "What doesn't?"

"The smell of Paris. You French are so fastidious in some things. You wash your gutters every day and yet the smell of your sewers still rises above the ground. You should have watched where you were digging your metro tunnels."

"And you need to watch your mouth, you insolent fucking *rosbeef*," thought Gerard. Aloud he said, "I have a story to tell you."

"A story? A story is no good to me, old son."

"A true story. About a cop, about the most wanted man in Europe - and about a document containing a secret."

"I think," said Becker, "we should walk."

"No, Englishman, I have a better idea. I am hungry. That little red-fronted *café* down there serves good food. If you want to hear what I've got to tell you, you will buy me the most expensive meal on the menu."

That day, for the first time in his life, Claude Gerard dined in Maxim's.

‡

59. Flic

Mercredi 24 Octobre

It could have been worse, concede Paul Richer. Much worse. On the other hand, it could have been better. Much better.

The man who, last year, had goaded him to the point of violence and even resignation was now his lodger! It had lasted more than a week, of course, as both of them had known it would. Claude had attempted a reconciliation with Mathilde but had been rebuffed, and apparently she had now taken the brats from their place in Levallois and had gone off to relatives on the west coast. Regrettably, before going she had changed all the locks in the apartment so Claude could not make a furtive trip back to claim any meagre rights he may have left.

It had to be admitted that Claude was more than generous with his rent contribution, and his nocturnal snoring did not penetrate through to the bedroom. So Richer had little to complain about - apart from the fact that he wanted his privacy.

That evening Claude was due in late (with instructions to pick up a fried delight from *Au Petit Comptoir* in the Place du Tertre on the way), so Richer relaxed listening to music and stroking Chivas, grateful there was no cooking to do.

Only after one side of Jean-Michel Jarre, two of Sylvie Vartan, and three cognacs, did he realise that time was getting on. Claude was late. Wonder what crisis there was tonight?

He went into the kitchen and began to prepare himself an omelette, beating out the tensions of the day as he whipped the three eggs in the bowl.

The telephone rang.

Turning the music down, he picked up the receiver. "Richer."

The voice was muffled and distant, the line poor and cracking. "Bruno."

"Well, have you been getting yourself talked about! Greetings *mon brave*. Any news?"

"We must meet. I have something for you."

"You have? Where? When?"

He told him.

"Come alone."

"Of course."

The connection was cut.

In a vehicle down on Rue Caulaincourt, someone removed headphones, thought for a moment and then spoke into a radio. Instructions received, the car started up and pulled away.

‡

60. Flic et...

The Arc de Triomphe is a curious, almost unfriendly, place at night. Tourists are not allowed up to the top of the Arc come dusk (on the assumption that they would not be able to see anything anyway once the powerful floodlights were turned onto the monolith), but the island in the middle of the Etoile, the Place Charles de Gaulle, still attracts people in the darkness to admire Chalgrin's illuminated masterpiece and the tomb of the unknown soldier underneath.

Having left a note for Claude to say he was going out, Richer took the metro, changing at Pigalle to Ligne 2 Diréction Porte Dauphin, and alighting at Charles de Gaulle Etoile. He crossed the island by the ornate subway, throwing a couple of francs to the busker in the tunnel (love was still such an easy game to play, yesterday).

There were upwards of fifty people on the island, walking round Napoleon's magnificent arch, mostly couples arm in arm, huddled against the fine drizzle that had taken a day to drift west from Luxembourg. As always, two uniformed *agents* patrolled the place, their sole duty on this shift.

Standing on the island of the Etoile, one experiences a strange auditory effect. Traffic moves in frantic disarray round the Place well into the night, yet from the island itself the traffic noises are muted, almost distant, not really there, as if the island at the top of the Champs Elysée is removed from reality.

The meet was a typical piece of Mesrine stage-management, reflected Richer. In the middle of Paris, right under the noses of two *flics* who patrolled with nothing to do except survey the passers-by, and at night when there were fewer people around and more chance of being noticed.

He looked around. So, this was where it would end, where his association with Mesrine would conclude. He couldn't say he was sorry. Like the old man of the sea, Mesrine had been on his back for a long time.

Richer turned up the collar of his raincoat as he walked round the Arc, passing a hopeful tourist trying to take pictures in the dark with his box camera, passing the young couple kissing, passing the more mature couple admiring Etex's reliefs of Peace and Resistance on the western side.

Richer stood in front of the tomb of the unknown soldier and lit a cigarette, cupping the flame of his lighter against the cool breeze. As he smoked he stared down the Champs Elysée, the red rain-washed rear lights of the vehicles descending on the right, the yellow beams of the headlights approaching on the left. Far down at the other end of the avenue were the diffused lights of the Place de La Concorde.

Come on, Jacques, come on. Hurry. Hand over the document and we need never meet again.

A gust of wind blew into his face, the weather turning worse by the minute.

He stood looking at the vehicles, even at this hour still streaming round the Place, but because of the peculiar numbing of the noise they seemed far away.

After a while one of the *agents* approached, rubber cape blowing in the increasing wind.

At the same time a car started to come round on the inside next to the island.

"Monsieur, you are waiting for someone, yes?" The agent asked it politely, respectfully, but with the smack of authority.

The car slowed down. Richer saw it over the *agent*'s shoulder.

Richer pulled out his identity card. The young *agent* frowned at it and then saluted casually. "*Excusez-moi, Monsieur l'Inspecteur.*" As he saluted he stepped in front of Richer and simultaneously his *kepi* flew off his head. He tried to grab it. "*Merde alors!*"

"Don't worry!" A few quick strides and Richer had the rolling hat in his hands. As he turned back he noticed the vehicle speeding away into the traffic heading south on the Champs.

"Bloody wind," he commented to the young *agent*. "Here - " He went to hand over the *kepi* and then stopped, puzzled. His finger on the inside of the hat was not where it should be. He looked down. His finger was poking through a hole in the back of the hat. There was a similar one in the front.

A bullet had passed clean through the *kepi*.

Christ, Christ, Christ, *Christ*. It was not possible. The car. The bullet was meant for *him*. If the *agent* had not got in the way and spoilt the aim. But why? Who would want to kill him?

The gun had probably been silenced, but it would not have been heard anyway due to that strange effect of the island. The *agent* had not noticed anything untoward, merely thanking his superior for retrieving his *kepi* and hurriedly placing it back on his head. He would notice it later, of course, and the roof would fall in, but he would not remember the Chief Inspector's name or what he looked like, and he might not even link the two things together.

Richer rushed along the subway. He did not notice the busker rising and he cannoned right into him, knocking his collecting cap from his hands, coins scattering noisily.

"*Pardon - "* Richer stared at the busker's face.

The busker smiled. He reached into an inside pocket.

Instantly Richer slammed him against the wall, pinning his hand in his coat. "No," Richer whispered urgently. "Not here. It's blown. Some other way, Jacques." Aloud he shouted, "Get out of the fucking way!" and hurried on.

He took the outside escalator of the Champs Elysée entrance to the metro.

Leaping over the waist-high ticket barrier, he headed for Ligne 2 Diréction Nation. From near the ticket booth, somebody watched him.

The smell of the metro system rose to meet Richer as he jogged nimbly down the escalator. A few people waited on the opposite platform, none taking more than a natural casual interest in him. Behind him, a *clochard* was stretched out on a bench, snoring noisily.

For something to do, he put two francs into a confectionery machine and pulled the first drawer to hand. A packet of scented *cachoux* was delivered. He put them into his pocket.

There came the high-pitched whine of an approaching train. *Bon.*

The train came from the right, on the opposite platform.

Merde.

Illuminated faces looked out of the carriage windows. In the yellow first class compartment he could see a busking puppeteer.

Almost at once the sudden cool draught preceded his own train, thundering in from the left. His carriage was half empty, but he stood by the doors, scrutinising the handful of others who entered: a pair of lovers, a youth, an old veteran, a dubious-looking eastern European from over Belleville.

After changing at Pigalle, he eventually arrived at Lamarck-Caulaincourt. There was no lift waiting at platform level so he ran up the stairs, the run reducing to a breathless trot after five flights.

He emerged into the now heavy rain, feet splashing up the steep stone steps from the station into Rue Caulaincourt. He turned immediately left past the Hotel Roma. The street was deserted save for a cruising cab which accelerated once it saw he had no interest.

Bearing right past the shuttered Co-Op, he entered Rue Lamarck and began the ascent up the *butte de Montmartre.*

‡

61. Flics

Claude was in, feet up, watching some foreign American film on the television. The smell of smoke and fried food enveloped Richer as he entered.

Claude looked around. "Bloody hell, you look a state. Blowing up out there?"

"And then some." Richer pulled off the raincoat. His pants were wet from the knees down, clinging.

"Chicken and chips in the oven," Claude swilled from a can. "And a few beers in the *frigo*. You look as if you could do with them."

"I'll make it a cognac first." Richer slid out of his shoes and went over to the cabinet. "Want one?"

"Sure, why not? Successful meet?" It was half-asked, Claude more interested in the goings-on on the television.

"Meet?"

"You said in your note."

"*Ah oui*. Like shit. Bastard snout didn't turn up."

"Huh! Thought it was a strange time of day."

"You been in long?"

"An hour. Must have just missed you on your way out."

Richer stood Claude's cognac on the arm of his chair and went into the kitchen. Chivas looked up from a bowlfull of food, mewed and carried on eating. Richer's food smelt good as he pulled it out of the oven with the aid of a glove. "Why were you late?" he called. "Something new on?"

"Eh?"

"Something new on?"

"Had to see the British Ambassador. Informally. Could only fit me in this evening, while he was dressing for some bloody ball or something. Been receiving less than kind letters from some farming co-operative up north, about our turkeys. And my car broke down earlier so I had to use the metro. I'm getting like you."

"Cars are no good in Paris for our work, I've told you." Richer knocked back his cognac and put the glass in the sink. He transferred his food to a plate and went back into the *salle*. "Any calls while I was out?"

"Mm?" Two men were shooting at each other on the television.

"Any calls while I was out?"

"No. Expecting any?"

"No, no. Just wondered." He forked a piece of chicken into his mouth. It was hot.

He went back to the kitchen for a beer and stopped in the doorway, staring at the cat still eating his food. He looked down at his own food. He looked back at Claude Gerard. He frowned.

The cat's bowl was full. Why would Claude, who had really taken to the animal, settle down for an hour before feeding him?

He touched the oven. It was luke warm, as if it had only just been turned on. Yet his food was hot, as if it had just been bought.

"Paul," called Claude, eyes fixed on the television. "What's the English for arsehole?"

Richer turned in the doorway. *"Trou du cul."* His eyes were burning into the back of Gerard's head. *"Trou du cul."*

‡

62. L'exécution

Jeudi 25 Octobre

At 23:00 that night, Veronique Lensens and her fiancé Michel pulled into the driveway of the Lensens' home near Fontainbleau. Because of the wind and the rain, Michel drove as close to the front door as he could so that Veronique could be in the house in two quick steps.

They had already had sex that evening, so they just kissed goodbye and Veronique nipped smartly out of the car, waving as she closed the front door behind her.

Michel reversed the car then drove off back down the driveway. It was as he was pulling out onto the road that he looked in his rear view mirror. He slammed on the brakes.

Veronique was running back down the driveway waving frantically. Had she left something in the car?

She was running strangely, as if she had one shoe off and one on. She would catch her death in that flimsy dress in the rain, silly girl. What had she left behind? He looked on the floor of the car and on the back seat but could see nothing.

Only when he wound down the window did he hear her mad, hysterical screaming.

‡

63. Flics

Vendredi 26 Octobre

The story caught the late editions of that morning's papers.

MESRINE'S REVENGE

Chief Prosecutor and wife die in hail of bullets

"We have been asked to assist in the hunt for Mesrine."

Commissaire Fleury-Goujon threw down the paper and watched the faces of the men seated in front of him. Claude Gerard's showed surprise. Paul Richer's was blank.

"*We* have?" asked Gerard.

"Giscard is positively doing his pieces after the Lensens murder. He has repeated that it is Minister Bonet or Mesrine – and it's no idle threat. One of them will have to go. Rumour has it that he just favours Mesrine. But only just. Paris is being saturated. Every known associate of Mesrine is now being watched and tailed twenty-four hours a day. Every known haunt is staked out. His family can't have a crap without somebody counting the number of turds. Bouvier has taken overall control, as you know. He says he is getting close, that it is only a matter of time."

"If Bouvier thinks that's all there is to catching Mesrine, then he's an optimist," said Richer lowly. "Mesrine's made mistakes recently. But he is a professional. While the entire force is watching his family and friends, he could be up to all manner of things free of police interference. Remember, he is always one thought ahead of his pursuers. He will not let himself be caught. But then the combined mights of the BRB, BRI and OCRB are not out to *catch* him, are they?"

The Commissaire did not respond to the question. "Our involvement is to warn all embassies and other foreign interests. Security is to be trebled. If, for any reason, Mesrine or anyone who looks like him or anyone who even looks suspicious sets foot in any area under BCP control we are to be informed immediately. For example, he might go to a South American embassy for a visa. Naturally he is not to be detained by them but if they can delay him until Bouvier gets there, all the better. But *no* chances are to be taken. The man is a killer, remember that."

"They should have shot him when they had him in La Santé," said Gerard. "Liaising with every one of our clients is going to take time."

"Which we don't have. Phone them all. Speak to your usual contacts. *Allez, messieurs.*"

When they were at the door, the Commissaire called Richer back. "Paul, one more thing if you please."

"See you back there," Richer said to Gerard, who nodded and walked quickly away.

Richer closed the door and came back in. He said, "It wasn't Mesrine."

The head of the OAS raised an eyebrow. "You don't think so? He always swore revenge on the man who put him away for twenty years."

"I know it wasn't him. Mesrine was with me last night."

"Ah. I see. So you have the document?"

"No. We were interrupted. And I know who by."

"Who?" asked the Colonel.

"The same people who murdered Lensens. The people who do not want the secret to come out. The people who, it seems, want to get the document and silence anyone who has read it."

"Or who knows the secret."

"Yes."

"Which means we are in danger."

"*I* am. You should be safe. No one knows you know."

"How did the British find out? Or need I ask?"

"Most organisations have a mole," said Richer. "We have a rat in ours."

"What are you going to do? I can have him moved."

"No, it's too late for that."

"More drastic action?"

"That shit is not worth it. The damage has been done now. The savages from the northern island are on the warpath. No, let me play this my way. Mesrine has the document. We are only one step away from having it in our hands. And when we do, *mon Colonel*, the British won't dare come anywhere near us."

Back in the office, Gerard was tucking-in to a mid morning *pain au chocolat*. A greasy bag containing its brother sat on Richer's desk.

"*Merci.*" Richer nodded at the bag as he came back in.

"What did Fleury want you to stay on for?" A piece of *pain* fell off the end of Gerard's snack straight into his ashtray.

"Just one of my cases. The Irish in Vincennes."

"The one Bauer's been handling?" Gerard picked up the fallen morsel, blew on it and popped it into his mouth.

"Have you seen the report? He's done a good job."

"That's because he's got two good superiors to teach him."

"Right."

"Do we really have to phone *all* our contacts?"

"That's what the chief say. Better. Sod's law says the one place you don't phone is the place he'll turn up."

"Bloody Mesrine. There must be a quicker way to catch him. Are there no grasses? Does nobody know nothing? Somebody somewhere must have contact with him."

Richer shrugged and tore open his bag. The phone rang.

"Coffee?" Gerard helped himself to one of Richer's Gitanes.

"Just had some."

Gerard went out, closing the door behind him.

Richer picked up the phone. "Richer." His voice echoed hollowly down the line.

"Bruno. *Printemps*. One-thirty. Walk about. I'll find you."

The phone buzzed and he was gone.

Richer was gone when Gerard returned with his coffee. Gerard sat down and unlocked his right hand desk drawer. Inside a red light flashed on top of a small tape recorder. He rewound the cassette and pressed *Play*.

He heard his own voice saying, "Coffee?"

The rest of the tape did not take one minute.

At the end he grinned, went over to Richer's desk and began to eat the abandoned *pain*.

Back at his own desk, he rewound the tape and once more listened.

He looked at his watch. It was midday. That gave him ninety minutes. Plenty of time.

He picked up the phone.

Fifteen minutes later, Gerard poked his head round the door of the Inspectors' office.

"Bauer, can I have a word?"

Out in the corridor, Gerard took the young inspector by the arm and asked, "How would you like to be the most famous *flic* in the whole of France?"

‡

64. Flics

Au Printemps is one of the three large department stores in Paris, at that time sharing the market with Galeries Lafayette and Samaritaine. It was the equivalent of Selfridge's in London, Macy's in New York and Penney's in LA.

At this time there were three Printemps in Paris. One was in Place d'Italie and another was at Nation. But whenever anyone simply referred to 'Printemps', it was the one in Boulevard Haussmann they meant.

Printemps, like the Galeries Lafayette (its immediate neighbour and rival on the boulevard), is a complex of more than one building, each with a varying number of floors stretching over a wide area. It was a ridiculous place for a meet. But, like the Arc de Triomphe, well in keeping with Mesrine's unpredictability and cunning.

A gusty breeze was blowing from the west as Richer crossed the road from the Opéra and walked up Haussmann. As always, the Boulevard was crowded. He passed the kerbside stalls, the suitcase men selling dolls that swam in a basin of water and those damn mechanical birds that you wound up and threw and which were supposed to fly but never did when you got them home. Past a morose-looking donkey holding two panniers of lavender across its back, past the pathetic sight of an Algerian mother sitting on the ground with a sleeping child in her arms (mouth open, teeth rotted to stumps) and a begging message written on the paving in front of her. Past the *bona fide* sellers of curtaining or food or the latest product from *Ronco* you could not possibly do without, in front of the shop's windows.

It was as Richer passed the woman selling hot, gooey *crêpes* that he became aware of the commotion outside Au Printemps. Almost at the same time, he heard the sirens as the black police vehicles appeared from everywhere. Whistles blew. People either fled in panic or stayed to gawp.

He ran, pushing his way through the milling crowd, shoving aside fur-clad madames with their green and white Printemps carriers. *"Pardon, pardon, pardon,"* he mumbled. *"Police."*

He stumbled off the kerb opposite the side entrance to the store in Rue Caumartin, and a uniformed *agent* shouted "Hey, get back! You!"

He thrust his ID in the air as the *agent* came towards him.

"Oh, pardon monsieur!"

Keeping the identification held high, Richer passed the two men now guarding the entrance and went through the double doorway into the store.

There was not much pandemonium, simply sheer confusion. People tried to leave but were restrained, in some cases forcibly, by the officers on the inside of the doors. By the souvenir counter on the left, a woman had fainted and was being tended to by a member of the staff.

"What's up?" Richer held his card in front of the nose of a young officer. "I was just passing."

"Mesrine. Tip-off - *Non, non, monsieur,* you must wait - " He blocked the exit of a grumbling customer. "Upstairs on the second floor, record department."

Richer ran up the escalators. There were fewer people on the *premier étage*, mostly queuing to give details to notebook-loaded *agents*.

Up another flight. A burly plainclothes officer guarded the top of the escalator on the second floor. He nodded at Richer's card.

"*Où?*"

"*Là-bas.*"

He dashed down to the other end of the floor, through the book department and into the record section. A rack of budget-label discs was lying sideways on the floor and, just beyond, a pair of feet jutted out from behind the counter. By the way nobody was taking any notice of the prostrate figure, its condition was obvious.

Richer rounded the edge of the counter. It was not a pretty sight. The chest had been blown away to leave a bloody red puddle, and there was something maroon caked onto the carpeted floor. He looked at the staring face. It took a few moments to register.

It was Inspector Bauer.

Back on the *rez de chausée*, Richer moved through the throng of people, past the perfumiers' islets. At the door at the far end where he had come in, he asked the *agent* "What happened to the woman who fainted?"

"Ambulance."

"And the salesman who was treating her?"

"Went with her."

"*D'accord.*"

‡

65. Voleur

The ambulance pulled into the square in front of the Hôpital Saint Lazare and stopped in front of the entrance. The driver alighted, curious as to why Eric, his colleague inside, did not open the rear doors. Lazy shitehawk.

The driver did it himself. He supposed *he'd* have to carry the patient in as well -

But the patient was not there. Neither was the man from Printemps who had insisted on accompanying her ("The good name of the store, sir."). But Eric was. Laid out. Fast asleep. Peaceful as a lamb...

‡

66. Flics

Richer hurried up Rue Lamarck.

Nodding at the *concièrge,* he took the steps two at a time, knowing that the twelve flights up to his apartment could be walked in quicker time than the old lift would take.

He stopped at the top floor, fighting to control his breath. God, he was getting old. Still, if this went wrong now, age was the last thing he had to worry about.

He listened at his own front door. There was no sound from inside.

Gun in his right hand, he turned the key with his left.

He crashed in, gun in the firing position. In a rush, he kicked open the doors to each room, making a hell of a racket. There was a screech as Chivas fled behind the washing machine.

No one was there.

He relaxed. He went to pick up the telephone, then thought better of it. He'd been caught like that just a couple of hours ago.

The bar by the Lamarck-Caulaincourt metro station had a few clients at the *zinc* and three sitting down. Richer ordered a *café cognac* and some *jetons* for the telephone, and took his drink with him over to the instrument.

The first call was Claude Gerard's last chance. Richer was giving fate a final opportunity to prove he was wrong

A meek, mild sounding woman answered the Levallois number. She was surprised at Richer's guarded enquiry as to the whereabouts of her husband. But surely he was on detached duty in Lyons for two or three months? Richer cluck-clucked, what a fool he was, hadn't been thinking, and terminated the call.

So Gerard had lied about everything. Madame Mathilde Gerard had just confirmed it. There was no family split. Gerard had moved in to keep a closer eye on him.

The second call was to Saussaies. "Chief Inspector Richer direct for Commissaire Fleury-Goujon."

It took a few moments then the Commissaire's voice said, "Hello?"

"Is someone there, sir?"

"Yes. A few."

"Tonight. The butcher's."

"Thank you."

The head of the OAS was on his own in the room above the butcher's shop in Belleville.

"Gerard came clean," he said as soon as Richer entered. "Admitted tapping your phone, admitted sending Bauer to intercept you and Mesrine. Implicated you to the hilt. Said you were a crook, an accomplice, Mesrine's mole. It is because of you that Mesrine is always able to be one step ahead of the police."

"The man is a *con*. He's dead meat."

"Oh, most certainly," agreed the Colonel. "But not yet he isn't. When you rang I had Bouvier, Devos and Broussard in the room with me and Gerard. Gerard had carefully planned it with witnesses. He's basking in the glory."

"Even though one of his inspectors was killed?"

"Honourably. In the line of duty."

Richer's nostrils flared and he punched his right fist into his left palm as he walked slowly across the room.

"So where does that leave me?"

The Colonel shivered. It was colder inside this room than outside. "You can come in and clear yourself."

"Or I can finish this assignment."

The Colonel paused, turning up his collar. "And how will you do that?"

Richer stopped pacing up and down and turned. "Mesrine is the most wanted man in Europe. The British are on the rampage and they don't care who they kill. Anyone who even comes near the document - and that means near Mesrine - is marked."

"Yes?"

"I am going to find Mesrine before either the police or the British do."

‡

67. Voleur

Jacques Mesrine gave Sylvie a final kiss, slipped out of her saturated sex, and rolled off of her. He lay back, a thin film of sweat on his brow. Sylvie snuggled up under his arm, one breast resting softly on the edge of his stomach, the nipple still hard.

Mesrine was not so much puzzled as resigned. Resigned to the fact that he had been right all along. The Captain's phones were monitored. Either that or the Captain had betrayed him, and that was an idea that was simply unentertainable.

He had the document. He had read it a hundred times. The secret it contained was explosive. Too explosive, perhaps, even for the OAS. In his opinion it should be left undisturbed and the document itself should be destroyed. But that was not his to decide, the Captain knew what he was doing.

But how to get the document to him? This had been the potential thorn all along. But now, with any arranged meet the subject of a barnstorming by Bouvier and his crew, it was going to be an impossibility.

Telephones were out. He would have to find some other way of contacting the Captain.

‡

68. Flic

"You have no knowledge of Mesrine's whereabouts? Or is it just that you don't want to tell the BCP?"

"Inspector Gerard, if we knew we would tell our fellow enforcement officers, common cause and all that." The voice on the other end of the telephone belonged to Sergeant Maurice Goise of the BRB.

"Of course you would. What is your last trace?"

"Printemps today. We *think* he is holed up somewhere in the eighteenth. But we can't be sure. We have checked everywhere. He must live in the sewers."

"Or right under your noses."

"*Monsieur l'Inspecteur!* It is nearly midnight. Why don't you phone back in the morning and speak to my Inspector? You never know, we might have something by then."

"You know something Sergeant?"

"*Monsieur?*"

"You lot are about as useful as a cunt to a eunuch." Richer slammed down the phone and left the booth.

‡

69. Le motard

Samedi 27 Octobre

Gilbert Pascal had been a government outdoor messenger, a *motard*, on the d'Orsay-Elysée-Saussaies route for a number of years. As with all government jobs it was not well-paid, but he enjoyed it; it was a responsible position to have to carry important documents between the three most powerful buildings in France. And besides, since his retirement from the police, it was either that or the dole queue.

That day, as every day except Sunday, he set out from the Quai d'Orsay on the first of his two morning runs. Turning his motorbike right onto the Pont d'Alexandre III, he crossed the Seine, sparkling in the autumn sun, and drove into the Avenue Winston Churchill.

The first thing he noticed was the girl's panties.

She was bent over the engine in the rear of her Volkswagen, orange mini-dress risen high to reveal her white panties pressed tightly into her crack. His immediate thought was that she must be a very, very cold young lady; the waist-length, armless white fur jacket she was wearing would not even keep her titties warm. Even he felt a chill and he was dressed in his usual black leather outfit.

She turned at that moment, seemed to pick him at random, and waved at him to stop.

It was against regulations, of course. It was written down that he was to stop for nothing but normal traffic signals. But she looked hopelessly at him like a lost kitten and it was obvious she needed help. And she did have lovely thighs.

Pascal pulled up behind her. *"Bonjour mam'selle.* You are in need of assistance?" He parked the bike and climbed off, adopting the firm, authoritative attitude of his police days.

She was wide-eyed and innocent with the prettiest of smiles. *"Oh monsieur, s'il vous plait,* it just stopped! I do not know what is wrong. I do not understand these things."

"It might be your big end," said Gilbert Pascal with a leer. "May I look at it for you?"

He did not notice that further up the road, from the Avenue Charles-

Girault by the side of the Petit Palais, a motorbike identical to his own, with an identically leather-clad rider, pulled out into the Place Clemenceau and manoeuvred through the traffic into the Avenue de Marigny at exactly the same moment that he should have done…

The substitute rider passed beneath the golden trees by the side of the Palais d'Elysée and moved quickly across the small Place Beauvau and through the ornate gates of the Ministère de l'Interieur. The guard on the gate let him through without so much as a nod. He was right on time.

The rider parked in front of the entrance and skipped lightly up the steps. He did not remove his helmet, but he did raise the visor to reveal the dark, deep-set eyes. In his hand he held an envelope and a bulky package.

"*Bonjour,*" said the clerk on duty without actually looking up from the paperback hidden under the desk.

"*'Jour,*" said the rider. "Can't leave it. Special Personal for Chief Inspector Richer."

The clerk looked up, bored, irritated at being disturbed. "Who?"

"Richer. Chief Inspector."

With a sigh, the clerk pulled over a large black book and began to thumb through the pages. "He's in Saussaies. Room four hundred and forty-two. Know the way?"

"Sure. Thanks."

He did not know the way, never having been in the complex before in his life, but it was common sense to presume that if one kept turning right one would come out at Saussaies eventually. The first priority was to get away from the duty clerk. The next was to get to the fourth floor where Room 442 would be located.

Out on the Avenue Winston Churchill, the hapless young lady moved closer to Gilbert Pascal until her body was actually touching his.

"You can see what it is?"

Pascal sniffed, casting a sideways glance at the huge breasts which were within stroking distance of his right hand. "I'm not used to these foreign cars. Nevertheless, I think I might be able to help you."

She sneaked a look at her watch. Five minutes. She had been told to give it fifteen.

Bending with him into the engine, she manoeuvred her face close to his, knowing he would get the full blast of her *Rive Gauche* perfume and *cachou*-scented breath.

"Is there anything you can do for me?" she asked innocently. "What's this hole for? It's all wet…"

‡

The substitute Pascal could not hurry overtly. But years of practice in deception and disguise had given him the ability to walk at speed while giving the appearance of partaking in a leisurely stroll.

He went wrong twice but eventually made his way through the maze of interconnecting corridors to the Saussaies building. He now carried his helmet in his hand. He would be conspicuous with it on, and nobody would recognise him, this being the last place anyone would expect to see him.

Several people passed him by, no one taking even minor interest in him.

He found Room 442, knocked and entered.

Jacques Mesrine came face to face with Claude Gerard.

"It is the petrol," concluded Pascal. "After all that, you are out of petrol!" He scowled but then softened as Sylvie pouted in regret, a schoolgirl awaiting her spanking.

"Petrol? But I never thought! So I just need a little something put in?"

"You could say that." Pascal could not keep his eyes from the mammoth bust straining against the confines of the dress. Her bare arms were goose-pimpled.

"Look," he said. "I've got to go, I'm on business. But wait here and I'll bring a couple of litres with me on my way back. That should see you okay. I'll be about half an hour."

"And you will put it in for me?"

"You bet."

"Monsieur, you are too kind..."

"Chief Inspector Richer?" asked Mesrine, emphasising his nervousness, a humble messenger where he had never been before.

"Gerard." He remained seated, hardly giving the messenger a second look. "Richer is on sick leave. You can leave it with me."

"Yes, sir." He handed over the bulky package, keeping the envelope. "I hope it is nothing serious, sir. The Chief Inspector, I mean."

"Why?" Gerard put the package down on his desk.

"Oh, nothing sir, nothing. *Merci monsieur, au revoir.*"

As he turned to the door, Gerard's voice said "Hey!"

Mesrine turned slowly.

"Haven't I seen you before?"

"Probably sir, I deliver every day."

"Ah." Gerard nodded then ignored him.

Mesrine headed for the nearest exit, being careful not to rush. He was pleased. Not only had he found out that Richer was not around, but his incursion into the very heart of the Interior Ministry and the *Sûrêté* would go down in the annals, a further addition to his remarkable legend.

The bike, which he had stolen earlier that morning, could be left in the yard. It would not start attracting attention for at least half an hour.

Helmet on, he nodded at the *agent* on duty at the Cambacérès exit and strolled out into the crisp October sunshine. He removed the helmet as he doublebacked down Rue Penthièvre. Turning right into Avenue Delcasse, he descended into the Miromesnil metro station.

Pascal arrived in the courtyard of the Interior Ministry just as Mesrine left via the Cambacérès exit. He frowned at the bike parked in his usual spot, and went inside.

Gerard had a telephone call, so he did not get round to considering Richer's package until the messenger had been gone ten minutes.

After terminating the call, Gerard picked up the package and felt it. Then without hesitation he ripped it open.

It was a book.

It was *Instinct de Mort* by Jacques Mesrine.

Gerard stared at the picture of the author on the cover. It took five seconds for him to realise he was looking at the face of the messenger who had delivered it.

Then all hell broke loose.

‡

70. Flic

Richer crushed out his twentieth cigarette of the day and immediately lit another. Room 55 of the Hotel Roma stank like a crematorium on overdrive.

He had checked into the hotel on Rue Caulaincourt, just five minutes from his apartment, late yesterday evening. Provisionally booked in for three nights, he had the option of a longer period if required.

Unaware of the adventure happening at Saussaies, he had spent the best part of Saturday getting nowhere with his telephonic enquiries of various police sources as to the whereabouts of Mesrine. As he was a marked man and could not reveal his true identity, he had continued to take a leaf out of the Duchess of Windsor's book and refer to himself as Gerard.

There was a lot of hot air, but he had come to the certain conclusion that the police - even under Bouvier - were running round in circles and barking up their own *trou du cul*.

He was booked into the hotel under the name of Gerard also. He could not risk being identified now and hauled in - however innocent (or not) he may be. His ID and anything identifying him as Paul Richer had been left in the apartment. All he had were the clothes he stood up in and his gun.

From late afternoon he had been closeted in the room, thinking of the past. Remembering back fifteen years to the old days, recalled with fondness if not affection. Occasionally he interrupted his musing to write a name on a piece of paper. In the end he had four of them.

Four names that might be able to help him achieve what the entire combined might of the French police forces had failed to do.

Four names to help him find Jacques Mesrine.

‡

71. Flics

Dimanche 28 Octobre

"And Bouvier has given me full authority to pursue this angle," concluded Inspector Cordelier of the BRB. "Officially we do not see anything coming of it. Unofficially we hope to God it works. Mesrine *must* be found this time. No near-misses, no might-have-beens, no cock-ups. Or *all* heads will be on the block, even at our level."

The men he was addressing murmured un-nice words.

"So, if there are no questions?" Cordelier waited all of three seconds. "We'll get on with the job. Here is a picture, although I'm sure you don't really need one." He handed four copies to the nearest man of the quartet, who took one and passed them on. "Have them copied to all of your men."

There was a general nodding of heads.

"He must be located. But it must be stressed that under no circumstances is he to be intercepted. Report back. Don't try to be brave, don't do anything stupid. And above all *don't* lose him. Any questions?" Four seconds this time. "Then find him."

With a clatter of chairs, three of the group rose and left the office. The fourth man remained seated.

"Think it'll work?" asked Cordelier when they were alone.

The other man shrugged. "We've nothing to lose. If it doesn't work, it doesn't work. If it *does* work, we'll be heroes. We'll get Mesrine. Commissaire next stop."

"I hope you're right."

Claude Gerard smiled and looked at the picture that had been handed out.

It was a photograph of Paul Richer.

‡

72. Flic et belette

Mardi 30 Octobre

Richer played pinball in a bar in Rue Clichy, just ten metres to the south of Place Clichy, his third beer resting on the glass top of the machine. His face gave the impression of intense concentration on the game, but in fact he observed everybody who went in and out of the place. He was waiting for that one person he knew, hoped, *prayed*, would come in sooner or later.

He was desperate. The man he was waiting for was his last hope. Of the other men he had tried to trace yesterday, one was in jail, one was dead and the other was nowhere to be found. At least he knew that this time his man was alive.

He waited, playing the damn machine until he was sick of the infernal *ping-ping*ing. Three more beers and two crusty rolls were consumed, and the beer reappeared five times in the *cabinet*.

It was nearing 22:00 when he came in. Small and weaselly in a dapper fawn suit and undone sheepskin overcoat. On his right arm was a black girl, beads in her hair, dressed in a tight-fitting gold one-piece lurex suit, open to the waist. A *maquereau* with his lady come in for a drink before the night's work. They walked over to a table and sat down. Unasked, the barman began preparing two drinks.

Richer wasted no time, enough had flown past already. He came across smartly and sat down in front of them.

The weasel looked at him stonily. "This is a private table, friend," he hissed. "Piss off."

"Hello Lenny," said Richer.

The other man frowned. "Do I know you?"

Richer leant forward and said lowly, "You bet your sweet arse you do, Corporal."

"Eh?"

"The Army. Algeria. Constantine 58."

The weasel stared long and hard.

"The Army...?" Slowly, uncertainly, realisation, disbelief then acceptance crept across his face.

"C'mon Lenny, you know me."

"I *don't* believe it. Captain, wasn't it? Captain...?"

"Richer."

"Captain Richer. My godfathers! Yeh, I remember you. God almighty, rumour had it you were shot down an alley one dark night - "

"You know rumours, Lenny."

"Jesus! It's been twenty years!"

"And you're still as beautiful as ever."

"What you been doing with yourself?"

"Oh, this and that... business, you know how it is."

The barman delivered the drinks for Lenny and his girl, looked at Richer's half-full glass and slouched away.

"Oh, I haven't introduced you," Lenny smiled, showing a set of perfectly, and expensively, capped teeth. "This is my old Captain from the army. Captain, this is Lettice, my number one lady."

"Hello." Her voice was deep and more than a little inviting.

"*Enchanté mademoiselle*," said Richer.

"Very nice girl," Lenny tapped her knee as her thick red lips fellated the straw in her Campari and orange. "You, er, interested?" He indicated the girl.

"I'd like to Lenny, but I need to talk to you. On business."

"Of course, Captain, of course. Lettice go and powder your bum, love."

"What?"

"Vamoose, make yourself scarce. But wait for me. It's not opening time yet. Go on, be a good girl." He handed over a handful of coins. "Go and put some music on, then play with the balls on the machine. Metal ones will make a change for you."

She pouted but obeyed.

"Now, Captain," Lenny leant forward, all unctuous ears. "Business?"

"Extremely important and extremely urgent business. For the army."

"The army?"

"The Organisation."

"Ah!" Lenny nodded conspiratorially as Lettice's first choice, Bob Marley, reggaed from the juke box.

"Now, I trust you Lenny. The Organisation has been following your career closely."

"It has?"

"Believe it. Lenny Le Coq, one of - no, *the* - top pimp in Paris, receiver of stolen goods, angel in many a job, owner of a string of sex shops, producer of the filthiest porno movies on the market today - and many other talents besides."

Lenny looked pleased with the list of his accomplishments.

"We need you, Lenny. We want you to do something for us right now. For old time's sake. And for fifty grand."

Lenny smiled and shook his head as he said, "Captain, Captain. One of my shops takes that in a day. I don't want money. If I can help the Organisation, it will be a pleasure. *Gratis.*"

"You're a brick Lenny, always have been. I'll give it to you straight. We need to contact Mesrine."

"Christ!" Richer was sprayed with *crème de menthe* as Le Coq began to choke. His subsequent swearing caused many a head to turn. His consequent murderous glare caused them to turn back again.

"I know, Lenny, I know," soothed Richer as he wiped his face. "But he's working for us and we need to contact him quickly. Our usual lines have failed."

"Can't be done," Le Coq's voice was raspy and two octaves higher. He coughed.

"We *must* contact him. We don't want any address. He can come to us. Me."

"But Captain," he looked about to check that all heads were turned away and said softly, *"Mesrine!"*

"You can do it, Lenny. We have faith in you. And Mesrine will thank you too. I told you, he's working for us."

Le Coq rubbed his hands over his face, ending with a slow downward drag on his cheeks. He said, "You ask a lot, Captain."

"We wouldn't ask just anybody, Lenny."

Le Coq pulled an outsize cigar from his pocket, ripped off the end, lit up and started coughing again. He put the thing down. "Look, if - and only 'if' mind - I could even remotely contact your man, I *couldn't* ask him to meet. Supposing something went wrong? Suppose the *flics* were there? He's a marked man. Too hot to handle. I couldn't take the responsibility."

"Just get a message to him, Lenny, that's all. Say Captain Richer is desperate. Ask him if *he* has a message for *me*. That's all."

Le Coq tried the cigar again, blew out a cloud of smoke and became mysterious behind it. "Can't promise, Captain, can't promise. But, for the sake of the Organisation, I'll try. It might take some time."

"That's the one thing we haven't got. Tomorrow at the latest. Now, preferably."

"Merde alors. Look, I'll see."

"Thanks Lenny. The Organisation will be grateful. Meantime," Richer sat back, "the least I can do is buy you a drink."

Le Coq laughed. "Captain, that's the one thing you can't do. I *own* this place."

"This bar is yours?"

"This block is mine."

"Ah."

Le Coq swilled back the remainder of the *crème de menthe*. "I've got some calls to make. No point you hanging around, I might not have any news for you tonight. But in case I have... why don't you entertain Lettice for a few hours?"

Richer looked over at the tightly-clad golden rump, lightly trembling as she played the machine.

"For old time's sake," explained the pimp. "On the house. She'll know where to go. And what to do." He stood up and sauntered over, slapping the inviting bottom.

Richer could not hear above the din, but Le Coq appeared to be giving the black girl her instructions.

She turned to Richer and gave a bright, toothy smile.

Le Coq waved and went out.

Lettice came across. "Hello again." Her accent was thick West Indian. "My man tells me you and he go back long way." She ran a soft finger across Richer's lips. "He say you old frens. Any fren of my man is a fren of mine." She pulled the chair over and sat close to him. He had an uninhibited view of her dark cleavage. "What would you like to do?"

As Lettice stroked the back of his hand, Richer said "Know how to find a fox?"

She raised an eyebrow. "Foxes are hard to find. How about a pussy?"

‡

73. Flics

Inspector Cordelier of the BRB drove as slowly as he could in the maelstrom of traffic that occupies the Champs Elysée at night.

"Not a trace," he was saying. "Not a trace. Not only has Mesrine gone missing, he's taken Richer with him. Where *is* the bugger?"

Next to him, Claude Gerard wound down the window and deliberately chucked his cigarette-end at a passing motorcyclist.

"He'll turn up." He spoke with a confidence he did not feel. "Just a matter of time."

"Which we do not have."

"Hmm." Gerard wound the window back up. "That's the whole problem with you lot. No patience. If you're patient and don't rush into things, things have a strange habit of falling into place." He unwrapped a chocolate bar and began to munch.

Cordelier cast him a sideways glance. "You never have told me exactly what Richer's interest in Mesrine is. Only 'unfinished business' you said."

"Right." A brown drool rolled down Gerard's chin and was smeared against his collar as he turned his head, grinning.

Cordelier negotiated the intersection of Avenue George V. "Going to tell me?"

"Best that I don't, state security and all that. You just find Mesrine, don't worry about our side."

"What's going to happen to Richer?"

"Depends. There's others involved. He might go down for a few years, or he might be quietly retired. You concerned?"

"No, just that he's a cop."

"Don't start giving me any of that comrades-in-arms crap. That's how this whole thing got started."

Cordelier blew his horn at the same motorcyclist who had received Gerard's unsolicited gift. Gerard said, "Fancy a drink? Before you go home?"

"Best make it a quick one."

"There's a bar I know in Châtelet. I have something on the owner. We won't have to pay."

"Suits me. It was on you, anyway."

"And he's got this lovely young daughter. Only fifteen but she's got tits like pumpkins."

"Sweet fifteen and never been kissed?"

"Hardly. But not by me. Jail bait. Although sometimes when I look at her arse..."

"Makes you sorry you're a *flic*?"

"Makes me sorry I'm fifty years old."

They moved into the Place de la Concorde.

‡

74. Flic et poule

Mercredi 31 Octobre

His first thought when he awoke was that he must get up to get Claude's breakfast. His second was that he didn't have to, Claude didn't live there anymore. His third thought was that neither did he.

He opened his eyes to see the black girl standing in front of him, beaded hair falling over her shoulders. She wore nothing but a wicked smile.

As he stared at the hairless black body, he tried to remember everything that had happened, everything they had done together during the night. He couldn't. Only the highlights remained in his memory, and even of those there were too many for permanent retention. He still had her taste in his mouth.

"Good mornin'." She knelt beside him on the floor-level bed.

"Good... morning?" He raised his left wrist. It was bare.

She held his *Seiko* in the air. "Here, you left it on the edge of the bath. Remember? You didn't wan' to get water in it."

"*Ah, oui.*" He did not remember. It must have been those cigarettes.

"You didn't worry bout gettin' water in other things tho," she grinned.

As he put the watch on he looked at the face, then looked again. "*Midi moins quinze?*"

"Sho' is. What's wrong with that? You didn't get to sleep till gone five."

"Where's Lenny?" He made to get up but she pushed him back down and kissed his forehead.

"Said he would take a while, didn't he? He'll come when he's ready... He always does." She threw her legs across his arms and sat down on his chest. His view of her full brown-pink lips was uninterrupted. "Brudder, when Lenny tells Lettice to look after a fren till he comes back, Lettice does jus' that. *R*elax, baby."

She laughed as she moved herself down his body until she was atop his stomach. She bent forward. "So, how about breakfast?" The pearl white teeth flashed. "I feel hungry."

She bit into his neck as her other end opened and swallowed him whole.

‡

75. Flic et belette

They were both washed, dressed and drinking coffee when Le Coq hurried in. He was pale, harassed, sweating and he had obviously not slept all night. His tie was askew and his fawn suit would need to visit the dry cleaners *vitement*.

He stared at Richer from the doorway, just a suggestion of fear in his eyes. "You didn't tell me, did you Captain?"

Richer looked over. "Tell you what, Lenny?"

"You're a *flic*."

"What?" Lettice gasped, nearly dropping her cup.

"Lenny, you didn't ask. And you didn't need to know. Remember the army days? 'Need to know' is everything. It was irrelevant. I am working for the Organisation, like I said."

"It might be b - bloody irrevalent to you, but *Christ*! If it ever got out - "

"A *flic*?" mumbled Lettice.

" - that I had let my best lady entertain a *flic* for the night *and* in my own pad... my God, I'd never live it down."

"I fucked a *flic*?" Lettice seemed on the verge of collapsing.

"You entertained a Captain of your regiment, Corporal Le Coq. You got a message for me?"

Le Coq still stood with his back pressed against the door, as if Richer was some evil spirit to be kept at arms length. "Have I! It took a lot of meetings, a lot of calls... a lot of money - "

"My original offer stands."

"Forget it. But I got a message. He seems to want you as badly as you want him."

"Where is he?"

"Nobody knows. At least, somebody must, but it's all done by contacts and dead points."

"What's the message then?"

"What the hell does Mesrine want with a *flic*? There's rumour you've turned - "

"Lenny!"

"Tomorrow. Flea market at Clignancourt. *Midi*."

‡

Richer returned to the Hotel Roma in Rue Cauliancourt. He resisted the urge to go back to his apartment. The bastard Gerard would be long gone, but someone might be watching. The murdering Brits perhaps? He hoped Chivas was looking after himself.

In his room on the fifth floor of the hotel, he spent the night. Not with an insatiable black *poule*, but with a bottle of *Napoléon* and fifty Gitanes.

At 01:30, the empty cognac bottle rolled across the floor and Richer began to snore heavily.

‡

76. Flic

Jeudi 1 Novembre

He awoke with the enforced subconscious delicacy and abbreviation of movement that afflicts most human beings who know they drank too much the night before. It was two minutes before he realised, much to his surprise, that he did not have a hangover. It was a further thirty minutes before the pressure on his bladder forced him out of the bed.

Claude Gerard stumbled into the bathroom, did what he had to do, and went into the kitchen without washing his hands. Chivas mewed and rubbed himself against the naked human legs.

Gerard opened a packet of something and emitted a volcanic fart as he bent to empty it into the cat's bowl. It was three minutes before Chivas re-emerged from behind the washing machine.

With two three-day-old croissants and a bowl of *Bonjour* instant coffee and chicory, Gerard shuffled into the *salle de jour* and sat by the window to eat, looking out onto a cloudy autumn day.

Richer had obviously not been located during the night, he mused, otherwise Cordelier would have called him. But it was only a matter of time. Richer certainly wouldn't be so stupid as to come back to his apartment.

Gerard left the apartment at 11:00 and, seeing as his car was still out of service, strolled at an easy pace towards the Lamarck-Caulaincourt metro station.

He popped into the small Co-Op in Rue Caulaincourt to pick up a boxed cake and a half-litre of red wine for his lunch, then continued on over the road and walked down the steps to the station by the side of the Hotel Roma.

He mumbled banal pleasantries as he bought *Le Matin* from the newspaper seller, then walked into the station, used the last of his *carnet* in the ticket gates, and waited for the lift. A couple of young female tourists, packs on their backs, travelled down with him, studiously avoiding his vacuous, lecherous grin.

As he left the lift and headed for the Diréction Mairie D'Issy platform, he started to read the front of *Le Matin*. Then he heard a train arriving, popped the paper under his arm and ran.

The train was at the platform and the tone signifying closure of the doors was blaring. Gerard wobbled frantically down the flight of stairs from the lift level, but was too late. The doors clicked closed in front of him as he arrived puffing. *Merde.* Sooner the garage fixed his bloody car, the better.

As the train pulled out, he glanced across at the other side then looked down at his paper. Then his head shot back up again and his bowels trembled violently.

Paul Richer was standing on the opposite platform.

Quickly, Gerard stepped back into the cover of the stairway. Richer had not seen him, he was certain.

There was a light breeze, then a low rumble. *There was a train coming on Richer's side.*

Gerard turned on his heels and ran back up the steps. There were only ten of them, but he was out of breath when he reached the top.

As fast as he could, he ran across the overhead corridor connecting the platforms. As he turned to take the stairs down, he collided with an old man and dropped his wine. It smashed and blood red liquid began to roll down the steps.

"*Monsieur!*" gasped the shaken pensioner. "Are you all right?"

"Fuck off!" he snapped courteously over his shoulder.

The doors-closing tone sounded as he reached the platform. He stopped and gave a quick glance to his right. Richer must have got on further down.

The doors came together.

With a movement born of desperation, Gerard wedged his cake between them. The box crushed and chocolate gateau oozed from it and fell like globs of vomit onto the platform. But it had its desired effect. The doors reopened and Gerard nipped on.

There was cake squashed on his shoes, wine splashed up the legs of his *pantalon* as if he was experiencing some perverse male menstruation, and he was bent double trying to regain his breath.

More than one person from the carriage got off at the next stop.

‡

77. Flic et Voleur

The Marché aux Puces is situated on the northern perimeter of Paris, near the Porte de Clignancourt. On Saturdays, Sundays and Mondays it is a hive of bustle and activity, more like an eastern bazaar than part of the most sophisticated city in the world. The legitimate merchants have single-level open-fronted shops or normal open-air stalls. The illegitimate merchants have little tables, or suitcases, or, in the case of the Africans selling their wares, rugs on the ground.

On a Friday there would be some activity in the market as the stallholders prepared for the weekend trade. On Thursday 1 November 1979 it was deserted.

On the metro Richer changed at Marcadet-Poissonniers for Ligne 4 and alighted two stops later at the terminus at the Porte de Clignancourt. He walked north from the station, past the Stade Bertrand Dauvin on the left and under the flyover. The vehicles on the Boulevard Périphérique thundered overhead.

He was unaware of the portly, dishevelled figure who followed him cautiously but with surprising expertise.

The mesh gates to the market were closed but not locked, and Richer slipped inside. He was fifteen minutes early.

He walked, the blank impersonal faces of the shops on either side, blinds down, each identical, anonymous. Many of the walkways led off at right angles from each other, each with the same rows of shuttered establishments. Just to his left, a group of empty stalls were cluttered together. It was like a ghost town.

There was a movement to his right and Richer stopped abruptly, hand going to his right pocket.

A cat shot out from between two shops and ran across his path.

A smile fluttered across his lips. The cat should have been black, like his Chivas. It would have been lucky. But it was ginger.

He was now well into the market, surrounded on all sides by the identical shops. The sound of the vehicles hummed from out on the Boulevard.

A piece of last week's *Ici Paris* blew across the ground and wrapped itself around his right calf. He was removing it when he heard the voice.

"Hi there, big boy."

He span round.

The girl was ten metres away, near an empty stall. Short blonde hair, generously proportioned body, old raincoat over thick woolly, denims and boots, bag over her shoulder.

Richer said, "Hello, Sylvie."

She was surprised.

"Sylvie Jacquot," continued Richer. "Known latest sidekick of the man himself. The Bonnie to his Clyde. Where is he?"

He was answered by the press of cold steel against the back of his neck. "Ah," he said.

"Good afternoon, Captain," said Mesrine's voice from behind. "You will forgive me please, but it has been a long time and some strange things have happened recently."

Sylvie came forward and ran her hands over his body. She had been taught well.

She held up his gun, then, at a nod from the man behind, stepped back five paces, holding the weapon raised but not aimed directly.

"Thank you," said Mesrine.

The steel disappeared from Richer's neck. He turned slowly.

It was not Mesrine.

At least, it did not look like him. The man holding the shotgun was of the same build as Jacques, but he was old, heavy-jowled, hair thin and iron grey; even the eyes contained the lacklustre unenthusiasm of the aged.

Richer frowned. "Jacques?"

The old man laughed and spoke again with Mesrine's voice.

"Yes, Captain. Just one of my little friends. I have to be careful, things are very hot at the moment."

"It's incredible."

"Thank you, it is meant to be. Now, sir. Eighteen months ago you asked me to retrieve something. In the light of recent events, I must ask you if your request is still valid."

"Oh yes," said Richer. "You have the document?"

"On me, no. But it has been obtained. It is safe."

"You have read it?"

"*Oui.*"

"Then you'll know its implications."

Mesrine nodded tightly. "It is dangerous, Captain. Dangerous. The repercussions could be unthinkable. *Alors...*" The heavy jowls wobbled. "What is its value to the Organisation?"

"Jacques! You of all people! It can be used for blackmail, *mon ami*. At the most basic level. The Windsors of England are, to say the least, very rich. On a more quixotic level, if the Organisation possessed that document it could be very influential in any future matters of government it decided to take an interest in. We could *be* the next government."

"I thought we already were."

"Openly I mean. People would do a lot to keep the document hidden. Certain favours could be bestowed..."

The jowls quivered in a smile. "I understand, Captain. And I do not think I want to know. Did the British kill Lensens?"

"Yes."

"Then they're after me."

"I would think so."

"It is nice to be popular."

"When I have the document our contract will be complete, the favour called in and paid. You must then concentrate on your safety and freedom. Where and when do I collect?"

"Tomorrow. Be at the Porte de Clignancourt station. Fifteen hundred. We will contact you."

"We?" Richer turned to look at the girl.

"Sylvie is my lady," explained Mesrine. "My only lady. You can be the first to know, Captain. We are to be married."

Richer's left eyebrow rose.

"Yes. I am forty-three soon. Finally it might be time to hang up the Smith and Wessons." He laughed. "Can you believe it? Jacques Mesrine is going to settle down! It is true! We have bought an apartment somewhere out of town. I shall perform one last job for my pension, give a final interview to *Paris Match* as a farewell to my public, then I shall be heard of no more. No one will ever find me."

Richer kept his thoughts to himself. He said, "You have it all worked out. Amazing."

"She," nodded Mesrine, "is the amazing one." He slid the shotgun under his old raincoat. His voice changed completely to suit his character. He was not impersonating an old man, he *was* one. "*Sylvie ma fille*, let us go. We have taken up too much of this gentleman's time." He held out his right arm. "Help me, my child."

As they passed, Mesrine's voice came back out of the mouth for an instant. "Tomorrow, Captain."

Sylvie gave Richer back his gun, then the couple walked slowly away.

Would they be walking to happiness? Could Mesrine really retire?

Richer actually found himself hoping "Yes" to both questions.

‡

78. Découverte

Gerard was lost.

Each alley, each passage he turned down looked the same. He had tried so many that he was now completely disorientated, not knowing whether he was facing north, south, east, west or any point in between.

He flicked a piece of hardened cake off his left shoe. He had been no more than a hundred metres - half a minute, time-wise - behind Richer, but he had not picked up his trail since entering the market. Richer was here somewhere to be sure. But where?

He walked on carefully. At one point he thought he heard the sound of muffled voices, but he could not be certain. The hum from the motorway distorted all but the most direct sound.

He stopped at the intersection of four identical alleys. Each was long and narrow and at the end led off at right angles into another alley.

Suddenly there was a high-pitched screech, a wail from hell itself. His heart leapt as a ginger ball with legs on ran out from beneath a stall and disappeared through a broken doorway.

He steadied himself against the whitewashed side of a shuttered shop, chest banging. Fucking cat. He tried to fumble for a cigarette, but his hands were shaking too much.

He stayed there for five minutes.

As he was about to move away, he heard voices again, distinct voices this time, no mistaking. He flattened himself against the wall as much as he could.

He waited.

The voices became louder, though still muffled.

At the far end of the alley, two people passed by, a young woman leading a doddering old veteran. Who the hell...? They did not look his way.

Who were they? Should he follow? Or should he concentrate on finding Richer? They were probably of no consequence, just stallholders having a midweek inspection.

Nevertheless, he would just check the couple out. If he did not move too far from the gates, he would pick Richer up again when he came out.

He crept on swift tiptoe to the end of the alley, peeked around the corner, saw that they were just turning right further on, and followed.

He tried to make it a professional tail, but all he succeeded in doing was to make himself look an idiot as he zigzagged clumsily from doorway to doorway. Had they turned around, they would have seen him.

The couple went out through the gate and turned right.

Still thirty metres behind, Gerard quickened his pace. He half ran, his fat gut bouncing with each pace. He charged through the gateway, turned right and cannoned into Jacques Mesrine.

Gerard only saw the old man, bending down to tie his shoe, at the last moment. He bounced sideways off the old man's rump. He did not actually fall to the ground, but his balance was lost and the impetus carried him onwards, his feet stomping flatly. He flew with unerring accuracy towards the young girl. His face landed with a soft *whump* in the exact centre of her breasts.

The girl called out.

So did the old man.

Gerard regained his balance and continued on quickly, calling over his shoulder *"Pardon!"* without showing his face. He went down the Avenue de la Porte de Clignancourt and out of sight.

"You are all right, my darling?" The old man took the girl's arm.

"I - I think so," she panted.

The old man looked back. "Where did he come from?"

"Je ne sais pas."

"Alors, he was probably just a stallholder having a midweek inspection." He turned, the suspicious frown lingering. "He has gone. Clumsy idiot. Come we must not hang around."

They crossed under the motorway and, in character, walked slowly down the Avenue.

Some minutes later, Richer came out of the gates, crossed under the flyover and went down the Avenue. He did not take any notice of the man who came out of the car park on the other side of the road opposite the stadium, head over-exaggeratedly buried in an upside-down newspaper.

Richer and the man continued in tandem on either side of the Avenue across Boulevard Ney.

As soon as Richer had turned into the metro, Gerard flung the paper down and rushed to the top of the road to the left, past the railway line. The couple were a little way down. He looked up at the blue street sign. Rue Belliard.

His heart was thumping wildly. He would not have recognised the old man, of course, not in a million years. He was a master of disguise, after all. But inside Gerard's head the words they had called out to each other as he had crashed into them echoed with sparkling clarity.

The girl had called "Ja - !" Nothing, perhaps, in itself.

The old man had called "Sylvie!"

And that had settled it.

For as every cop in France knew, Mesrine's latest moll was Sylvie Jacquot. He had them.

By Christ, he had them! Of all the *flics* in France, it was Claude Gerard who had found them.

But did Richer have the document?

He stopped, looking back at the metro. Twice he started towards it and twice he stopped in a quandary. It was not an easy choice.

Finally, he turned his back on the metro and continued down Rue Belliard.

‡

79. La Fin

Vendredi 2 Novembre

All Souls' Day 1979 was crisp but bright in Paris, the waning autumn sun reflecting off the Seine and dazzling the *clochards* who still occupied the river banks despite the seasonal temperature. Soon these Parisian tramps would move inland into sheltered doorways or the parks or, if they were lucky, over the warm air vents of the metro. Some might even venture as far north as the Clignancourt metro and seek warmth there.

In fact a *clochard* was already seated on the sidewalk near that station, eating a *pain* and swilling back some anonymous liquid from a bottle inside a bag. Paul Richer noticed him as he ascended from the station at 14:50.

At last, thought Richer. At bloody last he was actually going to get his hands on the infernal and, for the Windsors of England, damning document. The secret which he had kept bottled up inside for what seemed like an eternity, would be his in writing.

He looked at the *clochard*, walked a little way on then looked again.

His heart stopped beating.

Jesus, no!

He recognised the man.

His first reaction was that the recognition must be because it was Mesrine. It was another of his disguises. It was Jacques waiting to hand over his prize.

But it was not.

It was somebody else. Somebody he had seen before. Recently. At Printemps. It was one of the sergeants of the BRB.

It was impossible. They could not have known details of his meeting with Mesrine. Absolutely impossible. How had they found him?

There was no time to analyse it. He could not now hang around at the top of the metro steps as he had intended. He would have to move.

Slowly he walked over to a newsstand, carefully watching the *clochard*. He bought the first thing he picked up, the pop magazine *Podium*, opened it and sauntered away, ostensibly reading.

He stopped no more than three metres away from the *clochard*, and it was then that he realised his error. *He* was not being watched at all. The man had not taken the slightest interest in him. Whilst munching and drinking the man was covertly looking to the east, down Rue Belliard.

Holy shit.

Operation Mesrine was obviously coming to a head. Somehow the criminal had been traced. Naturally he must live around here, that was why he had suggested the meets first at the *marché* then at the station. They had found him. There would be more of them around, like a plague of rats they would be more intense where the meal was to be found. Damn them all.

Deliberately, Richer dropped the magazine and, as he picked it up, looked down Boulevard Ornano to the immediate right. As far as he could see, to the Place Albert Khan, things looked normal. In the narrow Passage du Mont Cenis behind him, everything was quiet.

Giving the appearance that he knew where he was going, he walked forward past the *clochard* and to the right into Rue Belliard.

As Richer passed, the *clochard* casually pulled a walkie-talkie from the brown bag.

Separated from the busy Boulevard Ney by the railway line, Rue Belliard gave the impression of life going on as normal. But to Richer's trained and experienced eyes, it was anything but. The place was riddled with them. A man and a woman walking down the street, self-consciously holding hands; another tramp; a girl dressed louder than the biggest tart on St Denis; and, inevitably, further down the street, the van of *Gaz de France* and the men in overalls pretending to work in the road.

They had Mesrine. The trap was set.

Richer forced himself to walk normally, not to run. He felt like screaming. *No! Not now, please!* At least wait until Mesrine hands over the document. *For God's sake!*

He could not help appreciating the irony of the situation. Of all the *flics* in France, he must be the only one who did *not* know Mesrine's exact location. But chances were it was near the gas men.

He looked at his watch. Two minutes to three.

Down the road, just past the gas van, two people came out of an apartment block.

Inside the gas van, Inspector Cordelier of the BRB also looked at his watch.

"Let's go in *now*." He spoke irritably into a walkie-talkie.

"*Non,*" instructed the voice on the other end. "We agreed. Sixteen hundred. If he is not out by then, you may attack the building."

"But that's another *hour*."

"Patience, Inspector, patience. You have no further sightings of either of them?"

"Only the girl at thirteen hundred. She posted a letter, picked up some food, then went back."

"You have not seen Mesrine?"

"No. You're sure he's in there?"

"Positive."

Another voice said, "Any sight of Richer?"

Cordelier spoke to someone next to him, then said "Might just have been spotted near the station. Not confirmed though."

"*D'accord.*"

The first voice came back on. "You have all the exits covered?"

"Certainly. He cannot escape."

"*Bon.* Then I suggest - "

"Wait! Something is happening. There's movement. Christ. I think they're coming out! Yes, it's them - !"

"Are you ready, darling?" Jacques Mesrine pulled on the leather jacket and pressed down the edges of the false beard. He surveyed himself in the gilt-edged mirror, smoothing down his hair. "Your first visit to our new home."

"Perhaps you should carry me over the threshold when we get there?" Sylvie came in from the bathroom, tucking the final piece of blonde hair under the brown wig. She was dressed in a grey skirt and blouse. She too looked in the mirror.

There was a sniffing at her feet and she bent down and picked up the present Jacques had given her two days ago: a white poodle. "Fifi darling, Mummy's not going to forget you." She looked up at Mesrine. "Our first baby?"

Mesrine smiled as he checked his pockets. "You have the bag?"

"There." Sylvie nodded in the direction of the bed. "Do we *have* to take it? Nothing's going to happen."

"Insurance, my love, insurance. There will come a day - sometime - when I will no longer need such policies. But until then we had better be safe than sorry." He unzipped the holdall. Inside were six hand grenades and a pistol. In his jacket also he carried a gun.

He rezipped the bag and picked up their overcoats from a chair.

At the door, Sylvie scooped the dog under her arm and took one last look around. "I hate goodbyes."

Gently, Mesrine stroked her cheek. "It is not goodbye. The rent is paid for another month. There are still things to move."

She cuddle Fifi. "*Bien sûr,* but it is a new life."

"You have regrets?"

She shook her head. "*Pas du tout.*"

"Here," he tucked in a dangling curl of her blonde hair. "Soon we will not have to don these damn disguises every time we set foot outside the door. Soon we will live as normal people."

"I have no regrets, my love, it has been fun." She kissed him. "I am pleased. After the life I have had I ask nothing more than to settle down with the man I love."

"*Allons-y*," Mesrine smacked her on the bottom. "We have to meet the Captain down at the station, then it is Marly-le-Roi non-stop."

It was Mesrine without a doubt. He was bearded but there was no other attempt at disguise. Over his left arm he carried some coats, in his right hand was a holdall. Sylvie was at his side, frumped-up and bewigged. In her arms she carried a white bundle.

Mesrine opened a door of a BMW for her to climb in.

Richer thought of breaking into a run, to shout a warning, but instead he stopped and pretended to be surveying the delights in a *patisserie* window. What should he do? Jacques would have to come this way, it was a one-way street, and he would be heading for their tryst at the station. On the other hand, he could be intercepted immediately without time to hand over the document.

Richer could tell that the gas men had seen Mesrine. While one continued working in the road, the other climbed into the van. There would be other men and a radio transmitter inside.

He couldn't risk it. He moved, breaking into a run, no time for pretence now.

The BMW pulled away from the kerb and moved smoothly down the street. Inside, bag beneath his legs, seat belt on, Mesrine noticed how clear the road was. In fact, except for the gas van there were no other vehicles at all...

A strong hand grabbed Richer's arm as he was about to run into the road.

"Fancy a good time, ducky?" grinned the girl dressed as a whore.

"No." He tried to shake himself free.

"You're in a hurry aren't you, handsome?" The grip was firm, belying the overpowering smell of *Ma Griffe*.

"I'm one of you, you stupid bitch!" Richer pulled his arm up and down. "Richer, Chief Inspector, BCP!"

"What?" She was confused, not knowing what to do.

Still held, Richer looked down the road. The BMW was moving into third gear, picking up speed every second. No intercept yet. He noticed the driver look back at the gas men.

He pulled his arm again. "Will you let go of me, woman! *Jesus!*"

There was no alternative.

Six of her front teeth flew out as he punched her in the mouth. She went down like a cognac on a cold day, instantly and spreadeagled.

Richer stepped off the kerb, waving his arms frantically in the air.

Mesrine saw him and began to decelerate.

Across the road, another of the tramps pulled a gun from within his rags.

"No!" screamed Richer. "Don't fire, don't fire!" He reversed his action and furiously began to wave the stopping vehicle on.

Then he realised. The tramp was not aiming at the car. *He was aiming at him!*

He crouched down, hopelessly exposed in the roadway. "*Sûreté!*" he shouted, drawing his own weapon from his jacket pocket. "BCP!"

It confused the tramp sufficiently to stop him firing.

The car screeched to a stop. Mesrine frowned down at him.

Richer stood up, aiming over the top of the BMW with his right hand, holding out his left. "Get out of here, Jacques! Give it to me and go. Go on, go on, go on!"

"It is safe, Captain. Tomorrow!" Back wheels skidding and nearly hitting Richer, Mesrine sped off, the dog yapping on Sylvie's lap.

Richer was again an open target, standing in the middle of the roadway, aiming at the tramp who, in turn, was aiming at him.

What the hell did Mesrine mean, "It is safe"? Today was the final meet, the day of the handover. *Tomorrow?*

Cautiously he began to move backwards, gun still aimed. "I am Chief Inspector Richer," he called. "Where is Broussard?"

The tramp was perplexed, bewildered at why the Chief Inspector had let Mesrine escape. He watched as Richer lowered his gun, and he answered uncertainly "Up - up at the Porte, sir."

Richer glanced to his left. *Mesrine was heading in that direction.*

He began to run.

The tramp kept his eyes on him, fumbling inside his rags for his radio, desperate for instructions.

Officer Jacqueline Dinon, the one disguised as the whore, stirred from her momentary unconsciousness. As she opened her unfocused eyes, the first thing she became aware of was the blood flowing down the front of her lace blouse. With the astuteness of all government employees, she then wondered who was going to pay for the cleaning or replacement. Only as she wondered where the blood was coming from did she become aware of the pain in her mouth.

It all came back instantly. The man, the man who was trying to warn

Mesrine…

Richer ran. He could hardly breathe. His lungs could not get enough air. His legs slowed…

Dinon pulled herself into a sitting position and shook her head. She was aware that her jaws seemed to be locked together, and yet there were gaps where her teeth should be. Her eyes focussed. Further down the road, a man was running. *It was him!* The one who had hit her.

She groped for her handbag, pulling it towards her.

The tramp saw Dinon move as he got to his feet. Still talking into his radio, he headed across to help her.

Dinon withdrew her gun from the handbag and aimed it at the running figure.

"No!" shouted the tramp as he quickened his pace. "He's one of us!"

Richer stopped.

Dinon fired.

Richer bent forward to catch his breath. Something whizzed over his head and then he heard the bang. *Bastards*. He turned round, fired without aiming, and ran on.

His bullet hit the running tramp in the right eye. The top of the tramp's head exploded but the momentum of his run kept him going even though he was dead.

He fell heavily on top of Officer Dinon, spreading her beneath him, his bloodied face coming to rest on hers in a bizarre necrophilial kiss.

For a moment Officer Dinon was nonplussed. Then she gave a guttural scream, smelling the last breath to emit from the dead body. Then she fainted.

Mesrine was convinced they would be expecting him to turn left into Ornano or head straight across the intersection and continue down the main part of Belliard, so he wrenched the wheel to the right, onto the bridge across the railway.

As he turned onto the bridge, a lorry lurched out from Ornano, hooting loudly. It overtook the BMW and pulled across in front of it at the intersection of the Boulevard Ney.

Mesrine slammed on his brakes. "Sylvie! The bag! Quickly!"

"What?"

"A grenade, get me a grenade!" He tried to engage reverse but failed.

Sylvie leant over between his legs, fumbling one-handedly. In her right arm the dog picked up the atmosphere and whimpered loudly.

With a crunching of gears, Mesrine forced the car into reverse.

The tarpaulin on the back of the lorry flew back. Four men stood there, weapons raised.

"I can't undo the zip!" screamed Sylvie.

The BMW lurched backwards. Mesrine looked behind.

Richer ran round the corner.

Mesrine's car went straight into him, knocking his legs back, his face crashing down and splintering the back window.

Mesrine slammed on the brakes as the Chief Inspector bounced off onto the cobblestones.

Sylvie still groped beneath him.

The dog yapped.

Mesrine turned back and stared at the men in the back of the lorry. For an instant he was back in Chateau-Merle, it was 1944, and the men were Germans. Then he shouted, "Sylvie! Remember I love you!"

The men fired.

In all, twenty-one bullets smashed through the windscreen of the BMW, nineteen of them hitting Jacques Mesrine. The bullets were brass coated to get through the glass, and they exploded as they entered his body.

He jerked as the bullets hit, the seat belt holding him as a literally sitting target. Suddenly there was blood everywhere. A piece of bone bounced off the steering wheel.

Mesrine's hand gave a final twitch in the direction of the bag and that was it.

It was over. It had taken less than five seconds.

Thirty seconds later, a car pulled up next to the BMW. An arm stretched out from the window and fired a single shot into Mesrine's head. A *coup-de-grace*.

The car reversed back off the bridge.

All was quiet. Mission accomplished. Affair concluded. The men in the back of the lorry looked around, as if they did not know what to do now.

Suddenly the passenger door of the BMW burst open. Sylvie staggered out. Because she had been bending down trying to open the bag of weapons, all but two of the bullets had missed her. One had hit her right arm and one had carved a deep furrow in the side of her head.

What had once been the white, whimpering Fifi was now a red, dead object in her hands. Sylvie was confused, unsure on her feet, wig hanging half off to show blood-stained blonde hair below. She looked about at the police who were slowly, quietly converging from all directions. She spoke, almost to herself.

"A- animals! Y - you animals!" She looked at the mess in her arms and asked with the wide-eyed innocence of a child, "Why did you shoot my dog?"

Three paces away from the BMW, she collapsed in the middle of the road.

Claude Gerard stepped from the rear of the vehicle that had backed off the bridge. He looked to the right. Paul Richer lay in the damp gutter, one arm bent awkwardly up onto the sidewalk. Gerard walked over.

Richer's face was a mess and his head was at a curious angle. His eyes stared deadly, almost accusingly, at the back wheels of Mesrine's car. His mouth was open as if he was about to speak, words which would never now be heard.

Gerard bent down and quickly went through his pockets. Then, frowning, he went through them again.

Nothing.

Gerard stood up and then bent down again and closed Richer's eyelids. Then he hurried to the BMW and quickly frisked the bloody, lacerated cadaver that had been Jacques Mesrine.

Nothing.

Absolutely sod all.

"*Merde.*" He sighed heavily. He pulled out a grubby handkerchief, blew his nose and then wiped the blood off his hands. He nodded to the man in the front passenger seat of the car he had got out of. The man nodded back and got out, taking charge.

Gerard walked away.

‡

ÉPILOGUE

Thus ended Jacques Mesrine, publicly executed by the French Establishment. There was never any question of his recapture, he had embarrassed The Powers That Be once too often.

Even in death, Mesrine was allowed no dignity. While he lay, naked, bloodied and exposed, on the slab in the police mortuary, a notice on the locked door read 'Until further notice, Mesrine will not be receiving visitors.' Macabrely humourless, perhaps, but also necessary because there were literally queues of policemen waiting to scoff over the corpse of their enemy.

One week later, after the official gloating had been sated and as his mother and daughter began proceedings against the police for manslaughter, Mesrine was buried next to his father in the cemetery at Clichy.

Samedi 3 Novembre

Gerard spent his final night in Paul Richer's apartment haunted by the face of his dead colleague, staring at him from wherever he looked.

Come the morning, he was pale and tired. He settled for a breakfast of three cigarettes and a glass of cognac. Chivas the cat was nowhere to be found.

Gerard's things were easily packed into his old holdall, and he left the apartment finally at 10:30.

Downstairs, the concierge poked his head out of his door as Gerard shuffled by.

"Monsieur?"

"What?"

"Monsieur Richer, he is in?"

"*Non.* He won't be back for some time." Gerard walked on.

"Monsieur."

"*What?*" Gerard turned back, not concealing his irritation.

"If he will not be back for some time, perhaps you would like it?"

"Like what?"

The concierge held up a long, white envelope. "It is addressed to Monsieur Richer."

"Stuff it up your - " Gerard stopped with his mouth opening and closing like a fish. The holdall slipped involuntarily from his fingers. "G - give it to me." His throat had dried. "I'll take it."

"*Oui, monsieur.*" The concièrge handed it over.

Gerard stuffed it quickly into his inside pocket, like a boy about to be caught with a dirty book. He picked up his holdall and walked out.

Then he came back, wordlessly handed the astonished concièrge a hundred franc note, and walked out again.

His car was parked on the opposite side of the road. He had watched the mechanics from the garage in Rue Norvins fixing it yesterday afternoon, after he had returned from the carnage at Clignancourt and after his apologetic phone call to the British Embassy to explain that the document was unavailable, presumed lost.

Would *he* have a surprise for the *rosbeefs*!

Inside the car, he carefully unprised the flap of the envelope as if it would bite him. Slowly, with the tops of his fingers, he withdrew the contents.

There was no covering note, simply a letter and an attached sheet. The paper was unheaded. The letter was handwritten in English, with a sharp forward slope. Automatically he looked at the signature first. *'EP'.* It was dated 26 January 1938. It began *'My dear Mrs Warfield'.*

Gerard looked again at the date. That was certainly a strange thing to call her at that time.

'In accordance with our agreement…'

He read on.

Halfway through, when he realised the significance of what he was reading, his hand began to shake and he lit up a cigarette. So, Elizabeth was *his* daughter?

He finished the letter and started on the attachment. It was typewritten in English and another European language, simultaneously line after line. There were five signatures on the bottom. One was 'Edward Prince'. One was de Gaulle. One was Charles Bedaux. One was Roosevelt. The fourth was of another European head of state at that time.

He read it.

Jesus H Christ Almighty in heaven above…

As he was gingerly replacing the papers in the envelope, there came a tap on the window. He looked up. It was Ron Becker of the British Embassy.

Gerard wound down the window.

"Morning Claude, old stick," smiled Becker. "You all right? You're sweating?"

"I'm… okay." He still held the envelope in his hand.

"Well, if you say so. You don't look too well to me. I phoned your office, they said you'd be here. Just wanted to confirm our telecon yesterday. The document is lost?"

"I - I thought so. But..." Gerard held out the envelope.

"You've got it?"

"Came in the post, addressed to Richer. In the fucking post!" He shook his head. "Take it, for Christ's sake."

Becker took it, staring at it in amazement. "Good God, I never actually thought you would get it. You've read it?"

"Yes."

"I see. Well... great." Becker put it in an inside pocket then bent down as if to adjust his shoe. Then he straightened up. "Well... no more to be said. Till the next time. No doubt some other crisis will raise its head soon."

"No doubt."

Becker turned away.

"Can I give you a lift?" Gerard poked his head out of the window. "I'm going into work."

The Englishman looked back. "No. No - thanks. My car's down on Caulaincourt."

"Okay. See you, then."

"Cheers."

Twenty metres away, Becker turned and called, "Claude? Thanks!" He tapped his pocket.

Gerard nodded and raised his hand. "Fuck you," he muttered.

He watched the small Englishman walk to the end of the street and turn left into Caulaincourt. Cigarette between his lips, Gerard settled himself behind the wheel and switched on the ignition.

The vehicle exploded.

Lundi 5 Novembre

The High Command of the OAS sat together in the room above the butcher's shop in Belleville, a near-empty bottle of Calvados on the table.

"But of course we have no proof," finished the Colonel. "His apartments have been ransacked, his safety deposit boxes emptied. His family and all his known acquaintances have been turned inside out by Bouvier and company. Plenty has been found but nothing relating to the secret. Mesrine has taken the whereabouts of the document with him to his grave."

"So it was all arranged," mused the chain smoker. "De Gaulle, Roosevelt, Hitler and the Windsors. And brokered by that sadist Bedaux. Incredible."

The cap man tossed back his fifth brandy. "So the person now on the English throne - "

"Yes indeed," said the Colonel. "I don't believe the children know. Only the grandmother."

"*Why* didn't Richer tell us before? Goddamn it, he was duty bound."

"He was duty bound to protect us. All of us, including our other member."

"Will you tell the President?"

"I don't know. The knowledge is dangerous."

"Hell's teeth," the chain smoker flung his glass across the room. It smashed loudly against the wall. "We were within this much - *this much!* - of getting it."

"Do Bouvier, Devos or Broussard know?"

"No," said the Colonel. "I just told them I was interested in budget papers stolen from the British Embassy."

The cap man stood up. "That's it then."

The Colonel nodded. "It would appear so."

"He was a good man, Richer." The cap man pulled a scarf from his pocket. "Despite our differences." He undid the top button of his overcoat and wound the scarf round his neck, covering his priest's collar. "I will pray for his soul. And Mesrine's."

"Thank you." The Colonel and the smoker also rose.

The three men shook hands.

The cap man stopped, reaching out for the door knob. "I suppose there's no one else we can activate, just in case it's still around?"

"How many true Frenchmen are left?" The Colonel was slipping on his gloves. "Richer was right. Mesrine was the only one who could even get close to it."

The chain smoker raised a hand. "*Un moment, mes amis,* can you smell something?"

The other two men sniffed.

"Yes, Maurice," laughed the cap man, "that bloody camel shit you smoke!" He turned the door knob and leapt backwards grasping his hand. "Christ! That's hot!"

The Colonel jumped across and tugged the door open with his gloved hand. He fell back into the other men.

Flame crackled around the doorway and black smoke tumbled in.

The stairway, their one way out, was an inferno.

The three men turned towards the window, long ago boarded up. They looked at each other.

Mercredi 7 Novembre

On the day that Paul Richer was buried in Dannemois, a small village forty kilometres to the south of Paris in Essonne, the tall thin man from the British Embassy in Paris visited Clarence House in London.

The old lady, the 79 year old matriarch of the British Royal Family, had been forewarned of his visit. She had only one question when the envelope was handed to her. "Does anyone else know of the contents?"

The man coughed deferentially. "Er, no, ma'm. No one... alive. Your instructions have been complied with."

"Good."

"Except, of course, the Duchess of Windsor herself."

"*That* woman!"

Without opening the envelope, the lady tore it into small pieces and let it fall into a glass ashtray. She then took a cigarette lighter and ignited the pile in three places.

As the paper charred and curled in on itself, she said "Now. No one, except that person of no significance, knows. And she'll have no proof."

"No, ma'm."

"But she knows. There is nothing we can do about *her*, I suppose?" The lady did not look up from the cinders.

"I await your instructions, Your Majesty," said the man.

‡

In memory of
Jacques René Mesrine
28 December 1936 – 2 November 1979

.

THE WINDSOR SECRET

Ω

DAVID CULLEN

*"Anyone who knows the secret, dies. That's the point,
don't you see?"*
- Ron Becker,
Friday August 29 1997

Ω

Revenge is a dish...

Ω

Cast in order of appearance

Prince Charles - *ex-husband and heir to the throne of Britain*
Diana, Princess of Wales - *ex-wife, and mother of the future King of England*
Sarah - *Duchess of York*
Billy - *a butler*
Her Majesty Queen Elizabeth the Queen Mother - *keeper of a secret*
Ilich Ramirov - *The Contractor*
Wallis Simpson Windsor - *Duchess of Windsor and erstwhile keeper of a secret*
Sir Kenneth Dean - *The Catalyst*
Christina Cascianis - *Israeli Intelligence (and still a special lady)*
Stelios Grivas - *a ghost*
A Daughte - *(seeking knowledge and revenge*
Will The Cat - *a companion*
Eric Dejeune - *a prison officer*
Chaim Cohen - *Israeli Intelligence – and a Catholic priest*
Dr Daniel Salinger - *Medical examiner*
Teresa Cotton - *assistant to Christina Cascianis*
Melanie Nathanson - *Israeli Intelligence*
Barking Dog - *no point in having one and barking yourself*
Charles Fleury-Goujon - *Commissaire of Police, BCP Paris (retired)*
Pierre Jamo - *Chief Inspector of Police, BCP Paris*
Maurice Goise - *Sergeant of Police, BCP Paris*
Claudette Ibrahim - *Inspector of Police, BCP Paris*
The Secretary to Her Majesty Queen Elizabeth the Queen Mother
The Medical Consultant to Her Majesty Queen Elizabeth the Queen Mother
Ron Becker - *The Rag, British Embassy Paris*
Gisele Joudeh - *a Lebanese diplomat*
The Professor - *scary*
John Smith - *Head of Charles' People*
Camilla - *future Queen of England*
Veronique Chevalier - *a socialite*
Michel Chevalier - *husband and lawyer*
Henri - *owner of the best bar in Paris*
Gillian Colet - *Commissaire of Police, BCP Paris*
Eli Lucas - *a journalist*
Claude Dumoulin - *a paparazzo (one of many)*
Jack Jones - *Head of Betty's Men*

Madame Renée/Sylvie Jacquot - *still in love*
LouLou - *a tart, no matter which sex*
Concierge of 1 Rue Lamarck, Paris
Receptionist at the British Embassy, Paris
Concierge of The Ritz Hotel, Paris
Assistant Director of Security, Ritz Hotel, Paris
Henri Paul - *acting Director of Security, Ritz Hotel, Paris*
Emad 'Dodi' Fayed - *in the wrong place at the wrong time*
Her Majesty Queen Elizabeth II of England

Ω

FOREWORD

It was Lord Byron who said, "Truth is always strange; stranger than fiction." But why is it that we humans will readily accept fiction but always disbelieve the truth if it stretches beyond our own narrow perception of what truth is?

Truth is not history. And history is not truth. History is written by the winners, by those who survive to tell the tale (and who want, perhaps, to justify their actions). The real truth is often what the victors do not want us to hear.

And, unlike in fiction, life is not just three characters. Life is not just the hero, the villain, the girl or the guy. Life is a mêlée of people whose paths criss-cross with one another. Each day of our lives we cross the paths of hundreds, sometimes thousands, of people, lives touching, different people with different aims all coming together.

The previous stories – *The Eye of Makarios* and *The Mesrine Conclusion* – were unconnected. *The Windsor Secret* is a natural follow-on from both of them – but nevertheless it stands on its own, an alternative recording of historical fact.

Where does fiction end and truth begin? As Voltaire said:

"On doit des égards aux vivants; on ne doit aux morts que la vérité."

– We owe respect to the living; to the dead we owe *only* truth.

David Cullen

Ω

PROLOGUE

Christmas 1986
Sandringham, Norfolk, England

"You are a whore!" The raised voice coming from behind the closed door of the west-facing bedroom on the first floor was unmistakeable. A famous voice, an often-imitated voice, and identical to the voice of his mentor and idol Louis Mountbatten.

When the voice spoke in a normal, unstressed tone it was regal and refined. But nowadays it seemed to be raised constantly, always shouting, at least when his wife was about.

The servants going about their business in this, the Norfolk country home of the Sovereign, had heard it all before.

The couple had been married for five years, a marriage of convenience, the future King of England and the non-Catholic virgin with a lineage going back to King Charles I, chosen as a brood mare by his real – but sadly already married – lover.

There had never been love ("Whatever that is"), not from his side. As for her, she had convinced herself that this was the real thing, the true love of fairy tales, the Princess Bride. But even before the marriage – witnessed by the world five and a half years previously on July 29 1981 – she knew she was deluding herself. He had had many sexual partners, including her own sister, but she knew that he had love for only one woman – and that woman was not her.

By the time she stood on the steps of St Paul's Cathedral and watched the world cheering, she knew that she would never be Queen.

Dutifully she had born the children. The future King, William Arthur Philip Louis (how she hated those last two names!) on June 21 1982, and the surviving twin Henry Charles Albert David on September 15 1984. Perhaps it was because the other twin, the girl, had been stillborn that his hatred of her grew in intensity – he had so wanted a daughter. Or perhaps it was because he suspected that the twins were not his ("Look at the red hair. He looks just like him!").

But now he had somehow found out about Barry. It was stupid of her to think that she could get away with it, she knew she was watched everywhere

– but she had needed someone to listen to her, someone to understand her, someone to be kind to her... Someone to love her, even if only physically.

"Oh, a whore am I?" she retaliated. "I have had two men ever in my life. *Two!* If I am a whore, what does that make *you?* The man who sleeps with whomever he chooses? The man who has his mistress installed in the same house as his wife and children– "

"Oh do shut up."

"What's good for you is good for me. I am not having a marriage of three people."

"What do you mean? You are being hysterical. I am the future King of England - "

"You are a man. You are not divine. *You are my husband.* Tell me you are not fucking her."

"Do you really expect me to be the only Prince of Wales who never had a mistress?"

"*What?* So you are not denying it - "

"We are talking about *you*. You have been screwing your bodyguard – I have proof."

"Proof? Proof! What do you have? Tell me! Show me."

"I do not need to. Just tell me, how *could* you?"

"How *could* I? This coming from the man, the family, that is the coldest on earth. How could you ever understand, you're all automatons."

"So you are not denying it."

"You just prove it."

"I don't have to prove it. Why do you think he was transferred? I have had my suspicions for months - "

"Kind of you to even notice me."

" – but you have still been seeing him."

"Prove it."

"Well, you will never see him again."

There was a pause. Her voice was lower, calmer, as she asked, "Charles, what have you done?"

Quietness. Then Charles said, "I have resolved the problem. Commensurate with the threat posed."

"Threat?" Diana shook her head in disbelief. "What threat is he to you?"

"You do know that it is treason to screw the King's wife, don't you?"

"What are you talking about?"

"And you know the penalty for treason."

There was a smash, the breaking of glass. The bedroom door flew open and Diana ran out.

Sarah, the new vivacious, red-headed Duchess of York, was coming along the corridor. "Di?" she asked as she saw her friend running towards her.

"Darling, are you okay?"

Diana stopped in front of her, tears streaming down her face. "Oh, Fergie," she hugged her friend. "I can't stand it, I just can't stand it."

Sarah held up the bottle she was carrying. "Come up to my room, tell me about it. Let's have some wine. Andrew is still downstairs."

"No. No, I want to see Grandma. Is she still downstairs?"

"She came up about half an hour ago. Had a few."

"I must see her." Diana turned and ran back towards the southern end of the building.

Billy the butler was just coming out of the room as Diana hurried down the corridor.

"Billy! Is Grandma awake?"

"Her Majesty is reading, your Highness." The butler closed the door behind him.

"I must see her."

"I would rather she wasn't disturbed. I have just put her down for the night. She has, er, celebrated the season a little too vigorously."

Diana tapped on the door. "You mean she's pissed."

"Your Highness, I hardly think - "

But Diana had entered the room, purposefully closing the door behind her in the butler's face.

By royal bedroom standards the room was quite small but it was plushly decorated, reflecting the Jacobean style of the downstairs rooms.

The large bed was against the wall on the left, positioned so that the old lady – who preferred to sleep on her left side – had a view through the window and out over the west lawns when she woke in the mornings.

An antique brass bedside lamp cast a pool of diffused light over the bed and created an opulent penumbra over the rest of the room.

The eighty-six year old matriarch of the British Royal Family lay propped up in bed, pince-nez reading glasses on the end of her nose, *The Times* open on her lap. Her open mouth and closed eyes indicated that the affairs of the world were temporarily in suspension.

On the bedside cabinet stood a nearly-empty glass containing a centimetre of colourless liquid.

"Grandma?" Diana walked across the red patterned Persian carpet. "Grandma!"

The old woman's left arm jumped and she opened her eyes. For a moment she was confused, then her face softened when she looked at her caller.

"Grandma?" repeated Diana.

The old woman smiled. "I'm sorry my darling," there was genuine affection in her voice for her granddaughter-in-law. "I must have dozed off. I told Billy to go."

"Oh Grandma, I don't think I can stand it." Diana sat down on the edge of the bed.

"What is it dear? Is he being beastly again?"

"You don't know the half of it. That bitch is behind it, I know she is. He is always accusing me of things – "

"Does he still think Harry is not his?"

"Oh, he denies ever having said that. But it's still there. I can see it every time he looks at him. He never holds him, you know."

"Men are strange creatures, Diana. And there are none more strange than the men in this family. I have done my best, but they can be so cold, so unemotional. Even more than their position obviously requires. His father's genes don't help, of course. Here, take this will you?" The old lady closed the newspaper and moved it towards Diana. As Diana took it off the bed and folded it up, the old lady reached across for her glass. "Is the bottle there?"

Diana opened the door of the bedside cabinet, placed the newspaper inside and removed the familiar green glass bottle. "I don't think there's any tonic."

"Doesn't matter. A strong one will help me sleep."

Diana unscrewed the lid and poured the clear liquid into the proffered glass.

"You really must try not to let him antagonise you," counselled the old lady as she raised the glass and drank. "Until your marriage he was always the centre of attention. Now you have taken that away from him - "

"Its not my fault."

"I never said it was, my dear. But nevertheless, you have taken away his spotlight. You are a married couple, a prince and his princess, the future King and Queen. And yet the world craves only you."

"Loved by the world yet despised by my husband!" Diana put the bottle back in the cabinet and closed the door.

"He sees himself as a bit-player. He is not used to it – and, dare I say, he is not yet mature enough to cope. That's why he still consoles himself with his friend."

"But what about me?"

The old lady took another large mouthful of drink. "You were told it would not be easy. That he would not be easy."

"I know, Grandma, I know. But I was in love with him. Or at least I fooled myself into thinking that I was."

"And now?"

"Now?"

"Are you in love with him?"

Diana sighed. "He is my husband, of course I am. But the question is, is he in love with me?"

"You would be surprised. He loves you, in his own way."

"Well, he has a very funny way. Coldness and accusations, that's all I get from him. Do you know we haven't had sex since Harry was conceived?"

The old lady's eyebrows rose as she emptied her glass. In the last few minutes she had drunk two hundred millilitres of neat gin. She said, "He will come round eventually you know. He will acknowledge Henry as his, when he starts to grow and look like him."

Diana took the glass from her. She did not comment directly but she said, "It's not that this time."

"What is it? The twin again?"

"No, this time it is something different." Diana took the pince-nez off the old lady's nose and put them on the cabinet. "Do you remember Barry, my previous bodyguard? He was moved onto other duties just before Andrew and Fer – Sarah's wedding last July?"

"Not really, dear, no."

"Well, now Charles is accusing me of sleeping with him. Of having an affair."

The old lady closed her eyes.

"And," continued Diana, "he is threatening to do something awful to him."

Slowly, the old lady's eyelids re-opened.

"And did you?"

"What?"

"Have an affair with him?"

"An affair? No."

"Thank goodness. One should confine oneself to affairs with one's own class. So what is he threatening to do? Nothing rash, I hope."

Diana shrugged. "You know him. He might find it difficult to make up his mind on most things, but when he does…"

"Well we can't have that, c-can we?" The old lady's speech was now distinctly slurring. "The man has been moved on, he should now be left alone. Royalty is no place for vendettas." To her dying day she never realised the hypocrisy in those words. "We… we must get him to lay off. We all have our skeletons, our little s-s-secrets. Even I do." She nodded, speaking to herself. "Good heavens, if his Grandfather had ever known! But he never did find out. Thank goodness. That was so, so long ago now."

Diana giggled lovingly. "You have a secret, Grandma?"

The old lady suddenly looked at her sternly, and the smile dropped from Diana's face. "Oh yes, I have a secret. A secret that can never be told. People have died to protect it." Her eyes clouded as she thought back over the years.

"Too many people. Anyone who knows it has been killed. To my sh-shame I have even used it as an excuse for my own revenge. As if the secret wasn't horrible enough. If… they ever… found out… " She closed her eyes again and her breathing became deeper.

"Grandma?" Diana shook her shoulder. "Grandma?"

"Mm?" Half of one eye opened.

"Grandma," asked Diana. "What is this secret?"

[Police Sergeant Barry Mannakee was killed in a road accident in East London on May 15 1987.]

8 months earlier…

Thursday April 24 1986
Boulevard Suchet, Paris, France

At 02:00 in the morning the streets of the 16th Arrondisement in Paris are still and almost deserted. Occasionally a taxi might cruise past carrying home a resident of this most exclusive quarter of the French capital. Here and there a solitary figure may be walking, having missed the last metro. Once or twice a week revelry may be heard from within one or other of the fashionable residences, an all-night party which the givers could not afford but had to hold for appearances' sake; for even in this day and age, appearances among the super, nouveau or manqué rich were everything.

But the streets did not matter to the man now moving slowly but purposefully over the rooftops. He was dressed in a black combat outfit and black balaclava hood. The apartment blocks on the east side of the street were taller than the houses on this side, and that was an irritation. There were a few lights on in the apartments but if anyone was looking out they were unlikely to see him, such was his skill. But nevertheless he glanced up occasionally at the windows; if he saw anyone looking out, he would silence them later.

His face was still boyish at thirty-seven years of age, still belying the powerful body underneath it. The hair was longer nowadays, but it was still wavy and pushed back. Its natural colour was black, but underneath the balaclava it was currently dyed blond. He no longer wore the tinted, plain glass spectacles which he was wearing in that full face photo that always appeared in the Press whenever his name was mentioned – a photo which was now nearly fifteen years old. He had not worn the spectacles since he had lost his right eye in Amsterdam twelve years previously. But judicious use of contact lenses ensured that not only was his sensitive left eye shielded from irritating daylight but also that no one knew that he was half blind – not even the doctors that used to give him his six-monthly medicals in Moscow before he was cast off by his masters as not needed anymore.

Not that 'half blind' meant the same for him as it did for normal people. For this man had been trained from an early age. The Russian state had taken him into care at the age of eleven, and he had been subject to seven years of the most intense and specialised training to augment and enhance his already natural ability to kill things in the most inventive – and sometimes painful – ways. The use of one eye to this man was the same as the use of four eyes to normal men.

He reached the building he wanted. From around his waist he unwound the thin but incredibly strong micro-fibre rope and looped one end around the chimney stack. The other end he threw over the side of the building.

One tug on the rope to ensure it was secured, and then Ilich Ramirov lowered himself smoothly over the side of number 24 Boulevard Suchet...

Bessie Wallis Warfield Spencer Simpson Windsor lay flat on her back in the centre of the wide double-bed under the crisp white sheet and maroon and gold filigreed eiderdown. Her black painted hair was spread out roughly on the bolster. Her mouth was hanging open, but after three facelifts that had tightened her throat so much that she could swallow nothing exceeding one centimetre in width, her airways were too tight to permit any snoring. Her head was propped up by four pillows so that she was permanently in a semi-upright position, so that she could breathe. She looked like a queen lying in state – something history had decreed she would never be.

She was just a few weeks off of her ninetieth birthday (on June 19), and to many it was a surprise not only how she had lived to such a vast age but that she had survived at all after the death of her husband fourteen years previously. "Sheer bloody-mindedness," her arch enemy – and, tonight, her nemesis – in London had called it.

Ilich Ramirov stood by the bed, looking down at her. He had no time for consideration or sentiment, a contract was a contract and he had been paid very handsomely. But this was his first British royal – or, he corrected himself, non-royal. The Duchess of Windsor she may be, but fifty years ago it had been decreed that she was never ever to be royal.

He heard a sound from outside the bedroom door. He froze. As he heard the doorknob turning he took one step backwards into the lee of the ornate, solid-wood wardrobe.

A sharp, wedge-shaped crack of light penetrated the darkness of the room as the night nurse peeked in. She came over to the bed and tucked in the sheet and smoothed down a strand of the Duchess' hair. Quietly she went out again, never knowing that Death was standing just two metres away.

As the wedge of light vanished, Ramirov moved back out and over to the bed. They had told him to make it look natural – and those that paid the piper called the tune. He leant forward and with the gentleness of a parent holding a newborn baby he put his left arm around the Duchess' head and lifted her forwards. With his right hand he pulled away all four pillows and let them fall to the floor. Carefully he began to lower her back down.

Suddenly her eyes sprang open. She stared straight at Ramirov. He looked at her and stopped lowering.

Her mouth moved. The sound came out moments later, like an out-of-sync movie. "David? David, is that you?"

He said nothing.

"*David?*"

"Yes, Peaches." He knew that that was her husband's pet name for her. "It is me." He felt the bony neck in his hand relax.

"Oh, it – it has been so long. I thought you would never come back for me. You do still love me, don't you David?"

"Of course, my darling," he spoke softly. "You have always been the woman I love."

"Oh, David! My beautiful little man - "

Slowly he began to lower her again.

"Kiss me," she said. "Kiss me and tell me it will be all right."

He bent forward and put his lips on hers. Her perfume almost covered the rankness of her breath from all the medicines in her body. "It will be all right, Peaches."

"I love you, my David."

Her head touched the mattress and he removed his hand.

It took one minute and sixteen seconds for her to stop breathing.

Ramirov waited for fifteen minutes after her heart stopped beating before he lifted the head back upright and replaced the four pillows. She would be found later, a natural death.

By the time Ramirov had his leg over the windowsill, micro-rope in his hand, her spirit had left her body. He felt no other presence in the room, just a slight odour where the cadaver had vacated itself.

He looked over to the bed and said, "Welcome to history, bitch."

Faubourg St Honoré, Paris, France

At 03:28 the telephone rang in the plush office on the first floor of the British Embassy on Faubourg St Honoré. Normally nighttime calls would be taken by the Night Duty Officer in the MI6 room downstairs, but this extension had deliberately not been transferred at 'close-of-play' yesterday evening.

It was picked up after just one ring. The tall, elegant but exceptionally gaunt man said nothing as he held the receiver to his ear.

The voice on the other end said just three words, "It is done."

The gaunt man said nothing but he nodded gently as he replaced the receiver. The official notification would come through around 05:00, after the night nurse had made her next two-hourly check at 04:30. Then he would have to alert all the embassy staff. The Press Office would be busy and he himself would have to arrange the usual post-death necessities: the death certificate, the embalming, the coffin, the plane back to England (ironically somewhere she was allowed to return to only once since the abdication and exile in 1936, to attend her husband's funeral in 1972), the undertakers in the UK and even the burial next to her husband at Frogmore.

But for now he had time. He looked at his watch. She had said she wanted to know as soon as her instructions had been carried out. It was 02:30 in England and she would probably be asleep, but she would not take it kindly if he left it until the morning.

He picked the telephone back up, pressed the number for an outside line and then keyed the number for Clarence House in London...

PART ONE

Ω

FOUNDATIONS

Ω

Tuesday July 15 1997

Cyprus

Christina kept running. Running and running. Wildly at first, the pain in her head increasing with each stride until she thought she would pass out. The wide ethnic skirt entangled itself around her legs as she moved.

After half an hour her legs began to tire and she slowed to a walking pace, her breath coming uneasily. In a further fifteen minutes she had reached the village of Laxia. People seemed to be going about their business as normal, but there was an eerie quietness about the place. She accosted a villager and asked what had happened that morning, but the old woman just gave her a stony stare and hobbled on.

Christina came to the main Nicosia-Limassol road. The traffic seemed unusually thin, and what little of it there was was heading for Limassol, away from the capital. She had a nasty feeling that she knew exactly what was going on in Nicosia. Stelios had probably got embroiled in an attempt to overthrow Mouskos. She only hoped that he and Martinez had been successful, because such was the nature of their mission - to steal a diamond from the very person of Makarios - that they must either succeed or lose their lives.

Resting under a tree by the side of the road, she realised that her best bet lay back at the villa. Stelios would need her help - if he came back. *If it was ever Martinez' intention to have him come back.*

She accepted her thoughts with resignation. She had been near death too many times for the thought of it to horrify her any more, even the death of General George Grivas's son, her lover. But she must not run away. She must return to the villa to see what she could do.

As she arose a jeep thundered past her on the road, heading towards Nicosia. In the back she thought she saw one of the old EOKA members of the good old days, but the jeep had gone in a second in a cloud of dust, and she could not be certain. Not until days later did she realise that she had seen Nicos Sampson on his way to take up his short-lived Presidency.

She returned to the villa by the route she had come, half walking, half trotting.

Arriving back an hour later, the first thing she noticed was that the door of the place was ominously open, and there was not a sound from within…

Slowly, cautiously she looked inside. It took a moment for her eyes to adjust from the glaring sun outside to the dimness of the villa.

Then her hand shot to her mouth. *In the name of God, no!*

Her fears had been right.

Stelios Grivas lay on his back on the tiled floor, blood oozing from a gaping bullet wound in his chest. He was not moving and he was so, so pale. He was dead, he must be. She moved towards him.

Then something strange happened. Stelios opened his eyes. Smiling, he pulled himself up onto his elbows. "Hello, beautiful."

"Stelios?"

"He took the diamond, kid. That bastard double-crossed us, just like we thought he would." Carefully he got to his feet. Blood was flowing out of the hole in his chest, but he seemed not to notice.

"You are alive?" Christina could hardly believe it.

"Of course. It's not my time yet." He walked towards her. "I die later. Until then you must look after me. But we must contact our Controllers in Tel Aviv, let them know what happened. Come here, hold me - "

As he lifted his arms to embrace her, blood squirted straight outwards from his wound, spraying into Christina's face. She gasped as it went into her mouth and over her chin. She stepped back, tasting the heat of his blood, tasting the iron, tasting his life –

She sat up in bed choking, gasping for air. Her hair was matted with sweat, the bed sheet was saturated. Perspiration gleamed on her naked, fifty year old body.

"Stelios?" She looked around the dark bedroom. "S- Stelios…?"

But of course he was not there. It was the dream again.

No matter how many times she had it, it always seemed so real. She could smell Cyprus of 1974. She could feel the heat of Cyprus 1974. She could experience the pain of Cyprus 1974. She could hear the noise of Cyprus 1974 as President Makarios was overthrown and the island was divided, seemingly forever. She could taste her lover's blood…

She rolled over and grabbed her bottle of Evian from the bedside table. She went to put it to her lips but changed her mind and poured some of it over her head. Roughly she shook her still luxuriant long black hair, spraying water like a living fountain of Aphrodite.

This *was* still Cyprus. And this was one of the many properties she owned in the Hellenic Mediterranean. But this was *not* 1974.

It was 1997. Twenty-three years to the day since the Turkish invasion of Cyprus. Twenty-three years to the day since the island had been partitioned.

Twenty-three years to the day since Martinez – otherwise known as the Russian assassin Ilich Ramirov – had betrayed *Mossad Aliyah Beth*...

Ω

Friday August 1 1997

Montmartre, Paris, France

The woman stood by the window of the apartment and watched the lights of Paris twinkle on beneath her. To her right the view from the *salle de jour* was obscured by the huge whitestone magnificence of Sacré Coeur on the crest of the *butte de Montmartre*. But just to the east, where the Basilica did not extend, she could see at an angle over the ridge with a view sweeping across to the towers of Notre Dame and beyond.

She sipped her Pernod and smiled silkily as the tabby cat wound itself in a figure of eight between her legs. This apartment had always belonged to a cat. Many years ago it had been Chivas, the long-haired black and white. But in the late eighties Chivas had missed his footing on one of his nightly sojourns across the rooftops of Montmartre, and he had plunged to his death onto Rue Lamarck below.

As if the cat world knew that a vacancy had arisen, a few months later Will, the female tabby, had appeared from nowhere and had stayed. She was called Will because when the woman had first noticed the cat perched perilously on the tiles outside, she had invited her in and asked her her name.

"Weeow," the cat had replied – and so Will it was.

The woman had been eighteen when her father had died, murdered not too far away from here. Two other men had also been killed at that time. One of them, a Chief Inspector of Police called Paul Richer, had been working with her father. Richer had owned this apartment. By a perversity that had never been explained, Richer had left this apartment to her father in his will. Richer had been killed just before her father, therefore the bequest was legal – even if her father never knew about his inheritance. The apartment had gone to her mother, who – after much family discussion on what to do with the place and whether to sell it – had agreed to let her daughter move in. That had been seventeen years ago, and she had lived there ever since.

Mother had died three years ago, and she had inherited in her own right.

She lived in the apartment alone – well, just her and Will. Just like any modern woman, men had come and gone in her life. Perhaps, she reflected ruefully, there had been too much coming and not enough going!

There had been one brief marriage, when she was young, impetuous and foolish. But she had soon got rid of him. None of her men (and she blanched inwardly when she thought of the quantity) had been the sort she would want to spend the rest of her life with. None of them matched up to The One – her father. Daddy. The man who had been her idol. The man who had been killed seventeen years ago. The man who was murdered, executed because he was who he was and he knew what he knew. The man who had never been avenged.

Until now.

She had waited all these years She knew she would know when the time was right. And it was now. She could feel it in her very being. Now, her father was calling out to her. It was time the world knew the truth. Time the world knew why her father had been murdered. Time the secret he had discovered and been killed for was revealed.

The quietness of the *salle de jour* was broken by a sharp, singular *crack*. The cat jumped but did not run away. It looked up and watched as the blood dripped down onto the fur on its back.

The woman looked at the broken glass in her hand. She felt no pain from the deep, bleeding laceration in her palm. Her only thought was that thank God she had finished her Pernod – it would have been a shame to waste good booze.

She raised her hand in the air and watched as the blood ran down her arm.

Yes, it had been long enough. It was time.

Time once again that the world heard the name Mesrine.

Ω

Monday August 4 1997

La Santé Prison, Paris, France

Eric Dejeune put his master key into the lock of the solid steel door of cell CS1 at 06:34 that morning. The cells in the solitary confinement block of the prison were locked and unlocked individually each day, there was no central locking unlike the cells in the main block.

And no central locking, thought Eric, unlike the doors on his new Honda Integra which he was taking delivery of that day. He smiled to himself as he thought of his new toy. He hoped this would be a usual, uneventful shift, he wanted to leave promptly at 14:00. No short notice overtime required today, thanks – he was picking up his new baby at 15:00.

He pushed the cell door open, hand on the holstered gun on his right hip. You always remembered your precautions, as trained – especially after, eighteen months previously, you had witnessed one of your colleagues literally have his head ripped off by one of these terrorist madmen whom the taxpayers of France kept in safety and relative luxury in what was colloquially known as The Mesrine Wing here in La Santé.

But this inmate was all right. World-famous he may be, responsible for the deaths of hundreds, but he had never been any trouble in the three years he had been here awaiting trial. A nice bloke, really.

"Bonjour Carlos," said Eric amiably as he entered the cell. "And what plans do you have this fine summer's day?"

The figure in the bed did not move. Normally he would be awake, ready to exchange quips.

Eric was instantly alert. "Carlos?" Instinctively his right hand clicked open the holster and pulled out the gun. "Ilych?" Slowly he moved towards the bed. He stopped a metre away and leant forward, prodding the figure with his gun. "Hey, Ramirez! Time to get up."

Nothing. Not a muscle. *Not a breath.*

Holding the gun rigidly in front of him, Dejeune carefully, gently, took hold of the blanket with his left hand. With a snap he whipped the blanket and underlying sheet off the bed Then he crouched in the defensive position, gun in both hands, finger on trigger, just as it said in the book.

He looked.

Then he sighed. The gun lowered as he straightened up.

Shit. *Shit, shit, shit.*

Bollocks.

Well, his car would have to wait now. Sod's bloody law. It was unbelievable. Today of all days!

The prisoner on the bed lay with his eyes open, jaw slack, tongue protruding, face frozen in agony. Ilych Ramirez Sanchez, also known as Carlos The Jackal, once the most feared man in the world, was as dead as a coffin nail.

Across The World

Time was, the death of the man who kept the world in fear in the 1970s and 80s would have warranted a News Flash on all major global television networks, maybe even an interruption of the scheduled programmes. But by 1997, Ilych Ramirez Sanchez – Carlos The Jackal – was a thing of the past, a hark-back to a bygone age when terrorism was in its infancy. His involvement in – and usually masterminding of – such things as the 1972 Olympics Massacre, the overthrow of Cyprus' President Makarios in 1974 and the 1975 kidnapping of the OPEC oil ministers in Vienna – were now consigned to history, fiction and movies. Terrorism in the 1990s had moved on, atrocity after atrocity laying the foundations for the ultimate crescendo in 2001.

So the death of Ilych Ramirez Sanchez warranted no higher than the sixth item on Sky News and Fox News; on CNN it was item seven; ABC did not mention it at all. The bulletins were near-enough identical: the famous full-face picture (round chubby face, tinted glasses, hair black and wavy and pushed straight back), a Lufthansa jet being blown apart and a ten second shot of the gunmen in the Olympic Village in Munich in 1972.

Of the millions of people around the world who saw the news items, three had extreme reactions.

In Athens, Greece, Christina Cascianis burst into tears.

In Florida, USA, Ilich Ramirov was convulsed by paroxysms of laughter.

And in Tel Aviv, Israel, Chaim Cohen picked up the telephone.

Ω

Tuesday August 5 1997

14th Arrondisement, Paris, France

By their very nature, post mortems are brutal procedures. The effective skinning, carving and eviscerally-emptying of what was once a human being is for the strong of stomach only.

The autopsy on Ilych Ramirez Sanchez was particularly rough. No one, after all, would be claiming the body. It would just be put, piece by piece, into the furnace. Even as The Jaws were cracking open the ribcage, Dr Daniel Salinger could see that the heart had simply exploded. Not unknown. A natural death.

But nevertheless, Dr Salinger performed a full autopsy. The growing cult of Human Rights in the late 1990s, even here in France, meant that even someone like this *ordure* on the slab in front of him must have his final mortal examination meticulously documented.

Four hours later, just before the last piece of the body was thrown into the furnace, Dr Salinger picked up a pair of surgical scissors and did what he had been requested to do.

Through France

It was a filthy habit.

Dr Salinger had seen more deaths caused by these little sticks, had cut open more tar-encoated lungs, than he could count. But still he took the last *mégot* from the packet of *Disque Bleu*, put it between his lips and lit up. He only just succeeded in holding in the cough. He was glad he had given up smoking years ago.

As the *TGV* train thundered through France from Paris to Lyons, he put the empty packet back in his pocket, thought better of it, pulled it back out again and threw it on the seat opposite.

A casual observer would have been curious as to why it was a *Disque Bleu* packet that went into the pocket but a *Gauloises* packet that ended up on the seat opposite. But there were no casual observers. There were just four other people in his part of the carriage: an old married couple (the man asleep, the woman reading a magazine); a young woman (headphones on, eyes closed, heading bobbing up and down to her music); and a business man (studying some papers).

As the train slowed towards its destination, La Part Dieu station in Lyons, Dr Salinger stood up and stretched. Wobbling with the movement of the train, he made his way forward, went through the internal doors and waited by the exit. Soon he would be checking in to the Carlton Hotel, and tonight he would have the finest meal on the menu at La Mère Brazier on Rue Royale. Tonight he would enjoy the most expensive wine available.

He was, after all, one million francs richer.

Back in the carriage, the old woman reached across and picked up the *Gauloises* packet from the seat. She placed it in her handbag and then went back to reading her magazine.

Under five hours later, the *Gauloises* packet was in Tel Aviv.

Ω

Wednesday August 6 1997

Troodos Mountains, Cyprus

"He iss gone, Stelios. At last, after all this time, he iss in hell where he belongs." Christina looked two metres to her right. "General, your son hass been avenged. *We* haf been avenged."

The sun beat down from the impossibly-blue sky. Even up here in the mountains – where it would start to snow in three months – it was hot. But the forty Celsius heat was well-tempered by the altitude. Down on the coast, the tourists would be sweltering and dropping.

The graves were in a sheltered clearing, in amongst the pine trees, well away from the main road. It was peaceful and naturally scented by the pines. Birds sang. Not many people now knew that there had once been a house on his spot. The house where the General had died on January 27 1974. Just two days after his death, the house had been razed by the Tactical Reserve Force of President Makarios. All but two people had died. At the time of the attack Christina and her lover, the General's son Stelios, had been higher up the mountain.

The summer Christina and Stelios had spent together had been... eventful. They had been on a quest, but they had been betrayed. Betrayed by the man whose death had been announced last week. By a man they knew then as Martinez. Only after Stelios' death had she discovered the true identity of the traitor: he was to become known to the world as Ilych Ramirez Sanchez, a Venezuelan idealist whom the Press would call Carlos The Jackal. In fact he was a Russian called Ilich Ramirov.

By that time she had also discovered that Stelios, a Cypriot Greek half-Jew, was also an agent of Israeli Intelligence. She had begged *Mossad Aliyah Beth* to let her help them find Ramirov. Initially they had refused. But over the years they had tested and utilised her, starting with little 'errands' until, many years later, she was trusted enough.

Ramirov had dropped out of sight at the end of the 1980s (it was even reported by some that he had died), cast adrift by his true masters upon the collapse of the USSR.

But the Jews never forget.

Information was gathered, analysed, retained, *remembered*. Israeli agents all over the world watched and waited. Like with the Nazis, the Israeli patience was long.

When Ramirov was kicked out of Syria in 1994, the Israeli machine was kicked back into life. Ramirov went to the Sudan where he thought he would be given sanctuary. But he was not. An Israeli tip-off to the French, a French 'word' with the Sudanese, and Ramirov was arrested in Khartoum on August 14 1994.

And watching in Sudan when he was arrested, and again in Paris when he arrived under heavy security, twenty years after the betrayal in Cyprus, was Israeli agent Christina Cascianis.

Officially General George Grivas, Head of EOKA and sworn enemy of Archbishop Makarios III, still lay where he was originally buried in the grounds of his house in Limassol. To this day the grave was tended by EOKA supporters, not all of them old.

Only a handful of people knew that the General had occupied the grave for little under a year. Upon the death of his son, he had been moved to the joint grave up here in the mountains, *his* mountains.

Christina knelt between the unmarked graves in the small clearing. Leaning forward, she ran her hands simultaneously over both the rocks underneath which the dead father and son lay.

"It iss over," she said to them both, speaking in English for Stelios' sake, her accented Greek voice deep and mellow. "Now we can at last get on with our lifes." She turned to the rock on her left. "Stelios, iff only you had not left me. Think where we could haf been now. Think what Cyprus could haf been had you lived. The island would be united. We could haf had children..." Her eyes clouded.

Then she said briskly, "But, my dear, I yam too old for that now. And anyway you are nott here. And I never wanted children with any off the others."

She opened the small plastic bag she had brought with her and, as she did every month when she visited the graves, she upturned it and sprinkled flower petals over the two rocks. This month it was oleander, so she was careful not to touch the petals.

Then she stood up. It was time to go. "It iss over," she said again. "At last we can all rest in peace. I love you, my darling. I will see you next month." She turned and walked away.

Two metres underneath the rock on the left, the bones of Stelios Grivas began to scream.

PART TWO

Ω

ASSIGNMENTS

Ω

Thursday August 7 1997

Athens, Greece

Christina arrived back at her offices just off Platio Omónias at 11:00 the next day, travelling straight from Eleftherios Venezelos airport. Her assistant, the slim, dark haired Australian Teresa Cotton, was already at work as were the three office staff. Telephones were ringing. Business was good at *Cascianis Properties*.

Teresa was used to the Director's monthly trips to Cyprus – she owned six properties on the island (and another twenty around the Mediterranean) – so it was only right that she should make regular visits to inspect them. A hands-on approach. Good business practice. She did not know the real reason.

"Anything?" smiled Christina as she sat down behind her desk.

"The boys are handling the rentals," Teresa reported. "Corfu and Crete are now fully booked for the high season."

"Good, so is Cyprus."

"On the purchase side, there are another two properties about to come up in Campania - "

"Really? This is good. I would like more property in Southern Italy."

"I've e-mailed the details to you."

"Good girl, thank you."

"And Alex called. He will be in Athens next week. He asks if you could call him." Teresa raised her eyebrows as Christina smiled. She asked, "You two getting serious?"

"Serious? Alex? No, he is just a friend."

"A *friend*...?"

"Well... a girl has needs you know."

"Are the rumours about him true?"

"Rumours? What rumours?"

"About his wealth. About his account at Bank Christina and the regular deposits he makes?"

Teresa screamed as a handful of paperclips came hurtling towards her.

"You coarse child!" scolded Christina. "Pick those up and get back to your work! Wretched girl! I will haf you deported."

Three minutes later, smiling quietly to herself at the thought of the sex she would be having with Alex – at 35, fifteen years her junior and with appetites to match his age – she opened *Outlook Express*.

There were eight e-mails in her private account. Two of them were spam and five were from friends.

It was the eighth one that made the smile fall from her face. It was untitled. The sender address said *david5758@templenet.com*.

She hovered her mouse arrow over the message. Did she really want to see this?

Her right index finger moved and the message appeared on the screen. Just three words.

CONFESS YOUR SINS.

Ω

Saturday August 9 1997

Santuario del Carmine, Sorrento, Italy

"Bless me, Father, for I haf sinned. It hass been... many yearz since my last confession."

The inside of the wooden confessional in the south transept of the church of St Mary the Most Holy of the Carmine was musty, tainted with the breath – the sins – of the many penitents who over the years had sought absolution for their human frailties in this dark, claustrophobic upright tomb. The church was over 400 years old – and that was a lot of sins.

Only faint spears of light entered from the priest's side, through the grill that kept identities hidden, the sinner known only to God.

Christina could smell the priest's breath as he spoke. "And what have you to confess, my daughter?"

"Haf you got all day?" thought Christina. But out loud she gave the prearranged reply. "My search for justice hass made me many enemies."

"Vengeance is mine; I will repay, saith the Lord."

Christina waited on her knees in the darkness of the confessional. Outside she could hear the hardly subdued voices of the mostly English and German tourists wandering around the church, admiring the Neapolitan baroque-style architecture and the huge tapestries on the walls. Even though she was kneeling on a small hassock, her knees were beginning to hurt.

"It was not him," said the priest softly, speaking in English with the sibilant hiss of his real race.

"What wass not him?" asked Christina, puzzled.

"The death, in Paris - "

Christina stiffened.

" – The body. It was not him."

After a moment she said, "How do you know?"

"We have suspected the trick for some time," explained the priest. "But until now we have not been able to prove it. We obtained a hair sample from the body before it was... disposed of. The DNA does not match the blood he left behind in Amsterdam."

"But hiss fingerprints - "

"Can be forged. False prints can be worn or grafted. Or base records can even be changed. You know what the west's idiotic police and security forces are like. But the Amsterdam DNA we have kept to ourselves all these years. And it does not match up. The man held in prison in France was not him. It never was him."

Christina was perplexed. "But I wass there when he was picked up in Khartoum."

"Yes."

"And I was there to see him off the plane in Paris."

"But you were not on the plane."

"*What?*"

"We think that was where the switch was made."

"But how could that possibly have been done?"

"Collusion."

"But he wass cuffed and manacled, surrounded by French agents - " Christina stopped as realisation hit home. The face on the other side of the grill said nothing. "So," she said slowly, "the French let him go...?"

"Yes."

"But why?"

"Who knows? This is the French we're talking about."

"My God." Softly.

"It has been done many times before. Churchill, Stalin, Roosevelt, Makarios – even today, Saddam Hussein. They were all known to use doubles. An effective ploy. The public sees what it wants to see, it believes what it wants to believe. If it is told that Roosevelt met with Churchill in the Hamptons, if it is shown a photograph that purports to be Roosevelt and Churchill meeting in the Hamptons, then Roosevelt and Churchill have met in the Hamptons. Carlos is arrested and taken on a plane, therefore it must be Carlos that is taken off that plane."

"I know how it works." There was a hard edge to Christina's voice. "But why are you telling me this? I haf not had contact with Tel Aviv for two yearz. Ramirov iss not likely to come after me."

"No, he is not one for vengeance. He would not consider you worthy. I am telling you this because you were instrumental in his capture. Or rather in his non-capture. You failed. And we, my dear, *are* ones for vengeance. As of this moment, Agent Cascianis, you are back on active duty."

"But I am fifty yearz old!"

The priest ignored her protest. "As before, our worldwide network will be at your disposal. You were recruited twenty years ago with one ultimate goal. You have not achieved that goal. You have not given us a return on the investment we made in you. As Jews, we do not like that.

"Achieve your goal, Cascianis. Find him. And this time end it once and for all."

Circolo dei Forestieri, Sorrento, Italy

Christina sat alone at a table on the wide terrace of the *Circolo dei Forestieri*, looking out over Sorrento's Marina Piccolo below. Her eyes travelled across the blue water of the Mediterranean to the huge, imposing bulk of Mount Vesuvius on the other side of the Bay of Naples.

It was the height of the holiday season, and very soon the Foreigners' Club – the restaurant, café, bar, nightclub, and tourist information centre that had been one of the main hubs of Sorrento's holiday industry for over 40 years – would be filling with lunchtime diners.

But at 10:30 she had the place almost to herself. There were a few early clients for cappuccino (maybe with a slice of delicious lemon cake), and over on the other side of the terrace a group of about a dozen newly-arrived vacationers sat in rapt awe of a holiday company rep giving her introductory spiel (and hoping to sell some lucrative local tours) for probably the fiftieth time that season.

The sun was high in the sky behind her – soon for the three hours of midday it would be impossible to sit out in. Even now the heat was increasing minute by minute, and although she wore just a sleeveless low-cut blue and white cotton dress, she had made a point of sitting at a table with a sun parasol.

She was waiting for the next contact. The 'priest' had told her where to go on leaving the church, and he had said she would be contacted almost immediately.

Her espresso was delivered. The waiter, wearing the name 'Tony', put her *conto* underneath the small wooden block on the table. A small, wrapped piece of dark chocolate sat against the cup on the saucer, and Christina took it out of the foil packaging and popped it in her mouth.

"Christina?"

She looked up. The woman was around fifty, shoulder-length red wavy hair falling from under a wide straw hat, large sunglasses covering her freckled face. She wore a loose red and green open flowered blouse with the top of a dark green one piece swimsuit showing underneath. A loose elastic-waisted red skirt fell to her calves, stopping above cream espadrilles. A straw bag was over her shoulder.

Christina took it all in, especially the friendly face, and then said "My search for justice hass made me many enemies."

The woman smiled. "Vengeance is mine; I will repay, saith the Lord." She sat down. "Hi, I'm Melanie." Her accent was straight English.

Christina nodded. "Excuse me iff I seem confused. This iss all a bit of a shock."

"I understand. It must be. It was for me, too."

Christina looked surprised. "You know him? Martinez? Sorry, I still use that name. *Ramirov?*"

"Oh yes, I know him." Melanie thought back over the years and of what she had done for Israel. "I thought you'd captured him. Then, like you, I thought he was dead."

"But how – " Christina stopped as the waiter came up behind them. She asked, "Melanie, can I get you something?"

"Er – cappuccino, please."

The waiter nodded, wrote on his small pad, and departed.

"But how the hell am I supposed to - " Christina made bunny ears with the index and middle fingers of both hands "'find him'? He could be anywhere in the world. It iss not like he just escaped from jail five days ago, he hass been out there all this time, all these yearz. It iss impossible."

"Do you not want to be the one who finally finishes him?"

"Until an hour ago I thought I was."

"And now?"

"Now?" Christina sighed. "That bastard ruined my life. I should have shot him when I could, instead of handing him over to the French." She looked across the bay at the sleeping giant of the volcano. "He should be dead. And yess, I would like it to be me that does it." She turned back. "But we have to be realistic here. I am fifty yearz old. I am not the young girl I wass."

"Neither am I," Melanie smiled.

"I would not know where to start."

The cappuccino was delivered and a second *conto* was slipped beneath the wooden block.

"Things are different nowadays," explained Melanie as she undid the packet of sugar and emptied it onto the froth. "Technology is advancing at an astonishing rate. Previously we had to use people on the ground. Tails, phone taps, you name it. Remember we found Ramirov for your Stelios before?"

"You were involved in that?"

"I had... some input, yes. Well all that with people on the ground is old hat. Nowadays you can trace anyone – and I mean *anyone*, even if they do not want to be traced. It is still not easy, but it is much more sophisticated."

"What do we need?"

"A computer."

"A computer?"

"And the technology which only we have. Even the mighty US is way behind us." Melanie reached out and took Christina's hand. "You want to find Ilich Ramirov?"

"Oh, *yes*."

"And this time finish it once and for all?"

Christina nodded, biting her lower lip.

"Then we shall do it," said Melanie with firm conviction. "We might be older but we are still trained operatives. And now we have the resource."

"But why us?"

"Tel Aviv trusts us. And they are Jews. They believe in an eye for an eye. They believe in the right of revenge. The right for you to avenge our agent Digenis – your Stelios Grivas."

Christina's eyes filled. Then she waved over the waiter.

"*Signora?*" asked Tony.

"You don't," asked Christina, "happen to haf a cigar, do you?"

"*Prego, signora.* What kind?"

"Something long, thick and utterly disgusting should suit me just fine," she said.

Ω

Sunday August 10 1997

Capodichino Airport, Naples, Italy

At 10:00 that morning Melanie and Christina met up as planned in the food court upstairs in the departure area of the airport.

The two women had gone their separate ways after their meeting at the Foreigners' Club yesterday: Melanie back to her hotel (the *President*, high up on the cliffs) via a brief spot of pre-arranged confession in the *Santuario del Carmine*, and Christina back to the *immobiliare* on the Corsa Italia to finalise a property purchase (she still had a business to run).

Christina spent the night at the *La Solara* hotel out on Via Capo (enjoying the legendary hospitality of owner Ugo di Maio and his staff), and in the morning her pre-ordered taxi collected her at 08:30 for the ninety minute journey to Napoli.

At 11:00 the women boarded the Alitalia plane for the 30 minute flight to Rome.

Fiumicino, Rome, Italy

Being an internal flight, there were no formalities at Leonardo da Vinci Airport, and the two women were in the unmarked, untraceable embassy Fiat Cinquento twenty minutes after landing.

"Can we talk detail now?" asked Christina as they moved out into the traffic on the A12.

"Sure," said Melanie. "No one to overhear us now. And the car is clean."

"So, we use a computer?"

"Yep."

"And this computer can track down anybody in the world?"

"Give or take. With the right knowledge. *Hey! Up your Mama!*" She gave the finger to a grinning, unhelmeted youth on a Vespa.

"And what knowledge would that be?"

"You'll see."

"This must be one hell of a computer. Must be huge. Where is it? Underneath the Coliseum? Beneath St Peter's Square?"

"No, it's in my apartment. It's my laptop."

Via Catalana, Rome, Italy

Melanie's apartment was in an old block dating back to before Il Duce. While Christina showered, Melanie made up a spare camp bed in the *soggiorno*. When Christina came out of the bathroom, wearing just a towel, a pair of fresh cotton day jammies (white T shirt and blue gingham shorts) were awaiting her. Then it was Melanie's turn to shower and change, into red day jammies.

While coffee brewed in the small, basic kitchen, Melanie removed her *Compaq* from a shelf and took it over to her coffee table.

"Don't know why they call these things laptops – that's the one place you can't put them. More than five minutes and they burn your bloody legs off!" She plugged the machine into the mains for constant power, and connected another wire into the back.

Christina's eyes traced the second wire to another socket in the wall. To the casual eye this looked just like a telephone internet connection – except Melanie's phone was plugged in on the other side of the room. This connection was stand alone and dedicated. Melanie saw her looking. "Ever heard of Broadband?" she asked.

Christina shook her head.

"Not many people have. But you will." Melanie left the computer to warm up and went back to the kitchen.

Christina looked at the thirty-eight centimetre screen coming slowly to life. She wondered how the hell this little machine was going to help them locate one person in the world. She said as much to Melanie when she returned with two cups of coffee and an opened packet of Grisbi crème biscuits.

"Barking Dog," the Englishwoman replied.

"Excuse me?"

"We have had it for a while now." A Grisbi crumb stuck to Melanie's chin, but she did not seem to notice. "It's more than a program. I suppose you could call it a *development*. Nobody else has it to the extent that we do. It gives us the technological edge – and therefore the information edge – over all our enemies."

"I can't imagine Saddam and Assad having huge IT resources." Christina reached over and brushed the crumb from her colleague's face.

"Thanks," said the Englishwoman. "You would be surprised. Even Arafat in his poor little bombed-out compound has technological resources that would amaze you. But I said *all* our enemies."

"All?"

"This is far in advance of anything even the Americans, Russians or Chinese have."

Christina raised her eyebrows, trying to conceal her doubt. "So how does it work?"

"Why have a dog and bark yourself?" smiled Melanie.

"Sorry?"

"Barking Dog. Why should we gather and store information when others will do it for us?" Melanie saw the confusion on the Greek woman's face and she rubbed her arm. "We have developed an instant universal hacker. Our little baby gives us access to *any* computer, any network, any server, any hardware, any software, *anywhere*. Even in space. We don't need user IDs, passwords, code words or whatever. Barking Dog has already done that for us and has by-passed all security, firewalls, defences, you name it. And afterwards the host has no idea we have even been there. Barking Dog leaves no trace. Like a thief in the night." She laughed. "I sound like a saleswoman, don't I?"

"But if this effer got into the wrong hands...?"

"It would not work. It would be useless. 'Hands' is right." Melanie held up the first two fingers of her right hand. "Ever heard of biometric access?"

"Er, no."

Melanie put her two fingers on what looked like a second mousepad on the computer. Slowly she ran them across the pad twice.

The screen flickered and began to metamorphose.

"Welcome to Barking Dog," said Melanie. "You now have access to every computer in the world." She turned to the Greek woman. "So, where shall we start looking? More coffee, hun? This will take some time."

Ω

Monday August 11 1997

Rue Le Regrattier, Île St Louis, Paris, France

"You are not Susanne."

The old man with the hideously scarred scalp and face manoeuvred his wheelchair back from the front door of the apartment so that the nurse could enter.

"*Susanne est en vacances,*" explained the woman as she came in. "She told you last week she was going away, don't you remember?" She spoke with the slightly condescending attitude of nurse to patient, but with just a hint of the coquette.

"Did she? I am sure you are right."

The old man wheeled himself into the salon and then turned to face the nurse. Even in his eighties, he could appreciate a pretty woman. And this one was indeed *belle.* She wore no make-up (which he found attractive), and the figure underneath the plain white button-through nurse's dress looked perfect – at least to an old man like him. He detested the skinny-Minnie look of the young women nowadays. Real women should have curves – and this one had them. She was not big, but the curves were in all the right places. He glanced down at her legs; they were clad in black hose. He might have imagined it, but did he have a long forgotten feeling in a long forgotten part of his anatomy?

"And you are?" he asked.

"My name is Florence," she smiled as she set down her case. In front of her she saw a man dressed casually but elegantly in fawn *pantalon* with a matching jacket over a white shirt, a front of respectability and culture, maintained despite the disability. A lightly patterned dark brown cravat around his neck harked back to another time – his time, which was long ago now.

His scarred and crimson head looked raw even after all these years, and there were about three strands of hair brushed over the top of it. The scarring continued over his forehead and down the right side of his face.

"*Et ma belle Florence,* you have come to give me my bed bath, no?" The watery old eyes twinkled.

"I don't think that is in the contract," she scolded. "How are we this week?"

"*We?* Well, I don't know about you but I still live. I suppose that makes *ça va*."

"Do you want me to take you for your walk?"

"Time was, if a beautiful young lady like yourself was alone with me in my apartment, going for a walk would be the last thing on our minds."

"Time is, not was, m'sieur. Come, where do you keep your blanket? An hour in the fresh air will do you good."

Le Jardin des Tuileries, Paris, France

Although it was a fine Parisian Monday and the sun shone, he was still dressed in jacket, shirt and cravat and now had the blanket over his legs, suffering from the permanent chill of age. A wide-brimmed hat covered his face from the casual passer-by.

She had wheeled him for twenty minutes, much to his annoyance. When she was behind him he could not admire her shapely body. She was just a disembodied voice, talking in the condescending *'nous'* format. "Are we too warm in that jacket? How are we feeling now we're out?"

Finally she parked the wheelchair alongside a seat in the Tuileries Gardens, facing the eastern pond. She sat down next to him. She smiled. "There now. Let us spend a little time here and then we will go back."

"Susanne usually reads to me," he said. "My eyes, they are not very good with words nowadays."

"Well, Susanne will be back next week. I have nothing to read to you. How about if we just talk?"

He sighed, "Yes, let us talk then *ma belle.*" His hand reached out and patted her knee. She made no move to remove it. "Tell me about yourself," he said.

"Me? Oh, I'm not that interesting. I will tell you about myself later. Maybe when we get back to your apartment you can get to know me better."

His heartbeat quickened. Had he heard her correctly?

"Tell me about *you,*" she said. "Do you mind talking about it?"

"About what?"

She motioned with her hand to her own face. "Your accident."

"Accident! Pah!" The old man raised his croaky voice. "This was deliberate. Eighteen years ago. They tried to kill us all. But I survived. They thought they'd burned us all to death, but I was saved. Trapped under the beam." He sniffed ruefully. "The same beam that broke my back also saved my life!"

He stopped talking as a group of Japanese tourists passed by. His hand was still on her knee, and now she covered it with her cardigan. Was it his imagination or did she jog his hand higher?

"We only have the medical background at the agency," she explained. "No history of the cause of the trauma. But Susanne mentioned you were a policeman?"

"I was a Commissaire. I had my own section, the BCP – *Bureau de la Co-opération Politique*. I set it up." His grip on her thigh relaxed as he reminisced. "It is still going strong today…"

"And this happened to you because of case you were working on?"

The old man said nothing. His chin shook gently and drool rolled slowly from the corner of his burnt mouth. The nurse reached across and wiped it with a tissue. Liquid filled his already watery eyes.

Then he said resolutely, "*Oui et non*. I do not wish to discuss it further."

She was quiet, looking at the children sailing their boats on the pond. She turned to him. "Do you want to go home?"

"*S'il te plait.*"

She re-tucked in the blanket. Instead of taking the wheelchair brake off with her foot, she leant forward to do it manually. As she bent down her face was only centimetres from his. "Now *you* can get to know *me*," she said.

Rue Le Regrattier, Île St Louis, Paris, France

When they re-entered the apartment a red light was flashing on the old man's telephone, but they both ignored it. She helped him remove his hat and jacket and then offered to make them coffee, but the old man refused. "Let us have a cognac, there is a bottle over there."

She went over to the wooden drinks cabinet and retrieved a bottle of *Otard*. He admired her rump as she leant forward. "So tell me about yourself," he said to her bottom. "You said I could get to know you better."

She turned back, smiling. "*D'accord*. It is only fair. But first you tell me just one last thing, Colonel."

The smile dropped from his face. Nobody had addressed him like that in eighteen years.

"How did you know - ?"

"I know a lot of things, Colonel." She was standing in front of him, legs apart. She had undone the bottom two buttons on her dress. The bottle of *Otard* was in her hand. "You are Commissaire Charles Fleury-Goujon. You were also Colonel and Commander-in-Chief of the OAS. My father died for you."

"Y- your father?" Fear mingled with lust as he stared at her left thigh.

"They were all working for you. Trying to find the secret. And they all died."

Instantly he was transported back eighteen years. Slowly, he said "It – it was not my fault. It was Richer. And that meddling fool Gerard. We were so close to getting the secret."

"What is the secret, Colonel?"

"What?"

"The secret. What is it?" She straddled his useless legs and sat down on his knees, the dress riding up her thighs. The brakes were on and the wheelchair remained stable.

He looked between her legs. Although she wore the black pantyhose, he could see she wore no other underwear.

"The secret?" He was drooling again. "How should I know? Richer would not tell me. He said it was for my own good that I did not know."

"But you were attacked."

"Afterwards. The British were mopping up, they obliterated the OAS High Command - just in case we knew."

"Just in case?" She took the cork out of the bottle. "That must be some secret. For the British to kill you all *just in case* you might know."

His right hand shook as he gently touched her inner thigh. It had been such a long time since he had touched a woman. He said softly, "We never knew - " Then he stopped. He took his eyes from her sex, squashed inside her tights, and looked at her face.

"Your father...?" he said thoughtfully. Then his head jumped backwards. "Oh my God. You look like him. *Him?* I didn't think - "

"What you think does not matter, Colonel. It is what you *know* that matters. What is the secret everyone must die for?"

"I don't know."

"What can be so terrible?"

"*Je ne sais pas.* If I did, do you think I would be a lonely old man living here?"

"The Brits would not have killed you all otherwise."

"They did not kill *me*."

"As good as. They certainly kept you quiet. You know the secret and you will not tell me." She noticed his eyes go back down to between her legs. "You want this, don't you?" She moved her hips back and forth against his useless legs. "Would you like to try?"

"A – a man of my age can only reminisce. And dream."

"What is the secret? Tell me and you can touch me. Would you like to kiss me there? To taste me? You know you want to. I will let you. Just tell me. What is the secret?"

There was deep regret in the watery eyes. "Not even for your delights, *ma belle.*"

Abruptly she stopped moving. "Do not *'ma belle'* me, Colonel."

"What do you want me to call you?" he sneered. "*Ma poule?*"

"Call me Mesrine."

He took a deep breath. "Mesrine," he said the name to himself.

"So, you won't tell me," she said pleasantly as she stood up, and Charles Fleury-Goujon looked at a woman's sex for the very last time.

"No." Gruffly, defiantly.

"Well, it does not matter. You have had eighteen years more life than my father, so we can at least rectify that."

"What do you mean, you little whore - " He lashed out with his arm, but she had stepped out of reach and had moved behind him.

Then his raw scalp began to rage as he felt her pour the cognac over his head.

"What - what are you doing?" He shouted, hands grasping for the wheelchair brake lever.

From her bag she produced a lighter and a bandage.

Fleury shook his head as the alcohol stung his eyes. He released the brakes and tried to turn towards her.

Calmly she lit the bandage.

"For my father," she said, and dropped the bandage onto his head.

She did not stop to see Charles Fleury-Goujon engulfed by flames for the second time in his life. As his screaming got louder and louder and she began to smell meat cooking, she calmly picked up her bag and left the apartment, closing the front door after her.

The Colonel was just a screaming fireball in the centre of the room. He pushed himself up off the wheelchair, but his useless legs crumbled beneath him.

The screaming stopped as the fireball settled on the floor, a living cremation.

And then the fireball began to move. Slowly, it rolled across the room. Could a whimpering be heard? It stopped by the table near the door. Bit by bit the fireball raised itself up. A human hand stretched upwards and outwards from it. It grabbed the telephone and brought it crashing down onto the floor.

Trembling, blistering, the fingers keyed a seven digit number. From the fireball came an inhuman sound. "Me- Me- Mer. Me- Me- Me-. Mesrine! Mesrine! Mesrine - "

Then the sound stopped.

The hand poking from the fireball twitched once violently and was still, succumbing to the flames.

The final twitch of the hand knocked against the telephone, which began to play the message on the ansaphone. A message which fell on dead ears.

"Allo? Allo, Monsieur Fleury-Goujon? This is the Saint Marie Nursing Agency. I am sorry but Susanne will not be with you today. She has not called into the office. I don't know what can be wrong with her. Regretfully we have no other nurses available at such short notice, but if you would care to call us we can arrange for somebody to visit you tomorrow. *Merci bien, monsieur, bonjour."*

Rue des Saussaies, Paris, France

Chief Inspector Pierre Jamo was alone in the Inspectors' Office of the BCP suite at 11 Rue des Saussaies when the telephone rang. He was halfway through reading a report about a Brazilian diplomat with transsexual proclivities, so he reached for the receiver absentmindedly.

"Jamo."

At first it just sounded like interference on the line, a crackling sound. Then he heard, "Me- Me- Mer. Me- Me- Me-. Mesrine! Mesrine! Mesrine - " It stopped suddenly and was followed by a gurgling sound. It was a human voice, definitely. But the gurgling following the words was inhuman. Then that too stopped abruptly. Then the call was disconnected.

The black haired, fortyish policeman frowned at the phone in his hand. What the hell was that?

Since the débâcle many years ago which had led to internal treachery and the consequent deaths of both the Chief Inspectors of the BCP, all incoming calls were recorded. Although nowadays there was only one Chief Inspector in the unit (*lui-même*), because of the diplomatically sensitive nature of the BCP's work, the tradition of recording incoming calls had been maintained. It was a fact known only to the Chief Inspector and his Commissaire – therefore giving the additional bonus of it being a management check on the staff.

What the staff did know was that all calls inwards on the unit's direct lines were automatically caller identified. Jamo picked his telephone back up and keyed the General Office.

The veteran Sergeant Maurice Goise answered.

"Maurice," said Jamo. "The last call to my line, a minute ago. Do we have a number?"

"I will look for you, Chief Inspector…" Goise was back within thirty seconds. "I have it here."

"Alors, try it for me will you? And get me a name and address."

"D'accord, Chief Inspector."

Jamo pressed the cradle on his telephone and then let it pop up again. He keyed the four digit security number known only to him and the Commissaire.

An automated, computerised female voice, deep and authoritative, said "Please enter your personal identification number."

Jamo pressed six figures.

"Please enter the extension number required."

He keyed his own four digit number.

"Please enter the number of hours required, maximum forty-eight."

He keyed 1.

There was the merest pause, and then the voice said in a more disjointed fashion. "There have been – *three* - calls on this number in the last – *one* - hours. Press five to hear the first call. Press three to listen to the next call."

Jamo pressed 5 and heard the beginning of a call he had received from the Vietnamese Embassy fifty minutes ago. He pressed 3. The next call was from a picture framers up on Boulevard Haussmann (he had left a Robert Heindel print to be reframed a couple of days ago). He pressed 3 again.

The voice said, "Call received at - *fifteen forty-three* - hours, - *Monday August Eleven.*" A pause. Then came the crackling sound. Then, "Me- Me- Mer. Me- Me- Me-. Mesrine! Mesrine! Mesrine - " Then the gurgling.

Jamo pressed the back arrow on the handset and listened to the message again. Then again. And again.

The voice was high. Was it male or female? It sounded old or distressed, or maybe both. Probably male then. "Me- Me– Mer." It could have been the personal pronoun, but it was more likely to be the preliminary attempts to utter the word that followed. "Mesrine! Mesrine! Mesrine - "

There was no mistaking it. *Mesrine*. The surname of the most notorious criminal France had ever produced. *Jacques Mesrine*. The man who, eighteen years previously, had been working on an assignment for Chief Inspector Paul Richer of the BCP, even as the combined mights of all the Police forces of France were hunting him. It was a mission that had ended up with both Paul Richer and his colleague Claude Gerard dead, and Mesrine executed publicly by Bouvier and his crew.

Despite internal enquiries, it had never been discovered what exactly Mesrine was doing for the BCP. There were rumours it was something to do with the British, but there was no conclusive evidence. All the protagonists had died in November 1979. The BCP Commissaire at the time, Charles Fleury-Goujon, knew only that Richer was engaged in recovering some jewellery stolen from the American woman, the so-called Duchess of Windsor. Richer had been working to his own agenda. And then, ironically, three days after the deaths of Richer and Mesrine and two days after the death of Claude Gerard, Fleury-Goujon had been paralysed and severely burnt in a fire at a Masonic lodge meeting up in Belleville.

They must have been crazy times…

The ringing of the telephone snapped Jamo out of his reveries.

"*Oui?*"

"Goise, sir. I tried the number but I cannot get a connection. It might have gone out of service or something. But I have the name and address for you. The call came from a telephone situated at 15 Rue Le Regrattier in the 4th, on the Île St Louis. The subscriber – wait for it – is our old friend and Commissaire, Charles Fleury-Goujon."

Jamo was quiet.

"Sir?" said Sergeant Goise. "Chief Inspector?"

"Mm? Yes, thank you, yes."

"Quite something after all these years, old Charlie Boy ringing. I wonder what he wanted? Did he leave a message on your Voicemail?"

"Yes, er, oh it was nothing important. Silly bugger didn't leave his name, that's why I asked you to check. I think the old boy was just getting nostalgic."

"I remember him well," reminisced Goise. "Shame, what happened to him. He was the first and the best of our bosses. Not like that career minded bitch we have now."

Jamo thought of the recently-appointed Commissaire Gillian Colet, 'The only woman who can travel further on her back than standing up' as she was known around Saussaies. But he decided to say nothing. He humphed and put the phone down.

From his top drawer he withdrew his new-fangled mobile telephone. He extended the aerial, managed to get into his ten number phone memory at the third attempt, located the person he wanted and pressed the green 'Call' key.

After ten seconds the person at the other end answered. As always on these things, it was a bad reception.

"Inspector Ibrahim," Jamo raised his voice. "I want you to get down to the Île St Louis. Rue Le Regrattier. Number fifteen. I will meet you there." Jamo looked out of the office window at the top of the Palais d'Elysée two blocks beyond. Still on the telephone he said, more lowly "I think history may be calling us."

Rue Le Regrattier, Île St Louis, Paris, France

The street was quiet. Although the summer sun gave a warm evening ambience, its rays touched only the upper parts of the old buildings on the west side of the rue at this time of day and did not reflect downwards to street level.

Pierre Jamo sat in his dirty white Fiat Uno and surveyed number 15.

There were no ambulances about, no bystanders, no gawpers, no commotion to indicate anything had happened here today. It was just a quiet street on the elegant Île St Louis.

He climbed out of his car and smoothed his short, cropped black hair. His grey suit jacket (which had seen better days even when better days had seen better days) hung open above his white, open necked shirt. His shoulder-holster and gun could be seen clearly.

He looked up as he heard a noise from down the road. A Ducati M900 motorbike turned in from the Quai de Bourbon and roared the wrong way down this one-way street. It stopped with a squeal of brakes, double-parking next to his Fiat.

Jamo raised his eyebrows as the person in biking leathers, boots and red crash helmet climbed off the bike.

"Nice of you to turn up," said Jamo with Gallic dryness.

The rider removed the helmet and ruffled the short brown hair beneath.

"Hello Chief. What's the panic? Where's the fire?" quipped Inspector Claudette Ibrahim.

The front door to the building was unlocked and the concierge was out. There was a distinct smell of someone's dinner permeating the entrance hall.

There were two apartments on the *rez de chaussée*, and the one they wanted was obvious by the added ramp leading up to the front door.

"I had a phone call an hour ago," Jamo explained. "Traced it here."

"You had a phone call and you needed to trace it?" queried Claudette, rubbing her short hair again to let it breathe after its session under the helmet.

"A strange phone call. Didn't leave his name. You know who lives here?"

"*Mais non*, of course not."

Jamo knocked on the door. "Have you heard of one of our old Commissaires, Fleury-Goujon?"

Claudette frowned. "Name rings a bell."

"You were probably still at school - "

She smiled.

" – or at least at the Academy." Jamo knocked again. "The first Commissaire of the BCP. Commissaire!" he called. "*Sûreté!* Bay-Say-Pay!"

"*Ah mais oui!*" Claudette unbuttoned her leather jacket. Her shoulder holster was visible above her black T shirt. "Wasn't he the one who was done in that fire?"

"That's him." This time Jamo used his fist on the door instead of his knuckles. "Commissaire!" He turned to Claudette. "Try the other apartment, will you?"

Claudette went over and knocked smartly on the identical door on the other side of the hallway. She looked back at Jamo. "Also he was in charge when those Chief Inspectors were killed."

"The Mesrine affair," nodded Jamo.

"Oui. La Conclusion." She knocked again. Nothing. "It seems everyone's out on a Monday evening."

"Well, someone around here is cooking - " Jamo stopped. He turned back to the door. *Oh my God.* "We need to get in." He pushed against the door. *"Now!"* He stepped back two paces and rammed his shoulder against the wood.

"Get out of the way." Claudette pushed his chest with her hand. "Mind." Her booted right foot slammed into the door, and it flew open with a splinter of wood.

The smell of cooking tumbled out to meet them.

"Commissaire!" called Jamo as they both entered with their Glock 17 handguns drawn. They stood either side of the salon door to the left. Jamo reached out, looked at his partner, turned the handle and pushed the door open.

Claudette crouched down, gun in both hands pointing in front of her, peering into the room The smell was now overwhelming. Then she said "Oh fuck," and stood up. Jamo looked over her shoulder.

On the burnt carpet near the door lay what could have been a discarded, barbecued pig, well done and crackling. The mouth was open as if it had been spit-roasted, but there was no apple in it. The flesh was so dark, it could have been honey-basted. But at the lower end of the object was the evidence that this was not an indoor feast.

Lying where the flames had not reached were the bottom of two human legs, encased in *pantalon, chaussettes* and brown formal men's shoes.

"In the name of Mary," said Pierre Jamo. He pulled a packet of *Gauloises* from his pocket and then, noting Claudette's look of disapproval, put them away again. Perhaps this was not the right place and time to light up.

"Is this him?" she asked.

"How the fuck should I know?" he replied. "He doesn't quite match his 'Class of 79' picture in the year book any more."

"What's going on, Chief?"

Jamo noticed the telephone on the floor near the body.

"I think," he said. "We may have a problem."

Montparnasse, Paris, France

"So you are leaving it all to the *Police Judiciaire*," said Inspector Claudette Ibrahim in a slightly mocking tone.

"What else can I do?" reasoned Chief Inspector Pierre Jamo. "It is a murder. It is their territory. We are the BCP. The *Bureau de la Co-opération Politique*. Unless the murder has a diplomatic involvement, it is not ours to investigate."

"But he was our ex-Chief, isn't that enough?"

"He hasn't been our Chief for eighteen years. He was just a retired old man, a civilian."

She sighed. "I know you are right. The poor bastard. Burnt to death twice! What about this Mesrine thing?"

"I don't know. What I do know is that Mesrine has been lying in his grave next to his father up in Clichy for eighteen years too. If he was going to come back and seek revenge, he would have done it long before now!"

"Perhaps it was just a dying thing."

"What was?"

"The Chief. You know, how some people when they're dying see a tunnel with a bright light at the end of it and people waiting for them. Perhaps the Chief saw Mesrine."

"Hardly a loved one!"

"Maybe it's different for us *flics*. Maybe we see all the people we've put away!" She chuckled. Then she said reflectively, "Or all the people we've killed."

"Well that's something you and I won't have to worry about for a long time. You got anything pressing in the morning?"

"Nothing pressing."

"*Bon.* Then you don't have to go home just yet."

"Not just yet."

She turned towards him on his bed and they began to kiss.

Ω

Tuesday August 12 1997

Clarence House, London, England

The matriarch of the British Royal Family was now ninety-seven years old. But despite her vast age, her mental faculties were all intact – there was not, and would never be, any hint of senility. Physically she was beginning to suffer the debilitation of old age (much more than the public realised), but her muscular and skeletal condition was still that of a person twenty years younger.

God, fate and history would decree that she had almost another five years to live, that she would live for over a full calendar century and see in the new millennium.

But she did not know that.

That day she thought she was dying.

Respiratory problems, palpitations and hypertension had given her a series of 'funny turns'. The last one at lunchtime that day was so bad that she had passed out. She had awoken in her bedroom with her consultant, a nurse, her junior secretary and Billy the butler standing around her bed.

As with all unconsciousness, the hearing was the last to go and the first to come back. So her return to the land of the living was not immediately accompanied by any physical movement or other outward signs, and the people around her bed did not know she had returned. Not that it would have mattered if they had, they were having a normal conversation about the patient's condition.

The actual conversation went as follows:

"What is Her Majesty's condition?" The secretary.

"Satisfactory. There is nothing to concern us," her consultant. "She is not dying yet! Such things must be expected. She is strong and will outlive us all! And don't be afraid to tell her I said so when she wakes up. I have given her a mild sedative."

What Her Majesty heard in her wakening state was:

"Her Majesty's condition?"

"There is concern. She is dying. Be strong. Don't tell her."

And that was why three hours later, when she was alone and fully conscious, she summoned Sir Kenneth Dean to her bedchamber.

Sir Kenneth Dean was a tall, elegant but exceptionally gaunt man, a product of pre-war Eton. The position of 'Senior Secretary' and the accompanying knighthood were created for him eleven years previously as a reward for services rendered to Her Majesty Queen Elizabeth the Queen Mother.

He had duties, of course, mostly the supervision of security surrounding HM. But he would have been the first to admit that the position was virtually a sinecure.

Now he attended Her Majesty, as requested. At four o'clock, "Just after tea."

She was sitting in her high-backed armchair in her bedroom, looking out over the inner garden.

"Ma'am? You asked for me." Sir Kenneth maintained the deference and respect due to the old lady, but he held none of the squirming obsequiousness of most of her lackeys.

She did not turn around or move her gaze from the window. "Sir Kenneth, I think we might have a problem again."

"Ma'am?"

"You have been good to me over the years. Loyal. You have not asked questions."

"It has never been my place, ma'am."

"But have you not ever wondered? All the killings in France in 1979? Then that troublesome woman in 1986? You carried out my instructions, yet not once did you ask the question why."

"I am your loyal subject, Your Majesty. I do as you bid. And besides…"

"Yes, Sir Kenneth?"

"I believe a secret should be a secret, Your Majesty."

"Quite." She went quiet. A bird in one of the trees seemed to be preoccupying her. She still did not look at him. Then she said, "I have been foolish, Sir Kenneth."

He came over and stood next to her chair. He also faced the garden. It was as if they were both having a conversation with the window.

"I should be the only one who knows the secret," continued the lady. "I should be taking it to my grave with me. But a few years ago, I was foolish. In a moment of weakness… I told someone. I told them something that no one but I should ever know. She has not mentioned it since, not in ten years. But now I am nearing the end of my life, I cannot take the chance that the secret will be known after I am gone. *That cannot be allowed to happen.* I deeply fear that there has to be one more death before mine. Do you think you will be able to take care of it for me again, Sir Kenneth? *Lord* Kenneth?" Now she looked up at him.

He did not look down at her. But he said, "As you command, Your

Majesty."

Highgrove, Gloucestershire, England

At the same time as Sir Kenneth Dean left the bedroom of the Queen Mother, and fifty kilometres to the north, His Royal Highness Prince Charles Philip Arthur George, Prince of Wales, Knight of the Garter, Knight of the Thistle, Knight Grand Cross of the Order of the Bath, Knight of the Order of Australia, Companion of the Queen's Service Order, Privy Counsellor, Aide-de-Camp, Earl of Chester, Duke of Cornwall, Duke of Rothesay, Earl of Carrick, Baron of Renfrew, Lord of the Isles, Prince Great Steward of Scotland and eldest son of Queen Elizabeth II, was contemplating two reflections.

One was his reflection in the window of his downstairs drawing room here in Highgrove House. He saw the future King of England, dressed casually by his standards in green corduroy trousers, hideous beige check shirt and – of course – a brown tie. He was shorter than people imagined, only 175 centimetres. Not as tall as his idol, beloved mentor and great-uncle Louis Mountbatten – but everything else about him was an impression of, a tribute to, the man he wished had been his real father, the man murdered by the Irish on August 27 1979. It was the imitation of the Mountbatten regalness, the demeanour, even the vague what-a-bore-it-is-to-make-my-muscles-move-to-talk way of speaking, that gave Charles his stature not his height.

The second reflection he was contemplating was not visual but mental. He had been separated from his hysterical, suicidal, unstable, whore of a wife for nearly five years now, and divorced for one. But she would just not go away. She had been stripped of her royal status and outcast by the court. If he had his way, she would be outcast from the country too – exiled, like Uncle David. But of course, exile was for royalty and she was no longer royal. And he could not deny her access to the boys, not in this day and age. Time was, a King could solve all his problems with just a word…

Things had gone from bad to worse since the divorce. He had never expected (but he had hoped) that Diana would retire somewhere with the pension he gave her, play the dutiful 'Mother of the Princes' and fade quietly out of the public gaze. But he had not expected what had happened. The full public exposure of her betrayal, the Bashir interview – the listing of her lovers, both marital and post-marital. Even a rugby player, in the name of God! Grandma always said one should confine one's affairs to one's own class. But these weren't affairs. It was just sex, deliberately cuckolding him over and over, again and again and again.

But now she had gone too far. She was fucking another *Muslim*, for

Christ's sake. The mother of the future King of England, the future Head of the Church of England, had her second consecutive Muslim lover. Diana had been with him since they had managed to persuade Khan that his health would be better served by ending his relationship with her. She had jumped from one to the next without pause, and Charles' 'People' had been watching them every step of the way.

Four weeks was a short time for one of her flings. But the more the Muslim got his feet under her bed (Charles sniffed in irony), the harder it would be to get rid of him. And the longer it went on, the more chance there was of Diana falling in love with him like she had with Khan and many of the others. She was fickle. She might even *make* herself fall in love with him, just to defy everybody...

Behind Charles stood the man who had been shown into the room fifteen minutes ago. The chunky, unshaven, rough-neck known as John Smith looked uncomfortable in the suit and tie he was wearing. It was not his real name, of course – but there were some things even the next King of England did not need to know. 'John Smith' would adequately suffice for the man who was the Head of 'Charles' People', the man who was the most ruthless, cold, callous and intelligent object the Special Boat Service had ever produced.

What he had to tell Charles had knocked the wind right out of the Prince's sails. Silly really, thought Charles, it was only the natural consequence of what had happened already – he should have expected it. But the spouse was always the last to know, whether he was King or pauper.

Emad 'Dodi' Fayed was going to ask Diana to marry him.

Well, that just could not be allowed to happen.

The princes could not have a stepfather – especially a playboy Muslim stepfather.

Had it been just that, it would not have been an insurmountable problem. Money would not have worked, not with the Fayeds. But other methods of persuasion had been effective on others in the past. He was sure Emad and his father were considerate of their health – especially if, say, an inherited peerage was offered to the father ('services to shopkeeping').

But it was not just the proposal of marriage. John Smith had imparted other news, gathered from phone taps and other listening devices on the Fayed boats and at their properties worldwide.

Charles turned from the window. "And there can be no mistake? No doubt?"

John Smith shrugged and spoke with his London accent. "There's always room for doubt, sir. Especially where – er – these things are concerned. But there is no doubt about the information as gathered. Done by our own fair hands."

"But this cannot be. It is just untenable. It cannot happen."

"I believe it already has, sir."

"Unbelievable," Charles said again. He looked confused. "She – she must have done it deliberately. There is no need for these things to happen, not in this day and age."

"She always was a wilful little girl," said the third person in the room, dragging on a cigarette. "A stupid child."

"But *pregnant?*" pleaded Charles. "And by a Muslim? It – it cannot be. Something must be done."

"Yes sir," said John Smith.

"The question is *what?*" Charles looked towards the third person for guidance.

She took another drag on her *Dunhill*. She looked at him through the smoke.

"What do royals always do?" asked Camilla.

Boulevard Exelmans, Paris, France

Ron Becker was stark naked when his girlfriend arrived home at 22:30. It was not directly intentional, but sometimes Serendipity smiled on mere mortals. He had just showered and was drying himself in the salon while watching English football highlights on the TV when he heard her key in the lock. By the time she had entered the salon, he was standing there facing the door, towel over his shoulders and outstretched, flashing his goods at her, an inane grin on his face.

Gisele Joudeh seemed less than impressed. She chose to ignore his exposed dick which, it has to be said, with its south facing inclination seemed to be ignoring her also.

"So this is what you get up to when I am on lates!" she frowned, her French perfect but with the hint of a Middle Eastern accent. "Watching football!" she smiled.

Becker let the towel fall and she came over and embraced him. "Hello Princess," he said warmly in English, his London accent just the acceptable side of cockney. "Didn't think I'd start without you, did you?"

"*Con,*" she said affectionately as she went into the kitchen.

Theirs was that sort of relationship, two strong but disparate personalities. He the short, stocky Cultural Affairs attaché at the British Embassy – where he had been stationed for the last twenty years. She the slender, classy PA to the Head of the Immigration Section at the Lebanese Embassy, six months into a two year tour of duty.

They had met at 'an embassy do' four months previously and had hit it off instantly, a fortysomething male and a thirtysomething female alone in Paris. She had moved in with him three weeks later, into his seen-better-days apartment in the Boulevard Exelmans in the nevertheless still desirable 16th Arrondisement. It was a move of convenience for both of them: he needed help with a recent savage rise in the rent, and she said she wanted somewhere with more comforts than the small garret in Malakoff. And the sex helped as well, of course.

They were a strange and unlikely couple – but often that is the best combination for a successful relationship. They were both fluent in several languages, but she steadfastly refused to speak to him in anything other than French, and he refused to speak to her in anything other than English. Naturally they both understood each other perfectly, but they got some strange looks in shops and restaurants.

Ron strolled into the kitchen as she prepared a snack of salami and that morning's bread. "Chelsea scored three times today," he held the fridge door open for her. "Do you think I will?"

"That is all you English think about!" she complained, but there was minx in her voice. "Football and sex! What is it with you barbarians? Anything to do with balls! Are you so base?" She removed some duck pâté from the fridge.

South facing Mister Willie (or Monsieur Guillaume) heard the conversation and began to take an interest.

"Straight and true, us Brits. At least you know where you stand with us."

"I know only too well where you stand – mind your *verge* in the door!" She closed the fridge. "*Imbécile!* Look at it! Pointing at me! That is disgusting. Still," she reflected, "if it is here it might as well make itself useful."

She scraped some of the smooth pâté onto her knife, grabbed him in her left hand, and spread the pâté over the helmet.

"Now," she said, satisfied. "That is much more pleasing to a hungry lady."

She was about to close her mouth over the end of his penis when the telephone rang.

"Ron Becker."

There was the smallest of pauses before a very familiar voice said, "Hello, Ron. It's been a while."

Becker's face dropped. "Mr Dean? I'm sorry, it's Sir Kenneth now, isn't it?"

"How are things over there in France?" asked the smooth, deep voice.

"As usual, sir. There's always some problem or - "

"Ron, I need your help again."

"You do?" He looked down at Gisele, who was continuing with her meal.

The pâté was cold.

"We do."

"I see. Do we need to meet?"

"This time that would be... inadvisable. You remember the gentleman who assisted us before?"

"Yes."

"It is a job for him. For the same reasons as before."

The damn secret that must be hidden at all costs. Becker did not let Sir Kenneth hear his sigh. "I understand."

"I will send details in tomorrow's pouch. As quickly as possible, Ron."

"O-okay, sir."

"Is everything all right, Ron? You sound distant."

"Well, considering I'm having pâté sucked off my knob by a French-speaking Lebanese diplomat, I'm not too bad at all," he said to himself. Out loud he said, "It's not the best connection, sir."

"I can leave it with you then."

"As always, sir."

Ω

Wednesday 13 August 1997

Faubourg St Honoré, Paris, France

The Diplomatic Pouch arrived at 16:00 that day, the same time as it did every day. It used to come by plane, nowadays it came on the 09:50 *Eurostar*.

In his office on the plush first floor of the British Embassy, Ron Becker received the plain manila A4 envelope at 16:23. His name was written on the front, nothing else.

The envelope felt very thin considering it contained instructions for a hit. Usually there were full biographical details, family history etc.

Neatly he ran a carved wooden paper knife across the sealed flap. Inside there was just one item, no covering note. It fell out, face down, onto Becker's desk. He pulled the flap of the envelope wide, upended it and shook it in case there was anything stuck inside. There wasn't.

Casually he turned the item over, wondering who the unlucky bastard was this time.

The shock made him stand up involuntarily. His chair fell backwards onto the thick light blue carpet with a muffled *whump* and he grabbed hold of the desk to stop himself falling.

He stared at the item on his desk. They had to be kidding, of course. He gave a little nervous laugh. Then he grabbed the envelope and looked at his name on the front to make certain he hadn't been given something that was meant for the Press Office. Then he shook the envelope again, but it was empty.

They must be joking.

It was a photograph of Diana, Princess of Wales.

Ω

Thursday August 14 1997

Sarasota, Florida, USA

Ilich Ramirov could not help but appreciate the irony of the situation.

Ilych Ramirez Sanchez – Carlos The Jackal – had always been fictional. A cover character invented when the world's press became aware that there was just one co-ordinating and unifying force behind the global terrorist atrocities in the nineteen-seventies. Ilich Ramirov was, and always had been, a Major in the *Komitet Gosudarstvennoi Bezopasnasti*, the KGB. Cast off by his Russian masters on the fall of the USSR, he became a freelance. For a while he lived in freedom in Venezuela, foraging into the northern hemisphere when his special talents were required. He had gained a certain perverse respectability and was employed as necessary by governments and royal households.

After his arrest in Sudan in 1994, the deal with the French had been simple: he would not go to jail. They would let him go or papers he had left in discrete safety deposit boxes around the world would be released. These papers gave an audit trail of proof of the French government's involvement in the SAC (*Société d'Action Civile*) and the Order of the Solar Temple, and in the 'disposals' of many 'enemies of the Republic' (including the Domenici and Markovic affairs) which still continue in France today. If he was to die in French custody, the papers would be released also.

So he had been switched on the plane taking him to Paris. His double – a brainwashed stoolpigeon who thought his family in Venezuela would live in luxury forever more (paid for by the French) – was substituted.

On arrival in Paris, Ramirov had simply stayed in the WC of the plane until party and prisoner had left and then, dressed as a cleaner, he had disappeared into the night.

The French got what they wanted: the capture of the most famous terrorist in the world. He got what he wanted: continued freedom. His activities were, of course, severely curtailed (he was supposed to be in prison, after all) but that suited him perfectly. He was less than happy with the way things were going in world terrorism – there seemed to be just one fundamentalist cause now, a cause his Russian Communist heart did not agree with (the tens of thousands of his fellow countrymen killed in

Afghanistan still rankled with him) – and his 'capture' gave the perfect excuse for the retirement of Ilych Ramirez Sanchez.

Ilich Ramirov Martinez, on the other hand could continue with his freelance activities. Right now, the irony was that if 'Carlos The Jackal' was dead, he could release the papers he had on the French and blow their cosy, selfish, murdering little Gallic world sky-high.

The French knew that, and in an official panic they had issued a statement that it was not Carlos The Jackal that had been found dead ten days ago, but his cell mate (a cell mate in solitary confinement!). Carlos lived, they said, and would face trial for his sins sometime in the future.

Yeh, right.

That morning, Ramirov shopped at Casa Italia on Constitution Boulevard as he did twice a week, exchanging pleasantries with proprietors Raj and Nita, and left with his wine (*Prunotto Barolo*) and imported *caciotta al tartuffo* (cheese with truffles) at 10:15.

At 10:55, after two more errands, he pulled into the driveway of his house on Sweetmeadow Circle, garaged the Ford Maverick and settled down with his coffee and that day's *Sarasota Herald Tribune* out on his lanai at 11:10. It was a hot Floridian summer's day, and he would not be able to spend too long outside.

He removed the cosmetic contact lens from his blind right eye and laid it on the table. He read better without it.

At 11:20 the fax machine in his downstairs office suddenly came to life with a whine.

Ramirov inclined his head and frowned. His normally accurate sixth sense had not given him any forewarning of this (although his scarred right shoulder had been aching more than usual recently). The only faxes he received were redirected on a circuitous route from the number in Venezuela via Tokyo, Mumbai, Vienna and Vancouver. Irritated, he neatly folded his paper, placed it on the poolside table and walked back into his house.

His irritation was soon assuaged.

The first thing to come out of the fax machine was a copy of a bank credit transfer advice confirming the transfer of five million US dollars into one of his thirty-one bank accounts (the one at the Bank Melli Iran in Dubai). He raised his eyebrows, and his mess of a blind eye began to water. His terms were a fifty per cent pre-payment, so someone was paying for something big.

He picked up the credit transfer advice to let the next item come out of the machine smoothly.

The machine seemed to tease him as the paper came out oh so slowly. The print head was on overtime. He saw the beginnings of a photograph. The top of someone's head began to appear. *Was that a tiara?*

And then he began to laugh. And laugh. And laugh. They had to be joking!

In the name of Christ and Allah, another one of them! He thought back to 1986 and shook his head. Did they want him to kill all the females of that stupid family?!

Ramirov did not know that halfway across the world, the fax that he was at that moment holding in his hand was about to make two other people laugh too. This time it was a laugh not of amusement, but of triumph.

Via Catalana, Rome, Italy

It had taken them five days.

Five days of cruising the world from the small apartment on the Via Catalana. Five days that had started off in awe, fascination and delight from Christina, but which soon turned to shock, horror and downright fear as the implications of Barking Dog had been brought home to her in graphic detail.

Every network, every website in the world was open to them. Every computer could be accessed *even if that computer was not turned on*. Providing it was plugged into an electrical source and was connected to a telephone line, it was theirs.

Just on a sample basis they had randomly accessed the computer of two schoolteachers in Riverside, California (they now knew everything about Charles and Tracy Slaughter, their two kids Charles Junior and Sara, their financial status, everything – even the fact that they were ardent Dodgers supporters); then they chose a Reserve Army Captain and his family in Canberra, Australia (Ben Digan had a weekend off from active service and was going to visit his granddad Bob); and a school for handicapped children in India (Asha Niketan in Bhopal run by Irish nuns, Sisters Christopher and Philomena).

The power at the Israelis' fingertips was endless – and the implications terrifying.

In their hunt for Ramirov, Melanie and Christina had started with the obvious: his name, and all conceivable versions of it. There were thousands of hits on 'Carlos The Jackal' and 'Ilych Ramirez Sanchez', but not one on 'Ramirov'.

They had then played what they thought was their trump card: Ramirov's DNA. But trump it did not. There was not one match in the world.

Then they had tried various forms of interrogation regarding people with one eye. There were over two million hits on the internet alone.

It was then that Melanie suggested they let The Professor make all the enquiries and collate all the information for them.

Who the hell? "The Professor?" queried Christina.

Melanie explained that it was another Mossad resource. A small country like Israel with limited universal intelligence resources needed all the technological assistance it could get. The Professor, a facility emanating from Tel Aviv, could do the work of two thousand human minds – at once.

Ramirov was just one thing. Whether it be terrorism for his original Soviet masters or his latter occupation as freelance advisor and assassin, he was, simply, a hired gun. The Professor would collate and analyse data concerning all international terrorist events and high profile deaths since... they put in 1974... to see if there were any links or trends.

The only snag was, The Professor would keep wanting answers to questions. It needed to be told directions to go in. Which meant that either Christina or Melanie would need to be at or near the computer at all times.

The women had taken it in turns, three hours on, three hours off.

For five days.

After three days, The Professor reported six events where 'someone had got away', either in fact or rumour:

1) THE ATTEMPTED KIDNAPPING OF THE BRITISH PRINCESS ANNE IN 1974 (RUMOUR).
2) THE MURDER OF LOUIS MOUNTBATTEN BY THE IRISH IN 1979 (FACT).
3) THE ASSASSINATION ATTEMPT ON POPE JOHN PAUL II IN 1981 (FACT).
4) THE DEATH OF PRINCESS GRACE OF MONACO IN 1982 (RUMOUR).
5) THE DEATH OF THE DUCHESS OF WINDSOR IN PARIS IN 1986 (RUMOUR).
6) THE BOMBING OF THE WORLD TRADE CENTRE IN NEW YORK IN 1993 (FACT).

The Professor asked for further refinement. The women went for the majority involvement in the list: the British.

The Professor accepted the further instruction – and went quiet for two days.

As Melanie prepared dinner that afternoon and Christina sat reading a thriller by the up-coming American writer Harlen Coben, the computer gave one small electronic beep. The Professor was reporting back.

"Mel!" Christina called. She was wary of touching the machine.

The red-haired Brit came in, wiping her hands on a tea towel. "What have we got?" She sat next to Christina on the couch and pressed two buttons on the laptop.

1) 1974. KIDNAP OF PRINCESS ANNE, LONDON. FAILED.
2) 1979. MURDER OF LOUIS MOUNTBATTEN, SLIGO, IRELAND. SUCCEEDED.
3) 1986. DEATH OF DUCHESS OF WINDSOR, PARIS. SUCCEEDED.

LINKS:
A) ALL MEMBERS OF BRITISH ROYAL FAMILY (QUERY ACCURACY 1986);
B) EVENTS CARRIED NO KNOWN ADVANTAGE FOR ANY GROUP (QUERY 1979);
C) ALL SINGULAR PERSONS;
D) POSSIBLE STOOL PIGEONS ARRESTED FOR 1974 AND 1979. 1986 CONSIDERED NATURAL BUT MANY WEBSITES QUERY THIS;
E) PERPETRATORS KNOWN TO HAVE BEEN CONTACTED BY FAX.

UNUSUAL FAXES:
1) NSA RECORDS SHOW ONE FAX SENT FROM BRITISH EMBASSY DUBLIN TO NUMBER IN VENEZUELA TWO WEEKS BEFORE 1979 EVENT;
2) NSA RECORDS SHOW ONE FAX SENT FROM BRITISH EMBASSY PARIS TO NUMBER IN VENEZUELA TWO WEEKS BEFORE 1986 EVENT.

That was the end of the analysis. Melanie pressed 'Page Down' but the screen did not move.

"NSA?" queried Christina.

"National Security Agency," explained Melanie. "American."

Then another page popped up on the screen.

FURTHER INFORMATION:
FAX SENT FROM BRITISH EMBASSY PARIS ON AUGUST 11 1997 AT 19:00 HOURS TO SAME NUMBER IN VENEZUELA. ATTEMPTING TO OBTAIN COPY.

Both women were quiet. "Oh my God," said Melanie softly. "I think this is it."

"It can obtain a copy of a sent fax?" Christina was astonished.

"It piggy-backs onto the American Echelon satellite surveillance system. You didn't think faxes, e-mails and phone calls were secure, did you?"

"Well, I neffer thought," Christina shrugged.

"They listen to and read everything. Wait! Here it is."

Up popped another screen showing the top half of a fax sheet. It was a bank credit slip, a little indistinct because of all its electronic incarnations, but showing a deposit of five million US dollars into a bank account.

Melanie scrolled down. The second half of the first page came into view, and then in slid the second sheet of the fax.

They frowned. What was that?

They both realised at the same moment that it was upside down, and they both turned their heads sideways.

It was a neck wearing a necklace. Then came the chin, then –

They looked at each other aghast.

"Does this mean what I think it meanz?" asked Christina.

"Even The Professor can't tell us that. He links, he informs," explained Melanie. Then she said, "And it looks like he has just informed us that our man has been contracted to kill Princess Diana!"

PART THREE

Ω

PROGRESSION

Ω

Friday August 15 1997

Rue de la Pompe, Paris, France

Veronique Chevalier had never worked in her life. She had never needed to. She had been born into money. Daddy had been a bigwig *advocat*, rising to become a Chief Prosecutor in the Interior Ministry or something – she didn't really know and she didn't really care. He had kept her and Mummy very 'comfortable' at their country estate near la Ferté-Alais in Essonne. She was his only child (although there were rumours of a bastard daughter somewhere, a mistake with one of his mistresses), and she had been spoilt since birth.

She had married Michel Chevalier seventeen years ago. She had married him at Mummy and Daddy's behest. She had been twenty-five and had had numerous 'fiancés', and Mummy and Daddy had thought it best that she 'settle down'. And she would do anything to please Mummy and Daddy, because the only thing she loved more than them was their money.

Michel Chevalier had simply been her fuck friend at the time. He too was in law, a divorce lawyer, and nowadays he was away a lot – but that did not matter because Veronique was proud of the fact that not even for one of her seventeen married years had she been faithful to him. And poor Michel knew nothing of her infidelities, he was an unknowing serial cuckold.

Perversely, Mummy and Daddy had died four days after her and Michel's engagement. Murdered in 1979. But Veronique had inherited everything and, to please their ghosts, she had gone ahead with the marriage to the hapless Michel anyway.

Today Michel was away (again), and that afternoon she had spent four hours being pleasured by Didier, her black stud from Marseille. So at 18:00 that evening she had a warm, contented glow to go with her bruised inner thighs, twinging rectum and still damp and swollen sex.

When her 'gentlemen friends' visited, she always gave the maid the afternoon and evening off, so she was alone in the apartment in Rue de la Pompe when the doorbell rang.

Still glowing with thoughts of Didier, she walked across the large hallway and opened the door.

"*Bonjour.*" The person standing in the doorway was a jolly, fresh-faced woman in her thirties, brown hair cut in a bob around her un-made-up but nevertheless pretty face. She wore a knee-length pink floral dress which seemed *un peu* too loose on her. She carried no bag – something only a woman would notice, as Veronique surely did.

"*Bonsoir?*" Veronique allowed the one word to carry her query.

"My name is Charlotte Fleury. I'm from Apartment 16," explained the caller. That explained her lack of bag. "Three down and sort of two across."

Veronique smiled. The building on Rue de la Pompe was one of the more internally-complicated of the 1980's apartment blocks of the 16th. "How can I help you, Madame – er - "

"Charlotte."

" - Charlotte."

"The concierge gave me your name, I hope you don't mind."

"The concierge - ? Look, *excusez-moi*, please, won't you come in Charlotte?"

"Thank you."

"My name is Veronique."

"I know."

Veronique led the way into the salon, a bright modern room with huge windows and an admirable view eastwards.

"Would you like a coffee? Or an aperitif perhaps?"

"*Merci.*" Charlotte shook her head. "I'm sorry to disturb you. You must think it a bit of a cheek - "

"*Pas du tout.* What can I do for you?"

"I was chatting to the concierge and I mentioned the trouble I was having with my ex-husband – I asked him not to let him in if he ever turns up here again, that sort of thing, you know. And he said I should consult a lawyer, about a divorce. He said that Monsieur Chevalier was a lawyer...?"

"*Ah, je comprends.* Please, sit down." Veronique indicated an ivory leather armchair to the left. "Are you sure you won't have a drink?"

"You are very kind," Charlotte smoothed her dress beneath her as she sat down. "*Oui. D'accord.* I will. *Café, s'il vous plait.*"

"I have some on." Veronique left the salon, turning left in the hallway.

Alone, Charlotte gazed out of the window. She could see the top of the Tour Eiffel above the Palais de Chaillot, beyond the older buildings over on Avenue Paul Doumer. She could actually make out the people up on the top floor of the tower, the *troisieme étage*, where Eiffel had his little apartment.

"*Et voila,*" Veronique came back in carrying a silver tray which she set down on the central glass table. There were 2 cups, spoons, a sugar bowl and a large silver coffee pot. Charlotte turned back from the window.

"So you will be divorcing your husband?" asked Veronique as she poured.

"I have no choice," explained Charlotte. "The man is a *bâtard*."

"Aren't all men?" Veronique sat down in a matching leather chair, facing her guest.

Charlotte frowned and smiled at the same time. "But you are married."

"So? Men have their uses, true. But I am so glad Michel is, what shall we say, *un mari du weekend*. If we were together all of the time I would have killed him long ago!"

Both women laughed.

"Can't live with them..." began Charlotte.

"...can't live without them!" finished Veronique. She was warming to her neighbour. "So Charlotte, you want my husband's advice regarding your divorce?"

"I know it's a bit of a cheek, me calling on you like this - "

"*Pas du tout.*"

"Is he here, your husband?"

"*Non*, he is up in Normandy until Friday." (Thank God, said her nether regions.)

"I thought we could do things amicably."

Veronique gave a rueful hmph. "There is no such thing as an amicable divorce, my dear. No matter what anyone tells you."

Charlotte put down her cup. "Don't I know that. I was married once, for a short while, a long time ago."

Veronique nodded. "So this is your second marriage?"

"No, once bitten and all that. I am finished with men. No one comes close to your first man, don't you agree?"

Veronique frowned. "I am sorry. I am confused."

"No, no, it is I who should apologise. When I said we could do things amicably I meant you and me."

Veronique just shook her head in puzzlement.

Charlotte stood up, picking up one of the small coffee spoons as she did so. "I should explain. I have entered your apartment under false pretences, and for that I apologise. But it was better than trying to explain my real purpose to you standing in your doorway."

"I'm sorry? *Je regret* - "

"Oh there's nothing to regret. I hope..." Charlotte was standing next to the older woman, looking down at the top of her expensively-styled head. Veronique looked up.

"You are Veronique Lensens, correct?" asked Charlotte.

"*Je m'appelle Veronique Chevalier.*"

"I don't care what you are called now. You were born Lensens, *oui*?"

"I don't understand, what is it you want? Not a divorce?" Absentmindedly Veronique was twisting her cup around between her hands.

"You are Veronique Lensens," continued Charlotte. "Your father was Chief Prosecutor Robert Lensens. He was murdered eighteen years ago, along with your mother."

Shock showed on Veronique's face. "What have my parents to do with you? I don't understand. In fact, I think I would like you to leave please."

Without warning, Charlotte's right hand slapped savagely across Veronique's face, knocking her head to the right. Veronique gasped, her hand going to her cheek.

"Shut up. I am talking," Charlotte's voice was cold. "Let us do this amicably. Just tell me what I want to know and I am out of here."

A small needle-thin trickle of blood appeared from the left side of Veronique's mouth. She started to get up but a surprisingly strong hand on her shoulder held her in the seat.

Charlotte bent forward and spoke into her right ear. "Your father was murdered because he knew something."

"My father was murdered by that thieving scum Mesrine - "

The hand shot to her throat, nails pulling the skin and digging into the flesh so tight that blood instantly appeared. "THAT IS A LIE!" snarled Charlotte. "A damn, damn lie that has been perpetrated for eighteen years! Your father was not murdered by Mesrine, he was murdered by the British." She squeezed the older woman's throat.

Veronique tried to speak but only a croak came out. Her face was turning maroon.

"You want to talk to me, huh?" said Charlotte as she eased the pressure. "That is good. You are a good girl."

"My... my..." Veronique was fighting to get her breath and speak at the same time. "My father was murdered by Mes - "

"NO, NO, NO!" Her head was slammed into the back of the chair again and again and again. The cup fell from her grasp, spilling coffee dregs onto the carpet. "You stupid woman! That is what they wanted you to think. So that they could hunt him down and murder him with justification. It was THE BRITISH that murdered your parents. They killed your father for what he knew. Can't you understand?"

Veronique's face was screwed up with fear and pain. Charlotte kept her hand where it was, silently staring at the other woman. Then she let go, leaving five distinct bloody finger marks dented around the neck. Veronique gasped for her breath.

"I know it is hard for you," Charlotte's voice sounded quite sympathetic. "To be told the truth about your parents' death after all these years. But you had to find out sometime."

Veronique continued to gasp, unable to speak even if she wanted to.

"Now," continued Charlotte, as if chatting to a friend. "Just to clarify.

Jacques Mesrine wanted a document. A document containing a secret. A secret which the British wanted to repress at all costs. Your father possessed the document and kindly gave it to Mesrine. But your father knew the contents of the document. Therefore the British killed him. And shortly this led to the death of Mesrine also." Just for a moment Charlotte's voice caught in her throat as memories of her father flashed into her mind. Then she said, "And I think you know the contents of the document too."

Veronique was totally dumbfounded. She looked bewildered, scared, in pain and confused all at once. Blood was trickling down her chin. She was thinking back over the years. To her meeting with Mesrine. To his sexual violation of her, the most erotic experience of her life as his tongue poked between the cheeks of her bottom... To the contents of the document.

"What is it?" Charlotte's simple question snapped her out of her reverie.

Veronique looked up, rubbing her neck "What is what?" she asked softly.

"The British secret. The secret our fathers were murdered for. What is it?"

Veronique was now totally subdued. "I don't know," she mumbled.

"That is not the answer I want. I know you know." Curiously, Charlotte was looking intently at the silver coffee spoon in her hand. She spoke to it. "Just tell me, that's all. We can still be friends."

"All – all I know is that it concerned the British Queen. There was some agreement..."

"Think, *mon amour*, think. I beg you." Spoon in hand, Charlotte stared intently into the seated woman's eyes.

"I – I was young. I did not care. It – it was part of Daddy's collection. I wasn't interested."

"THINK!"

The shout made Veronique jump. A lady-fart popped from her bottom. She began to sob. "S – something about the Germans, Hitler and the Russian guy, I don't know. I DON'T KNOW! The Americans also..."

Charlotte was studying her face. "If I gave you time, would you remember more?"

"I..."

"Are you telling me everything? Sweet, sweet Veronique, are you telling me all?" Tenderly she stroked the other woman's hair.

"Please... I can give you money - "

The hand that had been tenderly stroking suddenly grabbed the hair painfully. "Money? MONEY? You think that is what this is all about? MONEY?" She pulled Veronique's head from side to side as she spoke. "You stupid, deluded, spoilt, selfish little bitch. This is about my father. This is about righting wrongs. I'll teach you about money - "

Charlotte's hand moved from the top of Veronique's head, to cover her eyes and pinch her nose at the same time. Veronique opened her mouth to scream. Charlotte pushed the head backwards and rammed the spoon into the open mouth. Both lips were sliced and immediately blood gushed out.

The spoon was pushed into the mouth sideways, rammed further and further back, into the throat. Veronique gurgled and tried to breathe in croaked, jumping gasps. She tried to close her jaws around the hand in her mouth, but her muscles had frozen. Her face began to turn from maroon to blue. Her hands pulled futilely at the other woman's arms.

Charlotte removed her hand. Veronique thrashed around on the chair like a mute marionette, legs kicking, her own hands grasping at her throat, trying to get into her mouth. Charlotte could see the spoon wedged sideways, pushing the skin of her neck outwards at both sides.

"I will not kill you," Charlotte spoke conversationally, avoiding the thrashing legs. "Let the ghosts of our fathers decide whether you join them or not." But she already knew the answer. Veronique's movements were slowing, her eyes were gaping, and her own nails had stopped digging into her own neck. She sat slumped in the chair, just an erratic, occasional jumping gasp getting air into the body.

Then the jumping gasps stopped completely, and the glazed eyes went dull. A damp patch appeared in her groin area.

Veronique Lensens died as she had been born. With a silver spoon in her mouth.

It was at that moment that the front door opened.

Sarasota, Florida, USA

Six hours behind time-wise, but at the same moment that the front door of the Chevaliers' apartment opened in Paris, Ilich Ramirov sat in the hot tub on his lanai and let the full-power jets massage his body. It was a hot and humid afternoon.

The chubby, boyish face smiled. Some might think that killing the most famous woman in the world was the toughest contract he had ever been given. But they would be wrong – so, so wrong. This was the easiest contract ever, and he was being paid ten million for it!

It was easy precisely because of the fact that she was the most famous woman in the world. He did not have to find her! At any given time, he could establish her whereabouts just by turning on the television or consulting the internet. That very day he knew she was flying to the Greek Islands with her friend, the *Tiffany* woman.

It was just a matter of when and where.

And how.

The British would want it to look 'natural', like they always did – therefore there could be no assassin's bullet from the rooftops, no point blank shooting or knifing in a crowd. But the definition of 'natural' was broad. Wallis Simpson had stopped breathing and had died a 'natural death'. The death of French President Georges Pompidou many years ago had been a 'natural death', the cyanide gas inflicted by Ramirov had been untraceable. Car crashes were 'natural', like the ones he had organised for Princess Grace and the police sergeant lover of his current target – and the one he had arranged for the toff James Hewitt which had been called off at the very last possible moment.

Choking could be 'natural'. Food poisoning could be 'natural'. Even a fall could be 'natural'. The possibilities were endless.

So he needed to play God. To decide which 'natural death' he would inflict on Diana.

With the skills of Ilich Ramirov, she could die 'naturally' anywhere. He would do it quickly, the British would like that. What was their expression? 'No sooner said than done.' They had said, now Diana would be done.

In preparation for action, he would now relax. Have a little fun...

Play God.

He looked across at the person sharing the hot tub with him: Candice, the fat black prostitute with the sagging tits and stretch-marked belly whom he had picked up on the Keys an hour previously. She was drugged up and smiling at him sleepily but lasciviously.

He raised his right foot and pinched her left nipple between his toes. Her areola was so big, it spread either side of his foot.

Her body had been washed clean by the water, but there were still crusty stains around her mouth where he had already used her.

"Again?" she asked. "My, someone is a horny boy. The fourth one costs extra."

"An extra thousand bucks for something special." He used his Texas accent. Flawless.

"What would you like? An extra thousand gets you whatever you want."

"Whatever?"

"Whatever."

He stood up in the tub, his massive (and impressive) erection rising up from the water like a surface to air missile. She smiled in admiration.

He moved towards her face and she opened her mouth in anticipation, closing her eyes. His dick touched her lips but went no further.

Suddenly there was a downward pressure on her head. *What the fuck?* She went under, the water gushing into her open mouth. Her eyes opened but they were stung by the water. She couldn't see. The water had instantly filled her lungs. She couldn't breath.

She began to thrash wildly, trying to get his hands off the top of her head. Her feet pressed against the bottom of the tub, trying to push herself upwards, but she moved not one inch against the pressure on her head.

She gasped again, but nothing happened, no air entered her body. Now her arms began to jump erratically, up and down, above and below the water. Splashing, splashing.

She wanted to scream but no sound came out. Her knees now buckled and she felt herself sinking further.

The pressure in her lungs was hurting, hurting, hurting. Her head was about to explode. He was killing her!

The roaring started in her ears…

Suddenly there was air, and she felt herself lifted by her hair out of the water. She was gasping and choking at the same time, small amounts of beautiful, beautiful air entering her lungs and being expelled in small, harsh gasps.

He grabbed her shoulders and span her around, forcing her to bend from the waist over the edge of the tub. She thought he was going to try the classic manoeuvre to expel the water from her lungs. But instead, as she lay over the side gasping for air, gasping for life, she felt his hands on her butt cheeks as he forced himself into her.

"Whatever?" he mocked.

Rue de la Pompe, Paris, France

Charlotte took her eyes off the body of Veronique Lensens and span round to face the hallway as she heard the front door opening. She had no time for surprise, no time for fear, no time even to swear. She had to act on pure instinct.

Lightly she skipped out into the hall. A man was just closing the front door behind him. The suit, tie, slightly receding hair and weak almost craven-looking face meant he could only be a lawyer.

"Michel," she said it as a statement, not a question, as she came towards him.

He frowned, confused. "*Bonj –*"

"I wasn't expecting you until the weekend." Charlotte jumped on tip-toe and her lips came up hard on his in a savage, drool-filled kiss. Her hands reached round and rubbed the back of his head firmly as her tongue poked into his mouth.

Being a man, Michel did not ask questions. He simply responded, his smoky breath forcing its way down her throat.

After thirty more seconds, she pulled away. Both their mouths and jaws were wet. She held his head in her hands, staring into his eyes. With firm, lust-fuelled sincerity she said, "I want you."

She grabbed his cock, which was solid beneath the suit pants. Then she moved her hand back up, and with both hands pressed hard on his shoulders, encouraging him down.

When he was kneeling on the floor in front of her, she raised her dress. She wore nothing underneath.

Michel gasped as he looked at her clean-shaven sex. He came very slightly in his pants.

"Kiss me," she ordered. "I want to feel your tongue."

Before he had chance to utter argument or thanks, she stepped towards him and rammed his head into her groin. Her hands held him there with surprising strength. She felt his tongue seeking for access.

She took one hand away from the back of his head, found the rim of her dress and pulled it down over his head.

To distract him, she moved her legs apart two centimetres to reward his probing.

Then, with the front of the dress over his head, she grabbed the rim in both hands and suddenly pulled herself away from him (shit, the bastard had one of her lips in his mouth!). She stepped round behind him.

Michel was kneeling on the floor with her dress completely over his head. She had the hem tight around his throat and was strangling him. She pulled harder and harder as she moved her left hand down over his face and pinched his nose.

He struggled but only weakly, thinking he was having the most bizarre, wonderful sex of his life with a complete stranger. Only when he realised he could not open his mouth to compensate for his pinched nose did he think maybe the sex game was going wrong. And by then it was too late.

As blackness overcame him and his lungs screamed, he ejaculated ferociously. He wondered what Veronique, his precious, wonderful, faithful Veronique, would say if she ever found out about this infidelity...

Ω

Saturday August 16 1997

Henri's Bar, Paris, France

Only *Le Figaro* made the connection. The other newspapers reported the deaths as straightforward murders, and they left the story for the inside pages. But Le Figaro topped them all.

HISTORY REPEATS

Socialite and husband murdered in bizarre family coincidence

Chief Inspector Pierre Jamo casually glanced at the story as he ate his morning croissant at the zinc of the bar at the corner of Rue de Penthièvre and Rue Cambacérès, opposite the back entrance to the Interior Ministry building. He went to open the paper, but then a word from the front page caught his eye and he closed the paper back up again, frowning curiously.

Had he seen what he thought he had seen? Where was it? Was his mind playing tricks?

He scanned the lesser articles on the page, especially the ones on the right near where he had been holding the paper. Then he looked again at the main story, his eyes moving up and down the columns. At first he could not find it, so instead of scanning he read the article in detail.

And there it was.

And he did not believe it.

He could not believe it. It was bizarre, as the paper said. More bizarre than even the editor of *Le Figaro* knew. But *coincidence?* No, coincidences were not pack animals. Coincidences despised each other. There was never more than one of them in the same place at the same time.

He sighed and pulled his chunky mobile telephone from his pocket. He went through the palaver of extending the aerial and got into his memory at the third attempt. He highlighted the wrong number, pressed green before he realised and then quickly pressed red. *Oh for God's sake, these bloody things.*

"Henri! Jetons, s'il te plait." He threw some francs down onto the counter as the elderly proprietor gave him the tokens for the telephone on the wall near the WC.

The old telephone had a dial, it was not even push button, and he connected in one attempt. It rang three times before she answered.

"*Oui?*"

"Inspector, I need you immediately."

"But I'm on lates today, I'm not in until - "

"Now. You have fifteen minutes."

"Fuck you."

"Not on duty, I have told you that before."

"Can't you - ?"

"Now."

Jamo hung up. He had never been to her apartment in the north of the city, their occasional medicinal fucks (done for mutual relief, no emotions involved) had always taken place at his place in Montparnasse. But he knew it would take her thirty minutes maximum to get in. Just enough time for him to finish his croissant.

And just enough time for him to start worrying what the hell was going on.

Rue des Saussaies, Paris, France

Inspector Claudette Ibrahim had a face on when she entered the BCP suite twenty-seven minutes later. She was dressed in her usual riding gear of T shirt, leathers and boots, and she had managed to apply some make-up (daytime eyeshadow and lipstick), but she was as pissed as hell for being called on duty a full five hours before her shift.

Jamo knew better than to try any pleasantries when she was in one of her moods, so he went straight into it.

"Have you seen the papers?"

"I haven't had time. Some bastard disturbed my morning." She thumped her red crash helmet down on her desk.

"Seen this?" Jamo tossed the folded *Le Figaro* over to land next to the helmet.

She looked at it and feigned astonishment. "Why, what is this?" The sarcasm could have been cut with a knife. "It looks like – what? What is it? Parchment?" She picked it up and felt it carefully. "No! No, it's paper! And what is this black stuff on it, it is coming off on my hand." She sat on the edge of her desk and began to remove her boots. She looked with a sneer at Jamo. "Which is more than certain people will be doing."

"Shut it."

She gave the main article a quick scan, mood satiated. She asked, "What is it? No political involvement, is there? The murder of a socialite and her husband." She pulled a pair of denim jeans from a rucksack, and slipped her leather trousers down.

"Read it carefully."

She did. Meanwhile Jamo enjoyed the view of her white G-string pants, the string actually invisible between her cheeks. He felt jealous.

Five seconds later she stiffened. "They're joking."

"I don't think so."

She read aloud as she pulled up the denims. "*Socialite Veronique Chevalier and her husband, society lawyer Michel Chevalier, have been found murdered in their apartment in Rue de la Pompe* – very nice. *Veronique, thirty-seven* – yeah, and the rest – *blah-di-blah-blah... Loving husband Michel... responsible for handling the divorces of many high society* wankers – *blah-di-blah. In a bizarre twist of fate, the parents of Madame Chevalier – Chief Public Prosecutor Robert Lensens and his wife Rosemary – were murdered together eighteen years ago by Jacques Mesrine. Monsieur Lensens was the Chief Prosecutor responsible for jailing Mesrine for twenty years, and he was killed in an apparent act of revenge just nine days before Mesrine himself was shot as he was being recaptured.*"

She lowered the paper slowly and looked across at the Chief Inspector. She said lowly, "Mesrine."

Jamo nodded. "Mesrine. Dead for nearly two decades, and now suddenly he's back. Our former Chief screams his name down the telephone before he dies in flames. Four days later a woman whose parents were murdered by Mesrine while he was involved with us is herself murdered along with her husband."

"How did they die?" Claudette raised the paper back up.

"Doesn't say. 'Thought to have been strangled' - "

"*But the police are not releasing details at this time...* Strange."

"Unusual, yes. But you know what this means, don't you?"

"I think I can guess."

"We can no longer leave it to the PJ. Somehow we – the BCP – are linked to this. But we have to find out. Why was Charles Fleury-Goujon killed? And why now? And why were Veronique Chevalier née Lensens and her husband killed? And how? And why now?"

"And," said Inspector Claudette Ibrahim, "who else is going to be killed?"

"And," said Chief Inspector Pierre Jamo, "why?"

They paused, Claudette giggling to herself at the dramatic moment. Then she said, "You know something, Chief?"

"*Quoi?*"

"You should have called me in earlier."

Sarasota, Florida, USA

Ian Ramsey, the first generation Texan of Scottish parents, left the house in Sweetmeadow Circle at 10:00. Ramsey was a man of medium height, long blonde wavy hair tied in a simple but smart ponytail at the back, complemented by a blonde goatee on his face.

He was a rich man whose money had come from oil (as any internet check would confirm), and he now lived off his investments.

His round face made him look a tad paunchy and overweight, a condition not helped by the loose beige linen shirt worn over the baggy multi-pocketed cargo pants. It was a perfect illusion which hid the tough, muscular and powerful body underneath.

Ramsey threw his back-pack into the trunk and climbed into the pre-booked taxi. Exchanging not one word with the driver, they set off for Sarasota-Bradenton Airport and his connecting flight before the long journey eastwards.

Ω

Monday August 18 1997

Athens, Greece

Ian Ramsey landed at Eleftherios Venezelos Airport, Athens, at 06:30.

It was four years before the seachange of September 11 2001 so, although immigration checks were made in accordance with the laid down procedures of the time, the Greek authorities did not check the names of arrivals against the passenger manifest of the arriving airplane.

Thus it was that the Texan Ian Ramsey left the USA on August 16 using his legitimate American passport, and the Greek Ioannis Rigakis presented himself at immigration at Athens using his equally legitimate Greek passport.

A cursory customs check of the returning national's one item of baggage revealed just clothing, shaving items, two books and sundry knick-knacks purchased in the USA and well below his duty free allowance limit.

No comment was made about the hand-wide, six centimetre deep tin of shaving soap in amongst the toiletries, and it was not even touched let alone opened.

Ioannis Rigakis reached the port of Piraeus at 10:30 hours.

Rue des Saussaies, Paris, France

"So run this by me again," Commissaire Gillian Colet stared hard at Chief Inspector Pierre Jamo, who stood before her like an errant schoolboy in front of his principal. Colet had that affect on men: if they were needed to advance her career, she was the coquette. If they were not needed to advance her career, she was a hard faced man hater.

A piece of her permanently-up-during-office-hours long grey hair had fallen down and it moved back and forth against her left ear. "An old man is murdered," she said. "He may or may not have screamed Mesrine at you down the telephone on the day he died. Four days later, a wealthy socialite and her husband are murdered. Eighteen years ago, *eighteen years,* this woman's parents were murdered by Jacques Mesrine. And you think there's a link. A link of which you have no proof, just supposition. And you want the BCP to take on an investigation of both murders."

"Yes."

"Why?"

"Charles Fleury-Goujon was our first, our original, Commissaire - "

"Need I remind you what the BCP is? What we do? We are the Bureau de la Co-Operation Politique. We are responsible for the protection of, liaison with and the general comfort and happiness of all foreign government interests in France."

"Yes, I do know that." Jamo's face showed no emotion.

"We do not investigate murders. That is for the *Police Judiciare*."

"I have a feeling that the murder of Fleury links straight back to the days he sat in this office."

"Proof?"

"Until I investigate, I have no proof."

"But we do not investigate murders."

"You know the rumours that Mesrine was connected to this office. That he was working for Richer and Fleury."

"That is all, Chief Inspector." Already she had picked up some papers from her In Tray.

"You're a fucking cow, you know. An incompetent *salop* who fucked her way into her job," mumbled Jamo as he walked back down the corridor to his office.

Claudette Ibrahim knew the answer as soon as he slammed through the door. "I take it that's a 'No' then."

"The bitch didn't even want to listen."

"I knew she wouldn't. I could have told you. I *did* tell you."

"*Oui, d'accord, d'accord.* Don't rub it in." He patted his pocket for his cigarettes.

"You know what your problem is?"

"Oh, here we go. Upward management again."

She came over and stood beside him. "Your problem," she reached forward and put her hands on either side of his face, "is that you are too nice."

"You didn't say that the other night when I was ripping you apart inside."

"Shut it. Your problem is that you have to do things 'the proper way'. Mister Missionary." She shook his head gently. "Why do you have to go through her anyway?"

"She *is* the boss," he said through puckered lips as she pushed either side of his face inward.

"She is the *bitch*." Claudette leant forward and pecked him on his protruding lips, then she let go. "I know, I know," she said as she went back to her desk. "I understand. You are the Chief Inspector, the chain of command *et cetera*. So we let it drop."

Jamo looked shocked. "Did I say that?"

Claudette looked up.

"Do you really think I'm going to let that bitch, who has never been on the beat in her life, tell me what to do?" asked Jamo. "The woman whose only qualification for office is that she fucks indiscriminately, men and women, whoever it takes to further her career? No way, Inspector, no way. We investigate. I hereby make it official. Let the PJ faff around, they don't know what we know. You and I will look into it from our angle."

"She'll have your balls." But Claudette was pleased.

"She will not. Currently my balls are in your court."

"Oh yes, you're right. I think I saw them in my drawer here..."

"Inspector!"

"Yes, Chief?"

"Remember the chain of command."

"Yes, Chief."

"I have it in my apartment. It has eighteen links, remember?"

"I know, Chief."

"How many did we manage?"

"Seven in the front and three in the back, Chief."

Jamo grinned. "Want to try for eight and four later?"

Le Marais, Paris, France

Les escargots are a cliché. Foreigners, especially those from the Anglo world, really think that those and frogs' legs are the staple diets of the French. In fact, a majority of French do not like either.

But Chief Inspector Pierre Jamo was not in the majority. He tucked into his plate of 16 snails swimming in garlic butter and relished every dripping mouthful.

Opposite him in the little restaurant in the Marais sat Eli Lucas, his oldest friend and, coincidentally, Chief Crime Reporter for *France Dimanche*.

Although controlled by the administrative unit called the *Sûreté*, the five police forces of France are effectively independent. Pride and jealousy are rife among the forces, and their dislike of one another is such that not only would it be unthinkable that they would co-operate with each other or give mutual assistance, but any request for help or information could well be met with disinformation or downright lies.

So there was never any question of Pierre Jamo asking for the co-operation of the *Police Judiciaire*. Instead, as in the past, he got his information from a much more trustworthy source: the French Press.

"It is strange, strange, strange." With his black hair and black moustache,

Eli had more than a touch of the Mediterranean about him. He spoke through mouthfuls of steak tartare, blood from his raw mince staining the corners of his mouth. "Veronique Chevalier suffocated to death on a spoon."

"On a *what?*" A snail shell clicked back down onto Jamo's plate.

"A spoon," confirmed the journalist. "A coffee spoon. It was found wedged in her throat. They had to slit her throat on the post mortem to get it out. A cutlery caesarean!"

Jamo grimaced at his friend's graveyard humour. "So they are sure it was murder? Not some bizarre suicide?"

Eli chomped on a piece of pink-stained lettuce. "What do you think, *mon ami?* If you wanted to kill yourself, would you really go to all the trouble of ramming a spoon down your own throat?"

"Probably not."

"And your poor rich husband is so overcome when he arrives home and finds you that he puts some textile over his head, jerks off in his trousers and then suffocates himself to death. And then, just for good measure, his ghost disposes of the instrument of death before the bodies are found."

"They have no idea what was used?"

"He suffocated for sure. Fibres were found on his head and in his lungs. Cotton, dyed. But from what, they do not know. Likeliest theory is that it was a sack or a cushion or something."

"And what about this thing about Mesrine, the fact that he murdered both her parents - "

"Allegedly."

" – all those years ago." Jamo poured more Merlot into their glasses.

"There's no connection. Just a happenstance. But we're running a 'Poor Veronique Lensens' piece on Sunday. Showing how some lives are just cursed – parents murdered by Mesrine, eighteen years on daughter and husband murdered by intruders. The place was ransacked, don't forget. There was no money or jewellery left in the house." Eli picked up his glass and washed down his steak.

"No other connection?" asked Jamo.

"With Mesrine? How could there be? Dear Jacques has been pushing up daisies for nearly two decades."

Montmartre, Paris, France

Thinking back over the demise of Michel Chevalier, she couldn't help but smile. Men. What stupid, dick-driven creatures they were. One hint of sex and they would do anything – even let you kill them.

She snuggled her face into the sensuous fur of Will The Cat, who rested contentedly in her arms as she looked out of her window onto the vista of

Paris below. Summer rain had cast a grey pall over the city.

"They are so, so naughty, my baby," she spoke softly into the cat's ear. "Why won't they tell me? I know they know. Is this secret so precious that they will all die for it? Surely not. Nothing is worth dying for. Daddy always told me that. Nothing."

She squeezed the cat and gently rocked from side to side, a little pout on her lips. For a while she was quiet. Then she made up her mind. She became business-like. "Right," she lowered the cat to her waist level and let it jump the rest of the way.

She went over to the bureau and opened a drawer, pulling out a manila folder. She placed it on her glass coffee table and sat down on her leather couch.

"Time," she said, "for the next one."

She opened the folder.

Ω

Tuesday August 19 1997

Largo Febo, Rome, Italy

A glorious Roman evening. The oppressive thirty-six degree heat of the day had waned to an acceptably hot twenty-six by 22:00.

Melanie Nathanson and Christina Cascianis sat at a table on the raised piazza outside the *Santa Lucia* restaurant and attracted admiring glances from many of the men (with or without their own female companions) who passed by on their *passegiata* around Largo Febo, the small square next to the Piazza Navona. Music drifted out from the restaurant.

Both women were dressed smart-casual. Christina was in a plain but fetching blue cotton dress, which displayed her still-fabulous-at-fifty legs to their best advantage. Melanie was in a green vest-style knitted top and off-white linen trousers, a colour combination that complemented her shock of natural red hair and suntanned skin.

The men who admired them had but one thing on their minds (this was Italy, after all) – and who could blame them? But they would have been stunned into disbelieving shock had they known the truth: that these women were two Israeli agents plotting the death of the most famous terrorist of the twentieth century.

"So how do we play this?" Melanie twisted her *tagliolini alla puttanesca* onto her fork. "Before, with Stelios, we used all our resources to locate and arrange the target for him."

"And that did not work for Stelios, did it?" After twenty-three years Christina could talk about the love of her life dispassionately. She took another mouthful of her *farfalle alle vongole*.

"That was bad luck. Some meddling Dutch policeman."

"True. But when we found Ramirov in Khartoum, it wass my team that did it."

"Equally true. But this time there is only a team of two. Us."

"So what do you think we should do?" Christina sipped her Verdicchio.

"I suggest nothing."

"Nothing?"

"No knee-jerk. Not yet. It's a different game nowadays."

"A game...?"

"Life is a game, hun."

"You think so?"

"With the whole world trying to throw a double-six. It's only the lucky bastards who manage it."

Christina smiled as she finished her dish. "I thought I had thrown the double-six with Stelios. Obviously I wass not to be one of the lucky bastards."

"Perhaps the great Gamemaster has realised his error and is now repaying us."

Christina put her fork on her plate and sat back. "How?"

"Well, we can't bring Stelios back - "

Christina said nothing.

" – but we have been given another chance for vengeance. We've been given that chance through a technology that was not even dreamt of back in seventy-four. A technology that nobody yet knows exists today." Melanie sipped from her glass of Barolo. Opposite her, the Greek woman lit up a cheroot. "We have found out that Ramirov's current base could be Venezuela. And it seems he has been contracted by the British to do something concerning Princess Diana. Look - "

Melanie stood up, went over to a vacated table and picked up a copy of that day's *La Repubblica*. She threw it down onto their table as she sat back down. "The Press is besotted with her. Diana is on the front of every newspaper, every magazine in the world. Now that she's hitched up with this Dodi Fayed, the Press are like sharks in a feeding frenzy."

Christina removed the cheroot from her lips and blew out smoke. "So we concentrate on Lady Di, not on Ramirov?"

"In a way. She is not our problem. But he is. He is coming after her. Where Diana is, that's where – sometime soon – Ramirov will be. We will simply wait for him to turn up. Then he will be yours."

"And this time," Christina signalled for the waiter, "there will be no arrest."

The waiter appeared.

"*Due espresso,*" ordered Christina.

The man turned and then Christina called him back. "Make them *doppio.*"

Ω

Wednesday August 20 1997

Via Catalana, Rome, Italy

"He can't be serious," said Melanie as she looked at the screen and read Barking Dog's response to their latest query. "He wouldn't do such a thing, would he? Would the great Ilich Ramirov be so unprofessional as to announce himself this way? I can't believe it."

"Ah, but remember," reasoned Christina, sitting forward and looking at the results displayed. "He does not realise he iss being traced. He thinks we think he iss in jail in France, following the death-of-Carlos-no-it-isn't fiasco last month. He thinks the world still thinks Carlos has been caught. And except for *Mossad Aliyah Beth*, it does."

"And I suppose we must not forget he is a man. As arrogant as they all are."

Christina grinned. "A genetic gender arrogance that hass played right into our hands."

And there on the screen it was. Barking Dog had ascertained that a certain Ian Ramsey had boarded a flight at Sarasota-Bradenton Airport in Florida USA last Saturday, bound for New York. At New York, he had changed onto an Olympic Airways flight direct to Athens.

The flight had landed at 06:30 on Monday morning. Greek Immigration showed no arrival for Ian Ramsey, but it did show Ioannis Rigakis, a native Greek returning from the USA.

The Professor had then taken over on request, and had linked the trip to Europe with Princess Diana in one nanosecond: the Princess was just ending a short break cruising the Aegean with her friend Rosa Monckton.

"I really can't believe it," Melanie clapped her hands together. "The arrogance, you're right. The great Ilich Ramirov has made the classic textbook error. Has he forgotten everything he learnt at Novosibirsk? He is using aliases *but he is using his own initials!*"

Christina nodded at the irony. "And he does not know that our baby here," she caressed the laptop, "can follow hiss every recorded move. But it does mean one thing," she looked up at the red head. "He hass locked on to Lady Di. We've got to move. And fast."

Island of Hydra, Greece

The man had long, wavy blonde hair, tied in a neat ponytail, and a goateed, chubbyish face which had obviously enjoyed copious amounts of moisturiser and other attention over the years. And there was a trace – just a trace – of eye shadow. He was dressed in sandals, three-quarter length white cotton beach pants and just-the-right-side-of-garish orange flowered shirt.

He sat in the guest lounge of the Hotel Leto, sipping his Metaxa and Coke, minding his own business. He had spent the day in the busy port area of Hydra Town, just two minutes down the road, overhearing, choosing, selecting. Now he was waiting.

And he didn't have to wait too long.

Claude Dumoulin, thin, balding and carrying two camera cases, walked into the lounge five minutes later and picked Ponytail up on his gaydar instantly. He came over and sat in a chair at the next coffee table along and ordered a beer when the barman approached.

Claude tried to make it look casual, as if he had just spotted Ponytail sitting there alone. He nodded. "Ciao."

"Ciao." Ponytail smiled with just a nano-hint of coyness. Was there a trace of invitation?

"You here on vacation?" Claude spoke in French.

"*Oui. Deux semaines.*" Ponytail was French too. Was that a southern accent? "*Toi?*"

Claude smiled. The instant familiarity augured well. "Working."

"Oh? What do you do?"

"I'm a photographer."

"Really? That's fascinating. Glamour? Fashion?"

"Press."

"Sorry?"

"I'm a Press photographer." The barman returned with his beer.

"You got some big celeb in town?" Ponytail was interested, but not too interested. His sipped his drink.

"None other than Lady Di herself. She's just left."

"Lady Di? She was *here*? Really?"

Claude looked around as if he was about to impart a secret. He leant forward.

"She was with a girlfriend, the Tiffany woman. Shame really, we wanted to catch her with her new boyfriend."

"We?"

"There's loads of us here – even The Rat. Diana's worth money."

"I love Diana, always have," said ponytail. "You work for an agency? Sygma? Gamma?"

"No, I'm freelance. Completely independent."

"What a fascinating life you must lead." Ponytail finished his drink and looked at Claude expectantly.

Claude took the hint. "Another?"

"I'd like that. But can we go some place?"

"Of course. How about we raid the minibar in my room?"

"Raiding," nodded Ponytail. "I like that."

Two hours later, Ian Ramsey quietly left Claude Dumoulin's room and made his way back to his own on the floor below.

When the police called in the morning he would be open and honest with them. Yes, he had gone back to Claude Dumoulin's room. They had had consensual sex for two hours, then he had gone back to his own room. Why were they asking?

Claude was *what?* Dead in the shower? Broken neck? Looked like he had slipped on something sticky on the floor of the shower cubicle?

Ponytail would be shy, almost embarrassed. The floor of the shower cubicle? That was one of the places he had come. You don't think Claude slipped on...?

The police would be grave, but in their hearts they would be thinking *fucking queers*, and it would be unlikely the investigation would be taken any further. After all, the deceased's passport, credit cards and copious amounts of drachma were in his wallet, untouched. Nobody heard any noise coming from the room. There were no signs of violence. It was an accidental, post homosexual coitus death. Happens.

And they would not even know that such a thing as Dumoulin's Press affiliation ID existed, let alone that it was missing.

Ω

Thursday August 21 1997

Whitcomb Street, London, England

John Smith, Head of 'Charles' People', sat at the small table by the door in the *Hand and Racquet* public house in Whitcomb Street, just off Leicester Square, and waited. A half full pint glass of Director's Bitter and the remains of a cheese and pickle sandwich were on the table in front of him.

No need for a suit today, he was wearing his black polo shirt and blue denims, and he felt much more comfortable for it. It was more *him*. He hated having to dress in 'shirt and tie' every time he went to see The Boss. What did a shirt and tie matter? Smith did not believe that 'Clothes maketh the man'; in his case, six years in the SBS, his daily two hour workout and his membership of MENSA, maketh *this* man.

But he had to keep The Boss happy. And that was why he was now sitting in this pub that had seen better days, waiting.

It had taken a full week for The Boss to make up his mind, and Smith's instructions had finally been given to him over the telephone that morning. The phone call had been vague – not only through circumspection because phone calls were not secure (even the word 'Squidgygate' made him cringe), but also because that was The Boss: vague. You had to second guess him, work out what he really wanted. And Smith knew what The Boss really wanted this time.

Smith was surprised at his orders. The Boss had been separated from his wife for five years, and was now divorced. But he still kept a critical eye on her activities. He haunted her. Or was it her who haunted him? He was now with the one true love of his life, Camilla, and yet he could not shake off – or leave alone – the mother of his children.

Whatever. This time, to quote The Boss, she had 'gone too far'.

As usual, The Boss had procrastinated. But, in true regal style, he had taken counsel and he had decided what to do.

And it was John Smith's job to arrange it.

There were twelve people in the pub at 17:00, with more trickling in by the minute. At 17:05 the door opened and five more people came in: two couples and a man on his own. The man was wearing a light grey suit with an open necked white shirt underneath. He was of medium height, trim with close cut greying hair which gave away his military background.

The couples went to find a table, the man went directly to the bar. He looked around as his pint was being pulled, saw Smith and nodded.

The man was Jack Jones – a name as real as John Smith – and he was the head of the MI6 Royal Family Liaison Team, known around the corridors of Century House as 'Betty's Men'.

He came over with his pint.

"John."

"Jack."

"I got your message, thanks."

"Thanks for coming."

Jones sat down. "So what's going on that I shouldn't know about?"

Smith smiled. *Twat*. "The Boss has a problem. Wants it solved."

"And I can help how?" He took a large swig of his Stella Artois.

"Just a little info, Jack. The problem is nothing for you to worry about. That's my department."

"Does he want you to fix the next polo match again?"

"Nothing so serious. Al Fayed, the Harrods bloke."

"Yes?"

"Have you got a briefing pack?"

"I can get one. Six has been keeping an eye on him for quite some time, as you can imagine. Poor sod still thinks he'll be granted citizenship one day." Jones looked up at the door as a giggling group of twentysomething females entered.

"You got people on the inside?" asked Smith.

"Bound to. It'll be in the pack. Ouch, look at that."

Smith followed his gaze. He had already noticed the blonde with the stunning Amazon figure. "How soon can I have it?" he pressed.

Jones looked back at him. "Tomorrow. Shall I have it biked? This is official, I take it?"

"Don't bike it." Smith thought of what he had been ordered to do. There wasn't a fan big enough in the world to handle the shit that would be flying from this job. And not one turd of it was even to point in the direction of HRH. "I'll pick it up. St James's Park at ten?"

"Usual terms?"

"Of course."

"Fine."

Smith raised his glass and clinked the bottom of it against Jones' glass. "Thanks, Jack. You're a brick."

But Jones' eyes were already back on the blonde Amazon and in his mind he was already licking Stella out of her belly button.

Ω

Friday August 22 1997

St James's Park, London, England

This was a fine day in London, and John Smith was in St James's Park half an hour ahead of schedule. He sat on what was known in the business as 'Six's Bench', the fourth bench eastwards on the northern lakeside path after the bridge.

He let the warming-up-nicely rays of the sun caress his face as he sat reading his newspaper. If anybody had cared to look, they would have been surprised to see this rough-looking, and now unshaven, man reading *The Times*. He looked as if he would be more comfortable reading *The Sun*. But, of course, at that time *The Times* was bigger than *The Sun* (its conversion from broadsheet to tabloid was six years away), and therefore more useful for his purposes.

From the bag on his knees, he pulled a slice of old bread and began to break pieces off and throw them to the ducks on the lake. As usual, the mallards were in the majority. They were the yobs of the duck world, he thought. But streetwise and canny. Just like himself really.

A swan glided past, too sophisticated even to look in the ducks' direction. But not too snobby to catch the piece of bread Smith threw towards it. In Britain all swans are the property of the Monarch, and Smith gave a little nod of deference. "Morning Ma'am."

He saw Jack Jones walking across the bridge at 09:58. The MI6 man was also carrying a copy of *The Times*.

They exchanged pleasantries like old friends, and Smith offered Jones the bag of bread. For five minutes they sat there feeding the ducks and exchanging pleasantries.

Had he got off with the Amazon last night? No chance. But he had pulled her friend, the small brown-haired one with glasses. He was seeing her on her own tonight.

Were Chelsea going to win the FA Cup? Manager Gianlucca Vialli had done wonders with them this season.

When they both got up, bidding each other farewell. Jones went back over the bridge, Smith went north towards The Mall.

They each had each other's newspaper.

Inside the one carried by Jones was one thousand pounds.

Inside the one carried by Smith was a CD-ROM.

Back in his office in the St James's Palace complex, Smith wasted no time.

Computer booted, he inserted the disk. The machine took twenty seconds to find and start the right program to open it. And then up popped what he had paid for.

The MI6 file on the Fayeds was extensive *[in the coming years it would grow to such a size that it could not be fitted onto one disk, even in a zipped format. The file was code named Paget]*. It traced the history of the Fayed family.

Mohamed Abdel Moneim Fayed was born in the Bakas neighbourhood of Alexandria in Egypt in 1929, eldest son of a primary school teacher. He married into the wealth of the Khashoggi family and was employed in the Khashoggi import business in Saudi Arabia. He became financial adviser to the Sultan of Brunei in 1966, and then he came to Britain in 1974. In 1979 he purchased The Ritz hotel in Paris, and in 1985, with his brother Ali, he purchased Harrods department store in London, after a bitter battle with Tiny Rowlands (a bloody fight which at one point included Mohamed's arrest). Then came the 'Cash for Questions' scandal when Mohamed was accused of offering money to Members of Parliament Neil Hamilton and Tim Smith to ask questions in the English Parliament.

The file explained the persistent refusal of successive British governments to grant Mohamed a British passport. Ah, thought Smith as he read the reasons, that had never been made public. Still a spiteful pettiness by the British though, considering the sorts they *did* give British passports to.

The file had details and plans of all the Fayed properties around the world, even of his yachts the *Cujo* and the recently-purchased twenty million dollar *Jonikal* [later to be renamed *Sokar*].

The dossier was fair and factual – as would be expected from Six itself, but perhaps not from the biased Betty's Men. And it provided no explanation whatsoever for the constant demonisation and mocking of Mohamed Al Fayed by the British establishment and the British Press.

But, although it was good background, this was not what John Smith was after.

At first he thought it was not there. But then he found it. A small *Word* document tucked deeply between the plans of the *Jonikal* and a 30-page dissertation on the life of Emad (Dodi) Fayed's current (you're a bit behind there lads) fiancée Kelly Fisher.

It was a list of names. People whom he could contact if he needed to.

For British Intelligence had an agent in every Fayed business, every Fayed building throughout the world. They were all regular employees of Fayed, and they were paid substantial, six-monthly retainers by MI6 for their irregular services: keeping a watchful eye here, passing on information gleaned there, taking the occasional photograph (British Intelligence was experimenting with hiding cameras in mobile telephones and key rings).

This was good, thought John Smith. Very good.

He would need to make at least one of these people an offer they simply could not refuse.

Via Catalana, Rome, Italy

"Chris, come look at this," called Melanie from the *soggiorno*. "I think I need your help."

The Greek woman came in, drying her hands on a tea towel. "What iss it?"

"I know we missed her in Greece," said Melanie. "But I asked Barking Dog to scan Hellenic police networks, just in case there was anything reported. And look."

Christina leant on her colleague's shoulders and balanced her chin on Melanie's thick red hair. On the screen was a list of police communications made in the last five days concerning Princess Diana. The index was in the women's selected language of English, but the source reports would naturally be in Greek.

"Here, sit down," Melanie stood up. "Can you have a look at the reports? There's only ten of them. Is the drying-up done?"

"It's finished." Christina passed across the tea towel as she sat down.

It took only three minutes for her to read the Greek reports. "Nothing significant. Just reports noting the arrival and departure of the boat at the islands. The Press are following them, but there has been no trouble." As Christina turned to get up, her hand brushed against the Enter key. The screen changed. "Oh shit," she gasped. "What haf I done?"

Melanie peered at the screen. "Don't worry. You've activated The Professor. He will look for any wider links between my original inputs – Diana and Greek islands. There'll be nothing there."

But Melanie was wrong. Within two minutes she was calling Christina back into the room. In the kitchen, coffee was brewing.

"Chris, The Professor has found something. One link. A death on the island of Hydra one day after Diana stopped there." Even Melanie thought this was stretching things. "That's a link?"

"Let me read the police report," said Christina.

Melanie clicked the on-screen link, and a new page appeared. Christina read it.

"A freelance Press photographer named... Claude Dumoulin – what sort of a name is that? Mr *Windmill?* – slipped and fell in hiss shower at the Leto

Hotel. Broke hiss neck. No sign of theft or violence. An accident." She turned. "But Diana had left the day before. I don't understand. Iss The Professor trying too hard?"

Melanie shrugged. "He only does what he's programmed to do. He just reports. It's up to us to accept or reject the link. But I don't see how this... Hold on, hold on. We have no record of internal travel, but let's make some assumptions. We know Ramirov arrived in Athens on Monday. We have nothing since then, but we know he is after Princess Di. Di is cruising the islands. So naturally we assume he follows her – but it's hard to know where the boat will be going next. He can't quite catch up with her. Wherever she goes, he arrives there after her. She visits Hydra, he arrives there just after she leaves. Then the next day a Press photographer dies."

Christina nodded in understanding. "It iss hiss cover," she said it lowly, matter-of-factly. She was staring at the screen but her eyes were elsewhere, looking back twenty-three years. "He hass done it in the past. He assumes different identities." There was a small catch in her voice. "Mr Ramirov has become a Press photographer, a paparazzo."

"Time then," said Melanie, "for us to move. He's getting closer. And so are we. Log in to the Fayed websites. Find out where Diana is next. We need to be there."

Montparnasse, Paris, France

"So what do we have?" Chief Inspector Pierre Jamo sat at the small table in the kitchen of his apartment in Montparnasse and watched admiringly as Inspector Claudette Ibrahim cut sandwiches over on the work surface. Except for a dainty apron tied around her waist, she was completely naked. The small, shapely-but-rock-solid rump and muscular back were lightly tanned, without a bikini line.

"Salami and cheese," she turned, her taut breasts a perfect complement to the trim curves below.

"No, no, no – the case. Mesrine." Clarified Jamo as the plate was set down on the table and she turned back to get the pot of coffee.

"Work, work, work, that's all you ever think of!" she sighed in mock exasperation.

"Not always," he grinned.

"Sex, sex, sex, that's all you ever think of!"

"Inspector!"

"Sorry, Chief." She sat down and in her turn admired the hairy chest opposite her, above the hint-of-podgy stomach. There was a distinct bite mark above his right nipple.

"Mesrine. Let's go through it," Jamo folded a piece of loose salami and popped it in his mouth. "One, Commissaire Charles Fleury-Goujon."

"Charles Fleury-Goujon," said Claudette. "The original Commissaire of the BCP. Paralysed in a fire eighteen years ago in which two other men died. Officially it was a Masonic meeting. Unofficially, there are suggestions that it was a brotherhood far higher even than the masons."

"The Organisation. The OAS."

"*Oui*. Fleury and one of the two BCP Chief Inspectors at the time, Paul Richer, were involved in… what?" She paused to take a bite of sandwich. She spoke with her mouth full. "We do not know. Nothing has ever been proven. But it is thought it all goes back to Algeria in 1958. It is thought Paul Richer was a friend of Jacques Mesrine – a *flic* and the most infamous criminal this country has ever produced! It is all rumour, rumour, rumour. Speculation."

"So let's go both ways - "

"We already did half an hour ago. Have you forgotten already?"

"Stop it. Officially what do we have?"

She sipped her coffee. "Chief Inspector Paul Richer and Chief Inspector Claude Gerard were both involved in the final hunt for Mesrine. Gerard found him. Richer died apprehending Mesrine. Gerard was killed the next day."

"Not by Mesrine then."

"Maybe by his accomplices, his gang. Three days later, Fleury and two others were trapped in a fire at a Masonic stroke OAS meeting up in Belleville. The two others died, Fleury was paralysed."

"An accident?" Jamo picked up a sandwich and began to take out the salami and cheese.

"No proof otherwise. Faulty electrical wiring."

"Too many deaths an accident does not make."

She looked at him stone-faced. "Whatever. Tell me, was there any point in me making sandwiches if you are going to pick them apart?"

He finished his coffee and poured more into both their cups. "Unofficially?"

She watched him put the pot down and begin to eat the components of the dismantled sandwich. "In short, Mesrine was working on something for Richer and Fleury. They even helped him bust out of jail. Gerard just got in the way."

"Do we know what Mesrine was working on?"

"No."

"Do we know if he succeeded?"

"No."

"Don't know much, do you?"

"Fuck you, Jamo."

He gave a Cheshire cat grin.

"And don't even think about it," she warned. "Twice in one evening is enough."

"Who says?"

"Says the pussy you're poking. And as of ten minutes ago, we're on duty... sir."

"I like a subordinate who shows me respect."

"Its not only my respect I've shown you. For a Chief Inspector you do, surprisingly, have your uses."

"Is that all I am to you? A sex object?"

"Yes. Have I ever led you to believe otherwise?"

He looked at her tanned skin, the muscular shoulders, the pert small-nippled breasts. He said, "Move in with me."

Inwardly she winced. It was not that unexpected. Why did men always have to complicate things? She could have been cruel, but she let him down gently. "You know I can't. It's not allowed. We shouldn't even be fucking."

He sighed. "I know, I know. But it's a nice fantasy, *n'est-ce pas?*"

She said nothing.

Jamo sat back in the chair, running his hands down through his hair and over his face. "Do one thing for me, will you?" he asked with a touch of weariness.

"Chief?"

"Find out as much as you can. What was Mesrine working on? Who else was involved? How does Veronique Chevalier fit into all this. And why, eighteen years later, are people beginning to die again?"

Ω

Saturday August 23 1997

The South of France

The tall blonde woman in the striped pastel swimsuit screamed in fear and joy, and clung tightly to her companion as their jet-ski bounced over the Mediterranean Sea just off St Tropez.

The machine came to a stop and Diana swung her right leg over Dodi's shoulder, as if to emphasise his smaller stature.

They laughed. My, how they laughed.

They seemed oblivious to the army of photographers, snapping at them through 300mm lenses from the shore. Or others in small motor boats or on their own jet-skis coming as close as they dare, as close as Rees-Jones and the Fayed security boys, watching from the nearby *Jonikal*, would allow.

On the shore, paparazzo Claude Dumoulin trained his camera on the laughing couple. This Dumoulin was a chubby-looking man with a completely bald pate and a veritable forest of black hair poking out through his half-undone shirt. He was nodding gently, his head slightly inclined to the left, as he focussed on the happy woman with her leg in the air.

But there was no film in his camera. This was just pretence. If they had not wanted it to look natural, this would be a gun he was holding.

And right now her head would be splattered across the blue Mediterranean.

Fish food.

Ω

Sunday August 24 1997

Monte Carlo

From her position on the Place Beaumarchais, Christina watched the excited hoard of photographers clammering outside the Hotel Ermitage and Repossi's, the society jewellers. Diana and Dodi had arrived a few moments before.

She scanned the faces. None of them even looked remotely like Ramirov.

But she knew he would be around somewhere.

She could feel it in her bones.

But this was frustrating, waiting for him to show his hand – waiting for him to do whatever it was he was going to do to Lady Diana.

And what he was going to do was obvious: Ramirov wasn't a kidnapper, he was a killer. Diana was to be assassinated.

Christina and Melanie had discussed reporting the matter to 'The Authorities'. They had discussed it with Tel Aviv, and Tel Aviv had agreed with them: the murder of the English Princess was nothing to do with the Israelis. Their mission was the elimination of Ramirov. If they prevented the assassination, all well and good. Otherwise, tough.

The Fayed Camp in London were quietly leaking to the Press the couple's planned itineraries one or two days in advance. Barking Dog had latched on to the telephone calls and faxes from publicist Max Clifford's office. So the Israelis knew that today was Monaco, tomorrow was Portofino (the one in Corsica). After that had not been decided.

And where Diana and Dodi would be, so would be the paparazzi. And in amongst the paparazzi somewhere, they knew, was the world's most notorious and ruthless killer. Waiting to strike.

Ω

Monday August 25 1997

Rue des Saussaies, Paris, France

"We must approach it logically," said Inspector Claudette Ibrahim. "eighteen years is a lot of ground to rake over. Things can be buried deeply over such a length of time. Mesrine has passed into legend and memories fade. So I think we should start from the present and work backwards...

"Commissaire Charles Fleury-Goujon is murdered. As he is dying he phones this office – you – and screams 'Mesrine'. Presumably his killer's name. But how can that be? Has Mesrine come back from the dead. *C'est impossible.*

"*Alors,* Veronique Chevalier née Lensens is murdered in a most horrific fashion, choked to death by a spoon wedged down her throat. To me that sounds like revenge or torture. Revenge for what? Torture for what?

"The first suspect in such cases is the spouse. But Michel Chevalier is murdered too. He could have murdered her before being murdered himself, of course – but that's stretching things. The chances are the same person killed them both. Who was the intended victim? Obviously Veronique, because of the manner of her death. The husband's death was more simple, a straight suffocation. He probably just happened to be there. So let's put him to one side.

"Charles Fleury-Goujon and Veronique Chevalier *née* Lensens. What is the connection between them? Why, it's none other than the late, lamented Jacques Mesrine. Mesrine stole some papers from Veronique's father eighteen years ago, and then four days later came back and murdered the father and his wife. Revenge on the Chief Prosecutor who put him away for twenty years.

"But wait a minute. Does this *really* make sense, looking back at it? Why didn't Mesrine kill Chief Prosecutor Lensens at the same time as he stole the documents? Why come back four days later to kill him?

"Let's make an outrageous assumption. Let's assume Mesrine did *not* kill the Chief Prosecutor, somebody else did. Similarly, let us assume that Mesrine's so-called 'gang' did not attempt to murder Charles Fleury-Goujon three days after Mesrine's death. Somebody else did. Where does that leave us with Mesrine?

"Mesrine is working for Chief Inspector Paul Richer and Commissaire Charles Fleury-Goujon of the BCP. He is searching for a document for them. He finds it, in the ownership of Chief Prosecutor Lensens. He takes it from him. Before Mesrine can deliver it to the BCP, he is shot while being re-arrested. Paul Richer dies at the same time. Let's just pause there..." She looked over at Jamo, who was rapt.

She went on. "Is it all logical? Does it all make sense? *Mais oui*. It is known Richer was chasing after Mesrine's car when he died. Was Mesrine about to hand over the document to him? No document was found in the car, in any of Mesrine's houses or boltholes, not on his tart Sylvie Jacquot, nowhere. So where was it?

"Now then, let's leave that story there. Let us treat what happens subsequently as a new story.

"The day after Mesrine and Richer die, Chief Inspector Claude Gerard – the *flic* responsible for locating Mesrine – is killed in Montmartre. Why and by whom? We have assumed it was revenge by Mesrine's 'gang'. Let's now assume nothing of the sort.

"Two days later, an attempt is made to obliterate the High Command of the OAS, of which Charles Fleury-Goujon is Colonel-In-Chief. Fleury only just escapes with his life, but he is paralysed, finished. The others die.

"And then that is it. It all stops. *Finito*. So what unanswered questions do we have? Firstly, the document – where is it? What happened to it? What does it contain? Secondly, the murders of Lensens and Gerard and the attempted murder of Fleury. If we discount revenge, why were they murdered? What is the other main reason for murder? To keep people quiet. Why did Lensens, Gerard and the High Command of the OAS need to be kept quiet? Because they knew something. What? Where the document was? No. People would want to know that information, not have it kept quiet. So what did they know... What the document *contained*? Ah, ha! Now that is something someone might want kept quiet. Perhaps the document contained something that was worth killing for. Logical, *oui*?"

"*Oui*," nodded Jamo.

"But after all this, it all goes quiet. Lensens and Gerard are dead, Fleury is effectively dead. The document has vanished, the contents suppressed.

"And it remains that way for eighteen years. Then, out of the blue, Fleury is murdered – really murdered this time, in a way that suggests torture. Veronique, the daughter of the last man known to possess the document except Mesrine, is tortured and murdered too.

"Both tortured. Torture is used to extract information. What information? What is the link? *Bien sûr*, the link is the document, not Mesrine. They both have knowledge. What knowledge? The secret of the document.

"Suddenly, eighteen years later, the secret rears its head again. And those who know it, or *might* know it, begin to die. Who has started the killing again?

"And" continued Inspector Claudette Ibrahim, "what the fuck is this secret that brings death in its wake down the generations?"

Ω

Tuesday August 26 1997

Rue des Saussaies, Paris, France

"Utter bullshit," commented Commissaire Gillian Colet the next day when Jamo quoted Ibrahim's theories to her almost verbatim. "Granted Inspector Ibrahim presents a very good case, a thesis that would have earned her goods marks at the Academy. But in the real world it is bullshit. And, as I have said before and you know I do not like to repeat myself, we do not investigate murders."

"*Mais -* "

"If she is so confident of her ideas, perhaps she should share them with the *Police Judiciaire*. And perhaps she should join them. The BCP has its own responsibilities. The new boy Prime Minister of England is visiting soon, and we need every available member of staff to ensure his comfort."

"But - "

"That is all. Please get back to your work. Your BCP work, Chief Inspector."

Jamo slammed his fist down onto a thick pile of folders on his desk. "That's the last time that bitch humiliates me."

"I told you not to even try," said Claudette. "You are a fool to yourself."

"That is all the thanks I get?"

"You will get your thanks in five days time, I've got the plumbers in at the moment."

"Great. Well, we're not giving up. We've got that new guy from England visiting soon, and Lady Diana keeps popping in with her latest lover, but apart from that the summer workload isn't too bad. The mundane stuff can be handled by the sergeants. So, Inspector - "

"Yes, Chief?"

"Clear the decks. We've got some murders to investigate. Commissaire Colet can go fuck herself. And when we've solved this, I'll take it straight to the Minister himself."

Henri's Bar, Paris, France

"So we are agreed. Mesrine is the secondary link," said Jamo. "The document – the secret – is the first. Someone again wants to know the secret. And they will go to extreme lengths, even murder, to find it."

Claudette nodded as she popped the last piece of croissant into her mouth. They were at the *zinc* in Henri's Bar.

"What we need to establish," mused Jamo as he took a swig of his *vin rouge*, "is who would know the secret? Other than those who want it suppressed. Paul Richer, Charles Fleury-Goujon, and perhaps Claude Gerard, all knew it – and they are all dead. Veronique Chevalier née Lensens might have known it – she might have seen it in her father's collection. Dead. *Alors,* who else might know it?"

"We must go back," Claudette gave Jamo a look as he lit a *Gitanes*, but said nothing about it. "Back eighteen years. Who is still alive who might know the secret? Whose life might we save if we get there before the murderer?"

"Who, if anybody, would Mesrine have trusted?"

They both looked at each other and said simultaneously, "Sylvie Jacquot."

Ω

Wednesday August 27 1997

Rue Ponceau, Paris, France

Professionally she now went by the name of Renée, in memory of her lover, her future husband, her life, which had been taken from her so cruelly on November 2 1979. The day France had murdered Jacques René Mesrine. She had been shot and wounded at the same time, and their child – Fifi, the poodle – had died in her arms at the scene.

Jacques had been her future. She had been the future Madame Mesrine. They had been on their way to start their new life in Marly-le-Roi, but God had decided that they would never get there. Not only that, but God had decided that she would be left destitute as well – for Jacques had not changed his will. Everything was left to his family – she was not even mentioned.

When she was thrown out of hospital after ten days, she had nowhere else to go. Their apartment in Rue Belliard was rented, and the lease had expired. Their new apartment in Marly-le-Roi now belonged to his family. So back she went to her old apartment in Rue Ponceau – and back to her old life.

And very soon she was as popular as ever.

But that had been eighteen years ago.

Now she was in her late middle forties. The hair was still bottle-assisted blonde and the breasts – always disproportionately huge and with an horizontal suspension that defied both gravity and science – had grown even bigger with age.

But she was a realist. Experience was always required, but so was fresh meat. A few years ago, when she finally admitted to herself that her 112HH bra had mysteriously become too small to contain the girls, she had decided to make the natural progression upwards. To a business of her own.

She did not run a house, that would be too grand and she would need a 'sponsor'. But her telephone agency had been popular from the start. Firstly by word of mouth from her clients both past and present and then – in the more liberal nineties – by discreetly worded advertisements in various suitable magazines.

It was a good living, and she still ran it from her apartment in Rue Ponceau. Real estate which in 20 years had changed from being regarded as in the downmarket, whore-lined Rue St Denis area to upmarket, sought-after 'Paris Centrale'.

The doorbell rang. That would be her 14:00 interview, the new girl. She went over to the entry-phone.

"*Allo?*"

"*Bonjour, c'est Veronique Lens madame.*"

"*Bonjour ma belle,* come on up. *Deuxième étage.*"

Renée made one final check in the mirror on her way to the front door. Not bad, she thought, for a woman with a lifetime of adventure behind her – and enough men to fill the Stade de France (several times over).

Veronique Lens was a slim girl, long blonde hair (looked more *l'Oréal* than peroxide), dressed in a pretty flowered dress and small pink jacket, carrying a small, strapless handbag. She wore only light make-up. Surprisingly, she was older than Renée expected. She looked to be in her early thirties.

After introductory pleasantries, including a kiss, Renée stepped aside and admired Veronique's bubble butt as she walked inside.

"*Café, ma belle?*"

"That would be nice, thank you." Veronique had a low, very pleasant voice.

The kitchen and salon were open plan, an 'American Kitchen' as the Europeans liked to call it, so they talked as Renée prepared the *Maison du Café*.

"Please, sit down if you wish Veronique."

"*Merci.*" She sat rather primly on the edge of the armchair, legs together, bag clasped on her lap. The timid, submissive type, thought Renée. A lot of men liked that.

"You are," Renée came straight to the point, "older than I imagined."

Veronique smiled politely. "Does that cause a problem, madame?"

"Call me Renée, please. No, no problem. My agency caters for all tastes." She came in with a cafetiere, then went back for the cups. "Have you done this work before?"

"No."

"Then why, may I ask...?" Renée brought in two mugs.

"I am divorced," Veronique sighed, noting that there were no spoons. "The bastard cut me off without a *sou*. He disappeared. No matter what the courts may decide, he cannot be found and maintenance orders cannot be enforced. I need money."

"There are easier ways," Renée sat down opposite her.

"Sugar?" asked Veronique.

"*Pardon?*"

"Do you have sugar?"

"*Ah, mais non. Je suis desolée.* I don't take it, and I never think to have it in for my guests."

"*Pas de problème. Du lait?*"

"Neither."

So no stirring necessary.

Veronique sipped her black coffee. She said, "Yes, there might be easier ways – for some. But for me? Non. I was married to that bastard from an early age. I have a certain lifestyle to maintain. A certain circle to move in. I cannot be seen working the till in Monoprix for ten hours a day!" She laughed. "And what could be easier than fucking? Minute for minute, the most profitable job around."

Renée was looking at her appraisingly. Her naïveté, her keenness, reminded her of herself when she first started out. She nodded. "I will need to train you, to ease you in."

"As you wish, madame – Renée."

"May I see you?"

"*Pardon?*"

Renée moved her hands, indicating Veronique's body.

"Ah," Veronique understood. She put her mug and bag on the coffee table. Business-like she stood up and removed her small jacket. Then she reached down to the hem of her dress and in one fluid motion pulled it off over her head and dropped it to the floor.

She wore nothing underneath save for her high-heeled shoes.

She stood there in front of the other woman.

Renée was impressed. "You shave?"

"Obviously. My husband liked the little girl look."

"So do many of my clients. It is also more hygienic. Turn please."

Slowly Veronique turned a full three-sixty.

Renée nodded in admiration. "You have a superb bottom, *ma belle.*"

"Thank you. So I've been told."

"Please, put your dress back on."

"Before I do, can I ask you something?"

"*Bien sûr.*"

"Seeing as you've seen one of my little secrets," Veronique nodded downwards. "Could you tell me one of yours?"

"One of my secrets?" Renée laughed. "*Ma fille,* I have so many. We do in our profession. What subject would you like?"

The nude woman stood with her legs slightly apart, confident body language.

"I want to know *the* secret."

Renée frowned.

"The one Jacques died for."

It was as if Renée had been punched in the face. She was literally knocked back in the chair.

"Jacques...?"

"You are Sylvie Jacquot, are you not? His last lover - "

Renée was confused. "I – I was more than his lover. We were to be married."

"And they murdered him, I know."

Tears welled in the older woman's eyes. "He was my life. I had given up everything for him..." She looked up, frowning. "Who... Who are you?"

Veronique knelt down on the floor next to the chair. She took Sylvie's hands in hers. "You never met any of his family, did you? His children. He never introduced you."

"That – that was for the future. When we had settled in Marly." She could smell the gentle musk of the naked younger woman.

"But that was never to happen," said Veronique. "They had decided that. They killed him. But why?"

"Why?! He was Jacques Mesrine, the most wanted man in Europe."

"But was that reason to kill him?"

"What are you saying?"

"Have you never asked yourself why he was executed? Gunned down in the street like a wild dog. You lived with him. In those last months he was searching for something. For a secret. I know he found it. I want to know what the secret is."

Sylvie was crying, the newly reopened sores of her memories almost too much to bear. "I – I don't know. He never told me things. For my own good, he said. So I could never testify against him if he was re-arrested." She gave a sad, humourless laugh. "He always used to say 'What little girls don't know won't hurt me.'"

Veronique was gripping her hand tightly. "So you know nothing about the secret?"

"It was all to do with the Captain."

"The Captain?"

"From his army days. Captain Richer – how could I ever forget that name? 'For richer for poorer.' Jacques found whatever it was he was looking for. It was a letter or a document. To do with the British. He never let me see it. The day he was.... was.... he got me to post it to Richer. I never knew what it was." Her eyes had glazed with her memories. Her darling, darling Jacques. At that moment she wanted to die, to meet him in eternity.

Veronique just knelt there, holding Sylvie's hand, unconcerned with her nakedness.

Then Sylvie looked up. "And you are...?"

"I am a daughter out to avenge her father. A daughter seeking the truth.

Seeking to know why. Seeking justice." She raised herself off her haunches. "Let me tell you about myself."

Leaning forward, she began to kiss Sylvie Jacquot on the mouth...

Sardinia

The boat *Iliad* bobbed up and down on the gentle Mediterranean waves, making it difficult for the ten men lined up against the port side to take a good picture. About two hundred metres in front of them sat the *Jonikal*.

But never mind. This was Diana and Dodi Fayed. This was the romance of the century: the Christian Virgin Bride and the Muslim Playboy. The world's papers and magazines were paying fortunes, even for blurred shots of the couple.

Claude Dumoulin was at the end of the line of clicking crows, at the bow of the boat. To maintain his cover he had to appear to be one of them - he had even chipped in his five thousand francs share to hire the *Iliad*. But he knew nothing would happen today. There were no 'natural deaths' he could arrange out here – short of pulling Diana over the side in the darkness, like he had done with Robert Maxwell six years before.

Dumoulin was just keeping up appearances being on the boat. But he was a very, very patient man. He had five million US dollars worth of patience.

His opportunity would come.

He looked up as a helicopter flew over his head.

It would be recorded later that the helicopter was hired by photographer James Andanson [*real name Jean Paul Gonin, and himself to be murdered in 2000*]. In fact the helicopter was hired by Israeli Intelligence. The reason it hovered above the *Jonikal* was not to get pictures of the yacht and its occupants, but so that the passenger in the helicopter – a woman with stunning red hair – could get pictures of the occupants of the *Iliad*.

Ω

Thursday August 28 1997

Sardinia

"Barking Dog has checked all of them," said Melanie back at the Cervo Hotel in Porto Cervo. "And guess what? They all check out – except one."

"Yess!" Christina punched the air. "It iss Ramirov, yess? Do we haf him?"

"Hold on, hold on. We *think* we have him. Barking Dog has determined that this one is not a photographer, but at the moment we don't know who the mystery man is. Barking Dog is checking the world's ID databases."

"Describe him."

"Bald, for a start. And I mean really bald, not shaved. Chubby face - "

"Good."

"One seven eight centimetres, huge belly, hairy chest and – would you believe? – wearing a medallion!"

"Hmm."

"The Americans have Facial Recognition Technology, and Barking Dog has cuckooed into it. We'll know soon."

Barking Dog reported back seventy-two minutes later.

Melanie looked at the screen.

"FRT has given us six matches. All passport applications. All the same person, but with a series of different names and looks. Ibaldo Ronaldo, a Brazilian. Igor Rimski, a Russian. Ioannis Rigakis, a Greek. Ib Rahman, a Qatari. Ito Rennes, a Frenchman. And – ah here it is, hun – Ian Ramsey, a Texan." She sat back in the chair. "Mr Ramirov, you are ours."

"But haven't we forgotten something?" said Christina. "They've gone. The yacht has gone and the photographers have gone."

"I know"

"And we let them go."

"What were we supposed to do? Two middle aged women. Should we have gone to the gang of photographers and said sorry but please could you stay here in Sardinia until our computer identifies which one of you is not a photographer but an international assassin? It's no problem, Chris."

"You think not?"

"Ask yourself something. Why hasn't he done it already, Ramirov? Why hasn't he killed Diana?"

"I don't know."

"The Professor brought it to our attention. Princess Grace, the Duchess of Windsor. The Royals. Only *rumours* when it is the Royals. Why? Because the deaths seemed 'natural': a car crash, asphyxiation due to throat blockage in her sleep. Ramirov is planning a *natural* death for Diana. Something he cannot do at sea, unless he makes her fall overboard like he did with our agent Robert. He is waiting for his chance. And now we know where he will try it."

"We do? Where? How?"

"Their next itinerary has just been released. They are going to Paris for a night on Saturday."

Barking Dog provided the connection into all the world's databases. The Professor was the most powerful information link program yet devised. The systems were not prey to RiRo [*rubbish in, rubbish out*]. No human data input was required. The systems merely needed to be told what to do. They provided accurate information.

But then came the weakness. The information was provided to humans. It was up to the humans to interpret and analyse the results given.

And that was how, on August 28 1997, the Israelis made one huge, fundamental, glaring error.

Rue Ponceau, Paris, France

Inspector Claudette Ibrahim sat on her Ducati M900 outside 3 Rue Ponceau and looked up at the second floor windows through the open visor of her crash helmet. Her natural instinct to get things done, to get things sorted, was urging her to go and kick in the front door. However, her police training held her back. One unanswered cold call did not entitle her to force entry. Sylvie Jacquot might be out shopping. Or working.

Claudette wondered whether to leave her card in the letterbox, but she decided against it and started the bike.

As she drove off down Rue Ponceau and turned right into Rue de Palestro, she saw two local girls on the corner, dressed in the obligatory revealing outfits, doggies on leads, chatting in between clients.

Claudette smiled. No *salad basket* for you today ladies, feel free to continue your good work.

Rue des Saussaies, Paris, France

Claudette was back in the office when Jamo arrived at 15:00. He had spent the morning at the Vietnamese Embassy over in the 16th, mediating on a matter regarding a junior clerk at the embassy and certain sexual demands made by a senior consul.

"Good afternoon, Inspector."

"Afternoon, Chief."

"Any luck?"

"She wasn't in. I didn't leave my card."

"Best not to alert her. Don't want her running scared for no reason."

"The Bitch wants to see you."

"*Merde.* When did she call?"

"About an hour ago."

Jamo picked up the phone and keyed the Commissaire's number. "*Bonjour, salop.* Washed your fanny today?" He put the phone down. "She's engaged. I'll go along."

Commissaire Gillian Colet was off the telephone and was examining a folder on her desk, reading glasses on the end of her nose, when Jamo entered by invitation.

"Ah, Pierre. *Merci.*" She was being pleasant. Meant there was a job on.

"Commissaire," he nodded. She did not invite him to sit down.

"I've had the Minister on the phone. The British have contacted him. About Lady Di. You do know Lady Di?"

"Of course I do, you stupid bitch. She's only the most famous woman in the world." He actually said, "*Bien sûr.*"

"Apparently she's going to be popping in and out of France a lot. With her new beau, the Fayed boy. She was already in Paris last month, on 25th – but nobody except the Fayed security people knew about it. The embassy didn't know until afterwards."

"*Oui.*"

"The Brits cannot ask officially because Lady Di is no longer royal, and she has foregone official protection. But she does not know about the *unofficial* protection. They have asked that we look after her – discreetly – when she is here."

"I will need more staff."

"Which you cannot have. She spends a lot of time on the Fayed's yacht, so you can liaise with the local forces down on the coast. You have national jurisdiction, so there will be no problem."

"And here? The father owns The Ritz, does he not? And several other properties in the city."

"When she's here, you and Ibrahim look after her. No one else. It is unofficial, after all. When she is in the city, she takes priority over all other work. Understand?"

"Of course I understand."

She looked up at the edge in his voice.

"Do you know when she next plans to be here?" he asked.

"No. You find out."

"*D'accord.*"

"How were things with the Vietnamese?"

"Oh, apparently the junior clerk liked and welcomed the attention of the senior consul. The complaint was made by a nearby resident who could see their adventures from her window." He looked over at Colet's window and at her enviable view down Avenue de Marigny. "I told them to keep the blinds closed."

He turned, and as he neared the door the Commissaire said casually, "How are things with Mesrine?"

Jamo smiled to himself. He was used to her little management techniques. He turned. "This office has nothing to do with Mesrine."

She smiled triumphantly. "Good. Please remember that."

He turned to go and once more she called him back. "Pierre?"

"*Oui?*"

"You coming round tonight? It is appraisal week."

He thought of Claudette and her visiting plumbers. Might as well. "*D'accord,* Gillian," he said with a small smile.

"The Brits cannot ask officially because Lady Di is no longer royal, and she has foregone official protection," explained Jamo.

"I can accompany her while she is here," suggested Claudette.

"Oh yes, in your leathers and with your kick-the-door-in attitude, you'll make the perfect complement to her."

"I can be a lady when I want to be."

He smiled. "Don't I know that. No, we are to be discreet. She is not to know she is being protected."

"Disguise?"

"Maybe. We'll see. Liaise with the British, will you? See what they think, when she'll be here, *et cetera.*"

"What about Sylvie?"

"I'll try to see her tonight."

Rue Ponceau, Paris, France

At 23:00 the streets were as busy as ever. Rue Ponceau might now be 'Paris Centrale' rather than the sordid 'Rue St Denis District', but the girls still plied their trade in the time-honoured fashion.

Business was brisk tonight, the girls were busy, and Jamo was propositioned only once as he drove slowly up to number 3. The girl thought he was stopping because of her waving, and she walked up business-like but sensual as he opened the door.

"Hello handsome. Care to party?" She wore a black basque with open-nippled brassiere, suspenders and black stockings. A small G-string covered her play area. A large silver-studded black leather bag was over her shoulder. She had no dog, therefore the bag would contain – amongst other things – a gun or a knife.

"Not tonight, LouLou," smiled Jamo.

The girl frowned. She liked to try to remember all her customers, but this one's face escaped her.

"And," continued Jamo, "I don't like boys."

"Ah," the prostitute nodded, and the voice that came out was now purely masculine. "Now I've placed you. How are you, Inspector? What's it been? A couple of years? Come to pull me?"

"In neither sense," said Jamo. "And it's Chief Inspector now, I've moved on to other things. I'm not Vice any more."

"So I'm a lucky girl then."

"Know if Renée's in?" Jamo looked up to the second floor. The curtains across the windows were heavy, but there were no telltale cracks of light.

"Haven't seen her for a couple of days. But there's no reason I should. She only employs bitches."

"Now, now, young man. Behave yourself. Just because nature gave you an unwanted dick."

LouLou grinned and turned her back. "Want to poke your nose into my business?" the feminine voice returned.

Jamo gave the naked cheeks a firm slap, and the hermaphrodite ran off giggling down the road.

A man was just leaving the building (flushed but sheepish) and Jamo caught the front door before it could close.

Up on the *deuxième étage* there was no reply when he pushed the bell button. He waited a few moments and then banged with his fist on the door. "Madame Renée!" he called.

Nothing.

Now this was worrying. Claudette had failed to gain entry yesterday. There had been just the ansaphone on for two days. And what nobody but Jamo, Claudette and the perpetrator knew was that Sylvie Jacquot was potentially the next victim.

Potentially? Or now actually?

Jamo pushed at the door. Naturally it did not budge. Tentatively he tried his shoulder against it. Painful. Where was Claudette and her one-kick-and-I'm-in when he needed her?

Okay, he would have a go. If she could do it, so could he.

He stepped back across the corridor.

"Monsieur?"

The query came just as he was about to take off. He looked to his left.

Coming up the stairs was a middle-aged woman, bottle-blonde hair, massive breasts straining the stitching on her flimsy summer top, nipples protruding a full two centimetres from the tits and stretching the garment even further.

"Madame Renée?" Jamo fought to gain his composure and at the same time not to stare at the incredible mammaries.

"Oui."

"I wonder if I might have a word?"

"Who are you, monsieur?"

Wordlessly, in case of ears, Jamo produced his ID.

She glanced at it superficially and nodded, also silently. "Come in, please."

Her legs were clad in tight denim jeans, and she carried an overnight bag over her shoulder. Jamo nodded a mental *bonsoir* to her bottom as she passed.

Renée had washed and changed into a red dressing gown. She now prepared coffee in the kitchen as Jamo sat at the small table and admired the still-shapely middle-aged legs and, of course, the arse. He did not know that nineteen years previously Jacques Mesrine had sat at that same table and had the same thoughts. Carnality never changes.

Coffee made, Renée came over with the pot. Bowls and a basket of rolls and croissants were already on the table. At Jamo's querying look when she had first set them out, she had said "It is never too late – or too early – for breakfast, m'sieur. I eat when I want to, I eat when I need to. Join me if you wish."

Now Jamo broke a roll and dipped it into his coffee, enjoying the illicit feeling of breakfasting at midnight – and with a Madame as well.

"So, m'sieur," Renée was sitting at ninety degrees to Jamo, to his right, giving him an admirable view of her assets as the dressing gown dropped open at the cleavage and leg. "Which one was it?"

"Which one was what, madame?"

"The word you wanted."

"Ah. Pardon." Jamo placed another piece of soggy roll into his mouth and spoke as it dissolved. "It is something of a delicate matter."

"You wish to use my agency?"

"No, no, not at all. Not that I wouldn't. Another time, another place - "

"Another planet."

"Not that far," he smiled. "Madame Renée, it is an old matter. Something from your past."

It was her turn to smile as she put down her bowl of coffee. A small brown rim had been left on her upper lip, and Jamo wished he could lick it off. But she beat him to it with a tissue. She said softly, "Jacques."

"An easy guess, *n'est-ce pas?*"

"In some ways. He was taken from me eighteen years ago, and after the first two years things went quiet. I was left in peace. Now, it seems, the past has reawoken."

"Madame?"

"In a moment, Chief Inspector. What was your word?"

"I believe you are in danger, madame."

She said nothing and carried on eating.

He continued. "There have been killings recently. We have reason to believe they are connected to the matter Mes – Jacques – was involved in when he died. With my office, the BCP. Concerning the secret. It has raised its head again, and people are dying. One even said the name Mesrine as he died. As if Jacques had arisen from the grave seeking revenge - ridiculous, I know."

"If only."

"I believe you are in danger. You might be next on the killer's list."

"Why should I be on any killer's list, m'sieur?" she shrugged. "I have done nothing – nothing except to fall in love. I know nothing – nothing except that I know time does not heal. In my mind, Jacques is as alive today as he was eighteen years ago."

"That is the point, madame."

"What?"

"*Is* he still alive?"

She sniffed. "You are being ridiculous."

"I apologise. But someone is out there. They are searching for the secret – and they are killing."

Renée refilled their bowls and indicated the basket.

Jamo shook his head. "*Merci.*"

She looked at him, a sad, wistful look that proved – as if proof was needed – that she was still a woman in love. "I never knew what the secret was, he wouldn't tell me. Said it was for my own good. It now appears, all these years later, that my Jacques was right. There would be no reason for anyone to kill me. I do not know the secret. And I did no harm, to Jacques, to anyone."

Jamo frowned. He asked, "What are you not telling me, Sylvie?"

"What am I *not* telling you, m'sieur? Look within. Perhaps there is something I *am* telling you."

"You know who the killer is, don't you?"

"No, I do not know who it is."

"Is it you?"

"If I wanted revenge I would have taken it a long time ago. But they all died without any intervention from me."

"*Revenge?* The killer wants revenge? Not the secret? Or as well as the secret? I beg you to be open with me, Sylvie. I fear you are in great danger."

"I am in no danger."

"Tell me, please. What is it you are holding back?"

She glanced at the clock on the wall. "What I will tell you, m'sieur, is that it is now one o'clock in the morning and I am tired. I think your word is over. May I ask you to leave?"

Jamo was not pleased but he said, "Of course."

They stood up simultaneously. Sylvie's gown fell open and she made no attempt to cover herself. Neither did Jamo make any attempt not to look.

He produced his card from his pocket. "If you feel there is anything else you need to tell me, call me at any time. My mobile number is there also."

She walked him to the door. "All I wish, Chief Inspector, is to be left in peace. Despite what you think, history cannot repeat itself. Jacques is dead and," she gave a small, rueful laugh, "he has not come back to haunt us."

Jamo looked her up and down, from her head to her toes. He wondered how many men had been entertained by that magnificent body, both pre- and post- Jacques Mesrine.

"Take care, Sylvie," he said. "Madame Renée."

He turned and walked down the stairs.

Ω

Friday August 29 1997

Faubourg St Honoré, Paris, France

Claudette Ibrahim had dressed up for her 08:30 appointment at the British Embassy. Dressed up by her standards, that is. The leather biker's clothes and boots were gone, to be replaced by lightweight slingbacks, cream linen slacks and a simple white cotton T shirt. More care had been taken with her make-up.

"Claudette, hello," Ron Becker came down the grand staircase, and admired the tanned, taut arms as he shook her hand.

"It has been a while," Claudette's English was perfect. "How are you, Ronald?"

"Oh, mustn't grumble. Your new Commissioner keeping you busy?"

"Hence my visit. Your office?" She knew the way.

"Yep."

"And you. How are things?" She chatted as they climbed the stairs and made their way along the first floor corridor.

"Don't ask, my love. Don't ask. First we have a new government – always a concern, you never know what they're going to do. Cut backs in the Foreign Service and all that. And now we have this Diana business."

"Is she *ever* out of the newspapers?"

"Never. I think there was one edition of the *Daily Express* two years ago – a Monday, I think it was – when her picture did not appear. But since then she has been everywhere. Really the embassy could do without this. We get torn down the middle. We have our ambassadorial and consul duties and they do not include looking after an ex-royal who has given up official protection. On the other hand, certain parties in the UK remain concerned about her and we have to pander to their requests."

They had reached Becker's office and he closed the door behind them and motioned for Claudette to sit down. "Coffee?"

"Thank you, no."

"Do you mind if I smoke?"

"It is your office," she replied politely, shaking her head at the proffered packet. "I used to but I managed to give it up." She noted Becker's hesitation. "Please, go ahead. It does not bother me, I am past that stage now."

"You must have great willpower."

"Perhaps. When I resolve to do something, I do it."

Becker nodded admiringly as he lit up and blew a curtain of smoke between them. "So, Diana."

"Lady Di, yes."

Becker grinned at the old title by which the Princess of Wales was still known throughout the world.

"We can solve some of your problems," said Claudette.

Becker's guts moved. If only you knew, dear French *flicette* with your pert little poky nips, that the solution had already been set in motion.

"We have been asked by the Minister to provide official protection for her whenever she is in France. Our local agents will handle it when she is down on the coast. When she visits Paris, my office will handle it."

"Jesus, for God's sake don't let her know, she'll have forty fits."

"We will be discreet, of course. She will not know." Why was the Englishman staring at her like that? "When she is on French soil she will be under French protection. So that takes the weight off of you, *non?*"

"*Non – er, oui.* Yes. What, er, what sort of protection will you be giving her. How are you going to handle it?"

"That is what I wanted to discuss with you…"

Rue des Saussaies, Paris, France

Commissaire Gillian Colet was in a bad mood. A very bad mood. And that did not augur well for the man who now entered her office.

She waited until he had closed the door.

"And where the fuck were you last night?" she tried to repress her anger but her strained voice gave her away. "You said you were coming round."

"Gillian – " Jamo saw the frown. "*Commissaire,* excuse me. I had some urgent business. I could not get away."

"Police business, I trust?"

"*Mais naturellement - *"

"I would not like to think that your monthly appraisal was missed because of some private appointment." She stood up and came round the desk towards him.

"Of course not. I could not get away. I was with an informant for - "

Oh shit.

Colet stood in front of him, glasses still on the end of her nose. "Since when," she asked calmly, "does the BCP have informants?"

Oh hell.

Without warning, Colet slapped him hard across the face. "You bastard." She turned around, her back towards him.

"I am truly sorry."

"Not as sorry as you're going to be. You were with her, weren't you? Do you think I don't know the two of you have been screwing? Do you take me for an idiot?" She turned around to face him again. She had pulled her glasses off and Jamo could have sworn there was moisture in the corner of her left eye. "Do you really prefer a jumped-up little tomboy to me? A tart more suitable to the anti-riot squad than the BCP?"

"You approved her appointment last year."

"I didn't really have any choice, she applied – what the hell has that got to do with it?" She realised she was shouting. This was undignified. She stared at Jamo, breathing hard through her nose.

He said nothing. Was she going to follow-up on his informant gaff?

She gave one huge sigh, and then the vulnerable woman façade faded and the hard-faced bitch-Commissioner returned. She went back to her desk and sat down.

"Is the Inspector in?" she asked.

"No, she is visiting the British this morning. She will be Lady Di's protection when she is in Paris."

"Now that is a fitting use of her talents. I want to see her when she comes in."

"Why?"

Colet looked up. "I don't have to justify myself to *you*, Chief Inspector. If I want to talk to a member of my staff, I will do so. I do not need your permission."

"Of course not."

She started to sort through some papers on her desk.

After a moment, Jamo asked "Is that all?"

"Go." She flicked her hand at him like she was flitting away an irritating bug.

Down by his sides, Jamo's fists clenched. He turned to go.

Then, as usual, she called him back. "It really is appraisal time. As your rank no longer has staffing responsibilities, I will appraise Inspector Ibrahim this afternoon."

He did not say anything. He turned, then stopped with his back to her as she spoke again. "*Your* appraisal will take place tonight at ten o'clock. At my apartment. And this time you will keep the appointment. Do I make myself clear?"

Faubourg St Honoré, Paris, France

Inspector Claudette Ibrahim was two minutes into the five minute walk from the British Embassy to the Rue des Saussaies when her portable rang. This was the time before twee ringtone downloads, so it rang just like any other telephone.

She carried on walking down the Faubourg St Honoré as she pulled the phone from her bag.

"Allo?"

"Claudette, Pierre."

"*Oui?*"

"You still with the *rosbeefs?*"

"Just finished. I'm coming in."

"Don't. I need to talk to you, but I also need to get out of here. Before I kill someone."

"Ah now, let me guess. Couldn't be a certain Madame Commissaire, could it?"

"The fucking bitch."

"Ah, I was right then." She paused at Rue de l'Elysée until there was a break in the traffic. "Want an early lunch?"

What he really wanted was to take her back to his place and ram his frustrations out on her body, but he settled for the alternative. "Yes."

"*Henri's.* I'm almost there."

"I need a stiff one."

"That's my line, isn't it? *Deux grands calvados* and a litre of the coarsest red will await you, *mon roi.*"

Henri's Bar, Paris, France

The calvados was just a memory, as was half of the litre of red wine. Henri stood behind the bar, studying the football reports in *L'Equipe* and continuing his seventy year fight against his flatulence problem. Two old veterans of a similar vintage stood at the zinc and also participated in the farting bonding session. Old music (Claude François and Joe Dassin) came from somewhere, permeating the background.

Jamo and Ibrahim sat in a booth in a far corner. His anger was now abating, helped by a ten minute listening session by his colleague in which she had simply nodded and hmmd and hah-d, and generally agreed that Commissaire Gillian Colet was a *salop* of the highest order.

Claudette had an amused expression. "So let her give me my appraisal. I have no problem with that."

"She knows we're screwing."

She let the grin break across her face. "Really, how? You don't think she was watching when we stayed late that night - "

"God knows."

"She's only jealous. She probably wants to ravage you herself." Jamo said nothing. "After all, it's not often a girl comes across a true ten centimetres - "

"Hey!"

She laughed out loud. "I'll see her this afternoon."

Henri shuffled across with baguettes, cheese and two whole, raw, unpeeled onions.

With their alcohol entrées, the two police officers attacked the food with gusto. Jamo picked up an onion and bit into it like an apple, skin *et al*.

"How did things go with the British?" he asked.

"Excellent. Actually they're very pleased with us. Taken a weight off them. They cannot be seen to be protecting her now that she is no longer royal and has given up official protection. They are pleased to leave it in our hands."

"How will you do it?"

"We have also got to be discreet. But when she is on French soil she is under French jurisdiction, so we can do what we like."

"But how will you get close?"

"Well, it's not like she's under threat. The Irish won't be after her. But when she is in public she will have her own personal protection – *moi* – and she won't even know it."

She looked away teasingly and popped a piece of camembert into her mouth.

It was the first time in his life that Jamo had been jealous of a piece of cheese. "How?" he asked.

"How can I get close to Lady Di, and stay close to her, without flashing my ID? By flashing another ID!"

"What *are* you talking about?"

She rummaged in her bag and threw a plasticised card down onto the table. "It is genuine. They have a whole collection of them at the embassy. I just have to pick up a camera. Meet," she said proudly, "Mademoiselle Paparazza."

Rue des Saussaies, Paris, France

For every positive there is a negative. For every day there is a night. For every yin there is a yang.

So it was that for every good mood of Inspector Claudette Ibrahim, there was a reciprocal bad mood.

Her's occurred at 16:00 that afternoon, a cumulation of the last twenty minutes being appraised by Commissaire Gillian Colet.

Her work was good, Colet had agreed. Her investigative skills were sharp. She was worthy of her rank. But her attitude was simply not what was required in the 'diplomatic' BCP. The BCP needed negotiators, literal diplomats. Her brash, brazen attitude was more akin to the BRB or the anti riot squads.

And, announced Colet peremptorily, it was to the CRS Anti Riot Squad that Ibrahim would be transferred, straight after she had finished "this Lady Di business." Her probation in her rank was confirmed. Her probation in the BCP was over – she had failed.

And no, there was no appeal. She should expect to be moved by the end of September at the latest.

So for the second time that day, a member of staff left Colet's office with fists clenched and a desire to kill.

Jamo had gone home after the extended tactical briefing in *Henri's*. Claudette thought of going round to his place and thrusting her frustrations out on his body, but she settled for a solo return to Henri's where several more calvados and a packet of Camel awaited her. Given it up? You never give it up.

Back in her office, Commissaire Gillian Colet was pleased with herself. Both her senior members of staff sorted in one day. And Ibrahim's transfer might well stop them screwing – or if it continued at least it wouldn't be in-house.

The only in-house screwing around here was done at Commissaire level.

She wrote up the appraisal in Ibrahim's file. Nowadays, with line managers relieved of personnel duties, there was usually no need for them to see the formal report of their staff's appraisal. A verbal briefing usually sufficed. But this time she would take pleasure in letting Jamo see her full comments about his little moppet – and her dismissal from the BCP.

She would leave the file on his desk for the morning. Tonight, when he visited, she would not say a word – she hoped her mouth would be too full anyway.

Rue Vavin, Paris, France

As it was, Jamo found out about the dismissal at 17:00 – via a one-sided, foul-mouthed, 15 minute telephone tirade from Inspector Ibrahim.

He was furious, and his natural instinct was to invite Claudette around to comfort her (or at least to shag away her worries). But he could not. He had an appointment at 22:00 with The Bitch Queen, and the days were long gone when he could give both matinée and evening performances at different theatres.

So he just cluck-clucked as appropriate, promised to take the matter up tomorrow and wished Claudette well with her 'Lady Di business'.

When he put the phone down, he was pleased with himself. He thought Claudette would create when she was not invited round, but the thought seemed not to have occurred to her.

Now he had a few hours to spare, but he must remember not to shower or even wash.

For that was one of The Bitch's little secrets. The outward callous ice queen and the inward whore that was Commissaire Gillian Colet liked her men dirty.

Neuilly-sur-Seine, France

For a woman in her fifties, Gillian Colet had a reasonable body. Her breasts had grown pendulous with age, true, but the career spinster had no baby belly or stretch marks. She had two small love handles on her hips, and her thighs and upper arms were a little on the wobbly side. But all in all she was not bad.

Make-up applied, long grey hair down, washed and styled, she slipped into a diaphanous red silk kimono. Underneath she was naked save for a red silk G-string (she liked her men – her Dirty Boys, as she called them – to take it off with their mouths).

She had just put on some mood music when the doorbell rang. She looked at the clock on the escritoire: 21:45. Jamo was early. She liked it when her boys were eager.

At the salon door she gave one final look back to see that the place was tidy, and dimmed the lights to seduction level with the switch in the wall.

She undid the catch on the front door, but turned her back as the door slowly swung open. She knew he would like the view of her G-stringed bottom.

"Come in, *mon amour*," she spoke over her shoulder as she walked back to the salon. "Are you dirty?"

She heard the front door close and she could feel him coming up behind her. "Drink?" she asked.

She felt his hand touch her bottom. She smiled. He was keen. "Or do you want to just fuck?"

Now he was pushing her bottom, pushing her quickly into the salon. She almost ran with the pressure of the push, and she giggled. "My, my, you are eager. Has it been so long, Pierre? Doesn't the little tramp satisfy you?"

She wanted to throw herself down onto the settee and allow herself to be ravaged, but his hand moved from her bottom to her neck and held her tight. "Come on, Dirty Boy, do me," she encouraged, raising her head in desire.

Without warning, the kimono was ripped off her shoulders. It fell to the floor and she stood there naked save for the G-string. She closed her eyes and breathed heavily, lustfully, through her nose.

He was right up behind her now, she could feel his breath warm on her back.

A hand came round and grasped the left breast, squeezing the nipple forward in a milking motion. It hurt, but she loved it.

Then she felt the inevitable hardness pressing between the cheeks of her bottom, pressing insistently. She would not resist, she would give in willingly -

Wait a minute.

The dick was cold. It was hard and made of metal. And already it was four centimetres inside her.

"Damn fucking *salop*," said the voice in her ear.

She gasped and tried to turn, but it was too late.

Commissaire of Police Gillian Colet had no final thought. She was just aware of the fiercest and most painful and burning form of buggery she had ever experienced, and then she watched as her bowels and their contents and her womb shot out through her stomach and splattered over her settee.

She did not hear the bang of the gun. Shock killed her instantly, and the blackness of eternity had settled over her even before her legs had time to buckle.

Chief Inspector Pierre Jamo felt like a man going to his doom. Which was silly really, because it was not the first time he and Commissaire Gillian Colet had had sex. And it wasn't as if she was bad in bed – in fact she was very good, wanton and demanding, with no holes barred. But it was like the old simile: going with a promiscuous woman was like sitting on a warm lavatory seat – comfortable but you wondered who'd been there before.

As he stepped out of the small elevator, he heard a faint ringing from down the stairs. Sounded like a telephone. Then it stopped and the building was quiet.

He walked over to the glossy mahogany front door of her apartment and rang the bell. Truth be told, he was looking forward to the session with one of the wettest women he had ever been with. He smiled as his excitement stirred in his *pantalon*.

He rang the bell again. Perhaps he should get his Old Man out and have it poking at her when she opened the door? That would surprise the bitch who thought she'd seen everything. Mind you, the way he felt right now it wouldn't be pointing at her, it would be pointing at his chin! He undid his zip and pulled himself out.

He knocked on the door. Where was she? Usually she was right there waiting for him. He hoped she was wearing those G-string things. He loved the way they disappeared into the Grand Canyon of her arse. A fabric pathway into the valley of promise.

He looked at his watch. Spot on 22:00 as instructed. She would be pleased.

Now he thumped on the door. Come on baby, look what Daddy's got for you.

No reply.

This was unusual. Where was she?

And then he realised.

The bitch.

The complete fucking bitch.

She had stood him up. Because he had failed to come round last night, she had done the same to him.

The cow.

Okay honey, well it was your loss.

To prove he had been there, he popped his card through the letterbox and then turned away and walked down the stairs.

He had gone down two flights before he realised his dick was still poking out, although now just limply. Quickly he popped it back in and did up his zip.

Faubourg St Honoré, Paris, France

"Claudette? Ron Becker."

"Allo, Ron." The connection between the telephone on Becker's desk in the British Embassy and Inspector Ibrahim's portable was full of static. They could have been talking to each other from the other side of the world, not just five kilometres away.

"Sorry to call you so late," said Becker. "But we've just got news from our people that Diana will be coming to Paris tomorrow. She's in the south at the moment, on the Fayed's yacht. Her and Dodi-boy will be coming into Le Bourget in the afternoon."

"*D'accord. Merci.* Leave it with me."

Becker frowned. Usually the tough little minx from the BCP was chattier than this. Perhaps she was somewhere she couldn't talk. "Do you have everything you need?"

"Yes, thank you. I will be around her."

"Okay. And thanks once again for taking this off our hands." But the static had won its battle and they could not hear each other.

Montmartre, Paris, France

Unusually for a cat, Will liked having her ears touched. She sat in the woman's arms and let her ears be stroked upwards, at the same time twitching them as she stared at a pigeon on the roof tiles outside the window.

The woman absentmindedly stroked the cat's ears and thought of other things.

It had never been her intention to kill Madame Renée – Sylvie Jacquot. Why should she? Unlike the others, Sylvie had not been instrumental in her father's death, she had not influenced events. She was just a pawn, a woman who had fallen in love.

And yet her information had been the most helpful of all.

So now events would need to go in the other direction – the British. She had seen to the French, now the final vengeance was drawing near. She knew there was a man at the embassy who had been there eighteen years ago. Was he involved in her father's death? Either directly or indirectly? And did he know the secret? She now knew without doubt that the answer to both questions was yes.

Her father had discovered the British secret. His involvement with it had led directly to his death. Now she would find out what her father had known. It was Daddy's legacy.

And in return she would give him British blood.

Boulevard Exelmans, Paris, France

Ron Becker and Gisele Joudeh, the Lebanese diplomat, were lying side by side in bed. Gisele was asleep and Ron looked at her admiringly, enjoying the regal countenance and thinking warm – and naughty – thoughts about what they had been doing just half an hour before.

Ron could not sleep – unusual for a man who had just made love. It was the first time Gisele had failed to knock him out with her carnal skills. Ron was thinking of another woman, and not in a sexual sense (although many men had): Diana, Princess of Wales.

Were they really going to kill her?

He laughed inwardly. Of course they bloody well were, he had set it in motion, hadn't he? And once the Russian was on a tail, it was hard to call him off. The one fax number was the only way to contact him. If he had already gone off on the hunt, he was unreachable.

Becker had been responsible for many deaths before, it was part of his job. Particularly he remembered the carnage back in 1979. How many people had died all together? Personally he had pulled the trigger on Robert Lensens and his wife, had had Paul Richer in his sights (before Mesrine had unwittingly done the job for him), and had planted and primed the device that killed Chief Inspector Claude Gerard.

That had been the biggest and most concentrated glut of killings in his career. In fact, Gerard had been the last person he had actually murdered himself. Since then, he had either ordered, blackmailed or paid others to do it. There hadn't been that many (nowhere near three figures), but Wallis Simpson in 1986 had been the most high profile.

Until now.

This time it was almost regicide – or was it not regicide if one royal killed another? Was the old woman back in England really going to do it? Clearly, yes. And why was obvious. It could only be one thing: the damned secret. Somehow Diana had found out. And like the rest before her, she was to die.

His musings were interrupted by his mobile phone flashing on the bedside table. It was on silent, but it gave off a gentle vibration.

He pulled himself up and sat on the edge of the bed, reaching for the phone. Gisele still slept soundly.

He did not recognise the number and he carried the throbbing instrument out of the bedroom before pressing the green button.

"Hello, Ron Becker," he answered lowly as he walked into the *salle de jour*.

"Monsieur Becker? I am sorry to call you at such a late hour." The voice was female, accented. "This is Commissaire Gillian Colet of the BCP. We haven't actually met."

"Ah, Commissaire, good evening. A pleasure to talk to you. Even at midnight. What can I do for you?"

"It is about Lady Diana - "

"The Princess, yes."

"I wonder if I could come round to see you? I know it is late but something urgent has arisen. We believe there may be a threat to Lady Di while she is here."

Shit. Did the frogs know something? They couldn't. Impossible.

"Well, er, of course. I'm not at the embassy, I'm at home."

"I know. I am outside in my car, now. Can I come up?"

His eyebrows rose. "You are outside?"

"Forgive my temerity. It is very urgent I see you."

"All right, come on up. Ring the bell – the top one – and I'll buzz you in."

Becker waited for the knock on the door. He had never met Commissaire Gillian Colet, but he had heard a lot about her from Jamo and Ibrahim. Apparently she was a bitch and then some.

What *had* she got wind of? Couldn't be anything to do with HM's instructions. Only Her Majesty, Sir Kenneth Dean, himself and, of course, the contractor knew what was to happen. There could not have been a leak. It must be something else. Was someone else after Diana?

The knock on the door was firm but low, like the secret knock of a lover asking to be let in.

Becker opened the door, knowing it was not a lover.

But neither was it Commissaire Gillian Colet.

The woman was dressed in black leather. Becker's mouth dropped open. At first he could not understand. *"Claudette?"*

The body was that of Claudette Ibrahim, but the look in the eyes revealed someone else's soul within. She held a gun in both hands, and it was pointing straight at Becker's head. "Get inside."

"Claudette?"

"Inside."

Becker stumbled backwards as she came in and kicked the door closed behind her. "What the fuck is this?" he demanded.

"Are you alone?"

"Y – yes."

"The kitchen. Where is it?"

"Over there."

"Lead me."

"Now just a minute, I think you've got some explaining to - "

The gun touched against the exact centre of his forehead. Her nose was flared. "I have no explaining to do, Englishman. In the kitchen. Now."

Becker turned and led the way to the second door along the dim corridor. There were only a few lights on. He kept his arms by his side.

She flicked the switch for the overhead fluorescent. "Sit down at the table," she ordered. "Put your hands on the top, palms upwards."

"I don't understand - "

"Just do it. There is nothing you need to understand." She looked around the small kitchen as Becker sat down. Her eyes stopped on a liquidiser next to the microwave. She smiled and then shook her head. Reaching over, she took a large carving knife from a block and examined the end for sharpness.

"Inspector Ibrahim," said Becker. "I - "

"Do not use that name. That is somebody else."

Becker frowned then shook his head in bewilderment. He was completely confused.

She pulled out a chair, right-angled it to Becker, turned it around and straddled it. The gun remained pointed at the Englishman. "Now," she twirled the carving knife around in her left hand. "Tell me what you know."

In the bedroom at the far end of the corridor, Gisele Joudeh reluctantly allowed herself to wake up from a delicious post-coital sleep. She did not want to come round just yet, but her bladder was insistent.

She stretched and felt the empty place in the bed next to her. It took a moment to register. Then she wondered. Where was Ronald?

Becker was puzzled. How the hell did the French know about the hit on Diana? Had there been a lapse? Security was usually so tight. When the British wanted to kill, 'need to know' was enforced with a strictness unrivalled in any other area. A maximum of four: the Instigator, the Catalyst, the Rag, the Contractor. Sometimes Becker was the Contractor; usually, as in this case, he was the Rag. Third in line: the Queen Mother, Sir Kenneth Dean, himself, Ramirov.

"How did you find out?" he asked.

"That is your last question," said the woman who did not want to be called Ibrahim. "Do not ask anything more. Tell me what you know."

Sleepily, Gisele pulled herself up into a sitting position on the side of the bed. She could hear muffled voices. Did Ronald have the TV on? At this hour? Surely he wasn't watching filth again?

She stood up and stretched.

"I am but an oily rag," explained Becker. "You must understand that. I do what I am told. When my masters say 'Jump', I say 'How high?'. I don't ask questions. I do what I am told." He paused. The woman sitting opposite him, legs straddled over the chair, gun in one hand, knife in the other, stared at him silently.

"The order came through two weeks ago. Look, it probably won't happen in Paris, so you've no need to worry. You won't be compromised or implicated."

Still she said nothing.

He shrugged. "They have ordered Diana killed, what can I say?"

Claudette showed no reaction. Her face was stone.

"I don't ask why – that's how I've survived," continued Becker. "My God, the things I know! Look, Claudette, are you - erm - are you sure this is diplomatically correct - ?"

The movement of the knife was just a blur.

Gisele padded naked down the corridor. She would have her pee and then she would give Ronald hell for even thinking of watching porn after what she had done to him earlier – she could still feel his stubble burn on her inner thighs.

She was one metre away from the kitchen door when she heard the scream.

The knife sliced through the palm of Ron Becker's upturned left hand, pinning it to the wooden table. There was one squirt of blood that rose thirty centimetres into the air.

"Fucking hell!" he screamed.

Claudette grabbed his left wrist with her gun hand. "Be still," she instructed softly, calmly, almost sensually. "Your natural reaction is to jerk your hand. Do not. You will cause more damage."

"What the fuck - "

"I told you no more questions. You did not obey me."

"I..."

"Eighteen years ago," said Claudette gently. "You were responsible for the death of my father."

"*What?*"

"The Mesrine affair."

Becker opened his mouth, stunned.

"Your *father?*"

"He was killed because he knew your British secret."

"And you have come to avenge him, I suppose. How the hell did you become a policeman?"

She gave a little flick with her finger on the top of the knife.

Becker's whole body stiffened as pain shot up through his wrist. "*Shit!*"

"I want to know what the secret is."

"You're crazy," said Becker, and he winced in preparation for another flick. It did not come. "Anyone who knows the secret, dies. That's the point, don't you see? *I* don't know it. I just have to arrange the deaths of everyone who does. If I knew it, *I* would be killed."

"Who knows it? Someone must. Who is ordering the deaths?"

"England."

"What do you mean 'England'?"

"Her Majesty?"

"Your Queen?"

"No, she does not know. It's her mother."

"And she is the only one who knows?"

"Her and Di - " Becker stopped as he suddenly realised he might have made a big mistake. A very big mistake. The French did *not* know about the hit on Diana. And now he had told them.

"Diana?" said Claudette. "Lady Di? She knows?" She let it sink in. "Oh my God, and that's why you are going to kill her?"

"It has been ordered."

"You crazy bastards."

"I do as I am told."

"Only obeying orders, huh? Where have I heard that before?"

Becker was looking around, trying to find a way out, a way to stop this. "Look, your father, he was a criminal."

Her face turned nasty. "He was not! My father was never a criminal. He was a good man," she snarled into his face. "He - "

At that moment, a naked woman appeared in the kitchen doorway and fired at Claudette from two metres.

Rue Vavin, Paris, France

Pierre Jamo drove his Fiat Uno down Rue Vavin and parked as near as he could to his apartment block. The small southern part of the road was quiet at midnight, but down on the main Boulevard, Montparnasse was still humming.

He was still obsessing over that damn bitch Colet as he let himself into the building, walked past the shuttered concierge's lodge and pressed the button for the lift.

He wondered if he should call Claudette? Perhaps it wasn't too late to salvage the evening. She might still come over, if he asked nicely. Or perhaps she would invite him over to her place in Montmartre? He had yet to be granted the honour of screwing her in her own bed.

He felt for his portable, and then thought better of it. He would use the landline indoors.

He let himself into his flat quietly, so as not to disturb his fellow residents in the block. Throwing his jacket across the back of an armchair, he picked up the telephone. He knew her numbers by heart, both home and mobile. He keyed the seven-digit home number.

After ten rings he gave up. Either she was not at home or she was not answering. Perhaps she was asleep? Or perhaps she was entertaining someone? They had never agreed that their relationship was exclusive.

He stood with the phone in his hand, wondering if he should call her portable?

What the hell, he had nothing to lose.

He dialled the eleven-digit code.

Boulevard Exelmans, Paris, France

It all happened at once.

In real time it took just three seconds, but for the participants it played out in slow-motion.

Claudette was snarling into Becker's face when she was aware of the shadow in the doorway. As she turned to look, she saw the flash from Gisele's gun. She felt the heat as the bullet missed her cheek by one centimetre, and then felt hot wetness hit her as the bullet tore into Becker's head, blowing away the left side of his brain.

Claudette turned her gun and fired instinctively at the naked woman. At the same time she pushed herself backwards off the chair.

The bullet hit Gisele in the neck, and blood spurted across the kitchen wall as the Lebanese was thrown fully across the hallway, crashing into the wall and falling limply.

Claudette lay on her back, slightly winded. Then she raised herself up onto her elbows and looked from one body to the other. Becker was laying back in the chair, eyes and mouth open. Some of his brain was stuck to the wall. She spat as she realised some of his brain was stuck to her face also.

The naked woman – *who the hell was she?* – lay twisted in the hallway like a shattered rag doll. Blood rolled slowly from her neck, across her chest and down between the cavity of her breasts. A little further down, the body was pissing itself.

It was then that Claudette's portable phone began to ring.

Ω

Saturday August 30 1997

Paris, France

10:00 Rue des Saussaies

Chief Inspector Pierre Jamo strolled into the office. He was working Saturdays that week, and should have been in by 08:00 at the latest. But he didn't really care. He was pissed off. Blown out twice in one night. Once by the Bitch Colet and then by Claudette who had not been answering her phones. And now here in the office there was no one else around.

Claudette would be out on Diana patrol (and racking up some good overtime in the process), and the whore Colet never worked weekends if she could help it (what Commissaire did?). No doubt The Bitch would be expecting him to contact her and ask her where she had been last night, but he would not do that. He was not going to play her little game. When he saw her on Monday, he would pretend nothing had happened.

He entered the office carrying his staple breakfast of a packet of *Gauloises*, one croissant in a grease-proof bag and an espresso – all from *Henri's*. This morning it was a double espresso. Perhaps, he thought, he should have ordered a triple. He had had such a bad night, in fact he had hardly slept at all.

His disgruntlement with the two women aside, something else had been nagging at him. During his intermittent bouts of sleep, he had dreamt of two huge, disembodied tits wearing a peroxide wig. They had been speaking to him, trying to tell him something. During his frequent bouts of nocturnal consciousness, he had thought of Sylvie Jacquot, Mesrine's wife-that-was-not-to-be.

Something she had said…

He noticed a blue folder on his desk. He read the cover as he sat down and tore open his croissant bag. **Ibrahim, Claudette Maria**. It was her personnel file. He had not seen it before. There had been no need to, now that staffing functions on Inspectors and above were all handled at Commissaire level. Why was the folder here now?

He grunted. The Bitch Colet had put it there, of course. On the top would be Claudette's appraisal report of yesterday and – to rub salt into his wound – her dismissal from the BCP and transfer to the CRS Anti Riot Squad.

Jamo popped the last piece of croissant into his mouth. He opened the folder. He would not read The Bitch Colet's report, but he would sneak a little look at *l'histoire* of the woman who had been his fuck-mate for the last few months. It would be nice to know something about her.

He picked up his espresso.

It took one minute and fifty-three seconds for it all to fall into place. For it to hit home. For everything to become clear.

It hit him like an RER express train ramming into his testicles and disappearing out his arse.

The paper coffee cup shot across his desk, espresso decorating the folder in front of him.

Oh, Holy God.

Now he remembered what Sylvie Jacquot had said. Now he *understood* what Sylvie Jacquot had said.

"What am I not telling you, m'sieur? Look within. Perhaps there is something I *am* telling you."

Look within. *Look within.*

He stared at the file in front of him, now stained with a miasma of brown. Something *he* had said came back to him also. He had said that the killings were not directly linked to Mesrine, that the supercriminal was secondary, a bit-player.

How right he had been. Only until now he had not known why.

He read the page in front of him again.

Claudette Ibrahim. Married for a few months in her early twenties to one Joseph Ibrahim. A marriage that did not last, but she had kept her husband's surname. But before that she had been known by her birth name.

For Claudette Ibrahim had been born Claudette Gerard.

She was the daughter of Chief Inspector Claude Gerard, late of the BCP.

The third victim of The Mesrine Conclusion.

The man who had been blown up in the Rue Lamarck.

Eighteen years ago.

Because he knew the secret.

PART FOUR

Ω

CULMINATION

Jamo snatched up the telephone on his desk and thumped out Claudette's home number. After ten rings he pressed the bridge of the phone and then keyed her portable.

It just rang and rang. No response. She had probably turned it off.

Jamo hoped he was wrong about this. Surely Claudette was not a serial killer?

This was perverse. Had he actually ordered Claudette to investigate murders she had committed? Had he sent her chasing *herself*?

He sat back in his chair and puffed out his cheeks. He had been played. Well and truly played.

She had joined the BCP twelve months ago, a tenacious, pugnacious little Inspector promoted from the *Police Judiciare*. The BCP had been her choice. Naturally in her new post she had access to all the diplomatically sensitive files. Files going back to the inception of the BCP in 1974. All files. Files that would contain names. Including the names of all those involved in the Mesrine affair in 1979.

Literally the murders had been an inside job! She was out for revenge. And she was out for something else too: the secret. The reason they all had died then, the reason she was killing them all now.

Again Jamo picked up the telephone. He needed guidance. He keyed The Bitch Colet's home number. She would be pissed at being disturbed on a Saturday, but it would serve her right, payback for standing him up last night.

The phone rang. And rang.

No answer.

She could be away for the weekend, reasoned Jamo.

He put the phone down. He looked up a number in his desk diary and once more grabbed the receiver.

This time he got an answer. "British Embassy."

"Good morning, Mr Ron Becker please. This is Chief Inspector Jamo of the BCP."

"One moment, please."

Becker's extension rang. And rang. No response.

This time Jamo lost it. Damn and blast. Would nobody speak to him? He banged the receiver up and down on his desk in rage. The top of the phone flew off towards Claudette's desk.

Fucking hell.

He grasped the edge of his desk and fought to control his temper.

Slowly his furious breathing subsided to normal.

He fumbled in his jacket pocket for his packet of *Gauloises*. Nowadays this was a non-smoking building but, quite frankly, he didn't give a shit.

Right, he thought. Time to do things on his own.

10:35 Gare du Nord

The 06:25 *Eurostar* from London Waterloo arrived just a few minutes late (a track problem – 'refugees' – at Calais-Frethun).

John Smith, Head of 'Charles' People', smiled farewell to the neatly-uniformed hostess standing by the door and disembarked from the First Class coach.

He walked along the platform with his fellow travellers and was swallowed up by the throng on the concourse of the station.

Outside, he waited in line for a cab...

11:00 Montmartre

Time was, the streets of Paris would be empty in August. Over two-thirds of the city would be shut down for the month for the *'Fermeture Annuelle'*. But this annual *en bloc* taking of holidays had dwindled over the years, so that by the end of the second millennium it was respected only by the old folk, an anachronistic reminiscence, harking back to the good old days when there was order, structure, and it was good to be alive. Nowadays life was simply chaos and disorder.

So the streets of Montmartre were teeming with traffic, despite it being August. Saturday meant that there weren't so many lorries and delivery vans on the capital's crowded streets, but this was more than compensated by the hoards of tourists, wandering into the roads without thought, brains left at Immigration.

Jamo took the back way, going around the western side of the *butte* via Place Clichy and Rue Caulaincourt. He had found Claudette's address on file: 1 Rue Lamarck.

It took him two double-backs to find a parking space, and eventually he settled for the tightest of spots outside the Hotel Roma. From there it was a five minute walk.

The top bell button said Ibrahim C. He put his finger on it and left it there. Somewhere up above it must be ringing.

But there was no reply, no voice over the entry phone.

He pushed the bottom button marked Concierge and waited.

Shortly the door was opened by a cropped-haired scruffy young man, a student type. "*M'sieur?*"

Jamo flashed his ID. "Police. I wish to see Madame Ibrahim, I'm getting no reply."

"I think Claudy's away for the weekend - "

Jamo pushed past him. *Claudy?* "I'll find out for myself."

The concierge shrugged as Jamo began his trot up the stairs.

11:05 Gare du Nord

Half an hour to wait for a cab. Well, thought John Smith, glad to see that some things are the same in Paris as they are in London.

His turn came and he climbed into the old Renault. The driver was a woman in her sixties, grey hair dyed yellow, with matching teeth and slightly darker nicotine-stained fingers. Next to her sat an equally yellow-tinged white poodle, who took one look at Smith and decided it had something better to do – sleep.

"*L'ambassade de Grande Bretagne*," said Smith.

11:10 Montmartre

After two flights, Jamo wished there was a lift in this old building. After five flights, he thought of paying for one himself. After six flights, he wished he was dead.

He stood outside Claudette's door, bending forward, regaining control of his breathing. He reached for his *Gauloises*, took one out of the packet, stared at it and then put it back.

He rapped on the door. "Claudette?"

He could hear nothing from inside. "Claudette? It's me, Pierre."

This time he heard something. Sounded like a drawer or a door being closed. He rapped again. "Claudette! Open up!"

There were no footsteps inside, no sound of locks being unlocked or bolts being unbolted.

Okay, the last time she had to do this for him. This time he was on his own.

He stood back, lifted his right leg, achieved his balance and kicked mightily at the door.

It took three kicks, and then the door shot backwards, the old wood splintering around the lock.

"Claudette?" He had his gun in his hand as he eased his way along the hallway. The three doors were closed. "It's Pierre. Come out please."

He tried the door on his left. The bathroom. Empty.

Then he tried the one on his right. A bedroom. Bed unmade. An old stuffed Snoopy between the pillows. From the doorway his eyes moved over her dressing table: various perfumes and girlie things adorned the top. He gave an ironic grunt at the open box of Tampax.

Then he heard a sound again. Coming from the next room. Gun raised and pointing at the ceiling, he turned the door handle. Then he stood back as his push made the door creak slowly open.

"Claudette?" He peeked into the salon and then relaxed. "No, you are not

Claudette." He put the gun down by his side as he came in. "You must be Will, I've heard a lot about you."

The cat looked up at him from the settee and mewed. Then, as if she had suddenly remembered that she needed to, she began to lick her left paw with intensity.

"Where is she pussycat, huh?" Jamo came over and sat next to the animal. He stroked the soft red-tabby fur. "Where has she gone?"

His eyes were caught by a manila folder sitting on the coffee table in front of him. Cautiously he reached forward and flicked it open. Then he frowned and leant forward some more, fanning all the sheets out over the glass.

There they all were. Charles Fleury-Goujon, Veronique Lensens, Sylvie Jacquot. Photographs, biographies and, importantly, hand written comments. Comments on their links with the Mesrine affair nearly twenty years ago.

Jamo noticed there was something underneath the picture of Sylvie Jacquot. He moved the picture to find another one below. It made his jaw drop.

It was slightly blurred and had been taken without the subject knowing. The person was younger in the picture than he was now, but without doubt it was him.

Ron Becker of the British Embassy.

"Weow!" said the cat.

11:30 Faubourg St Honoré

John Smith paid off the cab and walked through the large black doors of the British Embassy and into the ornate lobby.

A plain-clothes security guard was on duty, but in 1997 one could walk, observed but unhindered, over to the Reception desk.

"Good morning, sir," the middle aged receptionist spoke in French. "Can I help you?"

"I'm here to see Mr Becker," said Smith, noticing how the receptionist's aura relaxed infinitesimally as she heard him speak English. "Mr Ron Becker. I'm from Special Branch, UK." He showed his ID.

The receptionist looked at it, but she knew better than to try to touch it.

"Mr Becker has not come in this morning, Mr – er – Smith. We don't know quite where he is. Would you care to wait or leave a message?"

It crossed Smith's mind to ask for the ambassador, Sir Michael Jay, but then he thought better of it. What he had to do was not for the ambassador's 'need to know'.

"You've no idea when Mr Becker will be in?"

"No, Mr Smith. Or indeed if he will be."

"Okay. I'll leave my number. Please ask him to ring me as soon as he turns up." He took a card from his pocket. "I can be contacted there."

"I'll see that he gets this as soon as he comes in. Will he know what it's about?"

"If he doesn't, he'll find out soon enough."

Smith turned and walked back across the tiled marble floor. He reached the front door and stood aside to let a man enter, a medium-height, paunchy, black haired man who, from his rosy cheeks, looked like he was in something of a hurry.

Smith went out.

The man hurried over to the reception desk, with the security guard looking at him intently.

"Good morning, sir," the middle aged receptionist spoke in French. "Can I help you?"

"I'm here to see Mr Becker," said the man. "Chief Inspector Pierre Jamo of the BCP."

11:40 Eastwards

John Smith decided to walk to his next destination. It was a fine Parisian summer's day and it would only take fifteen minutes.

He headed east along Rue du Faubourg St Honoré for the straight-line walk to Rue de Castiglione.

11:45 Henri's Bar

Pierre Jamo decided to walk to his next destination also. His walk would take just five minutes.

He headed west along Rue du Faubourg St Honoré and then cut up Rue de Duras. He soon found himself entering Henri's Bar.

Jamo was never one to succumb to the mawkishness caused by alcohol, but he was susceptible to anger – with or without booze. He was angry now. Where the fuck was everybody? Colet, Claudette, Becker. All missing.

"Two calvados and two glasses of paint stripper," he said to Henri, who grunted and began to place glasses on the *zinc*, shot glasses for the calvados not brandy bowls because he knew the policeman liked it that way.

"Tell me something, *Henri mon ami*," Jamo watched the calvados being poured. "What do you do when no one wants to speak to you?"

The old bar owner sniffed. "Doesn't happen in my job, m'sieur. Everyone talks to me. I am their counsellor, their psychiatrist. They all confide in old Henri. I could tell you some things, m'sieur! Even the men from your Department - "

Something occurred to Jamo. "How far back do you remember?"

"I have seventy years, m'sieur – and I remember every one of them!"

Jamo knocked back the first calvados in one. "A man called Claude Gerard, a Chief Inspector. Nearly twenty years ago. Remember him?" The second calvados disappeared like the first, and Jamo belched loudly.

"Claude Gerard..." Henri was looking at a point way behind Jamo. Eighteen years behind. "Oh, yes. He died, didn't he? Blown up in his car. It was the time of *Le Grand*, the great Jacques."

"What was he like? Gerard."

Henri's eyes came back to rest on Jamo. "What can I say, m'sieur? He was a regular customer. He was... How can I say this? A slob, a nasty piece of work. Excuse me, m'sieur." Henri went off to serve some new arrivals.

Jamo started on his red wine. *A nasty piece of work*. Did that mean he was a murdering piece of work? And had the murdering genes passed to his daughter?

He felt a trembling next to his right testicle.

For a second he thought it was the booze. Then he realised his portable was in his pocket. He took it out, still vibrating and ringing. He couldn't see who it was in the dim light of the bar – and he certainly wouldn't be able to hear with Dalida singing her stuff through the speakers.

Signalling to Henri to leave his wine where it was, he went outside, squinting as the sun hit him. He answered the phone.

"Where the fuck is my cat?" said a raised female voice.

11:55 Rue Cambacérès

"Claudette?"

"It was you, wasn't it? In my apartment. Did you have to kick the fucking door in? Will got out."

"I'm sorry, I – Where the hell are you? I've been trying to contact you."

"I've had things to do. Still have."

"I know, Claudette. I know about your father."

"That bitch left you my file, right?"

"Has it been you? The killings?"

"I just want to know why they killed him. I must know the British secret."

"Come in. Stop this nonsense."

"Nonsense! So my father is nonsense, is he?"

"I didn't mean - "

"I have a job to do and I will see it through. Did you know I'm being transferred to the CRS? Of course you do, I told you. Colet's last act as Commissioner."

"What do you mean, her last - " Oh God.

"There's a vacancy, *Pierre mon amour*. Could be yours."

Claudette was mad. Quite mad.

"But I tell you one thing," she continued. "If my cat does not come back, I'm going to put a skewer through your scrotum and kebab your balls while you're still alive."

She hung up.

12:00 Place Vendôme

John Smith entered The Ritz Hotel by its main doors on the Place Vendôme. His smart-casual fawn cotton trousers and blue open-necked shirt did not look out of place in the 4-star Fayed establishment *[there is no official 5-star designation for hotels in France]*, but his battered, lived-in face looked like it would be more at home in the back streets of Pigalle.

He went over to the Concierge desk. A smartly-uniformed grey-haired gentleman greeted him. *"Oui, monsieur?"*

"Bonjour. The Director of Security, *s'il vous plaît."*

There was just a momentary pause before the concierge asked, "Who shall I say is calling, sir?"

"A friend of Mr Jones. The Director knows him."

"Un ami de Monsieur Jones. D'accord." There was just a hint of reluctance – or perhaps suspicion. Then the concierge picked up a remarkably old – or *faux* old – telephone and keyed an internal number. He had a discussion with someone in rapid French, then he put the phone down.

"Je regrette, the Director is out, monsieur. His assistant will see you momentarily."

Smith nodded his thanks and moved away from the desk to let an American couple berate the concierge about the quantity of towels in their room (they were quickly referred to Housekeeping).

Smith looked around the elegant lobby, and was impressed. You've done a great job in restoring this to its former glory, Mohamed.

He waited.

"Monsieur, you were asking for the Director?"

Smith turned. He was expecting someone in uniform. What he saw was a fortysomething matronly woman, dressed in a blouse and trousers with just the right amount of class and elegance to make her fit into her surroundings perfectly. Of course, Smith thought, the Ritz Security Team would need to blend, not to publicise their presence.

"Yes," he said. "I believe he's out."

"At the moment, but we are expecting him back later. May I help you?"

"I'm just a friend of a friend. I was in Paris, and my friend suggested I pop in and say hello. Nothing important. But I go home tomorrow, so I thought if he was free later perhaps we could get together."

"Are you staying at the hotel, *m'sieur?*"

"Regrettably no. But if I give you my telephone number, could you ask him to call me?"

"Your phone works in France, *m'sieur?*"

"Yes, no problem." It works in places you couldn't begin to imagine, lady. He produced a card from his shirt pocket. It contained simply his name and mobile phone number.

She took it and read it. Then she said, "*D'accord, Monsieur... Smith.* I will see that Monsieur Henri Paul gets this."

12:15 Rue des Saussaies

Chief Inspector Pierre Jamo hurried through the Cambacérès entrance and took the nearest elevator up to the sixth floor. He walked through the labyrinthine connecting corridors until he came out in the building that was 11 Rue des Saussaies.

He heard the scraping of a chair from the General Office as he passed by, and Sergeant Maurice Goise caught up with him as Jamo was opening the door to the Inspectors' Office.

"Chief, Chief!"

Jamo continued on in with Goise behind him. "*Oui?*" He stood in front of Claudette's desk, staring at it, as if wondering what to do.

"They say they've left messages on your ansaphone, but they came though to me also. Apparently it's extremely urgent, although I can't recall them bothering us before."

"Jesus, Maurice," Jamo looked up. "Can't somebody else take it? I'm very busy. Give it to Inspector - " He looked at the empty desk.

"They were asking for you specifically, Chief. I asked them to leave me details but they wouldn't. They just asked that you contact them urgently. As if it was yesterday."

"If it was that urgent why didn't you phone me?"

Goise smiled and relaxed his shoulders. "You told me you were going to Henri's after the embassy. Nothing is so urgent to disturb a man's quiet time."

Jamo smiled also. "So what is it?"

"The Lebanese Embassy, Chief. They're asking that you call them right away."

13:00 Saint Denis

Saint Denis on the northern borders of Paris could at that time best be described as working class. True, the impressive Stade de France had given the area a much-needed boost in self-esteem, but it could not hide the fact that this area consisted predominantly of factories and social housing.

It was on the Rue des Poissoniers, outside a graffiti-daubed block, bed linen hanging out of the open windows of the apartments above, that the bald-headed man found what he was looking for.

People who live in social housing (the projects, council houses, call them what you will) soon learn the basics of security. You keep your doors locked at all times. Your windows, if you are on the lower floors, you keep locked at all times also, even if you are in. You only leave outside what must be left outside. If possible, cars and bikes should be kept in lock-ups.

The rider of this motorbike had a lock-up, and he was going there shortly. But first he had to leave his heavy parcel, which he had balanced perilously on his fuel tank all the way from Porte de la Villette, outside his front door on the ground floor. Leaving his engine running, he dismounted and bumped the parcel through the main doors to the building and over to his apartment just in on the right.

Just ten seconds after he had gone through the main doors, he came back out.

And his bike was gone.

13:45 Neuilly-sur-Seine

Jamo stood outside the door of the apartment of Commissaire Gillian Colet, as he had done sixteen hours previously. Only this time he didn't have his dick hanging out.

This time he had come prepared. He held a crowbar in his left hand, his Glock 17 in his right.

One knock on the door. No answer of course. She would never answer a door again.

The wood splintered, and he kicked the door open. The smell hit him immediately, and he gagged.

He tucked the crowbar under his arm, covered his nose and mouth with his hand, and quickly but cautiously went over to the salon door.

"Gillian?" His voice was muffled behind his hand. He pushed the door open with his foot, pointed the gun out in front of him, and went inside.

The sight was astonishing and disgusting. She had been blown almost in half. She was naked and she was kneeling on the floor in front of the settee. Her top half was on the chair, and it was connected to her legs only by a squashed mess of various glistening red entrails and gleaming white bone. It was as if she was expecting to take a lover doggy-style.

It was that final thought that did it. Jamo felt it coming and there was nothing he could do about it. With an inhuman roar he vomited with alarming ferocity over the body. Not once, not twice, but three times.

A total and utter waste of good calvados and Henri's *vin rouge* paint stripper.

14:45 Place de Clichy

The European Union is intended to be one big country – that is why the countries that belong to the Union are called Member *States*. One of the concepts of this mega-country is that once a person has crossed the frontier and immigration controls of one 'State' he or she is free to travel at will throughout the rest of the States – akin to travelling between one county and another in England, or one region to another in Italy, one state to another in the US.

Whilst to a degree this happens, the Member States of the EU still retain a normal record of 'foreigners' on their soil, usually by hotel checks. Visiting foreigners are required to hand over their passport at Reception, either for it to be retained for 24 hours or for a copy of the details page to be taken there and then.

A way round this is to be a native. Home nationals are required to present nothing at check-in, save perhaps for a credit card imprint.

So it was that French national Ito Rennes checked into the 3-star Hotel Mercure Montmartre just north of the Place de Clichy that afternoon. He was a pleasant man with a pronounced Normandy accent. His completely bald head was pink, and he made a point of explaining to the clerk that he was on his way home from his *vacances* motor-biking on the south coast and had decided to stop off in Paris on his way back.

How long would he be staying?

Just the one night.

Up in his room, Ito Rennes peeled of his biker's leathers and stepped into the shower. It felt strange to be in Paris where Ilych Ramirez Sanchez was supposedly awaiting trial for his crimes, just a few kilometres to the south, over the river, in La Santé Prison. He hoped the stool-pigeon enjoyed his lifetime in a French jail. At least the poor schmuck knew that his family in Venezuela were well taken care of - pity the prisoner had never thought to ask the definition of 'taken care of'!

Rennes laughed as he let the water cascade over his bald head and over his body. But, he thought, he would get the job done – here, today – and then be off. Two murders of royalty in one place was enough. Wallis Simpson eleven years ago and now Diana today. History was, literally, repeating itself!

He stretched out and slowly turned the shower knob to its maximum heat. The water became uncomfortable, but it was by no means scalding.

Then something strange began to happen. The bald head started to peel away under the hot water, as if he was being burned or had suddenly been afflicted by instant leprosy. Then the mat of hair on his chest began to fall bit by bit into the shower tray, with flesh attached.

Ito Rennes ran his hands over his scalp and pulled the skin away from his head...

Twenty minutes later, Ian Ramsey stood in front of the mirror. Looking back at him was another person. The man had cropped black hair, greying at the temples; his chest was hairless and he was several kilos lighter than Ito Rennes.

Ramsey smiled, felt in his toiletries bag and brought out what looked like a fifteen centimetre long black caterpillar. Using the tiniest tube of prosthetic glue, he stuck it on his upper lip, flexed it a few times and was content.

He went back to his toiletries bag and brought out his wide tin of shaving soap which had accompanied him all the way from the USA. He prised off the lid, then took the tin in his hands and unscrewed the top containing the two millimetre layer of soap.

He was left with a round metal object twenty-five centimetres in diameter.

Right, time to get rid of this little bitch 'naturally'. Then he could go home. He looked at his watch lying on the bedside table. She would be arriving about now.

15:15 Le Bourget

Le Bourget airfield is seven kilometres to the north of Paris. The Fayed jet touched down smoothly after its one hour flight from Olbia, Sardinia. On board were Diana, Dodi Fayed, their bodyguards, a few assistants and crew.

Meeting the plane were two vehicles from The Ritz Hotel: a Mercedes 600 and a back-up Range Rover. There were just a handful of photographers.

Diana, Dodi and his bodyguard would travel in the Mercedes. Henri Paul and Les Wingfield would travel in the Range Rover, together with the luggage.

By 15:30 disembarkation was complete, and the vehicles set off on their journey into Paris. Their first destination was a house now owned by Mohamed Al Fayed on a 50 year lease from the Mayor of Paris. It was a house where Dodi hoped to set up home with his future wife. It was in western Paris. Number 24, Boulevard Suchet, at one time the residence of the Duke and Duchess of Windsor...

On the edge of the airfield, a leather-clad figure in a red crash helmet watched the cars drive away. Then she climbed back onto her Ducati M900 and followed at a safe distance.

15:30 Rue de Berri

In their room in the Hotel California in Rue de Berri just off the Champs Elysées, Christina Cascianis and Melanie Nathanson looked at the laptop screen.

Over a secure link from Tel Aviv via Rome, Barking Dog was accessing the Interior Ministry server to discover all foreign nationals who had checked into Paris hotels in the previous forty-eight hours.

"If he does not use a hotel, we are sunk," said Christina.

"Oh he will, hun, he will," reassured Melanie. "You can bet on it. Hotels are impersonal places, especially the big ones. People come, people go. He wants to just slip in and out – as they say."

But Christina was uncertain. "What if he hass a private apartment or iss staying with someone?"

Melanie touched the Greek woman's knee. "I doubt Ramirov would have an apartment in a place where he has committed assassinations in the past. The Duchess of Windsor, Georges Pompidou, you name them. He *might* be staying with someone – in which case that person is dead, like that poor bastard in Hydra. It will be much easier for him to just stay in an hotel. Save all the hassle. He doesn't want to kill unnecessarily or draw attention to himself. He'll just use one of his many aliases – Hold on. Shit!" Melanie slapped herself on the forehead.

"What?" Christina frowned.

"Are we dumb cows or what? He won't be a foreigner checking in, will he? He will be a national, a Frenchman! We've asked Barking Dog to look for the wrong thing! We simply want all hotel check-ins."

"All hotel check-ins?" queried Christina. "For every hotel in Paris? For forty-eight hours? In August?"

"Yep," said Melanie, reaching for the keyboard.

"And how long will that take?"

"Several hours. If we want details of all of them. But let's pander to his ego again. Remember he's been using the IR initials. It will take Barking Dog a while to access the systems of every hotel in Paris, but let's refine our search to just one thing: his initials. Should take no time."

"No time?"

"Well, an hour or two maybe. Fancy going downstairs for a bit of a pamper meantime? The Health Centre looked empty when we came in…"

16:45 Place Vendôme

The Fayed party arrived at The Ritz Hotel having spent half an hour over at the house by the Bois de Boulogne. Diana had been impressed at the restoration of the house carried out under the supervision of Dodi's father.

While Henri Paul supervised the unloading of the luggage, Diana and Dodi went up to the hotel's Imperial Suite to relax for a couple of hours.

Outside, in the Place Vendôme, more paparazzi began to arrive: on foot, by car, by motorbike...

Sitting on her bike on the other side of the Place, Claudette watched the group of photographers grow and grow, like a swarm of bees attending their queen in the hive.

She hmmphed at her own simile. Sorry Lady Di, but the Brits had decreed that a Queen you were never to bee. She laughed. Her wit was as sharp as ever. But what about her skills? Somehow she had to get to Diana and both warn her of the imminent attempt on her life *and* get her to reveal the British secret.

Her Press ID would get her up to The Ritz doors, but no further. She could go in with her police authority, but would they accept it without checking? And if they checked, that would give away her whereabouts. Had Jamo put out a *Stop and Detain* on her?

This would take all her skill. She would make her move when the time was right.

Of one thing she was certain. Diana knew the secret for which her father had been killed. Tonight that secret would be revealed to Claudette Gerard.

18:30 Rue de Berri

At the same time as Dodi Fayed popped out from The Ritz to visit Alberto Repossi's Paris branch of his jewellery business just down on the Place Vendôme (concerning the ring from the 'Tell Me Yes' range that he had ordered for Diana), Christina Cascianis and Melanie Nathanson returned to their room at the Hotel California.

Christina had enjoyed an ayurvedic massage and Melanie had enjoyed a little private indulgence: colonic irrigation. Both women, of course, had had manicures and pedicures.

Melanie went across and opened the laptop. The screen immediately sprung into life. "Okay baby, show me what you've got." Melanie wiggled her hands.

Christina looked over the Englishwoman's shoulder.

Barking Dog's report read: **1 MATCH FOUND.**

"Yes!" Melanie snapped her fingers. "Ready for this?"

"Go for it." Christina was smiling in triumph.

Melanie pressed the Enter key.

19:00 Rue Cambon

The Ritz hotel's acting Director of Security, Henri Paul, watched as Dodi and Diana were driven away from the back entrance of the hotel in Rue Cambon. He knew that they were on their way back to Dodi's apartment at 1 Rue Arsène Houssaye, and that they intended to go out to dinner at *Le Benôit* near the Pompidou Centre.

Well, good luck to them. By using the back exit of the hotel they had avoided the paparazzi out the front, but word would soon spread.

Henri Paul was happy. Everything had gone well. Perhaps this would help confirm his post as Director.

Now he could go home for the night.

His hand touched the small business card in his jacket pocket. He had forgotten about it. Mr Jones's friend. He'd better call him. The British paid him well for his services, a hundred thousand francs a year, and he'd best not disappoint them.

20:00 Rue Arsène Houssaye

The Rue Arsène Houssaye is at the top end of the Champs Elysées, on the northern side. Dodi's apartment was on the top floor of Number 1.

At 20:00, amid a scuffle of security guards and photographers, the couple left the building for the short ride round into the Champs and down to *Sephora*, the classy perfume and make-up emporium.

By the time the Mercedes pulled up outside the shop, having been delayed by the traffic lights up at the Arc de Triomphe, a crowd had gathered, tipped off by the presence of the photographers that 'Someone' was arriving.

It was impossible for the couple even to get out of the car. Dodi said something to the driver and they moved off into the Saturday evening traffic on a circular route back to the apartment.

It happened very quickly, but Diana knew she had heard it.

The Mercedes pulled up back at 1 Rue Arsène Houssaye. The security men were pushing back a group of snapping photographers, and they were helped by Dodi's security man who leapt from the front passenger seat.

It was aural mayhem as the couple dashed the few metres from the car to the sanctuary of the building. The clicking of shutters, like some constant whirring machine, the shouts of the photographers' male voices, "Diana!", "Dodi!", "This way!", "Diana!".

Then she heard it. It was almost drowned by the male voices, but because it was a distinctly female voice it stood out. "Lady Di! I must talk with you! You are in danger!"

Diana looked around, but the security men had her and she was bustled inside the building.

21:15 Rue de Malte

The small bar in Rue de Malte off the Place de la République in east central Paris was off the tourist track and was frequented only by locals. This suited the Englishman fine, although one or two heads did turn when he ordered his beer and *croque monsieur* in good but accented French.

John Smith chose a small round table away from the bar and sat facing the front window.

He had just finished his *croque* when he saw an Austin Cooper pull up across the street. The man who got out was 41 years old, compact, balding, wearing glasses. He was dressed in a dark suit with a lighter shirt and tie. Smith recognised him from the file pictures: Henri Paul, acting Director of Security for The Ritz Hotel and MI6 informant (and doubtless informant for many other agencies as well).

Paul entered the bar and Smith stood up and waved him over.

"Mr Smith?"

"Mr Paul." They shook hands.

"Let me get you something," offered Smith.

Paul looked down at the half empty beer glass. "I will have one of those, thank you." His English was flawless. He sat down as Smith went over to the bar.

Two minutes later Smith was back with two beers and a bowl of garlic croutons. "Would you like something more substantial to eat?"

"No, no, I eat well at work." Paul sipped his beer. "What can I do for you, Mr Smith? Mr Jones sent you?"

"Mr Jones gave me your name," explained Smith. "But he did not send me. I am here on behalf of someone else. Someone with a problem."

"Problems can always be solved, m'sieur."

"Quite. But this problem is very delicate. That's why we're calling on your services. We need someone who can use the utmost discretion." He had read in the file that Henri Paul conducted himself with a certain hubris, a *parvenu* aware of the heights to which he had risen. Smith was pandering to it.

Paul nodded. "What can I do for you?"

"My employer is having trouble with his ex-wife. Big trouble. He has asked that certain, er, solutions are found to his problem."

"Solutions?"

"Solutions."

"And this lady, she is a guest at the hotel?"

"Oh yes," said John Smith. "Oh yes."

21:45 Rue Arsène Houssaye

Dodi was the first out of the building in Rue Arsène Houssaye. He leapt through the held-open back door of the Mercedes. Diana followed. She was dressed in a black jacket, a black body, white trousers and sandals.

There was the usual clamour, the usual noise, the rushing river of clicking cameras, now flashing as the night descended.

But then she heard it again. The female voice. "Lady Di! What is the secret?"

This time Diana stopped by the car door and looked around, but all she could see was a mélange of faces, cameras, flashes, arms. People pushing and shoving each other, frantic to get *the* picture of her.

"Lady Di!"

Diana turned and looked over the top of the Mercedes. A red-helmeted figure was sitting on a motorbike next to the car. The visor was up and two big female eyes looked at her. "You are in danger!" The person shouted. "We must talk. There is something I want to know!"

A hand reached out from the back of the Mercedes and pulled Diana inside.

The car door slammed shut and the car sped quickly away towards the Avenue de Friedland.

21:50 Rue de Malte

"That is the most preposterous thing I have ever heard," said Henri Paul.

"Then you've led a very sheltered life," retorted John Smith.

"But *Princess Diana*?" There was disbelief in Paul's voice. "How can it be done?"

"That I leave up to you. Here," from an inside pocket of his jacket, Smith produced an envelope and slid it across the table. "A bonus of fifteen thousand, over and above your usual stipend. Not bad for a few moments' work."

"But what work! And I don't know how I can do it."

Smith put his hand into his other jacket pocket and brought out what looked like a small glass bottle, wrapped in a plastic bag. "Use this. We know it will be diluted, but it will still be effective. She will never know."

"This is unbelievable. What if she leaves the country? I hear they might be going back to England tomorrow."

"If they do, then we will see to it there. But they are equally likely to shoot off on one of their holidays again. And we want to get this matter determined and over with. And you never know, Henri," Smith reached across and slapped the Frenchman on his shoulder. "You might enjoy it!"

There was a ringing from inside Paul's jacket. He pulled out his chunky portable phone and had a conversation in rapid French.

After the call was finished, he nodded his head, looking across at John Smith. "It might be sooner than you think, m'sieur. That was the hotel. The couple are there, and they want me back."

"Good. I'll be staying at the Hotel Keppler, on Rue Keppler. You know it?"

"I can find it. The Sixteenth?"

"Yes. Let me know when it has been done."

Paul stood up, the envelope with the money already in his pocket, the plastic bag in his hand.

"And Henri," said Smith, retaining his grip on the Frenchman's hand after they had shaken. "Be discreet. Nobody is to know."

"No one will know, m'sieur. I guarantee it. They will never find out it was me."

Henri Paul turned and walked out of the bar.

21:55 Place Vendôme

The Mercedes arrived at the main entrance to The Ritz. More photographers were waiting here on the Place Vendôme, and those who had followed the couple were fast arriving on their motorbikes and in their cars.

The entire security team of The Ritz, less the Director, formed a passage for the couple.

There was the usual shouting, clicking and shoving. As they walked towards the hotel, Dodi smiled, seeming to like the attention. Diana was casting her eyes over the mêlée, seemingly looking for someone.

They walked through the revolving doors.

Inside, up above them, the security cameras began to record history.

22:10 Rue Cambon

The Ducati M900 was parked just metres from the small service entrance of The Ritz in the three-metre wide Rue Cambon.

Claudette was certain Diana had heard her – she had even stopped at the sound of her voice – but the Princess had been dragged inside the car.

Now there was no time to lose.

She showed her police ID to the man just inside the door. "*Sûreté Nationale*," she said. "I must speak with your Director of Security immediately."

22:15 The Ritz Hotel

Dodi and Diana had intended to dine in the hotel's two-star *L'Espadon* restaurant, but because of the media frenzy outside and the staring heads inside, they decided to take their meal in the sitting room of their suite. The first course of scrambled eggs with mushrooms and asparagus was finished.

The second course of fish with vegetables tempura was being served (sole for Diana, turbot for Dodi) when Henri Paul rushed in.

"Sir, madame, excuse me."

"What is it, Henri?" Dodi did not looked pleased at the interruption. In the next hour he was going to propose to the mother of the future King of England, for God's sake!

"I'm sorry, sir. It's the police. Asking to speak to madame urgently."

"*What?* Oh for God's sake! Tell him to go away, we are eating."

"Yes, sir. And it is a 'her', sir. It's a police woman."

Diana looked up. "Is she on a motorbike?"

"Madame?"

"The policewoman."

Henri frowned. "Well, I presume she must be. She is dressed in leather."

"Tell her to wait. I will see her when we're finished.

22:59 The Ritz Hotel

Champagne (*Cristal*) was delivered to the Imperial Suite at 22:59. It was followed closely by Claudette, accompanied by Henri Paul.

"Inspector Ibrahim, madame," introduced Paul.

Claudette came over, only subconsciously registering the impressive high ceilings of the suite and the painted bas-reliefs on the walls. She took Diana's proffered right hand. "Your majesty." She looked at Dodi but no hand was offered.

Diana suppressed a giggle. "Call me Diana. It was you, wasn't it?"

"Me?"

"Out in the street."

"Yes, your – Yes. I must talk with you. It is - "

There was a bang and Claudette spun round, reaching inside her leather jacket.

Dodi had opened a bottle of champagne. He smiled. "You're good, Inspector. Sharp reflexes." He nodded. "Ever think of joining the private sector? My father pays handsomely." Was he being sarcastic?

"I might well need to, m'sieur." She turned back to Diana.

"And if that was a gun you were about to draw, you – Henri – are in trouble," sneered Dodi.

Paul did not react. He was used to Dodi's 'little ways'.

"Madame – Diana," said Claudette. "You are in danger. Can I speak freely?" Her eyes moved towards Paul and quickly back again.

"Please speak freely," said Diana. "Henri is a loyal and trusted friend."

"I have reason to believe that your life is under threat, madame."

"Are you sure? There are always nutters out there."

"It is more than that, madame. I have it on the utmost authority that an attempt will be made on your life while you are here."

"That is ludicrous," said Dodi. "Who by?"

"The British."

"The *British*? Oh come on, Inspector," sneered Dodi. "Do you really think the British would kill their own Princess?"

"It's Charles, isn't it?" said Diana thoughtfully.

"I don't know. But I have reason to believe there is an assassin out there."

Henri Paul walked over to the tall windows and looked down at the Place Vendôme. It looked like a crowd outside a Stage Door after a concert, waiting for the Superstar to appear. "Nothing will happen on my watch, I promise you," he sniffed.

He turned back around – and found Claudette pointing a gun at Diana's head.

23:00 Rue de Berri

In the Hotel California, Christina Cascianis and Melanie Nathanson were dressing up for a night on the town. At least, that is what it would look like. That was the alibi.

"You are sure it will happen tonight?" Christina was strapping a back-up Beretta and holster to the inside of her left thigh.

"He's here," reasoned Melanie. "Deaths on yachts never look natural – even if they are. Deaths in big cities – a dime a dozen."

"And we are just going to let him do it?"

"Grates, doesn't it?" Melanie was applying brown eye shadow (*Brun Aztèque* by Bourjois). "But Tel Aviv has pointed out that Ramirov is our mission, not Diana. The game must be played out."

"But could we not just stack the deck in her favour...?" wondered Christina.

They both looked at the laptop, thinking of the other information supplied by Barking Dog.

"Should we?" wondered Melanie.

"Letz," said Christina.

23:00 Rue Vavin

Pierre Jamo entered his apartment in Montparnasse and pulled off his clothes. They reeked of death and vomit.

Seven hours! He moaned to himself. Seven fucking hours the *Police Judiciaire* had detained him. And he had been the one who had found the body, the one who had called in the death! They treated him as if he were the murderer.

He had gone over his story again and again, with God knows how many people. He had an important meeting arranged with the Commissaire last night. (What about? That was BCP business, politically-sensitive, 'need to know'.) He had gone round to her apartment but had received no reply. She must have forgotten.

She did not turn up for work today. (A Commissaire working on a Saturday? Commissaire Colet often did. She was a very conscientious Commissioner.) So he went round to her apartment. Again there was no reply to his knock. But he could smell something. So he broke the door in. (He always carried the crowbar in his car.) Found her. Called the PJ.

That was his story.

And seven hours later they let him go home.

As pissed as sin, he turned the television on and went into the bathroom.

Ten minutes later, hair dripping, stark naked and with a towel in his hand, he stood motionless in front of the television.

The news bulletin was reporting Princess Diana's arrival in Paris that afternoon.

23:00 République

John Smith had stayed in the bar for an hour after Henri Paul had left, enjoying another three beers and chatting with the locals in his perfect but accented French. Now he walked north on the Rue de Malte and then turned west onto the Rue de Faubourg du Temple. He was satisfied. Job done. He had every faith in Henri Paul, fifteen thousand francs worth of faith, plus the one hundred thousand retainer Paul received each year from the British Security Services.

It was eleven o'clock on a Saturday night in Paris in August. Smith thought he might head up to Pigalle to celebrate – but then what if Paul succeeded sooner rather than later? He'd best return to the Hotel Keppler and wait.

He entered the Place de la République and trotted over to the metro. The musty popcorn smell of the subway system hit him as soon as he walked down the steps.

As he was on the *Ligne 9* train heading west, *Direction Pont de Sèvres*, he thought back to his meeting with Charles and Camilla two weeks previously.

"What do royals always do?" Camilla had asked.

They all knew the answer. The royals dithered, but then in the end they solved their problems.

There were conflicting reports about Diana's pregnancy. Her friend, Rosa Monckton, had reported that Diana had had her period when she was on holiday with her in Greece earlier in the month. If that was true, Diana could not be pregnant now.

But in contradiction, the US National Security Agency via their base at Menwith Hill in the north of England had listened to Diana telling another girlfriend on the phone that she was pregnant with Dodi's child *[the Americans were monitoring Diana because of her anti-landmine campaign and activities, which would threaten US defence industry interests]*.

So The Boss had ordered Smith to determine Diana's pregnancy status for certain. If she was pregnant, she would be 'persuaded' to abort the child – or it would live in a social 'iron mask' for the whole of its life, denied and rejected by the establishment, a lifetime Fayed lie. But that was a bridge that would be crossed only if necessary.

John Smith had asked Henri Paul to obtain a sample of Diana's urine. A simple plumbing problem in the hotel, a failure to flush, don't worry madame, Henri will see to it – and that was it. If the urine tests were inconclusive, she would be sedated via a meal or a drink and be examined by a tame doctor. She would wake up none the wiser, with just a slight feeling of a hangover.

And that was the only involvement of His Royal Highness Prince Charles Philip Arthur George, Prince of Wales, Knight of the Garter, Knight of the Thistle, Knight Grand Cross of the Order of the Bath, Knight of the Order of Australia, Companion of the Queen's Service Order, Privy Counsellor, Aide-de-Camp, Earl of Chester, Duke of Cornwall, Duke of Rothesay, Earl of Carrick, Baron of Renfrew, Lord of the Isles, Prince Great Steward of Scotland and eldest son of Queen Elizabeth II, in the events of August 30 and 31 1997.

23:00 The Ritz Hotel

"So much for your security," said Claudette. "Mr Fayed was right. A simple

ID was all it took to get me in here." She put the gun back in its shoulder holster under her jacket. "It's just as well I am a policeman."

Diana sat there graciously. Henri Paul stood there open-mouthed. Dodi's first reaction of fear had turned to bravado. "Oh, you are going to work for us, madame," he nodded. "We have a vacancy at Director of Security level." He looked pointedly at Paul. He had taken a breath to say something else when his cell phone rang. It was on the mantelpiece. He went over, picked it up and frowned. "I'll take this in the other room. *Henri, allons.* I'll be back in a minute, darling."

The sitting room door closed behind them,

"So what should I do?" asked Diana.

Claudette turned round from watching the men leave. "Diana, what is the secret?" she asked abruptly.

Diana was confused. "What's the *what?*"

"The secret. The secret everyone dies for. I must know it. My father was killed because of it."

"I don't know what you mean - "

"We haven't much time. Many years ago. That is why the British are going to kill you now. The royal secret. Please, I beg you."

"I don't know any - " Diana stopped. She looked at the Frenchwoman in front of her. There was pleading in Claudette's eyes. Desperation. Oh my God – a royal secret. She never thought it was real.

Her mind went back eleven years to that Christmas at Sandringham, her row with Charles (perm any year from eleven for that one), the solace she had sought with grandma, the Queen Mother.

But surely the old woman had been drunk? Surely she had been kidding?

"I... I never thought she meant it," Diana said hesitantly. "Are you sure? I never thought it was true. She told me about the deaths... Oh my God. Is *she* going to kill me? Is it her? Why? Why now?"

"What is the secret, madame? Please tell me."

"Inspector, it is not *a* secret," said Diana. "It is three secrets. Two in the past, one in the future. Each one building on the other. I don't think I should tell you..."

Claudette was a muscle-twitch away from re-drawing her gun. Then Diana said, "Oh, what the hell. Perhaps it is safer you do know. The more the merrier. The more the safer. They can't... kill us all..." She sounded uncertain. "The first secret is well-known. Wallis Simpson was a patsy. A cover-up for the affair of the century. David Windsor did not love her, she was the arranged bride to get him out of the country. It was the only reason he could abdicate. He would have to go if he intended to marry a divorcee. He could never be King. How ironic compared to today!" She paused briefly with her thoughts. Then she went on. "Because if he became King and was married to the barren Wallis, or indeed to anybody, his already-born daughter would never accede to the throne. But she did, and she's there to this day. The royal bloodline is pure. David Saxe-Coburg-Gotha, also known as David Windsor, and Elizabeth Bowes-Lyon. A love affair that lasted until his death. And their daughter Elizabeth."

Claudette said nothing, but her hand was shaking slightly.

Diana continued. "The second secret is an agreement. David Saxe-Coburg-Gotha was very proud of his German ancestry, his German blood. With the Teutonic English royal bloodline secure and his daughter destined to be Monarch, it was agreed that Germany would capitulate in 1945 – the war could have gone on for years, the German army was mighty. Do you really think the small little island of Britain was any match for them? But there is more than one way to win a war. The Germans had done what Britain wanted – annihilated over six million troublesome Jews. Before that, Zionism was a force in both countries – the Jews would have taken over the world. Has it never occurred to anybody that *Britain and Germany were effectively on the same side?* They wanted the same end-game. So did the Americans. They all wanted to make the world a better place – and they thought getting rid of the Jewish threat would do that. The fools."

She looked up at the Frenchwoman. "Hitler's assassination by his mistress was not in their plans. But the French, Yanks and Brits did not mind – he was a troublesome little runt. The plan was working. Britain's ruling family was, and remains to this day, German. Its bloodline is pure. And who really won the war? Who rules Europe today? Not France, not Britain. Fatso in Berlin, that's who rules Europe today.

"The third secret is the last part of the plan, very soon - "

The door opened and Dodi walked in.

"Can you believe it?" shouted Dodi. "Can you fucking believe it!"

Diana grimaced. She hoped he wouldn't swear like that in front of The Boys. Claudette turned to look at him.

"Do you know who that phone call was from? Fucking Israeli Intelligence. Israeli Intelligence! Some daft Jewish cow informing me that an attempt was to be made on your life tonight! Can you *believe* these people! The arrogance of them! And how did they get my number?"

Diana stood up. "What did you say to them?"

"Told them to mind their own fucking business. They even told me the man's name. A professional hit man, named Ramir something or other."

Claudette snapped back towards Diana. "Get away from the window now."

Diana ran over.

"Two independent confirmed sources," explained Claudette. She looked around. "Where is your security man?"

"He's ordering his staff to clear the Square in front of the hotel," said Dodi. "Onlookers are being sent back to the arcade on the other side. The Press can stay at a fifty metre perimeter – but he is checking all their IDs and noting their names."

"So you believe the Israelis then?"

"I believed *you*. Fucking Jews."

"You need to leave here," advised Claudette.

"What do you mean? We're safe here," argued Dodi.

"In a huge hotel? Anyone could get in. You need to be somewhere smaller."

"Listen to her, Dodi," advised Diana.

"Where do you think we should go?" he asked, and then answered his own question. "Ah, I know!"

"This is what we'll do," said Claudette.

PART FIVE

Ω

FULFILMENT

Ω

Sunday August 31 1997

Paris, France

00:05 The Ritz Hotel

Henri Paul returned to the Imperial Suite with a sheet of paper in his hand. "I have checked all their IDs and listed their names. They are all genuine press photographers."

"Let me see," Claudette took the paper from him. She read the list of twenty names. There was Christian Martinez, Romauld Rat, Stephane Darmon, Claude Dumoulin, Jacques Langevin, Laslo Veres, Fabrice Chassery, David Oderkerken and Serge Benamou amongst others. No Ramir – something. Well, there wouldn't be, would there?

"So it is agreed," Claudette folded the paper and put it in her pocket. "They'll be expecting you to go to the Rue Arsène Houssaye. That will be the decoy. The full car and back-up, full security, usual drivers – but you will not be in it. Also they'll be expecting you to go out the front. We mustn't disappoint them. Henri, go and tell them we'll be leaving soon. Dodi, call your bodyguards."

00:10 Place Vendôme

Diana and Dodi left the Imperial Suite, and the bodyguards and others followed. Downstairs, the Mercedes 660 and the Range Rover pulled up at the front of The Ritz. There was a mass movement and shuffling from the crowd waiting outside.

00:18 The Ritz Hotel

As the Mercedes 660 and Range Rover pulled away from the hotel, some paparazzi followed on motorbikes. At the same time Diana and Dodi waited in the small lobby at the back of the hotel. Dodi had his arm touching Diana's back. Outside Henri Paul pulled up in the black Mercedes 280S, licence number 668 LTV 75. He opened the car's doors and then came into the hotel.

After a few exchanged words, the group walked out the back of the hotel. Despite their best laid plan, there were seven photographers waiting outside, among them Jacques Langevin, Fabrice Chassery, Claude Dumoulin, Serge Arnal, Christian Martinez, Romauld Rat and his driver Stephan Darmon.

Henri Paul smiled at the photographers, almost challenging. *"Bravo, mes amis.* Tonight you won't catch us."

Trevor Rees-Jones climbed into the front of the Mercedes, Dodi and Diana climbed into the back.

Nobody took any notice of the female who left the hotel immediately after them. She went over to her Ducati M900 motorbike next to the wall and put on her red crash helmet.

At the same time at the northern end of the Rue Cambon, Pierre Jamo turned his Fiat Uno a sharp right from the Boulevard de la Madelaine...

00:20 Rue Cambon

The Mercedes pulled away from The Ritz hotel and headed south on Rue Cambon. Two or three of the photographers decided to follow. The others picked up their portable phones to call their colleagues.

One bike in particular was keen to keep up with the Mercedes...

Pierre Jamo squinted down the narrow Rue Cambon and saw the flashguns going off outside the back of The Ritz. He saw the Mercedes pull away, and a few motorbikes take off after it. One of them seemed very keen. It was a big bike, like a Ducati.

That was Claudette's bike.

Claudette Ibrahim watched Diana and Dodi go. She wished them well. Her job was done.

Diana had told her the Windsor Secret. It was shocking. The world had been fooled. Millions had died unnecessarily. But worst of all was the third part, the part that was to come early in the next century. Would they really attack New York?

What should she do with the knowledge? One thing was for certain, she was in danger. Mortal danger. If the Brits knew she knew...

She was looking south down the Rue Cambon as a white Fiat Uno shot past her. The car hardly registered with her. She was thinking about Lady Diana.

The Brits were going to kill one of their own – at least they were going to try to. But the decoy car plan should work. If not, the decoy destination should work, at least until the men from Harrods in London could get to the Press and blow the assassination plot wide open.

As for her, she needed to disappear. She had avenged her father, she had been told the secret. Time to start anew somewhere.

She fingered the piece of paper in her pocket, the one Diana had given her as they waited to leave the hotel. It was Diana's direct line telephone at her home in Kensington Palace, London. "Ring me," Diana had said. "If there is anything you want me to do for you. Ever. Ring me."

Claudette Ibrahim smiled and turned the ignition on the Ducati.

00:22 En route

The Mercedes turned right into the Rue de Rivoli. In his wing mirror, Henri Paul could see a few motorbikes behind the car. One seemed to be ahead of the others. There was also a white Fiat.

They passed into the Place de la Concorde and turned left with the traffic flow.

Paul smiled to himself. This is where they would be expecting him to turn right into the Champs Elysées. He put on his right indicator and then pressed his foot down on the accelerator.

The Mercedes shot straight ahead across the bottom of the Champs, heading towards the Seine.

In his mirror Paul saw two bikes actually turn into the Champs, but the closest bike stuck with him. As did the Fiat.

Pierre Jamo cursed. It was not Claudette, it was not even a Ducati, it was a BMW. He had gotten close enough to see that the helmeted, leather-clad rider was far too tall and chunky to be her. It was probably just another dumb paparazzo.

He would just get up close to the Merc to make sure everyone was all right inside and then he would go home. He really couldn't think straight anymore. He needed sleep.

The convoy of the Mercedes, the Fiat and the motorbike passed into the Cours la Reine on the banks of the Seine. They were travelling at 70 kilometres per hour, ten kilometres above the speed limit of 60 kph but by no means speeding. They entered the first tunnel.

The Fiat accelerated on the inside of the Mercedes. Jamo could see four people inside. They seemed normal. The couple in the back were laughing.

The motorbike accelerated on the outside.

They came out of the tunnel just underneath the southern end of the Avenue Franklin D Roosevelt.

In the Mercedes, Henri Paul was pleased with himself. The plan was working. Their destination was not Dodi's flat in the Rue Arsène Houssaye but the other Fayed property, 24 Boulevard Suchet, the 'Villa Windsor'. He would take a right up the slip-road before the Alma Tunnel. Then it was a straight route: Avenue Georges Mandel, Avenue Henri Martin, Boulevard Suchet. Simple.

The motorbike overtook him on the left.

Paul began to cruise to the right towards the slip-road, but he wrenched the steering wheel back as he saw a Fiat up by the side of him. There was a faint knock and a scrape as the vehicles touched.

It was too late to get to the slip road now, he would have to go down through the Alma Tunnel.

There was a thump and he saw something round on the windscreen.

In the back, the laughing Diana looked up at the beautiful lights on the Eiffel Tower across the river as they descended into the tunnel.

00:30 Alma Tunnel

On the BMW, Ian Ramsey pulled up level with the front wheels of the Mercedes. Steering the bike with his left hand, he reached down into a bag attached on the fuel tank between his legs and brought out what looked like the bottom of a large tin of shaving soap. It was a *Stunpet* – a combination stun grenade and limpet mine which would stick to any surface.

Ramsey turned his arm around and slammed the *Stunpet* on the windscreen of the car. Then he accelerated down into the Alma Tunnel, way ahead of the Mercedes now.

He began to slow as a Citroen and a couple of other cars passed, and then he pulled a small device out of his top pocket and pressed it.

The Mercedes entered the tunnel only 20 kph above the tunnel speed limit of 50.

Henri Paul only had time to register the round object stuck onto the windscreen. Then it simultaneously flashed and exploded. The flash had the brightness of seven suns and it instantly blinded Paul. The percussive explosion blew out his ear drums.

Instead of curving left with the road in the tunnel, the Mercedes went straight, clipping the right wall and then flying across the carriageway, spinning into the thirteenth concrete support pillar with an almighty bang and crushing of metal. It then bounced back off the pillar and span again, coming to rest facing backwards down the tunnel, the way it had come.

Ramsey slid the BMW to a stop, turned the bike around and drove back to the wrecked vehicle. The horn on the car was stuck and blaring. Smoke was rising from the mangled engine.

Beneath the airbag, the driver was squashed to a pulp, one of his hands jutted through the broken windscreen. The front passenger was held rigid by his seat belt, the airbag pressing against him. Where his face should be was a cascade of blood.

Ramsey pulled open the back, off-side passenger door. Over the other side, Dodi Fayed was stretched out, his legs broken and bent at a terrible angle. His eyelids were open but his eyes had turned back in his head. He was dead.

Near to Ramsey, his target was doubled up between the front seat and the back seat, her head between the two front seats. She had a cut on her forehead and was disorientated, but otherwise she seemed unhurt. She looked at Ramsey. She said, "My God, my God."

Ramsey flipped open the pocket on his leather jacket and withdrew a small, three centimetre long, one centimetre wide aerosol, like a perfume sampler. He took the top off and, clinically, dispassionately, sprayed something into Diana's face. She was not even aware of it.

Ramsey replaced the top of the aerosol and put it back in his pocket. Then he pulled out a few sachets of heroin and threw them into the car. Cosmetics. He closed the car door back over, and walked off back towards his bike as paparazzo Romauld Rat arrived with his camera. The smoke was still billowing, and the car horn was blaring incessantly, noisily, eerily.

Ramsey was half hidden by the smoke by the time he reached his bike. He looked back at the Mercedes. The colourless, odourless, cyanide gas had served him and his previous masters well in the past, notably killing Dr Lev Rebet in 1952 and used by Ramirov himself on Georges Pompidou in 1974. Diana, Princess of Wales, would be dead within the hour.

He straddled his bike and looked back one last time. He said, "Welcome to history, bitch."

Then he sped off out of the Alma Tunnel.

PART SIX

Ω

END-GAME

01:00 Rue Vavin

Pierre Jamo felt the bump from the Mercedes as he took the slip road up onto the Cours Albert 1er, but he thought nothing of it. Bumps happen all the time in Paris.

Across the Pont de l'Alma, he took the Avenue Bosquet. The streets were reasonably quiet at that hour of the morning, and he was pulling into Rue Vavin by 01:00.

That hadn't been Claudette on the bike, and he was happy that Diana and Dodi were all right. He'd seen them laughing in the back of their car.

But what had happened to Claudette, he wondered? Both literally and figuratively. What had happened to turn his talented, feisty, clever, *sexy* Inspector into a serial killer? Or had she been conning him all along? Was this yet another woman who had led him a merry dance, who had fooled him?

And where was she now? He had been tempted to go back to her apartment one more time but, frankly, he was just so damned tired. He would leave her to her fate. He did not owe her anything.

But, he thought regretfully, she was a damn good screw. 'Was' being the operative word.

As he was locking his car, he noticed one of his back lights was smashed. Shit, the Mercedes must have bumped him harder than he thought. More expense!

Normally he would walk up to his apartment on the third floor, but having exercised his legs today first in Colet's block and then in Claudette's block, he decided to take the lift.

The elevator was the old but effective see-through variety, with double concertina gates, going up the middle of the stairwell. It hummed loudly as it crept upwards.

As the lift raised his head slowly above the second floor and his apartment door came into view, Jamo frowned. For a moment he wondered whether he was back in Montmartre and not Montparnasse, and this was Claudette's place. Because the door to his apartment looked just like hers had after he had kicked it in – the wood around the lock was splintered. And the door was open a few centimetres.

Before the lift had clunked to a stop, Jamo had his gun in his hand. What the hell was this? Was it her?

He peeked into his hallway without touching the door. His lights were on and blazing. Whoever it was, if they were still there they were announcing their presence.

His foot pushed the front door open. He was pleased it did not creak.

The salon door was ajar, and the lights were on inside. Gun raised, he pushed the door open.

The room was empty. But now he could hear a sound. Running water. And something else. A buzzing.

The kitchen was off the salon, and the bathroom was beyond, off the kitchen.

The kitchen door was open, lights on, nobody there. The bathroom door was closed. That's where the noises were coming from.

Jamo turned the door handle and the door moved. It was not locked. Finger lightly but determinedly on the trigger of his Glock 17, he opened the door. The sound of the running water and the buzzing noise got louder.

Looking in, his eyebrows rose.

The gun lowered.

Claudette was standing there.

She was completely naked and she was using his mains electric razor to smooth out the stubble on her already-shaven pudendum. Next to her, water was running into a foam-filled bath, steam rising.

She looked up as the door opened and smiled in delight. "Hi, Chief!"

"What," he asked slowly, "are you doing here?"

"I didn't know what time you'd be back. I was making myself nice for you. Care to join me?" she nodded towards the bath. Turning the razor off, she rubbed between her legs. "Nice," she nodded. "Just as you like it."

"I have been looking for you," Jamo said carefully, cautiously checking the rest of the room with his eyes. "Lots of people have."

"I know. Now you've found me. But look, I'm unarmed as you can see, you can put the gun away." She came over to him and stroked the side of his face. As always, her pert, muscular, naked body was mesmerizing him. She took hold of the Glock and he released his grip. Carefully she put the gun down on the clothes basket.

"What are you up to?" he asked.

"I know I've got a lot of explaining to do," she pushed his jacket off his shoulders, and he could smell the warmth in her hair. She stood on tiptoe and lightly kissed his lips. "And I will, I will tell you everything. I will tell you why." Her lips were brushing against his as she spoke. "I have found out the secret." She pressed her lower body against his. "Ah, that's a better greeting for a lady. I know that's not your gun and I *know* you're pleased to see me."

Jamo felt her hands against his chest as she unbuttoned his shirt. He was rigid in his trousers, and thank God she started to touch him as she undid his belt.

"And I will tell you who I really am," she said.

"I know who you really are," he retorted as she pulled his trousers and underpants down and reached round and rubbed the hairy cheeks of his bottom. She was kneeling in front of him and his hard dick was banging against her face.

"Not today," she kissed his knob. "Today let's pretend I have another name." She rubbed him with her right hand, sucking on him. Then she looked up and said, "Call me Gillian." She moved away and stood up in one motion.

"Call you *what?*" Jamo was standing there erect, trousers and pants around his ankles, shoes and socks still on.

She giggled. "Gillian. She won't be using the name any more. Come, bathe with me." She beckoned with her finger.

"You little bitch." Jamo hopped across the room towards her, and she laughed out loud.

When he got within distance, she reached out, grabbed his penis firmly and used his own hopping momentum to push him into the bath. He went over the rim, bottom first, legs hanging over the side. Water splashed up and over onto the floor.

"Hey!" he shouted.

Gillian reached behind her and turned the razor back on. Jamo could see what was going to happen and he struggled to get out of the bath, but he was hampered by his tied feet.

She threw the razor into the bath.

It was as spectacular as she had expected. Cracks, crackles, smoke, Jamo jumping up and down, eyes nearly popping out of his head.

She did not turn the current off, it would probably blow eventually. She turned, and the last thing Pierre Jamo saw was her superb bottom walking away from him.

He did not live to see her turn back in the doorway, nor to hear her say, "You Parisians and your accidents in the bath. Will you never learn?"

Singing *Bordeaux Rosé* she went out and closed the bathroom door behind her.

01:15 Rue d'Italie

Ian Ramsey parked the BMW in the small Rue d'Italie down in the 13th, put the crash helmet on the seat and walked away.

It would be a long walk back to his hotel at Place de Clichy, but it had to be done. The authorities would have their hands full tonight but, if there were any eagle-eyed witnesses, they might – just *might* – be looking for an unaccounted for paparazzo on a BMW.

And he would not hail a cab. Someone on his own at this hour of the morning on this historic day, would be remembered. The night's events might even be on the radio already.

02:00 Rue Vavin

Claudette Gerard spent some time clearing all traces of herself from Pierre Jamo's apartment. No prints anywhere, no tell-tale girly items she might have inadvertently left behind.

After thirty minutes she went back into the bathroom just to ensure Pierre was dead. He was, well and truly. The bowels had vacated themselves into the bath, which was unfortunate – and smelly – but never mind, couldn't be helped. He had no housekeeper so, she realised, he might not be found for some while. Not until his absence from work was noticed. And who would notice that? She would not be there, and The Bitch Colet was dead. Old Sergeant Goise might start looking in about a week.

She laughed. Was she bothered?

04:00 Place de Clichy

Ian Ramsey reached the Hotel Mercure Montmartre at 04:00, having walked a circuitous route across the Boulevard de Port Royal (he saw a slowly moving ambulance and some police cars on the Boulevard, but he thought nothing of it)), past the Jardin du Luxembourg, across the river via the Île de la Cité and then along the various side streets up through the Bourse and St Lazare then straight up the Rue d'Amsterdam.

As he crossed the Place Clichy, he pulled out his cell phone and began to make a call.

With 305 rooms in the hotel, the front door and the Reception were always open. At this hiatus hour between night and early morning there were fewer people about, but he still walked over to the lifts unnoticed, talking softly on his cell phone. One or two late night travellers were returning (Paris on a Saturday night was still the place to be), and he had to share the lift with a couple of middle-aged women.

He used his phone conversation to ignore them and they ignored him as they travelled upwards, but the black haired woman burped as they passed the third floor and that started the red haired one giggling.

The lift reached the sixth floor, and Ramsey stepped out. He heard the lift doors close behind him.

"Yes, thank you," he said into the cell phone as he put his key card in his door. Then he was aware of running footsteps, muted on the carpet, coming towards him. He turned to find the two women who had been in the lift. They had identical Heckler & Koch P7 handguns with bulbous silencers, pointing at his head.

"Hello Ilich," said Christina Cascianis, pushing her gun against the back of his head and forcing him into the room. "Remember me?"

"There must be some mistake - " He lowered his hand holding the phone.

"None at all," said Christina as Melanie closed the door. "Not this time."

Christina shot him in the head from behind. The bullet went through the skull and took out his left eye, which was later found under the minibar. Christina stood over the body and emptied all thirteen of the 9mm Parabellum cartridges into his head, the body jumping with each one.

"Not this time," she repeated.

She spat onto the corpse. "For Stelios."

04:30 Rue Larmarck

The Ducati motorbike roared up the quiet backstreets of Montmartre and stopped at the end of Rue Lamarck. Claudette Gerard wondered whether Will The Cat had returned. She hoped so. She must leave Paris now and she wanted her baby for company.

She reached the top floor and thought of Jamo as she saw her broken front door. *Bastard.*

She went in and pushed the door closed behind her.

Then she heard a noise. In the *salle de jour.* Yes! She smiled. She had left the window open and Will was home.

She pushed open the door, and there was the cat waiting for her. She bent down and Will jumped into her arms. "Hello, baby."

"Hello," said a female voice.

Claudette's head shot up.

"Come away from the door." Over by the window was a small, elegant woman dressed in denim jeans and loose white silk shirt. Her dark hair fell down either side of her face, but it could not hide the large surgical dressing on the left side of her neck. She was holding a Smith and Wesson.

Oh, merde.

"Remember me?" asked Gisele Joudeh.

"Of course," Claudette stood up slowly. "You are Becker's girlfriend. I thought you were dead. Silly me. I am sorry I did not finish the job." Claudette kept her eyes on the other woman but mentally she was looking around the room. She was hampered by the cat in her arms.

"You are quite the charmer, aren't you" said the Lebanese. "Why did you hurt Ron?"

"I didn't, you did."

"You were torturing him, weren't you?"

Claudette frowned and tightened her grip on the cat.

"What did Ron say to you?" Gisele saw the grip tighten. "And please, don't make me shoot your cat, she is not involved in this."

"In what?"

"Do you know the expression 'honey trap'? The Brits were involved in something. Courtesy of Ron, I had learnt of their plans. I heard him talking to you about Diana."

"I just needed to know why my father died."

"Your father? What has that got to do with the death of Diana?" Gisele was surprised.

"The death?" Claudette was perplexed. "What do you mean death?"

"She was killed tonight."

Claudette shook her head. "She can't have been. I was…" She thought back to Diana and Dodi driving off in the Mercedes. How could Diana be dead?

She looked at Gisele and her eyes went blank. Stone-faced, she lowered her arms and the cat jumped down. In her right hand Claudette was holding her gun.

"Put it down," ordered Gisele.

"Fuck you." Claudette raised her arm.

Both women fired.

Gisele jumped to her right as she pulled the trigger, and Claudette's bullet thudded into the chair behind her.

Claudette did not move. She grinned at the Lebanese woman prostrate on the floor and she was on the verge of laughing. Then the hole in the centre of Claudette's forehead popped out a clot of blood and the crimson river rolled down between her eyes. She crumpled to the floor.

After a moment, the other woman slowly stood up. She brushed fluff and cat hair off of her denim jeans. She looked at the body on the floor and then gave it a tentative kick. Nothing except a twitching left foot. The Frenchwoman was dead.

Well, what was all that about? she wondered. Had it anything to do with her mission?

Gisele Joudeh, a member of the Lebanese Department of General Security, gave a final look around the room, and left.

On the floor next to Claudette, Will The Cat rubbed her nose against her mistress.

"Weow," she said.

Ω

Saturday August 30 1997

Sarasota, Florida, USA

In the USA it was still Saturday. It was 23:00 local time when the death of Diana, Princess of Wales, was confirmed on the networks. A tragic accident, cause by the picture-hungry paparazzi.

He nodded in satisfaction, turned the volume off on his TV and walked out onto the lanai.

The evening was hot but the humidity of the day had evaporated. He eased himself into his hot tub, alone this time.

Ilich Ramirov leant his head back on the marble edge and closed his eyes. He couldn't help but smile.

He had heard Ian Ramsey's execution on the cell phone – and he had heard who had done it. The Israelis. The damn, fucking Israelis. But his smile was one of "I knew it."

Ever since the stupid French had announced the death of Ilych Ramirez Sanchez – and had then hastily withdrawn the announcement – he knew the Jews would be after him. He had been left in peace for the three years they thought he had been incarcerated, but now they were onto him.

Well, damn them. They did not know that in those three years, he had created a brand. He had recruited the cream of the world's professional assassins and mercenaries, from the US, from Scotland, Ireland, Russia, Mexico and, yes, even Israel. A co-operative of callous, emotionless, highly skilled killing machines who would terminate anyone – for the right money.

Like 'Best Western' was not one hotel chain but a group of independent hotels, like 'Wimpy' was not one restaurant chain but a group of franchises, like 'James Patterson' was no longer one author but a group of co-writing authors, so 'Ilich Ramirov' was no longer one assassin but a group of assassins.

And did the pathetic Israelis really think that he would go on an assignment *and use his own initials?* The unfortunate 'Ian Ramsey' was his patsy, his stoolpigeon. Ramsey had served him well. He had completed his mission and he had lured the Israelis. Ramirov hoped Ramsey's heirs, whoever they may be, enjoyed the five million US dollars Ramirov had paid him.

As the warm water lapped against his chest, Ramirov felt a longing. His wished the whore Candice was with him. He needed a tangible celebration. To celebrate on your own was not to celebrate at all. And anyway, it would make him go blind – and he only had one eye left!

He reached for his bottle of *Coors* on the ceramic edge of the tub.

Now the Israelis really thought he was dead. That was good, and he wished he could leave it at that. But there was an old saying: once is happenstance, twice is coincidence, three times is enemy action.

The meddlesome Greek Christina Cascianis. Cyprus 1974. Khartoum 1994. Paris 1997.

Three times.

Enemy action.

He began to formulate his plans.

Ω

Sunday August 31 1997

Balmoral, Scotland

"Mummy," said Elizabeth, Queen of England. "Mummy, I'm sorry to disturb you but something dreadful has happened."

The ninety-seven year old matriarch of the British Royal Family slowly opened her eyes from the pretence of sleep. "Mm? Elizabeth? What is it?" She wished she was at Birkhall instead of the main house, but her cottage was being redecorated. So she had to go through with it.

"It is positively awful, Mummy. Diana has been killed. In a car crash. In Paris."

The old woman looked at her daughter, her beautiful pure blood Elizabeth.

So, it was over. The last person to know the secret had been expunged. It was a pity it had to be Diana, but it had to be done. And it wasn't as if she was a member of the family any more. Or royal. She was simply the carrier of the bloodline of the family. Provided William survived, the line would be pure. Henry would never be King, for obvious reasons.

What she had done, what she had had to do, would never be known. The secret was dead.

She pulled herself up in her bed and held her arms out. "Oh my darling," she said. "That is dreadful. Come, kiss Mummy."

Clarence House, London, England

Sir Kenneth Dean, Senior Secretary to Her Majesty Queen Elizabeth the Queen Mother, gently replaced the telephone on its receiver. Her Majesty had called to thank him for his speed and efficiency – and, of course, for his discretion. His promised reward would be forthcoming.

Dean sat back in his chair behind his desk in his small, austere office in the Queen Mother's London residence. He thought back over the years. Back to 1979 when they had at last obtained the documents that had been retained for over thirty years by Wallis Simpson, Duchess of Windsor. Documents that had kept the Duchess alive for so many years. Documents that had then been stolen. Many had had to die to retrieve the documents and protect the secret.

At that time, he was plain Kenneth Dean, Under Consul at the British Embassy in Paris (the knighthood and secretarial position were six months away 'for services rendered'). The documents had been retrieved and he had visited Her Majesty at Clarence House and had given her the sealed envelope.

He had watched as Her Majesty tore the envelope and contents into small pieces and let them fall into a glass ashtray. She had then taken a cigarette lighter, lit the pile in three places, and stared as the paper charred and curled in on itself, reducing to ashes.

But she had not looked inside the envelope before burning it.

Now, eighteen years later, Sir Kenneth Dean unlocked the bottom left drawer of his desk and pulled out an A5 envelope. He lifted the flap and took out the contents. Carefully he laid it on his desk.

He looked at the old sepia envelope with the royal crest and the initials E.P on the back. It was about time, he thought, that he found out why so many people had had to die.

He picked up the envelope and took out the two pieces of paper inside.

"It is absolutely black-and-white horrendous murder."
- Mohamed Al Fayed, 6 January 2004.

"There is not one drop of blood in my veins that is not German."
- David Saxe-Coburg-Gotha,
also known as David Windsor,
King Edward VIII of England.

Anyone who knows the secret, dies.

Now you do...

DAVID CULLEN

SHADE

There are no such things as ghosts

A Short Story

Written in 1971. Discovered in the vaults of a derelict house somewhere in the west of England in 2012.

SHADE – *(ancient use) a ghost or phantom.*

There are no such things as ghosts

I believe in ghosts. I have not always but since my night in that terrible, terrible house, I have had no choice. I *have* proof.

It was silly how it all started, and why I did it puzzles me to this day. Perhaps deep down in the grey recesses of my head there was some esoteric suicidal wish which I had not even acknowledged existed.

There were four of us: myself John, my beautiful fiancée of two months Pauline, my best friend Philip and his young wife Angie. Pauline and I had met just three months previously at a party given by some mutual distant friend. I had arrived late and when I walked into the room I was struck immediately by this fawn-haired vision sitting in a corner and gaily laughing at some banter. It did not take me long to wangle an introduction to her out of our host and for the rest of that evening we talked, danced and ate together, really quite oblivious to everyone else. To my incredulous delight I discovered that this pretty and charming girl had no permanent boyfriend.

At the end of the evening, we had arranged to meet again a couple of days later. Meet we did and it was then that the feelings started. Strange, unfamiliar feelings, feelings that grew more powerful each time we met (which quickly became on a daily basis). Feelings that hurt when I was not with her but which were the most wonderful feelings in the world when she was in my arms. After just one month I had asked her to marry me and she had accepted readily; our marriage was fixed for exactly one month from today.

Tonight was the first time Philip and Angie had met my darling and perhaps it was for that reason that I accepted the challenge, not wanting to look a coward in my future wife's eyes.

We had been two hours in the lowly-lit, warm, cossetted atmosphere of Philip's *very* exclusive Kensington restaurant in London. Now liqueurs were being served. Conversation had progressed from the formal introductions earlier to the light, amicable chatter of after dinner conversation. How it got round to ghosts and the supernatural I do not know.

Philip was expounding on his belief in spirits. Angie and Pauline's eyes were fixed upon him. Yes, I suppose you could say that I was jealous that another man was holding *my* goddess's attention. It was the jealousy that only comes in the puerility of a man's first overwhelming moments in love. Oh, what a fool I was!

The secure feeling of our private alcove table was almost womb-like, and yet as soon as Philip touched on the subject of the supernatural I could have sworn that the temperature of the place dropped a few degrees – and was that an icy finger that seemed to prod at my very soul?

"It is a fact," Philip was saying, "that ghosts – spirits of the dead – *do* exist. There have been too many sightings at too many different times by too many different people for it to be merely superstition. Throughout history people have seen ghosts. Some have been literally terrified to death by them. Others have been guided by them. There are many stories of the Second World War where the spirits of dead soldiers have returned to guide their comrades out of trouble. One incident I remember reading about happened after the war was officially over...

"A Lance Corporal was driving along in a Jeep on a quiet road in Normandy just two days after the Axis forces had surrendered. It was dusk and he was idly cruising along back to his unit when, standing directly in front of the Jeep, about fifty yards down the road, he saw a familiar-looking figure. He slowed the Jeep right down, and as he crawled nearer he recognised the figure as, of all people, his brother. Well, the Lance Corporal couldn't believe his eyes. He smiled and waved but the figure in front did not return the greeting. All the figure did was to raise his right arm, palm outwards, in a 'Stop' signal and move his head slowly from side to side. Well, the Lance Corporal pulled to a halt and leapt out of his Jeep, eager to embrace his brother. But as he went to go towards him his brother just simply disappeared. Gone. Just like that. Not there.

"The Lance Corporal was astounded and he stood still for a moment, leaning on the side of his Jeep, staring at the empty road ahead. He had been standing there for a good few minutes, puzzled, wondering if he had been seeing things, when about twenty yards ahead of him a rabbit ran out from some hedges at the side of the road. Suddenly there was an almighty explosion and the Lance Corporal was blown clear into the air...

"He awoke two days later in a military hospital. He was concussed but otherwise not too badly hurt. It was to be some months before he remembered all of what had happened and a further few months before he found out that his brother had been one of the last Allied casualties of the war *and had died six weeks before the Axis forces surrendered...*"

Our private alcove was silent. The music of the restaurant's resident jazz band seemed muted now, far away as if it didn't want to reach us here, did not want to disturb the moment. Again I felt that strange, cold, almost tactile atmosphere in the alcove.

My Pauline was the first to break the silence. She smiled and asked, "Have *you* ever seen any ghosts yourself, Philip?"

Philip returned the smile (so igniting another pang of jealousy in my heart). "Not in the flesh – if that's the right expression – but I have *heard* one. There's this old house I came across once on a hike - "

"Personally I think ghosts, spirits and all such claptrap are rubbish," I heard myself interrupt. Maybe I was rude but at least I'd broken the almost mystical spell that was being woven in the alcove. "Ghosts are simply figments of people's imaginations, instilled by tradition and the belief – the hope – of an immortal existence."

"So you don't believe in life after death?" asked Angie.

I finished my liqueur and gently laid the glass back down on the table. "I'm not saying that. Maybe there is, maybe there isn't a life after death. None of us knows until death actually happens to us. What I'm saying is, I do not – cannot – believe that people 'come back', in their same mortal appearance, same voice *and* wearing clothes, whether they help or do mischief. I have always believed in the maxim that you *cannot* go back."

"I have an open mind about these things," said my darling Pauline. "I have yet to be convinced one way or the other. Although I must admit that I do feel that there is something in what Philip says."

Philip was in the throes of lighting his pipe, and from behind the billowing smoke he said in his best Orson Welles voice, "Perhaps we can convince you, Pauline – or at least convince you by convincing our doubter here."

All eyes again reverted to Philip and he looked straight at me. "I was telling you about this house I came across on a hike. Well, that *is* haunted, and I'm willing to bet that if you spend just one night in that house, my friend, you will be convinced that there are such things as ghosts… just as I am convinced."

The ladies' eyes now turned to me. It was as if they were watching a tennis match and the ball had been well and truly knocked into my court. I was serving to save the match.

I could hear the music of the band slowly fading away, far off on another plane. All around us the life of the restaurant was going on as normal, the wealthy young and not so young of the 'swinging' Kensington jet-set enjoying themselves on a summer's night, the last summer of the 1960s. But here at our alcove table life had stopped in a man-made hiatus.

I looked at each face individually. There was curiosity in Angie's eyes, challenge in Philip's, and love, pure and simple, in Pauline's. I had no choice, had I?

"All right," I said. "I'm willing to be convinced. I'll do it."

Deuce.

There are no such things as ghosts

Exactly where the house was, I was not told. All that was revealed was that it was deep in the heart of a forest somewhere. It was the night after the challenge had been issued that Philip and Angie collected us in their Ford Granada Ghia and drove us to the place.

The rules were simple: I was to spend one night in the house, from 23:30 till about 08:00 the next morning. Philip had guaranteed that if I did that I would be convinced of the existence of ghosts.

We went under cover of darkness, all part of the plot so that I would not know my exact location and be tempted to make a bolt for it. All that I knew was that it was a four hour drive to the west of London.

The forest was as black as pitch and the headlights of the car illuminated trees, trees and more trees as we bumped along a roughly-hewn path just wide enough for the Granada.

Ten minutes into the forest, Philip pulled the car to a halt and I alighted, torch in one hand and a duffel-bag containing food and a flask in the other. Philip pointed behind me. "There's a path through there which leads to the house, couple of minutes, no more. This is as far as we will go." His voice echoed in the still night air.

I turned around and played my torch over the area, illuminating a narrow, unwelcoming pathway through the trees. I turned back and said goodbye to them all, giving my Pauline an extra long, extra firm kiss on the lips.

"We'll pick you up about eight in the morning," smiled Philip. As I turned, he said "Hey, John. Do you still want to go through with it? You needn't you know."

I looked at each of them. Pauline's face showed concern, but what would she think of me – what would *I* think of me? – if I pulled out now?

"See you in the morning," I said tersely and turned back into the forest.

There are no such things as ghosts

Although it was a warm summer's night, it was eerily cold in the forest as I stumbled my way along the very narrow path. It was deathly quiet, not even the hooting of an owl to keep me company, to assure me that there was life in this gloomy, tree-infested graveyard.

I trudged on for a few minutes and suddenly it was there. From out of nowhere the house had appeared, a black amorphous mass looming out of the darkness, turrets seeming to reach up into the heavens in the best Hammer Horror movie tradition. My torch beam played upon the outside like a spotlight on an empty stage. I decided to waste no time exploring the place. I would find the first comfortable corner somewhere, eat my food and then sleep till the next morning. I *would* spend a night in the horrible place, just to show them – and myself – *that there are no such things as ghosts*.

The heavy wooden front door hung half open on one hinge, the other having rotted through years of neglect. I manoeuvred my way past without touching it. Even so, the door still screeched a deathly greeting as I went in, as if it was an old family retainer announcing my arrival to the rest of the house.

Dust was thick on the floor and cobwebs occupied every available corner. The place had the horrid, dank, musty smell of years of disuse. The interior looked as if it had been decorated in various shades of brown and no other colour. It was grim to say the least. The beam of my torch highlighted a charred staircase to my right, the victim of a fire sometime, leading to the upper floors. I felt a strange compulsion to go up it, almost as if an unseen force was urging me to do so. But I resisted and turned to the left.

There was a door. Big, dark, wooden. As I approached it a wind whipped from somewhere and blew it open with a loud creak. It *was* a wind, it couldn't have been anything else. I was alone in the house. *And there are no such things as ghosts*. Are there?

Inside was a small, bare room, a room which had probably been the study or library in the days when this house had been alive. I smiled to myself as I thought of my turn of phrase: *alive*. Yes, this house had been alive once. Long ago. But now it was dead, so, so dead. At least the nasty smell was not in this room, for every single pane of glass in the two windows here had been smashed or broken by the passing of time, and the refreshing draught of the now cool night air was blowing in, fumigating the place.

Without further ado I settled myself in the dust of the far corner, from where I could keep a careful watch on the door. I unpacked my food and flask. I decided to eat in darkness to conserve my torch batteries. A very weak moonlight illuminated the room sufficiently for me to see that I wasn't pouring my coffee over the floor.

I had finished my food and was just repacking my empty flask into the duffel-bag when I heard it.

I couldn't believe my ears. It was far away but so clear that I could *not* have been mistaken.

"Joh-nny!"

It was a distant female voice, beckoning from far away. I stood up quickly, torch in my hand – as much for protection as for light – and strained my ears. Ten seconds later it came again.

"Joh-nny!"

I frowned. Surely not... this could not be real.

I found myself walking out of the room and towards the staircase.

"Joh-nny!"

It was a familiar voice and it seemed to be coming from somewhere upstairs.

I reached the charred staircase and began to ascend. I only distantly heard the stairs' creak of complaint, my full attention being on that voice. *Where* had I heard it before? Surely there was no one else in the house – but there must be. *There are no such things as ghosts.*

"Joh-nny!"

Then I knew it. It was Pauline's voice! What was she *doing* here? Hadn't she left with Philip and Angie? Hold on – was this a game? Were they ganging up on me?

My feet hardly touched the stairs as I leapt upwards. "Pauline, where are you?"

"Joh-nny!"

It seemed to come from the very attics of the place. How had she gotten up there? I ran onwards and upwards, past the first floor, past the second...

And then I saw her, standing at the top of the next flight of stairs. I smiled. "Pauline - "

Then I abruptly stopped running. She was standing there, beckoning at me, arms outstretched, smiling – *but it was not Pauline.* It was some unfamiliar young woman dressed in Victorian costume. The left side of her face was hideously disfigured and scarred, as if she had been severely burned.

"Joh-nny!"

The voice came from her but she was not moving her mouth. Again I felt a strong, unseen force pushing me forward, pushing me up the stairs towards her.

I shook my head, fighting the force. "No, NO!" I screamed. "You are not real!"

She had begun to walk, to *glide*, down the stairs towards me. I could see wisps of smoke rising from the burnt side of her face. I could smell charred flesh.

With all my strength I managed to tear myself away from the diabolic force that held me, and I ran back down the stairs.

"Joh-nny!"

Faster and faster I ran, along the landing, taking the next flight of stairs two at a time. I looked behind but she was still there, arms outstretched, beckoning me to her. She was walking – *gliding* – calmly, yet she was going as fast as I was.

"Joh-nny!"

The devil voice was penetrating into my very soul. "No, NO!" I screamed again, forcing myself to run faster, leaping down the stairs three at a time. I would not turn back. I would not look at her again.

Then it happened.

I heard the ripping, the creak and the definitive crack too late as the charred, rotten staircase gave way beneath me and I plunged downwards into blackness, into infinity, still hearing that horrible voice.

"Joh-nny!"

There are no such things as ghosts

The next thing I was aware of was that it was light and rays of sunshine were making inroads into the house through the broken front door. I could hear voices approaching from outside and I knew that it must be eight o'clock.

Waves of relief washed over me. I had done it.

Pauline, Philip and Angie appeared in the doorway. "John?" called Pauline. "Johnny?"

I smiled and rushed up to my darling and kissed her on the tip of her upturned nose. I was so happy to see her again.

But she ignored me.

"My God!" exclaimed Philip. The three of them rushed across to the pile of rubble and debris which was the collapsed staircase.

Pauline screamed as she saw my body lying there at a hideously twisted angle and quite, quite dead.

"My God," repeated Philip softly. "Oh Lord, no!"

So you see, now I *do* believe in ghosts. I have proof.

I *am* proof!

There are no such things as ghosts

Also available

DAVID CULLEN

THE LEBANESE COLLECTION

THE BAALBECK DECISION

THE BYBLOS DISCOVERY

THE BEIRUT CONFESSION

DAVID CULLEN
THE LEBANESE COLLECTION

Three full-length novels
featuring Captain Jihad Merhi of the Lebanese Internal Security
Force and Captain Fadi Lattouf of the Palestinian Civil Police

THE BAALBECK DECISION

What links a series of murders in the Bourj el-Barajneh refugee camp
with the assassination of Prime Minister Rafic Hariri? Merhi and Lattouf
race against time to prevent the event which will change Lebanon
forever.

THE BYBLOS DISCOVERY

'Sajida was right' - a cryptic message leads to murders in New
York and Lebanon and sends Merhi and Lattouf on a chase to find
al-Mahdi. Is the world ready for The Second Coming which could
blow the Middle Eastern order apart?

THE BEIRUT CONFESSION

As civil war rages in next door Syria, Merhi and Lattouf have to find
a spy in the security services - before the spy finds them.

ISBN 978-0-9559911-8-9

DAVID CULLEN

KNOCK ON MY DOOR

ONE LOVE, ONE LIFE - A THOUSAND DEATHS

"They say a lady should always have some secrets, layers which she allows to be peeled away only by the intimate few, a striptease that goes beyond the physical... The hard part is when the layers of your mind are stripped away also, level by level, until the very core of your being is exposed. And if that is attacked too, if the very essence of who you are is taken away, what are you left with? Nothing. So how far shall I strip for you? How far should I go? All the way?"

Based on true events, David Cullen tells the story of Carly, a woman who thought she had met The One to take her to heaven – and found herself in the depravity of hell itself.

**She thought he was the love of her life.
He thought he was the end of it.**

KNOCK ON MY DOOR
ISBN 978-0-9559911-3-4

also available as an eBook and on Amazon Kindle

David Cullen